The

LOCKSMITH'S
DAUGHTER

Also by Karen Brooks

Fiction

The Brewer's Tale

The Curse of the Bond Riders trilogy:
Tallow
Votive
Illumination

Young Adult Fantasy

It's Time, Cassandra Klein
The Gaze of the Gorgon
The Book of Night
The Kurs of Atlantis
Rifts Through Quentaris

Nonfiction

Consuming Innocence

The

LOCKSMITH'S DAUGHTER

KAREN BROOKS

WILLIAM MORROW
An Imprint of HarperCollins*Publishers*

P.S.™ is a trademark of HarperCollins Publishers.

HarperCollins books may be purchased for educational, business, or sales promotional use. For information, please email the Special Markets Department at SPsales@harpercollins.com.

Originally published in Australia in 2016 by Harlequin Mira.

FIRST U.S. EDITION

Library of Congress Cataloging-in-Publication Data has been applied for.

ISBN 978-0-06-268657-2

18 19 20 21 22   LSC   10 9 8 7 6 5 4 3 2 1

*This book is for Kerry Doyle and Peter Goddard,
beloved friends and extraordinary people
whom I'm so very fortunate to have in my life.*

*It's also for my partner in everything,
Stephen—the man who has always held the key to
my heart, and always will.*

There is less danger in fearing too much than too little.

—Sir Francis Walsingham

CONTENTS

PART ONE
The Colors of Night

Eumaeus: Forsooth, playing false is as much a game
men indulge in as women, sir.
Vagabond (King Odysseus in disguise): Aye, but it's the only
one where women are always victors.

—Caleb Hollis, *Circe's Chains*

. . . Also she must be more circumspect, and more careful
not to give occasion for evil being said of her,
and conduct herself so that she may escape being sullied by guilt
but even by the suspicions of it, for a woman has not so many ways of
defending herself against false calumnies as a man has . . .

—Baldassare Castiglione, *The Book of the Courtier:
The Third Book, Part Four*, 1528

ONE

*T*he old wherry glided up the bank and halted in the thick silt. With practiced ease the boatman leaped out, ignoring the splash of muddy water spattering his breeches and stockings, and dragged the craft as far up the embankment as his strength allowed. Twining the rope around his elbow, he slung the remainder over his shoulder, then turned and gave a curt nod.

Caleb nimbly jumped over the side of the boat and, fortuitously, onto some rocks. Finding his balance, he held out his hand to proffer assistance. I gestured for Angela to precede me and watched as she maneuvered her girth over the edge and onto the embankment. Grunting as he took her weight, Caleb held her while she found her feet. I looked back toward the opposite bank and London's licentious cousin, Southwark, where, for a few joyous hours, I'd been able to forget everything. Watching the first performance of Caleb's new play, *Circe's Chains*, I was once again Mallory Bright, daughter of the finest locksmith this side of the Thames, a woman with a future as promising as her name.

Melancholy unsettled my brief happiness the way the wind snapped the pennants above the Tower looming to my right. Clouds lumbered toward the battlements from the east, foretokening yet another late autumn storm. In the time it had taken us to cross the river the wind had become stronger, its bitter bite stirring whitecaps on the water. There would be wild weather tonight, and other ships and barges on the river were being battened down in preparation.

"If my lady is awaiting an invitation, one will not be forthcoming from this quarter." Caleb used the voice he usually reserved for the stage, catapulting me out of my reverie.

The boatman murmured something under his breath. I was sure I heard "popinjay," and bit back a wry smile. It was an apt description. In his parti-colored hose, peascod-bellied doublet, polished buskins and marten-lined cloak to keep the chill at bay, Caleb Hollis was a picture of sartorial splendor. The debts he incurred to maintain such style he saw as a matter of necessity rather than something to concern him. I admired the colorful picture he presented, even as his mouth formed a moue that would have done Angela proud. Yesterday had been Queen's Day, when Her Majesty's accession to the throne was commemorated, and the annual tournament, with its tilts and other entertainments, took precedence, postponing the opening of Caleb's play until today. Concern that patrons would still be recovering from the previous day's revelries and unlikely to attend proved unfounded, as the courtyard of the inn was crowded. After the play finished, and despite the consternation its themes caused, the troupe had been called back to the makeshift stage not twice but three times to resounding applause and stamping feet before the place emptied of all but the excited players, friends and hangers-on. Even so, Caleb forwent his moment of glory in order to keep his promise to my father. Ignoring my insistence that he stay and enjoy the praise due to him as both playwright and leading actor, he insisted upon seeing Angela and me across the river to Wool Quay.

"I'll be back anon," he'd replied to the entreaties of the troupe's book holder, his gaze lingering on the tankard of foaming beer being offered. "Please, crave his lordship's pardon."

The crush for watercraft at the busy docks at the Inn of Battle Abbey made me grateful for Caleb's presence. Able to hail the boatman with ease and assert himself so our passage was prioritized above others who also waited to cross, he ensured we were seated, warm and heading back to London before anyone realized their rights had been charmingly usurped. Shushing my protests that we were no more important than anyone else, Caleb gave an impudent flash of his dimples and, as we pushed away from Southwark's busy banks, begged us to review the play and his part. Though I had some reservations regarding the disputatious content and the potential it had for attracting undesirable attention from the authorities, who were always quick to pounce on those who dared to criticize the Queen and her council, it was no hardship. Caleb was among the most talented of those currently treading the boards and his reputation as a gifted playwright—albeit one with a knack for flying close to the wind—was becoming firmly established. Praise was the least I could offer him. Of all those I shared my home with, it was Caleb who most behaved as though the years I'd been gone were but the bat of an owlet's wing. It was he who picked up our friendship, developed over the many seasons he'd lodged within our home, where it had left off, and without the conditions attached to my other bonds. Indeed, I owed Caleb a great deal and hoped one day to repay him.

Still standing in the wherry, I continued to moss-gather, unaware of Caleb glaring at me until he waggled the fingers of his already outstretched arm and snapped them before my face.

"Out!" he said curtly. "Or do you intend to keep us waiting for what remains of the day?"

I flinched at the force of his words, and almost fell back into the boat. Caleb's hand shot out and prevented a tumble.

"Mistress, forgive me," he said quickly, shocked by my reaction.

Simultaneously surprised and embarrassed by my weakness, I quickly recovered and offered a small grin.

"'Tis naught, Caleb. Truly. Only you startled me." Before he could respond, I gathered my skirts, the burden of my Spanish farthingale and the yards of fabric sitting over it—never mind the pattens I was forced to don to protect my pumps from the feculence of the streets, Southwark's being even worse than London's—and levered myself onto the rock with all the refinement of a seagull. Disembarking was more a matter of strategy than grace, and I might well have fallen on my hindquarters were it not for Caleb's firm hold. As it was, swaying precariously before I found purchase, I chose my dignity instead—something I'd thought forever lost to me.

"God give you good evening," I said to the boatman and placed a coin in his gnarled hand as I stepped onto the sand.

The boatman displayed what remained of his brown teeth. "May God save you and prosper you, mistress," he said, pocketing the coin and coiling the rope he still held tightly. "I'd not be loitering if I were you," he added, indicating the sky. "You neither, sir," he said pointedly to Caleb.

Offering an arm to Angela, Caleb ignored the wherryman and we made our way across the pungent slurry. Workers operating a crane upon a nearby ship paused to watch. We must have presented an odd sight—me in my widow's garb, Caleb pretty as a peacock, and Angela, my mother's companion and my chaperone for the day, who was plainly but sensibly dressed and needed both of us to steady her. A surly shout ensured activity on the ship resumed. As if responding to the order, we crossed the final section of shale and broken shells quickly and scurried up the steps, past the dock and the warehouses lining this part of the river, toward the houses and the network of lanes and snickets.

"For all that London is my mistress, I care little for her perfume," muttered Caleb, screwing up his nose.

The city glowed softly in the fading light. There was something about sunset that, like dawn, changed the filthy streets of London into an altogether different place. The approaching storm threw a shimmering veil over the churches and shingle-roofed houses. If you held your breath and pretended the chimneys and forges gave up heavenly clouds instead of choking miasmas, and closed your nostrils so the pungent streets became instead bowers of dewy blooms, then London and the churning wide waters of the Thames could be whatever you wanted them to be. At least, that's what Papa used to say. Once I'd thought never to wander its cobbled alleys again, and thus every hearth's smoky billow, every stinking carcass hanging from a rusting hook, every ring of a hammer, every grubby child, toothless slattern or blue-smocked apprentice and every step upon its mostly crowded and fetid lanes drew from me only gratitude; a new appreciation of the place I'd grown up in and to which, God be praised, I'd been returned.

Earlier that day, as Angela and I had made our way over London

Bridge, I'd felt the same. I'd persuaded her we should walk to South-wark and Lewes Inn, where Caleb's play was being performed, claim-ing I wished to see the sights. In truth, cowardice had also been a factor. The route I'd chosen meant I was less likely to encounter folk I knew—one particularly—especially since I'd selected a time when the stalls along Little Eastcheap would be so crowded the passing of two women would go unnoticed. And I'd been correct. My day thus far had passed in a fanciful haze, offering an ease I'd not felt for a long time. I could almost forget the recent past and the dolorous present, and appreciate the city's glories as if they were new to me.

Only God, my Lord and Savior, knew how much I was akin to the prodigal son, and how great a wastrel. All that was needed for my par-able to be complete was for my father to embrace me. God knew, such an act was beyond my mother.

Pausing near Custom House, at the entrance to Water Lane, we said our farewells. Caleb was to quit our sight and, for the first time in over two years, I prepared to walk among those I had once called neighbors and who, I was certain, now waited to judge me. A thousand birds took wing in my chest. Sensing my mood, Caleb placed Angela's hand firmly upon my arm and held it there.

"Hold your lovely head high, Mallory. You've naught to be ashamed of and much to arouse pity." Though he gestured to my ebony garb, he was wrong. I was a sinner of the worst kind.

"I can remain by your side if you wish," he whispered, leaning so close his whiskers brushed my cheek, "but feel you should strengthen that backbone instead of allowing it to turn to eel jelly."

"Sirrah!" exclaimed Angela, her dark eyes flashing, her plump cheeks turning crimson. "You forget your place."

"Indeed, Angela," I reassured her, placing my hand over hers, "he remembers it."

Beneath Caleb's words lay deep concern, and I knew he meant to remind me of the person I once was, a person not inclined to fret over others' imaginings or to stand trembling before friends and strangers, but rather one who viewed the world as a dish created for my delecta-tion and thus to be savored.

With an attempt at a careless "See you anon," I spun away with a brittle laugh. Caleb, with a flourish of his cap and a deep bow, honored my pretense and left. I didn't begrudge him his celebrations, but dear Lord, I wished he'd stayed. His departure forced me to rally what strength I possessed. I sent a swift prayer heavenward.

"Let us get home," I urged Angela, my throat tight, my thoughts flurried.

We continued along the lane, dodging the urchins chasing each other and any poor stray cat that crossed their path. A couple of gentlemen on horseback rode past, and a group of apprentices leered outside a small alehouse, tankards in hand, nudging and whispering. So little had changed. More people, more noise, more grime. Yet I feared what this suggested. How could so little have altered when I had undergone the greatest of transformations?

We reached the main thoroughfare of Thames Street and its canny vendors, waiting till last light and the distracted air of those traveling home, who tried to tempt us with stale bread, strings of shrunken onions, panniers of warm smelly oysters, cold soggy pies and other unpalatable fare they'd failed to sell during the day. Angela shooed them away with a gaze worthy of Medusa, while I pretended not to see them. It hurt to manufacture an indifference I didn't feel. Times were always hard for those who relied on what came from the land and sea for their keep, especially within the city walls.

Up ahead, a pack of dogs barked as a butcher unhooked the gutted pig strung up outside his premises, a swarm of flies lifting from the gray flesh as he hoisted it over his shoulder and leveled kicks and curses at the hounds. Nearby, a flower seller chatted to an old sailor with a wooden stump where his left leg should be. We entered an area I'd once walked with confidence and I stayed close to Angela, who'd begun to hum the ditty drifting from a nearby tavern.

A wider thoroughfare than some, Harp Lane was lined with two- and three-story houses, many with shops at street level, all with upper stories canting toward each other over the lane. They were like old friends, intent on sharing the secrets of those within.

For all that much was unchanged, there were strange faces, too. People constantly drifted in and out of the city, but here also were the lingering effects of the plague, and of the earthquake that had shaken the city earlier in the year and sent Londoners scattering into the countryside.

Just as these thoughts entered my mind, Master Swithin Hattycliffe, weaver and local counselor, stepped outside his shop, hands upon his bulging stomach, his face upturned to the darkening skies. It had been a long time since we'd last encountered each other. Lost in his study of the oncoming clouds, he failed to see me. I hesitated just a second, then screwed my courage to the sticking place.

"God give you good evening, Master Hattycliffe." My voice was dry, odd.

Before he could reply, the door beside him swung open and out stepped the real reason I'd been reluctant to explore these streets: Isaac Hattycliffe, member of Gray's Inn and my one-time betrothed. He froze when he saw me.

Together, the men stared dolefully. Master Swithin's skin was pale and pitted and his eyes looked oily in the twilight. His son's gaze was like iron—cold, hard and unforgiving. There'd been a time when I had persuaded myself Isaac was moderately handsome. He was the wealthiest man of my acquaintance and, with a law degree almost complete and a prosperous business to inherit, possessed of unlimited prospects. He was considered a good catch—one I'd rejected in a public and shameful fashion.

Unable to speak, I nodded in his direction, trying ineffectually to impart so much with such a simple gesture. What could I say? I'd not only broken his heart but, worse, made him appear a buffoon. I was sorry for that, but dear Lord forgive me, I was not sorry we hadn't wed.

Isaac's lips thinned before he slowly and deliberately turned and walked back into the shop, slamming the door with such force it trembled in its wooden frame. At the sound, activity in the lane momentarily ceased; the chatter stopped and the flames of the braziers and the lamps dimmed. Eyes that had previously failed to notice my presence fastened upon me like gimlets, including those of the dog guarding the stoop of the house next door. A wave of whispers rose and fell. Master Swithin folded his arms and stared, a smirk tugging his mouth. I stumbled. Regaining my composure, I kept my chin up and, as we continued on our way, only the clop of my pattens and the swish of Angela's cloak could be heard.

Until a voice that once murmured ridiculous promises in my ear cried from a window above, echoing over the street, "Lock up your sons! Mistress *Blight* is back among us."

There were gasps followed by vicious and prolonged cackles. The looks became bolder, more appraising. Catcalls and taunts followed. Someone spat. Frigid cold then blazing heat replaced the blood in my veins. My vision blurred as tears began to well. I wanted to run, to be swallowed by the growing shadows. If it hadn't been for Angela's hold upon my arm, her muttered prayers, I think I would have bolted. I don't recall our next steps, but I gradually became aware the jests and attention had ceased and the lane's activity resumed. There was sing-song cheer from the alehouse, the screech of an alley cat and the caw of ravens winging their way home. My breathing steadied; my heart did not. This was guilt unassuaged—it would ensure I was punished over and over for my sins.

"Ignore that *bastardo* Hattycliffe," said Angela softly. "He is nothing more than a, what is it you say? A roaring boy—and all who live here know it."

I hesitated a second before responding, determined the wobble of my limbs would not infect my voice. "A coward and a bully he may be, but there's many would argue my actions created him—Mamma among them."

Mistress Blight. Dear God, is that how they see me?

We walked the rest of the way home without exchanging another word, aware of the gossip that would no doubt swell in our wake. Relief swept my body as the house came into view. I was a soldier returning from war, longing for the safety of those walls, even though the harbor they represented was only temporary.

On the corner of Harp Lane and Tower Street, our house was a fine three-story building with mullioned glass in all the windows and two parlors inside, all surrounded by a stone wall. The entrance was on Harp Lane, while access to Papa's shop was on Tower Street. His work-shop was at the rear, separated from the main house by a small yard complete with chickens and a greedy cow. Just before the intersection with Tower Street there was a big old creaking gate, partially hidden by a huge elm tree. Mainly used by tradespeople and servants, it had always been my preferred entrance and exit.

Once inside, I would pay my respects to Papa, to my lady mother, and then lock myself in my room and never venture out again . . . This outing had been a mistake, a terrible, wretched mistake. I should never have allowed myself to be persuaded. The play, for all its glory, was not worth it. Damn Caleb . . . and damn Papa for his acquiescence.

Just as I opened the gate, it was wrenched backward. In the gap, a grime-streaked face with large eyes appeared. It was my father's youngest apprentice, Dickon. Upon seeing me, he started, his neck and cheeks reddening.

"M . . . M . . . Mistress Mallory. I . . . I . . . I was just coming to find you."

"What is it, Dickon?" I asked and, casting etiquette aside, squeezed past him.

Leaving Angela to shut the gate, Dickon followed me then stopped, studying his feet, scraping them back and forth in the dirt, hands clasped behind his back, his blue shirt covered by his leather apron. Taken on by my father after I left, Dickon had heard the prate about his master's daughter and didn't know what to think when the subject of that tattle manifested as a living, breathing being. He had avoided me since I'd been home. Now he had no choice.

He swallowed a few times. "It's your pa. He needs you, mistress."

My heart gamboled in my chest. *At last.*

He locked eyes with me. He had lovely brown eyes, like our spaniels. "Thank you, Dickon."

A long, low rumble of thunder sounded. As one, we glanced toward the heavens. The chickens squawked and the cat, Latch, scurried along the branch of the elm, leaping onto the rear wall. The dense, dark smell of moisture clung to every surface.

"M . . . Mistress, I feel I should tell you—" Dickon paused and gulped, his head swiveling to follow the cat. "The master's not alone. There is a stranger with him."

I turned toward the workshop. Light flickered through the closed shutters, smoke billowed from the chimney. "A stranger? Who?"

Dickon shrugged. "A gentleman . . . nay, a nobleman. I've not seen him before. Master seems to know him. Not certain if I should be telling you this, mistress, but he's not been himself since the gentleman arrived. Not at all."

The earth opened beneath me, a great maw into which I would sink. *No. No. Please God. Had damnation come to visit me?* I resisted the urge to clutch the locket hidden beneath my dress. Instead, I rested my hand briefly over where it lay against my heart, cleared my throat, and pretended nothing was amiss.

"This man, he's been here awhile?"

"Since the bells tolled three at least. Master told us to leave the workshop, even though tasks remain unfinished, what with the holiday yesterday and all."

"I see." This time when I met Dickon's eyes, I saw something that reflected what lay in my own. Fear. I pulled my cloak tighter.

"Lead the way." I mustered the warmest smile I could, considering the cold wrapping itself about me. The first drops of rain struck.

"Nay, mistress," said Dickon, brushing water from his cheeks. "The master says I'm to stay in the house. You're to go alone."

The light was gloomy, the shadows growing. A gust of wind lifted my cloak, my kirtle, nipped my cheeks. The rain became heavier and still I didn't move. A flash of lightning ripped the sky.

"*Vai,*" said Angela, giving me a little shove. "You go, Mallory. You must obey your papa."

Indeed, from now on, I must. I promised. It was what we'd agreed, after all. A condition of my return. I would be a dutiful daughter.

Gripping Dickon by the shoulder, Angela maneuvered him before her, a shield against the weather. With one last reassuring look, she jerked her head in the direction of the workshop.

Left with little choice, I lowered my face and ran, wondering who this mysterious nobleman might be. The man who finally forced my father, a proud master locksmith, to acknowledge that he needed me still.

TWO

I paused outside the workshop, took a deep breath and entered. Arthur and Galahad, our two spaniels, scrabbled at my legs to attract attention. Trained not to bark lest they destroy Papa's or the apprentices' concentration, they were nonetheless active in their affections. I kneaded their ears and stroked their soft heads as I glanced around.

Papa was bent over the main table in the middle of the room. He raised a finger to indicate he knew I was there, and continued to concentrate on an object in front of him. As for the mysterious guest, of him there was no sign. Aside from Papa, the workshop and shop beyond were deserted.

Slipping the wet cloak from my shoulders, I studied the place where I'd spent a great deal of my youth. I had not graced its rooms since my return some weeks earlier. Everything appeared just as I remembered. So much so, I could almost persuade myself time stood still. The forge against the west wall glowed, its embers banked, its heat comforting. A pair of bellows rested next to it; the anvil squatted a few feet away. The larger tools sat in their holders nearby. Beneath the shuttered window was a bench strewn with instruments and bits of solid metal. An assortment of keys and barrels lay awaiting ward and tumbler cuts, their shanks gleaming in the soft light. Beside them were locks in various stages of completion, not yet dressed for the occasion. Papa's work stool was abandoned underneath the bench. The half-eaten remnants of a loaf, some cheese and unwashed tankards sat on a smaller table. Above a large cupboard on the far wall hung a series of keys and an unfinished master lock—the work of Kit Jolebody, Papa's eldest apprentice, if I wasn't mistaken.

Though it had been a long time since I'd sat at these benches and tested my competence, I knew locks and their workings better than most.

I'd never sought to acquire such knowledge nor the skills that attended it. Up until the age of seven, I was like any other girl of my station, learning to sew, dance, paint pretty pictures and correctly address folk of all ranks. What set our family apart, aside from Mamma's origins and stubborn adherence to the old faith, was that our house was blessed with books—wonderful books, full of stories, ideas and so much more. The second son of a gentleman, Papa, like his brothers, had been given a good education. Able to translate from the Greek and Latin, he would read me stories of gods, goddesses and the mortals who both loved and defied them. I also learned of King Arthur and his knights, the Holy Grail, courtly manners and tales of damsels in need of rescue by sword-wielding lords with noble intentions, holiness and grace. I would imagine what it would be like to be the object of such intense passion that a man would forgo his dearest friends and his sworn oath in order to serve the woman who'd captured his heart and soul. I would sigh into my pillow, clutching the cat or one of the hounds until they wriggled free. My days were crowded with such stories and my nights with the dreams and longings they inspired.

Then Papa read Thomas Becon's book *The Catechism*, whose pages argued forcefully for the education of girls. Becon believed girls must be as learned as boys so they might grow into virtuous women who in turn would teach their children the benefits of godliness and morality. According to Papa, one had only look at Her Majesty Queen Elizabeth to see such principles in action. She was clever as well as virtuous and godly and her children, the good folk of England, reaped the benefits.

So would I.

It wasn't long after Papa had finished Becon's book that Master Fodrake, a teacher, sought lodgings with us. Papa struck a deal— Master Fodrake could have rooms and food provided he taught me my letters and, much to my delight, to read for myself the tales Papa had related. It was Master Fodrake, then a man of middle years with a straggly beard, kind twinkling eyes and a voice so mellow and soft that listening to it was akin to being stroked with feathers, who brought William Lily's Latin grammar book into the house and used it to add the language of scholars to the Greek he struggled to teach me, as well as the Italian, French and English with which I was already conversant. Within months, I was able to read the marvelous orations of Cicero and, against Mamma's wishes, the magnetic verses of Ovid and Virgil. Master Fodrake, my tutor and oft-times instructor to Papa's apprentices as well, also brought the musings of Plato, Aristotle and the works of the Saracen philosophers into my little sphere. Insisting my mathematics must be beyond reproach, he introduced me to William Buckley's *Arithmetica Memorativa*, a series of Latin verses that taught the rules of mathematics—so my Latin and numbers were improved in one fell swoop.

But all this learning, this vast pool of knowledge in which I swam with such pleasure, didn't compare to having the attention of my papa. Mamma may have labored to bring me into this world but it was as if once this maternal duty had been accomplished, she was not obliged to fulfill any others. It was no secret Mamma longed for a son, but no matter how many times her womb quickened, aside from me no child, male or female, survived more than a few weeks. Believing that somehow it was my fault and that my presence precluded her being blessed with any other babes, her relationship with me became increasingly strained. To say it lacked the fondness I enjoyed with both Papa and with Mamma's companion, her cousin Angela, was to understate the coolness that accompanied our every encounter. Over the years Mamma became an ever more distant figure of judgment and disdain. At first I sought to please her, but, as I grew older, I came to challenge and ultimately defy her.

Did Mamma's remoteness drive me into Papa's workshop, to hover by his side as he made beautiful intricate keys and locks? Did I understand, even as a young girl, that my bond with Papa was at the expense of the one with my mother? I'm uncertain. In many ways I simply accepted that Mamma didn't hold the same fondness for me as Papa. It was the natural order of things and required no explanation.

I was my father's daughter. When I was with Papa, the hours became a solace, the workshop a refuge from the vexation my mere presence aroused in my mother. Indulgent, he would answer my endless questions, explain his techniques and allow me to file his carefully crafted keys to polished smoothness. At first he did it to humor a lonely child, but as he saw my enthusiasm and responded to it as a natural teacher does a willing pupil, these early lessons transformed into something more. My mornings were spent with Master Fodrake and my afternoons became Papa's. Mamma did not object nor change the manner of her dealings with me.

When I reached the age when I should have been learning how to run a house, make ale and perform any charitable works the parish required, I was not only burying my head in the work of the Romans and Greeks, I was also becoming adept at understanding the temperatures at which a forge must be kept in order to turn metal molten and make it pliable. When I should have been concerned with studying songs and perfecting my abilities with a musical instrument, I was learning how the instruments of a locksmith were used: the tongs, hammers, rods, stilettos, slim metal bars and bellows. Father would explain how someone who works with bronze, iron and steel or alloys must approach each task not only with respect for the material but with an awareness of the shape it would take. It was the master's role to understand what resided within the metal and to help it emerge. Only then could a locksmith bend the iron, for example, to the pattern in his mind or in the sketch before him. While the head held the Platonic and God-blessed form, the product of the hands was the imperfect earthly version. Though it never lived up to its heaven-sent ideal, it was incumbent upon the craftsman to seek perfection. I would watch as Papa sought to arrive at this destination daily. Though he believed he fell short, his many wealthy clients and the reputation he earned did much to counter that notion.

While fashioning keys and locks didn't require the strength of a blacksmith or an ironmonger, it was beyond my capabilities and sex—apart from filing the metal, Papa would never allow me to practice as his apprentices did. But testing the locks, seeing how resistant they were to the cunning of a lock-pick, this was within my ken and something Papa indulged. Lock-picking required an agility and firmness of purpose, a mind not shackled to the object itself and what it was designed to do, but to defeating the intentions of its maker. My nimble fingers and understanding of the workings behind the metal plates and elaborate escutcheons—the ornate frontispiece that often covered the keyhole—as well as the pins, springs and bolts, served me well. Undoing the locks, bypassing the wards and tumblers without the keys designed to open them, was something that came naturally to me. Being a girl proved no handicap—not while my skills were kept secret.

Before long, after the apprentices had retired for the night or were occupied with errands and other tasks, I was helping Papa test the locks his workshop produced.

It became a game between us—and as I grew older and more skilled, more often than not I emerged the victor.

Whenever Mamma saw my stained and calloused hands she railed at Papa before turning on me. Accused of taking no care over my appearance, of defeating her efforts to make me presentable and thus marriageable, I didn't argue. Instead of exclaiming over the silk and woolen garments she ordered so I would not shame her, the wife of a wealthy locksmith, in public, I would gladly cover the sumptuous fabrics and shuck on the leather apron and gloves of the trade, hiding my pretty skirts and bodice, tying back my long hair and tucking it beneath an ugly thick scarf instead of the fashionable coifs, caps and decorated bonnets designed to enhance my ebony locks. Shamefully, I sometimes paraded in this working apparel before Mamma simply to nettle her, but also to get her attention. With a slap across my face, or a hairbrush against my thigh, Mamma would demand I remove the filthy garments and, with loud prayers to blessed Mother Mary and all the saints, banish me from her sight.

In the privacy of my room I would smile through the tears, holding my hand mirror aloft, turning it this way and that in order to admire my strange ensemble before undressing. Mamma was mistaken in thinking I wasn't vain. I was. I relished every scald and scar, every broken fingernail, every scratch and torn piece of clothing. Her punishments became part of my achievements, a sign I wasn't the curse of a female instead of a male child, or God's punishment for her sins, but a skilled and useful person. Dressing in my best for church each Sunday, I wore the badges of my secret ability the way other young women wore their ruffs, embroidered stomachers, decorated partlets, satin kirtles and farthingales. My indifference to her perturbation, my stubborn refusal to capitulate to her desires, infuriated Mamma and saddened Papa, who loved us both.

"She's a young woman," Mamma would screech. "Not an apprentice to be enslaved to a craft."

Papa would agree, reaching for his ale, and grin. "No less because she wears leather over her silks."

"You only say so because when she dresses like this, she resembles you. She's like an actor in costume. But God in His wisdom knows, there'll come a time when she must cast this playacting aside and be the woman she was born. It's not a profession she needs but a husband. If we're ever to see her settled in this world, out from under our roof, it's by marriage. Lord knows she'll have enough trouble finding a husband looking the way she does, let alone possessing a man's mind and skills. It's not natural," she would cry and then, lowering her voice and turning her head aside, would murmur, "Nothing about her is."

Defiantly she would stare at Papa, cross herself in the papist way and mutter words that, if they ever reached certain ears, would see her loyalty to the throne questioned. Despite how she sounded, Mamma's objections were never about our sovereign lady; they were about the woman I was becoming.

The pain Mamma's words aroused became another piece of my armor—chinks were not allowed.

"Let her be, Valentina," Papa would sigh. "You're too hard on the child. What harm is there if, for the time being, she continues to find pleasure unpicking locks? After all, she's very talented."

"At unmaking what you fashion, sir. This is not a gift but a curse you have bestowed. You're playing at God. Making her in your image," scolded Mamma. "No good will come of it. The smithy is no place for a woman. Look at what happened to the last one known to work the forge—she crafted the very nails driven into the palms of Our Lord

Jesus Christ. *Mio Dio!* As if we women don't suffer enough penance for our sins. The catalog need not grow, and not with your daughter's name upon it."

In attempting to shield me from her wrath, Papa was actually providing Mamma with more ammunition.

"She's a locksmith's daughter, that's all, and cannot be accused of the charges you would lay at her feet."

Mamma made a noise of disgust.

Unaware of the effect of his words, Papa would continue to defend and even praise me, and I loved him for it.

"She is my Athena, my Hecate, and, like these goddesses, she's but the key holder. She holds the keys to my heart, the city that is my forged mind." He would laugh at his joke. Mamma didn't. "One day I will pass these keys to the man who deserves her. Not before, Valentina, so hold your peace."

Mamma would throw up her hands and stride from the room. If she spied me hiding near the door, she never acknowledged it. I would wait until she ascended the stairs then enter the room and my father's arms.

And so, as I grew older and spent more time with Papa, the arguments would circle. Despite my joy in Papa's pride, I could not fault Mamma in her concerns. It didn't take much to disqualify a woman from the marriage market. Stories of spinsters with harelips, six toes, eyes that stared in different directions, hair that fell out when combed and monstrous growths upon their bodies abounded—any night I spent in the kitchen with the apprentices and servants I'd be regaled with tales of good fortune and woe. That all these deformities and many more besides became invisible depending on the size of the dowry, business or house a woman brought with her to a marriage bed was not lost on any of us. Alas, my dowry was merely adequate, Mamma said, and it was up to me to make up the deficit by making myself more desirable. My skills and even my education, according to Mamma, did naught in that regard.

Unspoken, but louder for that, was the fact that in a world where appearances counted for so much, I was already at a disadvantage. Physically I was most unfashionable. Uncommonly tall, slender as a willow stick but with olive-toned skin and jet-black hair, I was most often described as ungainly and teased as the spawn of a blackamoor or a Romany. I looked nothing like Mamma, who had the fiery hair of our Queen, her creamy complexion and the voluptuousness of a woodland nymph. I'd taken father's height and build, but my hair, skin and eyes— which were a pale gray circled by dark rings (like a new planet glid-ing into our ken, Papa teased, while Caleb sighed at his poetry)—were my own.

"Your *nonna*, she had such eyes," Mamma would say bitterly, as if I'd not inherited a familial characteristic but a malediction. "Your *zio*, your uncle, he too had the dark hair of Romans," she would spit before once again rinsing mine in lemon juice in a useless effort to lighten it. If Papa's religion had allowed it, I knew she would have smeared my face with ceruse; anything to make my prospects more appealing.

It used to bother me that I didn't look like my parents, in the way that family are the first mirrors upon which we see ourselves reflected. As time passed and their faces wizened and their hair became sprin-kled with gray, I understood that any resemblance was fleeting. If God had blessed us with three score years or more, we all looked alike, as if we belonged to a much greater family—and we did, according to our parish priest, Reverend Bernard—the good Lord's.

I don't know exactly when I understood that Papa, who'd never anticipated passing on his craft to me, had come to rely upon the expertise I'd developed. Only that one day, as he summoned me to the workshop when Mamma was out on errands, and I unpicked the locks he'd placed upon a noblewoman's *cassone*, testing their strength, it struck me that this was what had happened—despite Mamma's efforts to prevent it, and Papa's denials. Just as he envisaged what lay within the metal he melted and shaped, he'd seen what lay within me and forged accordingly. Papa had raised a daughter and created a lock-pick.

And, may God forgive my conceit, there was a time I was glad that he had.

My education and talent with locks did not, despite Mamma's fears, prevent someone she deemed worthy seeking my hand. She'd been so proud the day Isaac and his father came to the house with their proposal. Bestowing a kiss upon my forehead, she'd dismissed Papa's resistance to the match and my overt dismay with callous indifference.

What if Raffe had not appeared when he did, offering sympathy and an alternative? What if Mamma had heeded my importuning and Papa's counsel that we wait and not force the betrothal to Isaac? Would things have been different?

Chiding myself for such thoughts, reminding myself the past could not be refashioned, I tiptoed over to open the workshop window. The tang of molten metal, the heady smells of leather, trapped smoke, male flesh and unwashed animals had made the room stuffy.

"Mallory? Leave the window." Papa's voice was gruff. "Come here."

I approached his side cautiously. Poised upon their haunches, as if anticipating adventure, the dogs were vigilant, their eyes shining in the light of the forge.

"Sir?" I said softly. "Dickon said you have need of me." Oh, how my heart sang to say those words. The workshop had been forbidden since my return. I smoothed my hands over the black I wore at Mamma's insistence. As long as I remained under their roof, it was to be in the colors of night; colors that supported the story she'd woven to explain my long absence. In this she would not be gainsaid.

I stood as close to Papa as I dared, certain he could hear the hammering of my heart. His arms rested on the table, either side of a *forziere*, a heavily decorated gilt-edged box. His hands were curled into fists, his eyes fixed upon the small chest.

"It's lovely," I said.

"Isn't it?" he replied absentmindedly, and it was as if I was nine again, learning at my father's knee, sharing the secrets of his craft, honing my skills.

Before I asked Papa where it had come from, I took a moment to study him. His thick pepper-and-salt hair was ruffled, his face pale, his dark eyes red-rimmed and his forehead creased with worry. Still wearing a leather apron, he had rolled the sleeves of his shirt to the elbow, exposing his sinewy forearms, the dusting of fine hair and the old scars. I'd barely seen him, let alone spent time with him, since he'd fetched me home. Though he'd deny it, and the admission pained me immeasurably, Papa had been avoiding me. I missed his company; I missed this, I thought, absorbing the workshop, the equipment, the smells.

Drumming his fingers on the table as he stared at the casket, Papa's agitation was palpable. I glanced around again, but could see nothing out of the ordinary, though the hair on the back of my neck began to dance to a discordant internal tune.

"Dickon said you have a guest—a gentleman—?" I left the sentence unfinished. "Is there a problem? Is there any . . . news I should know?"

Stepping back from the table so suddenly I had to jump out of the way, Papa ignored my questions and gestured to the table.

"Tell me, what do you make of it?" He swung away toward the forge, lifting a poker to prod the burning coals. I was left to examine the small chest.

Sorrow welled. Whoever had been here, Papa wouldn't tell me; worse, he could not bring himself to watch me work. No doubt recollections of happier times battled within him. With a small, sad sigh, I took off my gloves.

Pulling the candles closer, I unpinned my hat then tossed it to the side, and rolled up my sleeves. The bruises and scrapes that had once covered my arms—and so appalled Papa when he first found me, arousing in him tenderness commingled with rage that someone could do such damage to his flesh and blood—had all but faded. When I caught him checking, mayhap remembering, he lowered his gaze.

Large enough to be mistaken for a generous jewelry box, the casket had four panels and a painted lid ornamented with tiny iron gargoyles, one perched upon each corner. Jewel boxes were generally smaller but deeper, more feminine in their crafting; this was something else. Decorated with scenes from the Creation, the first panel showed Adam and Eve being expelled from the Garden, the serpent, and the Tree of Knowledge. The second told the tale of Cain and Abel. As I peered more closely, I noted that Eve was depicted with long red hair, white skin and an unusually high forehead.

Wiping my palms down the side of my kirtle, I was excited by what I was viewing, distracted by what this casket promised.

"This image of Eve, she's been designed to look like Her Majesty," I said. "Adam bears a close resemblance to the Spanish king, Philip." A tiny exclamation escaped. "And the serpent wears the face of none other than the Earl of Leicester." Father spun around as I examined the next panel. "And here"—I pointed—"Cain is King Philip also—and Abel—" My hand flew to cover my mouth. "Abel is Queen Elizabeth." I gaped at my father. "What game is this?"

My thoughts flew to Caleb's play, to the risks he'd taken with the barely disguised politics he had enacted upon the stage; the criticism he'd dared to level toward our ruler and the religious tolerance he sought to espouse. Here were the same people playing biblical characters. The message was clear. What was happening?

"I would it were a game, Mallory. Continue." Papa's eyes darted toward the gloom collected around the door of the shop.

My heart beat faster now. Heat suffused my cheeks. This was no ordinary object but one that spoke of something darker, more dangerous . . . something heretical. While this false *forziere* might have been regarded as a parody, an ironic retelling of Creation, it was also, when read a particular way, a call to arms—a Catholic call to arms. The scenes on the rear of the casket were similarly rendered—Elizabeth, Philip and other members of the Queen's court, some of whom I didn't recognize, replacing figures from the Old Testament.

Crouching until my eyes were level with the middle of the box, I studied the escutcheon and ran my fingers lightly over the surface. I tried to prise it away from the wood, but it remained sealed. Tracing the embossed metal, I noted the chasing and central plate had a coat of arms engraved upon it. I searched for a hidden spring. Agitating the metal with my nail, I managed to slip a finger beneath a section of filigree. Pushing it gently, there was a slight noise and then a piece swung aside to reveal a keyhole. Raising a candle, I studied the cloverleaf shape.

"Ah," sighed Papa. I almost leaped out of my skin. He was right behind me and I hadn't heard him approach. "I'd forgotten the ease with which you could accomplish that." I raised a hand to touch his arm, to share a remembrance, but lowered it again. I didn't want to alter the sudden intimacy this mysterious casket had created between us. For the first time since I'd come home, he looked me in the eye.

"I need you to open this."

My heart soared.

"I will." It was a vow. But, at the back of my mind, a small voice chimed. *Why does Papa need me to open what is within his compass?* Ignoring my reservations, I turned my attention to the task.

"Be careful," he said, his manner more like that of old. He strode to the other table and threw me an apron, which I caught deftly. Dragging his stool out, he offered it to me. "This is no ordinary container. Someone has gone to a great deal of trouble to ensure the contents cannot be easily accessed, that they remain secret."

Taking the stool, I sat and chose what I required from the selection of tools upon the bench.

The room had grown uncomfortably warm. I could feel a trickle of sweat between my shoulder blades and another leave my temple and begin to course its way down the side of my face. I swiped it with my arm. Outside, thunder growled and the dogs gave their own muffled retort. Using two long metal picks—both bent in such a fashion that to an untrained eye they looked like castoffs from the forge, one possessing a small hook at the end—I positioned myself so I could work the keyhole from below. Inserting first the hooked rod, I slid the other in past it. Satisfied they were in position, I began maneuvering them, turning my head so my ear was close to the chest. The rods teased the opening—one at the top and one at the bottom. I looked as though I were driving a miniature cart as I held the picks like reins, rotating them slowly, my hands steady, my breathing deliberately measured.

Just as my fingers began to ache from lack of practice, there was a sharp click. The buried wards in the opening of the keyhole gave and simultaneously the lid came ajar.

"I knew . . ." began Papa, then a figure detached itself from the shadows next to the door to the shop.

I let out a small cry and dropped the rods. The dogs leaped to their feet, baring their teeth and snarling. The rods rolled and clanged, emitting a tinny fanfare. The fire in the forge sparked, sending a cascade of orange into the workshop. The triumphant rain beat hard against the window as a man walked slowly into the light.

"You were right, Gideon," said a deep, clipped voice.

With the exception of a modest white ruff, the stranger was dressed completely in black. Wiry, with raven hair, swarthy skin, a graying beard and moustache, his lean face was topped by an ebony skullcap. Heavily hooded eyes appraised me quickly.

"You said you'd remain out of sight," said Papa, anger marching across his face. He pushed me behind him.

My eyes strayed from the man to the *forziere* and back to Papa. My insides were churning, my resolve to be calm melting away. Who was this dark man?

"Mistress Mallory," said the stranger, stepping around Papa and taking my limp hand in his. "It's a pleasure to finally meet you."

I found my voice. "I'm afraid, good sir, you have the advantage." I dipped a curtsey and tried to extract my fingers.

The man's lips curled and he glanced at Papa, who, with a shake of his head that bespoke surrender, moved aside and mumbled, "Mister Secretary Walsingham, my daughter, Mallory. Mallory, this is Sir Francis, a member of Her Majesty's Privy Council and an old friend."

The room swam, my vision blurred into a kaleidoscope of tangerine and indigo. Oh dear God. Papa's visitor, his old friend, wasn't just a noble. He was none other than the most dangerous man in all of England.

The man from whom no secret was safe.

THREE

Sir Francis Walsingham's name was known far and wide, if only to strike fear in the hearts of those who heard it. Including mine. But it was not just his name; his sepulchral appearance and raven-like manner whispered threat as well. No wonder Dickon had been overcome.

We stood before the casket—me, Sir Francis and Papa—in an unlikely tableau. Gradually the hammering in my chest subsided, the vise that gripped the back of my neck loosened. The dogs, sensing that the stranger in our midst posed no immediate menace, quieted. Their indifference allowed me to see him not so much as a figure of state authority come to cast judgment, but merely someone capable who'd sought professional assistance. Someone whom Papa named an "old friend." Why, then, had we never heard his name in our home? Why did he not feature in the stories of my childhood? Studying him beneath my lashes, I confirmed my initial assessment: capable and unpredictable. The Lord knows, there's a great deal to be feared from those qualities, depending how and for whom they're deployed. But I sensed no peril from this man—not this night.

Aware of my hand still in his, I tried again to withdraw it, but he held fast. Turning it over, he examined my palm with astonishing liberty, running one long ink-stained finger to the calloused tip and then twisting it back and studying my nails. My hands were no longer those of a master craftsman's privileged daughter, and had seen better days. I felt like a hind in a county market.

"That was expertly done." He nodded at the casket and released my fingers. Facing the table once more, Sir Francis fastened his arms behind his back and bent to examine the small *forziere* closely.

"May I?" he asked, indicating his wish to open the lid. I nodded.

Straightening, he lifted it. His face fell. Beneath the elegant satin-lined top sat another one made of the same dark wood as the exterior, only this one lacked decoration, except for two holes in the center.

"I see," he said, and went to place his fingers in them.

I grabbed his wrist. "Don't."

Papa groaned and placed his head in his hands. "Forgive her, Francis . . ."

"Why?" Sir Francis directed his question to me.

"If I'm correct—" I released him slowly and swallowed, flashing an apologetic look at Papa. Without ceremony, I invited Sir Francis to stand aside. As God is my witness, working with locks again, unraveling their mysteries, instilled in me something of my former self, the confidence I once wore as comfortably as my leather apron. "These finger holes are a false key. They won't open the casket. They're simply placed there to make sure anyone who tries cannot open this or any other."

Unperturbed by my bluntness, Mister Secretary's eyebrows rose. "Demonstrate."

I quickly went to the forge, returning with two pieces of kindling, each roughly the width of a finger. Placing them in the holes, I bore down hard then tried to extract them. There was a loud crack. Slowly, I withdrew the wood. The pieces were half the length they'd been, the ends shattered.

Sir Francis took a step back. Papa buried a wry smile.

"These kinds of safeguards are rare, but deadly," I said. "A spring makes the metal beneath snap like jaws. If these had been your fingers . . ." I held the pieces toward him.

"Quite." To Sir Francis's credit, he studied the wood judiciously.

Only the slight widening of his pupils revealed his surprise. "How did you know?"

I glanced at Papa, who gave a small nod. "I've seen two others. The first some years back." I indicated the casket. "The lock's design is Italian or Spanish. The other, well . . ." I hesitated.

"I made it for a Genoese noble," said Papa. "It was just as effective."

Sir Francis took the remnants of kindling from me one by one and touched the torn ends. "Possessed of such a device, how does one open the casket?"

"Like this," I said and, removing what remained of the wood from the holes with a thin file, inserted two bent picks, one in each opening. After rotating them once or twice, another spring clicked, and more of the ornate scrollwork sprang apart from the escutcheon. This time, the real lock was revealed. Deceptively simple from the outside, closer examination revealed it was designed to take a key with many ward cuts.

"I'm guessing you don't have the key?"

Sir Francis shook his head.

"Could you hold this candle just so, please?" I asked, and passed one to him before he could respond. "Don't let any of the wax drop onto the casket."

Lost in my task, I forgot to whom I spoke, only understanding as I bent to pick this lock that I'd ordered one of the most important men in the Queen's government around as if he were ten-year-old Dickon. Blushing to the roots of my hair, the heat was now unbearable. I could feel the brush of Sir Francis's suit against my shoulder, smell the spices emanating from his body as he held the candle in place. Alien to my senses, they were not unpleasant. Behind me, the forge coughed and one of the dogs scratched itself, its leg thumping against the floor. Outside the rain pounded furiously against the shutters. Papa remained motionless.

It took time, but finally, with a small twang, the catch sprang open. I withdrew my instruments and wiped a hand across my brow.

"There," I said, and lifted the lid, catching only a glimpse of what lay inside—a flash of ornate silk, a cloth of white lace, the twinkling silver and gold of a thick crucifix, the muddy richness of old embossed leather and the creamy perfection of lace—before the lid was slammed shut and the *forziere* snatched from the table.

"Was that . . . ?" The sight of a priest's tools—an alb, a chasuble and cross, the apparatus of heresy—here, in the workshop, stole my equilibrium. Wonder and terror coursed down my spine. Was this brought here deliberately? To threaten Papa? To torment him over his wife's recusancy? He used to pay all her fines . . . Had my actions and the cost made that impossible? I spun toward my father.

"May I thank you for the service you've provided, Mistress Mallory?" Sir Francis was suddenly formal and distant.

Papa gripped my forearm and squeezed. Hard. "That will be all, daughter. Go back to the house. Tell your mother . . . Tell her I'll be with her shortly."

"There's no need to mention this"—Sir Francis motioned toward the chest—"or my presence to anyone, Mistress Mallory."

I contained my curiosity, the questions I wanted to ask. Instead, resisting the urge to plead forgiveness for my mamma and her adherence to the old ways, to affirm they were not mine, despite my previous lodgings, my relations, I took off the apron, grabbed my cloak, threw it over my shoulders and, carrying my hat and gloves, went to the door. The entire time Papa and Sir Francis neither spoke nor moved.

"May God give you good night, Sir Francis, Papa," I called and, with a final curtsey, drew the door shut. Ensuring there was a mere crack, I forgot my recent vow to be obedient and, instead, remained where I was, pressing my face against the wood, turning so I'd catch anything they said. After all, had not this practice stood me in good stead for many a year? I was adept. I prayed the rain beating upon the thatch would fool them into thinking I'd scampered back to the house. Grateful for the small awning that protected me from the worst of the elements, I rolled down my sleeves and stationed myself for listening.

When there was still no exchange of words, I thought my ruse had been suspected. Rain fell steadily, gusts of wind forcing it to strike my arched back, ruining my ruff and dampening my hair. My gloveless hands fast grew cold and stiff. The shutters rattled. As I was about to flee to the warmth of the kitchen, the men finally spoke.

"Good, now, what do you think?" asked Papa in a voice I barely recognized, laden as it was with portent and sadness. "Can you find her a position?"

God-a-mercy, Papa was asking Sir Francis to find me employment. Like a little child who still believed in angels, fairies and the possibility of dreams, I'd persuaded myself Papa's talk of finding me work as soon as I had healed was a threat, a form of punishment for the worry and pain I'd caused and the shame I'd brought upon the Bright name. I'd never really believed he'd do it, not even when my wounds had mended. Yet, here he was, seeking work on my behalf with none other than Sir Francis Walsingham. His "old friend."

Tears of frustration and injustice rose. Is this why Mamma insisted I go to the theater? So Sir Francis could arrive unseen by me, so Papa and Mister Secretary could collude without my knowledge or objections? So together they'd arrange my eviction from hearth and home? Then why the mummery with the lock? Why did Papa want to show Sir Francis what I could do? What sort of employ was he seeking for his child?

"I confess, she's far more skilled than you led me to believe." Sir Francis sat upon the stool I'd recently vacated and put the *forziere* back on the bench, his hand resting lightly on the lid. "She's not what I expected."

Papa looked wistful. "She's not what anyone expected."

They exchanged a brief smile. "She looks well . . . considering . . ." said Sir Francis. Papa didn't reply. "You say she has languages?" he continued.

"Italian, French, some Spanish," replied Papa. "She writes in these as well as Latin and Greek. She reads as well as any learned man. Has a solid grasp of mathematics."

Sir Francis rubbed his beard. "She knows her letters? Mathematics, you say? Unusual for a woman, but may be of worth. And she can unpick any lock?"

"You saw for yourself. I've yet to find one she cannot open."

"Extraordinary." Sir Francis struck the casket with his knuckles and sighed. "I want to help, Gideon, truly I do. I want to help her."

"You must, Francis. If not you, then who? I've nowhere else to turn, no one else to whom I trust her welfare. Only you. I'd never have thought Mallory with all her learning, her headstrong ways, would be one to fall prey to a varlet, but I'd forgotten, for all her knowledge, she's also a woman, with a woman's heart and head, readily turned by pretty words and a fine pair of legs." Papa paused and heat sped through my body. Was that really me? I blinked and swallowed. It was. Once upon a time. The truth pierced me; my cheeks burned despite the cold.

"After what she endured and the rumors that accompanied her return, she needs to forge herself a new identity." Papa sat opposite Sir Francis and leaned forward on the bench, closing the distance between them. The tiny chest was all that separated them. He blinked rapidly.

"Your sight does not improve?" asked Sir Francis with sympathy.

What was this?

"It worsens daily," sighed Papa. He gave a hollow laugh. "The vagaries of age and profession; too long spent at the forge, an errant spark in my youth." My heart contracted as Papa pushed his knuckles into his eyes. "Part of me wishes it had been stolen completely so I didn't have to see what the scoundrel did to her; the conditions in which she was forced to live. Truly, it broke my heart into pieces, Francis—and when I thought it could not be shattered any further."

"Just so," said Sir Francis. "The knave did not pay dearly enough for his crimes."

Sweet Jesu. This man knew my sins, my fall from grace. What else did Sir Francis know? Why, when I had brought so much shame to my family, was Papa conversing so freely about me with his friend? My father, who was so private, had not only confessed a physical frailty about which I knew nothing, but saw free to reveal my disgrace. If I couldn't trust Papa to keep my degradation to himself, then who?

Hot tears welled. I dashed them away, determined to see as well as hear what unfolded in the workshop.

Papa shook his head. "Regardless of *his* sins, Mallory committed her own and, truth be told, as much as I wish it were otherwise, she can no longer stay here. Not now evidence of that man's . . . *attentions* has faded. Valentina . . ." He gestured as if trying to conjure the words. "Valentina cannot find it in her heart to forgive—not yet. She does not know the full extent of what happened, all the humiliations Mallory suffered." He let out a long, wistful sigh. "I thought, seeing Mallory again, how frail, how damaged and changed, would make a difference . . ." He shrugged. "I was wrong. Her very presence arouses Valentina's spleen and the doctor, my own brother, tells us it will do naught but delay her recovery. I will not allow that. I cannot. From the moment Mallory . . . left, shunned the betrothal Valentina arranged—"

Sir Francis made a dismissive motion with his hand.

"She went into decline, a condition from which she'd only lately begun to improve. Mallory's presence is not . . ." Papa had the grace to appear ashamed. "Beneficial. I would it could be different, that I could keep her here beside me. That I did not have to seek your aid again."

Again? What did that mean?

Sir Francis nodded gravely. "It will take time for what happened to be wiped from people's memories, and for the stain to be cleansed from her soul."

"It pains me, but she must find work, Francis. And soon. As much for herself as anything." He glanced toward the window. "My apprentices tell me the neighbors call her Mistress Blight. My daughter, Francis. My daughter. I would spare her such knowledge."

Oh, Papa, I would have spared you such knowledge.

Papa clasped his hands and shook his head sorrowfully.

I wanted to pound on the door, to shout at Papa not to listen to the names others bestowed on me, to retract his words and make Mamma see reason, but I couldn't. With all that had occurred as a consequence of my disobedience, I'd lost that right. I *was* a blight. Mamma's malady *was* my fault. Perchance my employment in a respectable household would restore her health; would re-establish good opinion.

Leaning against the doorframe, I hung my head; anguish tightened in my chest. I'd not only humiliated my family, besmirched the Bright name and impaired my relationship with Papa (and any hope of reconciliation with Mamma), I'd ruined any chance of a decent marriage and a family of my own. In God's eyes and those of my parents and neighbors, I was more than a fallen woman—I was a scourge, the blight they labeled me. How far I'd fallen, only my widow's garb, the golden band Mamma insisted I wear upon my finger and the story of the fictitious cousin I'd hastily wed prevented others from learning the terrible secret I had to keep. I sought the solidness of my locket. The real extent of my sins I could share with no one, except Caleb.

Caleb alone knew and he loved and forgave me . . . Caleb alone . . .

It was fitting that Papa sought to place me elsewhere, concerned by what my presence was doing to Mamma. I should be grateful he didn't simply throw me on the streets. I'd heard stories of young women being disowned by their families, cast out with no more than the clothes upon their backs, left to make their way in this cruel world. At least my parents hadn't rejected me in such a manner. Would they, if they knew everything? I pressed my face against the door, uncaring that the wood would leave an impression upon my cheek. The men were silent. The rain drummed against the shutters and thrummed along my shoulders. A log split, and the sound caused one of the hounds to growl sharply. It seemed to prompt the men to action.

A stool slid across the floor. "Her skills are unusual," said Sir Francis, rising. "They may yet serve a purpose. I need time to think, to talk to those whose judgment I trust. Leave it with me, Gideon, I'll see what I can do."

Papa stood and clapped his hand on Sir Francis's shoulder. "Know you, Francis, this is most important. It may be Mallory's only chance. Find her a purpose. She has talents, beauty, too, for all she sees fit to disguise it. Place her somewhere, anywhere, give her a fresh start, restore her confidence and with that the opportunity to make the future she's denied herself. God's truth, she must be gone. The sooner the better—for us all."

In that moment, I was reduced to nothing more than a living reminder of my own folly and defiance. With Papa's words, the consequences of my reckless decision two years earlier were made painfully apparent. Eloping with Sir Raffe Shelton had cost me not just my home, my family, the esteem in which I'd once been held, my dreams and hopes, but something I thought as everlasting as the sun or moon—my father's regard. It was more than I could stand. Sorrow welled from my stomach, filled my chest, weighted my legs and arms and threatened to spill from my mouth. I clamped a hand across my lips lest it escape.

At that moment Sir Francis lifted his head and stared straight at the gap in the door with those unforgiving eyes. I jumped back, slipping in my haste. I began to shake. *Please God, don't let him discover me. Don't let him wrench the door open and find me trembling like a wet cat.*

I picked up my sodden skirts and bolted down the path, my pattens kicking up mud.

Uncaring of the torrents of rain, the cloak falling off my shoulders, the hat and gloves crushed in my hands, I ran to the back door, slowing only when the merry voices of the servants, the apprentices, the clank of tankards and the scrape of bowls, reminded me where I was, what I was doing. Our servants were part of the family from which I was to be excluded, the life I was to be denied—the life that, God's wounds, I'd denied myself. Along with Papa's words, the sounds combined to bring home to me the extent of the price I was still to pay. I paused, my hand pressed against the door, my breath ragged, my chest rising and falling.

Tilting my head back, I opened my mouth and with eyes screwed against the icy, hard drops that pummeled my flesh, cried soundlessly to the dark, savage skies above.

FOUR

*C*omposing myself, I removed my sodden cloak and stepped into the kitchen only to be swooped upon by our maid, Comfort. Muttering darkly, she failed to notice my swollen eyes and no doubt red nose—or if she did, saw them as a consequence of the cold and wet. Plucking the heavy garment from my numb fingers, she pushed me toward the hearth, admonishing me for the state of my clothes, much as she did when I was a child.

Squeezing past the long table in the center of the kitchen, I shot a look at Papa's four apprentices sitting on a bench against one wall, a set of pipe organs. Kit Jolebody was the eldest and tallest, his golden head and thin neck rising above Matt Culpeper's dark locks, while next to him was the brooding Samuel Blackstone. At the end of the bench was little Dickon. Catching my eye, he bestowed a reassuring toothy grin. With the exception of Dickon, I'd known them all for years and had even shared lessons with Kit and Matt. Only Dickon was new to me, replacing Benedict Thatcher, who, having finished his journeyman period, had left not long after I did to start his own business in the south.

Conversation ceased and one by one the young men lowered their

heads and gazed blankly into their tankards of ale and empty tren-
chers until Comfort reminded them of their manners and they chanted
a "God's good evening," which I returned. Despite a common childhood and many a game between books and slates, as I matured, our
open exchanges were replaced by sidelong glances, murmurs or studied
indifference. Since my return they were even more discomfited to be
sharing a space with me, a situation no doubt made worse by what
had happened to our maid, Nell, and all the gossip surrounding my
disappearance and her dismissal. When it was discovered that Nell had
passed notes between myself and Raffe, Mamma let her go without a
reference. I had never thought that Nell, who'd been with us since she
was twelve and I was six, should pay for my sins. Every time I passed the
room she used to share with Comfort, or set eyes upon her replacement,
Gracious, guilt would enter my chest and march around tirelessly.

"Gone home to Kent," Comfort shrugged when I found the courage to ask. "I've not had cause to think of her these past years," she
added. Nor had I, which just made the situation so much worse. How
had I been so unthinking, so selfish?

The young men were tense, waiting to see whether or not I would
join them. Though the pottage our cook, Mistress Pernel, had prepared before she went home smelled wonderful, I'd no appetite or
desire for company this night and no intention of ruining what
sounded like a convivial repast. I'd barely shared a meal with the
household since coming home. With her health poorly, Mamma had
made a point of eating in her rooms and so, in order to avoid any
accusation of taking sides in a dispute that remained undeclared but
which seasoned household relations the way salt does a stew, Papa had
his meals brought out to the workshop. With the master and mistress
disposed to eating in solitude, the large room in which we used to
dine remained empty and cold; the practical Comfort refused to light
a fire just for Caleb and me. Instead, once the marks upon my face
had healed, she insisted we eat in the kitchen, along with the servants
and apprentices. When Caleb was home, I didn't mind perching on
one of the benches and sharing dinner or supper, letting the conversation wash over me. It reminded me of easier times. But when Caleb
wasn't there to punctuate the meal with stories and laughter, to draw
me out of my desire to become invisible, discussion became stifled,

wary, nothing like the gatherings of my memories. Before long, I asked to dine upstairs in my room. The relief on Comfort's face when I made the request, never mind the faces of young Gracious and the apprentices, would have been comical if it wasn't also hurtful.

Now as I stood by the fire, my hands outstretched, I was aware of Matt and Kit exchanging cautious glances.

I put them out of their misery and said, "I'll not be needing supper tonight, Comfort. Do not trouble yourself on my behalf." If I thought the audible sigh of relief from Dickon was my imagination, the cuff across the back of his head from Comfort confirmed my ears had not been deceived. Entering the kitchen from the scullery just as I spoke, Gracious almost dropped the basin of water she was carrying. Bobbing a curtsey, she lowered her eyes and hurried through the room. Matt snickered while Comfort simply shook her head and regarded me with narrowed but kindly eyes.

"There's pork and wild onions in it." She nodded toward the bubbling pot, trying to persuade me to change my mind. "And a fresh manchet to sop it up as well." She indicated the platter of sliced bread in the center of the table.

"My thanks, but I've no appetite." *Not for food.* "The excursion to the theater has all but exhausted me." I forced a smile. "I'll go to bed."

Comfort bestowed one of her looks that swept my entire frame and told me as loudly as if she'd shouted it what she thought not only of my attending the theater but also my refusal to eat when I was already "like a desiccated scarecrow, fit only for the pyre." I found myself strangely calmed. It demonstrated that, despite everything, she cared—not that her tone revealed this.

"Whatever mistress says," she said tersely, forcing Kit and Matt to sidle up the bench as she draped my cloak over the end, spreading the hem over the flagstones, and placed my hat and gloves nearby. "Though if you're to be venturing out more often now, it's sustenance you'll be needing."

Comfort had been urging me for weeks to summon the courage to leave the house and step back into the world. Until today, I hadn't heeded anyone's entreaties. What I'd overheard in the workshop indicated I'd soon have no choice. The thought made me sick to the stomach.

I bade the room a good night and left. Gracious reappeared

from where she'd been waiting outside and the buzz of conversation resumed. Confused and heartsore, I needed to think about what I'd heard, what Papa and Sir Francis had said—and not just about the prospect of employment.

Thus far, I'd been able to hide the way I felt about Mamma's indifference in the misplaced belief that Papa at least was partial to my return. After all, hadn't he rescued me? Hadn't he traveled the length of the country to retrieve me? Wept when he saw the condition I was in, the circumstances to which I'd been reduced? Hadn't he paid for the silence of the women who'd been forced to care for me? Yet his words to Sir Francis tolled in my head: *"She must be gone. The sooner the better—for us all."* They wormed their cruel way into my heart and splintered it painfully, exposing the reality of my situation: I no longer had a home.

Ascending the stairs to the first landing, I paused outside my mother's room and discerned Angela's muffled voice describing our day. I raised my hand to knock. Though Papa had asked me to pass on a message, and I'd mother's blessing to seek before retiring, I could not. Not this night. Requesting, let alone receiving what was insincerely given would be my undoing. Lowering my hand, I stood still. Ever since I'd been home, Mamma's manner toward me had further cooled, as if her emotions were contingent on the seasons and my presence presaged winter. Thus far I'd been able to pretend her attitude didn't nip at my soul like an icy wind. I'd not manage such mummery tonight.

Standing in the frigid hall, I recalled my reunion with Mamma. It was seven weeks since I'd returned, yet the painful emotions the memory evoked were still fresh. I did not need to add to my burdens this night. I passed by Mamma's door, guilt weighing every step.

The candle I carried almost went out as drafts swept across the staircase. Whereas I used to sleep on the same floor as my parents, since her illness my room had been given to Mamma to use as another parlor so she could entertain upstairs. My new room, though a corridor away from where the apprentices shared theirs, was a tiny space in the loft. The cold was bitter there, the walls and thatch inadequate to prevent its stealthy entry. My breath came in a fine mist as I climbed the dark, narrow steps.

I ducked under the lintel into my bedroom and shivered in the chill.

As I closed the door I savored the welcome darkness, the demonic shadows the candle threw against the bare walls. Listening to the howl of the wind, the lashing rain and the low rumble of thunder, I shut my eyes briefly and wondered how Caleb fared, if he'd avoided the worst of the weather. I imagined him carousing with his troupe, enjoying the attentions of his new patron, who could not help but be pleased with Caleb's efforts this day—both his words and his performance of them. A smile tugged my lips. Rain would not douse his spirits, no matter how heavy or how long it fell.

If only Caleb were here so I might seek his counsel. But he was not. I trimmed the wicks and lit two more candles—one in a sconce above the narrow bed, the other in an iron holder atop the battered chest tucked under the window. Kneeling by the hearth, I stacked some kindling, my hands shaking. The timber was dry and it wasn't long before the wood took and the pleasant glow of the fire illuminated the room. I eased myself up, noting with delight that my knees didn't hurt anymore and the dull ache banding my back had all but gone. Depositing the candle on the mantelpiece and spreading my hands toward the flames, I glanced toward the window. Rain cascaded down the frigid glass. One of the shutters had blown open. No servant tended this room. Gripping the window frame as lightning divided the heavens, I looked down upon the workshop. Blurred stars of light glimmered in the gaps in the wood. The evening already felt like a dream. Had I really opened that casket? Had I actually met Sir Francis Walsingham? Papa was either still conversing with his guest or biding his time before telling Mamma his plans.

What would she say? I could not imagine she would be anything but glad. Papa left me in no doubt as to how he felt.

She must be gone . . .

Running my fingers through a tangle of wet hair, lost in dark thoughts, I didn't hear the door open. It was only when a pair of plump arms slipped around my waist and the familiar smell of the flower Our Lady's Modesty assailed me, I knew who'd entered. I pressed my head against the soft body and relished the solace it offered.

"I heard your step outside your mamma's room."

"Ah. I believe the angels and their envoys themselves would not get past you, Angela."

She chuckled softly. "What did your papa want, *bella*? Is everything all right? You never came to see your mamma, to receive her blessing. She was worried." There was a mild rebuke in her tone; I knew who had been anxious.

I pulled away, a wry expression upon my face.

"Despite what you think, she does care, *bella*." Angela's voice was husky and sad. She hated that her cousin and dearest friend and the child she'd helped raise were always at odds—especially now. "May God forgive her, she just has difficulty showing you."

"I know." Why I said that when I wasn't certain, I'm not sure. Perhaps I needed to believe it.

Angela kissed the top of my head. "I've said this to you before, but you broke her heart when you left. Her greatest fear came to pass. She . . . she thought she'd lost you forever."

"I know," I repeated, my voice harsh this time as I tried not to dwell on the idea that Angela was mistaken and that such a possibility would only please my mother. "But she did not. And the moment I returned she wished me gone. You were there, Angela. You heard her. That I am still here offers her naught but constant unhappiness." I picked up the poker and began prodding the fire, which had all but gone out, sending sparks up the chimney. Smoke billowed into the room.

"It's not only her heart that's broken," I whispered, sealing my mouth against words that should never escape. Between coughs, I blew upon the wood, ceasing only when the crackle of flames announced the fire had taken again. I took a log from the pyramid next to the mantelpiece, heaved it atop the embers and clapped my hands to rid them of detritus. I stepped away, my face hot, my soul sore. I reached for a drying sheet and began to towel my hair.

"*Bella*, what is it? Tell me," said Angela, taking the sheet from my hands and tending to the wet strands of hair. Her kindness undid me. The tears I'd thought vanquished welled once more.

Angela tried to fold me in her arms again, but I held up a hand so she could not. "Don't hold me, Angela. I don't think I could bear it."

"Mallory?" She let her arms drop and, sitting on the bed, patted the worn coverlet beside her. "*Dimmi.*"

Tentatively, I joined her. I would talk this time—to Angela. Taking a deep breath, I began.

"I learned tonight Papa also wants me gone—the sooner the better."

"Learned?" She gently tugged a lock of hair. "Ah, you were listening where you should not again, weren't you?"

I nodded miserably, hiccoughing as a cry rose in my throat. Angela renewed her attentions to my hair, the combination of ruffling and smoothing strangely comforting.

"Is it possible you didn't hear aright?"

"I wish it were so. He has even deployed a powerful friend to help find me a position—and swiftly." My head fell into my hands. "Oh, Angela, I never foresaw a time when they'd be so accustomed to my absence that Papa and Mamma would wish me away from their sight altogether."

With a cluck that managed to express sympathy and regret, Angela put down the sheet and pulled me toward her, her lips against my hair.

"You gave them no choice, *bambina*. You left when they did not wish you gone, and with that . . . that man. And now . . . now they have no choice but to let you go again."

"No choice?"

"You left this house a child, now you're a woman grown. Twenty-one and a widow." I didn't contradict her. "You cannot remain beneath your father's roof, not anymore. You made your way in the world once, it would look strange, unseemly, if you did not do so again. As if you were hiding something . . ." She paused. Waited. I didn't utter a sound. "People will talk."

As if they hadn't already.

"This is about appearances, then? About what others will think? What they'll say?"

Angela gave a gentle laugh. "Is it not always? You heard Isaac Hattycliffe. Your papa and your mamma seek to protect your reputation, not to damage it further—"

"You mean no more than I have already."

Angela nodded. She would not insult me with platitudes. "They also seek to protect their own, and for that I cannot blame them. It was not easy for them. They had to work hard to placate those who were . . . offended by what you did. Some clients took their work elsewhere. Gideon found it hard to replace Benedict when he left. Dickon was not your papa's first choice, nor his second. They had to rebuild trust."

A whimper escaped me. Angela tightened her hold. Acting on a whim, I hadn't given my parents a choice then and now they had none either. I had disobeyed their express commands. Left without their blessing, without so much as a fare-thee-well. At the age of nineteen, a besotted innocent, I thought I knew better; that my choice of husband far surpassed Mamma's. How could a mere weaver's son compare, regardless of his prospects? Like the stories I so loved, I imagined the day would come when I'd invite my parents to my manor house as Lady Mallory, the elegant and respected wife of Sir Raffe. I believed my choice would make Papa proud and Mamma more so.

In that, and in so many other things, I'd been grossly mistaken.

From the moment Sir Raffe first encountered me, he played me for the callow girl I was. Fed me flattery and stoked my outrageous dreams with even bigger promises. Had he ever loved me? God knows, I thought I loved him.

Bottled up, not simply for the weeks I'd been home but, as God Himself knew, almost every day since I'd left, I cried the tears I'd denied myself. I wept for my lost innocence, for the pain and humiliation I'd endured, the hurt inflicted on my parents, the apologies and regrets that failed to compensate for my actions, for the lives forever altered, for those lost, and in weeping I found a kind of release. As the rain raged against the glass and the wind screeched through the gaps in the walls, I held Angela and cried my own torrent. Through it all, she held me in her arms, rocking me, dropping light kisses on my brow, my hair, stroking the tendrils from my face where they clung to my sticky cheeks.

I'm not certain how long my lamentation lasted, only that when it subsided, the fire had once more begun to shrink and the candles were lower. Even the rain had subsided to a steady trickle that promised a better morrow.

"One day, you will look back upon all this and wonder it had the power to torment you so," Angela said softly.

I sniffed and shook my head. Angela did not know. "I cannot begin to imagine what would ever induce me to forget."

Angela gave me a squeeze. "There's only one thing that has such power. *Amore, bella. Amore.* What else? Does not love conquer all?"

I choked and pulled away from Angela's embrace. "Love? Oh, Angela, love was what caused all my troubles in the first place." I shook my head dismally. "I've given up on love."

"Such a nonsense you speak," said Angela, tweaking my nose. "One does not give up on love."

"I do. It's nothing but a torment, it causes nothing but pain. The poets and troubadours describe it as a madness, and they're right. 'Falling in love,' they say. Tumbling into the abyss, more like. What happens when one falls but injury? I'm injured beyond all repair." I blew my nose on a kerchief Angela passed me.

"Ah, but love's arrow is a wound that heals all others, even as it makes another."

I gave a bark of laughter. "Love's arrow will sail over my head before it lodges in my heart." I wriggled away from her, pulling at my kirtle, the laces of my bodice. "Of that I'll make certain. I will duck." I imitated the action.

Much to my chagrin, Angela began to laugh.

I tried to ignore her chuckles but failed and laughed with her. I stared into the fireplace, placing one hand on my heart, the other on my stomach. My smile vanished. I'd been such a fool because of my heart, taken such a risk, destroyed lives. I would not be led by it again. It was too dangerous. If I had a choice, I would rip it from my body and throw it upon the flames like an offering of the ancients. Watch it sizzle and blacken until it was nothing but ash. The thought was oddly cathartic; if it was within my ken to do such a thing and live, I would. I put my thoughts into words.

"It would be much better"—I dried my eyes upon the kerchief—"not to have a heart for Cupid's arrows to strike in the first place."

"Alas," said Angela. "We all have a heart."

"Not me. Not anymore." I spun around to face her, slapping my breast. "I no longer have one."

She gave a gurgle of mirth. "You're no conjurer to magic it away. And why would you wish such a thing anyhow?" Joining me by the fire, Angela took the kerchief from my hand and flapped it toward my face to prevent my answer. "Of course you feel that way now, because it's drained of any emotion except sorrow. One day it will be ready for love again. Like your body and mind, it too needs to heal."

But the wound I'd sustained could never be repaired. Angela didn't understand, could not. No one could. I would not let them.

Stepping closer, Angela lowered her voice. "Not all men are knaves, *bella*. There will come a day where you will meet one who will make you forget the past, forget what pain you endured. Who will show you what love truly is."

It never occurred to me then to ask Angela how she could possibly know such a thing. In the fireplace scintillas of golden sparks latched onto the wood, turning into undulating flames. As I watched them, my mind wandered. The heart I denied possessing beat strangely as my thoughts turned to Sir Raffe, the man who, with his handsome face, head of flaxen curls, pretty turn of phrase and passionate kisses, had spun my heart and my head.

I glanced at the book sitting open upon the chest, Castiglione's *The Book of the Courtier*. It had been a favorite of Master Fodrake's and mine and was also one of Caleb's. Ostensibly about excellence and moral integrity and how to achieve this as a courtier, even if the king you served was a tyrant, it urged a gentleman to seem indifferent to the very thing he pursued—perfection. While written for men of a certain rank, I wondered: what if a woman was to do the same? What if a woman was to aim to be the best in all things, but without appearing to try? Didn't women do this often? Appear unaffected by events and those around them? Mamma and Angela used to speak of married women of their acquaintance and how they suffered their husbands, their lot in life, presenting a calm and even grateful face to the world, never revealing their true feelings. Then there was our neighbor, Dorothy Lamborn, who loved her husband so much that when he died of the sweating sickness she refused to rail and mourn, to hide herself away until such time as she could face the world again. She told Mamma that would dishonor her husband and their love. Instead, she went about her business as if naught was amiss, keeping her tears and sorrow inside. People talked, of course they did, but Mamma said she understood. Castiglione called such a thing *mediocrita*—a careful balance of opposites. Could I do that? Seek not to love or hate but to be content in a state somewhere between? According to Caleb, I'd no small talent for acting. Could the world be my stage?

I thought of Sir Francis and Papa down in the workshop. Couldn't

I, using the tools others provided—a job, shelter, wages, and all the learning Papa had ensured I received—mold myself into a different person? One for whom the ruinous past was not inevitably the scaffolding upon which my destiny would be built? Truth was, if I didn't do something, change the way I felt, the way others spoke of me, then Raffe, along with his lies and his malice and the dark road he had forced me down, would be the victor—even in his absence, he would govern my life. This must not be.

It didn't occur to me then to wonder why Mamma had spoken so freely of those women who hid their real feelings from others. It would be a long, long time before I learned why—and the knowledge would tear at the heart I sought to deny.

The rain beat against the glass as the fire warmed my face. Images of Papa hammering molten metal, the sparks flying about the workshop, filled my head. I was a piece of metal to be fashioned into a new shape. *Mediocrita*, the courtier's studied insouciance, would be my means.

Wiping my face, I gave Angela a tremulous smile. "You're wrong, Angela. I won't ever forget the past, but I won't let it dictate my future. I won't let it shape who I become."

I studied my left hand, the slim band of gold glinting in the firelight. Mamma had given me both a ring and a character: the grieving widow. Papa had urged a fresh start and sought the aid of an old friend.

I stared at the fire. Didn't the flames roar anew each time the hearth was swept and the wood stacked? I shut my eyes. The light continued to dance against my eyelids, certain, merry, strong. I was a Bright.

From this day forth, I would be Mallory Bright: the woman with a past and a future as well. There was equilibrium in that. There was *mediocrita*. And I would be a woman without a heart.

As if to contradict me, my heart beat beneath my locket. My fingers closed around the warm metal. But being without a heart didn't resonate with how I felt or with Castiglione's advice. Rather, I must be the woman who refused to reveal her heart, to show passion—toward anything.

Opening my eyes, I retrieved the kerchief from Angela and gave my nose a final, defiant blow. There'd be no more tears. From this night forward, I was done with those as well.

FIVE

As I sat in the parlor the following morning and watched the gray dawn cede to a cold, sunless day, the events of the night before crowded my head, thwarting any attempt to read and forcing me to recognize that governing my emotions was easier said than done. It would require much practice. Curled in what was known as Mamma's chair, Ovid's poetry open in my lap, the pages unturned. The fire crackled in the hearth, light refracting off the ewer and small cup of ale sitting on the table in front of me. A scattering of empty chairs and stools as well as low tables, some with pretty objects upon them, filled the space. Lavender had been sprinkled through the fresh rushes, giving the room a sweet perfume. Tapestries I'd gazed upon my whole life adorned the walls, a little more frayed and faded than in my recollections. I'd spent many cold and lonely nights over the past couple of years trying to recall each and every scene, every last thread, as well as conversations and meals that had taken place in their presence in order to transport myself back home again when the possibility of return seemed all but gone. Forcing myself to cease that line of thought, I listened to the sounds of the house. Wind rattled the shutters and shook the panes. Above me, floorboards creaked as Angela, Mamma or the servants moved about the rooms. Beyond the parlor, doors opened and closed, feet shuffled across rushes, voices rose and fell. Outside, bells rang, criers could be heard and the faint groan of wheels on cobbles could just be distinguished.

The conversation I'd overheard between Papa and Sir Francis played over in my head, and my anxiety ebbed and flowed. How did Papa know this man? To whom did the *forziere* with the deadly lock belong? What would happen to that person now the contents were discovered? Recalling Sir Francis's somber appearance, I shuddered. Why had Papa asked Mister Secretary for help? And in what other matters had he asked for assistance?

So many questions without answers, except those crafted by my wild imaginings. One thing above all tormented me. How could I not have noticed Papa's failing eyesight? There'd been no hint, no sign when he found me. Thinking back, we'd barely spoken on our journey home. Ashamed, I couldn't look at him or, when I did, it was only to turn away again lest he read what I tried to hide. The trip had taken days and during that time there'd been moments when Papa had mistaken a shadow for a beast, a distant plume of smoke for clouds. I'd thought nothing of it. Then there'd been that night at the inn near Nottingham where he'd missed a step and fallen to his knees, blaming it on the wine he'd consumed. Wrapped up in a mixture of remorse, relief and fear my secret would be discovered, I'd not heeded these things, accepting Papa's explanations when all the time he was concealing his condition. No wonder he'd asked me to unpick the lock for Sir Francis. Guilt consumed me. If I'd been at home, perchance Papa wouldn't be in this predicament. If he hadn't been so keen to express his disapproval by banishing me from the workshop, I could have helped, taken on extra duties; or ensured the apprentices did so, at least.

If I'd never left, he wouldn't have had to strain his eyes so much. Papa's poor vision was likely my fault, another sin to add to my growing inventory.

There was no help for it, I would have to persuade Papa to let Uncle Timothy examine him and see if anything could be done. Why, a pair of spectacles might help. The possibility Papa might also change his mind and keep me by his side was too delicate a notion to properly examine. I let it rest—for now.

I flipped a page, and the parlor door flew open. In tripped Caleb, sweeping an elaborate bow before throwing a sheaf of papers onto the table and casting himself into the chair opposite.

"How goes it, sweet lady?" he said and reached for the ewer. Without asking, he topped up my cup and downed the contents in a few swallows, releasing a satisfied sigh before refilling it.

"Better than you, I'd say," I said, removing my hand from my heart, which had leaped at his entry. "How were the celebrations last night? Was your new patron happy with the production? What time did you get in?" I closed my book. There was no point even pretending to read now.

"Pray, when did you become such a shrew? The sun has barely risen. Cease, my lady, and let this gentleman, who has only just crossed the threshold, rest his folly-fallen head with easeful silence and this medicinal—" He raised the cup to his lips once again.

"Is that not the cause of your affliction, sir?" I asked wryly, pointing at the cup. Caleb looked worse for wear. His eyes were red, his skin sallow and his attire appeared slept in. The smell of taprooms, beer, smoke and other odors wafted from him. I screwed up my nose.

Seeing my expression, Caleb brought his sleeve to his nostrils. "Ugh. I reek worse than a tanner's jakes. I blame Lord Nate, whom I rename the devil incarnate. He made me do it."

"Ah, your new patron," I said and gestured for him to return my cup.

"Aye." Caleb tossed back the remainder of the drink and gave the vessel over. I refilled it and sipped slowly. "Sweet Jesu," he continued. "The man is a libertine. First he gave me malmsey, then sack. I believe there was beer as well, before he persuaded me to drink a philter or two. Then he had the courtesy to abandon me for a pretty wench."

I raised my brows.

He chuckled before groaning and holding his head. If Mamma or Papa ever heard how Caleb spoke to me, they'd disapprove. I enjoyed the details to which no lady should be privy. It was a mark of our friendship, of the easy yet fond regard in which we held each other. He was the brother I never had, the friend and confidant I so sorely needed.

For certes, Caleb was taken with this Lord Nathaniel Warham. He might dub him the devil this day, but he'd also called him "dashing," "clever," and after his lordship purchased the rights to form an acting company and appointed Caleb a shareholder, actor and chief writer, he called him "a man of great taste" who had a story for every occasion. Unlike most nobles who gave their name, protection and funds to theater companies but little else, Lord Nathaniel watched every performance, attended rehearsals and made suggestions for improvements which Caleb, uncharacteristically, accepted with goodwill. Nor was the lord above drinking with the men—as the events of last night testified. Caleb said he'd even been to Lord Nathaniel's houses— a grand manor not far from St. Paul's and an estate upriver from Hampton Court. I hoped to meet this paragon one day, but with the possibility of my departure looming, I might be gone before the chance presented itself.

"A groat for your thoughts," said Caleb from the hearth.

"Only a groat?"

"If they're worth more, I'll give a fair price."

I half-smiled then frowned.

"What is it, Mallory?" Caleb crossed the room in two strides, drew up a chair and reached for my hands, holding them loosely in his own. "Is it your mother again? What has she said?" I shushed him, glancing nervously at the door. "Have you been weeping? You have, haven't you? Has someone offended you? You were safe walking home yester eve? Is it those dreams again? You have to stop holding yourself accountable. You must seek me out if you're distressed." Questions and injunctions poured out of him. I shook my head, trying to get a word in.

"No. No. Aye. It's none of those things. I know you care for me and I give thanks. But please, Caleb, no sympathy, not today. I prefer your scandalous tales. Show me kindness and, as I told Angela, the dam inside me may well break again." I drew a jittery breath, fighting for control.

Releasing my hands, Caleb sat back and adopted the voice of one of his characters, Master Toby Scrofula. "Very well. Hold nothing, vixen. Tell me all. What ails thee?"

I bit back a smile. God, I would miss Caleb. "Turns out, you're not the only one who might be leaving—the house, if not the town. Only

I fear my absence, unlike your tour of the shires, may be more than temporary."

I quickly filled him in on what had happened when I arrived home last night. When I said Sir Francis's name, Caleb let out a long whistle.

"Mister Secretary! Here?" His eyes widened as I confirmed it. "Why?"

I confessed how I'd lingered outside and listened to their conversation.

Caleb sank back further into the chair, his fingers gripping the arms. "So, Mister Secretary Walsingham, the Queen's spymaster, is your father's 'old friend.' Zounds. I wonder what that means? How do they know each other?" His eyes took on a familiar faraway look. "It's well known Sir Francis left England when Bloody Mary came to power, returning only when Her Majesty took the throne. So did your father. It's entirely possible they knew each other in exile."

"Papa has never made mention . . . not one word."

"You could ask your mother . . ." began Caleb, before catching the look on my face and pressing his lips together. "All right . . . perchance not. Still, how intriguing. I wonder what work, if any, he'll find for you? I wonder where you'll go? I know." He sat upright and pointed at me. "You'll be given to a diplomat in the Spanish embassy who'll fall for your Romany beauty and beg you to marry him."

A small noise of disgust escaped me.

"I'm allowed to dream," protested Caleb. "Especially since you stubbornly refuse to and insist on appearing like a drab. You may think you hide your beauty by dressing in such a manner, concealing your face and refusing to smile and shine in conversation like you used to. One has only to look beyond the dreary exterior and see the treasure sparkling beneath." He waited to see if I'd respond, and when I did not, he reached over and grasped my fingers. "You'll not bring him back by denying yourself, you know."

Oh, I knew.

Kissing the back of my hand, he released it and lifted the papers he'd brought into his lap and began to straighten them.

"He has daughters, Sir Francis." He scratched his head. "Some stepsons, too, though I believe there was a terrible accident. An explosion if I'm not mistaken . . ." He shuddered. "There was something about the younger daughter as well . . ." Caleb paused and examined his finger-nails. "I forget. No doubt he needs a governess. Imagine that: Mistress Mallory, Keeper of Mister Secretary's Children." He gave a bark of laughter. I returned a dry smile. "You might find yourself working for the most feared man in the realm."

"And angels will descend to dance for my pleasure and you might find yourself a respectable woman."

Caleb met my eyes, his twinkling. We burst into laughter.

Wiping his eyes, Caleb passed me a sheaf of paper. "So happens, I have work for you. I need to con lines for tomorrow's performance. Can you help?" Before I could answer, he went on. "I managed to convince Master David, our new book holder (if ever a man was born to hold the book, it's Master David), to loan me his copy of the play as well as the sheets with my lines." He waved the pages he was holding. "He told me if anything happened to that"—he pointed to my lap—"he'd cut my balls off and fling them into the bear pit. I'm not ready to be a eunuch and not pretty enough to play the woman's part, so watch what you do with those, my sweet lady."

I carefully perused what Caleb had given me. Covered in neat script from which lines, arrows and scrawled amendments blossomed in the margins, it was Sackville and Norton's popular tragedy *Gorboduc*. Familiar to Londoners, it told the story of two princes who, after their father divided his realm, fought over their share, setting off a chain of catastrophic consequences. With no single heir, there was bloodshed aplenty, families torn apart, misery, war and love. In other words, it was a marvelous story that captured the audience's imagination and spoke to the times. After all, our Queen had refused to either produce an heir or name a successor.

"Knowing your manhood is in my hands," I responded carefully, not daring to look at him, "I'll protect these pages accordingly."

Caleb gave an amused snort.

"I'm surprised you haven't performed *Gorboduc* before. It's just the type of work you like, agitates political sensibilities."

"Oh, I have. A few times in your absence. Though not with Lord Warham's Men, and only in minor roles." There was an uncomfortable silence. With false gaiety, he continued, leaning over and trailing his finger down the first page. "If you could read all the parts with the exception of the King's and the Chorus," said Caleb, getting down to business.

Glad for the distraction, I took another sip of ale and settled into the chair. The pleasure I took from pretending to be someone else was greater now than it had ever been, and I launched myself into the various roles with gusto, rising from the chair and moving around the room as appropriate, adopting diverse postures and voices. Lost in the world Norton and Sackville had created, I could be anyone but myself.

Absorbed in what we were doing, time flew. As we were about to start a third read-through, this time with Caleb attempting to recall his lines without looking at the script, he went to throw more wood on the fire while I refreshed our drinks.

"Gideon!" exclaimed Caleb.

I spun around. Standing in the doorway was Papa. How long he'd been there, I was uncertain.

Caleb dusted his hands and stood up, touching his bonnet. "God give you good day, sir. We didn't hear you."

Bestowing a warm smile, Papa shut the door and approached the fire. "Nothing to forgive." He patted Caleb on the back. "I was enjoying listening to you both. It's an excellent play. God give you good day, Mallory." He kissed my cheek.

"You too, Papa." I tried to examine his eyes in the daylight, but he turned his face away.

"When and where are you performing it?" asked Papa, moving to the table and bending over as if reading the sheets.

"Inn of Temple Courts on the morrow," said Caleb. "We rehearse from dawn," he sighed. "We intended to practice today, but I'm afraid the festivities of last night went longer than they should, so we decided to put an extra effort in tomorrow."

"Ah, yes, *Circe's Chains*," said Papa. "Angela said it went well."

Caleb glanced in my direction, his lips twisting slightly. I pulled an apologetic face. There hadn't been the chance to tell Papa about the play. Caleb knew that. Still, his voice had a slight chill when he replied.

"Better than I'd hoped. Can I be of service, Gideon?" he asked, pouring a drink and passing it to Papa.

Taking the cup and raising it by way of thanks, Papa took a sip. "Not you, Caleb. It's Mallory I need."

Caleb's astonishment matched my own and he turned slowly aside.

I kept my voice calm, calling on my resolve to be controlled. "How may I be of service?"

Papa flexed his fingers, finding them suddenly very interesting. "A locked chest has just been delivered—the workings are curious and I thought you might like to see them." He raised his face and for the first time since I'd returned, I was able to see his eyes clearly. Though the late afternoon sun struck his cheek, casting part of his face into shadow, it was evident his once shining chestnut eyes were dulled. A milky film had grown across one. Aware of my scrutiny, Papa blinked and lowered his head. "I believe it's Flemish, but I would like your view."

"Does it need unlocking?"

Papa nodded. "The key was lost in the crossing."

"Then let's open it and make a new one."

Papa slid the cup into Caleb's hand and turned to the door. "Caleb," he said gruffly by way of farewell, "I'll not keep her long."

Caleb casually dismissed me with a wave of his hand and mouthed *Go, go.* "I will return anon, your majesty," I said, dropping a small curtsey, allowing Caleb to see my delight before regaining my composure.

"And I will await your return, my subject," he said with a straight-faced bow behind Papa's back, raising his hand in a signal of solidarity.

Without another word I followed Papa, my feet barely touching the floor. Perchance Papa's loss of sight would work in my favor and, instead of sending me away, he would keep me by his side and allow me to be his eyes.

And if dreams were locks, we'd all possess keys.

SIX

*T*he chest and its numerous locks were not particularly interesting. Nor was the design Flemish but Spanish. A spring-loaded flap hid the main keyhole that was raised by pressing a trigger at the side of the chest. Once exposed, it was evident any well-made master key would open this lock and likely the others. Papa would have known this.

He stood by my side, silent, his breathing heavy. I wanted so badly to question him regarding his sight, Sir Francis, to plead with him to let me stay. Once I wouldn't have thought twice about posing such questions—or questions about anything. Artlessly, I could shock Papa with my queries, which ranged from why Plato had Socrates banish poets from his Republic, to why Mistress Shoemaker, the mercer's wife, had died while her child lived. Whereas Mamma would sometimes strike my cheek, appalled by my temerity, Papa would take it all in his stride and answer honestly and in detail. Thus I learned that Plato believed poetry excited the parts of the soul that steered a person away from rational thought and behavior. Poets fired the imagination, dealt in untruths and pretended to knowledge they did not and should not possess. When I said I wanted to be a poet, Papa laughed and said, "Don't we all." As for Mistress Shoemaker, Papa took his time to answer and when he did, it was in the kind of voice reserved for church and Sundays. He said, "Sometimes God calls mothers to His side," and that we shouldn't see it as a tragedy so much as a blessing because they were at peace with the Lord. "But what about the baby?" I insisted. "If going to God is a blessing, then why wasn't the baby, who is without sin, taken too?"

Papa stared at me and, instead of answering, folded me in a crushing hug.

When I'd asked Mamma this question, she hit me so hard I fell against the furniture. My curiosity sent her into a flood of sobbing that lasted for days. Angela later explained that Mamma had thought I was referring to the babies she had lost and why she had outlived them all. I would never, ever have dreamed of asking the question if I'd thought Mamma would interpret it in such a manner. But my apologies fell on deaf and hostile ears.

Why was life so contradictory? Why were people? I wished for the hundredth time they could be placed in chests protected by locks that were only opened to fulfill a particular purpose. How much easier everything would be. Instead, we human beings were all jumbled together like a washerwoman's laundry, impossible to separate, the dyes often running from one into the other, sometimes staining indelibly.

As I raised the pins in the lock one by one, wedging them in place with another piece of thin metal, the other tumblers clicked and the lid opened. I stood back as Papa lifted it, squinting slightly, sighing and grinding a knuckle into one eye. I opened my mouth to speak, then closed it again. The comfort of being able to discuss anything with my father, the closeness we'd once shared, was no longer available. I had to respect that. He would reveal his malady to me in his own time.

Much to my surprise, though I'd completed the task he'd given me, Papa didn't ask me to leave. Instead, he gave me a couple of keys to file, and I made no effort to hide my delight. Thus I passed the last hour or so of daylight in the position I'd once occupied every afternoon: by my father's side. In another part of the workshop, Kit tinkered with his master lock, while Matt and Samuel hammered freshly forged metal and Dickon was set to sweeping. Aware of their curious eyes, I bent to my task, basking in my father's approval. I would not risk spoiling that for anything, not even to confirm what I was now certain was true—that Papa was losing his sight.

That afternoon set the pattern for the following weeks. I spent my waking hours between the parlor and the workshop, my routine broken only by another trip to the theater (Caleb was brilliant as Gorboduc, though I thought his writing far superior to that of Sackville and Norton and told him so). Papa had me testing his locks and opening those of customers who'd either lost or damaged their keys. Twice I was summoned back to the workshop after dark and given much more complex locks to open. One evening it was a great sea chest that took up much of the space in front of Papa's workbench. I labored over it with my back pressed against a table. Another night, a leather cylinder containing rolled documents awaited my tools. Secured by multiple locks, it only required one to be unfastened to open the entirety. Problem was, if the wrong one was chosen, the cylinder would remain locked. Once I tripped the ward in the second lock, the rest unfastened. It was then I discovered that if the cylinder had been tampered with in any other way, a type of fluid that ate parchment (and potentially fingers) would have been released. Removing the sac of acid with the utmost care, I passed it to Papa, who took it outside for disposal. A man I'd never seen before and who, despite Papa's protestations that he should wait in the shop, insisted on remaining by my side while I opened both the chest and, a week later, the cylinder, took the items away (the chest with the help of hired men) before I could see the contents. Somehow, I knew these things had been opened for Sir Francis. The locks were not English; the chest had traveled far, and apart from the scratches on the wood and the battered iron bands ringing it, smelled of not just the sea, but of adventures and danger as well. The cylinder was more sinister still. Along with the complicated locking mechanism, it was carved with strange markings. When I asked Papa if we were opening them at Sir Francis's behest, he neither confirmed nor denied it. I wondered if the man observing would report to his master who was responsible for unlocking the items. For the sake of Papa's pride and reputation, I hoped not.

Lulled into a false sense of security, allowing memories of Sir Francis

and Papa's request to recede, my days fell into a rhythm. As we spent
more time together, Papa and I began to repair our tattered relationship. It wasn't that we exchanged words or discussed what had happened, it was more that the silences became shared blankets in which
we wrapped ourselves, content, able to predict each other's needs, just
as we had of old. Even the apprentices began to grow accustomed to
my presence and would forget I was there and talk openly. I made no
mention to Mamma of what I was doing. I knew she would disapprove. The way she maintained her distance when I greeted her every
morn and asked for her blessing each evening, I believed her ignorant
of the new arrangement.

The churning river slowed as ice clogged its currents and Christmastide approached. The house transformed, adorned in a kirtle of bay,
rosemary, ivy and holly, their perfumes mingled with wood smoke and
cinnamon from the kitchen. Carolers strolled the darkening streets,
their candles guttering in the wind, their lanterns steady. Evenings
became more companionable as Yuletide approached, replacing the
urgency of working shortened days and the effect of this upon business. Everything moved at a different pace, like the lazy motion of cogs
in a clock winding down. Legs of mutton and pork were delivered,
as were extra ale, wine and spices so Mistress Pernel could work her
magic. When Master Gib, our general help about the house, couldn't
be found, one had only to look in the kitchen, where he often sat sam-
pling his wife's brawn and pies. Likewise any of the apprentices, sent
on an errand, would often amble back via the kitchen, lingering by the
door hoping for a taste. It was so achingly familiar. Even Mamma's
indifference to preparations didn't have the power to dull the occasion
as it once did. Memories crowded my mind. Music, feasting, dancing,
singing, all of us cramming into church, blessing the neighbors, and
the sharing of wassails. There had been some good times over the years.

There had also been Mamma. I recalled her disregard for the
lovely lock and intricate, delicate key I'd so carefully designed and
Papa had crafted the Christmas before I left. Her disdain for my
efforts still stung. How she always turned her cheek as I stooped to

kiss her, muttering a halfhearted blessing. How she had excluded my name from her wassail, completely unaware of her omission until Papa sought to make good her mistake. Only, it was no mistake and all present knew . . . I'd simply fixed a smile to my lips and pretended the ache that plowed my chest wasn't there. The relief I felt when Mamma pleaded a megrim and retired to her room before the dancing was unbecoming in a child, and the resultant guilt staunched any joy I felt from her absence.

Then there were the two Christmases I spent with Raffe. Those memories were buried deep and I refused to allow them to surface. I was home. It was Yuletide.

Despite rumors of Catholic plots and King Philip of Spain planning a vast enterprise against the realm, especially now Portugal was within his grasp, the new year started peacefully. Within our household, murmurs of papists, recusants and those who would harm our sovereign or country were treated much like the fanciful stories I once read—as things that belonged only in the realm of the imagination or happened elsewhere. My fear of being sent away slowly faded, and I began to believe that this would be my life now—working with Papa, helping Caleb, running errands for Angela, exchanging gossip with Comfort, avoiding upsetting Mamma and becoming part of my family once again.

Thus, when the messenger pounded on the door in the second week of January with a note from Mister Secretary demanding Papa and I present ourselves at his house the following day, I was caught unawares and my heart, the organ I had sworn to cast out, quickened.

I'd been naught but a clay-witted fool.

PART TWO

An Exceptional Pupil

Between the years 1580 and 1590 England was exposed
to a greater danger from Roman Catholicism and its
adherents than it had ever been or ever was to be.

—Conyers Read, *Sir Francis Walsingham, Volume II*, 1925

Therefore, men have instilled in women the fear of infamy
as a bridle to bind them as by force to this virtue,
without which they would truly be little esteemed;
for the world finds no usefulness in women
except the bearing of children.

—Baldassare Castiglione, *The Book of the Courtier:
The Third Book*, 1528

SEVEN

SEETHING LANE, LONDON
Friday the 13th of January, Anno Domini 1581
In the 23rd year of the reign of Elizabeth I

*W*e left the house before the clock struck one the next day. Papa was dressed in his church best, while I wore my obligatory black, the wedding band tight on my finger, a thick cloak over my shoulders, my hood covering my coif. Kit was left in charge of the workshop and the apprentices given strict instructions. As we stepped from the shop onto Tower Street, Papa took my arm. I wrapped my hand around the sleeve of his doublet and drew succor from his woolen cloak brushing against me. It was almost like old times, except it wasn't. When the note arrived, Papa had simply said Sir Francis may have found employ for me, I should dress well and be ready on time. I tried to ignore the questions buzzing like bees in my head and to concentrate on our walk, to register each and every step, reminding myself that though my nerves were afire, I wouldn't allow them to show. Was I not embracing Castiglione's *mediocrita*, the studied nonchalance that was my preferred state?

Gray clouds slumped above and frigid winds buffeted us as we tucked chins to chests and swerved around shallow banks of black-ened snow. Caparisoned horsemen waded through the slurry and the

Christmastide leavings overflowing the street's central ditch, shouting at those in their way. A weariness infected the streets, despite the presence of scampering urchins and the occasional passage of a gentlewoman or well-dressed man. Not even the smells of baking and pottages bubbling or the grand facade of the Baker's Hall mitigated the gloom. In contrast to the day I first met Sir Francis, when everything had been bathed in gilded hues before the storm broke, today wore a patina of age and need.

Toothless women, some with frowsy children clutching their threadbare skirts, loitered at the entrance to Mark Lane. Men squatted with their backs against buildings, begging for groats, their filthy hands cupped in desperation, their faces pleading with passersby. Fumbling for a coin in the little purse that dangled from my wrist, I broke away from Papa and pressed one into a frail old man's palm. His mumbled blessing was quickly lost in the clatter of cart wheels and barking dogs. A group of vendors trundled by, and as I rejoined Papa, he offered a smile.

"Times like this, it's as if naught has changed," he said, taking my hand again and patting it into place on his arm. "You were always kind, Mallory."

I wished I could tell Papa that nothing had changed—that I hadn't. But that would be a falsehood and we both knew it. The old Mallory, the cocky young girl with dreams and hopes and a stubborn belief in the milk of human kindness, was gone. As, I feared, was her goodwill toward men—with the exception of Papa and, of course, Caleb. Still, that Papa could say such a thing kindled a warming flame of gratitude within me.

It took less than half an hour to cover the distance to Sir Francis's house, which lay at the top of the ridge in Seething Lane. Situated in the parish of St. Olave, not far from the church of All Hallows Barking, but nearer the junction of Crouched Friars and Hart Street, it was an imposing residence. A corbeled house rising to three stories with a steeply thatched roof, the lower section was half timber, half red bricks laid in a diagonal pattern. The top two stories were a combination of wood and whitewashed daub and projected over each other, as if the entire house was peering with more inquisitiveness than was seemly upon the street directly below. There was glass in all the mullioned windows, and lush velvet curtains were partially drawn across them. The land accompanying the house was of healthy proportions and the bare spindly branches of trees stretched over the high wall that protected it. Beyond the wall, the roof of an imposing mews and a series of outhouses and stables could be seen. The area outside the house was swept clean, the snow pushed into mounds at the sides. The polished front door possessed a large, beautifully designed lock that at first glance appeared to be made in the Dutch manner. As we drew closer, I recognized the work around the escutcheon, a series of exotic flowers, the tendrils of which extended into branches that transformed into spirals and scrolls. The keyhole emerged from this, a cloverleaf in a metal garden that required a folding key to open it. It was lovely. It was also Papa's craftsmanship. I glanced at him for confirmation. He gave a brief nod before rapping sharply on the wood.

Papa had been commissioned by Sir Francis to provide his locks and keys. How long had they known each other? What other projects might they have embarked upon together?

The nearby church bells began to toll the hour, the first note of a musical conversation that echoed over the city. From here I had a clear view to the Tower and to the Cage, a place of punishment where, even today, a wicked soul was slumped. The long shadow of the Tower's high stone walls was accentuated by the dismal after-noon light. The houses that rested in darkness at its foot appeared to huddle together, as if against the cold. Above the walls loomed the grand White Tower, its color not so much that of its name but rather the ashen pallor of the decaying heads on the spikes atop London Bridge. To the left of the fortress were open fields dotted with a peculiar mix of gibbets, stocks in which knaves languished, as well as laundry left spread over bushes to dry. Folk loitered, jeer-ing and throwing rotten missiles at the captives in the stocks, while scavengers with ribbed dogs searched the fields for wild fruit, herbs and anything useful that may have been thrown among the piles of refuse teetering in the wasteland.

Overall, it was a sorry view to greet from one's doorstep, and I won-dered how Sir Francis and his family bore the daily reminders of mis-ery, crime and hardship. Perchance they saw God's will enacted via secular justice, but as I saw a fight break out among the scavengers, the notion fled. These men and women only fought to stave off hunger and fill their stomachs. Did necessity make them varlets?

The dull reverberation of bells hadn't yet ceased when the door opened sharply and a man of some years ushered us in, locking the door behind us, the decorative folded key he used jangling against others tied to his waist. The hall was spacious, darkly paneled but also mercifully warm. A staircase dominated the far end, one arm ascending into the airy spaces above, the other descending into the shadowy ones below. Smells of lemon, orange and another fresh scent wafted in the air. Upon the wainscoting hung miscellaneous swords, a pike and halberd and a huge leather shield, as well as a coat of arms featuring a tiger's head. Next to that was a portrait of the Queen, elegant in a huge ruff and heavily embroidered garment. Her deep-set dark eyes, so bold in her pale face, appeared to latch on to me, and I found myself drawn to her again and again, wondering in a fit of fancy if she could see me. Below her portrait hung another of a woman whom I guessed might be Sir Francis's wife. She stared at us too, her painted eyes blank, her smile fixed. She looked neither happy nor unhappy—much like the Queen. Fronds of dried ivy were stacked on top of a cabinet, and a bucket of pinecones sat atop a stool—explaining the smell I was at first unable to identify.

From the rooms beyond came sounds of domesticity—the clash of pots, the excited bark of a dog and voices raised in conversation. There was a bright female laugh followed by a volley of coughs.

As we were led through the hall and into a corridor, I tried to get a sense of Sir Francis, his home and family, but the doors leading to other rooms were closed. The only sign of life aside from our silent guide was a large ginger cat that shot past, hackles raised. Papa and I were shuffled down some stairs, along another corridor, and ushered into a large windowless room filled with desks and tables piled with papers, scrolls and books. The walls were lined with cabinets and chests. The room contained at least a dozen men and was a veritable picture of activity. Two were engaged in an earnest conversation that ceased the moment we entered, before resuming. Quills scratched busily, papers were moved from one table to another, and candles burned—so many candles. The smell of lemon was strong, as was a bitter, pungent odor that may have been tallow. The air was thick with smoke. We were escorted swiftly through. I could not have described the men or their business, except to say it appeared urgent, important and cloaked in gloom.

At the end of the room was a door and after a smart knock we were bade to enter by a low, familiar voice. Our guide gave a small bow and indicated we should go in. With a tug of his doublet and a brief nod, Papa did so, and I followed.

Despite the numerous candles burning, the room was quite dark and it took a moment for my eyes to adjust. A figure rose from behind a large wooden desk. My chest constricted and I swallowed rapidly, sinking into a curtsey as Papa bowed beside me.

"Well met. God give you good day," said Sir Francis and gestured to the seats in front of his desk. "Punctual as always, Gideon."

"Some habits are worth maintaining," Papa replied as we seated ourselves.

Though the room wasn't small, it was very cluttered. Apart from the big desk covered with papers, quills, and inkwells as well as a coven of burning candles, there was a long bench against one wall stacked with boxes, each with its contents inked on the outside. One box was marked "Religion and Matters Ecclesiastical," another "Navy, Havens and Sea Cases," while still another was marked "Box of Examinations." Examinations of what, I was uncertain. Near the hearth, which burned merrily and provided much-needed warmth and more light, was a series of chests. One was open, and bundles of manuscripts and books poured from it. On the walls were maps of France, Spain and other countries whose identities were obscured by shadow; on a small table behind the door was a huge book titled *Book of the Maps of England*. Another portrait of the Queen hung to the left of this, along with a rather grand arras portraying a battle scene in which unicorns and satyrs also frolicked. Another chair rested near the only window, which looked upon the courtyard. Directly behind Sir Francis was an elaborate cabinet made from a dark, highly polished—but badly scratched—wood. Two solid doors and an enormous intricate lock protected the contents. I tried to identify the lock, but the light was too low to tell much, though there was something familiar about the patterning of the guard.

Sir Francis regarded Papa, then his eyes rested upon me. "Ah, I see you're admiring my cabinet. My clerk and brother-in-law, Master Robert Beale, insisted I have one. It's a fine piece of furniture, is it not? Italian. Cost a pretty sum, too." He spun around and ran his hand down its polished surface.

"It is indeed, Sir Francis," I remarked, my voice quivering slightly. The man made my teeth hurt and every breath was tight. I forced myself to appear at ease. "The lock especially—"

"You recognize your father's handiwork."

Ah, another suspicion confirmed. "I do."

There was a sharp knock. The man who'd admitted us earlier entered with a tray bearing a jug of wine and one of beer, as well two goblets and a tankard. He poured quickly and placed the vessels before us.

"My thanks, Laurence," said Sir Francis, pushing the papers at his elbow to one side to make room for his goblet, gesturing for Papa to take the tankard.

Laurence grunted "milord," and with a small bow withdrew and shut the door.

Sir Francis turned to face us, hands wrapped around his goblet. "Thank you both for coming," he said, his manners implying we had a choice. "Mistress Mallory, allow me also to thank you again for the service you rendered when we last met—'twas November, I believe."

Had it been so long ago? "It was nothing, my lord," I began, thinking how working with locks offered a respite from memory that was lacking in my other activities.

"I'll be the judge of that," said Sir Francis. "I propose a toast." He lifted his goblet. "To the locksmith's daughter and her fine skills."

"To the locksmith's daughter," repeated Papa with more force than I felt was warranted.

I sat mute, slightly uncomfortable as they drank. There was an undercurrent here that I didn't understand. I took a sip of the claret, enjoying the warmth coating my throat.

Sir Francis sank into his chair, his mind appeared to be working furiously behind his guarded eyes. "I know you're very curious as to why I summoned you here, Mallory—may I call you that?" I nodded. "Firstly, and this was very remiss of me, may I extend my sympathy for your loss."

For a moment my head swam, then clarity came. He was acknowledging my status as widow.

"Thank you, my lord." I could not meet his eyes.

"While they go to a better place, the death of a beloved is never easy to reconcile." His fingers brushed against a miniature of a young girl that sat upon his desk.

"I heard about Mary." Papa leaned forward. "Francis. I've naught to say except how very sorry I am."

Sir Francis bowed his head and, as if aware his fingers were revealing more than he wished, curled them into fists. "My dear, sweet daughter was but eight. Eight. She is with God now."

Caleb had made mention of Sir Francis's children. Dear God, the poor man had lost a daughter. My palms grew damp. The portrait showed a cherubic face with rosy cheeks and a pursed mouth beneath a frame of dark, lustrous curls. Sorrow for Sir Francis and this pretty young girl welled. I tried to push it away. I could not allow emotion to dull the lucidity I needed. My temples began to ache. My gaze returned again and again to that dear innocent face and deeper feelings rose unbidden : . .

"Now," said Sir Francis, striking the desk with the flat of his hand, banishing the sadness and forcing my eyes from the painting. "Let's to business. Your father asked me to help acquire you a position, Mallory. One befitting a widow of your education and skills."

Papa kept his gaze fixed upon Sir Francis.

"I've pondered this request very carefully and it seems the best way for me to be acquainted with your various talents is to observe them firsthand."

"My lord?" Every fiber of my being strained to understand, and dread lapped the edges of my mind.

Papa straightened. "What do you mean, Francis?"

"I mean, since I've been unsuccessful in finding her suitable work elsewhere, but knowing your request was somewhat urgent, I wish to employ Mallory as a companion for my daughter, Frances."

A sense of relief unfurled through my veins just as Caleb's words came back to me: "Keeper of Mister Secretary's Children." Not children, sadly, but child.

Before I could respond, Papa leaped to his feet. "No. No. This will not do. When I sought your assistance in this matter"—he glanced in my direction—"I never intended you to be her employer."

Sir Francis stood. The desk became a moat between the two men as they stared across the candles.

"Did you not?" There was a beat. "Believe me, if you hadn't emphasized how important this was, I wouldn't suggest it." Sir Francis's voice was tight, his words considered. "I do not expect Mallory to live beneath this roof. I merely wish to avail myself of her considerable talents . . . for the benefit of my daughter. She will remain with you. I would hope that would make you content; in this way, you're able to satisfy many needs and wants, including my own."

Papa's hands were screwed into fists by his side. Why did I feel as if another conversation was taking place beneath the one I was hearing? My eyes moved from Papa to Sir Francis. Tension made the men lean toward each other, though Papa looked as if he were trying to resist. Sweat dotted his brow.

"This is not . . . proper. Valentina . . ." Papa glanced at me again. "She will not like this."

My father was right. Mamma wanted me gone completely, not some half measure.

Sir Francis held Papa's eyes for a long time. "It's all I can offer at present, Gideon. Take it or leave it." Slowly he resumed his seat and rested his forearms upon the desk, twining his fingers together.

I didn't realize I was holding my breath until Papa swung toward me. In his eyes I saw despair, fear and something else. My heart leaped. What made Papa so afraid?

"Mallory—" he began, but Sir Francis allowed him to go no further.

"I would ask that you come to the house each day. You will work to improve my daughter's Latin and Greek and, when my daughter doesn't require your company, that of some of my staff as well. Once you are comfortable with your duties, you will be sent on errands about the city. For this you will be paid a small sum. Think, Gideon, it will do Mallory's reputation some good, will it not, for it to be known she is biding in good society? It will silence those who would spread salacious rumors, and add to her status." Sir Francis nodded toward my coal-black ensemble. "Add to yours . . ."

I twisted the ring upon my finger. 'Twas but another prop to shore up the deceit of my costume. But Sir Francis was right. When word got out that the Walsingham household had embraced me, other doors would open, gossip would quiet. What Sir Francis was offering was beyond generous, and a means to even greater opportunities.

"Papa." I brushed the sleeve of his doublet. He swung away as if burned. I blinked in surprise and swiftly withdrew my hand. Papa looked from me to Sir Francis and back again.

"It's the best I can offer—for now." Sir Francis gestured for Papa to sit. "I would not even consider it if other alternatives were available."

I couldn't understand what was amiss. To me the proposal offered a happy compromise between Mamma's desires, Papa's and my own. I could remain at home yet be gone from the house all day. Why Papa didn't leap at this, I couldn't fathom. Unless the good relations I'd felt had been restored between us were nothing but a mirage . . . I lowered my chin and waited; tried to render myself invisible.

Sinking back onto the stool, Papa released a sigh that came from his boots. "You're right, Francis. Forgive my doubts. It's a good offer." His tone suggested it may as well be a death sentence.

"If it pleases you, shall we sign a contract? Seal the arrangement," said Sir Francis.

"Soft," I began, half rising out of my seat. "Today? Now? Why such haste? When would I start?"

"What is your objection, mistress? The placement or the haste?" asked Sir Francis.

Remember, my inner voice hissed. *Nonchalance. The speed at which this is enacted does not alter the course.*

I gave a small shrug and resumed my seat. "Nay, my lord, I do not. I object to neither."

"I'll summon my secretary." Sir Francis rang a small bell. Moments later, a youngish man with straw-colored hair, glasses and pockmarked skin entered. "Thomas, you know Master Bright. This is his daughter, Mistress Mallory." Master Thomas bowed. "This is my chief assistant, one of my secretaries, Master Thomas Phelippes."

"Well met," he said.

Sir Francis continued. "Mistress Mallory will be joining the household. I would that you and Master Gideon finalize the contract expressing same."

"Very well, my lord."

"Gideon, if you would be so good as to accompany Thomas. I've taken the liberty of making a draft. Examine it and make any amendments you see fit," said Sir Francis, indicating my father should follow Master Thomas.

"Very good," said Papa. His face was pale. He didn't look in my direction.

I went to rise.

"Mallory, if you would remain," Sir Francis said, "I will supply you with the details of your new position and answer any questions you may have."

I looked to Papa. "I'll be back anon," he said and slowly followed Master Thomas from the room.

Once the door was closed, Sir Francis drained his goblet and stared at me. The candlelight turned his eyes into liquid darkness. "I've but a short time to speak freely with you, Mallory."

"My lord?"

"The contract your father is about to sign only refers to the services others believe you're being hired to render. What I wish to speak to you about, and what's not included, are the duties you will actually be performing—not for Frances, but for me."

EIGHT

Friday the 13th of January, Anno Domini 1581
In the 23rd year of the reign of Elizabeth I

Not one word of what I'm about to share with you must leave this room. This is between you and me." His elbows on the desk, Sir Francis leaned so far forward I could see where his servant had nicked the flesh on his left cheek trimming his beard.

"Of course, my lord." My throat was dry. I resisted the urge to seek the talisman of my locket. *Nonchalance.*

"Good. Now"—Sir Francis eased himself away from the desk, but his spine remained straight and his eyes never left my face—"before I tell you what it is you'll be doing, I need to provide you with a context."

"Very well."

"You're aware the Pope has renewed the Bull against the Queen?"

"I am."

"Gregory XIII exhorts Catholic subjects within England and beyond her borders to spurn their allegiance to Her Majesty. He claims she is no longer their true sovereign. He even promises that should one of them rise up and murder her, they would be pardoned such a grievous sin. They would be hailed a hero of the Church."

I knew this—we all did. The pamphlets distributed around Cheapside had found their way into homes, as had the words of the preachers at St. Paul's Cross and the gossip in the market, but the way Sir Francis spoke gave me a chill.

"The Pope, that spider of Rome, panders to Philip of Spain and the Guises in France, all of whom wish to see our Queen dethroned. But Gregory goes further. He is throwing coin and promises at any mad Catholic adventurer who'll indulge in heresy and treachery—the type of person who wouldn't think twice about murdering a reigning monarch." Sir Francis gave a bark of laughter. "Have you heard of the Jesuit seminaries on the Continent?"

"I don't believe so."

"With the Pope's blessing, Jesuit colleges have been established in Douai, Reims, Rome and more. Their sole purpose is to train English priests. Doctor William Allen, a traitor if ever there was one, runs them. Under the guise of godliness, under protestations that faith alone is driving their actions, the first of these priests arrived on English shores some years ago. It turns out they were just a drop in the ocean. Now the steady drip of Jesuit recruits has turned into a tide that threatens to wash away the souls of true believers. A royal proclamation was delivered only three days ago ordering all English students in foreign seminaries to return home, and the arrest of every Jesuit in England. It's now treason for these priests to be here, and for would-be priests to seek out these European seminaries." He lowered his voice. "You've heard of the Jesuits, Edmund Campion and Robert Persons?"

There were few who hadn't.

Sir Francis continued. "They arrived in England last year."

"You didn't arrest them?"

"No, we watched them, or at least we tried to. We weren't expecting that so many English families would be prepared to risk arrest and protect them. Acting upon the advice of his followers here, upon his arrival in England Campion had the gall to write to the Privy Council explaining his purpose in coming."

"You mean Campion's 'Brag'?"

"I do."

"It was the talk of the household when I . . . when I came home."

"It still dominates conversations in the taverns and streets," said Sir Francis, looking as though he'd bitten into an apple and found a worm. "Though Campion claims, most earnestly, he's not here to interfere with any matters of state or policy, I know differently. The government knows differently. The Council has been forced to address this 'brag,' as it has been dubbed, and show it for what it is and show the supporters of Campion for what they are."

"And that is?"

"Traitors. Traitors who utter papist lies. Campion would set father against son, mother against daughter. He cares not for English souls, despite what he writes. He's an agent of Rome and as such, he's our enemy. If his intentions were honest, why did he disguise himself as a merchant in order to enter the country? Why does he continue to flee the authorities?"

"Perchance he fears what would happen should he be caught?"

Sir Francis's eyes glinted dangerously. "And so he should. You heard that we have captured his mate, the student-priest Ralph Sherwin? Aye, such news spreads quickly. What is not generally known is that we've also arrested a group of Catholics in Lancashire. Some have been induced to talk. There are plans afoot, Mallory, treacherous plans—spearheaded by Allen, Campion, the Godforsaken Society of Jesus and that canting monk in Rome. Campion's so-called enterprise ends now. I'll not allow this Catholic kindling to light the fire of heresy in England. Not after what happened in Paris. Not after what your father and I survived." He closed his eyes and sighed. Just when I thought his anger spent, he turned a steely gaze upon me. "I imagine you know the tale of how, when Mary Tudor came to power, many of us were forced to flee the country and run for our lives to Switzerland, Italy and the Low Countries?"

I knew Papa's story—how he and his brother, my uncle Timothy, had left England after the "Nine-Days Queen," Jane Gray, was imprisoned in the Tower and it became evident that the new Queen, Mary Tudor, was determined to overturn all her brother Edward's religious policies and bring the country back under the yoke of Catholicism. A veritable flood of émigrés deserted England for safer religious climes in Venetian and Swiss territories, as if they sensed something in the wind. They were prescient. It was the Queen's unforgiving treatment of "heretics" that earned her the sobriquet "Bloody Mary." To remain in England was to risk being burned alive or tortured into recanting their Protestant beliefs. Hundreds met their deaths this way—many of Papa's friends among them.

It was while he was in exile in Padua that Papa met Mamma. I loved their story. She was the beautiful daughter of the successful black-smith, Baldassare Zucchero, and was courted by many. But it was the *Inglese*, the English gentleman, who won her hand. Papa had been studying at the university and sought the services of Signor Zucchero to make a lock for the chest in which he kept his books after a couple were stolen. He was mesmerized by the blacksmith's skill, the way my *nonno* crafted keys and locks not simply to secure rooms or possessions, but as works of art in themselves. Casting aside his studies, Papa, the youngest son of a gentleman lawyer who himself was the eldest son of a blacksmith and thus already reasonably skilled in the craft, begged my *nonno* to train him so he too might make these exquisite locks. So it was at the forge of my *nonno* that my father met his true calling and his bride. I was born not long after they wed. Papa always said meeting Mamma and my birth were compensation for his time abroad.

It was only once Queen Elizabeth had been in power for a couple of years, after swearing she wouldn't open windows into men's souls but would allow people to worship as they pleased, as long as they were loyal to the throne, that Papa returned to England. Uncle Timothy followed not long after to practice medicine. By this time Papa was a much-lauded locksmith.

The Queen had a reputation for being mercurial, and from what Sir Francis said, it appeared she had changed her mind and had now not only opened windows into men's souls but was demanding the view from each be identical.

"I was unaware you shared so much in common with Papa, Sir Francis. I didn't know you were in Padua at the same time." Once again, I wondered why Papa had concealed their relationship from me.

Sir Francis paused. "Your father and I share many things, Mallory. Our faith, friends, follies, even family—your uncle is my doctor as well." He drank. "Perchance you think me harsh? Unbending when it comes to Catholics?"

If I did, I dare not confess.

"Do you know the story of the St. Bartholomew's Day massacre?" he asked.

"When thousands of French Protestants, the Huguenots, were brutally murdered and the streets of Paris ran with blood? Aye, but only in part. Uncle Timothy was there. He does not like to speak of it. He was spared because he sought shelter at the English embassy in Paris."

"I was the ambassador who sheltered Timothy," he said simply.

My mouth fell open. Uncle Timothy had always said the ambassador risked his life offering sanctuary from the rampaging Catholics, not just to English nationals, but to many others. But why had he never mentioned Sir Francis by name? I regarded the man opposite with newfound respect.

"My family owe you much, it seems," I said softly.

"We owe each other. Yet your family has paid the debt to me many times over," said Sir Francis, dismissing everything again. "And now," he added before I could digest all he had told me, "I not only seek to extinguish one debt, but ask to be in yours."

Angela always said a wise person knew when silence served better than words. I hoped she was correct. In the silence that followed, my measure was taken.

"Watching you unlock that casket impressed me mightily. I've never seen something so complex done with such ease, let alone by a woman. It was not an easy task—it wasn't intended to be. But you managed to bypass the wards, to disable the pernicious traps. In case it was fortune that guided your hands that night, I sent two more locked objects to test your skills."

Another suspicion confirmed.

"Not only did you open them, you disabled the locks in such a way the owner never knew the goods had been disturbed. After we'd taken inventories and made copies of the contents, we were able to reseal them once more. Thus I've obtained the evidence I needed to uncover the latest nest of Catholics. You saw what lay inside the *forziere* that night. You understand what it signified." They were not questions. I nodded. "The sea chest you opened contained not only more priestly robes, but many seditious books intended to lure good Protestant souls back to the old religion and multiply the Catholic hive. Within the cylinder you opened, I found correspondence of the most treacherous nature between men I'd long thought trustworthy." For just a moment his guard dropped, and I caught a glimpse of a man tired beyond his years, on the verge of breaking. Almost.

"For years I've worked diligently towards the acquisition of information, Mallory," said Sir Francis. "Even before I was made the Queen's Secretary, I understood how important knowledge is, how the scraps my sources collect, the objects, orts and imitations, can together make a coherent meal. Few know how I glean my information, how I come into possession of others' secrets." He smiled, or at least his mouth did. "It's simple, really. I have men from all walks of life in my employ— from the basest criminals, double-dealers and servants, to the most educated soul and the most noble. Some do it for coin, others for faith and family, some for loyalty. Others seek adventure. Their sole purpose is to watch, listen, act when necessary and report it all back to me." He gestured toward the rolls of parchment, the overflowing boxes, the cabinet.

He began to pace the room as he talked. "From this I've discovered that men's words and actions, no matter their station, are not necessarily in accord. Following the tenet *video et taco* . . . you understand what I am saying?"

"See and keep silent," I said.

"Good. I've acquired a great deal of information, a lot of knowledge. That night I watched you unlock that casket, and through the tasks you've subsequently performed for me, I discovered something else." He paused before the window and gazed outside.

The day had darkened. The wind rustled the bare-limbed trees. Chickens, their feathers ruffled, ran toward their shelter, avoiding the muddy boots of a maid hefting a sloshing pail toward the house.

"Believing I saw all, the truth is, I've been half-blind." Sir Francis turned around. "My information network is incomplete and until I remedy that, it doesn't matter how many men I've working on my behalf, or the country's, or how many plots I foil. I'll never see the entire picture. Until I can make that complete, England and the Queen will never be safe."

"What are you missing?" I asked, my voice tight.

He stopped before me. The fire made one half of his face glow, his eyes stygian pools.

"You, Mallory Bright," he whispered. "You are the missing piece in my network."

NINE

SEETHING LANE, LONDON
Friday the 13th of January, Anno Domini 1581
In the 23rd year of the reign of Elizabeth I

I was a coney struck by a stone, unable to move. Yet a huge wave of excitement rose within me to wash aside the agitation and the guilt I'd carried for months. I was the missing component of this man's elaborate network of information?

Unaware of the hope he'd ignited, Sir Francis went on. "Mallory, I want you to unlock the secrets of those who would hide their true selves; not only those who whisper in the dark, but those who, like the men we apprehended, believe their heresy and treason, their seditious plots, are safe under lock and key. I want you to ferret out whatever it is they hide and give it to me so justice may be served and the realm and Her Majesty kept safe."

My mouth opened at the passion of his words; this, from a man who appeared so contained. Why, this was wonderful, preposterous— and Papa would never allow it. The wind left the sails of my imagination and my dreams deflated at the thought. Mamma would disown me completely. A young woman didn't do such things. Why, this was men's business. I could not. Must not.

Aware that Sir Francis's eyes hadn't left mine, I recalled the oath I had made to myself, that from here on I would assume indifference, even when none was felt. I wanted, I needed, to refashion myself, to make something of my life, and that required discipline. Was Sir Francis offering me the means to bring about the change I so desired? Weakness was a garment I would not wear again, regardless of my sex. Raffe had forced it upon me once; I would not don it afresh. I would stride forth boldly. Nonetheless, doubts assailed me.

Sir Francis's voice intruded. "Mallory, I want you to give my men access—to unlock doors, chests, secret closets." He rapped his knuckles against his own cabinet. "More importantly, I want you to help us discover what's being written in letters, hidden in jewels, in caskets such as the one you opened. I need you to open doors to those places currently closed to me. I want you to inhabit the spaces where men cannot tread. I want you to keep under watch those I suspect of possessing Popish sympathies, those who harbor Catholics, who foster traitorous thoughts. And, of course, you will pass whatever you learn on to me without their knowledge. I don't want them to be aware that the woman in their midst is a watcher, that their locks have been picked, their doors opened, their secrets discovered, read and copied; I want them to feel secure until I am ready to expose them."

Perhaps sensing my equivocation, Sir Francis leaned forward, his hand flat on the desk. "What I ask of you is risky, Mallory. Better than most, I know this. I want you to understand, not only would you be trusted with one of the most important jobs in the kingdom, helping to protect our sovereign and thus our country, but you would also be well compensated."

"I would?"

Sir Francis gave a curt nod. "Contingent on what you deliver, a tidy sum as well. And on top of what's agreed in the contract your father is signing."

Me, a woman, paid a goodly sum? Suddenly, what I was being asked to do was imbued with even more gravitas; it also solved another problem.

He began to tell me about the sums earned by his other agents. I confess, I barely listened. Casting aside the ethics of what I was being asked to do, I forced myself to focus on the recompense I'd receive— not just in shoring up the safety of my liege and her realm, which, in the scheme of creation, was priceless, but in coin. The notion that I, who'd been so dependent first on my father, later on Raffe, and then again on my parents, might one day be able to repay Papa what I owed, accumulate a dowry that would overcome my shortcomings, and even help my dearest friend Caleb escape the shackles of debt, was almost too much to grasp.

Aware Sir Francis was still talking, I snapped out of my reverie and gave him my full attention once more.

I drew myself up. "Sir Francis," I began. As much as I thrilled to hear his plans and his need of me, I'd fallen for this before and my heart swelled painfully against my ribs. Also, in fairness, I could no longer allow him to pursue this fancy. Truth be told, neither could I. "My father is much better equipped, has much better skills than I to assist you in such a formidable task. Mine are but a poor echo of his abilities."

"This might be true," said Sir Francis and, resuming his seat, he reclined slightly, lifted the goblet to his lips and took a long, slow draft. He wiped the back of his hand across his mouth and down his beard.

"Despite what you think"—he pointed at me—"your father, even knowing the foolish choices you made and what befell you as a consequence, wants you to be happy. He wants you to succeed by doing something fulfilling, something that makes use of your education, as unconventional as that's been. He wants you to put the past behind you rather than be victim to it."

I opened my mouth to protest, but the earnest look on Sir Francis's face stole my words.

"You speak of Sir Raffe." He inclined his head. "My . . . my late husband."

"Husband?" he asked softly.

My stomach churned and the bile of shame gathered in my throat. "You know the extent of my folly," I whispered.

"I know, Mallory. Just as I know the foolish whims to which women are particularly prone, I also know that the man was a knave fate treated far too kindly."

Fate, thy name is Mallory. I glanced up. "But—" I began.

"Why do you persist in arguing when you know what I'm offering is your chance, Mallory? Possibly the only one you'll get. Grasp it and make your father proud. Prove that the skills he taught you have worth. What better way to do that than to work for me, who wants you to succeed?"

I glanced toward the door. Only later, long after I'd left his presence and had the chance to reflect upon our conversation, did his last words puzzle me.

"What about your daughter? If I work for you, then what about her? Does she really require a companion? Or is that merely a fabrication to placate Papa? A role to obscure my real purpose? You made mention of improving the language skills of some of your staff . . ." When he didn't answer, I continued. "Papa would never permit such an arrangement. Not after . . ."

Sir Francis folded his arms and nodded approvingly. "It was no lie, Mallory. To all intents and purposes, you will be working for me as Frances's companion, as I made clear. I said I would like you to teach my staff and you will. You'll be introduced to Frances and you will spend time with her when she comes to London. She mostly lives in Surrey. You need not concern yourself on that account. You'll be able to answer any questions about your role in this house, dissemble with ease. However, my intention is that a great deal of your day will be spent studying the additional skills I need you to acquire in order to be an effective agent within my network; I doubt you'll have time to meet Frances until you've mastered those skills."

"Such as?" I asked.

"I already know you can gain entry to a lock, but I also need you to be able to mingle with people of all ranks and occupations, to move in diverse places without drawing attention to yourself. To watch, listen, learn and, when necessary, report, but in such a manner that should your words fall into the wrong hands, the recipient would be none the wiser. For that, you need to learn ciphers, and how to forge a signature, a seal or document. If you're as quick a study as I suspect, you may even have a knack for deciphering code."

I gulped. It was all too much. "What if you're wrong?"

"I'm unaccustomed to such a condition," snapped Sir Francis. Color flew to my cheeks. I must never forget whom I was with, and keep my doubts and fears to myself. Mamma's face loomed in my mind. Here I was considering working for a man who asked me to hunt down

Catholics and ferret out traitors, believing them to be one and the same. Did he know Mamma was a recusant, one of those who refused to give up their Catholicism for the Church of England? He must. Why didn't he mention it? Should I raise it?

Before I could say anything, he continued. "In return, as I said to your father, I do require you to teach certain skills to a select few of my men. It will be an exchange—you will learn their tricks, and you will teach them your lock-picking as well as improving their other languages."

"Lock-picking is not easy, sir. At least, not when the locks are of the caliber of those you've already sent my way."

"I never thought for a moment it was. I simply want you to impart the basics. There's an advantage to being able to access a locked room, a sealed chest." He motioned toward the papers spread over his desk. "There's much to be done, and most of it behind the scenes."

I thought of Caleb, the troupe, the activity that went on in the tiring room as the actors prepared for stage. The way Sir Francis spoke, this job was similar to an actor's in many ways—pretending to be one thing while really being another, dressing up, giving the appearance of stability, strength and coherence while all the time understanding their temporary nature.

"What do you say, Mallory? Do you agree to my proposition? Or do you wish to bide your time until I find you a less taxing post?"

My brows rose. "I have a choice?"

"I would not force what I prefer to be given willingly."

I lifted my chin and gazed at my prospective employer cautiously. Understanding relaxed his features; compassion rendered them paternal.

"Besides," he added, a small smile hovering at the corner of his mouth, "talented though your father might be, and as much as I might want his services, he's not a woman."

Ah, so that was it. No matter the praise for my lock-picking skills, or ability to read and write in different tongues, my primary talent lay in the fact I was born cloven, not crested.

"As a woman, you see things men do not," said Sir Francis, his words sounding as rehearsed as Caleb's lines. He had considered this appointment carefully. "What other ears may deem nonsensical or dismiss as mere prattle may have meaning for you. Females dissemble with impunity, as I've had good cause to observe in the last three years." He gave a wry grin; surely he wasn't referring to the Queen? "Though women carry no water, you're the conduits through which, I believe, I can influence events. In God's truth a woman is a dark continent to me, alien. Only another woman can be the guide I require, shedding light upon such a strange world." He laughed at his analogy. I began to imagine myself as a Francis Drake, replete with sword, ship and crew, shouting orders. "You will be Virgil to my Dante."

My fingers were knotted tightly in my lap. But then . . . was my sex my only advantage? Nay, Mister Secretary needed a woman and a lock-pick. I, Mallory Bright, fitted the bill. What would Mamma say? What could I say?

"Will you enter my employ and do this for me, for your Queen?" he asked. "Will you join my network and help me uncover the traitors in our midst?" He spread his arms wide; his eyes glittered. Above the faint sounds from the next room rose the voice of a young woman practicing her scales. A horse's hooves crunched the gravel in the courtyard and an ostler cried for assistance. Papa's murmurs also reached me.

Sir Francis smiled for the first time, and it lit up his face. He jerked his head in the direction of Papa's voice. "If you choose to accept my offer, you will not tell him. You will not tell anyone. It will be our secret."

I'd kept so many secrets from my father, betrayed my parents' trust—possibly irreparably. Could I do it again? What was one more? But this was so big . . . There would be no return if I were discovered. Yet, for all my misgivings, I could see how it could work, how under the guise of one duty, I could perform another, with no further damage to my reputation. What Raffe took from me, Sir Francis would return. No. *I* would return. Sir Francis was merely offering me the means to do so.

"Mallory, you made a choice that almost destroyed your life. Why not make one that will salvage the ruin it has become?"

I met those leaden eyes that reflected my own gray orbs. The clock tower began to chime the hour.

It was time to pick up the quill and make the first mark against the blank page that was my new life. "I say, aye, my lord. I am yours to command."

Sir Francis stood and gave a most solemn bow. I rose and curtseyed in return.

"Welcome to the Walsingham family," he said.

I gave a light laugh at his humor, but his eyes flickered and his mouth thinned. He did not seem amused. I'd made a blunder, and coughed into my fist to cover my embarrassment.

"My lord," I said. "Thank you."

"I do not require thanks, Mallory Bright, only loyalty," he said. "Only loyalty," he repeated, like a judge delivering a sentence.

TEN

HARP LANE, LONDON
Friday the 13th of January, Anno Domini 1581
In the 23rd year of the reign of Elizabeth I

*B*efore we reached home, Papa extracted a promise from me. I was to allow him to tell Mamma of the arrangement with Sir Francis.

"I'm not sure how she'll react," he said.

I wasn't certain either.

Comfort took Papa's thick cloak and folded it over one arm while he plucked off his gloves. She handed him an old rag and he sat on a stool and wiped his boots while I discarded my pattens and exchanged my pumps for the slippers Comfort passed me. The entryway was dim; only two candles burned, casting a pleasant light. The kitchen door was ajar, emitting a golden glow and the soft murmur of voices and the clatter of pans. The tantalizing smell of baking fish and spices drifted on the air. Hunger gnawed my insides. I'd barely broken my fast, I was so churned up over our visit to Sir Francis, but now my appetite had returned. Papa caught my look and nodded. He too was hungry.

Comfort grinned. "Mistress Pernel has outdone herself this evening. In honor of our guest, there'll be baked flounder and a lamprey pie."

"Guest?" asked Papa. "I wasn't expecting anyone." He passed her the rag and stood up.

"Excuse me, sir," said Comfort. "It be Master Caleb's patron, Lord Nathaniel Warham. He called to see Master Caleb. The mistress said we were to invite him to supper." She could barely conceal her excitement.

"Mistress Valentina?" Papa could not have been more surprised had the cat walked in wielding a sword and demanding a duel. "*Valentina* invited him?"

"Verily, sir. When Mistress Angela told her who'd arrived, she insisted he be brought to her parlor. Excuse me saying so, sir, but the man is so tall, he had to fold himself in half to fit beneath the beams. But he was so mannered and courtly. Mistress Angela said his visit cheered the mistress no end."

Stunned, Papa turned to me. "Well, well."

"She invited him to dine personally," added Comfort.

Papa's hands froze. My mouth formed a round O.

"Did she now?" he said finally.

"Caleb said his new patron is a man of extraordinary charm, Papa," I said, as much to reassure myself as my father.

"Indeed. He must be, or else he's possessed of powers to rival Doctor Dee." He looked toward the stairs. I knew what he was thinking. If Mamma was in such good spirits she would admit a stranger, albeit a lord, into her rooms, now was a good time to tell her of my situation. "Where's his lordship now?"

"In the parlor. Master Caleb is entertaining him."

Papa glanced at the door. Duty dictated he should greet our guest. There was a muffled burst of laughter. For certes, Caleb was entertaining.

Papa's gaze returned to the darkening stairs.

There was no help for it. As much as I wanted to retreat to my room and consider the implications of the day and what I'd agreed to do, I must put on a social countenance; I owed Papa that at the very least.

"I will attend his lordship, Papa. You go to Mamma." I placed a hand upon his arm.

"That is best," he said, patting my fingers. Like a soldier going to battle, he straightened the armor of his doublet before climbing the stairs. "I'll return anon."

Comfort and I watched him ascend, the stairs creaking.

"Comfort." He leaned over the railing on the first landing. "Bring some wine to your mistress's rooms, would you? The one from Gascony. And some food."

"Mistress said she would join us downstairs," said Comfort.

Papa tightened his grip on the balustrade. "I'm afraid she won't be; not any longer." Could Comfort hear the heaviness in his tone? Was the information he carried really so burdensome?

"Sir," said Comfort, looking askance at me.

Waiting until he rapped on Mamma's door, she whispered, "Bad news then?"

I paused. "For Mamma, it may well be." Would I ever be forgiven for the pain I had caused? I prayed every night it would be so, but it seemed God was not on my side. Dwelling upon this subject only led to dark thoughts, and I'd a guest to consider. I would not greet him with a long face, not the man who had changed Caleb's fortunes. I'd wanted to meet him and here was my chance.

"Be my mirror, Comfort," I said as I tidied my gown. "Reflect back any shortcomings." I bent my knees slightly so Comfort could see my face. "I've a noble to greet."

Pushing a stray hair behind my ear and tugging at my coif, Comfort's face softened as her eyes traveled my length, brushing snow from where it had caught on my skirts, and dusting my jacket.

"There," she said, stepping back. "You'll pass."

She went to open the parlor door. I grabbed her sleeve. "A moment." Worry caught me and stilled my progress. I placed a hand over my heart. It was as if someone had released a brace of pigeons inside my ribcage, unbalancing me. What was wrong? I'd never been so overcome meeting strangers before—not within the home. True, I avoided such encounters when I could, but when they occurred, I simply made myself as inconspicuous as possible. Why, even meeting Sir Francis had not caused such a reaction. This was another legacy of Raffe's, my preference to hide—in rooms, beneath clothes.

I inhaled deeply and exhaled, one hand pressed to my stomach. He must not be victorious in this. *Mediocrita. Mediocrita.* God help me.

"It'll be all right, Mistress Mallory." Comfort touched my shoulder. "When you choose, there's none can hold a candle to you." Before I could stop her, Comfort opened the door and announced me, as if this were a grand house and I its lady. What none in the room saw was the huge shove she gave me.

Tripping across the threshold, by the time the men seated by the hearth registered my entry, I'd regained my balance, though my cheeks were flooded with color.

"Mallory!" exclaimed Caleb, leaping out of his chair. I caught a glimpse of the man opposite him before Caleb filled my vision, approaching me with arms outstretched and a huge smile that I couldn't help but return, my anxiety receding slightly. The door clicked shut behind me. Dressed in some of his finest clothes, all velvet, beads, feathers and silk, Caleb was a picture.

"Why, look who has deigned to bless us with her presence, my lord, like an actor on cue—just as your part was being discussed," he said, taking my hands in his and leaning forward to kiss my cheeks. As his beard brushed against my ear, he whispered, "Wipe that glower from your brow. You will tell me what's placed it there later. For now, come and meet the Adonis in our midst."

Obediently I smoothed my forehead and turned toward his lordship—Adonis by any other name.

"Lord Nathaniel Warham," said Caleb. "May I introduce my dearest friend and daughter of the Bright household, Mistress Mallory." With a flourish, Caleb stepped aside.

Like a great sail unfurling, Lord Nathaniel Warham rose languidly from his chair, downing the drink in his hand as he did so, giving me time to register his extraordinary height. Why, Comfort was right. He was simply enormous! Possessed of broad shoulders and limbs of unnatural length, he all but touched our high ceiling. While his height was astounding, so was his clothing. Whereas Caleb was attired in splendor, Lord Nathaniel appeared to have wandered in off the docks or the servants' quarters on a country estate. His jacket, though of fine fabric, was old and threadbare. The lace cuffs of the cream-colored shirt beneath were stained, as was his faded damask vest. His woolen hose were black and likely of good quality, but the boots into which they disappeared were scuffed and dirty. Why, the man didn't even wear a ruff. His only adornments were the three sparkling rings on his fingers and a bent ostrich plume upon his battered bonnet. He wore a long rapier at his side; the pommel, loop guard and quillon were dented and the sheath housing it scratched.

If this wasn't enough, his beard was unkempt and his tawny hair needed trimming.

Standing before me, he gave a slight bow. His nose, Roman in design but flawed in execution, had clearly been broken. Beneath straight brows, a pair of golden eyes conducted their study boldly, without the stealth men usually adopt when examining a woman. As I took his measure, so he too took mine. Aware of the impropriety of our frank mutual regard, his eyes revealed nothing except depths of amber and honey. I looked away, self-consciously. Never before had I been in the company of such a one. Was he really a lord? Was the guise of an ordinary fellow something he adopted when visiting those of lesser rank? The thought made me bristle. No one I knew would enter another's house in such a state, without at least a clean shirt and boots—not even the apprentices.

I found his entire appearance offensive. Nonetheless, I must do my duty. Swallowing hard, I took a moment to compose myself before bidding him welcome, but before I could form the words he took my hand in his huge one, pulled me to him and, as was the accepted etiquette among many, kissed me soundly and lingeringly on the lips before releasing me with a low chuckle.

He spoke in a voice summoned from deep within, like the contented growl of a large beast.

"Mistress Mallory. I've heard a great deal about you. Odd name for a woman, Mallory. What were your parents thinking, bestowing upon a lady the name of a knight who fancied himself a poet?"

I could taste the sweetness of the wine he had been drinking. Did he not see my widow's attire? Did he not understand that his greeting was improper? From the twinkle in his eye, the rogue more than understood. He took pleasure in defying conventions. Fury swelled in my chest. *Mediocrita, mediocrita*, I chanted to myself.

Drawing myself up and resisting the urge to wipe my mouth, I forced a smile. "I imagine they never thought there'd come a time when a gentleman would pose such a question to its owner." His rudeness beggared belief.

There was a pause before Lord Nathaniel tipped back his head and laughed—not any ordinary laugh either, but one that issued from the heart, loud and long. His eyes crinkled joyously and it was then I saw the twin scars running down the right-hand side of his face, across his cheek and jaw. Another scar cleaved his brow, touching the corner of his eye before disappearing beneath his bonnet. I tried to remain impassive, but fie upon him, his laugh was contagious.

Caleb nervously released a rather high-pitched giggle and flitted between us, urging us to sit down.

Lord Nathaniel ignored him and faced me. "Well met, Mistress Mallory. Well met." He wiped his eyes and without waiting for me to welcome him, returned to his seat, reaching to splash more wine in his goblet. The anticipated apology never came.

He looked at Caleb, raising the ewer slightly.

"Ah, I will," said Caleb, pushing his vessel toward his lordship. He caught my astonished look and gave a small shrug. "Mallory, please, sit." The plea in his voice was impossible to resist. So was the hand he thrust against my back, propelling me toward the spare seat at the small table.

"I really should check upon Mamma," I said.

"Your mother is a fine woman," said Lord Nathaniel, lifting his goblet toward the ceiling. "*Italiana, si?*"

"*Si, mio signore.*"

"*Allora. Parle Italiano. Bene. Bene.*"

The man's accent was flawless and he knew it. But rather than enhancing him, it became another flaw. How dare he speak my mother tongue so well.

He watched as I gathered my skirts about me and Caleb poured the wine. "Northern blood if I'm not mistaken—the women are all beautiful there." He gestured toward me. "You look nothing like her. She is all fire and snow—you, you're midnight and—" He looked me up and down. Stiffening, my hands clutched the arms of the chair. The devil began to rise inside me. Who was he to be so free with his opinions upon a first meeting?

"Nate—" warned Caleb, sitting forward, trying to hide a grin. Why, he was enjoying this.

"And bronze. Like a warrior princess of old."

Somewhat mollified, I began to relax and accepted the brimming cup Caleb passed me.

"Or a Romany," added Lord Nathaniel, spoiling the effect.

"Drink," mouthed Caleb, before I could say anything. I glared at him.

This, this *boor* was the man Caleb had spoken of so glowingly? This disheveled, scarred and frankly impolite swaggerer with no notion of how to behave in polite company? In the brief time I'd been in the parlor he'd dared to kiss me, insulted my name and now my appearance. Oh, he was possessed of virtues—those of a churlish, dog-hearted cur. He was not only disrespecting me, but Caleb, my home, my family. Were we so far beneath him we didn't warrant any effort? Not even polite discourse?

I took a sip of the Rhenish, but decided I'd no longer participate in this farce.

"Caleb's right," said Lord Nathaniel, observing me with the studied indifference of a lazy house cat. "Your timing is impeccable. I was about to propose a toast."

"Oh, to what?" I asked, annoyed at the tremor anger lent my query. Two could play at this game; I turned slightly so my shoulder faced Lord Nathaniel and put the question to Caleb alone. I wasn't above being discourteous myself, not when it might teach the noble clotpole a lesson.

"To Caleb," said Lord Nathaniel, seemingly unaware of my snub. "I came here straight from the docks to tell him the good news. He's been officially commissioned by none other than Her Majesty to write a play about Francis Drake and his magnificent accomplishment. It will have its first performance at Deptford in April, when the old sea-rogue is knighted."

Forgetting everything, I embraced Caleb. "Why, that's simply wonderful. Congratulations." We struck goblets and Caleb jerked his chin in the direction of Lord Nathaniel. I pretended not to understand the signal and continued to address my conversation to him alone.

"Does that mean your troupe will perform before Her Majesty as well?"

"Indeed." Caleb's eyes sparkled. "And many more of the gentry besides. Is it not grand? And all due to his lordship, to whom I owe more than gratitude." As our cups lifted in another toast, Caleb pushed mine toward his patron's so all three vessels touched. Once more, I met Lord Nathaniel's amber eyes and felt a wave of aggravation flood my body. I began to pray Papa would arrive and break up this intimate party, send me to Mamma's side and free me from my social obligations. Filling the awkward silence, Caleb continued, "I thought Lord Leicester's Men would earn the commission. I was not alone in that belief."

Lord Nathaniel pulled a face. "Perchance, once. But the Earl is currently out of favor." He stretched his legs, unaware or uncaring that his boots rested against my skirts. I tried to move them out of the way, but it was impossible without shifting my chair. I wouldn't give him the satisfaction.

"And will remain so while his current marriage lasts," added Caleb.

"Unless an accident should befall *this* wife, I see no reason to predict an early end," shrugged Lord Nathaniel, and took a long drink. His foot moved back and forth, striking my shin. "My Lady Lettice is a woman of great beauty and wit."

As I attempted to move beyond the rhythmic touch of his boot, I pondered this exchange. It was no surprise the Earl of Leicester's marital arrangements were still the subject of gossip, but I was a little shocked his lordship would so readily disparage one of his peers. He may simply have felt at ease in Caleb's company, but I took it as another strike against his character.

The Queen's favorite for many years, Lord Robert Dudley, the Earl of Leicester, had endured at court where so many other men failed. The mysterious death of his first wife, Amy Robsart, who conveniently broke her neck falling down stairs many years earlier just as rumors began circulating that the Queen would have married Lord Robert if only he were free, quenched Her Majesty's desire for his company. Rumors of the Earl's complicity in his wife's death had dogged him ever since. Even so, he'd been loyal to the Queen—at least until just over two years ago when, without her knowledge, he'd married one of her own ladies, Lettice Knollys, who, it was said, resembled a young Elizabeth. Unable to forgive him, the Queen had banished the Earl from court. Only recently had he returned, without his wife, whose presence the Queen still refused to tolerate.

"One man's folly is another's good fortune, is it not?" laughed Lord Nathaniel. "Unlike the Earl, I'm a novelty whose gilt has not yet worn. I asked and she said aye." He chuckled. "It will not always be so easy. We'll make the most of what's sure to be a temporary setback for my Lord Robert. Her Majesty is wont to forgive him what she won't in others—even a wife. So here's to our company's chance to shine." Raising his goblet, Lord Nathaniel smiled. "To Caleb Hollis and . . . what is the title you've bestowed on your forthcoming masterpiece?"

"Drake's Hind," said Caleb.

I stared at him in horror. *Drake's Hind?* Oh dear God. "You're not calling your new play *that*, are you?" I blurted. "You can't!"

"Why not?" said Caleb, rising slightly to strike Lord Nathaniel's goblet before bumping mine and falling back into his seat. "Drake's voyage is a story of setbacks, loss, death, doubts, random plundering, a growing following, treachery from those you least expect and so much more. The man showed pluck and succeeded where most believed he'd fail. If nothing else, it will earn a laugh or two. What say you, my lord?"

"I think, like all your scribblings, it might earn more than that. I'm inclined to agree with Mistress Mallory—you must rethink your title lest you risk offending those you seek to please, including Her Majesty. My credit at court will last awhile yet—yours, I'm not so certain. Particularly after *Circe's Chains*."

My misgivings on that score were well founded. Attracting the attention of the court did not always bode well, and certainly not for the likes of a writer who dared to criticize the Queen. Why, only last year Master John Stubbes, a local publisher, had lost his right hand for daring to express his views about the Queen's proposed marriage to the Duke of Anjou in a pamphlet distributed throughout the city and beyond. News of how Sir Francis interceded on the writer's behalf, to commute a certain death sentence to the loss of a hand, had reached even my ears. I recalled my dismay that mere words, not deeds, could attract such punishment and offered fresh prayers for my own salvation. I also sent up a swift one that Caleb might be spared such attention.

"Still," said Lord Nathaniel, "is it not the role of entertainment to offer a challenge to those in authority, to prick the conscience? The Queen enjoys such frolics immensely, and gives preferment to court- iers who support them."

"Your patronage of our troupe was timely; the good fortune you have brought me is beyond reckoning." Caleb grinned.

"'Twas only what you deserved, my friend," said Lord Nathaniel. "I was fortunate that when I returned from the voyage with Drake, Leicester or one of the other companies hadn't yet seduced you."

I studied Lord Nathaniel from the corner of my eye. For all his uncouth behavior, he seemed genuine in liking and supporting Caleb—and watching his back as well. The scars upon his face showed that he was not only a drinker, but also a fighter. I would not have been surprised if they were the consequence of his talent to offer offense. He treated others with such . . . what was it? Not contempt exactly, but a carelessness that bordered on disrespect. Few among the gentry would tolerate such treatment, even from one of their own. How he managed to remain in one piece at sea for three years was indeed a mystery.

Lord Nathaniel tossed back his drink and helped himself to yet another, topping up Caleb's goblet as if he were the host, but failing to offer me any. Not that I would have accepted. I'd no desire to share anything with this man, let alone the companionship of a drink.

Caleb took a hefty swallow, dabbed at his mouth with a ker- chief and, picking up the jug, added to my goblet. I could not help myself and bestowed a warm smile upon him before addressing Lord Nathaniel. "Perchance you're right, my lord. In that regard, it's the playwright's duty to please and offend—"

Caleb broke in. "One just hopes to do more of the former and less of the latter. If we worried about such matters, not a word would be written, not a player would dare take the stage. Drake will enjoy the title's jest at his expense and that of his detractors, I assure you. Marry, the play will have to receive the blessing of the Master of Revels before it's performed."

Lord Nathaniel nodded. "I don't need your reassurance or that of Sir Edmund Tilney, my friend. I know your words will amuse and bemuse. Here's to Caleb whom God has blessed." He stretched over the table and smacked Caleb's goblet hard with his own, slopping some of the contents over the table and my skirts.

"Zounds," said Caleb, putting down his drink and making a poor attempt to mop up the spill. Lord Nathaniel laughed. *Laughed.*

"Sorry, Mallory." Caleb gazed dolefully at the darkening patch upon my skirts.

"Do not worry yourself on my account, Caleb," I said, making a halfhearted effort to dab at the wine before giving up. I glared in his lordship's direction, waiting for an apology.

"Black hides a multitude of sins," said Caleb.

"Verily," I snapped, my anger not directed toward him but his drunken patron.

"If that's so, mistress, what are *you* hiding beneath those raven hues?" drawled Lord Nathaniel, heaving himself upright in his chair.

I froze and looked into the golden eyes fixed upon me, stripping away the barricades I'd erected and staring into my soul. A lump formed in my throat, checking the retort I wanted to give. My hands began to shake. Unbidden, tears dammed my eyes. Before I could gather my wits, the door opened and Papa entered.

Relief flooded me and, as he was introduced and conversation began to flow, I was able to regain my equilibrium. Almost immediately, Lord Nathaniel underwent an abrupt change. Before Papa, his manner was most courteous and solicitous, especially when he learned Mamma would not be joining us for supper. Why, no wonder this man patronized an acting troupe, for he'd missed his calling when he went to sea—it wasn't the deck of a ship he should be treading, but the boards.

I begged pardon to go to my rooms and change. I also wanted to see Mamma—well, "want" was maybe too strong a word. It was the right thing to do and, sweet Jesu, I needed to escape the present company.

The men rose and bowed and I curtseyed. As he escorted me to the door, Papa pulled me aside.

"Your mother is not . . . well, Mallory. She's asked to be left alone."

My heart quickened. "What's wrong, Papa? Was Lord Nathaniel's visit too much?" I was quite prepared to accord this man all manner of sins, including my mother's illness.

"Not his lordship—" He couldn't meet my eyes.

"Oh. I see."

"Nay, Mallory," sighed Papa. "You don't."

Not wanting to contradict Papa, I held my peace. But I could imagine all too well what was going on. My arrangement with Sir Francis didn't remove me from the house as Mamma desired, it merely shouted to the world I was not fit for marriage, only lowly employment. Mamma could not bear what this latest arrangement would do to her reputation.

The anger Lord Nathaniel's behavior stoked began to burn anew. I felt besieged.

"Don't be long," whispered Papa. "A woman's presence will sweeten the company tonight." He indicated the men.

Caleb and Lord Nathaniel were thick in conversation.

"I will join you shortly then," *and be as sweet as belladonna.* I bestowed a kiss upon Papa and closed the door behind me.

Slowly I mounted the stairs. What a day this had proved. First Sir Francis, then Lord Nathaniel, and now Mamma.

Excitement, disgust, anger and despair battled within me. How I wished I had a mother like those in the tales I loved or like my *nonna* had been to Mamma and her younger sister before she died; a mother to whom I could turn and confess my rage toward Caleb's patron and laugh at the obvious shortcomings of such a tall man. Or to whom I could confide my agreement with Sir Francis, knowing the secret would be forever safe. To whom I could confess all that had happened while I was with Raffe . . . Did such mothers exist or were they, like love, the stuff upon which foolish dreams were made?

As I passed Mamma's door, I hesitated and pressed my ear to the wood. I stilled my breathing, forced myself to be calm. At first I heard nothing except Angela's tread as she moved around the room. Then another sound reached my ears. Mistaking it for a cat's wail at first, I waited, leaned more heavily against the door, and listened. When I knew for certain what I was hearing, I withdrew in shock.

Backing away from the door, I fled up the last steps and into my gelid room. Angela had always said no good came from eavesdropping. She was right.

I never knew a mother's sobs could be so heart wrenching, so painful to hear. Unlike her acerbic words and cool behavior, her cries exposed the depth of her loathing, how desperately she wished to have me gone. I stood by the window, breathing deeply, ignoring the cold

that seeped into my bones as evening crept across the yard below. To
my left lay Castiglione's tome—my bible. I rested a hand upon the
cover, as if drawing strength from the contents.

Little did I know when I swore my oath what a toll the nonchalance
of *mediocrita* would take. I would not always possess the strength to
disguise my emotions, not when they were tossed by tumultuous seas
such as Mamma, or struck by unexpected storms like Lord Nathaniel and Sir Francis—never mind the constant guilt that attended me.
There was no shame in remaining in port until it was safe to venture
out again.

Consequently, I didn't return to the parlor that evening. Nor did
anyone come to find out why.

ELEVEN

HARP LANE AND
SEETHING LANE, LONDON
Sunday the 15th of January, Anno Domini 1581
In the 23rd year of the reign of Elizabeth I

*T*wo days later, I woke early and snuggled beneath the covers, watching the bands of light peeping through the shutters grow brighter as they traveled across the bed toward my face. When the morning bells began to toll I could delay no longer. It was time to face the day.

Still I hesitated, luxuriating in the illusion this was an ordinary Sunday, a Sunday like those before Raffe entered my life. I allowed myself to imagine what might have been. Would I be married to a weak-chinned lawyer, lying abed while he snored? Or swaddling a baby before heading to church? Or would some other swain who pleased Mamma and Papa have swept me off my feet? Or would I be plain old Mallory, innocent of the machinations and lies of men, working by my father's side, losing my head in books, testing locks and yearning for romance and adventure?

With a sigh of disgust that yet again my thoughts had led me along this weed-strewn path, I tossed back the blankets and swung my feet to the cold floor. Today was today and nothing I wished or thought would change that. And I was still plain old Mallory—Mallory Blight, if the neighbors were to be believed.

Shivering by the hearth, I patiently blew upon the embers, prodding them with the iron until they flamed, and then threw some kindling on top. I washed and dressed in a kind of daze, not wanting to think too far ahead lest the tiny mice inside my stomach nibble my insides away and I collapse in upon myself. The thought made me grin. Why, I'd been spending too much time with Caleb, my fancies were preposterous.

Thinking of Caleb led me to consider his patron. Since that first encounter with Lord Nathaniel, he'd occupied far too many of my waking hours. He was like no one I'd ever met before. His manner confounded me. Indifferent not only to his title and the rank it accorded him, he possessed no social graces, had treated me with little more than contempt, and yet when he chose, he could exude a certain rakish charm that Caleb, Papa and—from what Comfort said—Mamma had responded to. When he wasn't being insulting, Lord Nathaniel conversed with me in the same manner he did with Caleb. I could not help but be gratified by that, especially after being raised by Papa and relishing dialogues with Master Fodrake and Caleb. Too often men modified their words and the subjects they spoke of when a woman was present. We were judged weak-minded, less able to grasp problems or use our wits. Raffe understood women to serve one purpose only. Sir Francis saw my sex as a benefit to him; so did Papa. While it would be easy to assume Lord Nathaniel had much in common with Raffe and considered women to be chattels, the fact he saw fit to debate the suitability of the title of Caleb's play in my presence—and to discuss the Earl of Leicester—suggested his attitude might be more complex. Or was I being overly generous?

When Caleb had found me in the parlor yesterday, he'd made any number of excuses for his patron's behavior (he'd been at sea for years and was accustomed to the company of certain types of men; he wasn't used to women; he'd consumed a great deal of ale and wine) and assured me that over supper his comportment had been exemplary.

"One does not lose manners the way one might a glove or a shoe," I chided as his excuses continued. He was desperate that I should see the qualities he so admired in Lord Nathaniel. "Nor is respect a pump to be turned on and off at will. One either possesses it or one does not. I fear your Lord Nathaniel is in the latter camp."

"Oh, but he does, Mallory. He does," argued Caleb, launching into another defense. "Forget his attire, he came straight from the docks. I beg you give the man another chance."

I did not, could not care. As Caleb continued, I made up my mind that the less I saw of Lord Nathaniel Warham, the better. Regardless of what Caleb said, the man put me on edge. Not in the way Raffe did, where I felt I walked on a slippery precipice with broken glass on one side and a raging river on the other. Nay, Lord Nathaniel was not a danger except that he brought out the worst in me and aroused the passions I sought to tame. I wanted to strike the smug look off his handsome face; like a mother teaching a small child, I wanted to insist upon courtesy. If the gentry didn't display manners, then who would? Did we not learn from our betters? That's what Mamma, Papa and Master Fodrake had oft told me. All I learned from Lord Nathaniel was that a title and a bulging purse did not prevent a person from being a vexatious churl.

While I was at it, I would discourage Caleb from speaking about him as well. Just as I had excised Raffe from my past, I would remove all references to Lord Nathaniel Warham from my present. And I would not give that kiss he bestowed another thought.

What I was reluctant to admit, and what contributed to the affront, was that Caleb never asked why I hadn't reappeared for supper that night. Nor did he ask about my visit to Sir Francis. His head was filled with Lord Nathaniel and his new commission. I understood, but that didn't stop the little burn of hurt. It was as if Lord Nathaniel had supplanted me in my friend's heart.

I tiptoed down the stairs, slowing as I passed Mamma's rooms. I still hadn't laid eyes upon her since returning from Sir Francis's. When I asked Angela how Mamma fared, she held me tight and said not to worry. Mamma's malady was one she oft suffered and it would, God willing, ease with time.

I broke my fast in the kitchen, eating my manchet and cheese in silence while Mistress Pernel plucked a chicken, Comfort heated water and the apprentices wandered in one by one, bleary eyed, all dressed in their Sunday best, murmuring "good morrows" and "well mets."

It wasn't until I was in the entry hall, donning my thickest coat and gloves—the rare sunshine had done little to deter the chill in the air—that Papa joined me. Flashing what he thought was a smile, although it barely pulled his lips, he too had dressed for the outdoors. Angela, Comfort, Gracious, Master Gib and the apprentices also gathered. We'd attend church together before Papa and I would continue on to Seething Lane whereupon, once he saw me safely into Sir Francis's care, he would be the one to leave me.

Sir Francis was expecting me. When I arrived I was taken swiftly to his office, where a fire blazed and cups of warm spiced wine awaited. I sipped mine gratefully as he began to outline what he expected of me over the next few weeks. I wouldn't be meeting Frances today, or any day soon. She and her mother had departed for Barn Elms, their house in Surrey. For now, it was incumbent upon me to keep up the charade, to ensure my family believed I was indeed Frances Walsingham's companion and spent my days by her side. In order to answer any questions that might arise, Sir Francis made me recite what our activities would have been had his daughter and I indeed been together: reading, sewing, playing the clavichord, a tour of the house, dinner.

"This can be the pattern of your days for now. Just remember, Frances is quiet, studious. She is gifted musically and speaks French and Spanish passably well. Take from that what you must and weave a story." He glanced out the window. "Add that you enjoyed some mulled wine in the sunshine," he said, nodding toward the yard, enclosed by a high fence and its outbuildings and long row of stables. A table and bench sat near a small garden. "Keep it simple. Embellish only when necessary. Though, knowing your father, I doubt you'll be questioned. He trusts me to look after your best interests."

Verily, that was so. "What about Mamma or the servants? What if they should ask?"

"Then you will assuage their curiosity with a suitable story."

I nodded. The servants, like the apprentices, were more inclined to avoid me than seek explanations of my whereabouts and duties.

Angela and Comfort might inquire so I would ensure I'd something prepared that would satisfy them.

"If I'm not to keep your daughter company today, what is it I'm to do?"

"Come," he said, and led me back into the outer room.

The last time I'd been here, numerous men were hard at work, their activities wreathed in tallow smoke like the fog that sat over the river throughout winter; it had been empty when I arrived today. Now a solitary man occupied one of the desks, two flickering candles at his elbows. It was Master Thomas Phelippes, his small eyes behind thick glasses, his yellow hair dry and untidy. Soberly attired like his master, he looked up only when Sir Francis paused beside him. Closing his book, he climbed to his feet and touched his cap.

"Sir, mistress," he said.

"Master Thomas," I said, and dipped a curtsey.

He looked about as pleased to see me as Mamma. Pulling a stool over to the desk, Sir Francis bade me sit and began to outline what I would be doing at Seething Lane. Whatever I'd thought my role would entail, nothing prepared me for what I heard.

"Mallory, it's important as few people as possible know your real purpose. For that reason, I'm putting Thomas in charge of your instruction. For today, and every other Sunday, you will work here. My men rarely come to the house on the Lord's day. For the remainder of the week, you will be given your own room in another part of the house. Unless I summon you, there's no reason for you to enter here; as far as possible, I do not want you to be seen. You will come to the rear door at the specified time, and Laurence, Thomas or Robert will admit you. You are to report straight to the room you've been allocated and await Thomas, who will outline your lessons and duties. If and when it's required, others will be asked to instruct you as well. What you'll find is that each of my men has his own special skill. I want you to be familiar with all of them, as much as you are able, that is."

"Such as?"

"Thomas here is a master of code. He can both write and decipher the most complex of them."

A wave of excitement washed over me. "I'm to learn this at once?"

Master Thomas made a small scoffing noise. He was as surprised as

I was—or was "appalled" a more appropriate description? Sir Francis gave me an indulgent smile.

"Only what you can comprehend."

"Do you know what code is?" asked Thomas, shoving a book toward me. His indignation at being asked to teach me, and his doubt that I could absorb anything, were apparent.

I opened the book's worn leather cover and chose not to be offended by his manner.

"Ah, Erasmus's *In Praise of Folly*." I glanced back at Sir Francis, then at Thomas, who looked astonished that I recognized the title. Were they testing my knowledge of Latin? Before I could say anything, Thomas jerked his head toward the book.

"Turn to page thirty-three."

I silently moved one of the candles closer and turned to the page as directed. Instead of a page of prose, there were rows of letters neatly arranged in columns, followed by some symbols.

"Do you know what that is?" asked Sir Francis.

"Aye, I've seen this before. In a copy of *Stenographia* by the Abbot Trithemius." Incredulity crossed Thomas's face. I pressed on. "I purchased it from one of the book booths at the Royal Exchange." I'd been thirteen years old. Master Fodrake had been delighted. "It's a cipher of some kind." I looked at Thomas. "Is it not?"

Sir Francis chuckled. "That's exactly what it is." He reached over my shoulder and stabbed the page with a finger. "The letters in every second line substitute for those here in the first." His finger drifted across the symbols. "These are nulls, used when a word ends or to confuse a code breaker. We don't often worry about phrases or paragraphs, but run the message in continuous lines. My men are very skilled at deciphering these, Thomas especially."

"Sometimes," added Thomas, "particularly if you know to whom you are sending the code, a mere symbol will suffice—we can convey with a few symbols what would otherwise take sentences."

Sir Francis withdrew his hand. "I want you to learn to use this cipher, and others, so that when you compose your reports for me, only we can read them. This will be your first lesson and Thomas will be your teacher. Do you think you can do this?"

What was I to say? That I relished the thought of immersing myself in such a task? That writing code was akin to a game or learning a new language that only a few spoke? That to be included in such an enterprise when I was excluded from so many others was thrilling? I balled my hands into fists and forced myself to sound calm.

"I think so." Modesty. And *mediocrita*.

"Good. You will practice—with Thomas and me and, later, others. We will use the same cipher. Each night, you'll be set a page to translate—into English or another language before putting it into code—or a report to write."

"Is that all you want me to learn, Sir Francis?"

Thomas bit back a sound that might have been a groan.

"Oh, no, Mallory," said Sir Francis, folding his arms and looking down his long nose. "This is just the beginning . . ."

TWELVE

HARP LANE, LONDON
Mid-January to early March, Anno Domini 1581
In the 23rd year of the reign of Elizabeth I

And so it was. How do I describe the world into which I was plunged over the next few weeks? From locks and tools as familiar to me as my own fingers, I became an avid explorer in a new world, once more the best and most earnest of students.

It took me less than a week to learn the code I was first shown. Every night I was given a passage from a book or a letter to either decipher or turn into code. I accomplished this with no mistakes. Much to my surprise, I was also given responses to none other than Campion's "Brag" to put into code, the very letter the Jesuit wrote to the Privy Council to defend his presence in England. These included extracts from a pamphlet by William Charke and another by an Oxford theologian named Meredith Hammer. Both men took Campion to task and identified him as an enemy to be feared. I was given Catholic tracts to cipher, as well as parts of John Foxe's *Book of Martyrs* and many more works besides. Not only were these assignments teaching me to code and decode, they were lessons in the battle being waged between Catholics and Protestants.

Unable to believe there were no errors in what I handed to him each morning, Thomas set me more and more complex work. He even had me ciphering different languages. The results were without flaw. After two weeks, and a particularly difficult letter coded in French, he gave me what might have been a smile. Looking back at the paper I handed him, he nodded approvingly.

"Well done, Mistress Mallory. We may make a watcher of you yet."

Thomas accompanied me home one afternoon and insisted we go a roundabout way via Leadenhall Markets, where he had dwellings. Snow had fallen throughout the day, making our passage more difficult and sodden than usual. Clouds hung low in the sky, giving the streets and lanes an oppressive air and darkening the afternoon light.

Groups of heavily wrapped folk stood shivering behind stalls or before crackling braziers that sent sparks spiraling into the sky, and eyes followed their glowing ascent lest they land on thatch. I didn't think there'd be much danger of fire when everything was so damp. A few vendors tried to attract our attention, calling out their wares, stepping into our path, but their efforts were apathetic at best. Alehouses were doing a fine trade, with customers spilling out onto the road. Down the laneways, hammering could be heard, as well as voices raised in argument. Outside one inn, a row of men stood with their backs to the street relieving themselves against a wall; one kicked a cat that had meandered between his legs. Dogs and children dashed past, the cold making them fleet-footed, though I noticed Thomas's hand dropped to the sword at his side whenever anyone pressed too close. I'd lived in London long enough to be wary of pickpockets, but Thomas's weapon and the way his hand hovered above the pommel kept our purses safe.

Lamps were being lit and the night watchmen had taken to the street by the time we reached my gate. I turned to thank Thomas for his escort, wondering why we'd ventured so far out of the way.

"For tonight's undertaking," he began. Despite working with me so closely for a number of weeks, he maintained a distance between us. I was never to forget who was the master and who the student. "I want a full report of everything you observed as we walked here—the people, the buildings, the mood. Was anyone suspicious? If so, why? What conversations did you overhear? What were people carrying? Buying and selling? I want you to record everything."

I stared at him in consternation. "You could have told me this before we left Seething Lane."

"I could have," he said. "But what purpose would that serve?" He doffed his hat and, before I could reply, disappeared into the shadows, narrowly avoiding a gentleman on horseback.

"What purpose indeed?" I sighed, and opened the gate.

I labored long and hard over my task, burning candles well into the small hours and losing sleep. When I passed the report to Thomas the following day, I watched in silence as he read it. It was all I could do not to lay my arms upon the desk and rest my head.

Behind me, the door to Sir Francis's study was closed. I'd not caught sight of him in weeks. Committed to Parliament, he oft slept at Whitehall, where he had rooms. Knowing he'd be absent didn't prevent me from searching for evidence of his return. There was none. Yet I knew he was aware of everything I did, my strengths and weaknesses. Thomas wrote to him daily.

Minutes passed. The small fire burned, the candles sputtered and still Thomas read. After all, there were many pages to get through. What he hadn't known when he set me the task was that I had excellent recollection. As a lock-pick and an only child, my memory was both an essential tool and my finest friend.

So when I wrote down what I'd seen on our long walk to Harp Lane, I included the name of every single street and byway, the number of shops we'd passed and what they sold, the different stalls we'd seen and the roaming vendors, their panniers and baskets half-empty. I recalled the cow with the discordant bell and the thin, disconsolate maid leading it. I described in detail the clothing of the women lingering near the conduit in Cornhill Street, the number of children, the toys they carried and even the condition of the dogs scavenging among the ditches. The pigs being herded into the churchyard of St. Benet's didn't escape my notice either, nor the swineherd who, though he wore a grubby jacket and breeches, was possessed of a creamy shirt and hands that didn't belong to a farmer. With his cap pulled low, I couldn't see the cast of his eyes, but his beard was well trimmed, as was his hair. A finely dressed woman admitted him into the yard, looking over her shoulder as she clumsily hauled the gate shut. She was of middling years and, from the linen kerchief pressed to her nose and lips, uncomfortable with the odor of the swine.

I listed every church between Little Eastcheap and Harp Lane as well as the number of times the bells tolled. Admittedly, much of this was not something I knew simply from the afternoon's amble, but from years of living within the parishes. I even made note of the men dressed for a meeting at the Baker's Hall who spilled from the Queen's Arms as we passed, as well as the three wenches who, with décolletages on display, tried to delay them.

I saw money change hands, a pistol drawn and flourished, four boys spoiling for a fight and, in the darkening reaches of Love Lane, just as we passed St. Andrew Hubbard, two young women tugging each other's hair, spitting and wailing while a group of men and women urged them on.

All in all, I was pleased with what I wrote, and how I had ciphered it, but as Thomas continued to read, and his expression revealed nothing, my confidence began to retreat. What if this was not what Sir Francis or Thomas wanted? What if my woman's eye was not as discerning as a man's? Would he mock my observations? Discard them as the feeble ramblings of a dizzy-minded female? I'd grown accustomed to Thomas and his ways. He was unlike any other man of my acquaintance—Papa, Caleb, Raffe or Lord Nathaniel—and indifferent to anything but his work. I was not so much a person as another task to be completed. He hovered between treating me with barely disguised resignation and, lately, a little pride. As if I was a job well done.

I was so preoccupied, I didn't notice he'd taken off his glasses and begun to wipe them with a kerchief, his eyes still on the paper before him. He cleared his throat. My hands were balled so tightly in my lap, my knuckles were white.

"Well?" I asked hesitantly.

Thomas wrapped the metal ends of his spectacles around his ears, blinked and stared at me. He had the look of a disheveled owl, and I resisted the urge to reach out and flatten the tuft of hair sprouting from his head.

"Mistress Mallory. I have to say, this is exceptional."

"Really?" I sat forward. I hadn't known how much I wanted to hear words of praise from this clever man's lips.

"Really. I can scarce believe what you've noted; the detail you've given, and all without mistake."

My heart pumped so hard it hurt. I twisted the document around, the pages fanning beneath my hands. "The swineherd at the church—"

"Ah, you're quite right. He is not what he seems. I'm astounded you observed what you did about him. We walked past there swiftly as well."

I couldn't help it; I beamed. "And the women—the ones near the inn. I felt they weren't simply—"

"Aye, aye," said Thomas, turning the pages back to face him, picking them up and straightening them by tapping them on the desk. "They were not." He held up a hand to stop me talking further.

"Mallory—I may call you that?"

I nodded.

"This is quite simply remarkable. Not only for the insight and descriptions that would give our man, Charles Sledd, pause, but you have mastered one of the most difficult codes of all. I never thought I would say this, but I am impressed. Furthermore, I know Sir Francis will be as well."

I didn't dare speak.

"I think it's time we added some more lessons to the curriculum."

The report I wrote about our walk home to Harp Lane altered my relations with Thomas Phelippes. Whereas he'd begun instructing me grudgingly, simply because his master had ordered him, he now became my ally. He not only taught me because he had to, but also because he understood he had a willing and apt pupil. From ciphers (of which I learned three more—even using genuine documents from earlier in the Queen's reign, ones pertaining to marriage agreements, the movement of troops in Ireland and more besides), I graduated to being able to make and write with invisible ink. The juice of oranges, lemons and even milk sufficed, all of them being absorbed into paper until they could no longer be seen. Upon heating, the script, and thus the message, was revealed. It was an alchemy that was marvelous in my eyes.

At home I would take an occasional piece of fruit from the kitchen or a tankard of milk from the pail, carry it to my room and delight in practicing. Able to eat the pulp of the fruit, I'd only to discard the rinds. If I forgot to drink the milk, Latch would purr with gratitude.

Over the following weeks, other men with different talents were brought to my small room at the rear of Sir Francis's house in order to further my training. Without exception, they resented sharing their skills with a woman. They spoke in barely coherent sentences, refused to answer my questions, provided examples a scholar would be hard-pressed to emulate, and left before I was able to practice or ask them to repeat anything I didn't understand. Ungenerous with their time and knowledge, they wanted me to fail.

Of course, I made sure I would not. I redoubled my efforts. And I never breathed a word of complaint.

I'd no idea who these men were. They did not give their names and were not given mine. From their dress and my knowledge of the sumptuary laws, which prescribed which ranks could wear certain clothes, it seemed they came from all walks of life: from the nobility to gentlemen to those below them. Whether garbed in rich velvets, silks and brocades and carrying a pomander between their beringed fingers, or wearing stained leather, fustian and wool, these men would pace the room or perch on the stool at the very end of my desk. Others, clothed in dirty smocks and with ruinous teeth and breath, would leer at me over the desk, or sit with their arms folded, barely meeting my eyes. Most, however, were dressed like my father—cleanly and neatly, with an air about them of lawyers or merchants. What made them so interesting was that, over time, I came to understand that any one of them could be in disguise, for that was something else I was taught.

At first I thought it was as simple as donning a different outfit or fitting a wig. But, like the codes that appeared straightforward on the surface, there was much more to it than wearing another set of clothes or affecting an accent. Moving your body a particular way, altering the pitch of your voice, the tempo of your speech, the way you addressed folk, mannerisms, stride: all were essential to being convincing in a role.

Late at night in my room, I would practice becoming someone different—older and younger; saucy women and polite gentlewomen. Emulating those I saw on my daily walks, I would affect their facial expressions, their way of speaking and moving, becoming more confi-

dent and surprising Thomas with my skill. For certes, observing Caleb
and helping him con his lines as well as attending the theater meant I'd
had years of absorbing such talents.

What astonished me was how much I enjoyed it. I thought all joy
in wearing pretty clothes, using my smile and my eyes to express pleasure, show affection or interest, had gone for good. Drawing attention
to myself only led to pain. My false knight had taught me many things
about being a woman—a woman who existed only for one man's
notice. He noticed me with lips, fist or cock, depending on his mood.

Sir Francis and his men weren't undoing the lessons Raffe had
imparted so much as transforming them, encouraging me to use my
attributes, such as they were, to attract notice or, when required, to
pass without a second glance, to appear browbeaten and defeated. For
the first time since my rescue, I was able to draw on my experiences
and use them in a way I had never anticipated.

This went some way to restoring my confidence and helping me
reclaim who I'd once been, only tempered, honed and steeled—like
the locks Papa forged.

Locks were another way I was tested. Oft-times Thomas would
appear at my door, a padlock or small locked box in his hands,
requesting I open it. It was easy to bring my lock-picking tools to
Seething Lane as they fitted neatly in my purse. Thomas would watch
while I inserted the picks and sprang the various mechanisms, then
passed them over without a word. Indifferent to my skills at first,
Thomas could no longer feign a lack of interest as some of the locks
became more complex. One Sunday, when the house was all but
empty, the servants attending a late service, Thomas led me through
the place, making me unlock every door then relock them. Not once,
but thrice, we moved up and down the corridors, my speed increasing each time. The only exception was Sir Francis's study.

Without a word, he led me back to my room and passed me a letter
from an agent in France to decode. When he brought me a cup of ale
and some bread moments later, I knew he was pleased with my efforts.
In the short time I'd known him, I'd discovered Thomas was a man of
few words whose actions defined him.

I was also given lessons in geography, but not of our country or the
lands and seas around it—of what use were they, when a map told me

all I needed to know? It was the nearby streets and laneways, as well as those across the river, I was to learn by heart. Every exit and entry into the various churchyards, alehouses, inns and taverns was explained over and over, as were the tunnels beneath the city, holes in the walls, shortcuts from one parish to the next. I learned who could be paid to keep silent and who, for a groat, would talk. Crude line drawings were made which I was forced to replicate the next day and the next, drawing arrows to indicate how I would flee if pursued, where I would hide. I was told how to exit from the river without being seen, disappear over a rooftop, which houses were empty and regarded as "safe." Whom I could ask for shelter. Whom to avoid.

One day in late February, Thomas met me at the door of Seething Lane and, instead of welcoming me in, took me by the arm and walked me through the same streets I'd been studying, subtly pointing out the errant staircase, broken window, torn pigskin or almost hidden snickets by the river and the various hiding places. Sometimes, the ladder I'd been told about had vanished, the hole in the wall repaired, or a house believed vacant had occupants.

"Things change all the time; people move, die, marry, fall sick. Never take for granted what you're told. Never trust what is written. Never trust your eyes."

"If I can't trust my eyes," I said, looking around, drinking in the solidity of everything I could see, "then what?"

"Your head," said Thomas. "And your heart."

Thomas made sense. You could never trust your eyes with a lock. So many appeared to be one thing but were really another. Unpicking them, I relied on every sense but sight—touch, hearing, my sense of smell and even taste. I also relied on my heart—on an instinct that arose from somewhere beneath my breast and warned or encouraged me in a manner that couldn't be ignored.

Over the weeks I spent at Seething Lane in the company of watchers and intelligencers, I became so adept at falsehoods and subterfuge, so quick to invent stories or color the truth, my family had no idea I wasn't attending to Sir Francis's daughter but instead was embroiled in much darker and more mysterious matters.

THIRTEEN

*W*inter bade adieu and spring blossomed, and as the days grew longer and there was still light to spare once I arrived home, Papa began asking me to join him in the workshop.

With music in my heart, I obliged. I would test the locks he made, open jewel chests owned by ladies who'd lost their keys, or document boxes that had jammed. It was at those times Papa would ask politely about my day and accept my rather taciturn responses.

"Sir Francis treats you well?"

"I hardly see him, sir," I answered truthfully. "Parliament is sitting and he is otherwise occupied. Most of his staff as well."

Even Mamma, accustomed by now to my long hours and reconciled to the fact that my being a companion to Mister Secretary's daughter was nothing to be ashamed of, admitted me back into her presence. I was forbidden to discuss my employ (I sent a swift thanks be to Christ for that respite), but was allowed to say a prayer or sit quietly as she and Angela conversed.

My evenings were oft spent rehearsing Caleb's new play in the parlor. I'd help him con lines, acting out the different roles, entertaining the apprentices and servants as well as Angela and Papa.

Curious about what my job entailed, Caleb proved most persistent in his need for detail when we were alone. I would try to distract him by asking about the fortunes of the troupe, his writing and even, on occasion and against my better judgment, Lord Nathaniel.

It was late March when news came via the town criers and the speakers at St. Paul's Cross that Parliament had passed stricter legislation against Catholics. There were to be crippling fines for hearing mass, and a year in prison for simply appearing at one. For saying mass, the fine was doubled, followed by twelve months in jail. For those who didn't attend the Church of England Sunday services, the penalties were increased as well. I worried how Papa would pay for Mamma's stubborn recusancy. Her nonattendance at church would no longer be viewed with tolerance and I feared what that presaged, a fear exacerbated by the work I was doing and the new and murky knowledge I was gaining.

But that was not the worst of it. Parliament also decreed that if anyone was caught converting to Catholicism, they'd be declared a traitor and sentenced to death.

The laws were the talk of the streets. The same day they took effect, I filled my time at Seething Lane donning different disguises, speaking only in Spanish, challenged again and again by Thomas as I played the part of a serving maid, a youth newly arrived from the Escorial, a lady's maid to the gentry and even a widowed gentlewoman—a part for which I had much experience. Satisfied with both my language skills and my convincing portrayals, Thomas bade me write a coded report of my day's activities for Sir Francis.

"He'll return from court tomorrow and will be keen to update himself on your progress," said Thomas. "I'm looking forward to learning what he thinks." He briefly placed a hand on my shoulder and gave a rough squeeze. "You have exceeded all expectations," he said.

"Thank you," I said. "Thank you."

We smiled at each other and his eyes began to look suspiciously dewy. Clapping his hands together, he barked, "Again! This time, in Italian." And so, another hour passed.

When I arrived home, a little later than usual, Comfort greeted me in the hallway. She took my cloak and gloves and promised to bring wine and some supper to the parlor. I went to my room to remove my hat, shoes and ruff. Papa was in his workshop with the apprentices, and Mamma and Angela were resting. Caleb was in Southwark, rehearsing with his troupe. There was no one to make demands of me. Ensuring the fire in my bedroom was stoked, I collected my copy of Juan Luis Vives's work *The Education of a Christian Woman* (a New Year's present from Papa), intending to enjoy the book and some solitude in the parlor.

Comfort, bless her, had left a jug of wine and a goblet on the small table by the window. The fire crackled, the room was lovely and warm. Evening shadows spread across the yard, chasing the chickens back into their coop and the heavy-stomached cat toward the kitchen. It would not be long before we were blessed (or cursed, as Master Gib would say, as he made room for Latch by the stove) with kittens. Pouring a drink, I sank into the chair, kicking off my slippers and curling my legs beneath me, imagining, with a smile, soft balls of fur and plaintive mews.

In the garden I could discern shy buds beginning to blossom on the trees. There were hints of violet and ivory, as well as coral and yellow. The vine that clung to the wall at the rear of the yard was also giving off new shoots. Spring was here and with it color and new life.

New life. That's what I too had been given. A fresh beginning, a novel way of being. For all that it relied on facades and fabrications, there was something real and meaningful about what I did, even though I'd not yet been asked to test the skills I was acquiring. Thomas felt I was almost ready. I did, too. But it was up to Sir Francis to decide.

In the weeks I'd been going to Seething Lane, I'd barely given Raffe much thought. Even the dreams that used to torment me no longer held the power they once had. Reaching for the locket nestled over my heart, I pulled it from my dress and squeezed hard. Well, all but one dream, one thought, but that was different. It was a dream of what might have been, had I not been so hasty, so gullible, so ready to defy my parents; so cowardly. And yet, despite the price I'd paid, here I was again, thwarting my parents' wishes. I'd agreed to be dutiful and obedient. While part of me reassured myself that this was still the case—had not Papa acquiesced to my employ and signed the contract?—another part called me to account: I was a fraud. Worse, I had a coconspirator of the highest order, one to whom I showed more loyalty than my own family.

But wasn't it all for a greater good? This was not to satisfy my own base desires nor to fulfill some childish fancy. This was for the Queen and country. It was also to atone for my great sin.

Why then did I feel more knave than hero?

Lost in a maze of thoughts, pulling tendrils of hair from their plaits, lulled by the wine and the warmth of the room, I did not understand that someone else had arrived until the door swung open and I heard Comfort's voice.

I rose quickly, the goblet still in my hand, and my book clattered to the floor.

Swooping to pick it up, the book held out before him, a smile upon his scarred face, was none other than Lord Nathaniel Warham.

FOURTEEN

*W*as it my imagination or was there perturbation on his lordship's face when he saw who was in the room? Ignoring my own sinking heart, I fixed a smile to my face.

"I'm afraid Caleb isn't here—" I retrieved the book from his hands.

"Good even' to you too, Mistress Mallory," said Lord Nathaniel, swaying slightly, managing in that simple phrase to both reprimand my lack of courtesy and exude a sense of goodwill, even though it rang false. He was no happier to see me than I him. It would be churlish of me to take offense, yet I had to fight hard to repress the feeling.

"Forgive me, my lord." I dropped the slightest of curtseys, aware of my stockinged feet, unruly hair. "I forget my manners. May God give you good evening."

"Finding you here, He already has," said Lord Nathaniel with all the sincerity of a Fleet Prison warder. Without waiting for an invitation, he threw himself into a chair, flashing me a grin as he did. "It's been a while, mistress."

Scurrying over with an extra goblet, Comfort poured his lordship a drink and handed it to him.

"Ah, you'd best be careful, mistress, lest you be accused of prophecy," he said.

"Prophecy, my lord?" Comfort stepped back abruptly, one hand upon her breast, her brow furrowed. Parliament had declared prophecy and casting the Queen's horoscope grave offenses. Anyone caught would land in prison. "I know naught of such things, sir."

"But, mistress, you read my mind." Lord Nathaniel winked and took a long draft of wine.

Understanding he was jesting, Comfort gave an exaggerated sigh of relief, chuckled and refilled his goblet.

"Thank you, Comfort, that will be all," I said. The last thing I wanted was his lordship cupshotten, though I suspected he was already well on his way. Not only had he been unsteady on his feet and keen to sit, but the fumes wafting toward me suggested an afternoon of imbibing, as did his slightly ruddy cheeks and distant stare.

Taking advantage of his distraction, I studied him as I resumed my seat. Unlike the last time I had shared his company, on this occasion he was very finely dressed. His cream peascod doublet, sewn with pearls and gold thread, was exquisitely pinked. Black velvet breeches, hose and boots complemented his ensemble, as did a modest ruff. Atop his tawny hair sat a black and cream bonnet replete with a large emerald feather that swept from his face to the back of his head. A jeweled brooch in the shape of an anchor fixed it there. Any appreciation of his fine apparel and the way it sat without a crease or fold, presenting—even I had to admit—a most becoming picture, was somewhat dimmed by his condition. Though he'd not anticipated seeing me, how dare he call when he was blathered by drink? We might be locksmiths, but were we not worthy of the same consideration he'd extend to a courtier? No polite man would presume to intrude upon a gentleman's house in such a state but would retire to either an inn or his own company—preferably, his bed. Yet, here he was in our parlor in Harp Lane. The man's arrogance knew no bounds.

Resigned to dealing with him until Caleb found his way home or Papa appeared, I sought my slippers with my toes and shuffled them back onto my feet. Comfort retreated to the hearth, pretending to tend it while chaperoning us. Though I was regarded as a widow, neither the family nor I could afford another slight upon our—my—reputation.

The silence stretched out. The fire crackled merrily. Lord Nathaniel sipped his wine. I placed my book upon the table. Across the yard, smoke billowed from the workshop and there was the faint ring of metal being struck. Aware of Lord Nathaniel's groggy regard, I began to color.

"I know not how long Caleb might be, my lord."

"There I have the advantage. He's already en route. I went by the inn where the Men had just completed rehearsals only to be told he'd departed. I came by river and am surprised he's not already here." There was a pause. "I wish to discuss the new play with him."

"You're referring to *Dido's Lament*?"

"I am. The Master of Revels, Sir Edmund Tilney"—he drawled the name—"pulled me aside while I was at court." Uncrossing his legs, he sat forward in his seat. "Seems Lord Warham's Men are developing a fine reputation and now the Queen has selected Caleb to celebrate Drake's accomplishments, his other work is drawing attention as well; not all of it the kind he would wish—nor would I as his patron, for that matter." He stared at a spot over my shoulder and then, slowly, raised his drink to his mouth. I'd long held fears about Caleb's temerity, his desire to pluck political threads and see where they unraveled, and it seemed those fears were being realized. Lord Nathaniel looked into his goblet, which appeared to be empty. Again. "Mighty fine wine, this." I gestured to Comfort to pour him some more. "*Dido's Lament* could be a great play, if only Caleb is careful," said his lordship, watching the ruby liquid splash into his vessel.

The tragic love story of Aeneas and Dido and the settlement of Rome was a rollicking tale of lust, greed and desire as well as invasion and treachery. Using Virgil's *Aeneid* as inspiration, Caleb had longed to bring it to the stage. It would cast a critical eye over Romish interests in Europe and the New World, and English ones as well—and thus explored questions of faith. It was no surprise the Master of Revels urged caution.

I searched for something to say. "For all that he has a marvelous grasp of words, I fear 'careful' is not in Caleb's lexicon."

"In that you're correct, mistress," said Lord Nathaniel and, with his golden eyes fixed on mine, raised his drink. "Perchance between us we can urge him to embrace such an unfamiliar state, especially in light of the new punishments offered to those who defame the Queen. I would Caleb keep both his meager wages and his ears."

I nodded. "I would sooner see him in his room upstairs than resting in a pillory."

"I would sooner him alive than dead."

My heart flipped. "Disparaging Her Majesty, even in jest or the fiction of a play, could incur such a sentence?"

Lord Nathaniel stretched out his long legs. He made the chair appear ridiculously inadequate. I wondered if he had special furniture made to accommodate his size. He'd need special chairs, stools, a bespoke desk. And what of his bed? That would require additional length and width. My face grew hot. I forced myself to concentrate on what he was saying.

"Aye, a second offense now means death to those so convicted. There are many among the Council keen to test the effectiveness of the new laws. In fact," he said, reaching for the ewer and helping himself to another drink, sloshing some wine onto the table in the process, "I believe you work for such a man."

My heart constricted in my chest. *Nonchalance*, I reminded myself. Reaching over, I slid my book away from the red puddle spreading over the table, and gestured to Comfort to wipe up the mess. My mind galloped. How did Lord Nathaniel . . . ? Oh, of course. Caleb. Swiftly cleaning away the wine, Comfort took the ewer to refill it, muttering she'd return anon. I waited till she'd left.

"You speak of Sir Francis." I was pleased how even my voice sounded.

"Mister Secretary. Indeed, I do. A friend of mine, and my family's as it happens. Loyal to a fault. To the throne." I wondered how praise could sound so ambiguous, so like a criticism. "Caleb tells me you've a position in the household." Lord Nathaniel's face was inscrutable. "What I know of Sir Francis is that he doesn't admit just anyone into his home lightly. Why, it's common knowledge he runs a network of intelligencers from Seething Lane—and Barn Elms. Couriers, too. His stables are legendary, are they not? You must be an extraordinary woman to be employed by him. Possess many hidden talents; something Caleb oft hints at as well. I cannot help but wonder what those might be."

I drew my breath in sharply. Did he think me Sir Francis's whore?

Or did he mean something else? Was he alluding to my real employ with Sir Francis? But how could he know? That was a secret between myself and Mister Secretary. Not even Thomas, or Sir Francis's brother-in law Master Robert, or any of his other agents knew what Sir Francis intended with me. Not even I knew. How could this man? He could not.

Zounds, but the insult was obvious and stung. The drink he'd consumed could not excuse him. That he awaited until Comfort was no longer present to say such a thing was another mark against him. I would not be spoken to in such a manner. He might be a lord, but his ill breeding was apparent. Let him think what he wants. I remained silent. What did I care? This man was nothing to me.

I willed Comfort to return. I began to wonder what was taking Caleb so long. If he'd indeed left the inn as Lord Nathaniel said, then he should be here by now . . .

"Well?" insisted Lord Nathaniel. "What say you, mistress? Assuage my curiosity, I beg of you."

"I say," I began slowly, determined to steer the conversation in a different direction, "curiosity proved fatal to a creature with many lives to spare, suggesting it's not a healthy state for a man who has but one."

Lord Nathaniel gave a bark of laughter. "I didn't ask for a parable, mistress. I asked for an answer."

"Then here is my answer, sir. I am companion to Sir Francis's daughter and sometime teacher to select of Sir Francis's staff whom he wishes to be more fluent in the languages of both our allies and enemies. To consider anything else is mere fantasy. Caleb is not only a master with words, but with fictions as well. He has created a story with me as his heroine. I would not believe all he told you, my lord; at least, I would not take it as truth."

Lord Nathaniel shook his head slowly, the smile fixed to his mouth altering till it took on the appearance of a sneer. "You play with me, mistress. I prefer straight answers to my questions, not rehearsed ones. They're preferable to mealy-mouthed lessons or female dallying."

I drew myself up. "I assure you, my lord, I do not offer a lesson— mealy-mouthed or otherwise. Nor do I dally. Play is for children or actors such as those you patronize. It is not for the likes of me."

"Is it not?" asked Lord Nathaniel, tilting his head. "I think all women capable of playing a part when it suits them. I'm sure your woman here would agree." His arm swept toward Comfort, who, entering the room with a refreshed ewer, stopped short.

"Me, my lord? I neither agree nor disagree, not with my betters." Shutting the door, Comfort approached and, before I could prevent her, refilled his lordship's goblet.

Comfort never shied from offering her opinion, solicited or not. Aware of the kind of woman she was, the type of servant she would be—loyal, honest and forthcoming—Lord Nathaniel leaned over and cocked his head toward an oblivious Comfort, his golden eyes glittering dangerously in the candlelight, his smile broadening, his meaning clear.

"I rest my case," he said as she returned to the hearth. "The woman is as fine a player as any of your sex." He took a long drink. "She says what she believes men wish to hear and thus conceals her true nature."

A small flare of anger burned in my chest. "She is merely loyal."

"There is nothing *mere* about loyalty, mistress." Rising to his feet abruptly, Lord Nathaniel joined Comfort by the fire, and turned to face me. His head grazed the ceiling and the flames threw his broad figure into silhouette. Comfort moved aside quickly, taking up a position near the door, her gaze traveling from me to Lord Nathaniel and back again. I looked at her once then fixed my regard upon his lordship, praying my beating heart, my shaking hands, were not obvious. *Nonchalance*, I inhaled. *Nonchalance,* I exhaled.

"Women may be forbidden from treading the boards as professional players," continued his lordship. "But they exit the womb masters of the profession. The entire globe is their stage." His arm swept the room, his wine splashing onto the rushes. "Their every utterance is a line delivered to a guileless audience who believes the part they play is the truth, the lines they utter are gospel. They don or discard marvelous costumes for whatever role is required, caring not whom they bewitch, whom they lure with their fictions. They pretend feelings they don't possess, speak words that come not from the heart, but the head, and so shore up their performance and remain convincing in every regard. Until the curtain falls and their lies are exposed and the disappointed audience is either trapped or ordered to exit—oft-times before the play has concluded."

He paused to take a long swallow of wine and I stared at him, blinking. Why, the man was more affected than I first thought.

"All of you are as changeable as—" He sought an apt comparison, and at that moment the wind chose to rattle the shutters. "The weather; nay, a weather vane, swinging one way then another," he finished, throwing back the last of his drink and pushing past his chair to refill his goblet again. Comfort went to aid him, but I shot out my hand to stay her.

How to respond to such a speech? Not only to the offense it offered but also to the evident pain that lay behind every single word and shocked me with its rawness. I smoothed my skirts and waited till he'd seated himself again. What a strange conversation to be having. He fell back into the chair and looked dolefully into the goblet, then raised his chin and locked his eyes upon me. I was not certain what he saw as he blinked, sniffed and blinked again.

Who had so poisoned him against womankind? What had made him so bitter as to read every action, every word of a woman as a mere performance that ruined trust? In my experience, it was not women who performed in such a way. On the contrary . . .

Against my better judgment, I challenged him. "Could the same not be said of men, my lord? Do not men also play their part— whether king or pauper? A great lord such as yourself, or the night soil man pushing his barrow through the city? Why accuse one sex of pretending when both are equally capable if not culpable? And for their own ends."

Frowning, he leaned forward. "What do you mean?"

"Truly, if women play a part, so do men. But perchance you misread genuine discourse as false. Or have you considered those who do engage in such theater may have a sound reason? Could it be an armor they wear, a means of protection against the whims of fortune or even their own folly?"

Lord Nathaniel fell back into his chair, laughing so hard its front legs left the floor and I feared he would tip over. The chair quickly righted itself, flinging his lordship forward again. His laughter never stopped.

"Mistress, mistress, you are grossly misguided in your appraisal. I've yet to meet a woman who means what she says, who is what she seems or has just cause to deceive—there is nothing safe in being false." Putting down his goblet, he searched for a kerchief, dashed it across his eyes and blew his nose lustily. "There's no cause to justify it."

I'd had enough. Standing, I picked up my book. "Then, all I can say, my lord, is you've clearly met the wrong type of woman."

"Ah. And there you have it. Accused by your own mouth," said Lord Nathaniel, pointing at me and chuckling.

"What do you mean, my lord?"

"Are you not a woman? Have I not met you?"

"Allow me to put an end to your evident disappointment." Filled with self-righteous anger, I forgot to curtsey or take leave of our guest. As I reached the door, I turned. "Comfort, see to his lordship's needs. I have duties to attend to."

Without waiting for an answer, I swept from the room, his lordship's laughter ringing in my ears.

FIFTEEN

*Y*our progress is most pleasing, Mallory." Sir Francis lifted the piece of paper before him. "Thus far, it seems there's no skill you haven't mastered. Thomas is generous in his praise and, let me tell you, that's very uncharacteristic of him."

My cheeks grew warm as Sir Francis placed the page back on top of the pile to his right and smoothed it with the side of his hand.

We were sitting in his study, and I had been waiting as patiently as I could while he read the reports painstakingly written by Thomas, Master Robert and the other men who'd been summoned to teach me various techniques, most of whom I could not name and did not expect to see again. I enjoyed the pleasant flutter beneath my breasts Sir Francis's praise elicited. Apart from Papa and, more recently, Thomas, no one had given me a kind word or any encouragement for so long, and I wanted to savor it. Chiding myself for being so needy, I concentrated on Sir Francis instead.

In the flickering candlelight, he looked tired. Parliament had been sitting since January, working out the new Statutes of Recusancy, the terms of which were already being discussed in the streets, inns and

alehouses and by London firesides. How these would change people's
behavior remained to be seen. Though I knew they were introduced to
deter would-be converts to popery and to counteract the Jesuits who
came to our shores intent on stirring up religious fervor for the old
faith and undermining the loyalty of the Queen's subjects, part of me
feared what these stricter laws would mean. I couldn't help thinking
of Mamma and her refusal to relinquish her Catholic ways. Though
her religion was no longer sanctioned by the state, she would never
do anything to hurt the Queen. She loved Queen Elizabeth and oft
spoke of Her Majesty in glowing terms as a woman of whom all her
subjects could be proud. In her mind, her loyalty to the Queen and
her loyalty to God were quite separate—the one did not lessen the
other, and she obeyed both in her own way. When I had listened to
Thomas and Master Robert over the past few weeks, and became privy
to some of the correspondence uncovered between the Scottish Queen
Mary, imprisoned though she was within our borders, and her fervent
supporters—many of them English nobles—it was evident that not all
Catholics felt the same way. Yet I wondered whether these latest laws
would bring unity or widen what Sir Francis believed was a growing
schism, one that was reinforced by the Pope, Spain, France, the Jesuit
colleges abroad and their allies—allies who lived among us. Those Sir
Francis called "the enemy within."

Sir Francis rose to his feet, bringing me back to the present. "I think
it's time I tested your skills in the outside world. It's time to put you
to work."

A shaft of excitement followed by fear impaled me, forcing me to
absolute stillness. After all the weeks of memorizing ciphers, the endless practicing, the accounts of treachery undone by the smallest piece
of information, all the keen observation and collation of facts, I would
no longer be an onlooker but a participant. Certain that the thundering in my ears must be echoing about the room, I waited.

Sir Francis took a key from around his neck, careful to keep it
enclosed within his palm, and turned to the great black cabinet behind
him. He bent and slid back a panel to reveal the keyhole. I saw him
glance over his shoulder to see if I was watching, so I politely turned
aside, despite my curiosity as to how the cabinet opened. I could not
help it. Was I not a lock-pick at heart? Wasn't this one of my father's

creations? In the silence of the room the click of the key turning once, twice, was distinct. Tumblers lifted with the barest of whispers, bolts slid back. There was a flick of a wrist near the side of the cabinet. So, it was a combination lock—three latches, two turned with keys, one with a knob. Clever. I'd no doubt the locks would have precautions built in as well, to deter would-be thieves. Papa favored ink that stained fingers or powders that caused convulsions. Forsooth, if that was my cabinet, with such dangerous contents, I would ensure it had many safeguards.

Drawers of different sizes and neatly arranged shelves were briefly revealed when the doors were finally opened. Sir Francis withdrew a seal from one of the drawers. I caught a glimpse of bound documents, the flash of a ring, more seals carved from wood and metal, and leather-bound pocketbooks. One book stood out from the rest—also leather bound, it was sizeable, with leaves of paper protruding from the covers. I wondered what secrets it contained.

Sir Francis looked at the small seal and grunted, then locked the doors of his cabinet. I made sure I was facing the fire by the time he turned his attention back to me.

"Mallory. I want you to take this and show it to a man." He dropped the small metal seal into my upturned palm. Written upon it, in code, were two Latin words: *De Mora*.

Seeing my frown, Sir Francis chuckled and pointed at his face. "The Queen refers to me as her Moor. She has nicknames for most of us on the Council, some less flattering than others. The point is, the man you'll show this to understands whoever is in possession of it is to be trusted. In return, he'll give you some documents that you'll bring safely to me. Am I clear?"

"Aye." I took a deep breath and released it slowly. "To whom do I give it? Where? When?"

"Patience," said Sir Francis. "Shortly, you will leave the house and walk to St. Paul's. Once there, you will buy some fruit from one of the many vendors, I care not which one, only that you fill the basket you'll carry. When that's done, you'll head to the north door. By eleven of the clock, you're to ensure you're in the bookshop called the Talbot in Paternoster Row. The door will be locked, the owner absent, so you will have to gain admission yourself. Once inside, find the book entitled *Descriptions of England* by one William Harrison, and hold it in your hand. Only then will you be approached. A man will introduce himself as Master Rowland Russell. Show him that"—he pointed at the seal—"and take what he gives you in return. Do not answer any questions or ask any. Do you understand?"

I nodded, holding the seal between cold fingers as if it were made of fine glass and might shatter. "What about the vendors at St. Paul's? Do I speak to them?"

"You may pass the time of day, act as you would when attending market. Disguise your voice; perchance do something with your attire so as not to attract attention—black draws the eye in this city of color. Thomas tells me you excel at this."

I lowered my head in acknowledgment of the compliment, already piecing together an ensemble. A gentlewoman? A maid to one?

"After you've received the documents, you will go to the Knight's Arms, drink some ale, have something to eat. After that, I want you to walk to St. Gabriel's and give alms to the poor." Opening a drawer in his desk, he reached in and passed me a small purse.

"Would I not be better coming straight back here?"

Sir Francis shook his head. "I have to make sure you're not followed. While it's unlikely anyone will suspect a woman, I have to be certain those watching Master Rowland disregard you as a likely courier. Hopefully, by meandering through the streets, stopping for a drink and a meal and heading to church, you will allay any suspicion. Only after you have done this, and the men I have tracking you are certain you're not followed, will you return."

"I'll be observed as well."

"On this occasion. Not only to ensure the safety of the cargo you carry, but your own. How you act, how you play your part, will also be reported. This is a test, Mallory."

Bowing my head in acknowledgment, I swallowed the lump forming in my throat. My thoughts went back to the conversation I'd had with Lord Nathaniel only the evening before. I'd denied being the kind of woman who played a role, who pretended to be something I wasn't. Yet here I was, about to do so boldly and with no small degree of elation. As one of Sir Francis's agents, I had to protect not only myself, but his entire enterprise, by erecting a facade. This was what I was hired to do, it was not how I lived my life. Yet the more I considered it, wasn't it something I did on a daily basis? Not for the reasons Lord Nathaniel claimed, to gull an innocent in order to achieve a selfish end, but in order to protect myself from further harm. It was why, months ago, I'd sworn to abide by Castiglione's instructions for the perfect courtier. I pretended to a calm I did not always feel; nonchalance, though initially alien to me, was becoming easier to embrace. I was simply trying to achieve a braver version of it. I was trying to reclaim my old self.

I was also protecting myself from . . . from what? The various passions that once undid me. Why then did Lord Nathaniel's observations sting? Was he right? Was I playing others false by not being true?

"Today you'll be accompanied by Thomas's servant, Casey. Folk are accustomed to seeing him about."

Relief washed over me that I was not being sent on my own.

"Now," said Sir Francis, rising and pacing the room. "Repeat my instructions back to me."

Despite being desperate to know what information Master Rowland would be passing, I refrained from asking and instead began to repeat what I'd been told. I'd no right to know the content of the documents. I was but the means to an end—the conduit through which the water of information flowed. But that didn't stop me being curious, or thinking about Lord Nathaniel's admission that he was curious about me.

Pushing Lord Nathaniel and his evident pain and bitterness toward womankind out of my head, I focused on my task. If I'd but one life to stake on curiosity, I'd wait until it was something worthy.

Casey's age was impossible to discern. At first glance, with his cap pulled low over his features, the skinny limbs protruding from his jacket and his middling height, he could have been a young apprentice or junior servant. But when he raised his face it revealed lines that ran from the corner of his nose to his mouth, a scar above his scant beard, and eyes that saw everything and conceded nothing. Never mind the calluses on his fingers and the ink stains beneath the nails—it was clear Casey was no boy but a seasoned man of the streets. Knowing he would be beside me for my first mission gave me additional confidence.

We left Seething Lane and headed north, turning into Hart Street, then Tower Street, joining the market crowds wandering up to Corn-hill Street before reaching Cheapside. I carried a basket over my arm, and though the day was rather warm, I'd chosen a green dress and a large bright shawl to wrap around my shoulders, pleased it tailed down my back and over my hips, hiding much of my sleeves and bodice. A bonnet completed my ensemble, and I hunched slightly to reduce my height and shorten my stride. I kept my head bowed and remained close to Casey, who matched his step to mine. We could be mistaken for a husband and wife, two servants of a good house, or even, if one didn't look too closely, mother and son.

The smell from the butchers' stalls lining Cheapside was pungent. Blood, offal and all manner of refuse flowed from the tables where freshly slaughtered carcasses were hung on huge hooks to drain or flung upon blocks to be dismembered. The dull thuds of blades hewing through bone and gristle were percussive, interrupted by the loud conversation of the men, their calls to attract custom, the clink of coins and the banter of buyers. In the dark alleyways and ginnels, the plaintive bleats of animals could be heard, as if they knew what was in store. I maintained a stoic expression and forged ahead, as if it were my practice to pound these streets each day, seek out fare for my household and barter with a ruddy-faced and grime-covered butcher.

I was glad when we reached the conduit and turned into Walbrook Street. Casey steered me into the smaller lanes, away from the press of bodies, carts and horsemen, taking us past St. Pancras. Vendors stood beside stalls or outside shops crying out their wares; women lifted ripe fruit from laden baskets, tempting passersby with cries of "oranges and lemons," "apples for sale"; strings of onions dangled, plump radishes, gray oysters, drooping coneys and pigeons by the brace. Still others sold ribbons, lace, cloth, iron nails and candles.

Groups of goodwives sat on their stoops plucking birds while they chattered, barely pausing to lean over and restrain a straying toddler or to box the ears of a naughty youth. Dogs barked, hens bobbed and clucked underfoot, pigs snuffled through the used rushes dumped in the ditches, oblivious to the boots tramping around them. Horsemen forced their way through the throngs, some using their crops to make the passage easier, curses following in their wake. Men gathered outside alehouses, some sitting at makeshift tables playing cards or dice, a beaker at their elbow. Tobacco smoke mingled with firewood, all of it adding to the odors that hung over the area like a pall.

Above, the tower of St. Paul's rose, a beacon as Casey darted down dank laneways, led us up cobbled streets, across an overgrown garden and over a broken piece of wall. Finally, not far from the Star Inn, we emerged onto Watling Street. Progress slowed as we joined the many entering St. Paul's through St. Augustine's Gate. The bells had rung ten of the clock a long time ago. I'd no idea how much time I'd left to buy fruit and reach the Talbot.

As if reading my mind, Casey leaned close.

"We best make haste, mistress, lest we miss the hour."

Increasing my stride, I began to use my shoulders and voice to clear my passage. I paused only to buy some fine-looking Seville oranges, though not before making sure I complained about the price. Thus supplied, I set off for the north gate.

Just outside, along Paternoster Row, was the bookshop called the Talbot. I crossed the street just as the bells began to toll eleven of the clock. I kept calm, maintained my pace and drew out my picks, relying on Casey to cover my activity. Swiftly I had the door unlocked. The clanging of the church bells was so loud, the one above the door could scarce be heard.

Casey and I slipped inside. I shut the door and drank in the familiar space. This was a shop I knew well. With Master Fodrake by my side, I had spent many a coin here.

Dust, cobwebs, leather, parchment and ink pooled to create the special fragrance of a room that housed books. I inhaled its magical scent and felt my troubles lessen. Lanterns burned brightly upon the front desk and on two tables. More hung upon hooks on the walls. There was not one unguarded flame, which was just as well: there were not only books but numerous maps, scrolls, stacks of documents and quills of all shapes and sizes scattered upon every surface. As expected, there was no sign of the owner, though it was quite possible he was buried among the debris together with his family and any assistants he might have had. The thought made me smile. Loosening my shawl,

I searched the titles positioned upon two tables near the counter running along the back wall. A doorway that led to the rear was open but remained dark. Whomever I was to meet remained out of sight, watching and waiting. Casey, unperturbed, took up a position near the door and folded his arms. I ran my finger along the spines of the books, quickly scanning the titles. Then I realized I was leaving a trail in the dust. I needed to cover my tracks, not announce them.

Descriptions of England was not there. I moved toward the two shelves against the opposite wall. It was only as I began to peer among the tomes that I noticed the quiet. The bells had ceased to ring and I still didn't have the title in my hand. Was I about to fail in this simplest of tasks? To put paid to my watching career before it had even begun? Just as I was about to ask Casey to help, I sighted it, leaning against one of Tacitus's volumes on Caesar. I snatched it up, dust showering me as I opened it and checked the title matched the spine.

"Always a good thing to do," said a voice at my shoulder. "Check before you buy."

I jumped, but had the presence of mind to give a light laugh. "Oh, aye," I said in my best northern burr. "Would not do to seek Homer and come home with Virgil, me pa always said."

"Your pa sounds like a very thorough man; though I be wondering at his wisdom, sending a young chit out to do a man's job—*Descriptions of England* is a weighty read that may confuse the female mind and cause all sort of conniptions."

Bristling, I bit my tongue. I didn't have to wait too long to find out who he was.

"I be Master Rowland at your service," he said slowly, doffing his bonnet and looking me up and down.

With all the gravity I could muster, I extracted the seal from my pocket and held it out to him.

Master Rowland took it between thumb and forefinger, twisted it around and ran a fingertip over the words. "I see," he said, and dropped it back into my palm. "Wait here."

I didn't dare move, though I glanced over at Casey, who was busy studying a map on the wall.

Master Rowland returned. "I'm not comfortable with this. But I know my instructions. You unlocked the door and you carry his sign."

He passed me a sheaf of papers tied with leather binding. "Take this to your . . . pa. He'll know what to do and where to find me, and he'll want to find me after he reads such gripping material."

I placed the papers under the fruit. As I did so, I understood why I'd been told to purchase it. Sir Francis knew what he was asking me to retrieve was bulky and would need to be hidden.

"What be your name, mistress?" asked Master Rowland.

I met his eyes. They were shiny in the light of the lanterns.

"I too know my instructions, sir," I said and, as he chuckled darkly, dropped a small curtsey. Without a backward glance, I left the shop, Casey following. I didn't lock the door behind me.

We retraced our steps, making sure we did everything Sir Francis said, from having luncheon at the tavern to stopping at the church and presenting the vicar with some alms. We sauntered back to Seething Lane and, if we were followed by friend or foe, I was unmindful, though my senses were alert to a familiar face, or even a strange one, recurring. Prepared to write a detailed report of everything I saw, only once did I think the old man with the missing tooth was the same one I'd seen near All Hallows. It was possible, just as it was possible there was a perfectly reasonable explanation for his presence begging for coin upon the steps of St. George's. Nothing untoward happened; our journey home, much to my ease but also some little regret, was uneventful.

We slipped through the gates at the rear of Seething Lane and into the house, using the door reserved for Sir Francis's many employees. Casey disappeared before I reached my room. I'd been told to wait and once he knew I'd returned, Sir Francis would find me.

When I entered, however, he was already there. The fire had been stoked, and candles and a lamp were lit.

"Mallory," he said, coming forward. He held out his hand. Mistaking his intention, I almost put my own in it until I understood he wanted the documents. Reaching into the basket, I handed them over.

I removed the shawl and unpinned the bonnet, placing them on the small desk, careful not to disturb the inkwell or quills that sat there, watching as Sir Francis untied the binding and began reading. His smile broadened as he skimmed over the contents, moving from one page to the next swiftly.

"By God, we have them now. All of them."

I wanted desperately to ask who, but remained silent and slipped into my chair. Finally, Sir Francis finished. He closed his eyes, breathed deeply, then opened them again.

"Do you know what you've brought?" His dark gray eyes sparkled. "What Master Rowland has uncovered?"

I didn't dare speak lest this confessional mood be broken. I simply shook my head.

"Contained in these pages are the names of the leading English Catholic families who have pledged allegiance to the Roman hell-goat and his devil spawn spat from the loins of Douai and Reims. Including the names of those who have given succor to the Jesuit traitors Edmund Campion and Robert Persons."

My hand flew to my mouth.

"You understand the significance of this. For months we've scoured the city and countryside searching for them, trying to put a stop to their secret midnight masses, their preaching and conversions, only to have them escape every time we came close. The priest-holes are empty or can't be found; the papist detritus has vanished, only the putrid odor of their stinking incense lingers. Families deny ever having seen them even though we *know* they were in their homes. Links to the throne, blood ties to powerful families, protect them from punishment and give their lying words the appearance of truth. But no longer." He slapped the pages. "Master Rowland has proven his worth yet again."

Sinking onto the stool, Sir Francis leaned an elbow against the desk and stared at the hearth. The heat of the flames reddened his face, as if he too were burning. His eyes were mirrors, the shadows beneath them bruised crescents. He gave a dry laugh that turned into a wheezing cough. As he tried to suppress it, it began to rack his whole body. He covered his mouth with his arm, his eyes began to water and his nose to run. Concerned, I rose and poured him a glass of ale. Stale and warm, it was nonetheless wet and he took it gratefully, as he did the kerchief I took from my bosom.

"Thank you. Thank you." The coughing fit slowly subsided. He wiped his eyes and nose. I waited a moment, then took the beaker back.

"Can I fetch you anything else?" I asked.

"My thanks. I'll be fine. It's simply the knowledge that I finally have what I've waited so long for. It ignites my humors. I'll ask your uncle to attend me later."

Sir Francis blew his nose, screwed the kerchief into a ball and seemed to consider his next words. He stared at me long and hard. I said nothing. Eventually, he spoke.

"The man you met today, his real name, at least as far as I know, is Charles Sledd. Rowland is one of his aliases. He's been invaluable to me—first on the Continent, and now here, in the city. It was Sledd who first alerted us to a grand plot between Spain, France and the Pope to assassinate the Queen. It is Sledd who, above all others, has kept track of the Jesuits swarming the country with treason in their hearts and murder in their cankerous souls."

Sledd. Charles Sledd. My work had been compared with his. My ears were pricked.

"Ever since we learned Campion and Persons were on English soil, I've had all my men focused on their discovery. I doubled the number, but with no success. The connections Sledd and another agent called Malyverny Caitlyn had in Marshalsea Prison, as well as those Sledd had made while attending the Jesuit college at Reims, enabled him to record the names of all the English families loyal to the architect of this papist enterprise, Doctor William Allen. A pustule on Satan's backside." He coughed into his fist. I didn't dare interrupt. Allen's zeal was only matched by Sir Francis's.

The thought shocked me. But whereas Allen sought to destroy what our sovereign and her Council and nobles had built, Sir Francis sought to protect it.

I wanted to understand. What I was hearing was both terrifying and thrilling. To think that we could live in this city, share meals with family and friends, walk the streets among our neighbors and attend church on a Sunday, never knowing who among those we knew, loved and trusted might harbor priests, might have murderous and heretical thoughts. There were those we called countrymen who would hand our sovereign and the nation she nurtured over to Catholic forces; hand the people over to those who would stop at nothing to convert us. Convert or destroy. It made me feel ill. I was filled with a burning desire to hunt them down, hurt them and, above all, stop them.

Sir Francis stared at me, a strange look on his face. Color infused my cheeks, breaking out across my neck and décolletage.

"It's all right, Mallory. It's right to feel indignation. These people, these papist scum, deserve nothing but loathing. They are like tiny insects infecting a host, entering at our most vulnerable points and eating away at our resolve, weakening the very foundations that uphold who and what we are. I want you to feel as I do, as my men do. I want you to be part of the retribution we'll enact upon all Catholic traitors—upon Allen's mission and those who would put the Scottish serpent in our bosom, Mary, on the throne. This is why finding Campion and Persons is so important. They boast of their presence, trumpet to all and sundry the hearts and minds they have won. They make us appear weak. As God is my witness, we will find them and, when we do, we'll shout from the turrets of the Tower itself, on London Bridge and at every gate in the city when we bring them down. Their bodies will be but carrion for the crows to peck at, pieces of meat for the rack and the executioner's ax. Their souls will be sent to eternal damnation."

I tried not to look away. For all that the thought of the Catholic traitors enraged me, the idea of treating their bodies in the same way the butchers of Cheapside did their animals was hard to stomach. An image of the rotting heads upon London Bridge swam before my vision. I swallowed, my throat thick.

Shaking the papers still clutched in his hand, Sir Francis gave a thin smile. A shudder ran through me and I hoped never to see that expression upon his face when he regarded me.

"And now Sledd has given us the means to find these priests. According to our Master Sledd, Campion has been traveling through Nottinghamshire, Derbyshire, Yorkshire and Lancashire. There's word he intends to deliver another of his ungodly railings to a printing press in Oxfordshire. It's there we'll catch him, Mallory. Catch him and destroy him."

"What of Persons?"

"Sledd believes he's still here in London. So do I. The time has come to make a noise, a great deal of it. Time to dislodge the rat from his nest."

Sir Francis rose. "You've done the country a great service today,

Mallory. You've passed my first test. Go home and think on what you did and what you learned. Tell no one. In the days to come, I'll have another test for you. One that may require more. Are you ready for that?"

Standing, I placed my palms flat on the desk. "I'm ready. I've much more to give, Sir Francis. Much more."

His hand shot out and, for a fleeting moment, I thought he might touch my face, but his arm dropped to his side. "I know you have. It runs in your blood."

"Papa—"

"Is strong and loyal, just like his daughter." His gaze lingered and I detected a note of sadness, of longing even. I began to feel a prickle of discomfort travel down my spine. For something to do, I picked up the shawl and began to fold it. I would change out of my dress and give my disguise back to Thomas on the morrow. I failed to notice Sir Francis open the door until the cold draft of the hall swept my legs.

"I bid you goodnight, Mallory," he said and left me alone with my thoughts and the small flutter of victory that, in a moment of sheer vanity, I felt I'd earned.

PART THREE
Little Cockered Bitch

And touching our Societie, be it known to you that we have
made a league—all the Jesuits in the world, whose succession and
multitude must overreach all the practices of England—cheerfully
to carry the cross you shall lay upon us, and never to despair your
recovery, while we have a man left to enjoy your Tyburn, or to be
racked with your torments, or consumed with your prisons.
The expense is reckoned, the enterprise is begun; it is of God,
it cannot be withstood. So the Faith was planted:
so it must be restored.

—Father Edmund Campion, "Brag," 1581

. . . Whereby she will be able to entertain graciously every kind of
man with agreeable and comely conversation suited to the time and
place and to the station of the person with whom she speaks,
joining to serene and modest manners, and to that comeliness
that ought to inform all her actions, a quick vivacity of spirit whereby
she will show herself a stranger to all boorishness; but with
such a kind manner as to cause her to be thought no less chaste,
prudent and gentle than she is agreeable, witty, and discreet:
thus she must observe a certain mean (difficult to achieve and,
as it were, composed of contraries) and must strictly observe
certain limits and not exceed them.

—Baldassare Castiglione, *The Book of the Courtier:
The Third Book, Part Five*, 1528

SIXTEEN

SEETHING LANE AND HARP LANE, LONDON
Late March, Anno Domini 1581
In the 23rd year of the reign of Elizabeth I

*I*n all the weeks I'd been working for Sir Francis, I'd yet to meet his daughter. While she remained in Surrey, I confess she'd lost a degree of significance to me, even though she was the entire rationale around which my employ in Seething Lane was built. So I was surprised when, in the final days of March, I was summoned to Sir Francis's study and informed I would soon be meeting his wife and daughter.

Taken aback, I hid my astonishment. "When will I have the pleasure, sir?"

"Why," said Sir Francis, not even raising his head from the ledger before him, "tomorrow. Come to the house at the usual time, await me in your room and I will fetch you to my good wife, Ursula, and daughter Frances."

There was something different about Sir Francis. His words were almost dismissive, angry even. It wasn't until I saw the slight tremor in his hands that I understood.

"Forgive me, sir, but are you unwell?"

"Unwell?" Sir Francis lifted his chin and sat back in his chair. "Why would you think that?"

Uncomfortable at the severity of his gaze, the tone he adopted, I dissembled. "I . . . I heard you sometimes have a stomach upset and I thought you seemed pale . . ."

"Oh. I see. I am well. Now, if there is nothing else . . . ?"

I hesitated. There was something else. "May I ask why I'm to meet your daughter and lady wife, sir? I mean, am I to commence the duties for which my family thinks I'm employed? Become your daughter's companion?" The thought of surrendering my little room, giving up the degree of freedom Seething Lane and the errands I was dispatched upon allowed me, made my heart sink to my boots. Until this moment I hadn't understood how much I savored my days here.

Sir Francis sighed and rested his hands upon the pages in front of him. He gazed at me, his head tilted slightly. "Would that be so bad?"

Coloring slightly, I tried to smile. "No, sir, I'm sure it would be very pleasant."

Sir Francis gave a wry laugh. "The reason you're to meet my daughter and wife is because next week you're to accompany us to Deptford for the knighting of Francis Drake."

"I am?"

"Aye. There's something I need carried to Deptford and something I need fetched and you're the perfect person to do it. No one will suspect the woman accompanying my daughter, no one." I opened my mouth to ask another question, but was prevented by his next words. "Now is not the time to discuss it. You will be properly briefed before we depart. Is there anything else?"

I swallowed the hundreds of questions wanting to fly from my mouth, stoppered my exhilaration and, with forced composure, simply shook my head and dropped a curtsey.

With a grunt, he made a dismissive gesture toward the door to hasten my leave-taking. "Be sure to wear something . . ." He lifted his head, swept me with his eyes. "Something impressive on the morrow. Mayhap it's time to consider casting aside the raven's colors."

Never before had he treated me in such a manner; referred to my dress let alone its shade. It was discomforting, to say the least. I drifted back through the outer room in a slight daze. All the desks bar Thomas's were empty. Sir Francis's intelligencers were busy elsewhere.

"Mallory," said Thomas, rising and bowing. "Are you quite well?"

His query so matched mine to Sir Francis, I gave a droll laugh.

"Only quite. I just found out I'm to meet Frances and Lady Ursula tomorrow."

"Ah," said Thomas, sitting back down and busily shuffling papers on his desk. "In preparation for Deptford."

"You knew?"

Thomas had the grace to look guilty. "There's very little I don't." He indicated the piles of paper littering his desk, the floor and every conceivable space. "You understand, I could not have warned you . . . Nor can I speak of Deptford. It is not how we—"

There was no point being cross. "It's all right, Thomas. You owe me no explanation." He was as bound to keep secrets as I was, even ones pertaining to friends. I stopped. Was that what Thomas had become? A friend?

The closed expression on his face made my position suddenly very clear. People who worked for Sir Francis didn't have friends. There was loyalty, but it was to the enterprise they swore allegiance, not to each other. Family and friends did not compare. What folly that even for a moment I believed it could be otherwise.

Anxious about the morrow, all I wanted was to make a good impression and not shame Sir Francis or my family. If I'd really been Frances's companion all this time, we'd be familiar with each other. As it was, we were strangers to be foisted upon one another for a very public royal event. What if she disliked me on sight? What if I found her repugnant? What did I know about thirteen-year-old girls?

I barely spoke a word to the servant assigned to escort me as I walked home, preoccupied by the Walsinghams and the realization that there was not one person outside the house I could call a friend; Caleb was the only one within it. Though he was so very dear to me, he had others beyond Harp Lane to whom he could turn. I had no one. Even Mamma could count Angela and Mistress Dorothy among her friends. Papa had many. When I left Harp Lane, I'd relinquished my few female acquaintances along with my reputation.

The truth was, for all I enjoyed what I was doing, the secrecy it required and its importance, I was also very lonely. But I deserved no better and, God knew, so much worse. I'd no right to complain.

Lost in misery, I failed to notice the extra horse in our stable or that

Comfort wasn't raising her voice at Gracious, who, as she flounced about the kitchen, was giddy as a girl around a maypole. Nor was she shrieking at the apprentices to keep their fingers out of the pots and their hands off the bread, but instead speaking in well-rounded tones.

I gave Comfort my cloak and gloves and decided I would approach Mamma for a loan of one of her dresses and ask Gracious to draw me a bath. Then I entered the parlor, and who should I find sprawled in one of our chairs, drink in hand, but Lord Nathaniel.

My face must have fallen because the smile with which he greeted me swiftly vanished, replaced by a startled look that transformed into one of grave offense.

"My . . . my lord," I began, curtseying. "I didn't expect to find you here."

"That was patently clear, Mistress Mallory." His voice was gruff. He stood and took a step toward me, holding out the goblet as if it were a weapon designed to keep me at a distance. "Perhaps you were telling the truth when you claimed to be beyond female artifice and facades. Nonetheless, you need to learn to school your features." He paused and swallowed some wine, unaware of the effect his words had. "Actually," he continued, putting the goblet down before swinging back in my direction, "it's fortuitous you've arrived while Caleb is fetching his manuscript and we're alone. There's a question I've been wanting to put to you. I'm curious as to why—"

I blame my perturbation at the thought of meeting my employer's wife and daughter. I blame the stark reality of my loneliness, my complicity in that state and the degree of self-pity this realization prompted. I blame the fact I was unprepared for Lord Nathaniel's frankness, his continued presence in the house and the irritation that came in its wake. But I cannot forgive what spilled out of my mouth next. Crossing the room, I stood before him, tilting my chin so I could peer straight into that arrogant face.

"And you, sir," I snarled, "need to learn to remember who and where you are. I'm not a schoolboy and nor are you a schoolmaster to harangue me. You're not my father nor my brother. How dare you treat me as if I were one of your ale-addled sailors, or one of your poor servants. School my face, indeed. You, sir, need to discipline your tongue. Though that would require you to do the same to your wits

and I'm persuaded you are only ever able to marshal half of them."
Words flew from me, anger making my voice deeper and louder than
I ever intended.

As he opened his mouth to speak, I wagged a finger in his face. Like
a virago in one of Caleb's plays, I dared to admonish Lord Nathaniel,
and not merely for the way he spoke to me. All his sins and those I'd
imagined got an airing. They ranged from his fondness for drink, his
sometimes slovenly attire, his swaggering and confident belief that all
women adored him and his rancid assumptions about the gentler sex,
to his expectation he was always welcome beneath our roof, regardless
of whether or not he showed us—me—courtesy.

God forgive me, I would have continued too had not Lord Nathaniel chosen that moment to grab the finger I was waving like a sword,
pull me into his arms and kiss me.

SEVENTEEN

I tasted the sweetness of wine upon his parted lips and the tip of his warm, liquid tongue. His soft beard grazed my cheek, as he drew me closer and closer still. His great, burly arms pressed me tight against his body, one hand burning the small of my back, the other holding my accusatory finger fast. Through the fabric of my skirts, I could feel the power of his legs encased in their woolen hose, the expansive strength of his chest as he pressed me against the jacquard of his doublet, flattening my breasts. I could never have imagined such a huge man could embrace someone with such gentleness even as he brooked no resistance. I was being absorbed, drawn into him, and for a moment I forgot where I was, who I was, my anger transforming into something that traveled in waves of heat throughout my lower regions before running like quicksilver along my arms and legs, exploding like a fiery sun on a summer's day in my very center.

Inhaling sharply through my nose as I melted into his body, a heady, musky fragrance that made my head spin, my stomach lock, consumed me. My traitorous lips opened further, my mouth receiving all he had to give.

The hand against my back moved up my spine to cradle the nape of my neck, long fingers loosening the tangle of hair, stroking, kneading, a thumb finding flesh and summoning sensations I'd denied myself in the false belief I'd no desire for such things.

His kiss deepened, his lips firmed and mine answered. He groaned into my mouth and with that primal sound, its echo rising in my throat, something within me snapped.

No. No. No.

I didn't know I'd spoken aloud until I managed to jerk my head away, to stare into eyes that looked upon me with such longing, I was snatched back into the moment and rendered temporarily mute. I ripped my finger out of the cage his hands had become and, with all the strength I could muster, slapped him across the face.

The effect was immediate. I was set free. Staggering back, I stared as thin red lines appeared on his left cheek, welling and widening as the blood began to flow. My palm burned by my side, the heat matching that traveling across my face and within my body as my veins became molten rivers that would not be cooled. I was reeling, confused. A fingernail was rent, the pain sharp. My legs began to shake beneath my skirts. I had to sit. I had to stand. I would not quiver like a wet cat. I would not retreat. Not again. Never again.

"How . . . how dare you," I hissed, my breath coming in short pants.

Kiss me, or elicit such responses?

Raising his hand to his face, Lord Nathaniel gingerly pulled it away, rubbing the blood staining the tips between his fingers.

"How dare *you*, mistress," he said, a note of laughter in his voice.

Taken aback by his evident humor, I renewed my attack. "Did I not tell you I wasn't one of your court ladies, bowing to your needs, demanding your attention, saying one thing and meaning another? Did I not say that I do not play with you, my lord? That I do not act?"

"You did." Lord Nathaniel reached inside his doublet, withdrew a kerchief and wiped his hand before daubing his cheek. "But you did imply I was a half-wit and that, my lady, is unforgivable."

His calmness was perplexing. The rage that had flooded my body and cast aside all sense began to subside. The marks on Lord Nathaniel's face glared at me, signs of my loss of control, manifestations of the very kind of behavior I despised in him. Oh, sweet Jesu. What had I done?

We stared at each other, only a pace or two apart. My chest was heaving. His was not. The fire spat, and footsteps could be heard above us. A door slammed shut somewhere in the house. The dogs issued a volley of barks outside.

Still we didn't speak.

I could take it no more. "What possible reason could you have . . . did I give you for taking such . . . such liberties?"

"You didn't," he said and picked up his wine. "May I pour you one?"

"I'd sooner you answer my question."

He filled a goblet and passed it over. I took it without thinking, my hand shaking, and sipped.

"Very well," he said. "But only if you promise to answer the question I intended to pose when"—he grinned—"circumstances altered." He touched his cheek again, wincing.

The enormity of what I'd done—struck a guest in our house, a lord, no less, Caleb's patron, and with such violence—began to dawn on me. Marry, the man had done the unforgivable, had, without invitation, violated the daughter of the house . . . No. He had not. It was but a kiss . . . a kiss I responded to like the shameless trull Mamma and the neighbors believed me to be, that Raffe had told me I was over and over.

I was not. I was a gentlewoman, a widow. Mistress Bright. He had no right. I gave him no cause. Not even the insult I offered deserved such a response. Or was Lord Nathaniel correct? Was this a facade I maintained which he, without effort, had dismantled? Had he shown me who and what I feared I truly was? A woman who couldn't control her passions?

"I've two reasons for . . . for interrupting you," said Lord Nathaniel, his eyes fixed upon my flushed face. "First and foremost, I wanted you to stop talking. Kissing you was the simplest way to achieve that."

I blinked. "I beg your pardon, my lord. I don't believe I heard you aright."

"Oh, you did. There's nothing wrong with your hearing. I wanted you to stop screeching at me like a harridan; leveling accusations against me as unwarranted as they were unasked. I thought a kiss would suffice. I was right."

Cold, hard fury staunched the heat more effectively than winter snows upon a flame. Quenched the doubts I'd allowed to well to the surface.

"You're wrong, my lord," I said coldly. "You didn't think."

Sitting down, he crossed his legs, lifting a thread from his hose and letting it flutter to the floor before looking up at me. My nails had left terrible raw marks upon his face. They almost matched the other, older scars. I wondered what talons had made those . . .

"No, mistress, I *did* think. I thought it would be very nice to kiss someone who could look so magnificent, so utterly irresistible when they were furious. I swear, your eyes emitted lightning, like Zeus in a rage." He drank. Slowly. He dragged the kerchief across his mouth, the red stains vivid on the white. "I was right. It was beyond nice. What wasn't so pleasant was the slap you conferred upon me for my efforts. I'll have to ensure I do better next time."

His eyes twinkled. Why, the man was a rogue, a blackguard who thought he could have his way with whatever woman he chose . . . and in her own home. Well, not this woman. I would not be won over so easily, nor by words he'd no doubt learned like an actor and rehearsed with many, many women after setting the stage for such a scene.

I put down my goblet and turned to him. "And you say that women play a part to attract a man, a husband? I say you stand accused of the same, only your intentions lack honor, sir."

Throwing back his head, Lord Nathaniel laughed hard. "I never pretended to possess any in the first place—honor or honorable intentions, mistress. Though, I find it ironic such an accusation springs from your lips, sweet as they be."

I felt my cheeks color again. Damn my flesh that it betrayed me so—and not for the first time this evening. Clearing my throat, I moved away from him, toward the hearth, forcing him to twist around if he wished to see me.

"My lord, I allowed you a question if you answered mine. Ask it, and I will quit your sight."

Lord Nathaniel smiled. "Very well, though it will dismay me to lose the privilege of your company, just when I am starting to enjoy it." I shot him a look that would have withered a fresh bloom. "You see, Mistress Mallory," he said, turning slightly and waving his goblet in my direction, "you're an object of curiosity to me. A young widow, a woman of learning, a person about whom Caleb does, even for a playwright, wax lyrical, swearing your virtues and talents are unparalleled. He supports your claims you're not fettered by those habits and mannerisms I loathe in other women, that you're not one to pretend or play. Forsooth, in the time I've spent in your company, I've had cause to doubt my own convictions regarding the fairer sex. I do but wonder then, how is it you claim to your family and friends, and even to me, that you tend young Frances Walsingham?"

My chest grew tight. "I'm afraid I don't understand, my lord."

He gave me his full attention and continued. "Oh, I think you do. My understanding is that Mister Secretary's family is in Surrey, at their estate in Barn Elms, yet you're in London. Unless you're taken by the wings of Hermes each day or saddle Pegasus, how can you possibly be a companion to Frances Walsingham when she is there"—he pointed to the furthest corner of the room—"and you are here?" His finger rooted me to the spot. "So who, I ask, is playing whom, mistress? What is it you really do when you go to Seething Lane each day?"

Damn his gleeking mind, it was as sharp as a Gray's Inn cleric's.

God must have been on my side, because before I could remind him I also taught languages to Sir Francis's staff, Caleb chose that moment to enter and I was spared having to answer. Unaware that anything extraordinary had happened, Caleb burst through the door waving a leather-bound sheaf of papers, continuing the conversation where he might have left off.

"Ah, Mallory. We were just discussing you." Dropping a kiss upon my cheek, he strode to Lord Nathaniel. "Here." He pushed the paper into his lordship's hands. "If Tilney wants more changes, he can make them himself. I never thought these words would leave my mouth, but I'm not only tired of *Drake's Hind*, but all hinds at the moment." With an abrupt laugh, he helped himself to some wine and threw himself in the chair I'd never had the chance to sit in.

Muttering something about being exhausted, I gave my apologies and left as swiftly as I was able.

As I closed the door, I heard Caleb say, "Go to, Nate, you and Mallory haven't had words again, have you? And what on God's earth have you done to your face?"

EIGHTEEN

HARP LANE, LONDON
Late March, Anno Domini 1581
In the 23rd year of the reign of Elizabeth I

HARP LANE, LONDON, AND
THE SHELTON ESTATES, DURHAM
Anni Domini 1578–1579
In the 21st and 22nd years of the reign of Elizabeth I

*I*t was pitch black when I awoke. My hair clung damply to my fore-head, my jaw ached from grinding my teeth, and my muscles felt tight and sore from fighting the demons of recollection. Tangled in the linen, I lay on my side, panting. Only the faint glow of embers revealed I was in my bedroom, not in the huge drafty room of my imaginings. There was no armchair in the corner, no sword resting against its torn fabric, no leather bindings coiled neatly on the table ready to hold me in place. All that was in my past. I lowered my arms that had been raised as if to ward off blows, untwisted the sheets, smoothed out the blankets, and climbed out of bed. Pulling the nightgown away from my sweaty flesh, I went to the window, cracked open the shutters and lifted my face to the heavens in the hope of a reprieve from the nightmares that crowded my head, blotting out the beauty of the firmament and leaving only darkness.

The darkness had a name: Raffe. Sir Raffe Shelton. I hadn't given him a proper space in my thoughts for weeks. Tonight my former lover saw fit to return with a vengeance.

Cool air flowed around me. The night was so still, so quiet. Nothing stirred except the memories I'd kept locked away deep inside. Roused by a kiss, a kiss I'd briefly allowed myself to become lost in—to, God forgive me, enjoy. Now, like the furies of old, they flapped their musty wings at the walls I'd erected to keep them at bay and demanded my attention.

I pulled the stool over to the window, lay my forearms along the sill and placed my chin squarely upon them, staring into the purple hues of the midnight hours, waiting until the darkness was transformed into familiar shadows. Only once I was certain I really was home, that this wasn't another mirage sent to taunt me, did I dare to go back and, once and for all, try and put my past to rest.

At the age of nineteen I found love, and by twenty-one had forsworn it. In two brief years I learned love was but a phantasm, a fool's paradise until we bit into the apple and saw the garden for the bed of thorns and stinking refuse it is. Love was merely a word used by men to beguile, seduce and deceive. It made the wise foolish, the cautious bold; it invited risk without thought of consequence. Unprepared, I'd been caught in its web and become drunk on its poison.

I thought I could only hate he whom I once thought I loved—that love and hate were two sides of the same coin, the extremes of passion. To my sorrow, I learned hate was not the antithesis of love. No. That status belonged exclusively to indifference. Love and indifference were perfect bedmates, one giving birth to the other.

All that hard-won knowledge lay in the future the day I met Raffe Shelton.

Excited as I was to accompany my father to the Royal Exchange, I was displeased by Mamma's insistence that I change into my best dress. Afraid Papa's goodwill did not extend to my tarrying, I conceded defeat only when I thought Mamma was on the brink of withdrawing her approval for the outing.

Angela assisted me out of my house dress and into my sapphire-blue kirtle and black-and-white bodice with silver pickadills sewn around the waist. Underneath, I wore a modest farthingale fashioned from whalebone, a gift from Mamma for my birthday just days earlier. Over the top, I wore another skirt gathered tightly underneath my bodice. It complemented my ensemble and revealed enough of the kirtle and leather boots to suggest both effort and some status. Once I saw my reflection in Mamma's mirror, I no longer resented having to change.

When Papa's oldest apprentice, Benedict Thatcher, saw me, he blushed brightly and appeared unable to wrench his eyes away. I had not received that kind of admiration from men before (or, as Angela insisted, I had not been aware of it)—apart from Isaac Hattycliffe, who showed his appreciation by bestowing a sloppy kiss upon me last Christmas before he returned to the Inns of Court, or Caleb, who would oft say my physical charms would be lost on those who adhered to the fashions (Caleb was not only biased, his flattery didn't count). Until I saw Benedict, a lad I'd all but grown up with, become awkward in my company, I had not realized the effect my appearance could have upon men, and I confess it made my heart skip.

We left at nine of the clock, and I held Papa's arm while Benedict walked ahead of us to ensure we avoided the worst of the mud and filth of the streets and crush of the crowds. The Royal Exchange had opened ten years or so earlier, and though I'd been once before with Master Fodrake, I was thrilled to be visiting this center of trade and industry again. Filled to the brim with people of all descriptions, from glass sellers and armorers to apothecaries and milliners, from peers to paupers, folk bustled about the open and closed stalls while vendors shouted for attention. Pickpockets moved nimbly throughout, the occasional shout evidence of their progress. Beggars camped in doorways, faces upturned, their dirty hands cupped.

We'd come to purchase gold Papa required for a lock he was fashioning for an Italian noble, and so we pushed our way through the merchants and their customers in the cloisters to head upstairs to the area known as "the Pawn." When I caught sight of a bookseller, I begged Papa to allow me to browse among the tomes. Possessed of a fine library as well as a fine mind, Papa was not averse to the idea— though Benedict was clearly appalled that we might lose ourselves in volumes of paper when there was precious metal to examine elsewhere. Soon Papa and I were opening slender leather-bound volumes, their pages printed and cut with great care, while Benedict sulked by the doorway. Searching for a copy of John Foxe's *Actes and Monuments of these Latter and Perilous Days, Touching Matters of the Church*, also known as *The Book of Martyrs*, an illustrated volume which told terrible stories of Protestant suffering under Catholic rule, I lost myself in other tales and times first.

The proprietor soon ended my indulgence; having found the book I sought, he wrapped and presented it to me. Papa was very pleased with my choice and told me I must read it to Mamma. He insisted I keep the coins I'd been given and paid for it himself. Thus, with angels still to spend, I left the shop intending to pay a great deal more attention to the contents of the stalls in the cloisters below when we departed.

The goldsmith, Master Cruikshank, was delighted to see Papa. Once Papa explained what he required, they soon agreed on a price. As he first weighed the gold and then placed it in a pouch, another gentleman accompanied by a squire entered the premises. Forced to wait, the gentleman at first appeared annoyed. Papa was in the midst of explaining to Master Cruikshank the style of the escutcheon he'd designed and how the gold would decorate the filigree and keyholes. Benedict contributed to the conversation but, as I already knew the pattern, I studied the newcomer and his servant instead.

A bill posted on a pole in the center of the shop advertised a forthcoming performance by the Earl of Leicester's Men at The Theatre. As I pretended to study it, I was afforded a good view. Of my height (which still accorded him some stature, as I was unusually tall for a woman), the gentleman had a fine head of flaxen hair combed back beneath his bonnet and cut to sit neatly above his white ruff. His beard sat close to his face and framed a wide mouth that grimaced as his squire bumped against a table and knocked a goblet over. Assuring him no harm was caused, Master Cruikshank righted it while continuing to chat to

Papa, asking him questions about the lock and for what purpose it was designed. In his element and delighted with the price he'd been charged for the gold, Papa's explanation was more detailed than usual.

The subject of the conversation clearly aroused the curiosity of the gentleman, who wandered nearer to listen. I noted his fine mustard doublet, the slashes along the sleeves revealing the white of his shirt. His breeches were in the Venetian style, cut to below his knee. I was marveling at the design of his shoes and wondering at the cost of the leather when I became aware that I too was the object of scrutiny.

Meeting the gentleman's eyes, I glanced away quickly, looking back toward his feet but studying a knot in the rushes as if it held the mystery of the universe. I became uncomfortable, knowing my performance was so weak it would shame Caleb.

"Ellis," said the man to his squire. "See to that, would you?" He pointed to the spot I was staring at. "I do fear it's causing the lady some distress."

My head jerked up and I caught the faintly mocking look, but also another akin to that on Benedict's face earlier. Was it admiration I detected? Or had my new dress also given me new conceits?

"Oh, I beg you, sir." I gave a small curtsey. "Do not exert yourself on my account, 'tis naught."

"Naught?" He folded his arms and stared at me boldly in a manner that made my heart beat faster and warmth flood my face and chest. "From the attention that"—he pointed to the rushes—"receives and the consternation it clearly arouses, I'd have said anything but naught." He turned his leg slowly and deliberately moved it into my line of sight, placing it on display.

This time, I countered his gaze with one of my own. God forgive my immodesty, but I turned my body and swayed my hips like a slattern. His eyes were twinkling now, his lips twitched. My face grew warm. Nonetheless, I raised my chin and observed his leg with a critical eye.

"Nay, sir, I was right the first time. 'Tis but naught."

At my riposte, the gentleman burst into laughter. Slightly high-pitched, girlish even, it was at odds with his manly appearance. Papa turned and looked from me to the gentleman and back again, brows raised. The gentleman apologized for his outburst and sought to allay Papa's concerns with an introduction.

"I beg your forgiveness for my unseemly exhibition, my good man. Allow me to introduce myself, I am Sir Raffe Shelton." Sweeping off his hat, he executed a bow that included me. Remembering my manners, I dipped another, deeper curtsey. One more befitting his status.

After that, Papa introduced me and Benedict and before I knew how it occurred, Sir Raffe was included in Master Cruikshank and Papa's discussion. As he asked questions revealing a keen understanding of locks and keys, Papa and Benedict responded enthusiastically. Master Cruikshank spoke of Papa's reputation and vast experience. Sir Raffe was impressed and did not hesitate to show it.

Within minutes, the knight organized to come to the workshop and discuss a commission with Papa. As it happened, he was in need of secure locks for his mother's chests; she was about to remove to his manor house in the north for the summer. Words flew around me, congenial, eager. Edging my way closer to Sir Raffe, I was able to smell the scent of roses upon his doublet, see the flashing jewels of the rings on his hands, and identify the markings on the peacock feather in his cap. His squire, Ellis, stood with his hands clasped in front of him, his head bowed. A bruise marked the back of one hand and it appeared he had a cut on his lip. I began to imagine Sir Raffe as a great lord needing protection or, better still, offering it to those in need.

As he listened to Papa his face was earnest. His body was designed for chivalry—hard and lean. Beside him, Benedict, whom I'd once thought handsome in an unconventional way, was clumsy and untidy. Even Papa appeared a lesser figure: suddenly his broken, blackened nails looked grubby; his hair was too long, his beard in need of trimming, his stomach distended. His clothes, which were of a fine cut, appeared ill-fitting and cheap. I became conscious of my own apparel. The velvet of my bodice felt patchy, the pickadills frayed. I resisted touching my hair, which fell from beneath my cap and down my back in a long black curtain, wishing for the umpteenth time it was the russet of Mamma's and that my skin was white like my maid Nell's. Through the shop windows I saw grand ladies pass in their dresses of ruby, gold and ebony, their creamy complexions glowing, their small pretty mouths pursed, their flaxen, chestnut and flame-colored hair statements of beauty that my ebony locks and Moorish complexion could never be. I hid my scarred hands behind my back, lowered my strange eyes and chewed my lips till they almost bled.

Appointments were made, farewells were bade, and all the time Sir Raffe never gave another glance in my direction. I know, because I could barely take my eyes from him. Yet, and I do not know how I was so certain, I felt as if he too was aware of me.

Master Cruikshank warned us not to linger for fear of cutpurses and rogues, but to hasten home. Only minutes earlier I would have objected, as my plans were so cruelly curtailed, but I didn't protest. I didn't even complain when we were caught in a downpour and my best dress was ruined. When I sat before the fire in the parlor and Angela dried my hair and asked what I thought of the Exchange, my replies were vague, my mind back in the goldsmith's shop listening to the dulcet tones of Sir Raffe Shelton, who'd shown me both a fine leg and a degree of attention I'd never experienced before.

My head was turned, my heart aflutter.

Sir Raffe began visiting the workshop day after day to ensure the locks he wanted were progressing. He would time his visits to match my hours in the shop, and would ask me numerous questions about locks and keys, affecting an interest in a subject that I knew so well. I was flattered. After two days, Raffe grabbed my hand and bowed over it, his fingers lingering upon mine. When he thought Papa wasn't looking, he included a quick but warm kiss upon my wrist. When Mamma was busy serving another customer in the shop, Raffe offered me a poem to my night-dark hair, sea-storm eyes and ruby lips. His poems were clumsy and poorly structured—how could I think otherwise, when I'd listened to Caleb's verses and been raised on the works of ancient masters? But where other men might have been offended by my laughter at their efforts, Raffe chuckled with me. Gesturing grandly, he would fish compliments from the ether, his cornflower-blue eyes sparkling, daring me to erupt with mirth, which I inevitably did. Mamma would usher him from my sight and admonish me not to encourage such a one.

"He is dallying with your affections, Mallory. He's not for the likes of you. He's a northerner, landed gentry. You're promised to Isaac and to Isaac Hattycliffe you will one day belong." Two days later, I was banished from the shop and exiled to the house.

Sir Raffe still managed to get his poems and messages to me. I would dream of my knight (as I now called him) and, daringly, of a time when we might be together. Was it Raffe who placed that seditious thought in my head, or did I place it there myself? I know not, but, as the number of his notes (delivered by Nell, whom his man had found among the servants at Cheapside markets) increased, so did their fervor, and the idea took root in fertile soil.

Raffe was an alien in a familiar country; a jewel that shone so brightly it made all others dim—especially Isaac. The prospect of being Mistress Hattycliffe, the wife of a weaver's son, a junior lawyer, suddenly seemed as dull as an unpolished key.

When Raffe first proposed we elope, I denied my growing affection and refused. Unaccustomed as I was to the ways of men, his ardor frightened me. One Sunday we met after prayers while Nell kept watch, and the promises he whispered as he pressed me against the church wall I took to be the truth. How could it be otherwise, when the Lord watched over us and he said such things upon His holy soil?

But there was something different about Raffe that morning, an edge of desperation in his words, a furtiveness in his attitude, that made me keep him at arm's length and voice doubts I didn't know I had. His kisses were hard that day, his manner forceful; his hands were not those of a gentleman. His eyes were too bright and I smelled wine upon his breath and sweat upon his clothes. I ran and sought the safety of my room, only to be called to Mamma's chambers not long after. When I saw Nell's tear-stained face, her flaming red cheek, and how she was unable to meet my eyes, I knew my assignations were discovered.

Mamma had beaten me before—I was no angel. I was a headstrong chit, as Mamma often said. But this day, she struck me soundly and repeatedly and made me swear I would never see the scoundrel Shelton again. Papa added his punishment to hers, taking the strap to my hindquarters in the same way he did the apprentices. I was humiliated, confused, furious. Sent to my room for two days without food, I brooded while I licked my wounds.

Perchance it was guilt at her betrayal that made Nell risk bringing me one last message from Raffe. She snuck into my room late on the second night of my confinement and found me curled on my bed, staring at the shadows the candle cast upon the arras. As she relayed Raffe's final words, I saw both salvation and, God forgive me, revenge.

"He begs you to meet him at the river, mistress. He gave me this for you." From her pocket she retrieved a small golden locket, which I slowly took, wide-eyed and reckless. Opening the clasp, inside was a curl of perfect yellow hair snipped from his own, a symbol of his love, his commitment to me. Tears welled and I held the locket close to my heart.

"He says . . ." continued Nell, kneeling by the bed so her words could be delivered straight into my ears, "he says to tell you if you come, never again will you be parted from his side."

I sat up, ignoring the pain of my bruised legs and buttocks. My eyes shone as I clasped the locket around my neck. Staring at Nell, I took her cold red fingers in mine and squeezed them hard. "You must not tell anyone, no matter what threats or promises are made. Swear on your soul you will keep these words in your heart and share them with no other."

"I do swear, mistress," said Nell, and fled.

And so I took leave of my home and my family and forswore my future as Mistress Hattycliffe, choosing instead Sir Raffe Shelton and the promise of becoming a lady of the realm . . .

In all my reading, all the stories that filled my head, where was the one about the knight who was a knave?

For all the wondrous vows Raffe had whispered in my ear, he neglected to mention the ones he'd made to his wife.

I found out too late that my Raffe, my knight, was in possession of a wife. Sickly, she was expected to pass into the Lord's arms any day, or so he said. Hence his mother had rushed to be by her side till she departed the corporeal world. Raffe had done his duty by his mother and married an older woman with lands and a generous dowry, though he'd felt no more affection for her than one might a milk cow. He was determined that when she passed, he would marry a woman of his choosing. I was to be that woman. Unable to risk losing me to another, he had brought me north to his estates so we could enjoy each other while we awaited the inevitable. Instead of entering the manor as his lady wife, I was accommodated in a small cottage on his lands near a stream, given two old harridans as my companions, and my understanding and patience were first implored, then demanded.

Stunned by the circumstances in which I found myself, horrified to find not only a wife but an ailing one he could so readily cast aside, and wanting nothing more than to return home and throw myself upon my family's mercy, I could not. As Raffe carefully and sorrowfully explained to me, my family would never take me back. In disobeying them so publicly, in choosing my own mate instead of the one they'd picked, I'd shamed them. They could no longer make a match for me, let alone a good one. The one attribute any respectable gentleman expected in a young wife was no longer mine to bestow, for, believing Raffe was my husband in every regard, I'd surrendered my virtue as proof of my love.

I needed Raffe just as, he said over and over, he needed me.

Ashamed, humiliated and understanding all my hopes rested not only upon the death of his wife but on his continued affection, I also knew I was doomed. I was the worst of sinners. I was nothing but a shameful trull who was fortunate to have Raffe and a roof over my head. How God did not abandon me, I do not know. I prayed every night for His forgiveness.

At first, I penned many a letter to my parents explaining my actions, begging their grace once I had a ring on my finger and the Shelton name. The letters were never sent. Once their ink was dry, they fed the fire as summer turned to autumn and the weather became grayer and colder. Alone most nights, I pitied my circumstances and even, at times, Raffe, whose ugly old wife clung to life and made his life (and mine) so miserable. Guilt would bubble up that I could be so cold, so callous, when another suffered, and I would pray fervently for her return to health, despite what that meant for me.

My days were spent with the ancient women, Agnes and Katherine, who cooked, cleaned and tended the house and garden, as well as laundering and sewing for the nearby village. They insisted I did my share, which I was content to do. Former nuns, they'd been taken in by the Sheltons, who I began to suspect were recusants. Another sin to add to my growing register. How Mamma would laugh. Her Protestant daughter in the care of papists. On occasion Raffe's squire, Ellis, would ride over with a haunch of meat, some fish, or a brief note from Raffe crumpled in his fist, filled with reasons for his long absences. Bruised and covered in scratches, Ellis wouldn't meet my eyes when I asked after his master and Lady Shelton. He would simply shake his head, shrug and leave.

Days passed into weeks and became months. Winter wrapped her frigid arms about the house and snow lay in deep drifts upon the fields, and still Raffe's lady wife didn't die. I began to grow angry—angry and bored. This was not the life I'd been promised, shut up alone in a dreary and drafty cottage with two Catholics who labored all day and prayed all night and did little else but criticize me. To escape their company, once the weather permitted and spring melted the snow, I enjoyed a daily walk. As it grew warmer, my ambles became longer until one day I trespassed where I had been told never to go. I mounted a green crest and saw, sitting in the sun amid a lovely flowering garden, a pretty woman with a babe upon her lap. From my hiding place behind a fallen bough, I saw a bonny child, whose chubby little hands escaped their swaddling and reached for a handsome young man who kneeled at the woman's feet. It was Raffe. The woman was his extremely healthy and very attractive lady wife. The child was his.

I'd been gulled.

Returning to the cottage, tears falling, sobs wrenched from my chest, I packed my meager things and demanded that Agnes and Katherine tell me the truth. Katherine told me that months ago it was indeed believed Lady Shelton was not long for this world. Unable to keep down food or drink, she'd taken to her bed and few thought she'd rise again. They were prepared for the worst. Much to everyone's surprise, her illness passed and the doctors announced another miracle: Lady Shelton was with child. Katherine believed it was the babe who'd caused the mother's illness in the first place.

Shocked by the extent of my recklessness, not knowing how to make it right, the only thing I understood was that I had to leave. But I also wanted to let Raffe know what I thought of his deceit and how much I hated him for it. Katherine warned me. Agnes shook her head. Perchance it was my pride, my stubborn need to try to extract myself with some dignity, that prompted what happened next. I wrote to him and forced Agnes to take the letter to the main house.

Raffe came as I knew he would. He sent Katherine and Agnes away and listened as I railed against him and threatened to reveal all he'd done, how he'd not only tricked me but dishonored his lady wife and his family name. Revenge would be sweet, I said, and my father would not rest until it was done.

When Raffe took me in his arms, I thought he meant to beg my forgiveness and still my tears. Yet my lunacy knew no bounds. I rested my head against his shoulder and allowed him to carry me to the bed.

I never saw him raise his hand, never knew a blow would sound so harsh nor elicit so much pain. When Raffe began to strike me, his fist clenched, his arm rising and falling against my chest, my stomach, my legs and arms, I screamed and fought back. I raged against his brutality. But he was a man, with a man's strength, and I was only a woman. I was unaccustomed to such treatment; he was practiced at meting it out, as I would learn over the following months from Ellis and even Katherine and Agnes. It wasn't until I was curled, silent, bloodied and shaking upon the floor, that he once again hoisted me into his arms and, with a bowl of water by his side, took off his ruff and used it to staunch the blood he'd caused to flow.

"Hush, hush," he whispered. "You're a naughty chit, Mallory. Look what you've made me do. Look at your beautiful cheeks, so swollen and red, your oh-so-kissable mouth all cut and bruised. Ah, now, my sweet, do not look at me like that. You should not threaten me so. Words such as those you uttered enrage me so I don't know what I'm doing. What did you expect? Am I not a man? No woman should speak to her man thusly. Aye, I'm your man and you're my woman. We are husband and wife in God's eyes, are we not? Hush now, hush now. It will be all right. You cannot leave me. I need you, and you need me too, Mallory. Who else would have you now? Who else would love you, care for you, but me?"

And so he placed me onto the bed and, as he whispered words alternately loving and degrading, tied me to its posts.

Oh, he saw that I was fed and occasionally bathed. Katherine and Agnes stayed with me in the cottage, but they didn't speak. I didn't understand why at first until I saw their bruised faces, their bloodied noses and eyes swollen and half-shut. Sometimes Raffe would send them away and stay the night, feeding me with his fingers, washing me himself. After, he would have his way with me, even as I recoiled from his touch. His ministrations oft shifted from loving caresses to painful pinches, punches and, if I looked at him askance, blows that rendered me unconscious.

When I awoke, he would press me to him, one hand upon my back, the other on my nape and would place his lips upon mine until I opened my mouth to his probing tongue. I could neither escape his hold nor, in the end, remember why I wanted to.

For, just like his lady wife, I was carrying his child.

Some memories were too heavy to carry. This night, after the confrontation with Lord Nathaniel, I chose to cease my dark recollections. Wrenching myself away from the window, I lit a candle and, knowing sleep would elude me, picked up Castiglione, flipping the pages till I found where I'd left off. I needed his words, not God's, tonight. For, in my hour of need, despite begging for mercy and acknowledging my sins, had He not forsaken me?

As I began to read, it seemed I was never to be forgiven. Castiglione's words both tormented me and reinforced a salient lesson:

> . . . According to universal opinion, a loose life does not defame men as it does women, who, due to the frailty of their sex, give in to their appetites much more than men; and if they sometimes refrain from satisfying their desires, they do so out of shame and not because they lack a ready will in that regard. Therefore men have installed in women the fear of infamy as a bridle to bind them as by force to this virtue, without which they would be truly little esteemed; for the world finds no usefulness in women except the bearing of children . . .

The absurdity and distress of those last words struck me. I didn't know I was crying until my tears struck the page.

NINETEEN

SEETHING LANE AND
BILLITER LANE, LONDON
Last days of March, Anno Domini 1581
In the 23rd year of the reign of Elizabeth I

*M*y introduction to Lady Walsingham and her daughter, Frances, occurred the following day. Exhausted from lack of sleep and the memories the night had visited upon me, I was ushered into Sir Francis's company and found my intention to speak of Lord Nathaniel and the question he'd posed regarding my duties swept clean from my mind.

No doubt part of the reason was due to the kiss the varlet stole . . . Though had he really stolen it? Stealing implied something taken against the will of the victim. Had I been unwilling? Memories of Lord Nathaniel's lips, the strength and hardness of his body against mine and the appetites he'd aroused, disturbed my dreams as much as anything else. Just as Raffe's face would appear, it was replaced by Lord Nathaniel's dancing golden eyes; the sense of terror, despair and fury at my inability to escape my circumstances was replaced by one of both pleasure and safety. Yet Lord Nathaniel had proved he was anything but a secure harbor. On the contrary, his curiosity was dangerous. In order to protect myself, I would endeavor to do all I could to avoid his company.

Hadn't I made that resolution before? And if a pinch of regret accompanied it, there was naught for it; I would have to increase my efforts. My employment depended upon it.

Sir Francis barely uttered a word as he brought me to the main parlor of the house, an austerely appointed room containing only four chairs with neatly embroidered cushions, a small table, and a credenza displaying gilt-ware. In a similar fashion to the entrance hall, the walls of the room were lined with dark wooden panels and rich tapestries, their scenes made more bold by the barrenness of the room. The scent of lemon, candle smoke and perfume lingered in the air. A large window overlooked the street and two horsemen passed outside just as a contingent of soldiers led a group of men in chains in the opposite direction, toward the north gate of the Tower. The clang of their irons rang in time with the clop of hooves.

It took a moment for my eyes to adjust; against the light pouring in the window the room's two occupants were silhouettes. After a moment I saw an older woman with auburn hair and hazel eyes sitting straight-backed in one of the chairs, some needlework held loosely in her lap. Opposite her was a young girl with long, straight chestnut hair and the steely eyes of her father. She had a book in her hand. They both possessed the pale complexions I envied, but only one smiled as we entered—the girl I assumed was Frances.

"Father!" said Frances, rising slightly from her seat, then, at a gesture from her mother, sinking back into it.

"May God give you good morning," said Sir Francis, lifting his wife's hand and pressing it to his lips before turning and kissing his daughter's forehead. "Allow me to introduce you to Mallory Bright, the young woman I spoke about. Mallory." He turned and beckoned me forward. I dropped a curtsey, bowing to both Lady Ursula and Frances. "She'll be accompanying us to Deptford on Tuesday. I promised her father she could come with us so she might see the play their lodger, Caleb Hollis, has written."

"So, this is Timothy's niece," said Lady Ursula cooly, indicating a seat. "Well met, Mallory." My back was to the street. The room looked different with the light behind me. Like Lady Ursula and her daughter, it was painted in brighter hues.

"Thank you, my lady."

My discomfort escalated as no one spoke further. Was it up to me to break the silence? I looked to Sir Francis, who watched his wife the way a hawk watches its prey. Ignoring her husband's gaze, Lady Ursula studied me frankly. I wanted to squirm, to ask what was amiss. I'd dressed so carefully that morning, with more attention than usual. My dress, borrowed from my mother, was clean, my hair washed and tucked away beneath my coif and bonnet. Was it my features she found offensive? Did she know I worked for her husband? Was she unhappy he'd employed a woman, or was there more at stake here? I simply sat and stared at my hands.

"Do you like the theater, Mistress Mallory?" asked Frances finally, her voice surprisingly deep for one so young.

"Please, call me Mallory." I turned toward her gratefully. "My friend Caleb, Master Hollis, has recently become a shareholder with Lord Warham's Men. He's a fine playwright and actor. It's his play that's to be performed in Master Drake's honor. I would not miss it for the world."

"The world? A grand sentiment, I'm sure," said Lady Ursula. "Only, you would be missing it had not my husband kindly said you could accompany us."

Abashed, I felt my face grow warm. "That's true. I'm very grateful."

"Frances has not been to theater before, have you, dearest?" said Sir Francis suddenly, moving from his wife's side to the fire and peering into the hearth, hefting the poker into his hand and prodding a few embers.

"No, Father, and, frankly, I've no desire to either. Theater is for . . ." She pressed her lips together, seeming to remember the company. "A playwright shares your house? Does not having a wordsmith living there distract you from God and His word?" Perched on the edge of her seat, her hands clasped in her lap, her face solemn, Frances resembled a preacher more than a young woman. She was slender and long limbed like her father, but in her icy regard, her bare tolerance for my presence, she could only be likened to her mother.

It was all I could do not to sigh. Lady Ursula was too like my mother for comfort. Two sets of disapproving eyes remained upon me. I knew not where to look, what to say. The room became smaller and smaller as my unease grew and I searched my mind for a reply.

I knew little of Lady Ursula except that Sir Francis was her second husband. Her first, Sir Richard Worsley, had died some years before, leaving her with two sons. Caleb had been right when he suspected there'd been more children. Papa told me they'd died in a terrible accident involving gunpowder the year after she married Sir Francis. This was a woman who had known great tragedy in her life, who had witnessed death, including the massacre in Paris. The lines etching her brow and puckering her mouth had been earned. Her eyes had witnessed so much and, like her husband's, could see through facades. Could she see through mine? And what about Frances? For certes, as lovely as she was, her stare was cold and hard.

A trickle of sweat coursed between my shoulder blades.

"Master Hollis's work will be a fine introduction to the theater for you, Frances," her father said. "It means you will see the best, the title notwithstanding. Will it not, Mallory?"

Grateful to Sir Francis, I tried not to gush. "Indeed, it will, sir. I've read the play and can attest to both its humor and drama. It's a fine tribute to a great man."

"Your bias notwithstanding," said Lady Ursula. "After all, the writer is, of your own admission, not only a mere lodger, but a friend." She made it sound like a folly.

I bowed my head, puzzled by her hostility as she continued. "It would not have been my choice for Frances's first experience of the theater, and while Nathaniel is trying to earn a reputation for having the finest troupe in London, it's a pity we have to travel to Deptford to see his Men. But Her Majesty is not to be gainsaid in this—or anything else, is she, Francis?"

There was an undertone to this conversation, and I could see Frances sensed it too.

"Oh, Mamma," said Frances plaintively. "If you had your way, I'd never leave the house."

"If I had my way, you would not be going to Deptford."

She glared at me as if responsibility for that decision rested on my shoulders. Perchance it did. Frances going to Deptford meant she was cast into my company. I was the problem here, though I wasn't certain why.

Picking up her needlework, Lady Ursula decided I was not worth any more of her attention.

"Truly, Mother, if you had your way," Frances went on, pretending to ignore her mother's manner, "I would not be going anywhere except to the church and then with a man of your choice. At least going to Deptford I get to see more of the world than Barn Elms. I also get to see Her Majesty." She sounded so like I did when I was her age.

Without raising her head, Lady Ursula countered, "You have seen more than most, child. And while you may not remember what we bore witness to in Paris, I cannot forget and would protect you from all our enemies and anything that would disturb the harmony of family and faith." She locked eyes with her husband. "Both without and within." Her voice was steady and firm.

He was the first to look away.

"Well," he said, before another word could be exchanged. "I'd best see Mallory gets safely home."

"Surely Robert, Thomas or one of the servants can see her to Harp Lane, husband," said Lady Ursula, as if I were a horse to be delivered to an ostler or a fish returned to the ocean. Only later did it occur to me that she knew where I lived. "As for you, Frances, you have your lesson on the clavichord to attend."

"Do you study an instrument, Mallory?" asked Frances.

"She is a woman with many gifts," answered Sir Francis. I tried not to show my surprise.

Frances's cheeks grew pink.

"Most of which our daughter need not know about," said Lady Ursula.

It was my turn to redden.

Rising from my chair, I curtseyed to both Lady Ursula and then Frances. "It has been a pleasure meeting you, my lady, Lady Frances." I would remember my manners even if they saw fit to abandon theirs. "I will look forward to next Tuesday," I lied sweetly.

Lady Ursula didn't acknowledge my exit, but Frances rose and followed me to the door. She was tall. We were almost of a height. "If I'm to go, mayhap you can take me to the tiring room so I might meet an actor. I've never met one before and would like to understand what motivates them to choose such an ungodly profession."

Overhearing, Sir Francis laughed. "Oh, but you have met one, many a time, dearest. His name is Baron Burghley, Lord William

Cecil, though I would hesitate to suggest *his* calling is ungodly." Sir Francis and his daughter seemed to find the joke very amusing.

Sir Francis was still chuckling when he brought me back to his study. Closing the door, he didn't invite me to sit, but went to his desk.

"I'm afraid while my wife and daughter are in residence, arrangements have to change—you can no longer come here each day. I think you can see why."

I could. Lady Ursula was a canny one. "If I remain at home, then it will raise suspicion . . . Why, only last night . . ." I paused.

"Hmmm? Last night . . . ?" said Sir Francis, not really listening, leafing through some papers.

Did I really want to reveal what Lord Nathaniel had said? Or would Sir Francis think me a hapless female, unable to deal with the most basic tasks without compromising myself and potentially his entire network? Much better to keep things to myself. I could handle his lordship's curiosity. Was I not an intelligencer, trusted with ferreting out secrets and keeping them?

God's wounds, I really had no choice.

"I was just thinking," I continued, praying my voice didn't betray me, "if I were to cease coming here, Papa would wonder why Mistress Frances no longer wanted me by her side."

"Indeed he would. That's why, for the time being, you will spend your days with Thomas and Casey at one of my other houses. There you'll learn what you need to carry out the task in Deptford." The candle flickered as he pulled his chair closer to the desk, almost going out before coming to life again. He gazed up at me for what seemed like an age, his eyes black pools.

"I'm to be trained?"

"This job requires a specific set of skills, some of which you're yet to acquire but which, as a woman, you'll have no difficulty learning."

"I see."

Sir Francis grinned. "No, Mallory, you do not. But you will. Now sit." He waited until I finished rearranging my skirts. "What I need you to do is not for the faint of heart," he said, his voice barely a whisper. "It's dangerous work. Many a seasoned watcher of mine would tremble."

Zounds. Was I really a woman? The very thought of danger made

my heart skip, lifted my worries and eased my doubts, the way words
of love once had. Mamma was right. I was unnatural.

"I'm ready, sir." I met his eyes and held them.

"I think you are too, so does Thomas. I want you to remember,
Mallory, what I ask of you is for the Queen and our country. Can you
do this?"

My back straightened, as if it were made of metal. Oh, if Caleb
could see me now. Without knowing what was being asked, I replied.
"I can, sir."

"Can you do this for me?"

His earnestness was not to be questioned. "Aye," I said. His look
made my heart soar with a mingling of pride and something else.

I was his creation. I must succeed for his sake as well as my own.

An hour later I was ensconced at a table in the parlor of a small house
behind the Fuller's Hall in Billiter Lane, not too far from the Ironmonger's Hall. Thomas had escorted me the half hour or so's walk
north of Seething Lane. The two lower stories of the house were made
of brick, while the upper two were wood. There was a lively alehouse
on one side and a pious Dutch family on the other. The houses opposite bespoke a mixture of wealth and poverty. One had been newly
roofed, the glass in the windows replaced and the front door freshly
painted. It was the property of a rich London alderman who, Thomas
said, lived there alone, his family preferring the country—not surprisingly, as the stench from the fullers nearby and the smoke from ovens
and furnaces was overpowering. Next door to the alderman lived a
night soil man and his laundress wife. They had five children, two of
whom were dressed in clean rags, dogs gamboling at their heels as they
played in the dirt outside while an older girl helped her mother in the
yard. Thomas said the oldest boys worked with their father and were
no doubt catching some sleep before it was time to go to work. Billiter
Lane, though long and narrow, was also an access point between Fenchurch Street and Aldgate, and was so noisy and crowded I marveled
that anyone could rest there, let alone sleep. The neighbors were slipped
a small sum now and then to take note of any interest expressed in the

house and its occupants and to deflect attention away from those who might frequent it.

We slipped inside, and Casey and an elderly woman met us.

"This is Mistress Bench, our housekeeper," said Thomas. "You'll not meet a more worthy woman." He never gave my name to the thin, ruddy-cheeked beldame. She wordlessly set about fetching us some ale and a haunch of cold meat and cheese.

While she gathered our repast, Thomas showed me around. I was struck by how ordinary the house was, how clean. A staircase led to bedrooms upstairs; downstairs were a number of rooms, most of them furnished with tables covered with paper, maps and quills and a scattering of stools, chairs and some makeshift pallets. A fire burned merrily in two of the rooms and the smells of baking and the clean scent of rosemary wafted in the air.

Seeing my nose raised in appreciation, Thomas gave one of his rare smiles. "She is an asset, Mistress Bench. I don't know where Sir Francis found her, but it's rumored she is related to Drake's privateer cousin John Hawkins, no less, a great aunt or some such. Verily, the woman is like a locked chest—nothing escapes her mouth—or this house, for that matter. She can be trusted, Mallory. You are safe here. Well, as safe as one can be in London in these times."

I stared after the slim-hipped woman as she put down plates of food, noting the strength of her chin, the veins that corded her neck, how knotted her fingers.

When we had finished eating, Thomas began to outline what it was Sir Francis wished me to do. Casey unfurled a map of Deptford on the table, and Thomas described the town, pointing out various landmarks. Situated upstream, on the southern bank of the Thames, Deptford was a deepwater port that had been chosen by the Queen's father, King Henry, as the site for his navy's shipyard. Since then, it had become a renowned center for ships and shipbuilding, providing anchorage for the royal yachts as well as the navy. The town was filled with naval officers and their families and boasted a goodly supply of shops, a central green and gardens as well as storehouses bursting with timber.

"At Her Majesty's command, Drake sailed the *Golden Hind* from Plymouth to here—" I watched his finger trail across the map to a dock.

"Now the town has become a tourist attraction as well, which works both to our advantage and against it." Before I could ask why, he pressed on. "This is the noble's house where Master Hollis's play will be performed, and this is the inn where many dignitaries are staying—others, like Sir Francis, will return to London."

Unable to wait any longer, I interrupted. "This is all very well and good, Thomas, and I will commit what I can to memory. But what is it I'm to do in Deptford?"

Thomas met my gaze. "While everyone is at the ceremony to knight Drake, you're going to steal some very important papers and replace them with a benign set of documents."

I sucked in my breath.

"It won't be easy, so time and a solid disguise are imperative."

"Disguise? What am I to be disguised as?"

"I'm afraid you're to become a person of questionable moral virtue, Mistress Mallory."

If I hadn't been seated at the table, I would have fallen to the floor. I quickly realized Thomas wasn't casting aspersions on my past, but was simply answering my question, and I composed myself.

"I see. And what does that mean exactly?"

"You'll be a boy pretending to be a woman."

Understanding dawned. "You mean an actor?"

Thomas flashed a grin of approval. "I do."

Oh, how Caleb would have railed against being called a person of questionable morals. There were many who looked upon the profession as nothing short of vagabondage and all who trod the boards as ungodly, without scruples or virtue or indeed any redeeming qualities. It wasn't just the Puritans who loathed the theater. Caleb oft spoke of the beatings his fellow actors had been subjected to, the mobs that attempted to have them evicted from the inns they played at, the frequent vituperation served from the pulpit toward actors and all who supported them. Fortunately, the Queen was among the latter and so most attempts to put an end to the profession failed, though some troupes had disbanded as a consequence.

"For what purpose must I be an actor, a boy?"

"So that you might board a vessel, enter a traitorous captain's cabin and there, steal the secrets locked within his chest."

I stared at Thomas with a mixture of disbelief and utter trepidation. "I hope you're referring to the wooden kind and not a flesh-and-blood one."

Thomas reached for the jug and poured an ale for me, then for himself. He passed me the cup and raised his own.

"That will be entirely up to you and how good a lock-pick you really are. If you are discovered, then I'm afraid the chest you open will be the human kind. This mission is a matter of life and death."

Perched on a stool watching us both, Casey remained quiet, his eyes on me. I stared at the map and back at Thomas. "Can you tell me why I'm stealing these documents?"

"To prevent war, Mallory Bright. To prevent war."

TWENTY

BILLITER LANE, LONDON

Last days of March to early April, Anno Domini 1581

In the 23rd year of the reign of Elizabeth I

I listened without interrupting as Thomas continued to explain, his finger traversing the map from the river and the pier where the *Golden Hind* was moored to the Upper Water Gate, where the vessel I was to board, *Forged Friends*, was currently docked. All ships weighing anchor had been forced to remain in Deptford, ostensibly to await the knighting of Drake, but this was merely a ruse to ensure access to the ship without arousing suspicion.

"The captain, Master Alyward Landsey, is someone we've observed closely over the years."

"Is he a Catholic traitor?"

"Catholic? I don't think the man knows God or much cares for His laws or blessings. But he is a traitor, a traitor who worships coin and kneels at the altar of those who pay the most. In this case, it's the hell-hated Spanish. He would sell state secrets to them and bring ruin upon our Queen and country."

Thomas sat back, folding his arms. "You've heard of the Levant Company?" I nodded. "Last year, a gentleman named William Harborne, from the very same company, brokered a treaty on behalf of the Queen with the Ottoman Empire."

I gasped. "The Queen negotiated with barbarians?"

Thomas nodded. "Well might you be surprised. The treaty was signed with none other than Sultan Murad III himself. Harborne and others learned that what the Turks want more than anything, and what the Pope has expressly forbidden them to possess, are munitions. They'll pay anyone prepared to deliver them very, very well. Our treasury is in dire need of funds. Who better placed to meet our savage friends' desires than our very own Levant Company? If, at the same time, our needs are met and our treasury is filled, is that not fortuitous? Harborne managed to reach an agreement—all in great secrecy, of course. In return for a steady supply of guns and powder, we have a charter of privileges allowing access to all sorts of ports and goods throughout the Ottoman Empire. To the outside world, it appears as though all the Sultan wants is the hand of English friendship. There are only a few who know the real situation. Unfortunately, one of those people betrayed us and sold the information to Captain Alyward. We have it on excellent authority he intends to sell the same information to those in the Escorial—to King Philip himself, which of course means Rome and the Guises. This cannot happen."

"You say this Landsey is no Catholic yet he would catapult us into war with them?"

"He's the most wretched of humans, a vile, despicable creature. Godless, masterless too—except, as I said, to whoever holds the fattest purse or, it seems, provides the prettiest boys."

Thomas almost spat the words. I was astonished at his vehemence. "Boys."

"Aye, the man is a sodomite."

My disguise started to make sense.

"Drake's knighthood has been chosen as the perfect time to switch the documents he possesses with something much less harmful."

Thomas outlined the plan. My heart hammered, my flesh grew cold then furiously warm. Outside shadows lengthened, the clamor of people and animals continued in the street and cannons thundered distantly on Tower Hill, but I barely registered any of it as I became drawn into the task, a task that would require my skills in disguise and as a lock-pick. I would need to show more temerity and courage than ever before.

Once Thomas finished, he asked if I had questions. I had hundreds, but stopped myself lest he think me ill-suited to the mission. I shook my head. He left the parlor and returned moments later with a rather worn but ornate lady's jacket, embroidered shirt and skirt as well as some very finely made, if old, hose, and passed them to me.

"This is your disguise. It's one of Leicester's Men's costumes. Designed for a tall lad, it should fit. Mistress Bench will help you change and make any necessary adjustments." Summoned by the mention of her name, the elderly housekeeper appeared in the doorway and beckoned me to follow.

I returned some time later completely self-conscious in my new attire. Any indication I was a boy dressed as a woman was lost by the revealing nature of the gown. It was scarlet and the cream stomacher didn't so much cover my upper chest and press my stomach flat as squeeze my waist into an impossibly narrow span and push my small breasts into mounds that threatened to burst the dam of the too-low neckline. The skirt was wide, split at the front to reveal a slashed cream underskirt providing immodest glimpses of my woolen hose, gartered above the knee. If I moved too swiftly, my thighs were also exposed. I slunk into the room, head bowed, and sat upon the stool, gathering the skirts about me as if they were a blanket to cover my shame. Mistress Bench had undone my hair, allowing it to spill down my back.

"It will be assumed you're wearing a wig," she said. "No proper lady would be seen with her hair so." No proper lady. I fitted the bill.

Casey's jaw had fallen open. Thomas gazed at me with a critical eye, frowning above his glasses.

"That will never do," he said and, without ceremony, pulled me to my feet. "You skulk into the room like a chastised dog. Mistress Bench, your help, if I may? Now, Mallory. Listen, watch and learn—your life may depend upon it."

Two more unlikely teachers you'd never find and yet, between them, as the bells tolled and the hours wore on, Thomas and Mistress Bench patiently showed me how to move like a boy pretending to be a girl. Mistress Bench, with more flair than I would have guessed, taught me how to distract a man, taunt and tease so he became flustered and lost his better judgment. I practiced on Casey, who turned redder than a cockscomb, and we fell about laughing until Thomas, in that righteous tone of his, reminded me this was no laughing matter but Crown business.

"A country's fate is in your hands, mistress," he said. "*Our* country's." After that, I didn't even smile unless it was for an ulterior purpose.

For the remainder of that day and most of the next, I learned how to separate myself from the Walsingham family prior to the knighting ceremony (Sir Francis would assist with that), which ship to board, the captain's name and his physical description should I encounter him, his background, how many crew were expected on deck, who would be at the celebrations, and the time I'd have to accomplish my task (all of which I had to repeat over and over to Thomas's satisfaction). I practiced how to walk, talk and act as if beneath the layers of clothing and hair was a boy accustomed to the stage and performing as a woman. A boy who was also accustomed to paying visits to men who paid for his time.

My greatest relief came when I learned that while I'd have to enter the captain's cabin alone and open the chest, Thomas would accompany me to the ship. He would adopt his regular alias, that of a merchant, Peter Halins, and would act as a procurer who'd found me at Captain Alyward's behest. It was a risky strategy, but no more so than the rest of the mission.

Breaking for some ale late Sunday afternoon, I was dressed in the garments Thomas had handed me the first day, only now I wore them as if I'd been born to them, enjoying the bright colors, the lower neckline, the lack of a ruff; I liked the feel of my hair about my shoulders and waist, of being able to push my sleeves up and show off my forearms and cross my legs—something Thomas and Mistress Bench encouraged me to do.

Thomas looked drawn and tired. There were dark shadows under his eyes and when he pushed his glasses further up his nose, his hands shook slightly. At the end of each day, once he had escorted me home, Thomas would return to Seething Lane either to do more work or to fetch papers to take back to his lodgings in Leadenhall. The man was dedicated. The least I owed was the same commitment.

Captain Landsey, I learned, was a corrupt soul who abused his power, was careless with his loyalties and above all, cruel to those who were weaker than him.

"It's believed his crew tolerate his proclivities providing the boys look like women," explained Thomas. "That way, they can remain willfully ignorant of his depravity. So Landsey insists the boys come on board wearing dresses and behave as if they belong in one. It's been simpler for him to sate his lust among the acting profession, where boys are used to wearing skirts on- and offstage—at least, until they're in the privacy of his cabin." I didn't ask how Thomas knew so much. He was one of Sir Francis's men, after all. "With Warham's troupe performing in Deptford, and the boy actors involved in *Drake's Hind*, never mind those from other companies who'll come to see the performance, we couldn't let this opportunity pass. Furthermore, Landsey has been given an invitation he dare not refuse: a place aboard the *Hind* while Drake is given his honors and at the feast and performance to follow. While he's absent from the ship, the crew will be encouraged to take liberties about town, leaving only a couple of resentful watchmen to guard the ship and the captain's cabin. And thus, *alea iacta est.*"

"*The die is cast,*" I whispered. Now everything Thomas and Mistress Bench had me do made sense—especially the idiosyncratic things, like leaning my forearm on the table, taking small simpering steps, then striding with my hips thrust out slightly. I was learning to be both boy and wanton girl. Smoothing my hands along the skirt, I looked down at my sorry décolletage. It wasn't hard to believe I was a boy in woman's attire. My lips twitched. "I see why I was chosen for the part."

Thomas followed the direction of my gaze and quickly turned away, his cheeks pinkening. Casey, who loitered in the doorway, sniggered. "Mall . . . Mistress . . . no. I mean, that's not true. You were chosen because . . . because . . ."

"There is no one else," I finished.

"Quite."

"Well, then, let's ensure I'm perfect in the role, shall we? Enough to persuade Captain Landsey should I have the misfortune to encounter him."

Thomas rose. "Let's pray you don't."

How Caleb would laugh at me, Mallory Bright, playing at being an actor, albeit a boy who was also a strumpet. Not for the first time, I longed to confide in him, to seek his guidance about playing my role. But, like everything I did, this too was a secret, and one I must keep lest Sir Francis's enterprise be undone and the safety of Queen and country compromised.

TWENTY-ONE

*M*aster Gib escorted me to the river at dawn, where I met the Walsingham family. We boarded a hired tilt boat and made our way downstream toward Deptford just as the sun heaved itself over the horizon, its beams piercing the clouds and turning what had promised to be a grim day into a pleasant one. Despite the early hour, the river was crowded as Londoners used whatever means possible—wherries, barges, sailboats and ketches—to travel east to witness the elevation of the most successful privateer in the country to a knighthood.

From Devon lad to wealthy peer—if Drake could do it, any man could. It was inspirational.

Under the canopy of the boat, my cloak tightly fastened, a black bonnet pinned securely to my coif, I sat beside Frances and appeared to listen as she chatted about Master Drake and what was known of his humble beginnings and nautical achievements. Her father added an occasional comment. Thomas appeared to be wrapped in his own thoughts. Beside me sat Lady Ursula's maid, Joan, an unassuming thing, and next to her was another one of Sir Francis's secretaries, Master Francis Mylles.

Though we shared a bench, Frances kept a distance between us. My feeling of being excluded wasn't helped when Master Mylles's new wife, who was seated opposite, mistook me for Frances's sister. Sir Francis and his daughter burst out laughing and Lady Ursula corrected her with no small degree of disdain. Aware of the eyes upon me, I prayed my cheeks were not flaming. After a while the gaffe was forgotten and I was able to think ahead to what I had to do.

Casey had ridden to Deptford at cock's crow and delivered the clothes Thomas and I were to wear to the inn. Beneath a blanket in the basket upon my lap were the papers Sir Francis had brought to Billiter Lane the day before. I tried not to clutch the basket too tightly. It wasn't easy.

Around us, the cries of watermen rang out as they navigated the current. The sweet melody of a lute floated by from a nobleman's boat, and above us gulls cawed and hovered. Folk gathered along the banks, knowing something momentous was to occur. Behind them, the road east was filled with people going to Deptford. The houses gradually thinned until there was nothing but open fields, trees, flocks of sheep, grazing horses and oxen. The human river flowed parallel to ours, filled with riders, carts and groups of people.

Thomas gave me a reassuring nod and turned his attention to the conversation. The further we drifted from the city, the fresher the air became; the wind, cool but gentle, still carried memories of the rain that had pounded London the past few nights.

I barely felt it. God knew, I'd rehearsed my mission often enough these last few days, and mostly without error, but today it had to be perfect—I had to be. The night before, Thomas had bestowed an alias upon me—one Sir Francis had invented. I was to be Samantha Short. I practiced my new name, sounding it in my head, tasting it on my tongue; I wondered if, when I donned my disguise, I would feel different. For a brief span of time, I would no longer be Mallory Bright, but Samantha Short. Sam. SS. She would be both like me and not like me. For a start, she was a woman who was also a boy, possessed of an imaginary past, not a real one filled with happiness, boredom, reckless pursuits, terror, deceit and pain . . . at least, not yet.

Samantha Short was also, like me, a lock-pick, an intelligencer, a watcher. And she would be watching carefully lest Captain Alyward Landsey—privateer, mercenary and traitor to the Crown—make an appearance.

For all that I tried to concentrate on the task ahead, other thoughts interrupted. Though I'd not seen him since the day he accosted me in the parlor and asked the question that had set my mind awhirl and pierced my growing confidence, his wicked golden eyes, strong arms and warm, searching lips would oft intrude and send ribbons of pleasure and trepidation running through me. Damn Lord Nathaniel's inquiring mind and merry eyes. Damn his mouth.

Laughter erupted around me and, without knowing the cause, I joined in, feeling my spirits temporarily lift even as fear and excitement of what awaited grew.

Due to Sir Francis's position within the government, he and his family were welcomed aboard Drake's ship so they could witness the ceremony at close quarters. The *Golden Hind* was a three-masted galleon, and the hollow eyes of its many guns stared out at the assembled crowd, a reminder that this ship and its crew had survived three years at sea and dared much to bring back vast riches. The sails were reefed and ropes coiled and pushed to the edges of the deck, creating a space where the official guests milled. Some of the gentry had gathered on the poop deck, gazing at those below and along the pier. Forced to remain on the quayside with the rest of Sir Francis's staff and hundreds of well-wishers, I scanned the growing crowd. I could just make out the figure of Drake. Not as tall as I imagined, he was resplendent in black and tan velvet, an extravagant hat with a huge white plume angled on his head. As he walked with a proprietorial air among the favored, he shook hands and laughed often. The sun shone her blessings upon the man and the day.

The morning wore on and more nobles joined those on the *Golden Hind*. Lord Burghley and his son, a crookbacked young man, ascended the gangplank, followed closely by none other than Lord Nathaniel, who was accompanied by a young, splendidly dressed woman. Standing head and shoulders above the crowd, Lord Nathaniel made Drake appear tiny. He took up a position behind Sir Francis and bent forward while the two exchanged a few words. Straightening, he peered at the shore. He nodded in my direction and my heart, damn it, leaped. I pretended to ignore him, lifted my chin and concentrated instead on Frances Walsingham, who was sharing a laugh with Lord Nathaniel's companion. I wondered who she was and then pushed the thought from my mind. What did I care? Even so, my eyes were drawn again and again to the man beside the young woman, and heat traveled through my body.

"Are you quite well, mistress?" asked Thomas quietly.

"Quite," I said, certain my face was red.

"Then cease fidgeting so."

Only with the arrival of Her Majesty, perched upon an ornate golden chair in a glass-sided boat draped in the green and white colors of the Tudors, did my agitation ease. A volley of trumpets and cries from guards who tried, unsuccessfully, to force the surging crowd back, announced her arrival. Aided by a mature gentleman of some girth, the Earl of Leicester, some whispered, the Queen stepped onto the dock to resounding cheers. Around me, people fell to their knees, heads bowed in obeisance as she moved across the pier and onto the gangplank. I had only ever seen her as a distant figure either upon a caparisoned horse riding through the streets of London or aboard her state craft as she glided along the river surrounded by courtiers. The opportunity to peek and see her at close quarters was too great to resist. Raising my head discreetly, I studied this woman, my liege and Queen, for whom I would risk my life today.

Her arrival was met with gasps of awe, and it was no wonder. Her dress was a magnificent concoction of gold, white and sparkling gems sewn into a damask so thick and covered in such rich and ornate embroidery—peacocks with dazzling feathers, vines twining around their splayed feet, miniature suns blazing, all stitched in threads that glittered and flashed in the sunlight. Some in the crowd covered their eyes lest they be bedazzled. Her Majesty was both a moving tapestry and like a celestial object fallen from the heavens into our humble midst. Her skirts were so wide and so heavy they almost felled those kneeling closest to the path her Gentleman Pensioners made through the crowd for her. I was too far back to catch the scent, but she raised her pomander to her nose often, inhaling its sweetness. The gauze ruff framing her face was so fine yet so firmly starched that its lace points reached the height of her flame-colored wig. But it was the face beneath that burnished hair that compelled my gaze.

Some of my earliest recollections of Her Majesty were the paeans written to her beauty. Courtiers across Europe penned poems to her eyes, her lips and the way her face invaded their dreams and eclipsed all others. Songs and sonnets were written in her honor; foreign princes begged for her hand, offering all they had and more, swearing their hearts would be broken if she said no. Visitors to our house who'd been to court spoke wholeheartedly about her charm, her wit and her talents. Children were both comforted by stories of her strength and magnificence and cowed into obedience with threats of her all-seeing command.

Now, at last, I was able to behold her for myself.

Every last one of them—from Papa and Mamma to the finest troubadors and bards—had lied. Papa, who'd been to court, who'd made locks for many of the royal coffers and the offices at Whitehall and fashioned an exceptional device for the Queen's rooms at Greenwich, had filled my head with pure fancy.

Her Majesty was nothing but a grotesque parody of womanhood. Wrinkled like a beldame, she was stick thin, her flesh capturing the powder and creams in which she was liberally doused. Her whitened cheeks were sunken, her dark eyes were cold and lifeless stones that scoured the people at her feet but didn't see them. The brows arched above her deep-set eyes were almost nonexistent. God forgive me, but the men who set such store by my Queen's grace and beauty were either bewitched or engaged in gross falsehoods.

Only her hands, one clasping an elegant fan, the other raising the pomander to her nose, suggested something of those lyrical descriptions. They were long-fingered, creamy, beringed and elegant.

Upon sighting Drake, who waited for her on deck, hat in hand, poised to bow long and deeply, Her Majesty flashed a smile exposing blackened teeth quickly covered by thin, reddened lips. The effect was repulsive, and as her mouth closed I felt a flare of sympathy. My Queen was but a woman. 'Twas her power and station that, like a glamor woven by a sorceress, kept the men fascinated and in awe. If she were but one of us here, squashed upon the dock, she'd earn no more attention than a stray dog.

Helped onto the deck by Drake, Leicester and one of her Gentlemen Pensioners, she paused and, finding her feet, bestowed a slight bow of her head. Only then did the higher-ranking officials waiting on the quay seek to follow her on board. They surged onto the gangplank, each struggling to gain the most advantageous position, when a great crack resounded. The crowd froze, holding its collective breath, then with a wounded groan and a shudder, the wood of the gangplank shattered. There were gasps of horror as men, women and some children were flung shrieking into the shallow, muddy waters below. There they floundered in the stinking sludge, their finery ruined, calling to God. Their cries for help mingled with the shouts of dismay—as well as laughter and jeers—from the quay and the ship.

The Queen turned to observe the cause of the commotion, surveyed her subjects, then turned back to those on the ship; her frown signaled her disapproval that her arrival was upstaged by commoners.

I didn't have time to watch any more. Thomas plucked at my elbow, whispered "Come," and wove a path for us back through the masses, away from the quay, toward the row of taverns, offices and houses behind it.

"We'll take the advantage such a distraction provides."

Before long we were at the Raven Inn and ensconced in a room where, while Thomas turned his back, I quickly donned my costume. Thomas had me repeat my instructions, and it helped keep my attention away from the riot taking place in my stomach. Imitating Caleb's gentle northern burr, I hoped to give my alias an origin far from my own home.

Thomas also changed. Now he was dressed in a dark brown cloak of wool and a plain hat and doublet that nonetheless shouted quality. In every inch he looked the conservative but wealthy merchant he pretended to be, someone accustomed to dealing with privateers and fulfilling even the most ungodly requests.

"Good," said Thomas as he inspected me. "Good. The accent is a nice touch," he added, his tone a little uncertain. "You can hold it? Very well. Now, find somewhere to hide this," he said, and handed me a dagger.

Light in my palm, it had an ornate handle and a short but deadly looking blade. Turning aside, I tucked it into the hose of the boy's garb I wore beneath my skirts, trying not to consider its implications. To my peril I knew what it was like to be defenseless before a man, and I never wanted to be in that position again. I blessed Thomas for his foresight.

He pulled a small flask from his doublet and forced it into my hand. "Drink."

I didn't need to be told twice. The liquid scorched my throat and filled my center with much-needed warmth. Thomas took a long swallow and pushed the cork back in.

"Ready?"

I nodded, unable at that exact moment to find words as the cold steel pressed against my thigh.

"Let us be gone, then," he said, and once more took my arm.

Moving through lanes and back streets, it didn't take us long to reach the place where the *Forged Friends* was anchored. We passed some pigs, a gaggle of geese stalked by a mangy red cat, and an old woman foraging in someone's garden. The sounds of cheers, whistles and clapping grew fainter the further we got from the main dock. Most of the ships were midriver and appeared abandoned. The only other craft moored at Deptford were at Middlewater and Upper Water Gates—our destination. A couple of old men sat outside a ramshackle alehouse but paid us scant notice. Nonetheless I couldn't help glancing around, feeling eyes upon us, hearing footsteps tracking ours. I saw no one.

As soon as we left the protection of the alleys, Thomas and I commenced playing our roles. We slowed our pace, Thomas gripped my arm tighter and I adopted the slight swagger I'd perfected, swinging my hips, but striding wide. A lone guard sitting upon the bow of *Falcon's Fury* at Middlewater Gate twisted around to watch us pass, his long, thin pipe drooping from slack lips, before deciding we posed no threat and turning again to face the river, drinking his smoke in solitude.

"No turning back now," said Thomas under his breath, his mouth barely moving as we approached the *Forged Friends*.

"Aye," I whispered, and was glad we'd no choice.

"Oy, there," called Thomas in a voice I'd never heard him use before. "I be after Captain Alyward, if you please."

Uncurling from the base of a mast, a sailor of middling years with a weather-beaten face, a filthy neck scarf and all but the thumb and forefinger of his right hand missing, stood. "And who would you be?" he sniffed, studying Thomas, then me, before releasing a huge gobbet of spit on the deck.

Trying not to recoil, I raised my chin and stared at him defiantly, swaying slightly from side to side, as if I'd had one too many ales.

"That be none of your business. I was told to bring this"—with a roughness I didn't expect and that made me stagger, Thomas pulled me forward—"trull to this ship for the pleasure of one Captain Alyward."

The sailor stepped to the rails and squinted. "The captain don't . . . oh. Right." He looked me up and down, screwed up his nose and spat again. "I don't know nothin' 'bout no . . . trull . . ." He scratched his head, his cap caught only by his ear. Without another word, he walked away. A small noise of protest escaped my throat.

"Steady," said Thomas.

I glanced behind. Nothing appeared amiss and yet . . .

"Wake up, you cankered excuse for a codpiece." The sailor kicked something on the deck hard, and a loud groan was followed by a series of expletives.

"Wha' you want, you onion-pocked pizzle?" The voice was thick as tar. "I told you to leave me be."

Out of the muddle of canvas and rope emerged a grizzled old man. What remained of his hair jutted out from the sides of his head; his nose looked like a rock had been thrown at his face and lodged there, serving no other purpose than to keep his ears apart. Bending down, the first sailor muttered something and the other sat up and looked past his companion to study us further. There was a long cackle followed by a wheezing cough.

"Not for the likes of us to question," said the old man. "That's betwixt 'im"—he gestured with a shaking finger at me—"the capt'n"—he jerked his thumb in the general direction of the *Golden Hind*—"and whatever God the devil-shat cock-sucker worships, cause it sure as Satan's missus ain't ours." With one last look in our direction, the old sailor lay back down on the deck and pulled the canvas over him.

The first sailor gestured for us to board. There was no plank, just a gap, the rails and the river seething below. Thomas didn't wait for a second invitation, but gripped the railing and vaulted across before turning to help me.

"Dunno when his Cap'nship will return, but you can wait in his cabin," said the sailor, jerking his chin toward the stern.

Was it really going to be this simple?

"But you," said the sailor to Thomas. "You can wait back there." He pointed to the pier.

"I will wait here," said Thomas, and planted his feet firmly on the deck.

"You'll do as you're damn well told," said the sailor, drawing a long dagger from the sheath at his hip and thrusting it into Thomas's face. "I may have to put up with the likes of him, but I don't have to suffer your kind what profits from 'em." With great relish and a lot of noise, he spat on Thomas's boots.

Holding up his palms in appeasement, Thomas threw a leg over the side. "Very well, yer cursed skainsmate. But I'm not moving from the dock. Not till the coin is in my fist and my lady friend is on my arm."

The sailor shrugged. "Suit yourself." He waved the dagger at me. "Go, get outta me sight. Lady friend my arse," he sniggered.

I didn't wait to be told again. I crossed the deck and entered the captain's cabin.

The smell was overpowering. I gagged as odors of shit, sweat, rotten food, stinking feet and linens swamped me. I held the door open until I had my stomach back under control. The cabin's bank of windows was closed, and below these, striped with sunlight, was a bed crowded with soiled sheets and pillows imprinted with stains I couldn't begin to identify. In the middle of the room stood a table awash with goblets, ewers and even a gold plate streaked with grease and gnawed bones. An overflowing jordan sat against one table leg, the leaking contents drying on the wood. The floor was littered with furls of paper, dollops of wax and clothes—not all were men's clothes, either. The walls held an array of weapons—guns, swords and some sharp-looking instruments that would inflict terrible pain. There was also a whip with leaden shots sewn onto the ends. I dragged my eyes away. At first glance I couldn't see the chest but, as I scanned the room again, it was evident the huge pile of clothes at the foot of the bed hid something larger. Holding my breath, I shut the door, latched it and then, with my basket firmly on my arm, leaped on the bed and opened the windows. Even the stench of the Thames around Deptford was better than this hedge-pig's quarters. The *Golden Hind* had sailed the world and maintained an air of orderliness. This vessel appeared to have sailed in a jakes and absorbed something of the territory. What kind of man lived like this?

The kind that sold secrets to Spaniards, betrayed his Queen and country, and swived young boys in a room a pig would be ashamed to call a sty. I wasn't here to judge his living standards or his habits—that was for God.

Still on the bed, I scurried over to the edge and began to throw off the clothes, shuddering as my hand stuck to bits of fabric, their odor thrown in my face.

Beneath the clothes was a lovely old sea chest. Large, with a hinged lid, it was covered in ornate iron decorations. A single padlock sat on the front. Leaving the basket on the bed, I clambered off and, with care, squatted before the chest and ran my hands lightly over the trace work on the outside. As I suspected, this wasn't simply decoration. Buried at intervals along the iron were keyholes. Small, they required a different key to open each one. I'd only ever heard of these treasure chests; they were rare and costly. Made by the Germans, they were also strong and cunning and said to outwit the best of lock-picks.

Would it be the one to best me?

I reached for the basket and from beneath the blanket took out the leather roll containing my tools. A shout outside made me clutch my chest, but it was only an oarsman calling to the sailors. This wouldn't do. *Nonchalance. Nonchalance.* Samantha must adopt this as her mantra if we were to succeed.

A simple twist with my pick opened the padlock. Unfastening it, I laid it on the dirty wood. That was the easy part. Now, to tackle each of the hidden locks. First, I dragged the chest away from the bed, grateful a shirt was caught under it, making my efforts relatively soundless. Then, I shut my eyes and trailed my hands over every inch of the iron. Altogether, I counted twelve separate keyholes. Twelve. I glanced at the door. This would take more time than I'd allowed or Thomas expected. I would have to work fast. I began at the back, inserting my picks, shutting out the caw of gulls, the slap of the water as it hit the hull, the low conversation of the sailors outside and the distant babble of voices. I also tried to shut out my fear that the captain would return.

It didn't take long to open the four locks at the back. They were easy, which instead of appeasing my anxiety, elevated it. There was something I wasn't seeing here, I felt it deep in my core. Pushing on, the two locks on either side proved no trouble either. It wasn't until I tried to open the four on the lid that I encountered my first obstacle. One of the locks refused to give. It simply would not open. It didn't matter how deeply or shallowly I inserted my picks, how slowly or fast I turned them, what tricks I used to defy the mechanism; the familiar click and wheeze of tumblers moving never occurred. Sweating now, I even forgot the smell of the room as I sought to open the chest. Leaving the locks temporarily, I focused on those I could open.

Finally, there were only the two on the lid remaining. Passing my hands over the chest again, I wondered what I'd missed. My instincts had been right. This had been too easy. The German who'd designed this chest knew it would keep precious possessions safe from the likes of me. The sun passed behind a cloud and I drew my hands away, falling on my heels, wiping the back of my hand across my brow.

Think, Mallory, think.

I glanced at the original padlock, the one that had rested against the chest and been so easy to open. Picking it up, I hefted it in my hand, examined it closely. It was heavy, beautifully formed. Perfectly symmetrical, it was engraved with an anchor which, when the padlock was placed back exactly where it had lain, sat in the exact center of the entire chest . . . The exact center. I stared at the chest, at the way the iron formed a bed for the padlock to rest in.

That was it! Returning the padlock to its original position, I locked it once more. Putting my picks back into the keyhole, I pushed down instead of twisting them and lo and behold, the lock sank into the chest slightly. There was the welcome sound of springs releasing around the chest. The other keyholes were false, a distraction.

Unlocking the padlock, I lifted the shank free, lay the whole thing on the floor and, praying fervently, lifted the lid.

Exquisite fabrics, golden goblets with bejeweled stems and strings of lustrous pearls met my gaze. Shoving them aside, I buried my hands, my fingers urgently probing. There were leather-bound books, a sheaf of what appeared to be deeds to land tied with string, and a highly polished caliver in a sheath. I began to think Sir Francis may have been mistaken when my hand struck what I was looking for. Extracting the documents carefully, I held them aloft. Papers tied with a leather binding, a letter at the front, a seal at the bottom. How Sir Francis had known this detail, I wasn't certain, but the description was perfect, as was my substitute, which I quickly pulled from the basket. I wondered what I was replacing the originals with as I returned everything I'd taken out. Closing the padlock, I was relieved to hear the tumblers grind back into place. Standing, I pushed the chest into position before strewing the clothes higgledy-piggledy over it.

I threw off my woman's garb, rolling up the skirts and bodice and placing them in my basket, covering what I'd stolen. Casting around for something to toss out the window, my signal I'd finished, I spied a broken piece of plate. Hurling it out the window, I heard a splash.

Then I waited.

It wasn't long before there were raised voices. I took one more look around . . . had I forgotten anything? Hefting the basket into my arms, I opened the door and strode onto the deck.

"Get over here, now, lad!" shouted Thomas. "We've been duped."

Standing on the pier beside Thomas, his arm draped around a rather disheveled young woman, was the man whose fine appearance belied the state of his quarters. There was no doubting who it was—the description was perfect: Captain Alyward Landsey. A pristine ruff framed a face that, though clean, resembled a punched chaff bag. His well-cut doublet clung tightly to a body that was well fed and sin-soft. Swaying back and forth, screwing up his eyes as he tried to look first at Thomas, then me, it was clear the captain was drunk.

"What's going on? Who's that—?" He raised the jug clutched in his hand toward me.

The first sailor pointed at me then Thomas, his words a jumble. The older sailor was trying to extract himself from the canvas. I didn't have long.

"Duped? You come here demanding your prog be let on board. I tell you, sir, he says this was your orders," insisted the first sailor, leaping over the side of the vessel, stomping up the dock and prodding Thomas in the chest.

Thrusting the sailor away so he fell on his hindquarters with a yelp, Thomas turned to the captain.

"Well, there's clearly been an error. My humbl'st, Cap'n." He bowed deeply to Captain Alyward, who still had his eyes on me. "Come on, lad. We'll be on our way." Thomas held out one hand while gesturing wildly with the other for me to climb over the rails; there was a look of concern on his face.

Keeping one eye on the old sailor who was hauling himself to his feet, I threw the basket to Thomas, who caught it deftly and backed away.

"What's that?" asked the old sailor, who'd finally found his feet and was shuffling toward me. "What's in that there basket?"

"Hold!" called Captain Alyward to the sailor on the pier, who'd not only found his feet, but drawn his knife again. The old sailor also stopped in his tracks. The younger one did so grudgingly.

Shoving the young woman with him into the other sailor's arms, Captain Alyward came forward and placed a thick-fingered hand on Thomas's shoulder.

"If there's been an arrangement to which I'm the beneficiary, I want to know about it," he drawled. His voice was effeminate for a man's and his words slurred. "Who might you be?" He looked at me, trapped on the deck, licking his lips. "For certes, you're one of the prettiest morsels of flesh I've seen in a long time. A dark beauty, tall, too. If your width matches your height," he said, rubbing his crotch in an obscene manner, "I'll not complain."

Surprising me with his agility, he leaped over the railing and onto the deck. Before I could move out of arm's reach, he grabbed me. I tried to jerk away, but failed.

"Good, good," he chuckled, holding my wrists tightly. "You keep that up and you'll keep me up." He gestured to the sailor on the pier. "Ned, bring the other one." He began to drag me toward his cabin. "The wig you're wearing is a nice touch. You can leave that on."

Oh dear God, I forgot to put my cap back on and hide my hair. My feet slipped on the deck as I was dragged toward the stinking cabin. I began to fight harder, the captain laughing all the while.

"That's it, a fight's what I like." Wrapping an arm around me, he tried to lift me off my feet. I could feel his excitement prodding me in the back. The old sailor turned away in disgust, while the younger one lifted the other girl—who was a young boy—over the ship's railing.

"Release him at once," shouted Thomas from the dock, the basket clutched against his chest. "Sam, Sam!" he cried. "This is not part of the deal."

Redoubling my efforts, I kicked and struggled, then slammed my head back, connecting with the captain's chin. There was a yelp and a gurgle of laughter. Why, the bastard was enjoying this. That made me furious. Throwing the jug to the sailor, he brought his other hand to my chin, tipping my head back so he might kiss me. I could smell the wine on his breath, see the great pits in his skin, the slug-like tongue. Despite his expensive attire, he smelled of sweat, ale and his foul cabin. Allowing him to tilt my neck so far, I became compliant in his arms; then, as his hand loosened, I grabbed it with both of mine, brought it to my mouth and bit hard.

He let me go, the hand I'd bitten flying to his mouth that was already filled with blood.

"Why, you little bastard," he grinned, his teeth red. "Come here. I'll teach you a lesson you won't forget in a hurry."

I slipped the knife from my breeches and held it before me. "Hold, Captain. As my friend there says, there's been a mistake." I kept my voice deep, jerking my head toward the boy, who stood wide-eyed and bewildered. "I'm afraid I don't share."

Swinging a leg over the railing, I paused, measuring the distance. Thomas ran toward me. The captain stepped closer.

"You won't regret it," he said, smiling wider, his hands fussing at his breeches. I glanced down, knowing what he was about to do.

Before he could pull out his cock that was straining against the fabric, I leaned over and drew the blade sharply across his fingers, narrowly missing his member. Blood flowered. With a yelp of fury, he let go his laces and lunged at me.

I tried to jump, but the captain grabbed a handful of hair, yanking me back. My knife flew again, cutting the locks he held. I toppled backward toward the dock, bracing myself. Thomas, bless him, caught me.

Panting hard as I found my feet, Thomas picked up the basket and backed away.

"Why," said the captain, staring at the long dark strands in his palm. "That be no wig. This be . . . what are you? Lass or lad?" His anger deepened. All signs of drink and lust disappeared. "What trickery is this?" He shoved his now limp cock back in his breeches and drew his sword. Blood dripped from his fingers from the cuts I'd bestowed.

"I told you," I said, standing my ground boldly, ignoring my heart straining against my ribs, "no trickery. I be a special one. So special, I don't share—but you may have that keepsake"—I jerked my chin toward his injury—"to remember me by. Be thankful I didn't take one of my own." I drew my knife across my groin to reinforce my point.

Sheathing the weapon, I slapped Thomas's arm and together we turned and ran as fast as we could up the pier, disappearing into the lanes.

"You little cockered bitch," roared Captain Alyward. "I'll have my way yet. You'll see."

The other sailor called something, but I couldn't distinguish his words.

Shouts of pain, confusion and fury followed, as did the heavy knowledge that I'd potentially ruined everything.

TWENTY-TWO

*T*hat was close," said Thomas calmly when we reached the safety of our room in the Raven Inn. "Your hair confounded them."

Touching the area where I'd been forced to cut the hair from my scalp, I winced—and not just with pain. "Until the captain mentioned it, I didn't realize I wasn't wearing my cap. I'm sorry, it's unforgivable. The chest took longer than expected to open and I was in such a rush to get out, I forgot I had to hide my hair. Zounds." I began searching through the basket. "I can't find the cap." I stared at Thomas. "I must have left it on the ship."

Disappointment swamped me and, putting the basket down, I sank onto the end of the bed, my head in my hands. "I've ruined everything, haven't I? They know I'm a woman . . . Captain Alyward . . . he'll know something is terribly amiss. I mean, he held me, I hurt him . . ."

"Pfft," said Thomas softly, putting a hand on my shoulder. "You managed to get the papers and, in the end, that's all that matters. Though," he added, "had you taken the souvenir you threatened, there'd be many a lad thanking you, methinks."

I glanced up at him. With his glasses restored and his yellow hair uncovered, he looked more like the man I knew. I wanted to believe him, but I'd panicked and, in doing so, made a grave error that had put both of us and our mission at risk. It wasn't good enough, and I knew Sir Francis would think the same thing.

"Cast it from your mind," demanded Thomas, releasing me and undoing the hooks on his jacket. "It matters not they think you a woman. What matters is that they don't know whom you work for or why. You maintained your disguise even when parts of your costume failed. You did well. Now, get changed and compose yourself. We've a play to attend."

With our backs to each other, Thomas and I slipped into our usual clothes, leaving the ones we'd used for the innkeeper, who worked for Sir Francis, to dispose of. This time I made sure to tuck all my hair beneath my bonnet, smooth the sleeves of my jacket and ensure my skirts weren't rumpled. Thomas chatted as we changed, assuring me that despite what had happened and the consternation aroused, Captain Alyward was unlikely to look in the chest.

"It's why Sir Francis chose you, Mallory. You may have been imprudent, exposed yourself as a woman, but the last thing the captain would expect would be for his impregnable chest to be opened—let alone for the papers to be stolen. After all, what woman could do such a thing? What the sailors saw, and what Landsey will believe, is that we were a pair of opportunists—a procurer and his trull, not agents. Should Landsey look in the chest, he'll see the papers you put there and all will be well, so wipe that frown from your brow and fix a smile to your pretty face. This is a day of celebrations and despite what has happened, we've reason to join them. The mission was successful."

Thomas was right. There was no point bemoaning the forgotten cap or anything else. The day wasn't over yet, and I still had a role to play and papers to transport safely to London.

If Sir Francis felt I'd jeopardized the mission or was concerned I'd been in grave danger, he never said so. The morning after Deptford, I sat in silence in his office as he read the report I'd labored over throughout the night. When he finished, he stared at the pages and then raised his head. I touched my coif. The hair I'd sacrificed during my escape was barely noticeable. Nonetheless, I was glad my head was covered and evidence of my misadventure hidden.

"This is very thorough, Mallory. You do not attempt to exculpate yourself, but readily acknowledge your mistakes. Mistakes, which, I'm relieved to know, Thomas feels didn't imperil the mission—on the contrary, he said your adherence to your role and steady head saved it. The fact you have the documents"—he held out a hand, and I extracted them from my basket and passed them over—"proves him right. All in all, you've done very well, Mallory. Very well."

Once more, I glowed in his praise.

"It's time for me to acknowledge that fact." He opened a drawer, pulled out a purse and passed it to me. "For your pains."

Though small, the purse was weighty in my palm. It was my first proper wage as a watcher. Was I such a tickle-brained minnow that I wanted to open it then and there and count my coin? Instead, I placed it in one of the hanging pockets inside my skirt, patting the gratifying lump.

Sir Francis rose and, with his back turned, unlocked his cabinet. Placing the documents I'd stolen inside, he withdrew a large book, the one I'd noticed before.

He cleared a space and placed the unruly tome upon his desk.

"Do you know what this is, Mallory?"

"No, sir." Curiosity lured me closer.

"This," he said, his fingers resting gently atop the leather, "is what I call *The Book of Secret Intelligences*." I almost gasped. Thomas had mentioned it. The book was regarded with a mixture of reverence and mystery and though I had longed to know what it contained, I never thought I'd lay eyes upon it, let alone have Sir Francis show it to me.

"Within it are the names of all my agents, their aliases, missions they've undertaken, and the keys to all the codes and ciphers currently in use. It also records all Catholic plots and assassination attempts and our efforts to foil them."

I tried for *mediocrita* and failed. My mouth fell open and my eyes grew wide.

"You can imagine what would happen should this ever fall into the hands of our enemies."

I could. Bedlam. War. Death.

Sir Francis undid the ties that bound the book, lifted the top cover off, leafed through a few pages and pulled one half-covered in writing to the fore, smoothing it with his hand. He dipped his quill in the inkwell and waited for the nib to fill.

"I do not enter anything or anyone into the book lightly, Mallory. It's a privilege to be thus recorded. Whoever is listed has contributed something of significance to the government; to the realm. I do this so that those charged with protecting the country after you and I are gone might know what action was taken, what sacrifices were made, how great the threat was that we faced and who risked themselves to combat it. I write so they can use this information to ensure our land's continued safety. Build on what I've started."

He gazed at me with great warmth, almost pride. "Now is the time to add your name and alias to my list, to inscribe what you have done on behalf of the realm, in defense of the throne. Make you a part of history. You're the first woman ever to be officially employed as part of my network—thus you're the first female agent to be listed in this book."

I held my breath and watched as his long and elegant hand added my name to the parchment.

Placing the quill back in the inkwell, Sir Francis gave a half-smile. "Later, I will record what you did and make a synopsis of your report. The first of many." He leaned over and blew gently on what he'd written before reaching for some sand and throwing it over the page. The dark ink was quickly absorbed.

"Sir, forgive me, but why are you telling me this? Surely, that"—I pointed at the book—"must be one of the most important books in the country, the greatest secret you hold."

Sir Francis stared at me strangely. "One of them, aye." He shook the page so the excess sand dropped to the rushes. "Why would I not tell you? Are you not one of my agents? Do you not work in the best interests of the country? Do you not do my bidding?"

"Always," I said. "But—"

"But?" He lay the page down again. "What? Out with it."

"Do Thomas and Master Robert know what's in the book?"

"Thomas and Robert, aye."

"Casey?"

"Casey, no."

For some reason, that knowledge made me feel better. I was being accorded a privilege. Sir Francis was entrusting me with something imbued with such importance that only his closest associates knew about it. Warmth toward him blossomed within me. I smiled.

"There are a few others as well," conceded Sir Francis. "Though their names are contained therein, none have ever read it." Aware of my eyes upon the sheet, he placed the leather cover over it. "Until I'm buried, none ever will. I simply wanted you to understand the esteem in which you are held, Mallory. By Thomas, and by me."

"Thank you, sir. It means a great deal." The peculiar itch that accompanies tears began to worry my eyes. I refused to show my feminine weakness at such a time. Damn my womanhood! Coughing, I searched for a kerchief to cover my mouth and sought to explain my watery eyes. "The sand," I said as Sir Francis passed a brimming goblet to me. I swallowed gratefully.

Sir Francis occupied himself with sharpening another quill while I regained my composure. "So," he said, when my kerchief was tucked away and my eyes dried. "Are you ready for your next task?"

"I am."

"Now that we've removed the danger posed by Captain Alyward's voyage, it's time to refocus our energies on capturing the priest Campion and his Catholic confederates. I'm using every resource available to track them down."

"How can I be of assistance?"

Rising from his desk, Sir Francis went to the many boxes stacked against the wall. Rummaging among them, he continued to talk.

"We know Campion is traveling about the countryside. I've men in Yorkshire, Derbyshire, Lancashire and anywhere else we get a sighting. Ah, here it is."

Turning, he passed me some sheets of paper. They were covered in code. "This is an exact copy of Sledd's latest work, *The Intelligences of the Affairs of Englishmen in Rome and Other Places*. It's a detailed description of every priest, their companions and servants who have set out from

Reims to come to our shores. Read it and memorize it." Returning to his seat, Sir Francis filled his own goblet and took a long drink. "You must be able to recognize a Catholic traitor by sight."

"This is the other dossier Sledd composed that you and Thomas spoke of some weeks back."

"Aye. Sledd began it a couple of years ago when he crossed Italy and France posing as a courier for William Allen and the pernicious priests who accompanied him. He not only copied much of the correspondence he was entrusted with, but wrote down everything he observed. Like you, he has a great eye for detail. From his earlier work, we know which English families are suspect; which ones are sympathetic to the priests. Now we learn who the men they hide are. I'm hoping by reading that, you'll have some sense of the danger Campion and his papist peers pose and understand how important it is we find them."

"I do not need to read this to understand that, sir."

"No. I believe you don't." Sir Francis gave me a warm smile. "Well, Mallory," he said, breaking the moment. "Take it to your office and be certain to return it before you depart this evening. That dossier must not leave the house."

I was being dismissed. I stood, the pages firmly in my hands. "That's all, sir? I'm to read and memorize these?"

Sir Francis levered himself to his feet. Our faces were almost level. "It is what you must do before I set you to work again."

"What kind of work?"

"You're about to put into practice everything you learned from Thomas and Mistress Bench. The day after tomorrow, I'm sending you into the streets, into businesses and houses. You will become not only my eyes and ears, but as Samantha Short you will learn all you can about the mood of the people, gauge what damage Campion, Persons and their foolhardy heretical supporters have done. I want to know what men and women are saying, what they're thinking and dreaming; more importantly, what they're hiding."

I took a deep breath and released it slowly, silently. So, it was to begin. My own enterprise.

Sir Francis stepped forward and took my hand. "Do not doubt yourself. Deptford proved you're ready. I need you to be. I need all my troops on the ground. As of today, your training is officially over. From this day forward, you're a spy, Mallory, a watcher. Remember, you're my secret weapon in this Godforsaken war. And now is the time to deploy you. Are you ready to take up arms?"

My shining face was all the answer he needed.

TWENTY-THREE

*U*pon arriving home and learning from Comfort that Mamma was asleep, Angela abed, and Caleb in his room writing, I shucked off the tiredness I felt after a day of trying to memorize lists of names and descriptions (mole above lip, red hair, two teeth missing from the right-hand side of the upper jaw, speaks fluent Italian) and, taking a ewer of ale from the kitchen, along with two cups, some bread and cheese, I slipped into the workshop. There was no sign of the apprentices. As I entered, the dogs ran to my side, tails wagging; Papa lifted his head from the key he was filing and bestowed a warm smile upon me.

"Mallory!" He waved me over. "I've not seen you since before Deptford. Come, sit and tell me what's kept you so busy you neglect your papa. And, while you're here, I want a full account of Drake's knighting."

Pleased he was in such a jolly mood (and wondering what had occasioned it), I deposited a kiss upon his brow. I put the food and drink down, paid the dogs attention, poured us both an ale and dragged a stool over. While I broke the bread apart and cut a piece of cheese, slipping the dogs a piece each, Papa talked.

"I swear, Caleb gave an account of the ceremony that can scarce be believed." He shook his head and chuckled. "I need you to verify it. Did the gangplank really break and toss the good citizens of London into the river?"

"It snapped like kindling," I said between mouthfuls.

Papa paused, holding the file ready above the key. I couldn't help but note he was completing tasks a first-year apprentice could do for him.

"And what of the Queen showing her garter and giving the sword to the French Ambassador, de Marchaumont, so he might knight Drake? Tell me these are but figments of Caleb's bountiful imagination?"

Laughing, I quickly downed some more food and took the file from Papa so he might enjoy our repast while I elaborated. Understanding they'd receive no more titbits, the dogs let out huge sighs for such small creatures and ambled back to their spot by the forge, curling upon each other.

"I'm afraid it's all true, Papa. Every last bit. Not even Caleb could have invented such a scene—a scene completed only by the Queen's purple and gold garter, which she then gave to de Marchaumont as a keepsake."

"A royal garter indeed," Papa grinned. Encouraged, I added to Caleb's story, grateful to Master Robert and Francis Mylles, who had provided me and Thomas with all the details of what we had missed at the dock. Able to sound as if I'd borne witness to everything, I was also able to entertain Papa with a vivid retelling of Caleb's play, which I had seen.

"It was a fine tribute and for certes, the Queen and Sir Francis appeared to enjoy it." As did other members of the audience, I thought. Unbidden, an image of Captain Alyward came to mind. Much to my horror, he had stumbled into the crowd during the performance, pushing his way through, clapping and laughing as if naught was amiss. I recalled the pockmarked skin, the receding hair beneath the bonnet, the pale, listless eyes that roamed the crowd as much as the stage. No doubt searching for another boy to quench his appetites. His eyes simply passed over me as if I didn't exist. I was a woman, so to him I did not.

"It doesn't seem to have attracted the opprobrium that *Circe's Chains* did," said Papa. "At least, not from what I hear."

"Nor what I believe *Dido's Lament* might," I added.

Papa wiped his hands on a rag, lost in thought. "I worry about that lad sometimes. He wears his sympathies upon his sleeve too oft of late. Now is not the time to be leveling criticism at the government nor offering a platform for Catholic beliefs, even imaginary ones. I said much the same to your mother. Tried to convince her to at least act as if she has abandoned the old ways." He sighed. "Not that she listens, either. It troubles me and I wonder where her stubbornness might lead."

I didn't admit that I worried about the same thing. Not a day went past when I didn't expect either Sir Francis or Thomas to make mention of Mamma's recusancy. As yet, the subject had not been raised. But they must know. Were they not spies who watched everything and everyone?

"Do not worry too much on Caleb's account, Mallory," said Papa. "For all it appears otherwise, there's naught too grave behind Caleb's verses. For now, he attracts audiences and coin; enough to keep anyone in his profession content and debtors from pestering him. Lord Nate has said he will keep a close eye on him and ensure he comes to no harm. If he has to, he'll insist he amend his works to reflect the government's position rather than inflame it."

Papa had spoken with Lord Nathaniel? This was reassuring and perturbing. Caleb had enormous respect for his patron, aside from relying on his goodwill for a living. Papa must think highly of him to confide his concerns. What did he see in the man that had thus far eluded me?

We worked in silence awhile, Papa passing me another key when I completed smoothing the first. Voices and laughter carried from the house. The dogs clambered to their feet, their slumber disturbed. The apprentices were back.

I rose and let the dogs out. They scampered toward the house, barking. I shut the door.

"What do you think of Lord Nathaniel, Papa?" I asked lightly, returning to my seat and stroking the key to locate the rough points in the metal. "You must have faith in the man to discuss Caleb with him."

"What do you think, daughter?" asked Papa, a smile in his words. He knew me too well.

"Me?" I kept my eyes on the key. "I don't—think of him, that is. Much." My cheeks began to burn. "Hard not to. He takes up so much space, after all."

Aware of Papa's fond regard and quiet chuckle, I refused to look at him, hoping his poor eyesight meant he would not detect the color flooding my face.

"I think," began Papa slowly, "he is a good man, but one cast adrift."

"What do you mean?"

"I don't mean, as many do when they use such a term, a sailor without a ship, floundering on dry land." He thought for a moment. "I mean, he has nothing to anchor him."

I shrugged. Lord Nathaniel wasn't the only one lost.

"Do you know his story?" asked Papa. "Has Caleb said anything?"

"Only that there was a terrible tragedy—that his brothers and mother died while he was at sea."

"Aye, they did. One after the other. It was unexpected and very sad. But not before he became the center of a huge scandal."

"Scandal?" I knew naught of this. "What kind of scandal?" My heart squeezed. I imagined a beautiful woman with red hair, soft white skin and large breasts . . . A noble's wife, a courtier's sister . . .

I waited while Papa refilled our cups and made himself more comfortable. "It was the talk of London for a while. Oh, you were too young to know or care. You were content with the locks and Master Fodrake and I was happy you were. But the Warhams were a well-known family. Three strapping sons, a father who was the favorite of King Edward and a mother who was a great beauty. Later, there was a daughter as well."

"What happened?"

"All in good time. You need to understand why something happened, not just that it did."

I sighed. It could have been Master Fodrake speaking. I put down the key and ran a wet finger around the plate, collecting crumbs.

"You've noted what a figure Lord Nate cuts. Well, even by his family's standards, he was a big lad. By the time he was at Oxford, he'd developed a reputation."

Why didn't that surprise me?

"Wherever Lord Nate went—the tavern, the theater, court, college—here or in Oxford, there was trouble, terrible trouble."

"What kind?"

"Fights, scuffles, brawls. It was easy to assume, being the size he was, Lord Nate caused them. Before you think the worst, it wasn't Nate, not always. It was often others—other lads and men. Because he's so big, you see, boys saw him as a challenge, as a way of gaining esteem from their peers if they fought him or, even better, if they bested him in a fight. Grown men were not above challenging him either . . . Young Lord Nate couldn't go anywhere without someone threatening to punch him, or worse, draw a blade, wanting blood, wanting to wound him and see the giant cower. When he was younger, he used to try and talk his way out of fighting, but when he did, they called him craven and struck him anyway."

My stomach flipped. "How do you know this, Papa?"

Papa raised a finger to silence me.

"But what happened in Oxford changed everything. You see, Lord Nate was involved in a duel—a duel he was lucky to survive. The other man did not. As a consequence, he had to leave the country. Thank the good Lord his father was dead by then so he never knew. Lord Nate's oldest brother, Jonathan, using his father's investment in the Muscovy company, bought Nate a commission with Francis Drake. So, this scholarly lad, who loathed fighting but had a reputation for it, who'd killed a man in a duel, was sent to Plymouth and forced aboard the *Pelican* to voyage around the world. They said it would be the making or breaking of him. It was all that kept him from justice. His family never knew if they'd see him again. As it was, his mother and brothers never did, nor he them, but not in a way anyone anticipated. He returned to all that now remains of his once large family—a sister, a lovely young chit, they say. Like her mother."

I didn't know whether to feel pity for Lord Nathaniel or despair that his sister was left to suffer his faults. "What was the fight over?"

Papa took a swig of his ale, wiping his hand across his beard. "What these kind of fights are usually over. A woman. Lord Nate was in love; the woman betrayed him with another man who boasted of his conquest and claimed the resultant child as his own."

"A child?" The workshop grew dark.

"Aye. Only this man, a tutor, was a distant cousin of the Earl of

Leicester's. If Walsingham hadn't intervened, I think Lord Nate would have been sent to the Tower or worse."

Now I knew how Papa had learned the tale. Not only that, but Lord Nathaniel and Sir Francis had a connection and a history as well . . . The knowledge made me uneasy. Sir Francis had a long reach.

"As it was, hardly anyone expected Nate to return from that voyage. So few of the men did. Even so, I believe him when he says he intended to do the right thing by the woman. She refused him. Found someone of higher rank than a third son and thus lied about her babe's conception. Broke his heart. I wonder how she feels now he's a lord, and a wealthy one, too . . ."

"What happened to the child?" My voice was barely a whisper.

Papa thought. "It died before it was a week old."

The room suddenly felt small. I tasted metal and a foul odor filled my nostrils.

"Lord Nathaniel told you this?"

Papa twirled his cup on the bench, watching the patterns it made in the fine metal dust.

"Some of it. He comes here quite often, you know, to the house. We're men; after a few wines, a few ales, there's not much we don't discuss. I think he's had to endure a great deal. Had his trust shattered many times."

He waited for me to speak. I didn't know what to say. Buffing the key with renewed purpose, I reflected upon what Papa had told me. It explained his lordship's distrust of the female sex; his conviction we were out to gull men. The woman betrayed his heart; he lost a child. No wonder he felt the way he did. Not that his assumptions were just. The bad behavior of one should not tar an entire sex. But his attitude was understandable.

Didn't I want to hold all men to account for Raffe's sins? In denying my heart, wasn't I doing the same thing? The small voice in my head was persistent.

"There's something else you might want to know, Mallory, before you judge my lord."

I welcomed Papa's intrusion. "What's that?"

"You've seen the terrible scars on his face?"

"It would be hard not to notice."

Papa nodded. "Happened while he served under Drake. Turns out, Lord Nate was protecting a black woman who'd been brought aboard for"—he picked up a key and began rubbing the surface vigorously—"the sailors' pleasure. He insisted she be released. One of the men decided to punish Nate after he set her free on some islands in the south and attacked him while he was abed. There was a dreadful fight and Lord Nate almost lost his eye and his cheek was cut very badly. The other man—" He shrugged. "Let's just say the fish were well fed that night."

"Did Sir Francis tell you this, Papa?"

Papa dropped the key, the noise loud in the silence of the workshop. "He and others. This kind of tale has a habit of being repeated," he said slowly. "It's not something Lord Nate discusses and it put him at odds with Drake and some of the crew."

"They're not on good terms?"

Papa picked up the key and resumed polishing it. He shook his head. "Drake, for all his bluster, has few friends, Mallory. He might have made the Queen rich and tormented the Spanish until they bayed for his blood, but he is a pirate at heart, a pirate who plunders and obeys the rules of the sea before those of the land. Men like him make enemies, for all that he might claim to have mates."

"Much like Lord Nathaniel, then," I said slowly, uncertainly. Pity stirred. Pity and admiration.

Papa's tales of this man, a man I knew, behaving with such gallantry and courage unsettled me. It felt as if the floor had shifted beneath me and I'd lost my footing.

"Perchance." Papa was cautious. "But for entirely different reasons. Lord Nate, for all his . . . how do I put it?" He put down the cloth. "Brusqueness? His ability to rub folk up the wrong way? Oh, I've seen him put a squire at ease with one word and enrage another with the next. Likewise, a street vendor or a lord. But he's a man of honor, of duty. He's the type of man to which others should aspire, yet he's seen as a threat, for too often he holds up a mirror to those with less noble aims and exposes their weaknesses and petty cruelty. They like him not. No, Drake and Lord Nate may have sailed together, but they're as far apart as the ends of the earth. But let me tell you this." Papa held the key to the candlelight, polishing it until it shone. "I know whom

I'd want to call friend, and it isn't a braggart sea captain with a newly minted title."

Sleep eluded me that night. Images of Lord Nathaniel again invaded my dreams and memories of his lips my waking moments. I tried to replace his face with Raffe's, to remind myself that men, regardless of who they were and what was claimed for them, were not to be trusted. I well knew the real intentions buried under the false words. Eventually, like a slave freed from his irons, they would burst through with unexpected violence. And it was women who paid the price. Always.

Yet he'd fought a duel and been forced to quit his family, his home and his country; he'd had his heart riven, and he'd released a slave. A woman. A blackamoor. He had placed her needs above those of the crew; her dignity and honor above his own safety. He was a traitor in the men's eyes and he suffered the consequences.

Tangled in my blankets, I tried to toss these thoughts aside, thumping the pillow for good measure.

Damn the man. Damn his eyes, his mouth, his nobly won scars. Damn his honor.

PART FOUR
Avenging Angel

. . . Also she must be more circumspect, and more careful
not to give occasion for evil being said of her, and conduct
herself so that she may escape being sullied by guilt but
even by the suspicions of it, for a woman has not so many ways
of defending herself against false calumnies as a man has . . .

—Baldassare Castiglione, *The Book of the Courtier:*
The Third Book, Part Four, 1528

Who seeks by worthy deeds to gain renown for hire,
Whose heart, whose hand, whose purse
is pressed to purchase his desire,
If any such there be, that thirsteth after fame,
Lo! Hear a means to win himself an everlasting name.

—Sir Francis Drake, 1583, first attributed to him by
Caleb Hollis in *Drake's Hind*

[English Protestants who refuse Catholicism] shall be
searched and sifted out as the good corn is
from the chaff and be put to fire and sword.

—John Hart, delivering a sermon in Reims,
Sunday the 17th of April, 1580

TWENTY-FOUR

BILLITER LANE AND
ST. KATHERINE COLEMAN, LONDON
Mid to late June, Anno Domini 1581
In the 23rd year of the reign of Elizabeth I

*D*espite having once defended myself and womankind from Lord Nathaniel's accusation that we played parts to hoodwink men, I found myself embracing my dual identities of obedient daughter and intelligencer, and the latter's requirement I play many roles. The irony of my situation didn't escape me. But I also worked hard to avoid Mamma's scrutiny. As a dutiful daughter I sought her blessing each day, but we barely exchanged words otherwise, and I would leave her room with no small feeling of relief. Once at Seething Lane, I would adopt whatever costume and manner was deemed necessary to fulfill my mission that day—goodwife, slattern, lady's maid, gentlewoman, flower seller, milkmaid, and many others. I would leave the premises a different person to the one who entered them.

In mid-June I received orders that required me to maintain the same disguise for a protracted period. It was as my least favorite of all the roles I'd been asked to assume—a laundress's assistant. I was to work for the woman directly across the road in Billiter Lane. It had

come to Sir Francis's attention she had customers who bore watching.
I was to be the watcher.

I was introduced as a young drab with no family but some experience in laundering (which was the truth), and so I went to work for
Mistress Bakewell. Dressed in ragged fustian, shabby boots and a torn
cap upon my head, my main duty was to pick up or deliver clothes to
various establishments. Sometimes it was a merchant's house, at other
times a gentleman's. On occasion I was forced to wait in the kitchen of
an inn while maids were sent to collect the laundry. I entered the homes
of mercers, jewelers, booksellers, ironmongers, bakers, brewers, and, in
Lombard Street, even a knight. In the bigger houses, the housekeeper
was summoned to check that what I'd returned met the exacting standards of the mistress or that what was being given to me was correctly
accounted for. Forced to wait, I would retreat to a corner, sometimes
able to enjoy a small ale, while around me the business of the house
continued. I kept my eyes and ears open, yet as the days passed, I heard
nothing of import. Not a whisper or a murmur, nothing worth sharing
with my master or Thomas. I learned of the death of a beloved child, of
unwanted pregnancies, of brutal mistresses and lecherous masters—as
well as kindly ones; of gentlemen tardy about paying their bills, of
illness, fights and infidelity. I entered houses where the servants were
slovenly and indifferent and others where loyalty and cleanliness were
paramount. But what use was this information to the good government and soul of England? When I dropped exhausted into bed each
night, I began to believe I was wasting my time.

Enduring the taunts and shoves of men and boys as I walked the
streets, my arms laden with bags of clothing, I became adept at returning insults, at kicking out at the urchins who tried to tug a piece of
fabric from my bundle. I wasn't always successful and twice I managed to lose all I carried, soiling dirty clothes further and ruining a
perfectly clean batch as well. Mistress Bakewell was not above offering
a scolding and a box on the ears before ordering me to remove the
stains. Unable to reveal who I was, my face flamed at the injustice of
it. I began to loathe the work, its tedium and the weariness that followed. As the days turned into weeks, I was ready to throw myself on
Sir Francis's mercy, confess defeat and beg another role, admit I was
unsuited for such labors. Then everything changed.

It was late June and the days were growing longer and the air warmer. London filled with the usual folk seeking the pleasures and entertainments only the season and such a city could provide. The crowds each day grew worse, the smells even harder to bear, and it wasn't long before rumors of pestilence began. This day I was waiting for the laundry of the vicar of St. Katherine Coleman. I'd delivered and picked up laundry from the vicarage a few times and was loitering near the back door, downing a cup of very good small ale and stroking a friendly cat who curled itself about my legs. A courier rode into the yard, his horse kicking up gravel, forcing the ostler who ran after him to fling his arms up and protect his face. The vicar was sent for immediately. The courier refused to come inside, instead pacing and inspecting his surrounds. He cast a quick look in my direction and turned away.

"Ah, Master Hamon," said the vicar, also peering around as if this wasn't his home but unfamiliar territory. "What brings you here?"

"Great news, sir, great news."

"Come this way, then," said the vicar, waving him toward the church. I hoisted the cat into my arms and, ensuring the ostler was distracted by the courier's exhausted horse, sidled up to the corner of the building so that I too might hear this great news. The men were but a few feet away, their heads close together.

"As God is my witness, vicar," said Master Hamon, ripping his cap from his head and wiping his forehead with the back of his sleeve.

Of no great height, Master Hamon sported a close red beard and had a wart tucked in the corner of his nose. Dirt from the road streaked his face. From the look of his horse and the filth on his clothes, he'd been riding awhile. Younger than the vicar, he was attired in livery I didn't recognize. The insignia appeared to be a fox; the colors were a muddy brown and burgundy. He had a bulging satchel slung over one shoulder.

"They were strewn all over the benches in St. Mary's." Master Hamon unhooked a flask from his hip and took a long swallow as his other hand rifled through the satchel, extracted a pamphlet and gave it to the vicar, who took it with a shaking hand. He glanced around. I withdrew slightly.

"It was brilliant," gasped Master Hamon. "No one saw or heard a thing. The students filed into the church and began to read them before they could be prevented."

"A miracle," said the vicar. The vicar's name was Mark Forwood. In his midthirties, he wore a cap to try to hide his balding pate and robes to conceal his soft body. Neither succeeded. He'd paid me scant attention in the past. I recalled that he hadn't been long in London, and was purportedly in search of a wife, though the staff felt that eventuality was most unlikely. I'd assumed it was because his tastes lay in different directions and had dismissed the gossip. Now I began to see him in a new light. Where did he hail from? I couldn't remember. Cursing that I hadn't paid more attention when the servants talked, allowing my disgruntlement to make me lax in my duties, I focused on listening to the men now.

Holding the pamphlet close, Vicar Forwood scanned the contents. "*Rationes Decem*," he chuckled, turning it over. "Well, well. Campion is unstoppable."

Thunder rolled in my ears. Campion? There could only be one Campion. Edmund, the seditious priest. What had he composed now? *Ten Reasons*. Was this another "Brag"? I pressed the cat closer to my chest, his purring increased and I leaned further forward.

"I came as fast as I could, Father."

"You've done well, my son," said the vicar, his eyes still held by the words in the pamphlet.

The courier patted the satchel slung over his shoulder. "I'm under instructions to deliver as many of these as possible to whoever is"— he scanned the yard, and I quickly withdrew into the shadows— "sympathetic to . . . the cause."

"Aye, aye," said the vicar quickly in a tone designed to silence the man. "Good work, Hamon. Here." There was the rustle of a robe, the clink of coins. "Go, go. Tell the others we'll meet at the usual place, at the usual time. There will be much to discuss, much to pray for. And God be with you. God be with Campion, the brave soul." He made the sign of the cross and touched the courier's head in a blessing.

Aghast at what I'd witnessed, I scurried back to the kitchen door and placed the cat gently on the ground as the courier hailed the ostler and remounted his horse. Master Hamon trotted out of the yard without a backward glance. I entered the kitchen before the vicar saw me, the words I'd heard going around in my head. At last, I'd something of worth to report. Something momentous.

I couldn't leave the vicarage quickly enough. I delivered the laundry to Mistress Bakewell, purchasing an orange from a stall in Mark Lane on the way, and without a by-your-leave, left her and entered the house on Billiter Lane from the rear. I asked Mistress Bench for paper and a quill. While I remained composed, perchance there was something about my tone because instead of asking why I was back so early, she fetched the items, as well as a cup of ale and a fresh manchet. I then asked her to send for Master Thomas.

I prepared my orange juice, then wrote steadily. The noonday bells sounded and still I wrote, page after page, drawing on my memory to recall every word, every gesture, including complete descriptions of both men and even a rough drawing of the courier's sigil. I signed it SS and, allowing the juice to be absorbed completely, folded the paper and sealed the pages with wax.

When I was certain the wax was dry, I sat back in my chair and shut my eyes briefly, hoping I hadn't omitted a single detail.

Sunlight streamed through the window, warming my back. Rivulets of perspiration trickled down my neck and my smock clung to my back. Noise carried from the alehouse next door; a hammer rang against metal. I opened my eyes. The click of the front door followed by voices in the hall brought me to my feet.

"Thomas," I said, and bobbed a curtsey with no small relief as he entered the room.

He gave a small bow. "God give you good day, Mallory. I believe you have some news to impart?"

Mistress Bench nodded at me from the doorway before disappearing into the kitchen.

"For certes I do, Thomas, and a report for Sir Francis." I indicated the pages. "Suffice to say, Edmund Campion has been busy."

Thomas took a seat and poured himself an ale. I was disappointed he didn't appear nearly as excited as I'd hoped. He gestured for me to sit. I was unable to take my eyes from him. He said, "You have heard of his latest tract, *Ten Reasons*?"

I tried to contain my surprise. "H . . . how do you know?"

Thomas drank, removed his hat and wiped his brow. "Zounds, it be sultry out there." He tapped my report with one finger. "We wouldn't be doing our job if we didn't know, Mallory. News reached us yesterday. Sir Francis is livid. Campion has outwitted us again. Waiting until the scholars met in the main church at Oxford to defend their theses, he had his latest pamphlet scattered about the benches—it was widely read, this *Rationes Decem* you heard of."

"Not only heard, I've seen it too—though only from a distance," I added quickly. "But please, go on. What is it?"

Thomas cocked a brow. "It's an audacious piece of Catholic propaganda which must be destroyed. It purports to be an explanation of the Catholic faith and traditions. Well, it may be. But what it's really designed to do is to remind those faithful to the old ways to hold fast against the government, to remain loyal to the Pope and to persuade the weaker minded to revert to the old religion. Whichever way it's viewed, it's illegal and demonstrates Campion's utter disrespect for our country and our laws. He has acted right under our noses. Four hundred copies were made. Four hundred were left for the scholars to find and discuss."

"I . . . I've reason to believe there may be more."

Thomas lowered his ale and gave me his full attention. "Oh? What convinces you of this?"

Quickly, I told him what I'd seen and heard.

"And this is in your report?" he asked, nodding toward it.

"All of it and more."

Thomas stood. "Today, you've justified the faith Sir Francis put in you tenfold." He leaned toward me. "My faith as well. Now, get to and remove those garments. You're a laundress no more. Sir Francis must know what you've heard."

"We're going to Seething Lane?"

"No. Whitehall. But not before I send a courier to alert him to our arrival and the importance of the information we carry."

My heart leaped and I swiftly did as requested. I was again Mallory Bright alias Samantha Short, agent, engaged in the worthiest of enterprises—saving England from the Catholic scourge.

TWENTY-FIVE

LONDON AND WHITEHALL
Late June, Anno Domini 1581
In the 23rd year of the reign of Elizabeth I

𝒲e traveled to Whitehall on a two-man wherry Thomas hailed for us just down from the fish markets at Billingsgate.

Surviving the rapids churning around the starlings that stood midstream at London Bridge was no mean feat, and the boat almost tipped twice; my fingernails broke as I held fast to the edge. Fortunately, the rest of the journey was uneventful. If it hadn't been for what I carried in my basket and Thomas's reaction to it, I might have enjoyed the river, the wherries and tilt boats maneuvering between fisherfolk, gliding from east to west and along and against the currents. Sunset transformed the sky into ribbons of orange and mauve, deepening into the royal colors of indigo and gold on the horizon. Above us, flocks of birds wheeled before speeding away like arrows.

As we left London Bridge behind, the crowded, noisy riverside with its cramped streets and fog of forges and ovens slowly transformed into the serene and splendid gardens of the palatial houses of Baynard's Castle, Whitefriars and the Strand. The grandest building of them all, the Savoy, was being rebuilt after years of neglect, and scaffolding clung to its exterior.

Whitehall Palace drew near. Vast in scale, it was more like a small city than a monarch's palace. Thomas saw my expression and put his hand over mine.

"It can be overwhelming. We'll meet Sir Francis on this side of the bowling green. There's a house owned by one of the nobles we use for such purposes. We will get you home late, but hopefully not so late it causes your parents concern."

What sort of daughter was I becoming? I hadn't given Papa or Mamma a thought. Slightly disappointed I wouldn't get to see more of the Queen's primary residence, I was relieved Thomas couldn't read my mind; that he didn't know how neglectful I was or how much I'd become Sir Francis's creature—one who could put duty ahead of family with nary a care. It was something no obedient, dutiful daughter would consider.

As we disembarked from the wherry, Thomas ordered the men to wait, tossing them some groats to silence their grumbling. He took my arm and escorted me across the grounds, nodding to the pikeman who watched us pass. A jumble of buildings of different sizes, Whitehall was nothing like I imagined. As we walked, Thomas provided a commentary, pointing out the King's Gate, the Queen's Privy Gardens and the apartments Her Majesty used when in residence. A large church could be seen in the distance, and the offices of the Chancery; further away again was the old royal chapel of St. Stephen, where the House of Commons met. I tried to take it all in, wishing I could sit and gaze upon the women and men wandering past. Some looked at us with frank curiosity, others were completely aloof, but almost all were dressed in clothing the like of which I'd rarely seen: velvets, luscious damasks, silks, pearls, sparkling jewels, feathers—all drowning in a cloud of perfume as we passed by. There were enormous stiffened ruffs and peascod doublets that resembled bloated fish about to burst. Bent men and aged women walked with vigor, chattering and whispering, flapping fans and waving kerchiefs. The clash of swords and the faint strains of music could be heard in the distance. The drum of hooves made the grounds shudder. Thomas gestured toward an area to our right.

"Practicing jousts for the Queen, no doubt," he said with a sniff. Like his master, he didn't approve of too much frivolity.

He paused outside a rather large house. A guard with a halberd stood to attention and, when he saw us, he opened the door and stepped aside. Thomas indicated I should go ahead of him, and before I could get my bearings I was being led along a dark corridor. Thomas rapped sharply on a door and entered. Inside sat Sir Francis. He rose to greet us. Clearly we were expected.

"Mallory, it's been some time. You're looking well. Perchance discontent suits you?" His tone was gentle, but the message was clear: my frustration at being a laundress's assistant had reached his ears.

Blushing furiously, I turned my attention to my basket. I prayed the news I was about to impart would compensate for my childish response to the role I'd been assigned, believing it was unworthy of me. Shamefaced, and feeling more than a little betrayed by Thomas, to whom I'd confided my feelings, I sank quietly onto a stool, the report in my hand.

"This is it?" asked Sir Francis, taking it from me.

"Aye."

"Speak to it, then," he said and, walking around to the other side of the desk, he sat down. Thomas stood beside me.

Without missing a single detail, I reported the scene I'd witnessed. Uninterrupted, my tale only took a few minutes. Sir Francis leaned back in his chair, steepled his fingers beneath his chin and stared at a spot on the table.

"The papist scoundrel is more clever than we gave him credit for. We believed there were only four hundred copies; that the outbreak of seditious material was containable." He slammed a fist on the desk, the action propelling him to his feet. I almost shot off my stool.

"Damn the priest. God damn his rotten soul to hell."

The loathing in Sir Francis's words astounded me. He was usually much more circumspect.

I took a deep breath and released it slowly, passing my report to Thomas who, unsealing it, held the pages over a candle so the writing became visible.

"And you are certain the courier had more pamphlets?"

"As certain as I can be, sir. He had a bulging satchel, and the vicar said he was to organize a meeting among sympathizers. I assumed that meant other Catholics."

"Correctly, I would guess." Sir Francis strode to the window and stared out at the small garden. Only then did I see a black puppy frolicking and a young girl, whose face seemed familiar, tossing a ball for it to chase. Where had I seen her before? Sir Francis spun on his heels and came back to the desk. "You've discovered something not even my finest recruits have uncovered, Mallory—a means of locating the nest of traitors here in London, most likely those responsible for hiding Campion's superior, Robert Persons, as well."

My discomfort began to abate and a tiny spark of warmth flared in me.

"We recently intercepted a letter Persons wrote to the rector of the English College in Rome that revealed he's aware Charles Sledd is searching for him and he knows about the raids we've been conducting. As a result, he's gone to ground and all our efforts have failed— including searches of the houses of those whose names and addresses you provided over the weeks. We've uncovered nothing to connect the households to Persons or Campion. But now, now we're a step ahead. Persons won't know we've gained knowledge of another papist meeting about to occur in London—one based on this pamphlet and its distribution." Rubbing his chin, Sir Francis walked slowly to his chair and sank into it, lost in thought. Thomas and I exchanged a look.

"Right," said Sir Francis. "Here's what we'll do. Thomas, alert our men to this latest information. Circulate a description of this courier; let's see if we can find out who else Master Hamon visits, and who else has these pamphlets in their possession."

"Do I give orders for their arrest?" asked Thomas.

"Not yet. I want them identified and observed. Closely. I want Hamon watched as well. We know from whence he came—you did well to describe the fox on his livery, Mallory. It's the Tresham crest. Known recusants who swear they mean no harm." He scoffed. "I want Hamon to leave London and return to his masters believing he's delivered his message safely. I will have him followed and Sir Thomas Tresham watched very, very closely."

The scratch of Thomas's quill as he made notes filled the silence.

"It may be," continued Sir Francis, "that Campion, the wretched caitiff, will go to the Treshams, and when he does . . ." He closed his hand in a tight fist. "We will crush him." He gazed at his fist, as if the priest was already in his grasp. "In the meantime, I want this so-called vicar, what was his name?"

"Forwood. Mark Forwood," I supplied.

Sir Francis nodded. "I want him arrested and taken in for questioning." Pulling out a piece of paper from a drawer on the other side of the table, he dipped a quill and began to write. "Give him to Norton," he directed Thomas as he wrote. "Tell him to hold back nothing. I want names, I want places. By God," he said, as he signed the bottom and tossed sand across the ink, shaking it off and folding the letter, "I want Campion and I will have him. We are close, so close I can smell him."

Tilting the candle with one hand, he dropped some wax on the fold. Rifling in the drawer once more, he pulled out a seal and pressed it into the warm wax.

Satisfied it was dry, he passed it to Thomas. "Give this to Norton and tell him to show it to the lieutenant of the Tower. He has my full authority to do what needs to be done."

Thomas pushed the paper into his doublet.

Unable to wait any longer, I leaned forward. "And me, Sir Francis, what do you wish me to do?"

"I need you to be a laundress's assistant a little longer."

"Then that is what I will be," I said, any reluctance gone.

Sir Francis gave a flicker of a smile. "Tomorrow I want you to return to the vicar's residence and learn what you can from the staff. After that, there will be many places I will need to send you. You have provided us with a key, Mallory. Now, I want us to find the lock so we may open this chest of Catholic worms." He stared at me. "Who better to help us find the right lock than a locksmith's daughter?"

Who better indeed. I couldn't help it—my chest swelled and my eyes gleamed. I drank in the look Sir Francis bestowed, one not unlike that I used to see on Papa's face long ago . . . A cloud briefly dimmed the sun of my accomplishment.

"Do you see now why I set you to the work that I did?" asked Sir Francis, taking me by surprise.

I lowered my eyes. "I do now. Forgive me, sir."

Behind me, Thomas gave a little grunt.

"Not all the work I set my agents is exciting. In fact, most of it is tedious and dull. It requires patience, patience and the ability to know when something important is heard or seen. You have experienced the tedium but now you also understand it can reap rewards."

"I do."

"Very well. I want a full report from you every day—as detailed as this." He slapped my report with the tips of his fingers. "Until Campion is caught, none of us will be safe. He seeks to rouse insurrection of the most terrible and bloody kind. We are all that stands between England, the Queen and anarchy. We will not rest until he is caught and an example made of him. Am I clear?"

"Aye, sir," Thomas and I replied in unison.

Smiling, Sir Francis nodded. "Farewell, and with my blessing." He gestured to the door. "Mallory, if you could wait outside? I would like a word in private with Thomas before he departs."

Curtseying, I bade Sir Francis a good evening and left, my heart singing, my soul stirred to battle. It was all I could do not to run to the river and demand the boatman row me back so I might don my disguise and become the laundress's assistant again immediately. I would keep eyes and ears peeled and woe betide any Catholic sympathizers or plotters. *Samantha Short will see you, expose you and ensure you're punished for your wicked sedition.*

So caught up was I in the imagined wrath I would bring upon all betrayers, I wandered into the hall and out a different door and found myself in the garden. While it must have been the one I had seen from Sir Francis's room, this was a different part of it. The sun may have been waning, but it was still balmy. There was a fountain gurgling, beds of colorful flowers humming with bees, and paving meandering away from the buildings. Seated upon a bench beneath a tree, the dog at her feet, was the young girl I'd seen from the window. Stroking the dog's ears, she was singing while it listened, its head cocked. It was such a lovely scene, I paused and drank in its simplicity, trying to recall a time when I was like that, ignorant of the ills of the world, dreaming of nothing more than finding someone to love.

Sorrow welled. Not wanting to disturb the girl and still trying to place her, I backed away, intending to head indoors. As I turned around, I slammed straight into a body and was only prevented from falling by a pair of burly arms.

"Why, Mistress Mallory, what on God's good earth brings you here?"

I looked up and into the dancing eyes of none other than Lord Nathaniel Warham.

TWENTY-SIX

*M*y lord, you startled me." I was unable to move, I was held so closely and tightly.

Lord Nathaniel didn't speak, just gazed as if he'd never encountered my species before. Outfitted much like the other gentlemen I'd seen perambulating about the grounds, he looked every bit the courtier and seemed so grand, so obviously a part of the palace, I was caught off guard. A lady's tinkling laugh could be heard, followed by the cheers of some men. It broke whatever spell had bound us.

"I would perform the usual courtesy," I said, finding my voice again, "but since you seem determined to prevent me—" I stared pointedly at his hands upon my arms, "I'm unable."

He released me so swiftly I staggered, and he bowed. I took the opportunity to place some distance between us, glancing over my shoulder toward the garden where the young girl still sat with the pup, oblivious to us. My mind was awhirl as I curtseyed, thinking how to explain my presence. What could I say? I was given no time.

"Sir Francis is not known for bringing family to court," he drawled, having recovered from his astonishment at seeing me. "Pray, how do

I find you here? Has Mister Secretary gone against the grain of his own sowing? Is young Frances about?" He looked around as if the girl in question might magic herself into our presence. "If so, I know someone who'd be very pleased to see her again." He nodded in the direction of the bench. Ah, that's where I'd seen the young girl before: Deptford. This was Lord Nathaniel's sister, Beatrice.

"You find me well, sir," I said. "I can see for myself you're in fine health. Now I must make haste. May God give you good day." I went to pass him.

"Not so fast," he said, blocking my way. "Ever since I asked you many a month ago why it is you tarry in London when your charge is at Surrey and you evaded answering, I've been most perplexed. I find you a puzzle I must solve, Mistress Mallory. You're a curiosity that teases my mind and I like it not. Now I find you here, at White-hall, when I also happen to know Mister Secretary is attending, by all accounts, very important business and in this very house." His arm encompassed the building. "So, I ask again, Mistress Mallory, what exactly is it you do for Walsingham?"

"I . . . I . . . find your questioning impertinent, sir, and really none of your business."

"'I find your questioning impertinent, sir, and really none of your business,'" repeated Lord Nathaniel. As far as mockery went, it was perfect. If I hadn't been so stunned, I would have laughed at how well he mimicked my voice.

"Which is it, then?" insisted Lord Nathaniel. "Impertinent, or none of my business?"

Rage tinged with anxiety that the truth would be uncovered tied my words in knots. They exploded from me. "How dare you, sir. Who do you think you are to interrogate me, to prevent my passage and, lest we forget"—I lowered my voice, my finger drawn back to jab him in the chest—"disrespect my person!" I withdrew my digit quickly lest he repeat what he had done the last time he held it.

"Oh, trust me on that score, mistress, there was nothing disrespect-ful about that." He ran his thumb along his lower lip and moved closer. "On the contrary, I respect you greatly."

Papa's words flew into my mind. *I know who I'd want to call friend, and it isn't a braggart sea captain.* Oh, how could this man be so full of contradictions? Why would he see fit to rescue a slave but torment me? What had I done to deserve such unasked-for attention? Did I not assiduously avoid his company? Aye. Most unsuccessfully.

I took another step back. Looking over my shoulder, I saw where my escape lay and spun on my heels. "Ah," I called out merrily as I crossed the garden, giving a small skip and wave. "You must be the Lady Beatrice." I almost tripped over my skirt in my haste. The dog broke away from its mistress and ran toward me, tail wagging, tongue lolling. Long-haired, with floppy ears, it was an adorable little thing.

Beatrice slowly stood and brushed off her fine skirts. She regarded me curiously and dropped a hasty curtsey. "Aye, I be Beatrice. But I'm afraid you have the advantage, mistress I know not who—oh, Nate!" she cried as her brother strode forward, her face lighting up. "I was wondering where you were—you were an age. Merlin and I were growing bored."

"My humblest, Beatrice, I was detained longer than expected." Lord Nathaniel kissed his sister's cheeks. Diverted for a moment, the dog greeted Lord Nathaniel, who patted it, before it turned its attentions to me.

Delighted, I dropped to my knees and Merlin leaped into my outstretched arms, wriggling joyously. "Merlin. What a fine name. I'll bet you're a wizard with that ball." I fondled his ears, reaching for the ball at Beatrice's feet. Aware of two sets of eyes upon me, I continued, my attention fixed on the pup, who began to mouth the ball in my hand. "I have two dogs just like this, only they're called Arthur and Galahad."

"Oh," said Beatrice, breaking away from her brother and kneeling beside me, rubbing her dog's coat. "You must love Malory's *Le Morte d'Arthur* as much as I do to name your dogs so! Nate likes the tales of the knights and the grail too, though he'll scarce admit it. Fancy that, Nate," she laughed. "Someone else who adores Malory!"

There was an awkward silence, broken only when Merlin jumped and tried to lick my face. Chuckling, I held him at arm's length as his tongue scooped the air. "My papa is especially fond of the work as well. In fact, I'm named after him."

"After Malory?" asked Beatrice, wide-eyed. "Your name cannot be Thomas . . . Is it Malory?" When I nodded, she stared. "But, that's a man's surname—" She put her fingers to her lips. "Forgive me, mistress."

Casting a look up at her brother, I smiled. "There's nothing to forgive; it's been pointed out to me before." Lord Nathaniel had the grace to look away. "You're quite right. It's a man's surname, only mine is spelt differently. It has two *l*s."

"Mallory . . . I like it," said Beatrice, and propped on her heels. "I know who you are. You're Caleb's muse."

"Muse?"

"That's what he calls you, isn't it, Nate?" she asked, unaware of her brother's growing discomfort as he stood behind her. "He talks a great deal about you. And I remember, he said you have a most unusual name and that it suits you." She regarded me as if I were the subject of a portrait and she the commissioned artist. "It does."

Now it was my turn to be uncomfortable. "And I imagine you're named from Dante?"

"Aye, *The Divine Comedy*, though, I have to say, when I first read it, I failed to find much comical about it."

I nodded. "The humor can be difficult to discern, but it is peculiarly Italian and the nuances are often lost in translation."

"Caleb said you speak Italian."

"I was born there. I'm English really, but Italian was my first language. My mother tongue."

"Forgive my tardiness in not introducing you," said Lord Nathaniel, who'd been observing our exchange with growing bemusement. "Any effort to do so now is redundant. Nonetheless, Mistress Mallory Bright, may I introduce my sister, the Lady Beatrice Warham."

We both lowered our heads in acknowledgment and shared a smile.

"Mistress Mallory is a gifted linguist, Beatrice," said Lord Nathaniel, "among her other talents." My head rose swiftly. There was no sarcasm in his tone or attempt to embarrass me. "Perchance one day she can help you improve your Italian."

"I would love that," said Beatrice. "Would you, Mistress Mallory? Would you help me? *Non sono molto bravo a Italiano*."

"*Brava,*" I corrected before I could prevent myself.

"Oh, that's right. For a lady," Beatrice giggled, tilting her head back toward her brother. "I forget sometimes." The devotion in her eyes

was matched only by that in his. My heart felt heavy. Really, she was
the most enchanting young woman and it was hard to believe she was
Lord Nathaniel's sister . . . Except, when he looked at her like that . . .
When he ceased the baiting and the mockery, why, he was a different
man. Perchance the stories about him were true. Perchance Papa and
Caleb saw much that I was blind to.

What I would give to be regarded in such a way, to share such a
bond. But the work I did, the life I'd chosen, denied me this.

Beatrice rose and resumed her seat upon the bench. Lord Nathaniel sat beside her, resigned to the fact he would not be able to continue
his questioning. I studied them, with Merlin now firmly ensconced on
my lap.

Slender as she was, you could see Beatrice would be tall. Her hair
was the color of sunshine and tumbled down her back in waves. Her
eyes were large and slightly darker than her brother's, hazel flecked
with green, only hers lacked the tired cynicism his always displayed.
Her skin was pale, her cheeks rosy. She slipped her hand into her
brother's huge one and flashed me a smile that lit her entire face. I
found myself returning it.

"Why, Mistress Mallory, when you smile like that I can see the
beauty of which Caleb boasts," said Lord Nathaniel softly.

My smile froze and fell. I stared at Lord Nathaniel in shock. Coming from this man's mouth, such a compliment meant more than most.

"Only when she smiles?" said Beatrice, nudging her brother. "Why,
I think Mistress Mallory to be one of the loveliest women I've ever
seen. Far lovelier than—" Beatrice clamped her hand over her mouth.
"Forgive me, Nate, Mistress Mallory, I forget myself too often of late,
as Nurse reminds me. Oh, aye, I have a nurse, Mistress Mallory, even
though I am far too old at fourteen for such an encumbrance." She
giggled again. "Don't mistake me, Nurse is most beloved. She calls
herself that—an encumbrance. Both she and Nate want me to have
a companion, and Nate says I may have a woman of my own choosing, lest I be shackled with a bore or a harridan—or worse, someone
who is likely to train me in the use of womanly wiles. Isn't that right,
Nate?" She tossed back her head and laughed. "It's all right, I don't
want anyone like that, either. Nate doesn't want someone around who
makes me or him"—she bumped him with her shoulder—"miserable.

He says there has been too much misery in our lives of late and that women suffer it more than most."

Lord Nathaniel said that?

Her smile dissolved as her ready words conjured memories to which I wasn't privy. Her sweet face became troubled, her bright eyes dimmed. Dear God, I wanted to leap to my feet and take her in my arms, comfort her in a way I'd no right to even imagine. Lord Nathaniel slipped an arm around her and pulled her closer.

"What do you do here, Mistress Mallory?" she asked, seemingly in an effort to push away the glum thoughts filling her mind. "At Whitehall? I begged Nate to bring me while he paid court to Her Majesty as I'd not been before. Is it not magnificent?"

"Funny," said Lord Nathaniel, a grin forming as he sat forward on the bench, his sister forced to move with him. "I was just asking Mistress Mallory the exact same question."

Lifting Merlin off my lap and surrendering the ball, I stood, brushing the grass from my skirts. "It is indeed, Lady Beatrice. I'm here because I work for the Walsinghams."

"Oh," exclaimed Beatrice, her hands coming together. "You mean Mister Secretary? Frances's father? I always think he looks like one of the ravens from the Tower and just as likely to swoop. He terrifies me."

Instead of admonishing his sister, Lord Nathaniel threw back his head and laughed. "He terrifies me too, sister."

This time, I couldn't stop myself, and joined in. Partly because the idea anything could terrify this giant of a man, a man who stood up to lustful sailors on a ship, who fought duels over women and won, was so preposterous.

That was how Thomas came upon us, sharing a joke at his master's expense—my master's. On seeing him, my mirth died.

"Thomas," I began as he came toward us.

"My lord," he said, bowing to Lord Nathaniel, who rose. "My lady." He swept his bonnet off and paid Beatrice a courtesy as well.

"Thomas Phelippes. To what do we owe your presence here at Whitehall?" asked Lord Nathaniel.

"Why," said Thomas without missing a beat, "to Mistress Mallory, who I've come to escort home. Mallory?" he said, gesturing for me to lead the way. "If you will forgive us, my lord, my lady, our boat awaits."

"Oh, by all means, don't tarry on our behalf," said Lord Nathaniel affably. "In fact, why don't we accompany you to the river?"

Before either Thomas or I could protest, he took a position beside Thomas, allowing Beatrice to walk behind with me.

Accompanying Beatrice was no hardship as she was as well spoken and well read as she was well mannered, for all the apologies she proffered regarding her unguarded tongue. I found her candor refreshing, her observations erudite, and if I hadn't been so concerned about trying to overhear what was being said between Lord Nathaniel and Thomas, I would have thoroughly enjoyed her companionship.

It wasn't until we reached the dock and bade farewell that two things happened to discomfit me. The first was, instead of accepting a simple curtsey from me, Beatrice threw herself into my arms and planted a kiss on my cheek and whispered, "I wish you were my companion." As she stepped away she looked at me with such imploring eyes, my heart was almost pulled from my chest.

"So do I," I responded without thinking, placing my fingers over my own lips in a gesture that matched hers. We smiled at each other from behind our hands.

Observing the exchange, Thomas frowned and jumped into the boat, an arm outstretched to assist me. Taking my forearm to aid me over the side, Lord Nathaniel used the opportunity to murmur in my ear. "That's twice you've evaded me. It won't happen again. I will have my answer, mistress. You may have bewitched my sister, but I will know your true purpose."

Passing me to Thomas, Lord Nathaniel released me and stood on the wooden pier, his sister beside him. There they remained, smiles fixed, Beatrice waving until they were dark specks against the burnished skies and my ribs ached from the pummeling my heart gave them.

Sir Francis believed he sent me into danger each time he bestowed a task. But Campion and all the Catholic plots bubbling away in England were naught. With Mister Secretary, only my body was at risk.

With Lord Nathaniel Warham, and now his lovely sister, my heart was under dire threat—something I had promised would never happen again.

TWENTY-SEVEN

ST. KATHERINE COLEMAN AND BILLITER LANE, LONDON
Late June, Anno Domini 1581
In the 23rd year of the reign of Elizabeth I

*A*rriving at St. Katherine Coleman the following day with a basket of clean and folded laundry over my arm, and with the admonishment I'd received from Mistress Bakewell for running away the day before still ringing in my ears, I found the vicarage in an uproar. An impromptu meeting was taking place in the kitchen. Servants and people I'd never seen were crowded into the space, all talking at once. The room was sweltering, the air sour and close. I maneuvered my way inside and placed the basket on the floor in the far corner and stood in front of it. My entry was barely noticed.

"Middle of the night, I tell you." A sturdy woman sat at the long kitchen bench, wringing her hands, her eyes swollen.

There were calls for quiet and the vicar's cook, Goody Clara, was asked to speak. "They burst in here," she pointed upstairs. "Broke the door down, they did, and without care for anyone or anything. They had swords and pistols. One held a thick block of wood that he kept striking into his palm. Dragged the master from his bed. His *bed*." She crossed herself; others followed suit, murmuring and shaking their heads.

"Jim's disappeared," said a short man with one eye.

"So's Robbie and Em," added another voice. "Took their belongings and fled before the cock crowed."

The servants nodded gravely to each other and there was more dark muttering and an odd rhythmic clicking. There were servants, yes, but also neighbors crammed onto the benches, parishioners as well as some other folk I couldn't place. I paid close attention to their features, their clothes, anything that could identify who they were, their trade. There was the butcher from two doors down. An elderly man and his wife, cordwainers; she was clutching a small statue. Near the hearth two gentlewomen were weeping, and a burly-looking ostler from the nearby inn comforted the young one who I'd seen calming the courier's horse yesterday. Maids from the inn were also there, holding each other tightly.

"Mistress Roach was apoplectic," said Goody Clara, referring to the vicar's housekeeper. "I had to give her a sleeping draft to calm her."

"Whatcha give her?" asked a woman who was dwarfed by the huge man sitting beside her. I peered around the person standing next to me and saw the woman from across the road knitting as she spoke, her needles clacking, the strange sound explained.

"The usual, women's milk, juice of a lettuce, flax and such," said Goody Clara.

Sage nods of approval followed.

"What's going to happen to him?" asked a young boy, his voice alternately high then deep. He tugged his cap, sniffed and looked around. "To the father?"

"What's gonna happen to us?" asked a shrill voice. I couldn't tell who'd asked, only that it was a woman and she was scared. They all were. I could smell it.

Apart from the rhythmic tap of the wooden needles, there was silence. A child wailed, and was quickly shushed by its mother.

I watched and waited.

"Will he tell, do you think? Are we for the gallows?"

"Shush your mouth, George Cooper, you don't know who be listening." A large older woman with a stained cap upon her gray curls and pouches under her eyes shook her fist at Master Cooper and glared fiercely at everyone in the room.

"Don't you go shushing George, Goodwife Mabel. He's only saying what we all be thinking. We all be friends here as the good Lord knows." It was the young deacon, Harold Pinchwhite. He placed a comforting hand on her shoulder and she lowered her fist. His name described him this morning. Even in the poor light, his face was drawn, his eyes red rimmed. "We must have faith. In each other, God, and in Father Forwood. He would not betray us. Are we not his flock? Do we not have this—" He reached into his pocket and, much to my horror, pulled out a copy of *Ten Reasons* and waved it around. Folk began to cross themselves, to murmur Pater Nosters. Afraid I would be discovered, I did the same, grateful to Mamma that the gestures and words were not foreign to me. "To remind us to hold fast," muttered Deacon Pinchwhite, his eyes screwed tight. "God will keep us in His tender care. Protect us from those who seek to destroy our faith, destroy us."

Opening his eyes, the deacon gazed out over the room. "I think we should offer a prayer for the vicar," he said, putting the pamphlet on the table and spreading it flat with his hands. There was reverence in his action and in the faces of those closest to him. I wanted to push through the people, shove the tract into the flame of the candle and watch it burn.

"He needs all the prayers he can get where they've taken him," said Master Cooper.

This time, there were cries from a few of the assembled.

"Bess's boy said Norton's been summoned," added Goody Clara.

"The rackmaster hisself," said the young boy breathlessly.

"Aye. He makes Satan seem benevolent," called out a man next to me. He turned to include me and I nodded. "He's stoppered up the passages and access to remorse, he has."

"I heard," added yet another, "he has no heart."

"None of 'em do. Why else would they pursue us so?" said Goody Clara. "We mean no harm."

Voices all began at once, some angry, others very frightened. I pushed back against the wall as those around me surged forward. Good God, they were all Catholics. Each and every one of them. Plotters and traitors, and yet . . .

As I inched toward the door, imprinting their faces upon my mind, their individual features, the color of their hair, the cut of their clothes,

I also saw people I knew—not directly, but of a kind. In their wide eyes, tangled fingers, the way they clung to each other in their despair, weren't these frightened, foolish people the same as those who lived beside us in Harp Lane? Simple folk, who lost or brought children into the world. Who suffered illness and celebrated good fortune. Who sold their wares at Cheapside and hailed us upon the river. Who shared walls with the houses in Billiter and Seething Lanes as well. Were they not Londoners before they were Catholics? Or did their faith make them something so strange, so different, they were no longer recognizable as English? As humans?

I saw no traitors plotting to bring down a queen, only desperate people; people whose world was in disarray and who felt threatened. Who prayed to the same God, only differently. Did this make what they were doing illegal?

It did. It made them criminal as well.

We mean no harm.

Perchance, but they caused it nonetheless. I had to report them. I had to tell what I saw. But could I not also write what I felt? That maybe, just maybe, these Catholics, unlike Campion or Persons or whoever else came to our shores from the Continent, did indeed mean no harm.

I could. I would.

Waiting until after the prayers were said, the rosary beads tucked away again, I left the basket and, after clasping so many hands I lost count and promising to offer prayers to various saints, I fled. The short walk back to the house in Billiter Lane took an age, each step heavy with doubts about what I knew I must do. Duty called. I would report this. I must. Sir Francis relied upon me, trusted me. Was not loyalty what he demanded? Did not justice have to be served? My country, my Queen, needed me to do this. Why then did I feel ambivalent?

As the afternoon wore on, the clouds thickened and rain fell, lashing the windows and darkening the room so much I was forced to light three candles while I wrote my report. The air was humid and steamy and sweat streamed from my head and down my décolletage. Ignoring the way my hair and clothes clung to my skin, the reticence gnawing at my resolve, I continued, describing each and every one of those present. Where I could give a name and a trade, I did. If I knew where they lived and worked, I provided street names and directions. I recalled the questions asked, the words that were said—everything was included, down to the deacon's copy of Campion's tract, the appearance of so many rosaries, and the prayers that were uttered.

But I also noted their fear, their very understandable concern for each other, their sense of unity—not only because they were Catholics, but more importantly, because they were a part of a community that had been torn apart. I wrote of their lack of bellicosity as well. It was the least I could do. It was the most.

I sealed the report, then sat, my head in my hands, staring at what I'd done.

It was in this state that Thomas and Casey found me some time later.

"Mallory? Are you well?" asked Thomas.

I looked up. Thomas took a seat opposite me and waited. Casey poured drinks and slid a cup in front of me. I took it gratefully and drank. Thomas said nothing. His forearm rested on the table, his clothes were wet, his hair flattened on his forehead, the feather on his bonnet sodden.

"Do you ever doubt what it is we do?" I asked finally.

"Never."

"Not even when you know the Catholics are just simple souls who could never do the Queen any harm? Who love the country as much as we do?"

"If they did, they would not be Catholics," shrugged Thomas. When I didn't respond, he sighed. "Hark now, Mallory. They've had years of toleration and understanding, years of the Queen's goodwill, and what have they done? Naught but abuse that goodwill. Remember, they're not loyal to us, to England. They're loyal to that plague-poxed spider in Rome. Rome! They would welcome the Spanish King with open arms if it meant the old ways returned; they would take arms against you— you, who offer them sympathy and understanding—and put Scottish Mary on the throne. Oh, don't deny it, I can see it in your eyes, hear it in your voice—you care. Don't be such a fool."

I recoiled at his tone.

"Give them compassion when they wouldn't think twice about

burning the likes of you and me if it meant their faith was restored? Bah. Our blood is cheap in their eyes. It's for spilling. Don't be gulled, Mallory. What you saw were Catholics who'd been caught, who were afeared for their lives. They deserve nothing but punishment for their stubborn ways, their dangerous and misguided loyalty to a Bishop of Rome." His voice softened. "You're but a woman being asked to think and act like a man. I understand this is a struggle for you. Being feeble-minded, you cannot harden yourself; you seek a truce where there can only be war. Do not chide yourself. Your weakness is beyond your ability to control."

Though I bristled at his criticism, Thomas was right. I was a woman. But was I not also a courtier seeking perfection? A watcher? Was that not achieved by nonchalance? I was not a fool for feeling as I did, but for allowing my feelings to be seen. I glanced at the letter. Perchance what I'd written was also a mistake. I placed a hand on the report and pulled it toward me. I could rewrite it; remove my opinion.

Yet Sir Francis believed I brought a uniqueness to this work and could offer insights men could not. Lifting the report off the table, I hoped he still felt that way when he read it.

"Is that for Mister Secretary?" asked Thomas.

"Aye."

"Here, I will take it."

"I thought I might," I said, bringing it to my breast.

Thomas shook his head. "You are to go home. Your work for now is done."

With a sinking heart, I handed my report over.

I stayed seated even after Thomas left, staring into space, wondering what would become of the people who had gathered in the vicarage kitchen, the people I'd so painstakingly described. Their fates would now be decided by Sir Francis and his men.

I didn't join Papa in the workshop that night, or Caleb, though I could hear him reciting lines in the parlor and Angela laughing and clapping. I wanted no part of anything this evening, only my own misery.

TWENTY-EIGHT

*I*t was some time before I rose from my bed and pushed the shutters wide to gaze upon the yard. Night had not quite fallen and the sound of revelry on the streets carried. The evening air was oppressive, thick. Heavy clouds slumped above, blotting out the stars. Water dripped from the trees. The sparks from a fire spiraled skyward. Below, Papa still labored in the workshop, taking advantage of the longer daylight hours, Matt by his side. Laughter carried from the kitchen, the door open to admit the warm breeze. The dogs scampered around the yard, chasing Latch onto a hay bale. From her vantage point, she turned and threw punches with her paws, her tail and coat twice its usual size. Her kittens, born only a few weeks earlier, were safe with Master Gib inside.

I watched the animals play out the eternal war between their species and thought how like Catholics and Protestants they were—fighting as if they were born to it, not understanding how much they shared. They both had four legs, tails, fur, dependency on humankind. If only they cooperated, how much easier their lives would be. Even language need not be a barrier. Playful scraps aside, did they not share our house?

Our attentions? The food from our table? Alas, the battles between Catholics and Protestants were never playful but deadly serious.

With a head bursting with contrary thoughts, and knowing sleep would not claim me for a long time, I decided to concede to my mood and give my misery company after all. I thought to seek out Caleb.

Taking a candle, I went down the attic stairs and past the apprentices' room, then descended the staircase toward Caleb's. I knocked gently on the door. When there was no answer, I opened it an inch.

"Caleb?" He oft became so lost in what he was doing that he failed to hear a summons. The same thing would happen to me when I worked with locks.

Still there was no answer. I opened the door further and peered inside. There was no one there. Caleb's bedroom was about the size of my old one, generously proportioned, but with a sloping ceiling that meant you had to watch your head at all times. At least, someone of my height did. An image of Lord Nathaniel in this space made my lips twitch. The man would lose his head ere he turned. The room contained a bed, a desk tucked against the window and a hearth with a thick mantel upon which sat Caleb's sword and sheath. The shelves Caleb had built were stacked with manuscripts, scrolls and books that threatened to spill onto the floor. There was also an unfamiliar trunk with a great padlock on it. Perchance Caleb had purchased it for when the troupe traveled. I entered the room and crossed straight to it, lifting the lock into my palm. Heavy, with an intricate shank and two keyholes, it could have been Papa's work. Putting it gently back into place, I looked around. Candles burned on the desk, illuminating the paper sitting there. A quill was upright in its holder, the ink on the page freshly dried. Caleb cannot have gone far if he left candles alight. Perchance he'd gone to the jakes, or to fetch another drink. A tankard sat on the desk, as did a greasy, empty plate.

Unable to resist, I studied the lock again. For certes, it was an unusual design.

"So, does it meet your exacting standards?" drawled a voice.

"Caleb," I exclaimed, dropping the lock. It clattered against the wood. "You scared me out of my wits."

Closing the door, Caleb laughed. "I doubt anyone could do such a thing. You're possessed of the soundest wit I know." Raising the ewer

238 KAREN BROOKS

he carried in my direction, he picked the tankard off the desk, examined the insides, and began to pour. "I'm afraid I wasn't expecting company. I've only the one vessel, so we'll have to share." Ale splashed. "Here. Have some. It's a hot night."

I refused a drink and instead went to his desk.

"Is this *Dido's Lament*?" I asked.

He made an affirmative sound, his mouth full of ale. From the look of the notes in the margins and the extensive crossings out, Caleb was struggling to find inspiration.

I began to leaf through it. "How goes it?"

"I can scarce bear to read it, let alone share it with you."

"You may when you're ready," I said softly.

Caleb smiled. "I will . . . when it's ready."

"Where on God's good earth did you get that monstrosity?" I asked, indicating the chest.

"It takes up a fair bit of space, doesn't it?" Caleb threw himself in his chair and waved his arm toward it. "Arrived today. A friend of mine asked if I could take care of it for him."

"Friend?"

Caleb lowered the tankard. "I do have some apart from you, you know!" He grinned. "'Tis a nuisance."

Kneeling beside it, I ran my hand lightly over the surface. The wood was old and battered and badly pitted, and the iron bands girding it had lifted in parts. I nestled the padlock in my palm. It was weighty. The plate was described with tracery and the figure of a monk in long robes was prominent. The lock required two keys and, as I examined it, I began to suspect it may have been fitted with an alarum—possibly ink or even pepper which would spray in the face of a potential lockpick. Replacing it carefully, I rose and sat on the end of the bed. Caleb hadn't taken his eyes off me.

"That lock is not for the faint of heart."

"It looks serious," said Caleb, half-turning back to his desk. "Apparently, it contains many worldly things and then some."

"Did Papa make the lock?" I took the proffered tankard from him and swallowed.

Caleb glanced over and shrugged. He was sweating heavily; the heat did not sit well with him. I passed his drink back to him.

"I don't know," he said. "It's possible."

Losing interest, he shoved aside the pages on the desk and set the tankard down. Turning, he took my hands in his and drew me closer. Apart from the ink stains, Caleb had such nice hands. Long, elegant fingers with pink nails.

"Now, enough about locks and such. Tell me what you've been up to. I've not had the pleasure of your company for—what is it? Over two weeks. Not properly. You're like an exotic bird. There are rare sightings, but no real proof of your existence. I wondered if perhaps you'd thought to run away again." He winked. "No. That was unkind." He drew his thumb along the back of my hand. "You've been very busy, it seems. Too busy for an old friend. Look at the state of your hands."

I snatched them away. Being immersed in lye some days had made my hands red and sore.

"Never too busy for you. It's just—" I began, wondering where this was leading. I didn't know what to say. I had neglected him; neglected everyone. I reached for the drink again. I needed to wet my throat as my mind worked to answer his complaint.

"I oft wonder what it is you do, Mallory," he said quietly. "Ah, ah. Don't. Don't silence me with that pat response. You work for the Walsinghams? Bah! We both know that's not true."

"What do you mean? I do."

"I think you mean to use the singular but adopt the plural. What you should say is you work for *Walsingham*. Sir Francis. Only you cannot, can you? Like all who work for him, they're sworn to secrecy. What I want to know is, what is it you do exactly, Mallory? What possible use could Sir Francis have for a woman apart from the obvious?"

"Caleb!"

Caleb laughed. "I know you too well to think that, and Sir Francis is far too . . . let us say, pure in his tastes to take a mistress. So, pray, my friend, what is the nature of your work? I've seen you about London, a boy by your side or the man with the yellow hair—Thomas Phelippes, is it not? Why would you be gadding about with Sir Francis's trusted secretary if not for some nefarious purpose? Have you become a hunter of Catholics too? Is that why you are so concerned about the content of my plays?"

I regarded Caleb with consternation. Not only was Lord Nathaniel suspicious, but now Caleb as well.

"You would turn my reality into a great fiction." I swept my arm toward the unfinished play.

"You have to admit, your story would make a fine play."

I glared at him. "My tale is not for entertainment!" Caleb held up his hands in surrender. I let out a sigh. "Master Thomas and the boy of whom you speak, who is no boy but a man, are merely my escorts while I attend to my tasks."

Caleb held my eyes then turned away with a sigh. "Tasks? Such a simple word for complex duties. Seems I'm not the only one to compose fancy. If you cannot share the truth with me, your dearest friend, then I'd best get back to my task." Hurt, he began shuffling paper, shoving it between two pieces of bound card.

"Caleb." I placed a hand on his shoulder. He stilled.

"What?" He made an attempt to sound lighthearted, but I could hear the heaviness.

"Don't. Don't turn away from me. Not you. My only friend. Even when my family barely acknowledged me, you made me welcome. I trusted you with my darkest secret, burdened you in a manner no friend should. You still loved me. More, you did all in your power to build a bridge between before and after and help me cross. Please don't abandon me—not now." I took a deep breath. If I wanted to preserve what remained of our fond relations, of my dearest and only friendship, I had to tell the truth . . . Only, I could not, must not, reveal all.

"You're right," I said slowly. "I'm certainly not his mistress. But Sir Francis *is* my master." Caleb stiffened. "As much as I might wish, I may not tell you what it is I do for him."

Caleb relaxed under my fingers. He reached up and covered my hand with his own.

"Thank you," he said and twisting his head, he kissed the back of my hand softly. "Your secret is safe. Always."

"And yours? You would trust me with any you might keep?" I leaned over to touch the pages in front of him.

Holding his drink steady, Caleb hesitated. "I've always trusted you with mine, Mallory. You know that. When others would turn away, you embraced me. There's no one else with whom I would share the secrets of my heart. No one."

I wanted to say more, but chose not to. I kissed the top of his head and with one last look at the play over which he labored, went to the door. As I opened it, he spoke again. "Be careful, Mallory, won't you? Don't do anything that leads you into danger. Sir Francis is known to be ruthless—not only in pursuit of traitors, but with those he uses to uncover them. I could not bear it if you were treated poorly again."

He spun around, his blue eyes serious.

"I am safe, Caleb. Sir Francis would not risk me so. But I would say the same to you—choose your words with caution. Above all, stay safe." I nodded toward the play. I thought of Campion and his tracts—the damage they'd caused, the trouble yet to come. "Words are dangerous weapons in these times. If anything were to happen to you, it would break what remains of my heart."

We held our gaze a moment longer before Caleb turned back to his writing and I left with one last look at the chest and the big lock securing it.

As I returned to my room, I thought about this unnamed friend. Whatever was in that chest was of great import. Locks were bought for one reason and one reason alone—to keep valuables safe, and what could be more valuable in these times than secrets? Caleb might believe the chest contained his friend's possessions, but—a plague upon my newly suspicious mind—I wondered what this so-called friend was really hiding, and if Caleb knew what it was.

TWENTY-NINE

*O*n the 17th of July, the Jesuit priest, author of seditious pamphlets and traitor to the Crown, Father Edmund Campion, was found hiding in a house at Lyford Grange. There, Master George Eliot and Master David Jenkins, hired by Sir Francis to track the priest, found a veritable nest of heretics protected by a well-known Catholic family, the Yates. After the men first witnessed a mass, they also uncovered secret rooms and priest-holes, along with all the accoutrements of popery— altars, beads, crucifixes, books, pamphlets, Agnus Dei medallions— and some nuns disguised as household staff.

Along with Thomas, Casey and crowds of Londoners, on the 22nd of July I bore witness as the traitors—Campion and three other priests: Thomas Ford, John Collerton and William Filby—were brought into the city. Campion was mounted on a huge horse, his hands bound behind his back, his feet tied beneath the horse's belly, as he was taken to the Tower. Around his neck was a sign bearing the words "Edmund Campion, the seditious Jesuit."

The streets were lined with people, some cheering, others jeering and throwing missiles of rotten fruit and vegetables as well as ordure. Scattered among us were those who remained silent, shedding tears, muttering beneath their breath, raising their eyes to the overcast skies. I recognized some of the women who had huddled in the vicarage kitchen that day after Father Forwood was arrested, and I nudged Thomas and nodded in their direction.

Once Campion's escort passed, the crowd began to disperse. Some would celebrate the arrests, others no doubt would mourn what it signified; most just got on with their lives. We were among the last.

Thomas almost danced as we wended our way back toward Seething Lane. There was certainly a spring in his step. "Sir Francis will be eager to have our reports. I'll have them sent to Whitehall as soon as they're written."

"He is with the Queen today?"

"As his office decrees. Today and every other day," answered Thomas. "Her Majesty is more demanding than a wife."

I glanced at Thomas in astonishment. It wasn't like him to offer criticism of the Queen. He was accurate in what he said. It oft occurred to me that even I saw more of Sir Francis than did his wife or daughter, who were mostly ensconced at Barn Elms. I hadn't seen them again since we had gone to Deptford and, I confess, I wasn't sorry.

As we crossed the road, narrowly avoiding a courier cantering down the middle of it, the horse's hooves kicking up mud and spraying a poor carter unable to move away quickly enough, I wondered about marriage. According to what I'd been told, Mamma and Papa had married for love. It was hard to imagine of late, as Mamma kept to her rooms and I barely saw the two of them together, but I remembered scenes from my childhood where, when neither was aware I was looking, a warm embrace or kiss was shared. One of my earliest memories was when Papa received his first royal commission. Capturing Mamma in his arms, he danced her about the parlor as she squealed in protest, flinging back her head and laughing. From the gap in the door, I'd watched and smiled, longing to join in, but knowing instinctively, even back then, that if I had made my presence known, the moment would end. Though distance had grown between them, it wasn't only duty that propelled Papa to Mamma's rooms almost every night, had him protecting her from information that might disturb her, had him tolerating her recusancy. I'd never really thought about whether or not Mamma and Papa loved each other, despite the alteration in their relations. I'd taken it for granted that they did.

What about Sir Francis and Lady Ursula? I couldn't imagine them stealing a kiss, or dancing, or indulging in romance of any kind. Was theirs simply a marriage of convenience? Sir Francis had been wed before and his wife had died. Had she been his true love? Was Lady Ursula but a pale imitation of what he had once enjoyed?

And what of my experiences? Promised marriage, promised love and adventure, I'd been delivered of nothing but deceit and pain. The man for whom I'd forsworn my life and my virtue had betrayed me in every way. I knew that not all men were like Raffe; if anything was to blame, it was my judgment that was lacking. Around me was evidence of good men, of good marriages. Why, walking just ahead of us was a man escorting his lady wife. She was swollen with child, and his solicitous attention was heartening to witness as he helped her over a puddle, led her around a clutch of snuffling pigs and lifted the train of her dress when she ascended the steps to a house.

Among the vendors we passed were many married couples. Some laughed and shared conversation, others looked as trapped and unhappy as the beasts harnessed to their carts. We saw one woman attack a man with a broom, her voice shrill, his face flaming with embarrassment. Further on, a man struck his woman soundly across the face, causing her to fall upon the cobbles with a cry. I wanted to dash forward and help, but Thomas prevented me.

Gripping my arm, he hissed, "Leave it, Mallory. No good comes of interfering in such matters."

When I glanced back, I saw the man kick the woman in the ribs. She curled into a ball, but no one offered aid, no one protested. Shouting curses, he stalked off, leaving her in the street, the object of both scorn and pity. Anger flared. I was once that woman. I wanted to turn around and tell her to get up and leave. But where would she go? What could she do other than endure? If he was her husband, he was within his rights to beat her and worse. As the good Lord knew, they didn't even need to be wed for him to have mastery over her the way a sovereign did his people. All a man needed to own a woman was for her to surrender the only thing she had to barter—her honor.

Wrenching myself free of Thomas, my hand paused over the locket nestled between my breasts. Little did I know when I met Raffe the price I'd pay for my surrender. Daughters of Eve, women were doubly punished—for their choices and for those of their men. What was it Beatrice told me her brother had said? Women suffer misery more than most. Aye, not even rank and wealth could prevent the desolation men could inflict.

Peeved my thoughts were so bleak when they should be joyous—after all, wasn't Campion in custody?—I tried to push them out of my mind. Gazing about, I recognized the streets. We weren't too far from St. Katherine Coleman.

"Thomas," I began. "Would it be possible to return to Seething Lane via Father Forwood's parish?"

Thomas shot me a strange look. Casey stopped in his tracks.

"Why?"

"So I can see the results of our watching and reporting firsthand. I've heard there's been raids. That Catholics have been rounded up."

"Ah." Thomas and Casey exchanged a look. Pulling down his cap, Casey swung around and kept walking. We fell in behind him. "I'm not sure that's a good idea," said Thomas after a while.

"Why not?" I demanded.

"Because . . . because . . . you are but a frail woman and not equipped to deal with such outcomes."

I bridled. "Am I not a watcher? Wasn't it my work that led to this discovery? What outcome don't you wish me to see?"

Thomas regarded me dolefully for a few steps, then sighed. "So be it."

With a toss of my head, I picked up my skirts and matched my pace to his. Casey walked ahead, hands folded across his thin chest, appearing to watch his feet, but I knew those quick eyes of his would miss nothing.

As we turned off the main road and into the narrow lanes leading to St. Katherine's, lanes I'd walked with baskets of laundry, nodding greetings to the folk who lived there, a terrible sight awaited us. Not only was the street half-empty, but with every step, evidence of violence met my gaze. Doors were ripped off hinges, windows broken, the dark interiors of the houses left open to the elements. Almost every third house had been damaged in some way or left empty. Businesses were closed, their shutters drawn. While there were still children on the stoops of houses, they neither smiled nor waved. Forlorn, they stared out onto the road with hollow eyes. Distant crying could be heard. In the next street, the children fled at the sight of us. A few men gave defiant and morose stares, then turned and walked the other way, calling out warnings. Doors slammed. A baby wailed. Thin dogs barked, while pigs roamed among the detritus. A man with bandages across one side of his head and an arm in a sling limped past, refusing to lift his head. It was the ostler from the inn.

"Thomas," I whispered. "What's happened?"

"Justice," he said.

I stopped midstep. "Justice? You call this justice? Why, the neighborhood is ruined. The place is a shambles. The children . . ."

"They're Catholics; they are traitors. They get what they deserve."

The arguments I wanted to fling at him died. They were Catholics. I had heard and seen them with my own eyes. Had I not helped serve this justice? Dear God, this was a consequence of my actions . . . my report. But had I not emphasized these people were part of a community as well? They were English. They were like us, like me . . . This was not what I had anticipated at all. But what had I expected? I'd read reports of raids and arrests. They were but words on a page. This . . . this was real.

Ahead was Fenchurch Street. Much to my relief, activity there appeared normal: carters on horses, barrowmen crying their wares and pushing their goods along the cobbles, women stepping from houses, purses at the ready, urchins rolling hoops. Ahead lay St. Katherine Coleman.

Slowing as we reached the back gates of the church, I saw a young girl loitering, her eyes upon us. Beckoning her closer, I pulled a coin out of my purse.

"What are you doing?" asked Thomas.

"What I'm hired to do. Eliciting information." I was angered by his indifference to what we'd seen; what I'd caused. It wasn't only the Catholics who were paying a price, but all who lived here—godly, innocent souls as well. I had to make whatever sense of this I could.

"May God give you good day," I said to the girl when she stopped before me. Her curls were the color of roasted chestnuts, her skin sprinkled with freckles. Large green eyes regarded us solemnly. "What be your name?"

"Beth," she said, tilting her head and scratching it. "What be yours?"

Ignoring her question, I showed her the coin. "May I ask you a question, Beth?"

"Aye, mistress," she said. Her face and hands were clean though her skirts were filthy. "For that," she jerked her little chin toward the money, "you may ask me two."

Casey snickered.

"What's happened to the people who used to live in Grouse Lane?"

"You don't know 'bout the purges?"

I shook my head with what I hoped was conviction. "Purges?"

"Aye. That's what my pa calls 'em. Says we been purged of Catholic scum. Thanks to Sir Francis and his men, this neighborhood has been purified of sin."

"There were Catholics here, then?"

The little girl put her hands on her hips, regarding me as if I were a moon-faced loon. "Everywhere, says Pa. But not anymore. A while back, a bunch of big men came with clubs and swords and guns and took away almost half what lived here. Those who weren't taken have run away. Pa says they'll pay for their heresy in other ways."

"Your pa knows what he's talking about," said Thomas.

The girl eyed him suspiciously. "What did you say? Are you a papist?"

"Me?" laughed Thomas. "No. I'm on your pa's side, you cheeky chit."

"Your pa be ignorant and a traitor to his own," piped a voice. Another young girl, slightly older than Beth, came running over. She was followed by more children. They formed a half-circle around her.

"Don't you call my pa a traitor! He's no Catholic!" Beth stamped her foot.

"No, but he betrayed those he grew up with, those who helped him when your ma died, Beth Oldswain, who said masses for her soul, and using their own coin—have you forgotten what my gran did? And now she is in the prison and like to die."

"My pa betrayed no one." Beth walked up to the taller girl and gave her a huge shove in the chest. There were cries of approval from some of the children.

"If it weren't your pa, then who was it?" said the girl, shoving back. Beth staggered and fell on her bottom, crying out in pain.

There were cheers. Before the older girl could launch herself at Beth, I caught her. "Stop it. There's been enough fighting and sadness." The girl shook herself out of my arms and stared at me with resentment. "Surely now is the time to support each other, not scrabble and bicker."

Wiping her nose with the back of her hand, the girl spat. "Yeah, well, tell that to the snitch's girl." She pointed at Beth. "It's her lot caused that." She nodded behind her. "You can choose what you see and what you don't. We were fine till they blabbed. Lived beside each other for years."

"You're wrong," screeched Beth, still on the ground. Casey went to help her to her feet. "It weren't my pa. It was the avenging angel, sent from heaven to punish papists."

There were murmurs of agreement from some of the children.

"Avenging angel?" I asked. "What's this?"

Beth lifted her skirt, which had been torn in her fall, twining it around her fist. "The angel what watches over us and whispers in the Queen's ear, tells her who's loyal and who ain't." She took a step toward the girl, her neck craned toward her. "'Twas the angel, not my pa. The angel sees and hears and sends the men to punish Catholic sinners."

"That's enough, now." There was a clapping of hands and as one, the children spun around. Coming out of the gates of the church was a young vicar. "You heard the lady, go home. Now." As he gave one of the boys a clip over the ear for good measure, the children seemed to think twice about disobeying and then ran down the street, pushing and shoving each other, the argument clearly just getting started. Only Beth remained.

"Beth, you heard me," warned the vicar.

"The lady owes me."

The vicar struck Beth across the face. She cried out sharply, her hand flying to her cheek. "Don't you dare speak in such a manner to your betters."

Casey grabbed his wrist before he could hit her again.

"Vicar, the child speaks true," I said quickly.

I pressed the coin I'd tempted her with into her hand. "Thank you, Beth. May God be with you."

Biting the coin before it disappeared, Beth gave a semblance of a curtsey. "He is, mistress. We be loyal, me pa and me. Not like some." She stared in the direction of the other children.

"That's quite enough, Beth," warned the vicar. "Now, go before I take that money for the poor."

With a horrified look, she scurried away, disappearing between two houses.

"Can I help you?" the vicar asked. His eyes were wary though a smile was fixed to his face.

Thomas began to answer, when I interrupted. "We were on our way home from watching Campion led to the Tower and Beth was telling us about the purges."

"Oh, aye," he said, looking a little relieved. "It's been a terrible time for the parish. What with Father Forwood being exposed and half the congregation." He shook his head in a mixture of sorrow and amazement. "I've had my work cut out. Many were seeking indulgences, worried about their souls being stranded in purgatory. I refused, though they pleaded." He held up his hands, aware of how his words might be construed by strangers. "Of course, I don't approve of such nonsense. Papist rubbish. I remind them, all they need is God's word. He is on our side," he said, including us. "I mean, finding Campion and those other traitors proves He is, does it not?" He beamed benevolently. I attempted a smile. Thomas appeared pained. Casey was busy tying his boots.

"What's this about an avenging angel?" I asked.

The vicar drew closer. "Ah, the children mentioned that, did they? Aye, well, rumor has it among the good folk that God has sent an avenging angel to destroy all Catholics. They say he works for Her Majesty, for Sir Francis." The vicar forced a chuckle. "That's how they're explaining Forwood's arrest, Campion's too, and that of people they've lived beside in harmony all their lives, since good King Henry's reign and through so many changes to the faith. Everyone swears they'd nothing to do with these latest arrests, that they didn't betray their neighbors. You heard Beth, her father is among those being blamed. Yet, after all this time, someone told. Since no one has a sudden fortune to spend, despite Rose's accusation against Master Oldswain, then the next best explanation is the angel. They say no one can see him but he hears everything. Sees everything—right into your soul and whether or not it is Catholic or Protestant."

"I didn't know souls could be distinguished," I said quietly.

The vicar thought it a great joke and slapped his thigh as he laughed.

"Well, this angel can tell the difference. And it's making Catholics tremble—and not just in this parish." He peered around the street. "After all, death follows in his wake . . ."

We walked home in silence. I couldn't help but liken the parish to my own home. After all, did we not live with different faiths under the one roof? If not in harmony, at least without turning on each other. There was Mamma with her Catholic ways, Papa and I who followed the new religion, while Angela was somewhere between. It wasn't so hard to be tolerant, was it?

Not until we were back in my room in Seething Lane did Thomas speak again.

"You seem very reserved."

"I've nothing to say."

Color filled Thomas's cheeks. "You desired to see the penalties your work served on the guilty."

"I did." Bile rose. "I have."

He lingered a moment. "Will you put rumors of the avenging angel in your report to Sir Francis?" he asked.

"Should I?" I lifted off my bonnet and pulled off my gloves. I wanted desperately to wash my hands, my face, to cleanse myself of the streets, though there was not a mark upon me. "It's but a nonsense devised by the frightened. We accept divine justice much more readily than that delivered by man."

"But it should still appear in your report, if for no other reason than that Sir Francis needs to know you've been given another identity."

I froze, my bonnet falling from my fingers. "Another identity? What are you talking about, Thomas?"

Thomas regarded me in disbelief. "You're not normally so obtuse, Mallory. To whom do you think they were referring? Who else walks among them and sees and hears everything? Is it not you?"

"Me?" I lowered myself into the chair. "I took it to mean all watchers."

"As you said yourself, are you not one of us?" He rested his hands on the desk. "It's not the first time I've heard such gossip. We've

encountered mention of this 'avenging angel' in letters we've intercepted; though Catholics try to dismiss it as Protestant propaganda,
it has taken hold and shaken papists here in London to the core. It
matters not how it is. What matters is it's being said." He pushed
himself away from the desk. "Wipe that frown from your face, Mallory. You should be pleased. Zounds, you should be proud. You've
not only helped to bring Campion to justice, but single-handedly
you unearthed a nest of traitors. And this is just the beginning. The
battle for English souls has just begun and we've an avenging angel
on our side."

I struggled to find words. I knew what we were doing was right. It
had to be. But if that was the case, why did I feel so . . . wrong? Forcing a smile to my lips, I replied, "Of course I'll include mention of it,
Thomas. Do I not report all I see and hear?"

"Like an avenging angel." With a beaming smile and a pat on my
shoulder, he left.

I pushed aside my misgivings and the wave of guilt rising inside me
as I recalled broken windows, hacked-down doors and scared, grief-
stricken children. I pulled out a piece of paper, found a quill and, like
the good agent I was, began my report.

THIRTY

HARP LANE AND
SEETHING LANE, LONDON
July to October, Anno Domini 1581
In the 23rd year of the reign of Elizabeth I

*J*ust as the capture of Campion and his compatriots was being celebrated, and as debates raged over how best to extract information
from the heretics, on the 25th of July the Queen sent Sir Francis to
France. In his absence, I was forbidden to venture into London or
Southwark. My work with the laundress was terminated and I was
ordered to remain in my office. Thomas could make no sense of the
command.

"Are you an agent or no?" he asked. "I tell you, Mallory, he treats
you differently and not just because you're a woman. He has great
affection for you and seeks to assure himself of your well-being in his
absence." His tone was disapproving.

Though I'd seen no evidence to support this, the thought made me
accept my orders with grace. Instead of donning disguises, unlocking doors, listening and watching, I remained indoors and labored
through piles of documents, deciphering, translating and recoding,
my knowledge of Latin and French in particular being put to good
use. The letters from Sir Francis's extensive network all had one thing

in common: in addition to reporting on those they were sent to watch, they constantly pleaded to be paid. His agents were bordering on penury and unless they received funds from Mister Secretary, they would be unable to continue. When I brought these requests to Thomas's attention, he was dismissive.

"Sir Francis will pay them when they prove their worth. He's not the Treasury."

"Doesn't the Queen pay these men?"

Thomas gave a disdainful guffaw. "The Queen barely recompenses Sir Francis for all that he does, let alone provide extra for his network. Those men"—he flicked his fingers toward the letters I held—"are paid out of Sir Francis's personal resources, which, as you can imagine with the demands being placed upon him, are rapidly diminishing."

Seeing the expression on my face, Thomas continued. "You earn your wage, Mallory, unlike many."

Even so, apart from one purse months earlier, I too had not been paid. My dreams of accumulating even a modest sum were fading.

When he was not busy elsewhere, Thomas kept me abreast of what was happening with the Jesuits, especially Father Campion: how he was moved from the Tower to York House at Westminster. Sir Francis's brother-in-law and secretary, Master Robert, had been appointed one of the commissioners—interrogators by any other name—who would question him.

The city was still captivated by Campion; though he was under arrest, every word he uttered was reported. Each day, criers would impart the news from St. Paul's Cross, and people gathered eagerly to hear the latest and share what they'd been told. Arguments would often break out, as some felt that while Campion's arrest was fair, his subsequent treatment was not.

Placed on the rack, stretched so his joints dislocated and pain ruled his body, Campion would not repudiate his faith. "I'm being punished for my religious beliefs," he would cry, his every utterance faithfully repeated to the crowds.

Finally, after being racked twice, he revealed the names of the Catholic families who'd sheltered him as well as the various houses and places in which he'd left his books.

"It's not enough," Thomas would say. "Does he think us priests, that a confession suffices? He must admit his error of faith and then repent. Until then, his punishment still stands."

But Campion did not repent.

In early August, Campion also revealed the whereabouts of the secret printing press in Oxford that had produced the *Ten Reasons* pamphlets. It was owned by a Master Stephen Brinkley, and a few days later, Brinkley and his four assistants were arrested and taken to the Tower.

During this tumultuous period, my days were spent deciphering and coding at Seething Lane, learning of various sins and nefarious intentions, and the depth of some of the plots against Her Majesty and the government. My nights were spent at home.

It was at this time that I learned the fate of Captain Alyward Landsey. He had arrived in Spain and been welcomed at the Escorial, where he handed over the documents purporting to reveal the Queen's unholy alliance with the Turks. What he actually delivered was a list of the Queen's dresses—in laborious detail. Furious that he'd wasted their time and money, the Spanish threw the captain and his crew into the dungeons.

"And let's pray the seditious scum rots there," said Thomas.

I prayed he would too and was gladdened to think that not only had I contributed to the imprisonment of a traitor to the Crown, but that my mishap in Deptford had not ruined the venture.

After weeks of slumping clouds and relentless heavy rain, the skies cleared and the sun shone. Puddles dried, thatch steamed, cats lazed and, like the flowers that once scattered the fields above the Tower, folk emerged and turned their faces skyward.

Sir Francis arrived home from Paris, unwell and disgruntled with the way his mission had resolved itself. I didn't see him for two days and, when I did, it was only briefly. He congratulated me on the fine work I was doing and told me to continue until he required me elsewhere.

"While I've been away," he said, "those who helped Campion in his secret work have been rounded up. Prosecutions will begin shortly, so while I'm at Westminster Palace trying these men in the Star Chamber, you must carry on with what you're doing for, just as one plot is foiled, another rises to take its place." He gave me a dry smile. "I need you to continue to be my avenging angel."

"What do you think of this appellation?" I asked.

He chuckled. "Whether pertaining to you or not, you've earned it. It's apt. No one suspects the angel in their midst is a woman. You prove your worth over and over, Mallory. I could not be more pleased." He winced as he spoke, his hand flying to his stomach.

"Sir?" I half-rose from my chair.

"Sit, sit," he said. "'Tis naught to worry about. My usual malady. On second thought, ask Thomas to send for Timothy. I need my wits and my health if I'm to deal with these traitors."

I wasted no time and bade Thomas fetch my uncle, who came immediately. The next I heard, Sir Francis was by the Queen's side and fulfilling his duties. Nonetheless, I did not like this sudden onset of illness or what it boded.

At home, Kit Jolebody finished his journeyman year and became a locksmith in his own right, admitted to the Blacksmith's Guild. This meant his time under our roof was over and he would now find his own way in the world. Papa helped him secure a position in Canterbury and we farewelled him with a combination of joy and sorrow. When it came time to say goodbye, Kit held me close and whispered, "Look to your father, Mallory. His eyesight fails and he is too proud to admit it."

I held him tighter. "I know. But what can be done?"

Kit pulled away reluctantly. "Naught but have him concede his malady and trust Matty and your good self with more responsibility."

I nodded and squeezed his hand in gratitude. Matt, Samuel and Dickon accompanied him down to the river, no doubt stopping at every alehouse along the way.

Kit's words played on my mind. It was time to confront Papa and force him to acknowledge it might be time to cease making locks himself. But how could I say such a thing? Locks were how he expressed himself in ways he could not with words. The making of locks and keys defined Papa. Asking him to stop was akin to asking him to stop living. I had to think of a way to approach the subject, to persuade him to find a replacement apprentice and swiftly.

As it was, I didn't need to. The day after Kit left, Papa began searching for a new boy to take his place. Within a week, nine-year-old Simon Thatch joined us. A quiet boy with a mop of dark hair his surname described, he and Dickon soon became firm friends. I had a quiet word with Matt, who, though worried about Papa, was keeping a close eye on him.

"I'll see no harm comes to him, Mallory. You need not concern yourself on that score. Master Gideon is like a father to me, I owe him everything."

It both filled my heart and eased it to know Papa had such loyalty, such love. It didn't stop me leaving Seething Lane earlier whenever I could and heading straight to the workshop when I arrived home. With the evenings growing shorter, I was determined to wrench Papa away from his locks before he strained his eyes further with candles. We would work together for a while, but as soon as the shadows grew too long, I would suggest we retire. Although he protested meekly, I think Papa knew what I was about and, trusting Matt to supervise what remained to be done, he would join me in the house. Matt would catch my eye and nod approval.

Audiences took advantage of the unusual autumn sunshine and flocked to the Lewes Inn to see *The Scold's Husband* and another performance of *Gorboduc*. Caleb shone in the lead roles. As a treat for the household, he would often reenact scenes in the evening for Papa, Angela and me. The servants and apprentices would creep up from the kitchen when they heard his booming voice and find a space to sit on the floor, enthralled by the unfolding story. Sometimes Caleb would invite me to take a part, and it was during one such evening that we were joined by an unexpected visitor.

I didn't see him at first, as I was taken up in the role I was playing, the apparently shrewish wife of a foolish man who refused to accept she loved him, and as a consequence kept testing her over and over until his unshakeable belief she was the scold he believed her to be became a reality. Bemoaning her manner to all who would listen, the husband painted a picture of a discontented and cruel woman with a roving eye who made his life one long trial. Continually asking for reassurances of her affection, he would invite friends to his home and point out his wife's flaws, persuading them to interpret her actions as wanting. Reluctant at first, these men who first protested her innocence, even highlighting her fine qualities, soon joined the husband in criticizing her, further poisoning him against her. Despondent and helpless, the woman eventually turned upon her husband, unable to bear that no matter what she did, it was never right.

"Pray, husband, when my eye doth light upon another man, be it to wish him 'God's good day,' or 'Blessed eve,' you do but see a trull's beguiling. I know not what you wish me do—shut mine eyes and thus not see these men, even those whom you invite to our table?" I'd adopted a coarser timbre to play the wife.

"Were I blind to your ways," said Caleb, immersed in the role, "you sly temptress, you who do make a cuckold of me over and over, I would be the happier man."

"Then let me grant you this wish, husband, since all else I do brings misery."

Picking up a quill from the table, I pretended to stab Caleb in the eyes.

His hands flew to his face and, shouting, he fell to the floor and rolled around. "My eyes, my eyes. You fever-sent whore, you plague-ridden scold, you've rendered me sightless!"

Straddling his inert body, I looked down upon him. "Nay, husband. I'm no scold." By now, I was panting, the quill tight in my fist. It was no longer Caleb lying beneath me, but Raffe. I was no longer in the parlor, but back in the cottage in Durham. My voice was hoarse, the drumming in my ears loud. "Like a good wife, I've but granted your wish. Now you no longer need to look upon my sins . . . or those which your actions and false words forced me to commit."

Breaking out of his role, Caleb stared through parted fingers. "That's not in the script," he hissed. Speaking louder, he tried to sit up. "Mallory," he said. "Get off me."

Flushed, my hand trembling. I stepped away. Turning around, I faced our impromptu audience, unable to focus on anything. They were a blur of smiles and hands until, as the applause dimmed, I saw Lord Nathaniel.

Caleb jumped up and with an extravagant bow and flourish, swiftly took the part of the wise woman who delivered the epilogue. There was loud applause as he led me to the credenza and poured a drink.

"You take liberties with my work?"

I stared at him blankly. Behind us, encouraged by Matt, the apprentices scrambled to their feet, slapping Caleb on the back as they left, bobbing their heads and heaping praise upon us. Comfort collected the empty cups and shooed Gracious, Master Gib and Mistress Pernel from the room. Soon it was only me, Papa, Caleb, Angela and Lord Nathaniel left.

Caleb nudged me when I didn't answer. "You added, 'Or those which your actions and false words forced me to commit.' I like it, but I'm not sure it will find its way into one of our performances."

Dear God, I'd forgotten where I was. "I'm sorry, Caleb."

A look of pity crossed Caleb's features as understanding dawned. "Ah, Mallory, it's me who's sorry. I shouldn't have asked you to play—"

"What won't find its way into one of our performances?" Lord Nathaniel appeared at my elbow.

"Ah, Lord Nate," said Caleb, passing Lord Nathaniel a brimming goblet. "I was just saying it's a pity women can't tread the boards or Mallory might supplant any one of our troupe onstage."

"Any one of the boys, perchance, but as a man, she would never pass muster."

"My lord," I said, recovering quickly. "Am I not already halfway there? You pointed out yourself, I have a man's name."

"Aye, but not his appearance. You're far too lovely," said Lord Nathaniel.

I started and met his eyes, expecting to see irony there. There was only an earnest regard. I found my drink very interesting.

"You were most convincing in the role of wronged wife, mistress," said Lord Nathaniel quietly. "It would be easy to assume you draw from experience. I hope in that regard I'm wrong."

Before I could summon a suitable retort, Papa came to my rescue.

"My lord, to what do we owe the pleasure?"

"Ah, Gideon," said Lord Nathaniel with such warmth my discomfort began to dissipate. "I'm here to avail myself of your considerable skills."

"Really? What can I do?"

Lord Nathaniel reached inside his doublet. "I was hoping you could open this for me."

Papa put his goblet down and took a long, thin, beautifully carved box from Lord Nathaniel.

"Why, this is most elegant. A lady's jewel case if I'm not mistaken."

"Booty from your trip to the country, my lord?" asked Caleb.

"Of a sort. My lady aunt, whom I took Beatrice to visit as she's been most poorly, gave it to me. It belonged to my grandmother. I'm afraid I lost the key between York and home and need to access the contents."

"Well, let's attend to it immediately, shall we? Mallory," said Papa, "can you help? The lock is delicate and your fine fingers are much better suited to this."

Trying not to appear too eager, I dropped a curtsey. "For certes, Papa," I said.

"Upstaged by a piece of wood," said Caleb drolly, refilling his goblet and dropping into the seat across from Angela. "Not the first time that's happened. After all, I've performed with Will Kempe."

Promising to return, we slipped out through the kitchen to the workshop. Papa sped ahead to open the doors and light some candles.

Night was falling, the stars making a grand entrance, turning the firmament into their own sparkling case of jewels. Gazing skyward, I caught the scent of wood smoke and was surprised to note the chill in the air. My second winter since coming home was almost upon us. So much had happened in a year. When Papa delivered me from Raffe, little did I suspect what my life would become, whom I'd become. Just as I'd returned home a different person, the last twelve months, the people I'd met and the work I'd done, had enacted another kind of transformation.

Lord Nathaniel cleared his throat. "Though it's been a while since our last encounter, I've wanted to tell you how much you impressed my sister, Beatrice."

"Why, thank you, my lord. She aroused the same response in me. She's a most impressive young lady."

"I think so as well," said Lord Nathaniel.

Papa reached the workshop. Arthur and Galahad burst out and ran down the path toward us. "Oh dear, the apprentices shut them in again." I dropped to my knees as the spaniels jumped and spoke their displeasure, their little tails wagging furiously.

Lord Nathaniel bent and fondled both dogs. It wasn't so dark I couldn't see the expression on his face. Here was a man who liked animals. Warmth flowed from my center and I recalled a desire to share my concern about Caleb with him; to discuss it without revealing too much.

"My lord," I began, rising.

"Mistress Mallory—" he started at the same time.

We both laughed. "After you," he said.

"Please, my lord. I wish you to speak first."

"Ah, well, I know better than to disobey a scold's wishes," he said, smiling.

I returned the smile. I'd never noticed before how long his lashes were. How much darker his beard was than the tawny hair upon his head. Without his cap, his hair was thick and glossy in the evening light. My hand traveled to my own head, finding a long tendril had escaped. I twined it around my finger, trying to replace it in my coif. I waited for him to speak.

"Mallory," he began. "I may call you that?" I nodded. "I'm serious when I say Beatrice was most taken with you. Ever since we've returned, she has pestered me about approaching you."

"Regarding what?" I asked. My legs felt unsteady.

"I wonder if you might consider becoming Beatrice's companion?"

My insides flipped. This was most unexpected.

"Oh. But, my lord, I already have employ."

"Aye, but perchance this position might be preferable to what you have with Sir Francis . . . Forgive me, with the Walsingham family."

I wondered then how much he knew. Or was he guessing? He'd drawn conclusions about Frances. The man was no fool. He'd once thought me a woman who was duplicitous for her own ends. Did he still? A small flare of anger rose and died. Wasn't he right? If that was so, how could he want such a one for his sister?

"My lord," I began. "I'm beyond flattered and cannot think of any position I would rather take than to be by Beatrice's side, except I'm not free to do so."

"You need only give the word and I could speak to Sir Francis."

I raised my hands as if to stop him. Speak to Sir Francis? Dear God, no. My throat tightened. This was too swift, too sudden. I was not ready to let go the freedoms, the importance my work bestowed;

the sense of value and autonomy it gave me. Seeing justice served . . .
Only that had not afforded me quite the gratification I'd anticipated.
On the contrary . . . But it didn't matter how conflicted I felt in
that regard, I was not yet ready to forgo my position in Sir Francis's
network. I'd so much more I could offer, there was so much more I
could do. So much more to understand. Yet I could not offend Lord
Nathaniel.

"May I consider your generous offer, my lord?" I shucked Galahad
behind the ears. He rose on his hind legs and rested his paws against
my leg, thrusting his head into my hands.

"You may," said Lord Nathaniel. "But do not tarry. Who knows, I
may find another accomplished young woman with a brilliant mind
and quick wit whom my sister finds most endearing to take your place."
I'd not heard him speak in that tone before. He was teasing, flattering
and reassuring all at once. I gazed at him with fresh eyes.

"Mallory?" Papa called.

"Coming." Galahad leaped down and I gathered my skirts. "Locks
don't unpick themselves," I said to Lord Nathaniel apologetically.

Clicking my fingers so the dogs followed, I continued to the workshop, Lord Nathaniel beside me.

"Is there anything you cannot do, mistress?" he asked.

"My lord?" I replied.

"I see you perform one of our most popular plays like a consummate
professional who has spent a lifetime strutting the stage and tonight I
learn you also pick locks."

"I am a locksmith's daughter, it's not really so surprising."

"Nothing you do should surprise me and yet, you're a constant
source of bemusement."

I laughed. "I'm sorry to be the cause of such consternation."

"Consternation? Nay, I find myself delighted by surprises of the
kind you deliver."

Lord Nathaniel grinned and stepped ahead to open the door. I
passed under his arm, trying hard not to dwell on our conversation,
and began helping Papa light more candles, aware all the while of Lord
Nathaniel's golden eyes upon me.

The forge kept the room warm, but even so, in case unlocking this
small box proved difficult, I invited his lordship to sit close to the fire.

"I would like to watch you work, if you don't mind."

I did, but it would have been churlish to refuse. "As you wish," I said. Papa dragged a stool over to the workbench. Seated on the edge of the bench, his lordship looked like an eagle on a canary's perch, uncomfortable and ready to take flight.

The lock plate on the casket was of a beautiful design, Gothic tracery interwoven with a popular vine motif representing Christianity. I guessed it to be Flemish or French.

I bent until my eye was level with the keyhole, all the time aware of Lord Nathaniel, the proximity of his bent knee, the perfume of ambergris and musk emanating from his clothing. Papa passed me two rods and leaned on the bench. It didn't take long to open the casket. Hooking the bent rod around the tumbler, I pulled and pushed with the other straight one. There was a click.

"Ah, well done, Mallory," said Papa. "Is she not clever, my lord?"

"Aye," said Lord Nathaniel, lifting the casket into his hands. "Exceptionally."

Opening the lid, he sighed. Nestled in some purple silk was an exquisite necklace. Sapphires and rubies embedded in a lovely gold filigree dazzled. Lord Nathaniel plucked the necklace from its bed and let it slither across his palm.

"Why, that's a work of art, my lord," said Papa. "It was your grandmother's?"

"It was. She bequeathed it to my aunt who, having no children of her own, has given it to me with instructions I find a woman worthy of wearing it."

Lifting his hand so the necklace dangled, he looked at me. I held my breath.

"And you've found someone?" said Papa warmly. "Then you're a fortunate man."

"I have and I am," agreed Lord Nathaniel. He placed the jewelry back in the casket. "I wish to bestow this beautiful piece upon her soon. When I understood the key was lost, I thought my intentions thwarted, but you, Mistress Mallory, Master Gideon, have allowed my plans to go ahead. You have my deepest thanks."

His words took a moment to register. He'd found a woman? He was going to give her the necklace? Why was my heart beating so fast and my mouth suddenly sour? Color flooded my face. Rising to my feet, I picked up the rods and, moving away from the bench, restored them to their pouch.

I barely remember saying farewell to Lord Nathaniel or the manner of his leaving, only that I found I wanted to remain in the workshop, to continue to test my skills against the locks. After escorting Lord Nathaniel out, Papa returned.

"Are you well, Mallory?" he asked, watching as I inserted the rods into a complex padlock.

"Of course, Papa, why would I be otherwise?"

"I thought . . . That is, when you opened the casket for Lord Nathaniel . . . Well . . ." He shrugged, loitered for a few minutes, picking up a tool and putting it down again, lining up a row of shanks, then bade me goodnight and went to Mamma.

It was only after he left that I understood I'd lost the perfect opportunity to raise the issue of his eyesight with him. All my thoughts had been thrown into disarray. Opening the casket for Lord Nathaniel had unlocked something within me: a little door I'd worked hard to keep closed.

For the first time since I'd mastered lock-picking, the lock I was working on refused to open. I threw it down in disgust. Arthur and Galahad growled.

"It's all right, boys, it's all right," I said, staring at the offending item. I sat by the fire, placing my arms around the dogs' soft bodies, pulling them onto my lap. "Sometimes what is locked should never be opened," I whispered into one floppy ear. I thought of Pandora's box, which had released pain and fury upon the world. But didn't it also contain hope?

The soft radiance of the fire was comforting. My mind began to drift. I wondered about the woman who would receive such a beautiful gift, who had captured Lord Nathaniel's heart—"a woman worthy of wearing it," as his aunt had said.

I tried to consider what this creature might look like and an image of a bow-shaped mouth captured by Lord Nathaniel's lips danced in my vision.

Tightening my arms around the dogs, I shut my eyes so I didn't have to see how tawny my own skin looked in the glow of the forge.

I imagined this woman melting into Lord Nathaniel's strong arms, leaning against his hard body, running her fingers over his silky hair. Would he look at her with twinkling eyes, horrify her by speaking without thought or concern? Or would he be cautious, treat her with respect, not inflame her with his careless words? He would treat her differently to the way he had treated me—as he should. Why did the notion fill me with such despondency?

"Mallory Bright," I groaned. "What has become of you? Where is your nonchalance now?"

Whoever this woman was, I should have hoped she was as deserving as Lord Nathaniel's aunt intended. Only, damn my treacherous heart, I did not. I hoped she was ungrateful, demanding and as much a scold as the foolish husband of Caleb's creation believed his own wife to be.

THIRTY-ONE

*A*fter that night, his lordship became a regular visitor to Harp Lane, claiming he'd business to attend to with Caleb. When I returned of an evening I'd oft find him in the parlor, enjoying an ale with Caleb and Papa and sharing the latest gossip from court or news of Campion's impending trial. Instead of making excuses and escaping to my room, I found myself drawn to the convivial company on offer and began to delight in the verbal sparring and teasing that inevitably followed my arrival.

Work at Seething Lane continued and though Sir Francis was busy preparing for Campion's trial, he also sent me on various errands, dispatching letters and collecting correspondence, all in the guise of Samantha Short, who was variously a washerwoman, a lady's maid, a tavern wench, a baker's apprentice and a vicar's housekeeper. In each of these roles I not only received information to take back to Seething Lane, but was able to gauge the mood of the people, listening to ramblings by firesides and over a tankard or two. Tongues were loose in the market and it was oft while I was lingering over fruit or waiting for a haunch of meat to be cut that I would hear suspicious snippets, a name carelessly dropped, a blessing being bestowed that had no place in England. I noted and recorded everything.

My perturbation over what happened to the folk at St. Katherine Coleman eased. Being in a position to see and hear the degree to which Catholics undermined the Privy Council's principles and defied the law helped me to reconcile their punishments. Thomas was correct when he said they deserved their fates. They had made a choice and had to abide by the consequences. I persuaded myself they were not godly people; they were not loyal and therefore didn't merit my sympathy—no traitor did. Nevertheless, the sad and confused faces of the children tormented me.

Just as I thought Campion's arrest had quelled the Catholic rising, in a bookstore called the Gun I discovered more treachery.

An icy wind blew through the streets and I entered the bookshop, grateful for its warmth. The familiar mustiness still had the capacity to transport me to other places and times. My bonnet had been blown askew, and as I adjusted it I glanced at Casey, who loitered outside. The handful of men milling near the counter ceased speaking, moved apart, and began to comb the shelves as if searching for particular books. The owner, Master Barton Crashaw, swept up a pile of pamphlets and placed them out of sight. Suspicious behavior at the best of times. Upon seeing a mere woman enter, Master Crashaw relaxed and gave a small bow. The other men lurked nearby, trying to appear indifferent and failing miserably.

"God give you good day, mistress. May I help you?"

"God give you good day too, sir," I began. I'd been instructed to observe who was patronizing the shop. Pretending to peruse the carts across the road before ordering a new pair of gloves from the glover opposite had kept me busy for over two hours. I'd seen four men enter the Gun, but none leave. Their reaction to my presence, the concealment of the pamphlets, told me I needed to do a little more than simply watch. Moving closer to where the owner stood with his hands splayed upon the now empty counter, I offered a conspiratorial look. The men rummaged through the books on the shelves with a disingenuous air.

"Sir, I pray you can help me. I have recently read an account of the arrest of Father Campion by Anthony Munday and George Eliot—"

The men froze. Munday was one of Sir Francis's men, a gifted writer who, under orders from Mister Secretary, had written an account of Campion's arrest. It was wildly inaccurate, and Munday subsequently spoke with one of the arresting officers, Master George Eliot, and had the truth. A more accurate version was quickly produced and distributed. It distressed and infuriated Catholics everywhere, but especially William Allen in Reims, who wrote a rebuttal of Munday and Eliot's story in the futile hope it would aid Campion's case. Someone in London was flouting the law and distributing Allen's riposte, and Sir Francis believed he knew who that person might be . . . Dare I nudge and discover if his conjecture was correct?

"I found it . . . How shall I say?" I pretended to choose my next words carefully. "Do I dare utter what is filling my heart without risk of retribution?" I glanced toward the hovering men.

Master Barton studied me, then gazed for a long moment over my shoulder. "I'm a lowly bookseller, mistress. Retribution is not mine to give, only to receive according to the dictates of the good Lord."

I went to make the sign of the cross and froze as I began, turning the gesture into a brush of my chest. Master Barton saw my action and again peered past my shoulder. This time, he nodded slowly, responding to a silent command.

"Mistress, you will receive no retribution from this quarter, only understanding. Speak what is in your heart."

Releasing a tentative sigh, I leaned over the counter, lowering my voice. "Munday's narrative is disappointing; inclined to falsehoods and exaggeration. It will not help Father Campion or those disposed to . . . shall I say, offer sympathy? On the contrary . . ." I shook my head in sorrow.

"There are many who feel that way, mistress . . . or so I've heard."

"I as well. In fact, there are rumors of an alternate version of events, a version that's inclined to offer a more sympathetic retelling, only I cannot find it." I hesitated, then whispered. "You wouldn't know where I might buy a copy, would you, sir?"

Master Barton again received a sign from behind me. His cheeks became ruddier the longer we spoke. For certes, it was becoming close in the shop. He stared at me for a long moment and then, with an abrupt step back, retreated from the counter. "I'm afraid I know of no such version or where you might find such a work. But I've many other wonderful books available. Please, feel free to browse the collection. There are also many pamphlets, some of which might satisfy your . . . tastes."

Like air from a deflating bellows, the wind of my ambitions left me. With a slight curtsey, I thanked the owner and, spinning on my heel, went to search the shelves. What I wanted to do was leave, but that would have aroused suspicion and put the men on guard.

No longer able to see Casey, I walked the length of the shelves, reading the spines of the tomes, picking up a couple and opening them, faking an interest I no longer felt. I handled books on theology, education, domestic solutions, philosophical pondering, some poetry, Homer, Tacitus, and a very nice edition of Malory's *Le Morte d'Arthur*.

On a whim, I decided to purchase it. Had not Beatrice claimed to love Malory's tales? I would give her this by way of apology for refusing her brother's offer of employment. Meanwhile the men had returned to the counter and were involved in a quiet discussion. I approached slowly while fumbling in my purse, and they parted to admit me. I'd already noted their attire, the cut of the cloth, the quality of their boots. These were wealthy merchants at least, if not squires from outside London. My head high, I passed Master Barton the book.

He examined the cover, brushing the dust from it. "Unusual choice considering what you were after, mistress, if you don't mind me saying."

I gave a light laugh. "Indeed, sir, I quite surprise myself."

"Fanciful stories for naught but children if you ask me," said one of the men gruffly.

Astounded by his rudeness, I rounded on him. "I did not, sir." A pair of pale eyes looked me up and down.

"And I wasn't addressing you, mistress," he said and began to laugh. The other men chuckled. I turned my back upon them, bristling. More than anything I wanted to escape this place.

Master Barton wrapped the book. When he finished, I passed him the correct change.

"Winter'll be bitter this year," said a different gentleman, touching his cap by way of deference, perhaps making up for the rudeness of the other.

Uncertain if he was speaking to his companions or me, I simply bowed my head slightly.

"Aye, that it will. But just as the good Lord gave His son who rose from the dead, so too will this winter pass into spring and rebirth," agreed another. There were quiet murmurs. It wasn't only talk of the season that made a chill run down my spine. It was hard to reckon they were so bold in their talk. For was not winter the new faith, and the rebirth an allusion to the return of the Catholic one?

I needed to be gone. Taking the book, I thanked Master Barton and forced myself to walk calmly from the premises, aware of five sets of eyes boring into my back, the silence thick. *Nonchalance*, I chanted in my head.

Relieved to find Casey at the end of the row of shops, I fell into step beside him. "So?" he asked.

I shook my head. "If they're distributing Catholic tracts, and I believe they are, I could find no proof. Still, the place is certainly worth watching if not raiding."

"I agree, mistress," said Casey. "It doesn't feel right."

"They didn't mind their tongues in front of me."

Casey grinned. "They knew not an avenging angel was among them."

I looked at him grimly. "They did not."

We pushed our way through the crowds about St. Paul's, rounding a corner and escaping the force of the wind.

In my office at Seething Lane, I stood before the fire, my hands held out to catch the heat, my brain afire. Pouring a drink, I sat down to write my report, but ceased after only a few lines. Convinced the shop was a center of sedition, a meeting place of Catholics, I'd no proof. Leaning back in my chair, my arms outstretched before me, frustration rose. What good was a report of maybes and mights? Of "I think" and "I feel"?

My eyes alighted on the book I'd bought. Pulling off the wrapper, I ran my hands over the embossed cover. Fanciful, the man had called Malory's tales. Fit only for children. Well, I quite fancied reading one now, even if that did make me a child. As I opened the heavy cover, a slew of paper fluttered to the floor. Distressed I'd loosened the spine, I bent down to retrieve the pages only to find what I held was not from Malory's book, but was in fact a pamphlet: Doctor William Allen's rebuttal of Munday and Eliot's account of Campion's arrest and subsequent questioning.

With a whoop of triumph I smoothed out the pamphlet and began reading it. I was right. The Gun and Master Barton were distributing treasonous material. Defending everything Campion did and said, Allen's work was clearly designed to inspire Catholics to maintain the faith, abhor everything Protestant and decry the persecution being meted out to their Father Campion.

With the pamphlet propped before me, I wrote my report swiftly, then went to find Thomas. It mattered not that Sir Francis was at Whitehall with the rest of the Star Chamber, he needed to know about this.

Only this time, I wanted to be the one to tell him.

THIRTY-TWO

HARP LANE AND
SEETHING LANE, LONDON
The 29th of November, Anno Domini 1581
In the 24th year of the reign of Elizabeth I

*M*allory," said Sir Francis. He stood and waved me into his office. Piles of paper lay across his desk, a thick bundle before him. From the look of the quills and shavings, he'd been up during the night working on reports.

Less than three hours had passed since I'd shown Thomas my discovery and shared my suspicions. Mister Secretary must have ridden hard from Whitehall when he received the message. I could smell horseflesh and sweat.

"Thomas informs me you've something significant to impart. Make haste, I've left important business for this."

I wasted no time in passing Sir Francis my report and the offending pamphlet. He looked at the latter while, as I was trained to do, I spoke to what I'd written. When I finished, he sat back. It was a while before he spoke. I noted how tired he appeared, but he was also strangely alert.

"This"—he began, his hand hovering over my report—"couldn't have come at a better time." I glowed under his praise. "This"—he picked up the pamphlet—"is the proof we need. No doubt the papers you saw being removed from the counter were more of the same." His frown deepened as he gazed at the offensive words. "Seditious rubbish. Making a martyr of Campion when he's the greatest of sinners. Allen's words further implicate Campion and the other priests in plotting against Her Majesty, against England. Their duplicity and treachery know no bounds."

"What will you do?" I asked. His quiet fury made me timid, quenching my small spark of triumph.

"Do? For a start, we will put watchers on all those gentlemen you and Casey saw. We will also observe the shop, see who else patronizes it, discover where these pamphlets are being distributed. I also want to see if we can locate the press that printed them. More of this nonsense is bound to be peddled, especially after Friday."

"Why Friday?"

"Because that's the day Edmund Campion dies."

"The Commission has reached a verdict?"

Sir Francis's eyes flickered to his desk. "Aye, we have." Rising to his feet, he collected my report. "Stay here. This cannot wait. I will get Thomas to organize watchers at once. No doubt these men will bear witness to Campion's death, and perchance we can follow them from Tyburn."

Before I could reply, he left the room and shut the door.

I'd not seen Sir Francis so roused since Campion was caught. "Death" and "Tyburn" tripped off his tongue. Uneasy, I rubbed my arms. Thoughts of those rounded up from the parish of St. Katherine Coleman crept into my mind once more. I recalled the men, the women, the children, all of them frightened—but passionate, too. There were no plots being hatched, none that I heard, at least. Were they also to be put to death? Or had they confessed their heresy, recanted and, in doing so, helped to confirm Campion's guilt?

Had I ever really believed that my work wouldn't lead to this? If not for Campion, then for others? No. I knew. I understood. It was only now it had become a reality. Death followed in my wake. And with more to come, I was the avenging angel incarnate.

Voices rose and fell. There was the scrape of chairs, the sound of boots on the floor. With a sigh, I clasped my hands in my lap and waited, gazing around the room that had become so familiar to me over the past year. Little had changed. The pictures and tapestries on the wall were the same, the candles were in a perpetual state of melting, the view from the window was as bleak and gray as it had been the first time I'd sat here. Only the mounds of paper, the overflowing boxes, had grown in number. I reached out and touched one of the teetering piles on Sir Francis's desk and, to my horror, it collapsed, sending papers tumbling.

I managed to catch some and quickly tried to restore order, glancing from the door to the desk and back again, hoping I hadn't been heard. Laughter began to build within me at the impossibility of my situation. Imagine Sir Francis walking in and catching me with my arms full of his correspondence, no doubt laden with state secrets, and me explaining how an innocent brush, an almost loving touch, had demolished the pile.

Swiftly stacking the papers, it wasn't until the tower was complete again that I saw two stray pages had fallen down the other side of the desk—one onto Sir Francis's work, the other upon his chair. I ran around and put them back where they belonged.

I'm uncertain what made me linger and caused my eyes to alight upon the pages he'd brought back from the Star Chamber. Nevertheless, I began to read. Was I not a watcher? Someone who observed and interpreted everything around them?

What I saw was a long list of names, accompanied by physical descriptions, a personal history, and different dates, places and even times. This was familiar. Looking up, I quickly flicked to the front page. Of course, this was the original dossier Charles Sledd had compiled, which Sir Francis had given to me to read and memorize months ago. Yet now there were amendments, marginalia.

Unable to help myself, I kept reading. There were some crossings out and additions, not always in the original hand. Turning to the next page, I recognized Sir Francis's writing, Thomas's too. They'd made notes—perchance to help with their arguments at Campion's trial. Trailing my finger down the page, I continued reading, reassured as the voices outside the door continued unabated.

Then I saw a name I hadn't expected. Above a redacted name was scrawled "Edmund Campion, priest Jesuit." I frowned. It was the only entry among dozens and dozens that lacked a physical description and a biography. Without a doubt I knew his name had not been there when I first read this material. This had been added since.

I slowly sank into Sir Francis's seat as the meaning of this late inclusion dawned upon me. Campion had never traveled among the group of heretics Sledd accompanied throughout the Continent. For certes, he was already in England when Sledd embarked on his journey with Allen and the others. He was not part of their plots. Thomas told me Sledd hadn't even set eyes on the priest until two days ago when he testified in court. Oh, he knew the others listed here, and intimately. He'd been their courier, lackey and much more besides. Sledd swore the men whose names he recorded, whose conversations he scribed, were all willing participants in King Philip and the Pope's enterprise against England.

Now Sir Francis ensured Campion's name was included among them. And thus he ensured the Jesuit's death.

Darkness closed around my vision. My head swam. I'd been told the evidence against Campion was overwhelming. Why would Sir Francis need to falsify anything? I didn't hear the door open. I wasn't even aware of Sir Francis on the other side of the desk, watching me from the shadows, until I heard him clear his throat.

With cloudy eyes, I raised my head and tried to fix upon him. His black clothing and midnight hair made it impossible to distinguish his features. He blurred into the darkness. I didn't leap from the seat; I didn't tender an apology. I just remained where I was.

"The traitor must die, Mallory. If he doesn't, then all this"—his arm encompassed the room—"the suffering of innocents, all my men have done, all you have done, will be for naught." He proffered no excuses. He knew what I'd seen, and that I understood the implications.

"What about justice?" I said hoarsely.

"You think this isn't just? That a Catholic priest in league with the pox-riddled monk in Rome doesn't deserve to die? You believe his mission in England righteous?"

I didn't answer, and lowered my head and looked at the page. The words "Edmund Campion, priest Jesuit" shouted at me.

"He lies, Mallory. Everything that comes out of that treacherous priest's mouth is a lie. He refuses to atone, to acknowledge the error of what he's done. He is unrepentant. Why? Because he sees nothing wrong with breaking the law, with persuading good English souls to his cause, to Rome. And what is Rome's cause?"

"Death to Her Majesty," I said softly. "The ruination of the Protestant faith and the return of the Catholic one. Anarchy. War."

"Exactly." His tone changed. Sinking into the seat I'd so recently vacated on the other side of the desk, he folded his arms and waited.

"If what he's done is so wrong, then why do you need to lie about this?" I jabbed the page. "Why add his name to this list of plotters when his crimes do not require such intervention?"

"Damn it, Mallory, but it does. Have you not heard a word I've said? Do you not understand? Every minute he lives, every time he speaks or his words are published for others to read and discuss, he wins souls to his cause, and that means against England. We're not safe as long as this man breathes."

His hand snaked across the desk and found mine. It was limp and cold within his warm, tight grasp.

"I'm merely doing my duty, Mallory, just as you have done yours. Do you doubt Campion's guilt?"

I hesitated. "No."

"Should he be put to death like all traitors?"

This time, I took longer to answer. "Aye." *If that is indeed what they are.*

He released my hand. "Then you understand. I'm simply doing what is necessary."

I heard the splash of liquid. A goblet was placed before me. "Drink." He sat back down. "Think of it this way. Do you not tell falsehoods to your family in order to protect them?"

I bridled. "I hardly think it's the same."

"Is it not? In lying about what you do for me, aren't you protecting them from full knowledge of your activities? Are you not protecting yourself from their judgment? Are you not keeping the secrets we uncover safe so that those who would suffer if they knew, who would live in dire fear, can instead continue their lives in blissful ignorance?"

"I . . . I . . . I hadn't thought of it that way."

"You should. Not all lies are bad, Mallory. Intention is the key. You lie with good intent; you omit to disclose the full truth in order not to hurt those you care about. Do you not?"

My hand found my locket. "I have . . . I do . . ." How much did he know?

Sir Francis smiled. "Then you are just like me. We are one and the same, Mallory, just as I knew we would be. I too indulge in falsehoods on occasion, only I do it to protect the entire realm."

"But Campion will die because of your lie."

"What is the loss of a traitor if it means saving one good English soul?"

I didn't reply.

"You've admitted this is what he deserves."

"Aye. No . . . I don't know." I was confused. If Sir Francis could not deliver retribution honestly, then what was the point? What was the point of having laws? Of courts and judges and trials? What was the point of what I did? And yet I did lie, and for good reason, and not just to Mamma and Papa, either. I lied to protect myself. It was not right. It was not good. It was cowardly. Burying my head in my hands, I sat in silence. I sensed Sir Francis stand again. A moment later, I felt his hands upon my shoulders.

"I never said this would be easy, Mallory. We all, whether we're the sovereign or a pauper, battle with our consciences. It speaks volumes for the woman you are that yours rages—just as it did over the fate of those at St. Katherine Coleman."

I lifted my head. I felt so weary. The weight of Sir Francis's hands upon me were nothing to the weight in my heart. I wished I could unburden myself to someone, anyone. Once upon a time, it would have been Caleb or Papa . . . but no more. I was sworn to secrecy, to a life that precluded sharing. This work separated me from those I held most dear. I was without a friend, without a father . . . I couldn't even speak to Sir Francis about how I felt lest I come across as weak or, worse, as a traitor myself.

And yet, was it not the cruelest paradox that the very work that caused such anguish of the spirit also gave me purpose?

A groan escaped my lips. Sir Francis shook me gently and helped me to my feet.

"Look at me, Mallory," he said. Accustomed to obeying him, I did so. He seemed different. The candlelight made him appear dark and devilish, his beard forked, his eyes cold and hard. "I want you to go home; rest and calm yourself. Wait until I send for you again. Do not fret, it will be soon. Have we not more Catholics to bring to justice?"

He chucked me under the chin. I nodded. He waited as I returned to my usual position on the other side of the desk before resuming his chair.

"I need to return to Whitehall," he said. "Sentence has been delivered upon Campion and it must be carried out."

I stared at the page that would send Campion to the scaffold.

Sir Francis's eyes hadn't left my face. "You've done well so far, my avenging angel. Rest your wings." He gave a half smile. I rose, curtseyed and turned to go.

"Wait," he commanded. "Promise me you'll not go to Tyburn on Friday. I know your inclinations, how you insisted on walking the streets around St. Katherine Coleman. Your duty is done. You helped bring a traitor to justice, there's no need to see him punished. I would you soothe your conscience, not prick it with a thousand cuts. Am I clear?"

"Aye," I replied.

"You'll not go to Tyburn."

"It shall be as you say, sir." I left him knowing another lie had tripped off my tongue. I would go to Tyburn and watch the penalty I'd helped secure be meted out.

As his avenging angel, it was my God-given duty.

THIRTY-THREE

*B*etween my waking and leaving the house, dawn had broken and a thick mist had risen from the river and engulfed the city, shrouding the lanes, drifting through the streets, muffling the sounds of those joining the throng leaving London to witness Edmund Campion's execution. Anonymous gray shadows emerged out of the dense white fog before being swallowed again. With each step I took, I sensed rather than saw our numbers grow, all of us doggedly heading toward Tyburn; a mostly silent group marching toward death.

Sir Francis may have forbidden me to attend and, may the dear Lord forgive me, I may have given a solemn promise I would not, but discovering the alterations he'd made to Sledd's dossier had changed everything. I had to see for myself where those changes led; see the fate of this man who'd preoccupied my master and his men for so long, who'd preoccupied me.

I'd reached St. Paul's before I was aware I was being followed. As I was forced to a standstill by the growing crowd, a gentleman sidled up beside me.

"I did not think this would be your choice of entertainment, mistress." It was Caleb.

"Nor yours, my friend," I said quietly. "What are you doing here?"

Caleb stared at me, trying to think of what to say. "I heard you leave the house and followed. Why are you here?"

I considered my words. "I need to see if Campion's the threat I believe him to be, or the gentle priest he protests he is."

"Mayhap he's both," said Caleb.

Before I could respond, around us whispers rapidly transformed into cries.

"He comes! Campion comes!"

The mist began to disperse as the sun tried to bleed through the gray clouds overhead. The murmurs became a roar and the crowds formed a line on either side of the street. Tied to wicker hurdles—woven sledges that offered no comfort or protection—drawn by horses, the priest and his fellow conspirators appeared. Their feet were bound and elevated, close to the horses' rumps, while only interlocked straw lay between their heads and the cobbles. The city marshal, a group of armed constables and some dignitaries in their best attire accompanied them on foot and on horseback. Not once did they spare a glance for their prisoners, whose bodies were bounced along the uneven roads, their faces pale, bruised and swollen, their twisted and broken limbs evidence of what they had endured upon the rack.

I only knew which was Campion because some threw themselves onto their knees and offered prayers for his soul as he was dragged past. He was smaller than I imagined, thinner, and altogether unlike the monster my mind had created. He tried to turn his head and bestow a smile. A smile. His lips moved, but I couldn't hear what he was saying. There was a calmness about him and it had an effect upon those who saw him. The weeping eased; the praying grew less frenetic.

Falling in behind the horses, the crowd, now numbering in the hundreds, tramped purposefully. There was crying, some singing, prayers and jeers. Many chose not to speak, but to walk in what I could only describe as a respectful silence.

Caleb linked his arm in mine and I placed my hand over his forearm, grateful beyond measure that I wasn't alone. The sheer number of people, from all stations, was daunting. I'm not sure what I had anticipated, but it wasn't this.

We passed close to Newgate before exiting the city gates and heading toward St. Giles in the Field. Parklands of lush green filled with trees and flowering shrubs sheltered a small village replete with smoking chimneys, grazing cows and busy chickens. Residents poured out of their houses, adding their number to the throng. Children skipped beside the adults; some urchins tried to sell stolen scraps or demonstrate tricks for coin. Cuffed around the ears, pushed out of the way, they were not deterred from their efforts. Along Oxford Street, canny vendors set up carts selling refreshments and hot pies, as if this was a fair or a play. Caleb made me stop and we bought something to quench our growing thirst. I'd no appetite for food.

The sun parted the clouds, chasing the last tendrils of fog away and melting the frost on the edges of the road, which was becoming churned into mud by the traffic. The edges of my gown were filthy, my boots weighed by the soil clinging to their soles. Bells began to toll as we drew closer to Tyburn and the gallows, their music flat and hollow, a mournful dirge that echoed the growing dread in my heart. We shuffled into the open space, the horse-drawn hurdles and officials heading straight for the huge wooden structure in the center. Colloquially known as the Tyburn Tree, it could hang over a dozen at one time. The crowd from London joined those already gathered, pressing as close to the platform as they dared. Further back, carts led by donkeys, horses and oxen pulled over, entire families standing on top of them to gain a view. Noblemen on horseback were scattered among them, their features unreadable, their backs stiff. One or two faces were familiar, no doubt Sir Francis's men sent to report on proceedings. I prayed they wouldn't see me and pulled my hood further over my head.

Still more gathered to watch from the windows of the nearby buildings. I didn't want to examine these faces or any of those around me, to take note of what they looked like or what they wore; to see who among them might be traitors or priests. On this day, at this time, I no longer cared. I was not there as a watcher but as a witness. I wanted to be vindicated, but feared I would be condemned.

Sensing my growing ambivalence, Caleb placed an arm about me. "Are you sure about this?" he asked softly as we were jostled to make room for yet more spectators. A woman next to us openly worried her rosary beads, a short man next to her clutched a cross in his fist. I wanted to shut my eyes tight and unsee this evidence of popery. Whether it was because these people believed or whether it was an expression of support for the priests, I couldn't be certain.

"No, I'm not," I answered. "But I must remain."

Shouts from the front forced the crowd to shuffle back as officials tried to create space. The press of bodies, the smell of distress, fear and longing made it difficult to breathe. Caleb shoved a scented handkerchief into my hand. I put it to my nose and inhaled gratefully.

"How much longer?" I asked.

"I don't know. I think the Council would want this done swiftly." He stood on tiptoe and peered over the crowd. "I don't remember seeing so many here before." He lowered himself. "Though most be loyal to the Queen, there's a great deal of sympathy for Campion. He won many hearts with his eloquence, his protestations of innocence. They dare not draw this out. The mood could turn."

Untied from the hurdle and hauled roughly to his feet, Campion— along with the student-priest Ralph Sherwin and Alexander Briant, whose names had featured in reports that crossed my desk—were all but carried on trembling, stumbling legs up the stairs to the platform. Their gowns were torn and soiled, their faces streaked with dirt. While Campion was composed, his wide-eyed gaze uncannily serene, his companions had been crying.

A vicar came forward to offer prayers. Someone in the crowd booed and was quickly hushed. An official in a braided uniform ascended the gallows and, as the executioner placed a noose around each priest's neck and a leather hood over each head, he read from a long document. The crowd grew restless and much of what he said was lost. But we understood: these were the crimes for which these men would be punished. High treason. The worst of sins.

Whether it was because I hadn't eaten, or because of the mass of unwashed flesh around me or uneasiness about what I was about to see, my mind wandered, taking me back to where this part of my life began. I was no longer at Tyburn, but with Papa in the workshop, unpicking the dangerous *forziere* while, unbeknownst to me, Sir Francis watched from the shadows. Sir Francis knew so much about me,

about my family, and yet Papa had never mentioned him. If Mister
Secretary was spoken about, it was only in relation to his role on the
Queen's Council. Mamma never once said his name and for certes,
neither did Angela. But Papa and he were old friends, and he'd protected Uncle Timothy from the deadly wrath of the Catholics during
the St. Bartholomew's Day massacre in Paris. His acquaintance with
my family went back years. Yet I only knew of him in the remotest of
ways . . . Why? Now these men were going to die because of Papa's
old friend, a man who had the power of life and death. Who was Sir
Francis to us?

A mixture of groans and cheers flung me back into the present.
Caleb took my hand in his, squeezing tightly, his face pinched and
pale. Upon the gallows, the three priests hung, their legs twitching,
their shoulders rocking from side to side as they fought the inevitable
slow death they were being made to endure. Some in the crowd cried
and turned away. I could not. I forced myself to confront the grotesque
spectacle.

Below the platform, a large brazier was fed more wood, the flames
crackling loudly, the smoke rising to screen those upon the scaffold
before the wind spread it over the assembled people. Coughing, splut-
tering, even the guards on the gallows were overcome, waving their
hands before their faces, spitting into the crowd.

Before they lost consciousness, the priests were lowered until their
feet rested upon the platform. The hoods were ripped from their heads.
Dazed, their cheeks were purple and their eyes bulged, their mouths
opening and closing like fish on dry land. Inhaling deeply, they coughed
and gagged. One vomited upon his robes, earning a kick for his trouble.
I released the breath I didn't know I'd been holding.

The crowd surged; murmurs grew to shouts. Caught in the momen-
tum, against our will, Caleb and I were propelled forward.

Caleb's arm tightened about my shoulders. "Steel yourself, Mallory," he urged, trying to hold me upright.

Before I could ask why, a soldier stepped up and, drawing a long
dirk, cut Campion's robes apart, exposing his stomach and flaccid
cock. There was a flash, a spray of blood and a jubilant cheer, followed
by lifted arms, toothless smiles and war cries. The soldier raised his
hand from which Campion's mangled manhood dangled. The excite-

ment grew. Flinging back his arm, the executioner threw it on the fire. Then, like an actor onstage, pausing for dramatic effect, he swiped the blade across the man's stomach, his hand following the wound he made, reaching into Campion's very being and pulling out his innards. Staring in horror, unable to believe what I was seeing, gorge rose in my throat as a mass of bloodied intestines was extracted, slithering over the hangman's fingers like escaping eels. Campion arched his neck, shouting to God in heaven.

The priests on either side of him, seeing their friend's suffering, began wailing and struggling against their bonds, knowing they were next. One pissed himself, earning laughter and crude jokes from those below. The hangman held the strings of intestines aloft before casting them into the brazier. There was a cry; flames roared, sparks flew to the sky. The smell of cooked flesh tainted the air; a metal tang followed by the unmistakable odor of shit. I gagged, pressed the handkerchief to my mouth. Some women shielded their children's eyes; others stared agog.

Dear God. Dear God.

I began to pray that the suffering of all the priests would soon be over. *Pater noster, qui es in caelis: sanctificetur Nomen Tuum . . .*

Caleb joined me.

We weren't the only ones. Prayers were being chanted all around me—Pater Nosters, Ave Marias, the Symbolum Apostolorum. Cries of "martyr" were taken up before being howled down by those of "traitors" and "heretics." There was loud weeping, the rending of garments and tearing of hair. Some cackled and screamed in delight as another priest's cock was added to the flames, followed by his bloody innards. A fight broke out behind us.

I staggered as someone pushed past us, unable to watch any longer. I wanted nothing more than to follow—to run and never look back. But I owed these men my presence. I'd helped bring them to this point, to this gruesome, awful death.

Finally, Campion was lowered to the platform and I thought his ordeal complete. Surely, he was dead. But he was not. His head turned as it struck the wood and he stared with unseeing eyes out onto the crowd. Hands reached for him, some dousing themselves in the blood that flowed freely from his body. Others used knives and other instruments to cut pieces of his robe. Soldiers ran at these people with pikes and halberds, forcing them back. The government wanted nothing of Campion preserved, no relics for followers to gather around, over which a cult could grow.

Exchanging his knife for an ax, the executioner came forward again and, raising his weapon over his head, with a bloodthirsty cry began to hew Campion's body.

"Holy Mother and all the blessed saints," said Caleb, tears streaming down his cheeks.

I clung to him. "No. No."

Impossibly, Campion was still alive. His eyes were moving, his lips too, and yet the soldier hacked and hacked until the priest's shoulder and arm fell to the ground. The rain of blood and gore descended over the executioner and those below, and I heard the exultant cries of those wanting death and the desperate wailing of those who did not. The screaming and begging of the two remaining priests whose own lives were seeping away even as they watched Campion's end, his head lopped off, his body sawn into quarters, was too much.

Blindly, I turned and, pushing hard against those in my way, staggered through the crowd. I was crudely groped and shoved, my jacket torn, my purse taken. A whore, thinking I was interfering with a transaction, slapped me hard across the face. I paused only long enough to strike her back, feeling grim satisfaction when she fell. Behind me, Caleb whispered words of strength, of hope, mingled with prayers to God for the priests' immortal souls.

Before a cart filled with silent people, there was space. I dropped to my knees and retched. With one hand across my stomach, I leaned over and vomited the contents of my heart onto the barren ground. Caleb tumbled onto the ground beside me, crying openly, placing his arm around me, his cheek against my back.

How long we remained there, I don't know. We cared not who saw us or what they thought. Gradually, my heaving turned into deep, painful barks, as if I were clearing my soul.

Whatever I'd expected to see when I came to Tyburn, it was not what I'd just witnessed. I knew what hanging, drawing and quartering meant—why, I'd read vivid descriptions of terrible deaths in Foxe's *Book of Martyrs*—but that was very different to seeing it with my own eyes, smelling it, hearing it; dear God, tasting it. I wondered if the world would ever feel the same; for certes, I knew I would not.

Those cruel and bloody theatrics were the punishment I'd helped mete out. This was what my watching led to—the brutal evisceration of three priests. And this was what it would continue to lead to. Was I not in the business of catching those who planned treachery? Those who would convert us English to popery? I was. I retched again. Good God, I sickened myself.

I eased back onto my buttocks, pulling Caleb with me. He was a sorry sight. His ruff was flattened, his once gorgeous velvet doublet stained and torn. His bonnet must have fallen off in the crowd, exposing his dark hair, and his blue eyes swollen with tears. I touched my head. My bonnet was gone as well, my coif flung back. My hair was undone, tumbling over my shoulders and resting in the dirt. Running my hand down my cheek, there were raised lines that burned. I remembered the trull who'd lashed out. I examined my hand. There was blood beneath the nails. Hers. I felt no remorse.

"Are you all right?" asked Caleb as he sat in the dirt, uncaring that his beautiful garments were ruined. He wiped the back of his hand across his nose, looking more like Dickon than a leading actor and playwright.

I gave a dry laugh. "No. Are you?"

He shook his head and began to cry freely again through a smile he fought hard to maintain. I took him in my arms.

"I don't understand, Mallory," he murmured into my neck, his shoulders shaking. "I don't understand how we can be so . . . so . . . cruel, so barbaric to each other."

"I do," I whispered, and thought not only of the deaths I'd seen, but of Raffe Shelton as well. It was easy to be heartless when your peace was threatened, when you were genuinely frightened of what others could do to those you loved. Sir Francis had felt that way ever since Paris; Raffe had feared what I would do to his family. It was even easier to commit atrocities when they were enacted in the name of justice; when you believed you were working for the good of the realm, for the security of the sovereign and your people. It was easy when you didn't see the consequences and others performed the retribution for you. It was easy to be ruthless when you ceased to think of those convicted as human, and saw them as enemies. In that way, anything—any kind of action—could be justified.

Caleb and I were still locked in an embrace when the crowds started to move again. With a crack and creak, the cart in front of us began rolling along the road. We helped each other up and stood amid the milling folk—most heading back to London, others to wherever they'd come from. Some remained, determined to watch to the end; others still hoped to collect souvenirs. Sir Francis would have men ready to follow those who took anything away. The priests' body parts would be distributed to different parts of the country—their heads, no doubt, would be boiled before gracing the spikes atop London Bridge. A warning to all who would plot against Her Majesty and listen to Rome.

We began the long walk back. It was after noon. An icy wind came from the north, blowing away the stench of death and bringing heavy clouds with it. There'd be rain tonight, a cleansing shower to wash away the blood, but not the memories. I wondered how I would explain myself to Papa. He would assume I'd gone to Seething Lane. If I could just sneak back into the house and wash and change without anyone seeing me, my early morning departure might go unnoticed. But how could I ever hide the effect of what I'd seen? It was as if the images were burned into my eyes and their impact would show forever upon my face.

Just as we entered the city walls, a voice hailed us. Spinning around, I saw Lord Nathaniel approaching on horseback. From the expression on his face, he too had been at Tyburn. I don't know how I'd failed to notice him.

"Caleb—" he began, then he saw me. His dour expression changed to one of shock. Dismounting swiftly, he flung the reins of his horse to a young man and grabbed Caleb by the shoulder. "What were you thinking, man?" he shouted. "Allowing Mallory to attend such a grue-some display? Have you lost your wits?"

Caleb began to defend himself when I interrupted. "Please, my lord," I said. There'd been enough violence for one day. Even a raised voice set my teeth on edge. "Caleb didn't allow anything." I shot a look at Caleb, praying he'd keep mum. "He found me en route and tried to persuade me to abandon my intentions. I wouldn't listen."

Lord Nathaniel stared from me to Caleb and back again. Folk passed around us, angry we were blocking the way.

"Is this true?"

Caleb opened his mouth.

"You doubt my word?" I asked, anger flaring. I motioned to Caleb to remain silent.

Lord Nathaniel looked at me in disbelief, his eyes sweeping my filthy gown, my disheveled hair and missing bonnet.

"And yet you ignored his entreaties."

"God forgive me, I did."

He made a noise deep in his throat before taking hold of my chin and turning my face first one way, then the other. "You look as if you've been struck," he said. His fingers were gentle, his voice more so. I wanted to lay my cheek in his palm and take solace. Instead, I jerked my face away. I didn't deserve such solicitations.

"I was, though I gave better than I received."

Lord Nathaniel's eyes narrowed. "That I do not doubt." He glanced around at the milling crowd before locking eyes with me again. There was concern, a flicker of anger and something else. "Are you well, mistress?"

I took a deep breath. "I will be. The crowds were inflamed." I glanced at them now. "By what they have seen . . . The deaths . . . It was not what I expected."

He stared bleakly over the crowds. "Death does strange things to people, particularly gruesome ones. I'm not surprised the crowd is excitable." On cue, a roar erupted in one of the side streets and a fight spilled onto the main road between two men, clothes torn, hats missing, fists flying. A chant began as groups formed, urging them to hit harder, draw blood. Stepping between me and the press of people, Lord Nathaniel unsheathed his sword, clearing a space swiftly.

"I will see you safely home. Come," he said and, before I could protest, he passed his sword to Caleb and placed his hands about my waist, hoisting me into the saddle as if I were a child. He kept hold until I found my balance. Arranging my hands on the pommel, he pulled my skirts over the withers and took the reins.

"Her name is Bounty," he said, patting the horse's neck.

Walking his horse, he fell in beside Caleb, retrieving his sword and holding it before him as a warning to any who would venture near. No one dared. His squire, to whom I wasn't introduced, protected our backs.

Bounty was a midnight mare, with a long mane and glossy coat. Caparisoned in the Warham colors of burgundy, black and silver, the horse looked magnificent. I could have been a lady atop her had I not looked like a strumpet with my hair loose, my gown torn and my face marked. I drew stares, and not for good reasons.

In a daze, I allowed myself to be led, grateful my aching feet were being spared, wishing my heart could be so relieved.

Caleb said something to Lord Nathaniel, who looked over his shoulder.

"It will upset your father considerably to see the state you're in, mistress. Should he learn of where you've been," he said.

Surprised he would consider my father's feelings, I was also touched. "I would spare him that if I could, my lord."

Lord Nathaniel slowed until the horse drew level, then reached up and placed his hand over mine where it clutched the pommel. "I would have spared you as well," he said softly, before letting go.

Tingling beset my limbs, as if a thousand tiny bird feathers stroked my flesh. I found myself staring at the back of Lord Nathaniel's head, noting how he towered over Caleb and any who passed. Women paused to watch him, while he, oblivious, or perchance accustomed to the stares, took it all in his considerable stride.

Expecting censure from this man who didn't hesitate to speak his mind, I was surprised by his uncharacteristic gentleness. I expected him to give me a tongue-lashing for my stubborn-hearted defiance. I wondered what had changed in him. Why had he been at the execution? What brought Lord Nathaniel, a peer of the realm who, as far as I knew, held no particular position at court or upon the Council—at least not yet—to witness the death of the priests? Was it secular or religious duty? A mixture of both? Or something else entirely?

The man I believed a rugged and discourteous boor was proving to be more mysterious—and, I had to admit, interesting and compassionate—than I ever would have imagined. Aside from what Papa had told me, a tale that twisted my heart and made me rethink my assumptions, he was demonstrably thoughtful and kind. And not just to me,

I noted, as he scooped up a small puppy that had escaped its owner's arms. The little boy came running over and took the dog gratefully, the child's mother bobbing a curtsey and bestowing a lovely smile upon his lordship. He doffed his bonnet and bowed in return and she giggled in delight. Fire burned in my throat and I wondered where that came from. Was I jealous? Over his lordship? The man I once did everything in my power to avoid? Surely not.

Nonetheless, as I rode the remaining distance home, I was grateful his lordship's presence had given me something other than death to think about. All the same, images of Tyburn bubbled away, threatening to breach the wall I was trying to build against them.

"Nonchalance," I whispered. "Nonchalance." But it was difficult to summon even the appearance of indifference after what I'd witnessed. I doubted it was even appropriate. Some matters deserved anything but nonchalance.

THIRTY-FOUR

HARP LANE AND
SEETHING LANE, LONDON
The 1st of December, Anno Domini 1581
In the 24th year of the reign of Elizabeth I

At my insistence and much to his chagrin, Lord Nathaniel left us outside St. Dunstan's in the East so we might make our own way home. He objected strongly, but when I explained I wished to enter the house without being observed so I might both change and compose myself and spare Papa or Mamma worry—something his presence would trigger—he relented.

"What you saw today, Mallory—" he began, reaching toward me, a look of great concern upon his face.

He addressed me informally. I didn't correct him.

"The bloody executions, the behavior of the crowds—" he said. "No lady should bear witness to that and you will suffer for it. I would Caleb had not listened and taken you straight home. I know, I know." He raised his hands as if to fend off words I'd not yet uttered. "He'd no choice." He gave a small smile to remove any rebuke from his words. "You're an obstinate woman, for certes."

His tone was conciliatory, but his expression contradicted it.

"Nothing can touch the souls of those men now. Traitors or misled

Catholics, they are before the Great Judge whom we all face. Before Him they will find justice, whether or not one believes they received it this day."

My throat grew tight. His words were both reassuring and, because they dared to offer even a modicum of comfort, perilous. Yet he was only articulating what many would be thinking.

"Thank you, my lord. Your words offer some consolation where I thought none could be found."

He stepped toward me and for one wild moment, I thought he would kiss me. God's teeth, I wanted him to. I moved toward him then paused, barely stopping myself. Color filled my cheeks.

"See her safe, won't you, Caleb?"

"Aye, my lord," said Caleb, and meant it.

As soon as his lordship had disappeared up the street and into the crowds outside the church of St. Andrew Hubbard, Caleb turned to me. "You have won yourself a heart, methinks."

I stared at Caleb's twinkling eyes, the smile he tried and failed to repress. "I know what you're thinking, you varmint, so cease immediately. Lord Nathaniel expressed only what any gentleman would."

"Oh, so he's a gentleman now, is he? A far cry from how you once described him."

I stared in the direction Lord Nathaniel had gone, but there were too many people, too many horses, to see him. "It is, isn't it?" I murmured.

We turned and walked back to Harp Lane, choosing the back alleys so we didn't pass the workshop on Tower Street. We didn't speak again until we reached the gate.

"Thank you for being with me," I began. "You're a good friend. I . . . I . . . am so sorry you were. It was . . ." My voice petered out. There were no words.

"I could not permit you to suffer such a sight alone."

I lowered my head, then quickly raised it again. "Please, Caleb, don't mention what I did to my parents," I said, pausing outside the gate, trying to fix my hair, my coif, gazing in despair at the state of my skirts.

"What sort of lackwit do you take me for?" He regarded me strangely, then shook his head. "Your will is my command, lady," he said with forced gaiety. "If I had my way, I would never speak of it again, but I fear we must." He glanced down the street. Folk strolled about the cobbles, bargaining with fruiterers, drinking a pint outside the alehouse, stamping their feet to keep warm, chasing a dog or errant child, their conversation plumes of white that lingered briefly in the air. Oblivious to what had happened miles away, to the manner in which the three priests had died, their lives continued.

"All who stood there in that bloody square must speak of such violence, such desecration of the spirit. It's our duty whether we be reformers, Puritans or Catholics."

I threw my arms around Caleb and drew him close, just as the bells began to toll. Waiting until the last echoes died, I whispered, "If you must talk of it, then be careful how and to whom you do. It's not safe."

Caleb pushed me away and tipped his head to one side, his expression cautious. "You're assuming I would take the part of Campion and his peers in Christ, decry their fate?"

I didn't answer straightaway. I took in Caleb's wild eyes and pale cheeks. His perturbation was great, a sure sign he would seek the solace of his quill as soon as possible. I only hoped what he wrote would not see him meet the same end as those at Tyburn.

"I do. Am I wrong?"

"Aye and no. You're not. I would decry the fate of any who met such an end. I will write of what I saw, put words in my characters' mouths, ensure in the worlds I create least such . . . such barbarity doesn't happen again. I would argue for tolerance, that we embrace the Queen's dictum and not make windows into men's souls. Seems to me, whatever we do, wherever we look these days, we see traitors. I don't believe that's always the case, and would share this view. I know there are others who feel the same." He paused and I wondered, as he took my hands in his, if Lord Nathaniel came into his mind too. "I'm safe when I reveal my intentions to you, aren't I, Mallory?"

I thought of the way his plays were oft-times critical of the Queen and our faith, and of Catholics, too. Then I considered the locked chest in his room and wondered what was within it. I loathed myself for it. That was the way Samantha Short would think. When it came to Caleb, I was first and foremost his friend, his confidant. To be otherwise was to doom myself to a life of solitude and suspicion, of more of what we witnessed today.

He flicked my arm gently. "You're taking far too long to respond."

"Oh, Caleb, forgive me. You're safe with me. Always."

"There was a time, I never doubted. Only . . ."

"What?"

"You've changed, Mallory."

I moved to open the gate. "Have I? In what way?"

Now it was Caleb's turn to hesitate. "You're not the woman you once were."

"What was I?"

"Malleable."

With a kiss on my cheek, he pushed past me and entered the yard, holding the gate so I might follow. We snuck into the house as quietly as we could—the noises of the kitchen were loud—and moved swiftly into the hall. I daren't leave my grubby cloak or gloves in the entrance. The bottom stair creaked as I stepped upon it. Wincing, I shrugged an apology to Caleb, who'd ascended to the landing without making a sound. Why, he was lighter on his feet than Latch.

Comfort chose that moment to come out of the parlor, a tray balanced against her hip. As none of the candles had been lit, the hall was quite dim, and she failed to see the state of our clothes or the looks of dread upon our faces as she happened upon our intrusion.

"Well, well, where have the two of you been, pussyfooting around the house in such a manner? I thought you at work, mistress, and you the theater, Master Caleb. I was wrong in those assumptions, wasn't I?"

"Ah, not so much," said Caleb brightly. "For certes, I saw some macabre theater today."

I glared at him before we both muttered about change of plans. Comfort's eyes narrowed. Perchance there was something in our tone or awkward manner, but when we requested food and drink brought to our rooms, instead of insisting we fetch it ourselves, Comfort agreed.

Stepping closer, squinting to see me better in the shadows, she raised a hand toward my face. "Are you hurt, mistress?"

Dear God. Hurt, hollow, scraped from the inside and filled with a great dark emptiness. I caught her hand before she could touch me, folding my fingers around her hand.

"I'm but tired, Comfort. Weary of the world and seeking the privacy of my chamber." Upon seeing her expression, I added, "I fear I have a megrim coming; I've pleaded ill and come home." Not such a great lie. I was heartsore and sickened.

"Ah," she said. I'd given her something she could deal with. "I'll bring a posset and something for that mark on your face, too," she said, and then tried to see Caleb, who'd taken the opportunity to make his way further up the stairs. "Would you like some extra feathers, Master Caleb?"

"Not today, Comfort. Today I will read rather than write. Replenish the well of my imaginings. Adieu, sweet ladies," he said, and practically bolted up the stairs.

With a small smile for Comfort, I followed.

Voices drifted from Mamma's room. Angela and Widow Dorothy. They were heated, shrill. In no mood for an interrogation, afraid Angela might choose that moment to open the door and catch me, I moved swiftly past.

My room was still warm, the embers of last night glowing in the fireplace. Taking off my clothes, I brushed the worst of the dirt from the hem of my cloak and my skirts, hanging them out the window as I did so the evidence would not collect on the floor. I combed out my hair and tended the fire, happy only when it was crackling fiercely and throwing light and warmth into every corner. Staring into its depths, images from Tyburn arose and I saw naught but the brazier and the foul fuel fed to the flames, the executioner's arms streaked with blood. I shuddered. No heat would melt the frost accumulating in my soul.

Hot water was brought, a fresh soap and drying sheet, and a fine repast of warm pottage, cold chicken, soft cheese and manchet. Comfort even delivered a ewer of claret. Hovering in the hope I might explain my unkempt appearance, if not my state of mind, she soon gave up and waited only until I'd taken the posset. With a loud harrumph at my thanks, she left me alone.

I picked at the food, poured myself some wine and then washed, gently at first, but I soon began rubbing so vigorously that the flesh turned red and my arms burned.

With a cry of frustration, I threw the cloth into the bowl, dirty water splashing and striking the fire, the hiss reminding me of the morning. Dear God in heaven, nothing would ever be the same again.

That was not true. I sank onto the floor, my head in my hands. Lord Nathaniel was right. It would just take time.

Pushing my hair back, I sat up. Did I regret going to Tyburn? Regret was not the right word. I regretted running away with Raffe, but witnessing the priests' deaths? It was the manner of their deaths I regretted and wished I could change, not that they had died or that I beheld their final moments. I owed it to my work for Sir Francis, to my own conception of justice, to see where our watching and listening, all our detailed reports, led.

I'd seen death before, many times. Mamma's wee babes, precious little scraps of bloody flesh that never breathed. When Goody Kat next door died, I helped prepare her body. Oft-times the poor passed where they slept, propped against a house or church only to be found once their skin was cold, their eyes opaque, the following morning. The streets were littered with dead animals: cats, dogs, butcher's refuse, rats, their corpses pecked by hungry birds. Then there were the plague carts rumbling through the lanes, the white-blue limbs of the dead jutting from beneath the cloths thrown over their indignity. Aye, death haunted the city and our lives the way mist did the winter morns.

Then there was the death I tried not to think about . . . the one for which I'd yet to pay penance.

I sought my locket.

How long I sat, the memories crowding my head as the shadows lengthened in my chamber, I knew not. It was a cock's startled screech that brought me back to the present. The afternoon was growing dark, and fingers of dusk slowly claimed the room. I tried to read Ovid's poems, but my head was unable to contain their optimism after the doom of the morning. As I replaced the book on the table, Papa's voice carried across the yard, ordering something from the kitchen. Comfort replied and shortly there was the sound of boots on the path and pounding on the workshop door. The cow bellowed, a cat mewled, and the bells chimed across the city once again.

I didn't remember feeling so tired, so drained. Certain sleep would claim me, I instead lay awake, unable to cancel images of blood, the cheers of the spectators and cries of utter horror. The screams of pain and terror of the priests played over and over. Madness ruled for those hours, a devil-induced lunacy that had no place on earth.

I remembered when Master Fodrake and I read *The Iliad*. How Achilles slew Prince Hector and then, in an act of wanton cruelty, sliced his victim's ankles and ripped out his tendons and used them to tie him to the back of a chariot before dragging him around and around the walls of Troy so Hector's family might see his contempt for his enemy's corpse—and how much disregard he had for them. But the gods saw it too, and Achilles was punished for his lack of respect for the dead, who belonged to Hades. Achilles paid the ultimate price.

Would the men responsible for what happened today also be punished? Would I? The thought made me tremble. Yet it was no more than I deserved. Had I not caused their deaths as well? Helped unlock their secrets and expose them to the world? Instead of keys and metal, I'd used disguises and falsehoods.

I lay on my back, my hands behind my head, staring at the ceiling and the patterns the flames made upon the plaster. They undulated and twisted, much like the men on the scaffold.

Sir Francis knew what awaited Campion and the others. He'd endorsed it. The same punishment awaited all Catholic traitors. If this was so right and godly, if these priests deserved their fates, why then had Sir Francis seen fit to interfere, to guarantee the outcome by adding Campion's name to Sledd's list? If his rationale was that they were doomed the moment they stepped on our shores and defied our laws, then why add Campion's name to Sledd's dossier? Such an action undermined his staunch principles. It also undermined mine.

Though I didn't feel close to God this day, I prayed to Him for the strength to discuss this with Sir Francis. I also prayed for the souls of the three men who had died, and for Mister Secretary and his misplaced ideals. I prayed for Caleb, that whatever it was he was doing with that chest was not against Queen and country—I could not bear it if he were to meet the same kind of fate as Campion—and I prayed for Mamma, that she would see sense and give up the old faith. I prayed for Papa, that his eyesight would improve. I also prayed that, despite what I'd done and the many sins I'd committed, the lies I'd told, Papa would find it in his heart not only to forgive me, but to love me as well.

I prayed and prayed, yet it seemed my pleas went unheard. Screwing my eyes tight to try harder, it was only when a sob escaped that I felt the tears cascading down my cheeks and onto my pillow.

I don't know how long I cried, only that at some point sleep claimed me. My dreams were filled with wailing, overlayed with images of dismembered bodies, people at prayer, Agnus Dei; Mamma in her bed, clutching her rosary beads; Caleb weeping. Sir Francis's swarthy face appeared, calmly justifying his actions, extracting promise after promise from me; as I made them, I knew they would be broken. Even Raffe loomed, leering and larger than life, admonishing Papa, striking him with a whip, and tearing me away from him. Scarlet-stained sheets, lacerating pain, screams that rent my body and flesh, all merged.

The only respite from my nightmare was a solitary image of Lord Nathaniel, his huge hands around my waist as he lifted me onto his horse, a look of disquiet filling his golden eyes—and, truth be told, my heart.

PART FIVE

Who Looks to Us Women?

[The trial of Edmund Campion and fellow priests in the
Tower of London is] the most pitiful practice that ever
was heard of to shed innocent blood by the face of justice.

—Father William Allen, 1581

Indeed, I do not deny that men have arrogated to themselves
a certain liberty; and this because they know that, according to
universal opinion, a loose life does not defame them as it does
women, who, due to the fragility of their sex, give in to their
appetites much more than men and if they sometimes refrain
from satisfying their desires, they do so out of shame and not
because they lack a ready will in that regard.

—Baldassare Castiglione, *The Book of the Courtier:
The Third Book*, 1528

But whenever you pray, go into your room and shut the door and
pray to your Father who is in secret. And your Father who
sees in secret will reward you.

—Matthew 6:6

THIRTY-FIVE

*W*hen I arrived at Seething Lane the following day, Sir Francis was at Whitehall, as I'd half anticipated. Determined to wait for his return no matter the hour, I sat in my room trying to attend to my tasks as if this were simply another day and not a reckoning.

Overnight, I made the decision that if I was to continue to work for Sir Francis, I had to know the nature of his relationship with Papa, their shared history and why it was kept secret. Perchance in learning this, I could reconcile myself to what Sir Francis had done.

Restless, tired and disconsolate, desiring answers yet doubting how satisfying they would be and fearing the choices I may have to make, I decoded and ciphered the correspondence before me. Again there were letters requesting money from Sir Francis's spies in Paris, Northamptonshire and even Scotland, all of them requiring replies. There were two more intercepted from the Spanish embassy discussing the arrest of Campion and his sentencing. There were a number in French dealing with the impending collapse of the marriage negotiations between the Queen and the Duke of Anjou, one blaming Sir Francis outright, another pleading with the French court not to give up hope. There was even a ciphered report from an agent based in the Escorial that mentioned how King Philip had asked the Pope for a huge sum of money to fund the building of a fleet to attack England. I moved this letter to the top of my pile.

With every cipher I formed, every word I wrote, I couldn't help but consider how what I did would affect others. No longer was ferreting out secrets a game in which I was a master player. It had become a matter of life and death—potentially, a brutal and agonizing one.

With every passing hour my agitation grew, as did my determination to speak to Sir Francis. To gain from him . . . what exactly? Reassurances that what we did was right? That the priests deserved the manner of their deaths? That we weren't simply executioners, slaying people with quills instead of swords? That we were delivering God's justice?

Long after sunset, when the watchmen had begun roaming the streets, their faint cries reminding folk to seek hearth and home, Thomas came to my door. Concentrating on my papers, I didn't notice him at first.

"So, you determined to wait." He leaned against the doorframe, his arms folded. His hair was in disarray and through the dirty lenses of his spectacles I could see the dark shadows ringing his eyes.

"I told you," I said, my voice sharper than I intended. "I must speak with Sir Francis."

"I'm here to inform you he also wishes to speak with you. He's in his office and awaits your pleasure."

With a calmness I didn't feel, I replaced the quill in its holder, stood and smoothed my skirts. "Thank you, Thomas."

"Are you well?" he asked, gesturing for me to precede him down the narrow hall. Sounds of activity in other parts of the house carried. "You seem . . . different."

The second person to tell me that in almost a day. "Do I?"

"You're not as . . . contained as you usually appear. As if something's happened and upset your equilibrium."

I shot him a look he didn't return and chose not to respond. I suspected then he knew I'd attended the executions, a suspicion that was about to be confirmed.

We entered the main room. It was empty of Sir Francis's other employees; a couple of candles burned by Thomas's desk, the hearth crackled. Paper covered every surface, and the cabinets and boxes lining the walls also overflowed.

Thomas paused by his desk. "I think you know the way," he said.

Sir Francis's door was slightly ajar and as I approached I could see him through the gap. Unaware he was being observed, he sat behind his desk, a grimace of pain crossing his face as he reached for the cup beside him. He took a long drink and then refilled it. When he wasn't controlling his features, they wore a permanently worried cast, as if bad news was imminent. His frown was profound, the lines from his nose to the corners of his mouth deep grooves. Resting his head in his hands briefly, he sat back and rubbed his eyes.

I knocked gently.

His head shot up. "Mallory, come in."

I shut the door behind me, and bobbed a small curtsey.

"Ah," said Sir Francis, studying me as I took a seat. "It's true, then."

"Sir?"

"You attended the executions after I extracted a promise that you would not."

I met his gaze. "I did. I felt I had to, considering . . ." I let what was unsaid hang in the air.

"You mean the correction to Sledd's dossier?"

"Correction?"

His eyes flickered.

"Forgive my presumption, sir, but I would have thought 'addition' more apt."

He rose and stared at me before exhaling a long sigh.

"Why did you go to Tyburn?"

"I . . . I . . . I went because I felt that as one of your agents, someone who helped bring Campion to justice, I should."

"As one of my agents, your first duty is to *me*." He struck the desk hard with his knuckles. I jumped. "Your first obedience is to *me*. Yet you flagrantly disobeyed my order and broke your promise."

I lowered my head. "I did break it. But"—I said, raising my chin, fire in my belly—"I had to know. I had to understand why you altered the dossier, what punishment you guaranteed the priests by doing so."

"And?"

I tried to speak, but the words would not come. My lower lip began to tremble. "And so I went and saw them meet their . . . their ends. I saw them hanged," I swallowed. "Drawn and then quartered." I shut my eyes as if to cancel the memories. "I hope never to see such a sight again."

With a gruff noise, Sir Francis resumed his seat. "This is why I expressly forbade you. It was not a sight I'd wish on anyone, least of all you."

I found it hard to look at him. "I do not understand why Campion had to die like that."

"As a lesson to those who would walk in his steps. If such a death is not a deterrent, then what is?"

There was no arguing with that.

"You were not there," I said after a while, accusing him.

"No. I was not. I was with Her Majesty and, afterward, Lord Nathaniel." At the mention of Lord Nathaniel, I started. "It was his lordship who revealed your presence at Tyburn."

"Lord Nathaniel?"

"Aye. He was most displeased and saw fit to rebuke me that I would allow someone in my employ to witness such . . . such an event." He ran his fingers over some papers. "He said I needed to take better care of my servants, of my women." Offense radiated from Sir Francis. "My Lord Nathaniel was most direct on the subject."

I could only begin to imagine.

"What did you say?"

"What could I say? I remained mute. In principle, his lordship was right. What he didn't know was I saw no reason to doubt you. I believed you when you said you wouldn't go. I do not take many at their word."

I studied my hands.

"Mallory," he said softly. "Your promise is your bond to me. If you break it so easily, how can I trust you?"

I stared at him. "If you alter documents, how can I trust you or what you ask me to do?"

Sir Francis frowned. "Remember whom you're speaking to, child."

"Forgive me, Mister Secretary," I said quickly, lowering my head in a form of obeisance. My throat was dry.

Sir Francis snorted.

"Do you laugh at me, sir?" I grew hot.

"Aye and no," he said. "Truth be told, were you a man, I'd congratulate you and ask you to report what you heard and saw."

"Why do you not? Am I not your agent?"

"Aye . . . But you are—"

"A woman." I turned my head aside. I'd thought that, as a woman, I had qualities Sir Francis found useful and rare. Now he was just like other men, dismissing me.

"I hadn't finished," said Sir Francis quietly. I faced him again. "I was not going to say 'woman,' I was going to say I would not ask that of . . . someone like you."

The air grew close. I found it hard to breathe. The way he looked at me . . . He stood and walked around the desk until there were only inches between us. Leaning against the desk, he placed a finger under my chin, lifted it, and stared deep into my eyes.

Part of me wanted to run from the room and never come back; another part dared not move.

"What do you mean, like me?" I whispered.

He hesitated. "I mean . . ." he began, then he released me. "It matters not." Heaving himself off the desk, he went to the fire, picked up the poker and prodded the embers.

I released the breath I'd been holding. *It matters not?* What did that mean? The man was under no obligation to me . . . But what about my parents? What did he owe them that he cared about my well-being? Cared whether I witnessed the deaths at Tyburn? Why had Papa sought his help? Why had he never mentioned this man?

"Sir Francis," I began. "May I ask you something?"

"It depends," he said slowly.

"On what?"

"On whether or not I want to answer." He turned around, the poker in his hand like a weapon. Seeing my eyes widen, he rested it against the fireplace. "What do you wish to ask?"

"I . . . I want to know how it is that until that night I met you in the workshop, Papa and Mamma had never made mention of you . . . Why you never visited us despite being an old friend of Papa's."

His eyes took on a distant look, as if he were taking an inventory of the past and choosing which sections to share with me. He picked up his cup and swilled the contents a few times. His lips moved, the words so soft I barely caught them.

"Perchance it's time the truth was out." He raised his head and looked at me hard, as if seeing me for the first time. "You want the truth of my friendship with your papa?" There was a challenge in his voice.

"I would."

"Even if it means learning it was built on the greatest of lies?"

I inhaled sharply. What had I begun? I stared at him. I teetered over an abyss. If I took one more step, I would tumble into the void and there'd be no turning back.

"Even so . . ." I said faintly.

With a sigh that came from the very depths of his being, Sir Francis put down his cup and, much to my astonishment, dropped on one knee before me, like a nobleman paying court to his lady. He took my hands in his own warm ones, stroking my fingers, rubbing my palms with his thumbs. The actions were so unexpected, so out of character, I didn't know what to say. I stared at the cap perched on the back of his head, my breath coming quickly. The scent of cloves, lavender and a flat muskiness reached me. I wanted to pull my hands away, lift my skirts and run from the room, yet I did not dare.

Just when I thought he would not speak, he lifted his chin. He was such a serious person, with his swarthy skin and dark gray eyes that saw everything. A man who never stopped thinking; who knew his mind and the minds of others, oft before they did. A man who'd risen from nowhere to become one of the most feared and powerful people in the country.

"Your father and I were once the best of friends," he began. "So much so, when I left England during Bloody Mary's reign, I followed him to Italy."

So, their acquaintance spanned years . . .

"By the time I arrived, it was to discover that your father . . ." He chuckled. "Well, let's just say he'd met a fiery, beautiful Italian—a locksmith's daughter no less." His fingers tightened on my hand. "Valentina."

I rarely thought about Mamma being a locksmith's daughter as well. It was something she never wanted for me. The thought made me sad. She wanted no resemblance between us.

"Valentina had a sister."

"Lucia," I said.

"Aye, Lucia." Her name was a sigh upon his lips. "Lucia Zucchero— the sweetest of lights." He was no longer in the room, but back in Padua. "Upon meeting her, I fell in love."

I could not have been more startled had Sir Francis broken into song. "With my aunt?"

"I did."

"Papa never said. Never. Mamma neither."

He lowered his head and raised it again. "I loved her with all my heart. My love; my light." A look of sadness crossed his face; he dropped my hands and stood.

I wanted to offer solace, but was uncertain how. "Aunt Lucia . . . she died . . ." I gulped. "In childbirth."

"Aye. She did." He took a deep breath. "With my child."

Oh dear Lord. I had to resist the urge to throw my arms about him, comfort him. It would not be seemly. I knotted my fingers together in my lap.

I glanced at the picture of his daughter Mary on his desk. She had been eight years old when she died. Sir Francis had lost not only Lucia, his love, and the baby they'd conceived together, but his first wife, two stepsons and Mary as well. Why, grief had visited this poor man over and over.

Had Lucia lived, he would have been my uncle. Uncle Francis. A wild laugh began to build and I struggled hard to contain it. No wonder he cared what happened to me; no wonder Papa sought his help. They'd once been so close, loved sisters, been through so much pain and loss. Bonds would have been made, bonds that time would test but never break. Ensuring his daughter was not lost to him as well, Papa had sought Sir Francis's help and confided in him, his old friend.

But how was this a great lie that undid the truth? For certes, he loved, had a babe out of wedlock, but had he not paid for that sin in the most terrible of ways? Had not my aunt? Did Mamma and Papa blame him for Lucia's death and no longer want him in their lives? Had they expunged him completely until Papa felt he had no choice?

I waited for him to continue, but he didn't. His breathing, which had become ragged, steadied, as did my own. The fire spat and the two candles on the desk guttered.

"Thank you for trusting me with this, Sir Francis," I said softly. "I am so, so sorry. I will pray for you and my aunt and your child." He didn't move. Uncomfortable now, I searched for something to say. "I can assure you, your secret is safe."

He raised his head just as my eyes alighted on the miniature of Mary on his desk.

Following the direction of my gaze, Sir Francis reached for the tiny portrait and closed his fingers around it. "Pray? For me and Lucia? Aye, you do that, Mallory. I thank you for that. As for our child, pray for her too. But you have nothing to be sorry about." He gave a bark of despair. His tone became odd, harsh. "You see, despite what you were told, Lucia's child lived."

"Lived?" What was this?

I could no longer hear what Sir Francis was saying. A clamor began in my head, growing louder and louder. I drove my fingers into my temples, trying to ease the noise, prevent the intrusion of the inexplicable notion that battered the edge of my mind.

His eyes fastened upon me. "Think, Mallory, think." His words penetrated the cacophony in my skull. "Remember your training. Watch, listen, report."

I frowned, trying to recall everything I'd been told about Lucia, the babe, about our life in Italy. "Mamma and Papa said the little girl died with her Mamma. That was the reason they came to England—Queen Mary was dead and Mamma could not bear the sadness of having lost her little sister and her niece. She wanted a new beginning, even if it meant abandoning her home and faith."

Not that she'd kept that part of her promise . . .

"And . . . ?" urged Sir Francis. "What else? Remember, I said the child survived . . ."

I thought of all the times Mamma would exclaim that what I did with locks wasn't natural, *"Nothing about her is."* How she would call me *his* daughter, never her own. The distance she maintained between us, that Papa said existed only in my imagination, until the breach was so great not even he or Angela could deny it. How keen Mamma was to have me married and out from under her roof . . .

I thought of Papa asking Sir Francis for help in finding me employment. *You must, Francis,* he'd said. *If not you, then who? I've nowhere else to turn, no one else to whom I trust her welfare. Only you.* I'd been horrified he'd confided my secret, the truth of my behavior and loss of face to this man. The stranger he addressed as an old friend.

Then I remembered the boat ride to Deptford and how Master Francis Mylles's wife had carelessly remarked on the resemblance between myself and Frances Walsingham, assuming we were sisters . . . Sisters . . .

Oh dear sweet Jesus.

My eyes flew to the picture in Sir Francis's palm. His fingers had opened and I saw a pair of large eyes, dark hair and sallow skin.

The room grew suddenly smaller. My fingers clutched at my throat. No. No. It couldn't be. It wasn't possible . . . Memories rushed into my head, a dissonance of sounds and images. All the while Sir Francis stared at me as if he would steal my thoughts.

I gazed back into those dark orbs, looked more closely at the long nose, the swarthy skin and silver-streaked dark hair and saw only a mirror that, after all these years, reflected the truth back to me. A truth as implausible as it was extraordinary.

He replaced the painting on the desk, turned to face me and waited.

"It can't be . . ." I said. "How is it possible? Papa—?"

"Is not your father." Sour little words that held a lifetime within them. "I am."

It was as if a huge wall of water slammed into me, sucking me down into the depths of an ocean, rolling me about in its wake. I could not find my feet, I could not see the surface. I rose to leave and staggered but Sir Francis Walsingham, Mister Secretary, Queen Elizabeth's spymaster, caught me and with a slow deliberation I no longer wanted to resist, pulled me into his embrace.

"You're my daughter, Mallory Bright."

THIRTY-SIX

*T*he roaring in my ears, the spinning in my head as my world tipped upon its axis before righting itself again gradually diminished. I became aware of the press of velvet against my cheek, the beating of Sir Francis's heart, as rapid as my own. His long arms felt strange around me. His fingers splayed against one shoulder and he held the back of my head. I wasn't sure how to extricate myself without causing offense, but I needed more answers.

Sensing my discomfort, Sir Francis withdrew and, with a fleeting smile, poured me a drink. His hand trembled slightly as he passed it over.

"Here," he said, and then busied himself lighting more candles and tossing more wood on the fire. I watched him, sipping the claret gratefully. The warmth of the wine spread through my body but failed to soothe my mind, which was galloping like a horse on the green.

Sir Francis topped up his cup and mine before easing himself back into his chair.

"So, what do you want to know, my daughter?" he asked, his eyes crinkling. He appeared more at ease now, certainly more relaxed than I felt.

He called me daughter. It was a foreign word to come from his tongue. And yet . . . this man, Mister Secretary Walsingham, was my father.

Dear God.

"Everything." I sat back and tried to pretend my shoulders weren't tight, my neck held in a vise. I affected nonchalance—what else could I do?—and did it in such a way I would have made a courtier envious.

"Very well," he said. "But not before I send Thomas with a note to your . . . to Gideon, explaining I'm keeping you late and will see you home safe."

Home . . . Verily, I no longer knew what that meant . . . Grateful for his consideration and the precious time it allowed us, it was a few minutes before we were alone again. Then Sir Francis sat forward.

"Very well," he said. "I will tell you everything."

Words poured from his mouth, words that told a story. His story. My story. Not the one I'd been raised with, which I had repeated as one does a favorite tale, each retelling cementing the details further. What I had been told was but a fanciful account woven over the years, repaired occasionally when it frayed, but false. Even so, I loved it in the way the familiar is loved and the unknown feared. Listening to Sir Francis, I was forced to staunch the terror stalking me and to be brave enough to plant this new identity and allow it to take root. He began in the years before my birth . . . in Italy.

In 1553, along with many other Protestant exiles from Queen Mary's England, Sir Francis left his homeland for the safety of Italy and enrolled at the University of Padua. He joined his friends from Cambridge, the brothers Gideon and Timothy Bright, who were also students there. By the time Sir Francis arrived, Gideon had already met and planned to marry Valentina Zucchero, the gorgeous daughter of the locksmith, after he finished his degree. When he was introduced to Valentina's sister, Lucia, for the first time in his life Sir Francis fell in love.

"Where your mother was all fire and brimstone, Lucia was moon-light, stars and quicksilver." I was unclear whether it was his poetry or the look on his face that made me both uncomfortable and strangely excited.

Cognizant—as were all the English exiles—that changes were on the horizon at home, Sir Francis courted Lucia cautiously, torn between his love for this Catholic Italian woman and his own beliefs. For a brief time, England and its religious upheavals seemed far away, foreign even . . .

When news reached the exiles that Queen Mary was ill and the child she had thought she was carrying was but a phantom, there was jubilation. This could mean that her half sister, the Princess Eliza-beth, would succeed to the throne. If she did, the promise of England becoming a Protestant country became a reality once more. Duty was everything to Sir Francis and, knowing he would have to return to England but wanting to bring his lover with him, he asked Lucia to marry him. She agreed but, in order to placate her parents, who were ambivalent about losing both their daughters to Englishmen and Prot-estants, Lucia would only leave her homeland once he was established in England, once he'd found not only his place in the new regime, but a home for them as well. Summoned to England urgently upon Queen Mary's death by Sir William Cecil, Elizabeth's Secretary, Sir Francis was promised the seat of Bossiney and much more besides. "England needs you," Cecil wrote.

Sir Francis left Italy, intending to return as soon as possible, wed his love and bring her back to England with him. When he returned, months later, it was to the tragic news that Lucia had died. She had died giving birth. She'd kept the knowledge she was carrying his child a secret—not only from Sir Francis, but from her family as well. When Valentina discovered the truth, her sister made her swear not to tell a soul. Lucia hadn't wanted to alter her love's intentions; she believed them to be honorable. She believed him to be an ethical man who would keep his promises to her.

Sir Francis was grief-stricken; he was also riddled with guilt, for he'd returned to Italy under false pretenses. It wasn't to collect a bride, but to inform Lucia that he could no longer marry her. His circumstances had altered; with the change of monarch, his religious conscience had been reawakened. He was now promised to another—Anne Carleill, a virtuous Protestant widow with a young son—whose connections would advance his fledgling career under the new regime.

By then, Gideon and Valentina were caring for the babe . . . for me. Gideon had ceased his studies and was learning the locksmith's trade.

I could scarcely believe that the child at the center of these events was me. It was like listening to one of Angela's stories, or watching one of Caleb's plays.

"When I saw how much Gideon cared for you, how content you were, how much a family you'd all become, I knew I couldn't destroy that," explained Sir Francis. "I didn't know what I could offer a tiny babe, my bastard child—" He gave me an apologetic smile. The truth did not hurt so much as tie me in confusion. I was a bastard. "I was bewildered, heartsore. Confounded. I also had my betrothed to consider, and my new role in Parliament. I already had responsibility for my three cousins and was taking on Anne's son, Christopher, as well. My reputation as a principled, ethical man was growing. How would I explain you? How could I explain Lucia?" He paused and stared at a point on the wall behind me.

I remained silent.

"It was then I asked your father to keep you. He and Valentina had cared for you a long while; Gideon showed such promise as a locksmith and had taken to the craft with ease. I had a vague thought that once I was firmly established, I could perhaps send for you, adopt you as my ward and thus protect your name and status. Protect my own as well."

The irony of this was not lost on me. Hadn't I done the same? Done whatever it took to shield myself, and thus those I cared for, from judgment?

"But I needed time," continued Sir Francis. "Gideon readily agreed, allowing me that and so much more. I think he was already more than a little in love with you." A ghost of a grin flickered. "I gave him all the money I had and returned to these shores and . . . continued with my life. Gideon and Valentina followed a couple of years later. By the time they arrived and settled in Harp Lane, you were so much their child, you were his daughter—even in name, you were a Bright. You had his mannerisms, his way of speaking; he was besotted with you. I had a wife of my own, a career . . . neither of us wanted to disrupt things, reveal what was best left concealed. We agreed we would never speak of it. There was no need. As far as everyone knew, you were the locksmith's daughter and I had to be content with that." He met my eyes. "It was God's will."

God saw fit to take my true father from me? Snatch away my birthright? "God's will it might have been, but Mamma's?" I had to ask.

"Valentina did what your father wanted." Sir Francis turned away.

What you wanted as well. She was suborned. Sweet Jesus. It explained so much. Mamma's bitterness; the coldness in her eyes when she gazed upon me, the empty press of her lips upon my forehead; the mumbled blessings, forgotten wassails, her lack of maternal feelings. My heart was squeezed. I put my hand to my chest, unable to believe there was still air in my lungs. How much more did I have to hear? How much more could I take until I became just a broken possession? That's what I felt like—an object passed about until it was finally discarded.

Was that to be my fate?

This revelation made so much sense. Mamma was not my mother. She was only my aunt. Her sister, little Lucia, was my mother. Lucia, the one named for the light, the one I never knew but loved because our name rhymed with hers—*light bright, bright light*. In Valentina's heart I was merely her niece, and responsible for her sister's death. Tears began to flow. I made no attempt to check them. My true mother's memory, Mamma and Papa's sacrifice, all they had done for me, for Sir Francis, deserved this from me at least.

And what of Papa? Papa, my beautiful, wonderful, loving father was my uncle. My papa who took me though I was not his, who sat me at his knee, read to me, taught me, who protected me from Mamma's blistering tongue . . . was not my father. This man, this tall, sallow man from whom I took my hair, my height, my complexion, who had relinquished all responsibility for me, was my father.

I was a Walsingham. I was his blood. And I had thought marriage to Sir Raffe Shelton, a mere country gentleman, was a social advantage my parents could be proud of. It wasn't the Bright name I'd sullied through my actions, it was the Walsingham one. No wonder Sir Francis was keen to help Papa restore my reputation—it was his own.

Mocking voices rang in my head. I was being the dutiful and obedient daughter I'd promised to be after all. I was following in my father's footsteps, doing his bidding—with the exception of yesterday, when I had broken my word. No wonder he was so affronted.

I swallowed the laugh that built in my throat. My life was like one of Caleb's creations, a piece of theater in which my character was written for me and I but played her part. Mallory Bright, enter stage right. Exit, stage left. No wonder I took to watching and all it offered with such ease. I was most experienced in the art of deception—something Lord Nathaniel had accused me of and something I had vehemently denied. The man had been right all along.

"You may have remained with Gideon," said Sir Francis, measuring my every expression carefully. "But you've always been mine. I've watched you from a distance your entire life, Mallory; watched you grow into the lovely young woman you are, a learned one too."

"Not so learned that I didn't dash my future upon a foolish dream."

"You're not alone in doing that. You're but your father's daughter. Did I not seek to do the same?"

In following my heart and not my head, I'd simply repeated the mistakes (or truth) of my real father. Like him, I too was given a second chance. There was a strange synchronicity that must have pained my parents so . . . only, they weren't my parents. What did they care, really?

Something else occurred. "Raffe . . . It was you who found me, wasn't it? In that house in the village? I never understood how Papa managed it, but he didn't, did he? That was you as well."

Sir Francis nodded. "I'd heard of your"—he cleared his throat— "elopement. Oh, how I wanted to intervene, especially when I learned the knave's wife still lived. That she was with child."

My hand crept to my belly. How much did this man . . . my father . . . really know?

"But I promised Gideon I would not, you see. He was always reluctant to ask for help, let alone take it. I think he feared I would swoop in and whisk you away as I'd once thought to do. So, I promised to maintain my distance unless invited to draw near. Eventually, I could not wait. Without Gideon's knowledge, I set my men searching for you. When you were found, I went to Gideon . . . He in turn went to you."

It all made sense. Papa's reluctance to speak about how he knew where I was. "And my working for you? Whose idea was that?"

Sir Francis made a hapless gesture. "It was never really intended you would work for me, I was meant to facilitate employment. Gideon invited me to the workshop so I might witness your skills. He wanted to show me that despite what had happened, you were still a woman with prospects. It was a huge concession for him. Afraid of what I might do should I meet you face to face, he nonetheless allowed it to happen. As it was, the thing he feared the most never came to pass . . . until now. But I saw your potential, Mallory, how I might use your talents and keep you close at the same time. Get to know you."

"Why wait until now to tell me the truth?"

Sir Francis paused. "To restore your faith in me. To make amends for the falsehood you believe I composed about Campion."

"By revealing a secret that's been kept for over twenty years?"

Sir Francis shook his head. "It seems preposterous when you put it like that. I've wanted to tell you for a long time." He sighed and his eyes wandered to the picture of Mary. "A very long time. My greatest concern now is how you feel about . . . this." He touched his chest. "About me."

I felt suddenly shy. The little flare of anger, of defiance, had been replaced by awkwardness. This man was my father.

"I'm uncertain," I said. "I never imagined . . ."

"Of course not. How could you?"

Aye, how could I when the secret had been kept from me all these years? My hand went to the locket nestled between my breasts. We all had our secrets . . .

"I must speak with Papa."

"I thought you might wish to . . ."

"You would not want me to?"

Sir Francis uncrossed his legs. "It is up to you. But if I may offer some advice, it won't be easy for Gideon, or Valentina. They feared such a revelation would alter your relationship with them and would have kept the truth from you . . . I swore I would keep silent until they deemed otherwise. I've broken my promise. Something else we have in common." He cocked his head. "Has it? Altered your relationship with them? Your feelings?"

I wasn't certain of the answer. "I . . . I do not know." That was the truth. And yet, deep in my heart, I knew it transformed everything. The thought scared me. It also elated me.

Sir Francis moved the jug, picked up some papers and straightened them. "Has it changed the way you feel about . . . working for me?"

I thought about the deep disappointment I'd felt at discovering Sir Francis's interference with the dossier, my indignation that he would stoop to such measures and the shocking consequences. What did it say about me that the fury and the disappointment were no longer there now I knew he was my father? They had been replaced by a desire to understand, and in so doing perchance to excuse his behavior, see it as necessary. To think of it in any other way was too much. I opted for the lesser evil. My father was noble in his intentions. He had to be.

But what about the promise he made to my real mother; the one he was willing to break? I could not hold that against him; to do so would be to punish him for something all men and women were guilty of at one time or another—changing their minds. Ignorance of her state, of her death, should not make his decision to part with her worse. Did he not travel to Italy to tell her in person? No, it was the choices he made after he learned everything for which he should be held to account. Was I so contrary that while I wanted to resent him, to loathe his selfishness, I also, knowing him as I did, understood what drove him? Did not the same motives drive me?

Aware he was waiting for a response, I took a deep breath. "If anything, I want to work harder, to prove my worth both as your agent and your daughter."

"Ah, you have proved that over and over, my dear. I could not be more proud."

My dear. A smile tugged my lips.

"But I ask that you keep the nature of our relationship to yourself. Not until I'm ready to claim you openly and freely should you mention the truth of your birth to anyone else."

"You would do such a thing? Claim me?"

Sir Francis's smile broadened and may even have reached his eyes. It was difficult to know with the candlelight distorting his expression.

"I want the world to know you're my daughter—but when the time is right. I've already lost one, I'll not lose another."

Curse my wretched heart, it responded like a plucked instrument. Papa and Mamma were ready to disown me and all this man wanted, all my father wanted, was the right conditions in which to claim me. Then I recalled his haughty wife and saintly daughter.

"What about Lady Ursula and Lady Frances?"

"Do not concern yourself with them. They will embrace you." Under duress they might embrace me, but accept me, never. "Until such time, it is our secret."

Just as one secret is exposed, another takes its place. God Himself knew, I was good at keeping those.

Sir Francis stood, arched his back and grimaced. "Tonight has been a revelation in so many ways. I'm most impressed with the manner in which you've accepted what I've told you."

It was Castiglione he should be thanking. On the outside, I was all aplomb. If he could but see into my head, he would find a maelstrom of wild thoughts. Maintaining my hard-won assurance, I gave a small shrug.

"What we cannot change . . . I'm grateful to finally know the truth."

There was an awkward moment when I rose and curtseyed just as he bent to kiss me and his teeth struck the top of my head. We both laughed, lifted our arms, dropped them, then finally held each other.

We stepped apart and he examined my face. Was he looking for likeness or weakness? "Until I've a new mission for you, you'll continue to come to the house, decipher and decode. We'll carry on as usual."

As usual? Nothing would ever be "usual" again. From the expression on Sir Francis's face, the same thought crossed his mind.

"Good night . . . Father," I said softly. "May I call you that?"

He hesitated. "For tonight alone—in this room. And I will call you daughter." He shook his head as if astonished by the notion. I was. "Good night, daughter, and may God be with you."

I shut the door behind me as I left, then rested my back upon it, staring at the dark ceiling. "Sweet Mother Mary and all the blessed saints," I said, using a phrase I oft heard Angela whisper when she thought no one was about.

"Say that in the wrong ears, and you'll be on the next hurdle to Tyburn," said a voice.

My hand flew to my breast. "Zounds, Thomas! Do you live in the shadows? I didn't see you."

He rose from behind his desk. "Obviously. What are you doing muttering papist nonsense? Where did you hear that?"

I approached his desk, which as usual was covered in paper. A solitary candle burned at his elbow. I tried to see what he was doing, but in the dancing light the ciphers were incomprehensible dashes and squiggles. "Here and there. Speaking of which, why are you still here?"

"I'm to escort you home." Rubbing his eyes behind his spectacles, he lifted his cloak from the back of the chair. "You and Sir Francis must have had a great deal to discuss. You've been hours."

When I didn't respond, he shrugged. He knew better than to press. "Come along, your papa is waiting."

Papa. Father. The terms were laden with fresh meaning. Though Thomas used what was a common expression, I knew this was different. Papa did indeed wait for me. He waited because he knew something momentous had happened.

As we walked the chilly streets toward Harp Lane, discussing the aftermath of Campion's death, Londoners' reactions and news from the French and Spanish embassies, my mind was occupied by an entirely different matter. On my way to Seething Lane that morning I'd thought nothing could distract me from what I had witnessed at Tyburn. Nothing.

But something else had taken center stage, changing the lines I'd thought to deliver and altering the very nature of my performance. A new character had been introduced—my father—and altered all the roles, especially mine.

At the gate I farewelled Thomas and entered the yard. The light was burning in the workshop. I took a deep breath and headed toward it, my mind full, my heart an anchor that tried to restrain me. It was time for me to enter the next scene, and see how beloved characters now played their parts.

THIRTY-SEVEN

I've not known him to keep you so late before. Is something amiss?"
Papa continued to polish the key in his hand.

The dogs gave me an excuse to linger by the door as they bounded over to greet me. I patted their heads and rubbed their backs as their tails struck my legs, but I didn't know how to reply. For all that I likened my situation to a play, I was the actor who forgot his lines. For all that Sir Francis praised my poise, it began to desert me.

Seeing the man who'd pretended to be my papa for all these years, who'd nurtured me, taught me, protected me and, above all, lied to me with the best of intentions, it was as if a great scythe swept through my memories and ruthlessly lopped them down. They lay scattered, disorderly and fragmented, and I could not grasp one. They made no sense.

Back in Sir Francis's study, it had been easy to pretend to an indifference I didn't feel, a boldness that owed everything to artifice. To hear the tale of how I came to be, who I really was, was both exhilarating and fantastical. The repercussions were not yet apparent. But here, in the familiar surroundings of home, confronted with the person around whom my life to this moment had revolved, I suddenly understood that this was no play like those Caleb wove. This was real. This was my life.

As at Tyburn, this was no place for *mediocrita*. The man waiting for me to drop a light kiss on his forehead, rest my head against his shoulder and chatter about my day was not my father. He never had been. He may never have wanted to be. The role had been forced upon him. Tears began to well, pushed to the surface by a wave of anger and self-pity that took me by surprise with its fierceness.

Why hadn't Papa told me? Why had Sir Francis been the one?

With a deep sigh, Papa put the key and rag down. Lifting himself off the stool, he studied me. I gazed back, fighting to maintain control, to not feel. Then, with a long, sad sigh, he turned around and placed his palms on the bench, arms straight, and bowed his head.

"He's told you." His words were slightly muffled.

Even so, I heard them. "He did. Everything." My voice trembled. I caught hold of the alarm, the fury bubbling away inside me, and forced the wave of grief back.

In the silence the dogs' panting was like bellows, the crackle of the fire a roar. Papa said nothing. What was he waiting for? My tongue was thick, my throat dry. I wanted to beg him to tell me it wasn't true. To reassure me.

I said nothing.

Almost indiscernibly, Papa's shoulders began to shake. Two great tears landed on the bench, splashing upon the key resting by his thumb, his blackened calloused thumb, misshapen from all the years of crafting locks and keys.

Dear God, my papa was crying. Was it with relief or sorrow? I could not bear it. I could not. I staggered back against the door, the dogs growling, thinking it was a game. At the sound, Papa turned and in his eyes I saw all the pain building inside me made manifest. It wasn't only my life the truth had irreparably altered.

"Mallory," he cried, tears blinding him as he stumbled toward me, arms outstretched.

"I cannot. I can't. Stay away, stay away." I pushed him from me, opened the door and ran, as fast as I could, toward the house. I raced past the kitchen, fled up the stairs and into my small, cold room and locked the door behind me.

I flung myself onto the bed and prayed the darkness would swallow me once and for all.

My fear Papa would follow was unfounded and so, drowning in a well of misery, I lay upon my bed and wept a torrent. There was so much hurt and confusion to release. I cried for the mother I never knew and, in my mind, the father I had been denied. I cried at my foolishness in running away with Raffe, at the horror my fanciful dream became. I cried for all the deception and lies my life was built upon, and, lastly, for what I was beginning to understand would never be mine—a family I could call my own; a family built on common blood, mutual love and truth.

At some point during the night, I rose, left my room to empty the jordan, returned and made a fire before creeping back under the covers and crying myself to sleep.

I don't know what woke me, except as I rolled toward the comforting glow of the fire, my head aching, my nose blocked, my eyes flickering, I became aware I was not alone. I gasped and sat upright, my knees pulled to my chest, and swung toward the shadow seated on the edge of the bed.

"I told him. I told him that one day you would find out. He never believed me."

I don't know which shocked me more: the words the voice spoke behind the flickering candle, or the fact it was my mother.

"Mamma . . ." I released the breath I'd been holding and, as my eyes became accustomed to the wavering light, I was able to see her more clearly. I wondered when she'd become so shrunken, so gray. Her flame-colored hair was doused liberally with the frosty hues of silver; her smooth complexion had become tinged with broken veins, and an ashen sheen surrounded her lips and the folds of her nose. The lines around her eyes might be faint, but the ones between her brows deepened as she regarded me with a dangerous glimmer.

"How did you manage the stairs?" I asked. It had been years since Mamma had ventured into my bedroom and not once since I'd returned.

She gave a dry laugh that turned into a wet cough. I took the candle from her and placed it on the chest, then got out of bed. I put some distance between us and tossed more wood on the fire.

"I may be ill, but I'm not dead . . . yet. My legs work. *Allora*, I used them." Her voice was a croak. "We need to talk but I do not want your father to know."

Turning, I frowned. "Why not?"

"Because he asked me not to speak with you."

I took a deep breath and released it slowly. "Why?"

"Because he's afraid of what I'll tell you."

At that moment, I too became afraid. We stared at each other across the room, me with my back to the fire, Mamma propped on the bed.

"Sometimes," she said quietly, "when I look at you, I see Lucia. Mostly, I see him." She spat the last word.

"Sir Francis?"

"*Si*. The *bastardo* who killed my sister, your mother. The man who put his own needs above his child's, above the man he called his dearest *amico*." Only her accent betrayed her deep agitation. It was thick with barely disguised fury.

"Papa."

"You would still call him that?"

"I . . ." I gazed at her in astonishment. What else would I call him? *"Naturalmente."* My heart had taken on a life of its own, thundering in my chest. It was too strange—Mamma, in my bedroom, talking about Sir Francis, about my mother, her sister, Lucia.

She screwed the ends of the bedclothes into a ball. "Why did he tell you? Why now?"

"I . . ." How could I explain to Mamma it was because he had sensed he was losing my trust in his judgment and that he had sought to bind me in the only way he could—with the truth? "He felt it was time."

She threw back her head and laughed. Again, it became a cough. I swiftly poured an ale from the ewer, crossed to the bed and brought it to her lips, holding it steady so she could drink. She took a sip then waved it away. "I am all right. Do not fuss."

I lit some candles, sat at the other end of the bed and waited.

Drawing her rosary from beneath her nightclothes, she began to worry the beads. Uncertain whether she used them to further agitate me or from genuine need, I tried to focus not on them, but on her words instead.

"He felt it was time, did he? How convenient." She stared at a point in front of her. "Mister Secretary, this father of yours, for all that he appears to work in your best interests, his motivation is always the same. He looks to himself first and foremost. Lucia, God rest her soul, died before she could learn this and have her heart broken. I always knew when he bought this house for us, when he helped your father gain wealthy clients, that one day we'd pay for his benevolence—interference, that's what it was. Control. I knew. Would Gideon listen? No. He is too trusting. Believes in the good of human nature. Bah. I have seen the worst and Sir Francis—*your father*—is among them."

I began to defend him. She made a dismissive gesture. "Do not talk of him in this way to me. Despite what you might think, what he says, this man cares not for you. Do not be fooled by pretty words, Mallory, not again." I dropped my eyes. Mamma could never resist an opportunity to remind me of Raffe.

Rain began to fall, a dull drumming on the roof, thick drops striking the glass. We both looked toward the window before facing each other again. "Is that why you never loved me?" I asked finally. "Because I was not your daughter or because I was his?"

Mamma studied me, a strange smile playing on her lips. "Never loved you?" She gave a laugh. "*Mio Dio*, I never dared."

She beckoned me closer. I hesitated, uncertain whether her intention was to embrace or strike me. Her mouth moved but no words came at first, then I heard them, faint, as if she loathed speaking them.

"You have her eyes. Her beautiful star-dream eyes. Her hair as well. Ink black, thick, straight. *Allora*, Mallory, no matter what you think, the moment you were placed in my arms, my heart filled. Were you not my sister's child? Blood of my blood? But you were also his. So I feared what loving you would do. I was terrified of losing you—not like I lost Lucia, who I will see again in heaven, God willing. But because you were never really mine, I dared not lose my heart lest you be taken from me forever.

"When Francis asked us to keep you as if you were ours, said that he would stake no claim, I dared to hope. We came to England, we were given this house and we became a family . . ." She took another drink.

Never before had Mamma spoken to me like this. I didn't dare interrupt.

"But, we were family in name only—*his* name. Hovering over us like an avenging angel—"

I started. She had no idea how such a description affected me. My stomach twisted. Verily, like father, like daughter.

"I thought perhaps if I had a child of my own, it would be easier to forget the way you came to us; if I could give you a brother or sister—a cousin, really—I would allow myself to feel something for you. Alas, God in His wisdom gave me many babes, but took them all to His arms."

Her eyes were so full of sadness, it was hard to watch as she spoke. I wanted to reach out and hold her, but I could not.

"I blamed you for that," she said, without malice or anger. Her candor struck me with all the force of a blow. "I thought God was punishing me for not loving you, for not accepting His will and trying to create another being." She gave a bitter laugh. "Your papa said he didn't mind and I truly think he did not. 'Look,' he would say to me, 'we have a beautiful, clever daughter who enchants her tutor and all who come within her compass. What more do we want?' I was greedy, I did want more." She returned to her beads.

"You had him under a spell. There was nothing he would not give you; nothing he would not do for you. I knew it would end in disaster. I could not stop him loving you, but I could make sure you understood the world was not there for you to sup from endlessly. That there was harshness and hate, manipulation and deceit. Oh, there was deceit . . ." Her voice trailed away. "I told myself it was up to me to ensure you had discipline; that you understood your place in the family, and thus the world. I may not love you like a mother, but I tried to ensure you were taught what a daughter should know. Yet again, your papa undermined my efforts and introduced you to what no female child should learn."

"Locks," I said softly.

"Aye, that, and to write, to read and speak the language of the ancients. For what purpose? I would ask. Why do women need such knowledge? It is an empty dowry no husband wants or needs. Again, he did not listen. Part of me began to think he was deliberately making you unmarriageable so he could keep you himself, filling your head with stories and so much more besides. Master Fodrake was no better, the old fool."

I lowered my eyes. I hated that she could talk about Papa and my beloved tutor in this way.

"And then there were the locks and keys. Oh, you two had your own little language, your time together huddled over his creations. Excluded from these, I could only watch and mourn what you were becoming."

Despite the fire behind me, coldness crept into my bones and my heart. Listening to Mamma divulge all she'd kept hidden, as if I were her confessor, able to grant her absolution, was far more painful than I could ever have imagined. Despair lapped at my mind. I fixed a blank expression on my face. I would not let her see how cruelly her words bit.

"You were so very different to the other girls." This was no compliment, but an affliction to be mourned. "Where your papa took pride in your accomplishments, I was ashamed. No real daughter of mine would have been like that—like you. Your father thought he was making you in his image. I used to accuse him of it. Looking at you now, I was wrong. No matter what Gideon or I did or said, you're Francis's."

She leaned forward, peering at me. "You were always Francis's spawn." She said his name with such violence, I slid back along the bed.

Seeing my reaction, she nodded.

"Even now, it's hard to look at you. Some days, I cannot stand it." She sighed, the burden of these feelings at last lightening as it was passed to me. "It became so unbearable, God forgive me, I arranged to meet with Francis's wife, Ursula, and tell her the whole sorry tale. But then you ran away and I thought our troubles were over. I dared to hope we could wash our hands of you and Francis forever. Don't look at me like that. You accepted the truth from your father, why not from me, your *aunt*?"

I lifted my chin, determined to hear her out and not to let her see me weep. Aye, I'd accepted it from Sir Francis, but he did not loathe me the way my mamma—*my aunt*—(God, that made it easier) evidently did.

"But Gideon would not let it rest. Nor, it turns out, would Francis. He found you, did he tell you that? Of course he did. *Si*, he told Gideon where you were, that your knight had abused you terribly and you must be brought home. I told Gideon to leave you, that you'd chosen your path and you should be made to walk it, but he would not listen. When it comes to you, he never does."

The tartness in Mamma's voice, in her breath, was overpowering. The more she spoke, the more a sickly sweet smell, one I recognized from Tyburn, emanated from her. It was the smell of death. God forgive me, but at that moment, I wished it would come and strike her. I wished I really was the avenging angel people whispered of and that I could silence her for good.

I was wicked beyond belief. *Oh dear God. Please, give me strength.*

"I told him if he brought you back, you would simply go again—you were never ours in the first place. I forced him to agree to find you employment, anything to get you out from under our roof; somewhere I didn't have to see you." She began to chuckle, a harsh, hoarse sound. "What does he do? Turns to his old friend, Francis. I knew then we'd lost you for good. It was only a matter of time. Ha! Is that not what he said? It was time to tell you? *Si, allora,* the man makes us all march to *his* time. To *his* rules. He always has and always will. You as well, daughter of his or no. You're another pawn for him to move if and when it suits him in his game of politics and power."

Unable to stand it any longer, I rose from the bed and flung open the shutters. The air was cold and fresh. The rain fell heavier now, as if the sky itself was weeping.

"I don't have to listen to any more of this."

"Oh," she said, heaving herself off the bed and shuffling around to join me. She pulled my sleeve, pinching the flesh of my arm as she did. "You do. I haven't finished. Don't turn your back on me, Mallory. The least you owe me is respect."

Respect? Aye, I supposed I did. Against her will, I'd been raised by her husband, dwelled in her home. She'd given me clothes, food and the education she thought a waste—which, by running away like a feckless colt, I'd proved it was. Holding my head high, I faced her. I towered over her bent form. I might be cowering inside, but at least I stood tall.

Shivering by the window, her breath came in gasps. "While my heart cannot be broken—I prepared for this long ago—your papa's has shattered into a million pieces."

I closed my eyes. I recalled the teardrops landing on the bench, Papa calling my name, beseeching me to stay. Opening my eyes again, I nodded sadly.

"What do you want me to do?"

"Me?" She turned away with a noise of disgust. "It's not for me to tell you what to do. He's your papa, for God's sake. It's for you to *know*."

Wrath took hold of me then; a rage so deep and incandescent, it burst forth. "How should I know? He's not my father! He's my uncle, my guardian, and then only by the grace of God and Sir Francis. Nothing is as I thought. Nothing." I grabbed her arms and shook her. "You were so certain this day would come, the secret would be exposed. You were right. So, tell me what to do."

My chest heaved, tears welled behind my eyes but I wouldn't let them fall. Mamma went still in my grip. I released her slowly.

"No. I won't," she said. "But what I will tell you is this: who walked away from his education so you might have one? Who sacrificed his future and mine so you might have one?

"You weren't told that, were you? I didn't think so. Your papa took up locksmithing, trained by my father's side, so he might immediately earn money for the family thrust upon him by his so-called friend. Your *nonno* insisted my wedding be brought forward so we could hold our heads high. Ashamed of Lucia, that she gave herself to the *Inglese* before they were wed, a tale was spun of how they'd secretly married before Francis left. My papa would not allow her name to be said in his presence again. Lucia was dead to him in every way. Lucia was gone and so was what had once been my family, what had once been my future. I was to marry a man with prospects, a man who would enter the law, become a member of Parliament, mayhap even the Privy Council; does that sound familiar? *Si*, it should." She tapped the side of her proud nose. "Instead, what happens? Because of Sir Francis, because of you"—she jabbed a finger at me—"I, the locksmith's daughter, became the locksmith's wife." Her mouth twisted into an ugly shape, her eyes were flint.

"There's nothing wrong with that," I said.

"You dare say that to me?" Her voice was shrill. "The woman who this very evening rejected her papa? Fled to her room? You who is the daughter of Mister Secretary, a knight of the realm? Ha. Which would you rather be, Mallory? A Bright or a Walsingham? A locksmith's daughter or the daughter of the Queen's Secretary? I think you know the answer. After your little performance in the workshop, so does your papa.

"You think your life has been a lie?" She thrust her face into mine; her eyes were luminous, filled with unshed tears. "Well, you have made ours one. I thought when you ran away with that *bastardo* you made all we had done worthless. I was wrong. Today, you and your newly discovered father have made everything we have done mean nothing. You've rendered our lives, your papa's life, meaningless. Think about that, Mister Secretary's daughter. Think about that." She began to hobble to the door, a bent crone, twisted with thwarted hopes, lost children and the burden of raising another man's daughter, a girl she never wanted.

Pity knocked against my heart, but I refused to allow it entry. I didn't help as she struggled with the latch, her fingers slipping. She wrenched open the door.

As she paused at the threshold, the cold air from the corridor swept in, swirling her nightdress around her thin ankles.

"Though I may not love you the way I should, or you would hope, I do care, Mallory. Believe it or not, I do." Her words were a force that drew me toward her. Her next ones stopped me in my tracks. "Let me give you a word of advice. Trust not Sir Francis. Just like you, he's not what he seems."

"At least he wants me!" I cried, a child wailing for its mother.

"Wants you? Is he prepared to acknowledge you as his own?" I stared. "I thought not."

"It's not the right time . . ." I began, the words sounding weak.

Mamma shook her head. "It never is for Francis. Not when it interferes with his lofty goals." She waited for me to look at her again. "You still want to know what you should do?"

I nodded, the tears I'd tried so hard not to shed beginning to fall.

"Go, child, and never come back. There, I've said it. That is what you should have done before. It's what you need to do now. I will repair Gideon's heart. You—even without intending to, you only break it."

I heard her on the stairs before another door opened then shut with a firm click. I didn't move. I stood staring at the space where she'd been. It was a while before I closed the door. Breathing deeply, I tried to achieve nonchalance. In and out. According to Castiglione, by adopting the outer illusion of calm, an inner sense of peace would follow. It had worked in the past. I had to think. I had to work out what I was going to do next.

When Sir Francis told me I was his daughter, I'd had no thought for anyone other than myself. Though I recognized Papa and Mamma had made sacrifices for Sir Francis and me, I'd not understood the extent of them or the impact they'd had.

Papa had surrendered his future for the sake of his old friend's daughter. In doing so, he forced his wife to do the same. No wonder Mamma despised me. No wonder she hated Sir Francis. She blamed him not only for her sister's death but for the demise of her dreams.

Oh God. I almost destroyed my future when I ran away with Raffe, but that was nothing compared to what I'd already done. I'd ravaged Mamma's and Papa's lives through simply existing. Me and my father. My real father.

I was no avenging angel. I was a destroyer—of hopes, of dreams, of futures. I was the blight I'd been tagged, a curse that devoured everything in her path: Mallory Blight.

Mamma was right. There was no choice. I had to leave.

THIRTY-EIGHT

*T*he cock had crowed and Gracious had collected the hens' eggs by the time I finished the letter. Dressing with more care than usual, I threw my few belongings in an old burlap, then went hastily to Caleb's room.

Without waiting for permission, I knocked and entered. The room was dark and frowsting. Stale beer, wine and food as well as the thick smell of tallow candles and smoke lingered. Fumbling my way to the window I flung the shutters open, allowing light and icy air to pour in. Sheets of paper were strewn all over the desk and a number had found their way to the floor. Tucking the letter beneath my arm, I began to pick them up.

"Mallory," grumbled Caleb, sitting up in bed. "What on earth are you doing? Good God, woman, even the sun is still abed."

Placing the pages on the desk, I pulled aside the curtains, admitting the weak light from the gray mizzle and sat on the bed.

"I need you to deliver this," I said and held out the letter.

Caleb rubbed his eyes and beard before looking from me to the letter and back again. "Why, you're nicely prinked," he said, taking in my attire. "Where are you—?" He stopped, screwed up his eyes then scooted forward in the bed, bringing the sheets with him. "Mallory, sweetling. You've been crying. What is it?"

I placed my hand over his on my cheek.

"Please, Caleb, no kindness, no understanding. I can scarce contain myself. Call me whore, call me trull or caitiff, but do not ask what is wrong, for I cannot tell you—not yet. One day soon, all will be apparent."

Taking the letter slowly, he beheld it as if it had teeth. "You're not planning to elope again, are you?" he said, cocking his head to one side, hoping to elicit a laugh.

I bit back a sharp, bitter one. "Of that, I can assure you I am not. But I am leaving. That's also why I'm here. I wanted to let you know."

"Oh dear gods, Mallory, why? I mean, I always knew it was a possibility, but why now?"

I shook my head.

"Is it because of what we witnessed? Campion? Has Sir Francis said something?"

Oh, aye, but not what Caleb assumed. I shook my head.

"Is it her?" asked Caleb, his eyes narrowing. We both knew to whom he referred.

I took a deep breath. "Mamma? No . . . she has . . . naught to do with my decision." What an accomplished dissembler I was becoming. "It's the right thing, that's all."

"Does your father know?"

My father. I almost choked. "Papa will not be surprised, I think." I nodded toward the letter. "Once he reads that, he will understand. Please, reassure him he's not to worry. I know you can comfort him; you're like a son to him—the son he never had."

"And he is the kind of father I always longed for . . . But where are you going? What will you do?"

I pressed my fingers against his lips.

"Hush. Hush. I intend to go to Seething Lane. I'm not leaving London, Caleb. I will still see you—at least, I hope so."

Frowning, Caleb slid his hand from my face. God forbid, tears gathered on my lashes. "I will do as you ask. But Mallory . . . are you sure?"

Before I could reassure or explain, there was the sound of muffled voices below—Mamma and Angela. They were speaking in Italian. Caleb's bedroom was directly above Mamma's.

"I love Angela dearly," groaned Caleb, gripping the sides of his head with his hands, crumpling my letter, "and the sound of your mother tongue, but sometimes it's more than I can stand. They chittered all through the night—your papa was with them for some of it—and it made reading, let alone writing, an impossibility." It was no mystery what they would have been discussing. He waved a hand toward his desk, awash with parchment, books, half-empty cups and paper. My eyes traveled to the chest. It was still there. Caleb saw the direction of my gaze.

"You're leaving now?" he asked, hoping to distract me. It worked.

"Aye, before the house stirs too much."

"Zounds. Will your father have apoplexy when he reads this?" He flapped the letter.

"I doubt that." I stood. "Please, Caleb, look to him, won't you? And write to me care of Seething Lane. This isn't *adieu*, my friend. I will come to your plays, we will still see each other."

"I will hold you to that, Mallory Bright. I lost you once, but ne'er again."

Caleb threw back the covers and climbed out of bed. Still in his shirt and hose, he was a sight. Drawing me into his arms, he held me tight. "Whatever it is that's brought this on and come between you and your father—for I know of naught else that would drive you away again—it will be resolved, Mallory. I will make sure of that."

The sadness I'd kept at bay began to spill. Caleb's understanding and commitment to heal a breach I'd not deliberately caused, yet did not know how to begin to mend, broke me. I tried to push him away. He held me tighter.

"It will, Mallory. It just needs time."

"Like all things." I managed to extract myself. "But also space. That is what I am supplying. Just give Papa the letter and keep watch. Alert me if there is need."

With a flourish, Caleb bowed, his hair flopping over his forehead. "Your wish, et cetera, et cetera, my lady." The cheeky grin fell, to be replaced by a look of deep sadness. "Good God, Mallory, what am I to do without you?"

Depositing a kiss on his cheek, I left while I still could.

THIRTY-NINE

I caught Sir Francis as he was about to leave for Whitehall and begged a few minutes of his time. He invited me into his office, away from the curious eyes and ears of his assistants, shut the door and bade me sit.

"You look tired, Mallory," he said.

It could have been said of him as well. His skin was gray, his eyes dull and red veined.

"I . . . did not sleep well. I'd much to think about."

"Aye, us both." He smiled, but it was awkward, lacking in warmth. Sadness drew my mouth down. I don't know what I expected but it wasn't this—a meeting of strangers.

"You spoke to Gideon?" asked Sir Francis.

"I didn't need to," I said. "He guessed."

"Ah. He was always insightful." He shoved some papers aside and placed both elbows on the desk. "How . . . how was he?"

Shaking my head, I lowered my chin. I could not, would not say. To reveal Papa's hurt and pain would be too great a betrayal, even to this man . . . my father.

"I understand."

I raised my head. I believed he did. "Living at home has become, for the present . . ." Mamma's face swam before my vision, her bitter words. *I will repair Gideon's heart. You—you only break it.* "Untenable. I thought perhaps I could live with Goodwife Bench at Billiter Lane and work from there."

I gazed at him hopefully.

"Live at Billiter Lane? Mallory, I'm afraid that's not possible."

What remained of my heart sank into my boots. "Then what am I to do? I know I cannot live here."

Sir Francis coughed. "That you certainly cannot. What would my lady wife and dau—" He stopped, shooting me a look before turning away. "It would not be appropriate and would only increase the wounds I imagine Gideon feels; Valentina too."

And be impossible for you.

Scraping back his chair, he stood. "There has to be a better solution. Are you sure you cannot remain at Harp Lane?"

I didn't respond. The man who only last evening admitted he was my father could not, would not help me. Despair hammered my resolve. I'd stupidly believed that when he confessed to his paternity, Sir Francis would at the very least accept some responsibility for my well-being. It seemed I was wrong.

"I see," he said.

I feared he did not.

He began to walk around the room, rubbing his beard, smoothing his cheeks, his agitation obvious. Why had he admitted paternity if he wasn't also driven by a desire to improve our relations? I began to pray for a solution; that the man who'd confessed he was my father last night would see fit to help me today. All I asked for was assistance, not public acknowledgment of my birthright.

I watched him pace before the portrait of the Queen; her eyes gazed at me over his shoulder.

How fortunate was my sovereign. A woman of power, not dependent upon menfolk for goodwill, for security and a future. Why, she could reject a thousand husbands, earn the ire of her Privy Council for ignoring their entreaties and still command. With ships, captains, armies and Sir Francis's entire network of agents at her disposal, let alone courtiers who obeyed her every whim, Her Majesty ruled not only men, but the country, and kept the baying Catholic world at heel.

Oh, to be a Queen . . .

I recalled something Mamma said not long after I returned home after being rescued from Raffe. I'd gone to her room to receive her blessing before bed. More mellow than usual, she included me in her conversation with Angela, which, as it often did, centered on who was marrying whom in the parish.

"Enjoy your freedom while you can, Mallory," she said. "'Tis but an illusion. None of us"—she gestured to Angela and me—"are ever free. It is a dangerous estate for a woman. The sooner we shackle you to a husband, the better. You're not Her Majesty to deny God's natural course and refuse to be a woman or a wife. You're a mere female, one with a past and a sullied reputation who must needs take salvation—in the form of a man—where she can."

"Valentina, you do not mean that," said Angela.

"Don't I?" Mamma spat. "Do not all men use us for their own needs, whether it be to satisfy their desires, produce an heir, or look to their well-being? We're not God's servants. We are men's. Who looks to us, Angela? Tell me? Who looks to us women?"

Mamma's words echoed in my head. *Who looks to us women?* After all this time, I had the answer. If our fathers could not or would not, then we must look to ourselves. My eyes were drawn to my burlap, which had fallen open at my feet. Atop my belongings was the book I'd purchased for Beatrice. Again, my mind led me down the paths of memories . . . *I wish you were my companion,* Beatrice had said.

Had not Lord Nathaniel also raised the possibility? Offered me not merely a position, but an opportunity?

"Sir Francis," I said, rising so fast that he spun around. Should I have called him "Father"? It did not seem right. It did not describe our relations. "If I may? I think I have a solution."

"Oh?" He regarded me in such a manner, I knew he thought the prospect unlikely. "Please, enlighten me." He returned to his seat, rested his elbows on his desk once more and waited.

I remained standing and cleared my throat. "It so happens that Lord Nathaniel Warham is seeking a companion for his sister, Beatrice."

"I know her. She's a friend of Frances's."

I bowed my head in acknowledgment. "His lordship once asked if I might consider such a post. At the time, it was not feasible. But in light of recent events, and since I'm unable to find accommodation in one of your homes"—I didn't disguise the recrimination in my tone—"might not this solve my dilemma? Since I am not free to leave your employ as I am contracted, could you recommend me to him?"

Sir Francis's eyes narrowed as he contemplated my proposal. He no longer saw me, lost in the maze of his mind.

"Perchance you could write to Lord Nathaniel . . ." My voice petered out. I sank into my chair and waited.

Voices drifted through the door, as did the sound of footsteps and a loud bang as something was dropped upon the floor. Sir Francis didn't notice. Through the window behind him I watched an ostler placing a feed bag over the head of a fractious horse, holding him by the reins, putting his face close to one of the horse's ears as it resisted before calming and plunging its nose into the chaff. An older maid stopped to converse with one of the yard hands, who threw his head back to laugh at something she said. If Lord Nathaniel would not have me, the life of a maid might have to suffice . . .

"Placing you in Lord Nathaniel's house could work in a number of ways," said Sir Francis. Hope began to flower in my breast. "It will provide you with safe accommodation, respectable employment, and you'll be seen to be away from my sphere of . . . influence by Gideon and Valentina. I believe they would approve."

I didn't correct his assumption. Mamma would not care if I was sent to the Celebes Sea.

"It will give them time to adjust." His tone softened. "It will give you the same."

"I've no need of time," I said swiftly. The lies were dancing off my tongue of late. I was indeed becoming the false woman Lord Nathaniel had accused me of being, saying one thing and meaning another.

Sir Francis regarded me patiently. My glibness did not fool him.

"Whether you do or not, a post with Lord Nathaniel places you in the perfect position to do something for me. For your country."

Not yet ready to own me as a daughter, he would fain continue to use me as an employee. Mamma's warnings tolled. My shoulders became heavy. My temples throbbed. I pressed my fingers against them. This didn't sit well. Had I been too hasty? I opened my mouth to object, but before I could, Sir Francis continued.

"In the wake of Campion's death, the colleges in Reims and the networks they've established throughout England are seeking to recruit more souls. That renegade priest Anthony Tyrell revealed as much when we questioned him. The Guises in league with Philip and the Pope are pressing harder for the Queen's removal. Her assassination. They will stop at nothing to achieve this."

I inhaled sharply.

"Over the last months, hundreds of Catholic books and pamphlets have made their way to our shores, all designed to sway weak minds against Her Majesty and our faith."

"You've not seized them?"

Sir Francis hesitated. "Only a few. We've allowed most to enter the country, tried to follow them from the ports with the intention to find the source and monitor to whom they're distributed. Even though hundreds have arrived, thus far only a few have reappeared. Alas, despite our best efforts, we've been unable to discover where the bulk of them are being housed, or for where they're destined. We suspect they're in London. Whoever has them is either awaiting a signal to begin distribution or the arrival of someone who will take them out of the city. From here, there's no doubt they'll disappear into Catholic strongholds in the countryside—Northamptonshire, Oxford and further north— and be used to garner support for that viper in our bosom, the Scottish Queen. For that reason, we must find and destroy them—and destroy whoever has them. If Campion has taught us anything, it's the danger of powerful, persuasive words."

My heart hammered.

"I'm uncertain what this has to do with me, sir."

Sir Francis smiled, and this time it reached his eyes. "Oh, everything. You see, in the past, any Catholic propaganda was distributed by those traveling for business—merchants, tinkers, itinerant workers. They move from town to town, village to village, without arousing suspicion. If you recall, Campion himself pretended to be a jewel merchant."

Pushing aside thoughts of Campion and the overwhelming sadness and confusion that attended them, I focused on what Sir Francis was saying.

"Aware we're watching them," he continued, "the Catholics have changed tactics. We now believe they're using troupes of actors to spread their lies and sedition."

"Actors?" *Oh.*

"Have you heard of Yeardley's Men?"

I had.

"About two months ago, we discovered a priest among them. Posing as a stagehand, he was able to travel about the counties over summer, delivering masses and hearing confessions. We captured him at an inn outside Norfolk—his meager congregation too."

"Did . . . did the other players know?"

"If they did, we were unable to elicit a confession."

I swallowed.

"Needless to say, the Master of Revels withdrew their license. Those men will never perform again under that banner. What happened with Yeardley's Men has also happened with two smaller groups. This has alerted us to the importance of watching the troupes—those with licenses and those performing without. I've men positioned to gather information. If you take up a post with Lord Nathaniel, it would mean I have eyes and ears there as well."

"So, I'm to watch Lord Nathaniel?" I shifted on my seat, leaning away from the fire. I was becoming uncomfortably warm.

"You're to watch his *players*. I do not suspect Nate of harboring papist sympathies—or priests, for that matter."

I could not help but feel a modicum of relief.

"As for his men," continued Sir Francis, scanning a document he lifted from the many piles atop his desk, "I'm not so confident. It's them I want you to watch and report immediately if you see anything amiss. You know what to look for. You've been well trained. Aye, placing you with Nate could work very well—for all of us."

My thoughts flew to Caleb . . . the play he was writing . . . the plays he'd written. Thus far, he'd avoided arrest. But for how long? I couldn't forget what he said after Campion's execution, how it was our duty to speak out against atrocities, especially when they were enacted as justice. And how his characters would do just that.

Keeping my expression impassive, I nodded. "So, I will observe and listen to goings-on and report, no more or less?"

"No more or less. As companion to Beatrice, Nate will expect you to attend the theater. You can familiarize yourself with the players, their movements, learn what you can." Sir Francis began to twirl one of his quills. It was distracting. "Is not your lodger part of his troupe?"

"Caleb. Caleb Hollis." My throat was dry. "He's their principal writer and one of the lead players."

"Excellent," said Sir Francis, casting the quill aside. "Verily, he will be a fine source of information. Encourage him to discuss the men he works with, draw him out."

"If that is what I must do."

There must have been something in my tone, for Sir Francis shot me a strange look.

"Does this not please you, Mallory? Did you not suggest Lord Nathaniel yourself?"

"I did, but not so I might continue my duties as a watcher while beneath his roof. I confess, sir, this is not what I intended."

He looked at me sharply.

"But it's what *I* intend. Mallory, you asked for my help and as your current employer and as your father, even if he wasn't already inclined to offer you work, I'm offering it. I will write a glowing reference for you, such that Nate could not refuse your services—"

"On the condition I spy for you."

"Exactly. Those are *my* conditions."

Frustration, despair and a sense of how impotent I was to direct my own course arose. Even my father could not see it in his heart to help me, not unless he benefited from the arrangement. Only, it wasn't just him, was it? The country had the advantage; our sovereign lady. Nothing else mattered. As much as it pained me, I had to acquiesce. Agree and pray Lord Nathaniel never found out.

"As your employee, your watcher and as your daughter, I accept," I said, unable to meet his eyes. My disappointment in him, in myself, was too great.

I was ordered to spy not only upon a family from whom I sought employ and sanctuary, but upon my closest friend. The man who shared my deepest secret, who had witnessed Campion's bloody death with me, and whom, only two days ago, I had reassured was safe with me.

Then and there Sir Francis penned a letter to Lord Nathaniel and dispatched Casey, bidding me wait. I prayed with a fervor I'd not felt in a long time. I prayed that, if placed in a situation where my friendships were compromised, I'd have the strength to do the right thing—regardless of what I discovered. Did not my very own father, my flesh and blood, trust me to deliver us from Catholic evil wherever and whenever I could? Was it not what I wanted as well? To keep the country and all I loved within it safe?

What if it meant I had to make a choice? What would it be? I was no longer certain; just as I was no longer certain what was right and what was wrong anymore.

PART SIX
Only Silence Will Protect You

No crooked leg, no bleared eye.
No part deformed out of kind,
Nor yet so ugly half can be
As is the inward, suspicious mind.

—Elizabeth I, c. 1565

Oh wretched mother, half alive,
Thou shalt behold thy dear and only child
Slain with the sword while he yet sucks thy breast . . .

—Thomas Sackville and Thomas Norton,
Gorboduc or The Tragedie of Ferrex and Porrex, 1561

FORTY

*M*uch to my astonishment (and Sir Francis's, though he made an effort not to show it), less than an hour after the message was dispatched, Lord Nathaniel rode into the yard accompanied by his squire. Amid greetings, introductions (the squire's name was Nicholas) and the rapid exchange of news, Lord Nathaniel's eyes rarely left mine. Aware of his unrelenting gaze, I listened earnestly as my duties, conditions and retainer were discussed. Sir Francis explained that he was acting on Gideon's behalf, a falsehood he intended to make good by writing to Papa after I left. Throughout all this, my heart behaved as if it wished to leave my body. I could not hold a thought down. Between noting how fine his lordship looked and wondering why I'd never noticed quite how distracting the lock of hair that fell across his brow was, and fearing he would see into my soul and uncover the growing number of secrets harbored there, I longed to escape the close confines of Sir Francis's study.

I was not kept waiting too long. The bells chimed ten of the clock, their cry picked up and carried across the city. Nicholas lifted my burlap and carried it into the yard. The rest of us formed a procession behind him. The eyes of Sir Francis's assistants didn't dwell upon us—they well knew how to look without appearing to—but I could feel their curiosity and relief: relief that the woman Sir Francis had chosen to elevate was finally being restored to her natural place. Only Thomas's gaze lingered, and when he was certain no one was looking, he offered a salute, which I returned.

Sir Francis grasped my hand tightly in an unspoken message as I gave my second farewell of the morning. This caused no pain. Promising to write and visit when possible, I waved Sir Francis goodbye as I was led out of the yard by Nicholas, who'd surrendered to me his mount, a cream and fawn gelding called Tesoro. "That be 'treasure' in Italian, mistress," he informed me, completely unabashed when Lord Nathaniel laughingly told his squire he could not teach a language to someone who was already a master of it.

"Oh, I was but repeating what Lady Beatrice told me, my lord," he said, "it being her pony and all."

"I'm honored Beatrice would allow me her mount," I said.

"She insisted, mistress," said Lord Nathaniel, doffing his cap to a gentlewoman watching from the window of her house. "Anything to ensure your safe arrival at Warham Hall."

The light rain that accompanied me to Seething Lane just after dawn had dissipated, leaving puddles and mud for the horses to negotiate. I felt for Nicholas, whose fine livery was quickly splattered by the traffic as well as Tesoro's hooves.

In single file, with Lord Nathaniel leading, we passed the beggars gathered outside Father Bernard's church and made our way into Tower Street. The relief I felt when I saw Papa's shutters were closed was replaced by worry. I guessed the reason and hoped the apprentices would soon welcome custom. *Oh Caleb, Matt, please, please look to Papa.*

Heading west, we entered Eastcheap and threaded our way through a crush of folk—vendors, goodwives and servants armed with baskets seeking to purchase a range of goods, as well as criers waving pamphlets above their heads, announcing everything from a new play to an outbreak of influenza. A group of children wove their way between us following a pastor, and I was certain I spied one picking the pocket of an unsuspecting woman who had paused to engage the pastor—who,

on closer inspection, resembled a vagabond in stolen garb more than
a man of the cloth. A posse of lawyers in their dark robes strode past,
papers tucked under their arms, their faces inscrutable. The noise grew
as we traveled and for a while we almost came to a halt as carts and
other horsemen competed for space with those on foot. It wasn't until
we passed the London Stone, a great lump of rock in the middle of
Candlewick Street where beggars congregated, that our passage was
eased.

London's streets were one cluttered, continuous chorus. I appreciated the advantage of being on horseback and drank in the sights. It
wasn't until we passed St. John the Baptist and came into the relative
peace of Horseshew Bridge Street that I inquired about our destination. Caleb had mentioned that Warham Hall was in London, but I
didn't know where it was.

"Along here a little further, mistress," said Lord Nathaniel. "My
family built the house during the reign of Henry IV. We've lived
between there"—he pointed to chimneys rising above the rooftops—
"and our estates near Hampton Court ever since. Now it's to be your
home, too."

My home? Oh, how wonderful and equivocal that word had
become.

I had to tip my head back to regard his lordship as he sat atop
Bounty, his beautiful destrier. The horse magnified his height. His
considered tone caught me unawares, tripping the tears I'd worked so
hard not to shed.

"Thank you," I mumbled, and pretended to be distracted by the
flower seller approaching Nicholas, who refused her goods politely just
as Lord Nathaniel crossed the street and entered the manor grounds.

Warham Hall was situated on the corner of Knightrider and Cord-
wainer Streets, at the top of Garlyck Hill.

"Isn't it splendid?" said Nicholas as we followed his lordship through
the open gates.

To say the least, Warham Hall *was* splendid. A three-sided building
rising to four stories, it was a rarity in that, apart from the roof, it was
built completely from stone. Moss claimed the lower levels while the
upper ones changed color according to where the light struck them.
The roof was shingled and possessed two small turrets.

A flurry of servants was unloading half a dozen carts parked in the middle of the yard filled with barrels of ale, haunches of meat, sacks of grain, strings of onions, root vegetables, baskets of eggs, pails of milk and bales of hay. The carts were emptied swiftly and I was astonished at the quantity of goods and wondered how many lived under the manor's considerable roof. Amid the men scurrying to and fro stood an older, well-dressed man in livery directing where items were to be taken. There was chanting, shouting, whistling, the exciting barking of dogs and the cackle of a couple of stray chickens being stalked by two tomcats as well as pink-faced maids dodging the attentions of the men.

For all that the scene appeared to announce chaos, there was an orderliness to everything. It was as if the man in livery was conducting a group of musicians who all played different instruments that made a marvelous tune when commanded to play as one. It was not what I had expected at all.

Unaware of Lord Nathaniel at first, it wasn't until the man in livery gave a shout that caps were whipped off heads and quick curtseys and greetings extended. An ostler tore over to place a box on the ground for me to dismount upon before taking the reins from his lordship.

Lord Nathaniel helped me and then began to issue instructions to the liveried man, who was clearly his steward. I brushed off my skirts, aware of how untidy I must look. I should be the one carting milk and eggs, not being helped to dismount by the lord of the manor.

Holding out his arms, Lord Nathaniel gave a half-turn. "Welcome to Warham Hall, Mistress Mallory. This is Bede, my steward."

The thin liveried gentleman doffed his bonnet.

"And this is his wife, Mistress Margery." A woman of middling years wearing a plain coif and a beaming smile approached.

"Welcome, mistress. That your belongings?" She pointed to my burlap. Before I could answer, she gestured to a maid loitering nearby. "Take that to Mistress Mallory's rooms in the western turret. Above Lady Beatrice's suite."

The peach-cheeked maid dropped a curtsey and took the burlap from Nicholas. Master Bede cleared his throat and spoke before his wife could continue. "Lady Beatrice is eagerly awaiting your arrival, my lord."

"Ah, eagerly, is she?" His eyes creased and he flashed a set of very white teeth. Accustomed to his teasing, accusations or irony, I was unsettled by the warmth in his voice. I placed a hand across my stomach to steady myself.

"When did you last eat, mistress?" asked Mistress Margery, her eyes narrowing.

"Why, I . . . I don't recall." For certes, nothing had passed my lips that morning, I had been so eager to get away from Harp Lane and to Sir Francis. Once I'd arrived, he couldn't be rid of me quickly enough. Sorrow descended and I worked to shuck it off.

Mistress Margery made a little click that bespoke kindness. "Well, that won't do at all. Mary!" She hailed another maid. "Go to the kitchens and see to it that Master Connor whips up something for Mistress Mallory here. Bring it straight to the family parlor."

"Aye, Mistress Margery," said Mary, a plump young woman with dark hair and pitted skin. She disappeared down a corridor.

"Come then," said Lord Nathaniel. "Before Beatrice sends out a search party."

Without further ado, we left Mistress Margery and followed Master Bede. Servants passed us as we ascended a wide wooden staircase, pausing to doff their caps, bow or curtsey as their curious eyes followed our footsteps. Master Bede called maids and footmen to attention with little more than a look or a pointed finger. There was a variety of accents, different hues of skin, many sets of dark flashing eyes and several who looked as though they belonged on the docks rather than beneath a splendid roof. I wondered where these men and women had come from. There were servants who looked no older than Dickon and some who were bent with age but not above smiling at his lordship. Why, there was a veritable army of them. All the carts began to make sense.

As I tried to take in my new surroundings I realized that many of the men I thought servants were in fact workers hired to paint and repair parts of the house. Plaster was being applied on the first landing, patching a wall with many gouges. The huge lantern windows were being cleaned, while above, the cumbersome chandelier was in the process of being lowered to the ground. Painters were at work in some of the rooms we passed and a sharp smell permeated the corridors. In another area, hammering resounded as damaged wainscoting was restored.

"I've had to embrace renovations since I returned," explained Lord Nathaniel. "The house had fallen into disrepair." Master Bede gave a look of understanding.

We passed many tables and cupboards containing lovely objects—glass ornaments, a brass astrolabe, a bejeweled box open to reveal the long ivory-handled dagger within. Portraits adorned the walls, as did large tapestries depicting mostly Arcadian scenes. Candles burned in the darker corners and large windows admitted the gray light of day. The house was surprisingly warm, though the doors of many of the rooms that had fires burning had been left open, letting the heat escape. His lordship must indeed be wealthy if he could be so wasteful. Outside, the poor languished in churchyards and by the conduit; here there was heat and food aplenty. I wondered if Lord Nathaniel gave to his parish or if he alone benefited from such profligacy.

My doubts on that score were quickly assuaged. A few steps ahead, Lord Nathaniel and his steward stopped to talk to a workman who pointed at some paneling and frowned. Nicholas and I paused a polite distance away.

"Workers be grateful his lordship ordered the fires burn all day," said Nicholas, rubbing his hands together. "It gets mighty cold in here, what with it being such a big house and all."

I stared at Nicholas. "His lordship keeps the fires going for the workers?" I glanced into the nearest room. Sure enough, a fire blazed in the hearth, and a rather burly-looking servant tossed more wood on the flames.

"Oh, aye," said Nicholas, grinning and showing two missing teeth. "He remembers what it's like to be cold and says he wouldn't wish it upon anyone. Anyhow," sniffed Nicholas, "some of the servants aren't used to the cold, not being from here and all."

"They're from other lands?" Suddenly the dark skin of two of the men, their flat noses and tightly curled hair, made sense to me. Another had a copper complexion covered in large dark freckles. His eyes were such a pale blue they were almost white. He carried a tray and nodded at his lordship and broke into a huge grin as he passed.

"Oh, aye," said Nicholas, also acknowledging the man. "From all over. His lordship rescued some from slavery, like the blackamoor cook, Master Connor. His wife, Virtue, their young daughter, Missy, and the twins as well. Others sailed with his lordship and Drake— like him in there"—he said, pointing at the fellow tending the fire— "and me."

"You were on the *Golden Hind*?" I couldn't hide my astonishment. Someone less like a sailor I was yet to meet. Why, Nicholas could be no more than thirteen, mayhap fifteen. Gangly, with thin arms and legs and sunken cheeks, he looked as though a gust of wind would blow him over.

"Aye, cabin boy to Lord Nathaniel, I was. Thought London'd be the pearl in my oyster when we landed. That's what Captain Drake—I mean, Sir Francis—promised. That and a cut of the spoils. Turns out, like all his grand promises, the oyster was all shell. Came to his lord-ship asking for work only a few weeks back. He gave me some—and as his squire no less." He smoothed his hands over his livery with pride.

That explained why I'd only seen Nicholas recently.

"Lord Nate took many of us who couldn't get work. I counted over a dozen yesterday. Bless him, I say. Bless him."

Being in Lord Nathaniel's home gave me yet another insight into the man. He had power and all the accoutrements, yet he didn't abuse it in ways I thought natural to his kind. On the contrary, he helped those who were unable to help themselves. I wondered if that was the way he saw me—unable to help myself. A part of me railed at the notion. If so, I would prove him wrong. But his kindness in offering work to these men, and to those who had been slaves, showed a deep understanding of others' needs, and a charity of which I'd once thought him inca-pable. The man was a conundrum.

Lord Nathaniel beckoned us to follow and we rounded another cor-ner. The faint strains of music could be heard above the hammering and scraping. As we paused before a large wooden door, the notes of a clavichord rose and fell. Master Bede opened the door and stood aside so we could enter.

"Beatrice," called Lord Nathaniel, striding in as Master Bede urged me to follow. "I've brought someone."

The clavichord stopped just as a bundle of fur shot out, throwing itself against Lord Nathaniel.

"What is it?" asked Beatrice, rising quickly, her hands clasped at her bosom. The pup had grown considerably since I had seen it at White-hall, and Lord Nathaniel swung it into his arms and petted it.

"The companion of your dreams," he said and, for just a moment, I thought he said the woman of his dreams and my heart soared before, with a great thump, I understood his words and was shocked at the wave of disappointment that followed.

"Mistress Mallory!" Beatrice ran forward and took my hands. "Is it true? Are you here for me?"

Mustering the warmest smile I could, I squeezed her fingers. "I am, Lady Beatrice. All for you." And for Sir Francis . . . my father.

My smile widened as guilt at my deception deepened.

After a fine repast, which both Beatrice and Lord Nathaniel shared, we sat in the pleasantly appointed family parlor. The rain had begun to fall again and the light was dim; servants came and went to tend the fire and light more candles to dispel the gloom. Never before had I found company so pleasing. Beatrice was the delight I first thought and her dog, Merlin, a delicious scrap that shared himself among all three laps.

As the afternoon wore on, I was surprised Lord Nathaniel chose to remain. In my limited experience, men seldom sought female company unless they had an ulterior motive or it was forced upon them. But he made no effort to move. Slumped in a big chair, his legs outstretched, nursing a goblet of wine that was constantly filled by an attentive servant, he was a picture of contentment. The servant, a Welshman named David, appeared uncomfortable in such a setting and I was certain he must be another mariner Lord Nathaniel had collected. The assumption was confirmed when Master Bede asked him to fetch more wood and he inadvertently proffered a sailor's salute instead of a bow.

Beatrice saw it too and stifled a giggle. When he had left the room, she turned to her brother.

"Really, Nate, you need to buy new livery for some of the staff. David's seams are tearing, his arms are so thick. Every time he moves I swear I hear the fabric scream."

Lord Nathaniel smiled. "You're right. Bede, raise it with me at our meeting tomorrow, would you?"

"Aye, my lord," said the unflappable Bede. Ensuring we needed nothing more than another ewer of wine, he left.

"It's not only David's uniform we have to worry about," said Lord Nathaniel, frowning.

"Verily, many of the others are in need of new ones, if not urgent repairs—" began Beatrice. "Nate, why are you looking at Mallory like that?"

I was grateful Beatrice posed the question, for his gaze was raking me from the top of my head to the tips of my feet, filling me with discomfort.

"From the morrow, Mistress Mallory," said Lord Nathaniel, his voice slurring ever so slightly, "no more black." He tossed back his drink and signaled to one of the footmen for a refill. A young man darted over to the credenza, grabbed the ewer and crossed the room without spilling a drop. Watching the red liquid flow, Lord Nathaniel waited till his cup was full and then raised it to me. "You may have the most uncommon of minds, but you look like a crow carved in Walsingham's image in that getup. This house has seen enough darkness and misery. No more."

My cheeks flamed. The pleasant afternoon, such a relief from my recent heartache and all the confusing thoughts I'd had about Sir Francis—not to mention my new master—hung heavy. I felt like a fool. That he could speak to me like that in front of his sister, let alone the servants, who stared at me with a mixture of amusement and pity, confounded and humiliated me. I glanced down at my dress. I'd been more concerned about its cut than its hue. Though I no longer had to wear mourning, my year being over, black was both my living memorial and my penance. It was also my protection. Lord Nathaniel had endured far greater losses than I had, yet with the exception of our first meeting, he strutted about like a peacock dressed in emerald and sapphire tones.

Well, a pox on Lord Nathaniel. I could no more transform my clothes than turn lead into gold. I wouldn't use my meager savings for such luxury. Fortunately, Lady Beatrice came to my rescue.

"Good God, Nate. Honestly, where are your manners? Forgive my brother, Mallory. As the dear Lord knows, I'm still trying." Her fond tone allayed any sting. "You're not aboard the *Hind* anymore, brother, and this is not some motley crew you're addressing." Her words had no more effect than snowflakes upon a mountain; her brother calmly took another drink. "And if my memory serves me correctly, it wasn't only Mistress Mallory's mind you found uncommon . . . I seem to recall you making mention of her beauty too . . ."

Before I could think of a suitable retort, Beatrice captured my hands and drew me toward the seats by the window, linking her arm in mine. "We must plan to visit the theater and see my brother's men upon the stage. Caleb is your dear friend too, is he not?"

"He is," I said, grateful to her. I went on to explain our relationship, all the while aware of Lord Nathaniel behind us, now excluded from our company. The rain fell steadily and through the thick glass we could see the drops sliding down the panes.

"We'll make sure we're equipped with fine furs and rugs aplenty," said Beatrice, sitting down and indicating I should as well. "And pray for sunshine," she sighed.

The smell of roses and a spicy scent I couldn't quite name, but which reminded me of her brother, clung to her clothing—clothing that, like his lordship's, was exquisite in cut and fabric. To my untrained eye it looked as if it were newly tailored.

Leaning toward me, she began to talk quietly. "Don't let Nate bother you, Mallory—I may call you that? Thank you. And you must call me Beatrice." Adding water to her wine from a glass decanter atop the small table, she swilled the liquid a few times before taking a sip. She wriggled forward on her seat and went on in a conspiratorial manner. "Ever since he's been back, Nate treats everyone in the same unthinking way he did the sailors when he was traveling—many of whom now live with us as well. You know Nate was with Drake on his famous voyage? Oh, of course you do. I saw you at Deptford—you were with the servants on the—" She stopped and her cheeks colored.

Quickly recovering, she continued. "Why, Sir Francis Drake's wife, Mistress . . . I mean, Lady Mary"—she flashed a smile—"well, she told me Sir Francis was the same—'quite the boor' was the expression she used." Beatrice clapped her hands together in delighted shock. "She said it takes some time for men who've been at sea and become used to what passes for customs there to be restored to their former selves and civility." She paused and glanced toward her brother, who had found a deck of cards and was shuffling them. "You should have seen what Nate chose to wear when he first came home. Took me weeks to persuade him to visit a mercer let alone a tailor."

That was one of his sins explained.

"Aye," said Beatrice wistfully, "three years is a long time by anyone's measure and much can change—not just a man's appearance or manner." She sighed and lowered her voice further. "I'm sure you know, poor Nate has had to deal with more than most. Sometimes, I think he wishes he were back at sea." Her lower lip began to tremble. She raised her goblet to her mouth to mask it.

My heart went out to this young woman who had set her own grief aside to care for her brother. For certes, the loss of her mother and two older brothers in the space of a few years was a heart-aching trial for anyone to endure. Yet, while I felt great compassion for Beatrice, it was hard to summon the same feeling for her brother, especially when he made it so difficult by persisting in being . . . being . . . quite the boor. Indeed, Lady Mary had categorized him accurately.

But why should Lord Nathaniel have to tolerate the shades of mourning when they only raised painful memories? Perchance it was time for me to embrace color along with my new role, to cast off the past completely. My eyes drifted toward where he sat, carefully laying out a deck of cards. He looked particularly fine today in royal blue nether hose and a damask jacket of ruby with seed pearls upon the sleeves. His white shirt and ruff sat boldly against his sun-kissed flesh. He'd trimmed his beard since I last saw him, his hair as well. Suffice to say, it suited him. If I didn't know the man, I would have described him as dashing.

Beatrice noted my regard. "Still, I'm sure we could do far worse than find you a new wardrobe," she said. "I know a very good mercer and seamstress if you have no preferences?"

"It's not only preferences I lack, but coin."

"Oh, Mallory," said Beatrice, her hands coming together as if to capture a joke. "You'll not be out of purse for this. Nate will pay."

My cheeks colored. "But I'm not his . . ."

Beatrice began to redden. "Oh, Mallory, forgive me. I didn't mean to cast aspersions on you or your apparel. I'm such an ill-mannered wretch. First I mention Deptford and now I offend your sensibilities. It's to be our gift to you, as a way of thanking you for accepting the position."

Now it was my turn to color. Was I not here under false pretenses? Did I not have an ulterior motive? I must not forget my objective nor fall for this young woman's considerable charms. I'd work to do and pride to swallow. As for her brother, as I first anticipated upon meeting him, he would best be avoided for all sorts of reasons . . .

Summoned by my thoughts, Lord Nathaniel loomed beside us. "Are you embarrassing Mistress Mallory, Beatrice?" he said, causing both of us to jump. Beatrice clutched her heart and giggled.

"Shame on you," her brother admonished. "I thought that was my responsibility. Next she'll be accusing me of having coached you." Lord Nathaniel winked and sat down with us.

"You have no cause to ask forgiveness, Beatrice," I said. "I will be glad to take your recommendations and to accept your gift—both of you. As for your manners, Beatrice, I know who should be giving whom lessons." I looked pointedly at Lord Nathaniel.

"Ouch," he winced. "Her bark is mellow compared to her bite."

Beatrice rose and held out a hand to me. "Come, Mallory. Let's leave Nate to his business. Are you not required at court today?"

Lord Nathaniel frowned and a look of sheer displeasure crossed his face. "I'm expected."

"It's not so bad, is it, Nate?" asked Beatrice.

He lifted her hand and pressed it to his lips. "Compared to your delightful company, it's sheer torture. The women simper and prattle and play games that would make a trull blush. They assume men are but rutting goats with nothing better to do than butt heads over their questionable virtues and beauty. The courtiers engage in this folly when they're not pandering to the Queen and her tantrums, enhancing their range and longevity. I've no wish to be target practice for a shrew, even if she does wear a crown. I'm tired of it, Beatrice. So very tired."

Shocked by his honesty, I wondered how he dare say such things about our sovereign. I remembered how she had appeared at Deptford, so old and bitter, and recalled her indifference when the gangplank broke and people plunged into the river and the mud. She cared only that her pleasure was interrupted.

"You will not stay and amuse a jaded lord? Play a hand of primer?" he begged, gesturing to the cards.

Beatrice laughed. "How unappealing. We don't want a jaded lord, but one who appreciates our goodly characters and worthiness."

"You do not overestimate your virtues, sister?" Lord Nathaniel's eyes danced with mischief. It was the most boyish I'd seen Lord Nathaniel. His delight in his sister was apparent. I too grinned.

Beatrice struck his arm and turned her back upon him. "Come, Mallory. Don't feel sorry for the varlet. I'll show you to your room and we can get to know each other without heckling from this unapprecia- tive audience. You must tell me about your family."

If Lord Nathaniel hadn't chosen that moment to throw back his head and laugh, my misstep at Beatrice's words would have been noticed. As it was, her attention turned to him and they didn't see me pale. Zounds, the last subject I wished to discuss was my family. I resolved instead to question Beatrice thoroughly about hers. Mine would wait for another day, a time when I could evade with greater ease.

"May God give you good day, my ladies." Lord Nathaniel bowed before falling back into his seat. I had a feeling he wouldn't strike out for court for some time yet.

As we reached the door Lord Nathaniel called out, "Oh, and, Mis- tress Mallory?"

I spun around. "My lord?"

"I hope, over time, you'll see yourself as part of our family."

With a mumble and a curtsey, I left the room.

What a choice of words. Denied a place in two families, here I was being welcomed into a third. A little family composed of a boorish but kind lord, his sweet sister and a motley household of sailors and servants.

Mamma was right: I was unnatural. For, as I followed Beatrice upstairs, I found the offer most tempting.

FORTY-ONE

Curtains of shimmering, claret-colored fabric were half-pulled across a huge mullioned window and tumbled to pool upon the rush mats below. The bed had a fine coverlet, and there was a cabinet and a deep chest in which to store my few belongings. There was also a plush chair, a practical stool, and a table upon which sat a silver ewer and matching cups, as well as sheets of paper, a quill, a small pot of sand and an inkhorn. A fire glowed in the hearth and a washbasin and jug awaited. This was to be my room at Warham Hall. I inhaled the sweet scents of rosewater and violets and stared at Beatrice, who smiled and settled herself on the bed while I unpacked.

Beatrice had wanted to question me about my home, but my gift of Malory's *Le Morte d'Arthur* undid her. She turned the pages of the book almost reverentially and gazed at me with moist eyes.

"Thank you, Mallory. Though there's a copy in the library, which by rights means it's Nate's, this is mine alone and thus so very special." She stroked the book. "Why, this is one of the nicest things anyone has done for me in a long time."

"I find that hard to believe," I said, opening the chest and placing inside it my smocks, spare jacket, set of sleeves and hose, as well as some swete bags Angela had made filled with rose petals, lavender and orange blossom that would keep my clothes fresh when I wasn't wearing them. When Beatrice didn't answer, I glanced over at her. She hadn't moved but was staring at the book. I ceased unpacking.

"How could you not be the beneficiary of acts of kindness? You're so sweet natured."

She gave a shy smile and wiped her eyes with a kerchief she extracted from a hanging pocket. "Oh, I didn't mean to make myself an object of sympathy. It's just that, the last time I was given a gift by a woman, it was my mother . . ." She bit her lip.

I reached for her hand. "I'm so sorry for all you've been through, Beatrice. You are very young to have endured such loss."

She gripped my fingers in return. "What do you know?"

I stiffened. Did she mean that I could not know suffering? Then I understood it was not an insult but a genuine question, and I was overcome with remorse.

"I know a bit. From Caleb and my papa. My employ . . . my former employer, Sir Francis, made some mention."

"Sir Francis has been a good friend to us." She let out a long sigh. "Do you know, I've not spoken to anyone about . . . about what happened?" She gave a small, sorry laugh. "As if by maintaining a silence the pain lessens. It does not."

She was wise. *If anything, the pain festers.* I kept that observation to myself.

"Sometimes, I wish Nate would talk about it. But he chooses not to. He never has. You see, by the time he sailed into Plymouth, Mother had been dead three months. He only learned of her death when he made land. Same with Benet. It was such a shock for him. At least I was here, you know. Witnessed everything, and was prepared. As prepared as one can be to lose your brothers and mother."

"How did they die?" I asked quietly.

"Jonathan was first. He contracted smallpox. He was in the north when it happened. He never made it home—his squire died as well. Then Benet fell from his horse and broke his leg. His pain was terrible to see. An infection entered his body and no matter what the physicians did, it would not leave. He died at Braeside—that's our house on the river.

"Losing Jonathan then Benet so close together, and with Nate being gone, was more than Mother could bear. She took to her bed. Master Bede called the doctor, who declared her suffering a malady of the womb, and ordered her to be bled every other day. After a few months, she rejoined us. But then she began to complain of bruises upon her body and she developed a terrible rash. We thought she'd encountered a plant in the garden or something. When her gums swelled and her teeth fell out, I feared for her life. She was in agony. The doctor prescribed poultices for the swellings in her joints, they drank her urine and declared it foul, but the cause was not known. She died a few months later . . . Nate sailed into Plymouth three months to the day . . ."

My chest was tight, bursting with feeling for this brave young woman and her brother.

Then Beatrice told the story of why Lord Nathaniel had embarked with Drake. It was a version of what Papa had revealed to me. She spoke of the duel he had been involved in, and how on the voyage he had rescued the black female slave. She gave scant details, and I had an overriding sense that she was sparing herself as much as me.

"Nate wasn't always as he is now—so direct, so indifferent to the impact of his words and actions. I still see glimpses of the brother I remember—the one before the fights, the duel, the voyage and the terrible scars," said Beatrice. "Why, do you know he brought the cats from Drake's ship to live here? Much to Mistress Margery's horror." She smiled and shook her head. "He couldn't bear the thought that they might starve—not that he'd admit that. You'll see them around. The big red one is Bilge Rat and the one with one eye and half its ear missing is Barnacle."

"Nicholas mentioned that my lord employed some of the crew from the ship as well."

"Aye. When the sailors weren't paid what they were promised and Drake turned his back upon them, it was Nate who found them work. Many are here—others he employed on our estate. Lance as well. Have you met him? Sir Lance?" When I shook my head, she smiled broadly. "You will. He's Nate's closest friend. Known him since he was a boy.

"Don't be alarmed by the sailors, will you? I was at first. But they're like Bilge Rat and Barnacle. They look ferocious and ill made, but they too are kittens in lions' coats. I've grown very fond of them; Mistress Margery, too, though she'd never admit it."

"And what of your brother? How does he occupy himself now?"

Beatrice rose and went to the window. "That's the problem, you see. He attends court as the Queen demands, but as you just saw, he doesn't like going there. The only thing to bring him joy since he's returned is his patronage of the troupe."

"Oh, I'm sure you bring him more joy than anything." I meant it.

She turned and flashed a grin. "I think I'm more of a problem than a boon. Nate never expected to be lumbered with me. That's why your being here is so . . . so . . . pleasing in so many ways." She sank onto the end of the bed. "I didn't realize how much I missed female company until I met you that day at Whitehall. Nate had spoken about getting someone, but I resented the idea. I thought I'd enough to occupy me, and Mistress Margery, nurse Rebecca, and my maid, Alice, are kind. But it's this—" She touched her breast and then rested her hand on my arm. "This intimacy, the fellowship is what I've missed."

It was something I'd longed for my entire life, but never achieved. Perchance with this young woman I too could find a bond I was lacking. I'd once thought to have it with Raffe, but that had proved an illusion, and while I shared so much with Caleb, he was a man. Already, with Beatrice, our words felt unforced, natural.

Then I remembered what I was really doing here, in this room, encouraging her to divulge aspects of her life and heart. Why, I was a false friend. The idea made me ill. Unaware of the turn my thoughts had taken, Beatrice gazed wistfully toward the door.

"He's so sad, Mallory, sad and discontented. That's the other thing Mary Drake said. Once men get saltwater in their blood, they can't forget it. She said it's like a siren song that lures them away. She said he won't stay, he'll venture forth again and that it's up to me to shore up a future for myself, for the Warham name and fortune."

There was only one way for her to do that: marriage. It seemed young Beatrice and I had more in common than I first thought. Our destinies were to make suitable matches, the only means of saving us from unnatural futures as spinsters.

"Forgive me, my lady, but I wouldn't listen to Lady Mary Drake.

Methinks she talks of her husband and not your brother or any other man. I would heed his lordship, for there's no doubt he loves you and would be loathe to leave your side again."

Beatrice's eyes filled with tears and she tried to hide a sob. Hesitating only a moment, I drew her into my arms. Stroking her hair, I whispered nonsense, made soothing noises and all the while my mind was a-fever. As I gently rocked Beatrice, I considered the ease with which she'd opened up to me. The poor child was in desperate need of a friend. I made a solemn vow then and there, despite the mission Sir Francis had given me, that I would be the friend Beatrice so badly needed. Being a watcher, an agent, did not preclude such a role . . .

Or did it?

I pushed aside my misgivings and the tremors of disloyalty and doubt that gnawed at my resolve. I bade Beatrice dry her eyes and begged her to give me a tour of the house that, for the time being at least, was to be my home as well. It also served to deflect her curiosity about me.

And so the day segued into a pleasant evening and a quiet supper with only Lord Nathaniel, Beatrice and Nicholas for company. In the evening, Beatrice played the lute and then the clavichord, and proved to be most talented. Asked to accompany her, I declined, as my musical skills were sadly lacking. However I did agree to sing a madrigal with her, as I had a passable voice.

"You put the robins to shame with your harmonious sounds," said Lord Nathaniel when we'd finished and Nicholas had ceased clapping. "You are perfect together."

A compliment it might have been, but I attributed it more to the wine than reality. Beatrice's voice had a lovely tone; mine was too deep for a woman. But it didn't stop Beatrice looping her arm in mine and begging a refrain. Rather than argue I obliged, and so passed my first evening in my new household.

FORTY-TWO

*B*y the time I'd been at Warham Hall for a few weeks, Beatrice and I had settled into a routine. For certes, she was an even greater delight than our first encounter promised. As the days passed and the rain turned into a thick, silent snow as Yuletide approached, I found myself thinking that if I could have been blessed with a little sister, I would have wanted her made in Beatrice's image.

Even Lord Nathaniel's contrariness, which familiarity seemed to reduce to tolerable levels, couldn't spoil my joy in my new role. He was in demand at court as Christmas festivities beckoned, and sometimes days would pass without us seeing him or his squire. I found myself looking for him and feeling oddly despondent when he was absent.

A week went by before I met Lord Nathaniel's old friend and fellow officer on the *Golden Hind*, Sir Lance Ingolby. Filled with good humor, which Lord Nathaniel's moods could not dent, Sir Lance would oft remain of an evening, entertaining Beatrice and me. I didn't need to be one of Sir Francis's watchers to note the lingering glances Beatrice bestowed upon the handsome man, nor the way she curled her hair

around a finger and took pains to wear her best dress and cleanest
ruff when he was present. I only hoped that if her affection was not
returned, or if her brother disapproved, Sir Lance would ensure she
was not too bruised.

While our evenings were often spirited affairs, most mornings
would find Beatrice and me in the parlor reading French, Spanish and
Italian. I encouraged her to read aloud, and would then question her
closely, insisting she converse in that language, sharpening her fluency. After luncheon, we'd translate passages from Latin by some of
my favorite poets and philosophers. While her Greek still left a bit to
be desired, over the weeks it improved markedly and as a reward for
her hard work, I would reveal snippets of my family's history and we
would read chapters of Malory to each other while the sun disappeared
behind the horizon and we curled before the fire with mulled wine,
soft cheese and sweetmeats on a plate before us.

The more I came to know Beatrice, the more I loved her and began
to view our relationship as one that could not be sullied by my true
mission. Some days, we'd abandon books altogether and play music,
sew or, donning our thickest cloaks, brave the snow and cold and
browse the shops in the Royal Exchange or walk down to the river and
watch the swans and boats gliding upon the frigid currents. On these
excursions we were accompanied by two men who were clearly former
sailors. Their glacial stares and the way their hands hovered over their
swords kept any potential pickpockets at bay and prevented vendors
from bothering us—though the call of "hot pies" was most tempting.

As I was absorbed into the fellowship Beatrice offered, and experienced the affinity of her huge household, I reflected on my lack of any
real bond with my newly proclaimed father. Since being employed by
him, I'd sought different kinds of allegiances, the kinds that proffered
regard for what one did rather than who one was. Allegiances that relied
not on a shared past, but on present actions alone. Hadn't I given loyalty
to Sir Francis over my filial obligations to Papa? Hadn't Thomas become
a de facto Caleb? Being at Warham Hall reminded me how important
the communion between those who shared history, values and feelings
could be—even when there was discord. I savored every moment I spent
with the Warhams, even though they reminded me of what Papa and I
had once enjoyed—something I feared we might not have again.

Perhaps it was this fear that ensured I wrote to Papa daily. The first missive had been the most difficult to write. While I wanted to object to the way the secret of my birth had been kept from me, to pour out my feelings of betrayal mingled with gratitude, I stayed my heart and thus my quill, and chose instead to remain on safe topics. As an obedient employee, I also honored my master's decrees and maintained my reports. I was so afraid that if I didn't, I would lose everything. Sir Francis may have declared himself my father, but it became clear that this was to be in name only. The realization cut deeply, and if not for my devotion to *mediocrita*, I may well have succumbed to despair. In the blink of an eye I'd gone from having two fathers to having none, and I could do nothing about it. Tempted to put my feelings into words in my reports, I nevertheless resisted and maintained a formal tone, hoping my lackluster efforts at watching were not apparent.

Sir Francis wrote to me saying he understood the lack of information in my missives, but emphasized that as soon as the weather improved he was eager I should attend the theater.

> *The books have not yet left London and are either being distributed within the city or stored with the intention to disseminate them later. Find out what you can about Lord Warham's Men. Remember, you are my eyes and ears.*

How could I forget? In order to compensate for my laxness, I asked if we might invite Caleb to supper one evening. Beatrice was most enthusiastic.

"What a grand idea. It's been a while since Caleb was here. I adored his play *Circe's Chains*."

"You saw it?" I was surprised Lord Nathaniel would allow Beatrice to attend such a political piece of theater.

"Oh, a few times," said Beatrice, and began to recite some lines. "I'm looking forward to seeing *The Scold's Husband* again, too, and his new work, *Dido's Lament*. Nate thinks that play will be the making of Caleb."

Making or breaking.

We then had a long conversation about those who abhorred theater (Puritans mainly) and attitudes toward actors—however accomplished they were, if a company did not hire them, they were considered lay-abouts and regarded with suspicion. If they lacked a license, they were arrested as vagrants and flung into the Fleet prison.

"I think that's why Nate made sure one of the first things he did was to offer patronage to a troupe," said Beatrice.

I glanced at her. "You think he was rescuing them as well?"

"I do."

And so Caleb was sent an invitation, which he accepted readily. I knew he was an old friend of Lord Nathaniel's, and that they'd been at Oxford at the same time, but I didn't know their families had a connection as well.

"Oh, my family isn't the only one with Catholic skeletons in the closet," said Caleb, his eyes glinting in the candlelight as we sat around the dining table. He held out his goblet for refilling.

"Caleb!" exclaimed Beatrice. "That was years and years ago."

"What was?" I asked, feeling thick-headed and wishing I hadn't finished the last drink.

"It's not everyone can boast an archbishop in their family. Aye, Mallory," said Caleb, lowering his voice, "consider that. Our good little Protestants, Lord Nathaniel and Lady Beatrice, can boast an uncle who, once upon a time, was Archbishop of Canterbury—William Warham. Why do you think Nate was at Oxford? A veritable hotbed of popery. You have found shelter beneath a Catholic roof."

"He was a great-great uncle or something," protested Beatrice, half-rising as if to clear away Caleb's words. "Hardly counts. Anyway, Nate's no papist."

Enjoying her discomfort, Caleb laughed. "Does it? Count, I mean? Mallory, you'd know, working for Sir Francis. Isn't he suspicious of anyone with Catholic relations in their past as well as present? It doesn't matter what one claims to believe, it's the connections they enjoy—or don't—that condemn them." I glared at him. He had a point. It always bothered me that Sir Francis never mentioned Mamma's Catholicism. I now knew why. Just as he kept her secret, she kept his.

"She didn't work for *him*, silly," chuckled Beatrice, pulling faces at Caleb. "Well, not really. She was his daughter Frances's companion. You know I wrote to her and told her you're mine now and how fortunate I am." Beatrice beamed at me.

I choked on my drink. Caleb stood and slapped me on the back. With watering eyes, I raised a smile. "Did you? When?"

"Oh, two days ago, but featherhead that I am, I haven't sent it yet."

That night I'd something to report to Sir Francis after all, and only relaxed when I learned the next day that Beatrice's letter would be intercepted.

It made me aware of how thin my facade was. Lord Nathaniel had caught me out with his questions on more than one occasion. He already suspected I was never Frances's companion and had made his opinion clear. Why then did he allow me into his household, allow me to be with his sister? What had changed? Was he watching me watching him?

The thought was strangely exciting.

After his first visit, Caleb's presence became a regular thing. I was grateful for his company and the laughter he brought to the dining room and parlor. When Lord Nathaniel was home, we all enjoyed discussing his plays, Sir Lance included, and getting insights into his new ideas. Concerned how *Dido's Lament* was proceeding, and knowing his political inclinations, I only relaxed when Caleb whispered that in the current atmosphere, where suspicion bred suspicion, he'd decided to err on the side of caution.

"Truth is, his lordship warned me off; said playing with religious fire is how martyrs get burnt." He swept his arms down his sides. "The thought of my fine apparel being consigned to the flames was just too much to bear." As usual, Caleb was dressed in colors and fabrics that bordered on breaking every sumptuary law in existence and those yet to be invented. How he afforded such fine cloth, feathers and fur was beyond me. I felt yet another rush of gratitude toward Lord Nathaniel.

It was from Caleb I learned the things Papa did not reveal in his daily replies to my letters. He had become increasingly withdrawn, more likely to be found in his workshop at any time of the day or night. According to Caleb, Papa was becoming a recluse.

"He declines invitations, keeps his customers' visits to a minimum; why, he barely enters the house except to sleep and wash. I don't believe he'd even eat if Mistress Pernel didn't send Gracious to the workshop with food and drink. Angela tries to persuade him to eat, and mostly

manages, but he's fading away. Your uncle has been to see him and prescribed a purgative that kept him between his bed and the jordan for a
few days. He looked worse after that. I take ale down, try and draw him
out, but he's distracted, sad, and, truth be told, a little angry as well. I
don't know what happened between you two, Mallory, but I suspect it
needs no physic beyond your presence. Can you not pay a visit?"

Caleb might be right, but I was not yet ready to face Papa, nor
had he extended an invitation. Nor had Mamma. What could I say?
Where could I begin? For all Caleb said, no matter how tempted I was
to fly home and see Papa, Mamma's words were like an itch I could
not help but scratch. Papa was better off without me. He would grow
accustomed to my absence. One does to anything, or so I reasoned . . .

After Caleb left that night, I retreated to my room and reread Papa's
letters, wondering why he did not express his feelings. His letters were
descriptions of his days—the locks he was designing, the style of bow
upon a key, who had ordered what. But then, wasn't I doing the same?
I too avoided any words of the heart and filled my letters with hum-
drum details. A formality had crept into our exchanges, making them
strangely perfunctory. I initially believed that by writing and sharing
my tasks, I was demonstrating how much he was in my thoughts, how
much I cared. I was mistaken. I was further excluding him, slowly
excising him from my real life—my inner one.

And he was doing the same to me. Through denying ourselves the
consolation of each other's presence, we were either protecting our hearts
or splitting them so badly it would only take a single blow to break them.

In order to remind myself what was at stake, I worked upon my
latest coded report to Sir Francis. It was a list of all the players in
Lord Warham's Men, information I'd gleaned from Caleb and Lord
Nathaniel. Imitating Sledd's style, I included physical descriptions,
where they were from, and what I'd learned of the past of each. I kept
a copy to build upon every time I met the men, compiling, I hoped,
the equivalent of a dossier.

When I finished, prodded by the poker of guilt, I wrote to Papa.
I spoke of my day, asked about his, and was considering asking after
Mamma when I decided against it. I hadn't before and saw no point
in starting now.

It was an omission I was to regret deeply.

I spent Christmas at Warham Hall. Papa neither invited me home nor asked what I intended. I was too proud and too heartsick to beg to share his table just one more time.

At Warham Hall, the repast was grand and the chef Master Connor outdid himself. We spent the morning serving the staff, as was Lord Nathaniel's custom and a Warham tradition. I was delighted to be included as a member of the household and not a servant and thus able to wait upon those who looked after me. Lord Nathaniel took the role of Master Bede and ordered us about, never hesitating to fetch a drink, replace a broken glass or lift the best cut of meat onto a servant's platter. There were many toasts to his continued good health and the jollity was infectious. Beatrice played music and there was dancing and singing. Master Connor and his wife, Virtue, twirled their little children in their arms and passed them on to Mistress Margery and a portly man with bowlegs, one eye and three teeth in his head, which he flashed at one young babe chuckling happily in his thick arms while Missy danced around him. I hadn't seen this man, Gully, before, as he worked the yard. After some encouragement, Gully pulled a set of pipes from his pocket and played the sweetest ditties, lulling the room and bringing tears to the eyes of men I'd never have suspected of weeping. This heralded the end of the celebrations.

In the evening, normal roles were resumed and the servants returned to their posts and we surrendered our aprons and went back upstairs. Much to my disappointment, Lord Nathaniel left soon after to attend court, taking Nicholas with him. The Queen demanded her courtiers not only present themselves on Christmas Day, but bring a gift as well. Sir Lance, Beatrice and I were left to entertain ourselves.

Wassails were said, songs were sung and some subdued dancing took place. I sat with a cup of mead and would happily have drunk myself into a stupor. With bleary eyes I watched Sir Lance and Beatrice accompanying each other as they sang a carol, while servants swayed and yawned in the corners, their cheeks ruddy, their livery a little mussed. Sounds from the kitchens below indicated the revelry hadn't ended after lunch.

My mind began to wander and I thought of the presents I'd sent home for the New Year, ones I'd purchased when I was with Beatrice at St. Paul's and the Royal Exchange: a fine pair of gloves each for Mamma and Angela and, after some intense bargaining, a pair of wire-rimmed spectacles, not unlike those Thomas wore, for Papa. For Caleb, I bought a plumed quill and some ink that was so dark it would rival Master Connor's eyes. For Beatrice, I'd found a beautiful edition of Chaucer's poems. Knowing she'd attended so many plays, I felt she could more than manage the poet's earthy bawdiness. For Sir Francis, I also bought a book. Cheekily, I bought him a copy of Castiglione. I hadn't seen it on the shelves of his library at Seething Lane, though he could well have a copy at Barn Elms. Still, it had a beautiful black cover and the print was elegant.

I had small gifts for my maid at Warham Hall, Tace, and for the apprentices, as well as for Comfort, Mistress Pernel, Master Gib and even Gracious. I'd wrapped them and sent them off with a courier. For all that Harp Lane was only a short ride away, it could have been at the other end of the earth.

Though it would be days before they opened them, I wondered what they would make of their gifts, when it suddenly occurred to me that I'd overlooked a present for Lord Nathaniel.

As if summoned by my thoughts, he swept into the room. The music ceased.

"Nate." Beatrice rose excitedly from the stool and Sir Lance leaped to his feet beside her. "What are you doing home so soon? What a delightful surprise."

He bowed to his sister, then scanned the room. Spying me in my chair as I tried to rise and greet him, he marched over. "Mistress Mallory, I . . . I didn't expect you to be here."

"Pray, my lord," I laughed. "Where else would I be?"

His frown deepened and I wanted to wipe it from his brow. No, I didn't. I blame the wine, I wanted to kiss it.

"I'm afraid I'm the bearer of terrible tidings."

My smile fled. I blinked. "Oh?" Had he forgotten to buy me a gift too? An image of the beautiful necklace in the box flashed into my mind. Had he given that to the Queen? To his latest fancy mistress?

Lowering his voice, he held out a hand. "You must come with me immediately. You're needed at home."

The world stopped.

"Papa?"

Lord Nathaniel's look of pity increased. "I'm afraid it's your mother."

Am I Satan's beast incarnate that a wave of relief swept over me?

"Oh, Mallory." Beatrice rushed to my side as, in a daze, I took Lord Nathaniel's hand, found my feet and set my cup down.

"Very good." My head was suddenly clear. I could hear my breath, the beating of my heart. It had come to this. "I will go to her at once. I will go to Papa."

I don't recall Beatrice asking Tace to fetch my cloak, or Mistress Margery ensuring I had gloves lined with otter fur to keep my hands warm and a scarf to wear over my mouth and neck, or being escorted into the yard. It was only as we rode out of Warham Hall that I became aware I was sat upon the withers of Bounty, Lord Nathaniel's horse, and that his lordship was behind me, his arms either side of my body and holding the reins. Mounted on a gelding, Nicholas rode ahead of us, a lamp in one hand, the reins tightly wound in the other.

Lord Nathaniel shouted directions, and Nicholas followed them faithfully, ordering some drunken revelers and trulls out of the way. A light snow fell as we rode through the mostly empty streets. Night watchmen, their lanterns held aloft, hailed us, but when they saw who it was venturing forth, they bowed and wished us Merry Christmas instead. Dark shapes moved down side streets and alleys, keen the light would not fall upon them. Shutters banged in the wind.

I was convinced I was in a dream, mounted upon a fine horse, a strong man at my back, riding through snowflakes. The soft light cast shadows that turned derelict houses into mysterious spaces, the arches and gargoyles atop the churches became promising havens of shadows and light where God awaited. The snow upon the ground filled the filthy ditches pristine white. I remembered a similar ride nigh on three years ago. It was colder, more desperate and so exciting. Then I rode into a new life. Here I was heading toward death. A death, God forgive my cursed soul, I'd wished for many a time.

I bit back a sob. Lord Nathaniel took the reins with one hand; the other he curled around my body and pressed me against him. For a moment I resisted, then melted into his solidness, reveling in the warmth of his chest, the way his chin grazed my hood. His arm squashed my breasts, which suddenly felt full, while his fingers gathered my waist to him. I felt safe, secure. Raffe had made me ride behind him, explaining it was so he could ride faster. I never complained about the cold upon my back, the snow collecting on my cloak that made it so impossibly heavy, or how my arms became lifeless, unable to grip him. I had ridden in fear of falling the entire way. Only later did I understand that it was because he was a poor horseman, something that became apparent when he hired a hack for me outside London's walls.

"I'm so sorry, Mallory," whispered Lord Nathaniel, "I daren't ride faster. I just hope we're not too late."

How could I tell him it wasn't possible to be too late? My mother had died years ago. The woman dying now was someone who had resented me with every breath she took, who'd never loved or wanted me. Like my entire life, this ride to her bedside as she drew her last was a pretense I maintained for everyone's sake—including my own. Would Mamma keep the facade going to the last, or would she expose me for what I was?

The weight of Lord Nathaniel's chin upon my head was a great comfort. If I hadn't been so selfish, I would have told him to set me down, that he didn't need to do this. He should be with his sister and his friend, at home. I could scarcely credit I'd thought ill of him so often and yet here he was, returned from court to escort me home in my hour of need.

Then it occurred to me. "How . . . how did you know about Mamma?"

"A messenger came to court."

"From Papa?"

"No. It came from Sir Francis. I thought you could tell me why. Verily, I was shocked to discover you didn't know. I didn't expect to find you at the house."

"I do not know."

Why hadn't Papa sent for me? Had our relationship so altered? Had he withdrawn his affection to such an extent that he would not want me by his side at such a time? I batted away the tears.

We continued in silence until we reached the shop in Tower Street. The gate was open, allowing Nicholas and Lord Nathaniel to ride in. Master Gib was waiting for us. He took the horses and ushered us toward the kitchen.

Inside sat the apprentices, Mistress Pernel, Gracious, who'd been weeping, and the dogs, Latch and her kittens. Caleb sat at the table, his head in his hands. Sadness filled the room. The fire crackled, a large pot spat and bubbled in defiance of the mood. Upon the table were tankards and jugs. A half-eaten loaf and some cold coney also sat upon a platter. As we entered, the company raised their heads. Caleb leaped to his feet and pulled me into an embrace.

"I'm so sorry, dear heart."

There were murmurs of welcome, of sorrow. When the others saw who accompanied me, there was a rush to stand and doff caps. Lord Nathaniel bid them stay.

Caleb released me and I went to thank the others. Before I could say anything, Comfort swept into the room. Her face was swollen, and tears streamed down her pink cheeks. When she saw me, her face brightened before she began to cry.

"Oh, Mistress Mallory, thank the dear Lord you're here. Come, come, I think she waits only for you. Forgive me, my lord, I must take the mistress."

"Go, go," said Lord Nathaniel. "I will wait here and pray." Once again he took my hand and squeezed it. "If you need me, I am here."

Caleb gave a reassuring nod and waved me to the door. It was all I could do not to drag him and Lord Nathaniel with me. But this was something I needed to do on my own: to say goodbye to the woman I called Mamma. My nemesis.

FORTY-THREE

*P*apa and Angela kept vigil beside the bed. Candles flickered on every available surface. The rood, usually hidden behind a plate upon the mantelpiece, was on full display. Scattered across the coverlet were Mamma's Agnus Dei, two sets of rosary beads, her worn missal and silver cross. As custom dictated, her hand mirror had been placed face down lest the living see their own image and follow the dead to the grave. Angela was reading from a prayer book. Papa looked up at my entry and gave a sad, weary nod before turning back to hold Mamma's hand.

With a heavy heart, I approached the bed. The curtains had been drawn back. Mamma lay propped up on the pillows, her eyes shut. Her face was pale and gray, and her hair, which had been brushed, spilled over her shoulders. Her lips were dry and bloodless; her breath loud, uneven and moist. She inhaled in one long, noisy effort before it was expelled. Not even the incense burning alongside the candles could disguise the smell of illness, of death.

As I went to touch her hand, I saw another man in the room. Of medium height, with dark hair and a clean-shaven face, he was dressed in the vestments for last rites. He stood near one of the bedposts and regarded me cooly, then began to chant from the open book in his hand.

Good God, it was a priest.

Horror rose only to be quickly doused. What did it matter now? Nonetheless, as I came closer, I tried to lodge his appearance in my head. How dare he show his face, repeat words that were forbidden? Wear such clothes? His presence in our house was a sign of growing papist boldness.

Angela gave a sob when she saw me and went to move in my direction. The priest glared at her and she subsided, responding automatically to his words, crossing herself.

Much to my astonishment, Papa did as well. I drifted closer and stood behind him. Resting a hand tentatively on his shoulder, I was about to remove it when he reached up and clasped it tightly in his fingers. It was all I could do not to burst into tears.

"Mallory," he whispered hoarsely.

"I'm here, Papa."

Mamma's eyes flickered open and she looked straight at me. A smile parted her lips and I began to respond, until I understood it was directed at Papa.

"She came for you, Gideon. She does her duty still. Did I not tell you?" Every word was an effort. Her free hand rose from the bed and rested upon what I first thought was a pillow beneath her breasts. It was her stomach. What ailed Mamma that her womb, barren of life to the end, was now swollen as if with child?

God, how can You be so cruel?

The priest's voice continued in the background. I wanted to hush him, to tell him to go lest I report his presence and have him followed. But I could not. If this gave Mamma comfort, if it helped reconcile her soul, then I would not interfere.

"This," she rasped to the priest, a bony finger pointing at me. "This is the one of whom I spoke."

Papa pulled me closer. "She has made her confession. Her soul is cleansed."

Mamma's head turned. "I'm not deaf, Gideon. My soul can never be cleansed. I've done great wrong in my life and no more so than to you both. Mallory, come here; I would speak with you one last time."

Releasing her hand and mine, Papa rose and offered his seat to me. I hesitated, and Mamma tried to laugh, but it turned into an effort to catch her breath. I sat quickly, taking the dry hand that lay on the coverlet.

"My bite has no teeth, Mallory. Not anymore."

Then you will just suck what little hope of redemption remains out of me.

I waited for Mamma to regain her breath. Angela tried to make her more comfortable, moving pillows, loosening the gown about her throat, but Mamma shook her head. *"Basta,"* she said. Enough.

Aye, for all of us.

She thrust her chin forward. The action emphasized the hollowness of her cheeks and the way her illness had wasted her flesh, rendering her little more than a skeleton. Whatever beauty she once possessed was now only in her eyes, and I looked into them as they held mine.

I knew what she wanted. "I'm sorry, Mamma," I began. "Sorry for what you had to sacrifice in order to give me a life. A life I chose to ruin. Forgive me, if you can."

Mamma's eyes were strange in the glowing light, softer and more than a little afraid. Was it fear of death, or was it me? Had I not just said what she needed to hear?

"I do not want you to apologize." Her body was seized by a fit of coughing, and I waited for it to pass. "What I want," she continued hoarsely, "is for you to forgive me."

I froze. Angela's hand flew to her mouth. Behind me, I heard Papa inhale sharply. None of us had expected this.

"There's nothing to forgive—" I began. With surprising strength, Mamma squeezed my hand.

"No. No. No more lies. I've not the time, or the inclination . . ."

Her eyes closed. It was some time before she spoke again. Papa, Angela and I remained gazing at her. The priest murmured in soporific tones, his voice rising and falling with the cadence of his prayers.

Mamma wanted my forgiveness? Why? She'd so clearly outlined what my presence had done to her life and Papa's. How, by simply existing, I'd destroyed their dreams. Was this her faith talking? Did she want forgiveness so her soul would rush to be with the Lord? So she wouldn't be sent to purgatory?

Why did I hesitate to offer forgiveness? When had I become so ungenerous? Mamma didn't deserve this. Not now. Nor did Papa. As we waited for Mamma to speak again, if she could, Papa placed his hand on my shoulder. I rested my cheek against it.

"If you cannot, I will understand." His words were faint but made any doubt I'd harbored flee.

Finally, Mamma's eyes opened. "Your tongue is still. Perchance forgiveness begins with the asking." She took a breath and it echoed about her struggling ribs. "I'm sorry, Mallory," said Mamma. Her voice was deep, quivery. "For not loving you, for not being the mamma Lucia would have wished me to be; that God wanted. For blaming you for destroying my life and Gideon's."

Angela gasped. Behind me, Papa groaned; his grip on my shoulder became painful.

"Bah. You did not do any of these things," she continued in a rush, as if she might expire before she was finished. "I did. I was the architect of my own folly, my own misery. Not you. *Allora, mio Dio* has, in His wisdom, shown me this." She drew me closer. Her breath was rancid, though her nightgown and bedclothes smelled sweet. Pushing the hair from my face, she caressed my cheeks the way I'd always longed for her to do, following the contours, tracking the tears that spilled, her eyes searching mine. "Lucia's eyes, aye, but also your father's." She gave a small smile that was nonetheless filled with the affection she'd denied us both. "Do not make the same mistakes I did; do not let the actions of others, of the past, decide your fate. Decide your own."

"How can I, Mamma?" The words were difficult, strangled as they were by the grief rising in my chest. "You said yourself, we women are doomed to be at the whim of men."

"*Si.* I did. But we can choose the men to whom we cleave, if not in heart, then mind. Learn from your mistakes in ways I did not. Your papa, bless him, equipped you to do that. Do not disappoint him. Do not disappoint me or my memory. Make amends for me as well." Lifting my hand, she held it to her lips. They were flaky, hot, but no less tender for that.

Mamma's face swam in my vision. My heart, so long deflated when it came to her, filled one last time, and it was as if all its wounds were repaired. I lowered my head against her frail chest, this woman who had battled to live so she might offer an apology. I understood and was quite undone.

"I forgive you, Mamma. I forgive you," I whispered.

I never knew if she heard, only that her hand became slack in mine. The chest beneath my ear grew still and quiet. Papa took me by the shoulders and slowly eased me upright as Angela let out a long wail. The priest came forward and closed Mamma's eyes. He anointed her with holy oil and said the final prayers. Held tight in Papa's arms, I watched. Angela joined our embrace and the three of us stood beside the bed, a trio of misery but, also, strangely, joy. With her last breath, Mamma and I had reconciled. The healing had begun. Mamma had ensured that.

At some stage, Papa left the room and, in the distance, the parish bell began to toll. One stroke of the bell for each year of Mamma's life. When he returned some time later, snow salting his cloak, he thrust something into the priest's hand.

"For your services, for the indulgences and candles. Go and God be with you. Our thanks and blessings as well. May you be safe."

With a nod and a final dark look in my direction, the priest made the sign of the cross toward Mamma's body, then toward Angela, and collected his cloak and left.

Papa watched him go, then went to the bed and with a look of utter desolation, stroked Mamma's cheeks. "You spent most of your life by my side, even though I broke almost every promise I made. How will I go on without you, Valentina, *amore mio?*" His voice cracked and he bowed his head.

Angela put her arm around me to prevent me going to him. "Let us leave him awhile. We can return to prepare her body. Comfort will want to help, no doubt Mistress Dorothy and some of the other gossips as well."

I nodded. If I spoke, the dam of weeping inside me would break.

"I will go to the others," said Angela, her face crumpling into a picture of anguish.

Taking a candle, I followed her from the room, shutting the door quietly. "I will come downstairs shortly. I . . . I just need some time to myself," I said.

Angela didn't question me, but descended to the kitchen. I went upstairs, to my old room. As I pushed open the door, the icy air wrapped itself around me. Without a fire, the room was bone cold and dark. Stumbling across the floor, I used the candle I was carrying to light some more. I sat on the bed and stared toward the window. The closed shutters looked back. Once, they'd appeared hard and unforgiving. Now I saw the grains in the wood, the places where splinters had lifted, creating textures that spoke of history, of changing seasons, other hands and times. Much like people, these shutters were weathered by their experiences.

Just like Mamma . . . bitter, brittle Mamma. Yet in ways I was only beginning to understand, she had been strong beyond measure. In her determination not to love me, to hide the reasons she could not, she had shaped the woman I'd become. She'd also set a path for me to follow, one in which she ensured Papa would be by my side.

The tears fell freely then and coursed down my cheeks. I cried for Valentina Bright, the woman I called Mamma but never really, until the last moments of her life, knew. I wish we'd had more time. That I could have been more generous in my heart toward her.

How long I sat there, I was uncertain. The bell ceased to toll, the house was quiet and I was so very cold. I rose and shivers wracked my body. I would catch a chill or worse sitting up here. I went down the stairs, lost in thought. A light flickered in one of the rooms on the next floor. There was a series of dull thuds. Caleb. I could do with his company, ask for solace and provide some. Tell him what had happened in Mamma's room and how, before a priest no less, a miracle had occurred.

FORTY-FOUR

I knocked quietly and pushed the door open. Caleb sat in front of the chest, a pile of books and pamphlets scattered around him. His eyes widened and his face paled when he saw me. "Mallory." Jumping to his feet, he began to push me out of the room, but not before I'd seen what he was sorting.

Multiple copies of *Motives Inducing to the Catholic Faith*—a seditious tract by Richard Bristowe—were strewn across the floor. There were many other publications as well.

"What are you doing with these?" I hissed.

For a beat, he locked eyes with me before throwing up his arms and backing away. I kneeled down and picked up a pamphlet.

"This is by the priest Nicholas Sanders. And what's this?" I asked, putting that pamphlet down and sweeping up another. I could scarcely believe my eyes. "Good God, Caleb. This is Bristowe's defense of Pope Pius V's Bull excommunicating the Queen. Are you mad? I thought this chest was your friend's?"

"It is," said Caleb miserably. His eyes filled. "I'm so sorry about Valentina, Mallory. I know you two didn't always have an accord, but she was your mother."

"No. She wasn't," I snapped. "Don't try and distract me. Caleb, what you have here is the work of heretics, of Catholics." I searched through the pile and uncovered writings by William Allen, Luke Kirby and other priests—some already on trial, others, like Bristowe, dead. These were the very books and pamphlets Sir Francis was turning London inside out to find. How dare Caleb bring such danger upon us? What devil-induced folly was this?

"If these are found here, not only will you be hanged or worse, but Papa as well. Caleb, how could you?"

"I tell you, it wasn't me." He sank onto the bed.

I stared at him. "Who then?"

He shook his head. "I promised never to tell."

"Caleb . . ."

"Oh, don't you 'Caleb' me. You refuse to break the promises you make to friends, to Sir Francis, so why should you expect me to break mine?"

I tried not to lose my temper, tried once again to affect an indifference I didn't feel. "If the chest isn't yours, then how did you open it?" I scooped the lock from the floor and brandished it.

"This is no ordinary lock, Caleb, don't try and persuade me otherwise. Unless you have the keys, and you assured me you did not, it will release a spray of ink or worse, identifying the lock-pick. You're not capable of picking this. Ergo, you are in possession of the keys. Ergo, the chest is yours and so are they." I gestured to the works on the floor.

I thought Caleb might try and deny my accusations, but he fell silent, staring at the offensive works, at the chest, at the lock in my hand. Anywhere but at me. My frustration mounted.

"Why open it *now*? Of all times, when Mamma's just died and the house is about to be filled with mourners? Did that priest make you? Or did he simply inspire you to be such a reckless fool?"

Caleb gave a strangled laugh. "It was the only way I could persuade him to come out of hiding."

"*You* found the priest?"

"I didn't find him. That implies he was lost. I knew where he was. I just had to convince him it wasn't a trap. That I wasn't one of Walsingham's men." He shot me a pointed look that I ignored. "I had to prove he was being summoned for a genuine purpose—a Catholic one. We needed him to perform the last rites. I took one of these"—he scattered the pages with a savage thrust—"as proof. I didn't know what else to do—" He stared dolefully at the material. "He couldn't come quick enough."

"So you knew what was in the chest all along?"

"Knowing who it belonged to, I guessed it was Catholic propaganda."

"Guessed? Surely you would know if you're a friend of this Catholic?"

"He's not my . . . it's . . . it's complicated."

I wanted to scream. Caleb lowered his eyes.

"Why didn't you tell me?"

"What difference would it have made?"

There was a long cry from downstairs. Widow Dorothy had arrived. I shook my head.

"I still wish you hadn't brought a priest to the house, let alone this . . . this material. I don't care whether you're storing it for a friend or an arch enemy." He shot me a strange look before turning away.

I sat on the floor and began to put the books and pamphlets back in the chest. "Caleb, you don't know what you've done. You've placed me in a terrible position. Are you listening to me?"

With an expletive that had no place in a house of mourning, he kneeled beside me and began to help. "I have little choice."

"You once asked if your secrets were safe with me. Caleb, it's not me you have to worry about. Sir Francis has his entire network focused on finding these. On finding who possesses them and to whom they're being distributed. Do you understand? He knows they're here, in London. He knows exactly what they are. He even suspects they're with a troupe of actors. His men are watching; they're waiting. All they need is for one of these to appear—" I shook one at him and he slapped it away. "Just one to be distributed and then Sir Francis intends to track it back to the source. To you. To Lord Warham's Men. To us."

Caleb stared at me in disgust. "I was right. You're one of his agents, aren't you?"

I didn't deny it. The time for dissembling was over. Mamma had decreed it. I had to choose. So I did. "I am."

Scrabbling across the floor, Caleb leaped to his feet, putting distance between us. "I thought I knew you, but I don't, do I?"

"What do you mean?"

"Mallory Bright, the woman with a Catholic mother, who shared with me how she lost her virtue to a rogue, bore his child, the woman who took a wrong turn in life and swore to head in the right direction. You've spun in circles and become lost. You're a spy, a turncoat. That's why you were at Tyburn, wasn't it? To see your work through to completion." He tore at his hair. "Oh dear sweet Lord."

A note of hysteria had crept into his voice. I tried to calm him. His arms shot out, warding me off.

"Who are you? I thought you were my friend."

"You dim-witted fool, I *am* your friend. If I was not, I'd run outside now, call the night watch and have you sent to the Tower. The very fact I've not done so must tell you where my loyalties lie. For all our sakes, Caleb, calm down. I need to think. We need to sort this mess out, before it's too late. We also need to pray that none of Sir Francis's men are following your priest and if they are, they remain unaware of what he took from this house, that he even entered it. If they know, we're all undone."

Caleb muttered something, but I ignored him and resumed picking up the books. "Don't just stand there, help me. The sooner these are out of sight, the better."

We piled the books and pamphlets back into the chest. The number of them was terrifying to behold. I imagined Sir Francis watching us, one of his men hiding in the shadows, upon an adjacent rooftop, ready to report everything back to his master: how his very own daughter was helping the enemy avoid justice.

Out of the corner of my eye I looked at Caleb, my dear sweet Caleb. My dandy, with his chestnut hair and dazzling blue eyes. The dimples that creased his cheeks and caught his beautifully groomed beard. I took in the fine cut of his clothes, the rich green of the velvet and whiteness of the lace at his cuffs, of his ruff.

"How much are they paying you to distribute these?" I asked suddenly.

"Me? Nothing. Well, not yet. I told you, I'm doing this for a friend. If and when it's removed, he'll pay me."

I took a deep breath. "How much is *he* being paid?"

Caleb closed the lid of the chest. "It cannot be reckoned."

"So you will benefit?"

Caleb began to laugh. "In ways you cannot begin to imagine."

I shook him by the shoulders until he stopped. "This is no time for mirth. When are you going to understand how dire this is?"

"Oh, believe me, I do, Mallory, I do."

"You're not a Catholic, are you?"

He didn't reply at first. "God is not on my side as you well know, Mallory—neither the Catholic nor the Protestant one. It doesn't matter what I believe, what I am. He punishes the likes of me. God of love? Not my kind. No, the only thing I've faith in is human nature—how ugly, beautiful and unpredictable it can be. Just when you're assured of one thing, something else arises to confound you." He began to chuckle uncontrollably. "Why, look at you. My friend, the spy. The Keeper of Secrets. How apt."

"Caleb, please!" I stamped my foot. "Dear God, I need you to be serious for once. Do you even begin to understand the risk that chest and its contents pose? I don't care whether it's yours or the Sultan of Turkey's—it's dangerous and its very presence marks us all."

Caleb's face fell. "It was never meant to be like this. It should have been collected long ago. Now I know why it hasn't been."

"But now it *is* like this. And we have to think of a way of getting rid of it before it's found."

"My friend tells me plans are afoot to remove it." Gathering my hands in his, Caleb regarded me earnestly. "Will you help us?"

"Us?" I sighed. "It seems I have little choice."

Time was I thought my loyalty to Sir Francis would always come before all else. That, like the courtiers, I could adopt *mediocrita* as a way of being. It was time to acknowledge I could not—not any longer. What was life, what was loyalty, without feeling? Without embracing passions and all they offered, good and bad? Without friends? Without family? I loved Caleb and would do anything to protect him, to protect Papa and Angela. I held him close.

"You stood by me when no one else would. You've kept my secret. Of course I will help you. It's my turn to repay a huge debt."

"God bless you, Mallory Bright."

"Someone has to," I whispered. Pulling away, I paced back and forth. "For now, the chest must remain." Caleb tugged his lower lip. "Neither it nor the books and pamphlets inside can be moved—not yet. If your friend tells you otherwise, let me know immediately. As to what we can do with them, I will think on it. Perchance we can relocate the chest, destroy the contents. Whatever we decide, we cannot act yet. It's too risky."

I looked him up and down. "For now, tidy yourself and prepare to play the finest role of your career."

"What's that?" he said, brushing his breeches and jacket.

"An innocent actor and writer, in mourning for the lady of the house. Put aside all thoughts of this"—I gestured at the offending piece of furniture—"that is, until I'm ready to tell you otherwise. Keep the chest locked and, whatever you do, do not open it again. And for God's sake, do not speak of what's inside it to anyone. Tell your friend to do the same. Do I have your word on that?"

"My word, my sentences, an entire page."

I reached for his hand. "Come then. It's Mamma who deserves our attention—not these . . . these . . . seditious tracts."

"Our prayers too," added Caleb, plucking a kerchief from an internal pocket and dabbing his eyes. "Only for now, I'm also going to pray she's watching over us."

"Better Mamma than Sir Francis," I muttered.

FORTY-FIVE

WARHAM HALL, KNIGHTRIDER STREET,
AND HARP LANE, LONDON
St. Stephen's Day, Anno Domini 1581
In the 24th year of the reign of Elizabeth I

SHELTON ESTATES, DURHAM
Anni Domini 1579–1580
In the 22nd and 23rd year of the reign of Elizabeth I

*L*ord Nathaniel had intended to banish stygian colors from his house once and for all, but with Mamma's death he was forced to endure the shade once more, even if it was only upon me. Without a word of protest, he offered nothing but sympathy and understanding for my loss, as did Beatrice. Both refused to accept their Christmas Day had been ruined.

Rising early, I returned to Harp Lane the following day, St. Stephen's Day, armed with food and wine, anything to distract the household from their grief. I wanted to reconcile how I felt now Mamma had passed. I also wanted to speak to Papa—about everything. Mamma, bless her, had made that possible.

Insisting I take Bounty, Lord Nathaniel ordered Nicholas to escort me. I left Nicholas in the kitchen with Comfort and Mistress Pernel, along with the fare I'd brought, which the apprentices fell upon when they came to break their fast, offering me a mixture of condolences and greetings. I went to find Angela.

She was seated before the fire in the parlor, and looked as though she'd barely slept. Her eyes were swollen and red, her cheeks puffy. When she saw me, her weeping began afresh.

Kneeling at her feet, I placed my hands upon her lap, stroking hers, which were twisting a kerchief into knots. "How will you cope?" I asked softly.

She took a deep shuddering breath. "*Allora.* I will be fine. Valentina is with God now. She would admonish me most severely for this." She raised the sodden kerchief and gestured to her face. "She has been fading for a long time and in so much pain. At least she suffers no longer."

I hadn't known she had been suffering.

Dabbing her eyes, Angela tried to give me a smile. "It's to the living I look. To you and your papa. Caleb too, God bless him."

"Is Caleb abed?" An image of the chest and its contents popped into my head.

She shrugged. "I don't know. He stayed with your papa and me for hours last night. We talked. He is a resourceful young man. You know he found the priest?"

I nodded.

"Valentina would have come back from the grave had she not been given the last rites."

I smiled at the thought. "And what of her burial? It's tomorrow, no? Father Bernard is content to bury her in the churchyard? Even knowing she was a recusant?"

It was Angela's turn to smile. "He's been given no choice. Your former employer made certain."

"Sir Francis?"

"*Si.*"

Of course, he would see to that, whether from a genuine desire to help or a sense of obligation, it didn't matter.

Promising to return, I left Angela and sought out Papa. He was, as I expected, in the workshop, sitting at the bench, his head in his hands.

As I quietly entered, the dogs rushed to my side. They sensed some-

thing extraordinary had happened and were extra attentive. Papa
looked up.

"Mallory." He rose and opened his arms.

I sailed into them, a ship returning to harbor.

We held each other tightly. "Are you well?" I asked finally, studying
him. His eyes were heavy and red-rimmed, his cheeks pallid, his beard
unkempt. The stale fumes of beer and wine lingered, and his clothes
were disordered.

"Well?" Papa scratched his face. "How can one be 'well' unless all
the humors in a body are in balance? Verily, I am not 'well,' Mallory.
But I am well enough considering I lost my wife just last evening and
my daughter weeks before." I tried not to react to his last words. "How
are you?" he asked, stroking my cheek.

"I lost the only mother I knew and, weeks before, gained another
father. I know not how I ought to feel except I too am not well."

We drew apart awkwardly. I began to regret coming, but knew I
could not postpone this any longer, that I must take advantage of the
opportunity Mamma had created—I owed her that at least.

I drew off my gloves and cloak, sat and looked around. The bench
was scattered with bits of metal, tools and cloths. The forge blazed,
keeping the room warm. Arthur and Galahad sat on the floor between
me and Papa, looking from one to the other, their tails wagging.

Papa began to run his fingers along the worktop. I placed a hand
over his, stilling them.

"I miss her so, Mallory," he whispered. "It's only been a night and
already all I can think of is the empty bed, the quiet room. How she'll
no longer be there to talk with . . . Sometimes, I'm ashamed to say, an
entire day would pass without me seeing or speaking with her, especially once she retreated to her room. The number of times I walked
past without saying goodnight, giving her my blessing or asking for
hers . . ." He sighed. "I would tell myself, there's always the morrow.
Now there is no morrow, not where Valentina is concerned. I'd do anything to have those moments back so I might make different choices."

I could empathize. "Guilt is a demanding guest and most unwel-
come." One that had visited me often of late. I leaned closer. "Is that
why you risked bringing a priest to the house?"

"She asked. Who was I to deny her final wish? I'd forced her to deny

herself so much. I even organized indulgences to be said. I have no
tolerance for such superstitious nonsense, but she was so afraid she'd
languish in purgatory, that her soul would not ascend to heaven . . ."

I nodded and withdrew my hand. We sat beside each other in
silence.

"Mallory," said Papa.

"Papa—"

Our eyes met.

"I thought in light of all that has happened," I began, "we should
talk."

Papa nodded. "Ignoring Valentina is not the only thing I'm ashamed
about. I should not have let you leave the house without an explanation. I should have sought you out, invited you back. It's not that I
didn't want you here. On the contrary. It's just . . ."

"Papa, you owe me nothing."

Papa smiled. "You're wrong, Mallory. I owe you everything. You and
Francis."

At the casual mention of his name, I stiffened.

Papa got some ale and brought it over. "That is why I want you
to know I understand your resentment, your anger, confusion, the
veritable cauldron of emotions you must be experiencing. I think, in
part, that's why I never wanted you to know. I guessed knowing would
cause more harm than good."

"Papa—" I began, but he raised a finger to silence me. "Please, Mallory, I need to say this."

I pressed my lips together. His pain was so apparent. "Go on."

He studied his cup a moment. "Now the truth is out, we have to
be pragmatic. As your real father, Sir Francis can give you what I
cannot—a good name, a good position. You won't have to work anymore, or try to rebuild your reputation. As a Walsingham, it's assured."

"Papa . . . I'm sorry, but I cannot remain silent. I've something I
wish to tell you." I slid off my stool and began to pace; the agitation I
felt at Papa's words would not allow otherwise. "Before I do, I admit
that when Sir Francis first told me I was his daughter, I imagined
where such a relationship could take me, how my life would change.
What I didn't understand at first, but Mamma made clear to me, was
what you both sacrificed for my sake—for Sir Francis too."

"'Twas no sacrifice—" he began.

"Now it's my turn to insist you let me talk," I said, touching his arm before moving away again. "I left the house believing you were better off without me. That you'd done so much already—not only raised and educated me, loved me—" Papa's eyes met mine and any doubts I may have harbored on that score were extinguished in his gaze. "But you also took me back and helped restore me when many parents would've abandoned their child. I felt you'd paid enough. It was time Sir Francis took some responsibility."

"Sir Francis helped me to find you. In fact, it was his men—"

"I know. He told me. But I also know it was you who came to fetch me, you who reminded me I was strong and believed in me enough to ask the one man you didn't want anywhere near me to find me work so I might build my confidence again."

Papa bowed his head. "I had to swallow a great deal of pride and fear."

"But you did. And for *me*. Papa . . ." I paused. It was time to discover if my suspicions were correct.

"What?" he asked softly.

"You know I was never a companion to Frances Walsingham, don't you?"

"I suspected as much . . ."

"You deliberately had me open a difficult lock in front of Sir Francis because you knew he would not be able to resist having an agent with such skills."

"That was my hope, aye."

I sat back down. "It was not misplaced."

"In you, my hope never has been. Do you remember me telling you about Anne Locke?"

"How could I forget? Her surname spoke to me. She was the woman who left her husband and went to Geneva so she might translate the works of the theologian John Calvin."

"You *were* listening. Aye, that was her. I used to tell your mother about her—I bought the books. My point was, being a wife and mother did not preclude a woman doing great and wonderful things. Being a woman should not. Mistress Anne wrote the same. She said—"

"By reason of her sex there were great things she could *not* do, but it should not prevent her from at least *trying* to do what she was able," I finished.

Papa nodded approvingly. "That was what I wanted for you, especially after what Shelton did. You needed to be able to do what little you could to redeem yourself, not through marriage, but through your own actions. I wanted you to remain here so I could protect you, but I knew that would not work. Francis could provide the means to help restore your self-confidence, your faith in your judgment and in others. Enable you, as Mistress Locke wrote, to do what little you could and more." Papa gazed at me with eyes filled with sadness, love and—I could see it glimmering there—pride.

It was not deserved. Not when he didn't know the complete truth about the girl he'd raised, what I'd done. Just as he lived in fear that should I learn his secret I would reject him, I too had one that made me tremble. Before I could change my mind, I took a deep breath and released it.

"I had a child."

There, it was said.

There was a flicker of something—anger?—in Papa's eyes. He grimaced and the crease between his brows deepened. It was only subtle, but he moved his hand from mine on the bench and his body shifted away slightly. Dear God. I swallowed. This is what I was most afraid of. I bit my lip, searched for my inner strength that now was fading fast. Nevertheless, the truth must out, regardless the cost. Hadn't Papa's secret been revealed? Had I not wished he was the one to tell me? I must stand by my beliefs—Papa must know. I must tell him.

"Mallory, you don't have to . . ."

"I didn't just bear a child," I whispered, holding my locket tight in my palm. "I killed him . . ."

When it had become clear that the baby was determined to stay, despite all the terrible things I'd done once I realized I was pregnant to try and expel it from my womb, I became reconciled. As the months passed and my stomach expanded and I felt the baby move, I began to love the life growing within me. Even so, I kept it from

Raffe. At my pleading, so did Katherine and Agnes. It had been easy at first. His visits had become less frequent and were mostly at night. In a darkened room, he simply pushed my skirts aside and had his way. To protect the child, I became more compliant, less argumentative. It didn't stop him striking me, as he'd begun to enjoy the beatings, the rapes. My humiliation excited him. Often he'd punch me just so I'd react. I'd learned the cost of that, so, with another life to protect, I did not. My shame intensified. I could barely look Katherine and Agnes in the eye, and I avoided mirrors, water, anything that could reflect my complicity and submission back to me. I took whatever he meted out with nary a whimper.

Raffe mocked my thickened waist, my swollen breasts, enjoying them in his own foul way, ignorant of what they signified—until he came to the house unexpectedly one day. He'd been hunting and drinking, carousing with his gentleman friends, and decided to pay a visit to his whore. That's what he now called me. Any pretense I'd one day be his lady wife had gone. Striding into the house, he caught me bathing. Upon seeing me in the tub, naked, my stomach on display for the world to see, my condition beyond any doubt, he went berserk.

When Agnes and Katherine tried to protect me, he lashed out at them with his riding crop and they were forced to cower.

Before I could escape, he pulled me from the tub, threw me to the floor and stared in horror at my swollen belly, my engorged dugs. I screamed at him, said the world would know what he'd done and nothing he did or said could hide the truth of this child from his mother or wife. He'd fathered a bastard and it would be known and he would be shamed; his wife would cut off his access to her money and he'd be a pauper.

I should have held my peace. Enraged beyond measure, he began to kick. At first it was my head, breasts and legs, but then he hefted his boot at my stomach, at our babe. My babe. I tried to protect the child and curled into a ball so tight Raffe's boot only struck my spine and buttocks. It was to no avail. He dragged me across the dirt floor, threw me face down on the bed and, as I bled from my nose, the cuts upon my cheek and arms, from between my legs, he had his way. Barely conscious, I remember him parting my thighs, thrusting himself deep inside, excited by what he'd done, aroused by my fear. Striking my arse repeatedly, he pinched the flesh, bit my shoulders and pushed me into the bedclothes so hard I could barely breathe. My womb was being squashed and I feared the baby would be suffocated. I begged him to stop, but he would not. Hot liquid splashed and I thought it was him. Withdrawing from me, he backed away.

Rolling over, I saw his manhood bloodied and limp. I followed the direction of his gaze and saw the carmine flood pouring out of me. I began to scream. Pulling up his breeches, he ordered Katherine and Agnes to attend me. Hurt and terrified, they could do nothing. My son was born hours later. Dead.

They swaddled him and passed my beautiful boy to me. His dark hair was plastered to his blue-white face. His eyes forever closed. I felt a rush of sadness so wide and deep that I would never know their color. His tiny little hands were clenched in fists, as if he'd arrived fighting a world that would have labeled him, and a brutal father who would have denied him . . .

Raffe entered the room then. A changed man, he'd tidied his apparel and his temper. He stood over me and studied the dead babe in my arms. Though I hadn't yet washed, I was dressed in a thick smock, a shawl over my shoulders.

Tears welled and his mouth trembled. "If only you told me. You know I can't deal with shocks like this. This"—he gestured to the boy—"this is your fault. If I'd known, if I'd been warned, then none of this would have happened. You should have told me. This was not your secret to keep."

The once-handsome face was full of recrimination and innocence, as if he'd played no part in this—the conception or the murder. I tried to reconcile my many failed attempts to take my son's life with Raffe's final successful one. I could not. Rage such as I'd never felt overcame me. Placing the baby down on the bloodied bed linen, I stood unsteadily.

"You're right," I said softly. "I should never have kept him from you. Please, my love, please forgive me."

He opened his arms, even though I could see the distaste upon his face at my state, streaked as I was with fluids and blood, bruised and cut from his attentions. As was his habit, he held me and whispered empty consolation. I wrapped my arms around him and, as I did, I drew the sword he wore at his side, and before I thought about what I was doing, ran him through.

Clutching his stomach, he backed away, staring in disbelief. "Why, you devil-cursed trull. You've killed me." He fell to his knees, blood pouring from between his fingers.

"A life for a life," I spat. I dropped the sword, grabbed my baby son and ran.

I ran across the fields, staggering, falling, getting up again. Covered in dirt, cold and weary, aching all over, I ran on and on, following the moon. Dawn broke, rain beat upon us, drenching my skirts, my shawl, my son's swaddling. Only darkness, when it fell again, shielded us, but I could not stop. Unable to see, I tripped and the baby fell from my arms, his little limbs, his head, striking the ground. Gathering him up again, showering him with kisses, I walked. I walked and walked until my feet bled and I began to have visions.

To stay awake, I told our child stories. So many stories. I told him about the great Odysseus and his ten-year voyage to return home from Troy. How, even after all that time, so many fantastical adventures and terrible catastrophes, his patient wife Penelope and his son Telemachus were waiting. I told him about the sack of Troy and how Prince Aeneas survived, how he escaped the Greeks and their allies and, after a long journey, including a trip to the Underworld, he founded Italy. I spoke of King Arthur and his valiant knights, his less than noble ones and his unfaithful wife, Guinevere. How Arthur never ceased to love them, believe in them, despite their fallibility. I whispered to him of the man he was named after, my beloved Papa and his witch-wife Valentina, who, despite her ways, was good and, I believed, kind. I told him of Angela and Caleb and the street where we lived. I named each and every apprentice, describing them in detail. My voice was hoarse as I spoke of good Queen Bess, her court, her many palaces, the marriages she rejected, the men she made. I imagined the man my son would have become.

Even when the words made no sense, I never stopped talking. I didn't want to sleep. I didn't deserve any respite from this nightmare of my own making.

Two days later, Agnes found me on the outskirts of another village, wandering in circles, babbling. She took me to the house of a beldame who asked no questions. I guessed she too was once a nun. Katherine awaited us there. Starving, thirsty, cold and filthy, I refused succour until I'd buried the baby. The women performed the last rites, baptizing and burying him in the one act. They said God would forgive them. Of me and my part in his birth and death they made no mention. Before I placed my tiny little son in the ground, I cut a lock of hair from his head and, opening the locket I'd been given by Raffe, I threw the strands it contained to the ground, grinding them into the mud, and replaced them with my baby Gideon's.

Only then did I collapse and slumber.

I found out later Raffe survived my sword thrust. Katherine had sent to the main house for a physician and said it was a riding accident; that somehow his sword had dislodged and stabbed him when he fell from his horse. My name and his dead son were never mentioned again. It was as if we had never existed.

Just over four weeks later, three weeks after I'd returned to the cottage with Katherine and Agnes, I was on my way back to London. As Papa and I rode past villages I hadn't seen in two years, stayed at roadside inns, ate, drank and slept, I swore I'd never mention my son either. His name would be preserved in my memory and in the little locket that would never, ever leave my heart.

I gazed at Papa with unseeing eyes. "I killed him, Papa," I whispered. "I killed him."

Papa stared at the ceiling, tears streaming down his cheeks. Lowering his chin, he slowly drew me into his embrace and held me so tightly I thought he would crush me. He made a sound I'd never heard before. Guttural, primal.

"No, dearling, you did not. Raffe did. That bastard killed the boy. He almost killed you as well." He groaned. "He killed my grandson . . ."

Papa's grandson. My son . . .

Though he never left my thoughts and appeared in dreams, I'd not spoken my son into existence before. What was it young Beatrice said? Keeping silent doesn't lessen the pain. Pretending nothing had happened, that a little life had not been cruelly snatched away, didn't either. Talking about him made my son real; made his loss—and Papa's—real too. I ached and the guilt that drove me, the hatred I felt for myself, poured from me in a torrent.

Finally, after what seemed an age, I withdrew from Papa's arms and wiped my face. My head pounded, my limbs were heavy, but my soul felt lighter than it had in over a year.

"I do not deserve such understanding, Papa," I sniffed.

"You deserve that and so much more. God forgive me I ever doubted you." His eyes were wet, his regard intense. I began to weep again. Papa bundled me close once more. My son had not only been denied a life, but a father. I was so blessed with this one. The man who would have been my little Gideon's grandfather, his *nonno*.

I didn't realize I'd spoken aloud until Papa stiffened in my arms.

"Does Francis know about . . . your son?" he asked softly.

I shook my head. "I don't want him to, either."

"Forgive me, but I must ask: does anyone else, apart from Shelton and the women?"

I stared at Papa. His urgency brooked no hesitation. "Caleb . . . I told Caleb." An acute observer, Caleb had guessed upon my return. When he asked, I simply nodded my assent without sharing the painful details, and thus told the crux of my sorry tale. The guilt, however, was mine alone to bear.

Papa gazed into space, neither speaking nor moving.

"Papa?"

"Mallory." He gathered my hands in his. "You must promise me that you will tell no one else of your loss. Promise me." He searched my face gravely, his fingers tightening around mine. "Others will not be so forgiving as me, as Caleb. We who love you. Should knowledge that you have borne a child out of wedlock—let alone that he died and in such dreadful circumstances—come to light, it's you who will suffer. Your reputation, which is only lately restored, the goodwill you've worked so hard to engender, would be lost like that." He snapped his fingers.

"I . . . I had no intention of sharing this . . ."

"Good. Do not. For regardless of Shelton's part, it is you, the woman, who will be called to account. Even the most considerate and understanding of men will find this tragedy impossible to reconcile without viewing you as guilty. It's unfair, unjust, but that's the way of the world. Only silence, only keeping this close to your heart will protect you—you and your boy's memory."

Aye, silence. And *mediocrita*. Acknowledge the pain, but pretend none exists.

"I promise, Papa." Truth be told, it was a relief to make such a pact. I reached for my locket. He may never be spoken of again, but he would never be forgotten.

When I had tucked my kerchief away, Papa led me to a stool, sat me down and hovered over me, unwilling to relinquish my hand.

"Thank you for trusting me, Mallory."

"It was never an issue of trust, Papa, but shame."

"I could never be ashamed of you." He kissed my hand.

Damn. Those tears began to fall again. "Why didn't you tell me about . . . about *my* birth?"

"I should have. I should have trusted you. Us. My biggest fear, Valentina's, too, has always been that we'd lose you. I was afraid that once you knew, you would cleave to Francis; forsake me and those who'd been your family for him and what he could offer."

Shaking my head, I gave a weak smile. I'd been tempted—not to abandon Papa or my family, but by what Sir Francis could offer, what his name could offer. But not for long. Mamma had been right about him. His work was more important than anything. I was more significant as an asset, a watcher, than as a daughter.

"You will never lose me, Papa. Learning Sir Francis was my father, working for him, made me understand something."

"What's that?"

"It doesn't matter who created me, whose blood flows in my veins or who I resemble. I'm your daughter, Papa. I always have been and I always will be."

We held each other for a long, long time without speaking, without weeping. Just drawing comfort and strength. I thought of my son, denied life; of Caleb, who was disowned by his father; of Beatrice and Lord Nathaniel, who were also without a father. I'd no need of two, not when I had this wonderful man to claim me as his.

As the sunlight won its battle over the rain, we sat together, as if we had just weathered our own storm. Side by side, we polished keys, quietly conversing about the last few weeks, about Angela, Caleb, Lord Nathaniel and Beatrice—even Sir Francis. We spoke about how we would remember Mamma and how, because of her final words, we now had a new beginning.

PART SEVEN

Great Is the Danger of Mastered Might

As by Aeneas first of all,
Who did poor Dido leave
Causing the Queen by his untruth
With sword her heart to cleave . . .
Jason that came of noble race
Two ladies did beguile
I muse how he durst show his face
To them that knew his wife

—Isabella Whitney, "The Copy of a Letter," c. 1567

Her Majesty to be depriv'd of life,
A foreign power to enter in our land:
Secret rebellion at home be rife,
Seducing priests, receiv'd that charge in hand
All this was cloaked with religious show
But justice tried, and found it was not so.

—Anthony Munday, spy for Sir Francis Walsingham, c. 1581

FORTY-SIX

WARHAM HALL, KNIGHTRIDER STREET, AND HARP LANE, LONDON
March, Anno Domini 1582
In the 24th year of the reign of Elizabeth I

*I*t was nearly three months since we buried Mamma one cold day in late December, but the time had passed quickly and the confessions her death had facilitated eased the life we now found ourselves living.

Guilt no longer pursued me like a rabid hound. At Papa's insistence I was trying to transfer the burning self-loathing I felt over my son's death onto Raffe. Papa could barely say his name without slamming his fist on the bench top or grinding his teeth. His reaction gave me grim satisfaction, but its rawness and intensity puzzled me. Raffe and what happened was in the past. The past could not be changed—a precept Papa liked to proffer to the apprentices and me to steer us out of dangerous emotional waters. Yet here he was, being tossed like flotsam on the tide. Only much later would I understand why.

As a belated New Year's gift Papa gave me one of Mamma's rings, a lovely gold and ruby creation he said she had always intended me to have.

"It once belonged to your *nonna,* and so is a family heirloom, too."

"I will wear it in memory of both my mothers," I said, and found myself astonished at the obvious revelation. Just as I had two men who were my father, I also had two mothers. I found myself twisting the ring upon my finger all day long. Each time I did, I would think of Mamma and her sister, the mother I never knew. Papa also gave me a bound book filled with blank pages. There was a metal faceplate on the cover that, when locked, sealed it so it couldn't be opened except by a beautiful small key he'd crafted.

"I made it for you," he said. "So you may record your deepest thoughts and feelings, something I believe you need to do, but without fear of them being seen by others."

"A book of secrets," I said.

"Exactly," said Papa and demonstrated the lock.

Now I could have my own *Book of Secret Intelligences*—only, unlike Sir Francis's, which contained the secrets of the realm and beyond, mine would hold the secrets of my heart. Slipping the key on the chain that held my locket, I smiled. All my secrets would be kept close to my heart.

That night, I made my first entry. I wrote about Papa and Sir Francis. I wrote about my son. After a little thought, I also wrote about Lord Nathaniel. The longer I spent in his company, the more I found myself considering him in a different light.

Along with a note expressing his deepest condolences, my Christmas present from Sir Francis was a sum of money for me to spend "on sundry items as I saw fit." I could not help but compare it to the present Papa had given me, but made sure that when I saw Sir Francis at Mamma's funeral, I thanked him prettily.

From his lordship I had received a superb fox-lined cape. Midnight blue, it was made from velvet. It was one of the most beautiful garments I'd ever owned. I tried to thank him, but it came out clumsily. I stopped and felt my face growing warm.

"Just as I thought, your eyes reflect the color."

I touched my cheek. What I really wanted was to touch his. When I explained I'd nothing to give him and asked if, when I found a suitable present, I could deliver it, he laughed and graciously accepted.

The gift that pleased me most was the one Beatrice received from her brother. It was an exquisite jeweled necklace nestled in a silk-lined box with a new key and a very familiar lock. Beatrice opened it and exclaimed with delight, insisting her brother clasp it to her neck immediately. Lord Nathaniel held his sister's shoulders and winked at me behind her.

"If you lose the key, I know a good lock-pick."

It wasn't simply because I recognized the jewelry and the role I had played in liberating it, but because I remembered how his aunt had asked that he find a woman worthy of wearing it. His choice was most appropriate, and I found myself floating about the house most of the day.

Lessons with Beatrice continued in earnest. Her fluency in Italian and Latin, as well as her skill with the clavichord, were things that, like a proud mother or older sister, I would oft boast of to Lance, Mistress Margery, Master Bede, Papa, Angela and, of course, her brother. Not that this was required. Since my mother's funeral, Lord Nathaniel spent less time at court and more at Warham Hall. Uncertain whether the loss of my mother had reminded him of the death of his own and thus accentuated his awareness of his responsibilities to Beatrice, or whether he determined to check the type of companionship I offered, he would oft sit in a corner of the parlor while his sister and I read aloud to each other, compared translations, and discussed poetry and philosophy in different tongues. Sometimes he would join in, and I discovered that Lord Nathaniel was no slouch when it came to foreign languages, having picked up a number of them while circumnavigating the globe. He was also far more widely read than I would have guessed, even for a man who once desired to be a scholar.

Whether or not he joined our dialogues, I was always painfully aware of his still presence, of his eyes upon us, upon me, and wondered what he was thinking. I found myself taking greater care with my dress and hair lest his lordship appear. It wasn't only Lord Nathaniel who intruded upon my lessons with Beatrice. Whenever he was present, the two ship's cats also decided the parlor was where they wanted to be. It was quite a sight, the huge, beautifully dressed man with impossibly broad shoulders, scars that would make a pirate wince and long legs, seated by the window with a large ginger tom on one knee and a mangy-looking black cat with half an ear and one eye upon the other. Sometimes their purring as he stroked them was such a distraction, Beatrice would bid them be silent. Ignoring her as they did every other human except their master, they continued their sounds of pleasure without a care.

At night my dreams would oft feature the cats, only I'd replace them upon his lordship's knee and his hands would not be stroking fur but flesh . . . I recorded my dreams in my little locked book. My "treasury of secrets and hope" is how I began to conceive of it.

I continued to write to Papa every other day, and every Sunday after church I would spend my free half-day with him, either in his workshop or in the parlor. Occasionally Caleb would join us, but I had the feeling he was avoiding me. If I hadn't been in the habit of attending the theater once a week and seeing him on the stage, I could almost have declared him a stranger. He even found excuses to avoid invitations to dinner at Warham House, declaring his writing kept him busy. I didn't believe him and felt he didn't want to face any questions from me about that Godforsaken chest. I sent him a couple of notes urging him to leave well enough alone, hoping he understood. He sent cordial responses and, in his own poetic way, told me not to concern myself, that all was well.

Well. That word again.

Forsooth, the chest and its contents played on my mind continuously. I wanted to ask Papa if he knew about it, if he'd made the lock, but if I was wrong and he hadn't, then I didn't want him to be aware of the danger sitting in his house. Papa had enough to consider without being alarmed by that. I would protect him, and protect Caleb as well.

To make matters worse, it was evident from the correspondence I received from Sir Francis that the search for the Catholic material continued unabated. Frustrated by the lack of success, Sir Francis assumed that whoever held it was waiting for the weather to improve and the roads to clear. He told me to step up my watching and be prepared to act immediately.

Justice will be swift and unforgiving, he wrote.

That's precisely what I feared the most. I had to do something about the chest and its contents, and soon. But what? Persuading myself that as long as the chest remained locked, the family would be safe, I pushed it to the back of my mind.

I also learned from Sir Francis that the Jesuit Robert Persons had fled back to France and was beginning to plot against the throne with deadly intent. More priests were arriving on our shores and thus far two had been found hiding in London. I could not help but wonder what had happened to the one who tended Mamma in her last moments.

As winter passed and the snows melted, revealing the dirty cobbled streets in all their glory, and the morning mists parted to admit a watery sunshine, Londoners appeared like butterflies emerging from a dark chrysalis, pale and wide-eyed. Soon the lanes, alleys and major thoroughfares were crowded and noisy again. The river was busy with boats, wherries and many a sail on its great pewter expanse, as well as swans followed by arrows of fluffy cygnets.

Stepping out into the spring fray, Beatrice and I, together with our maids and two of the guards appointed by his lordship to accompany us wherever we went, attended the theater as often as we could. Seeing Caleb in his element, I could briefly forget the risk he was taking and the danger to which he had exposed Papa and the household in Harp Lane. I laughed at *The Scold's Husband*, *The Mercer's Malady*, *King John and the Earl's Errand*, wept over the futility and tragedy of *Gorboduc* and the sorry, fantastical tale that was *Circe's Chains*, but it wasn't until I saw *Dido's Lament* at the Cardinal's Hatte inn on the 18th of March that all the transformations I swore had taken place within me were put to the ultimate test.

For it was while I was sitting next to Lord Nathaniel, who'd chosen this of all days to accompany us, caught up in the tragic story of Princess Dido and her love betrayed, that I saw the man who had once betrayed mine; the man whose son I had borne and lost and who, with all my ravaged heart, I wished I'd killed.

I saw Sir Raffe Shelton.

FORTY-SEVEN

*A*ware of Lord Nathaniel—his fragrant velvet doublet, the strands of glossy hair sitting just above his ruff, the rumble of his voice as he whispered to Beatrice—while I tried to concentrate on the action taking place below, I had the sensation of being watched. The inn was crowded; people were thrilled with Caleb's latest creation that had been so long in the making. Music blared as soldiers marched across the stage, confronting Aeneas and his crew as they sought to flee Carthage. All eyes were upon them, with the exception of a man almost directly opposite me. Seated above the stage, near the musicians, in a position usually reserved for the nobility or those prepared to pay extra to be seen, he stared at me, a frown upon his face.

Of middling years, with a strong build and square jaw, he was dressed in the height of fashion. The rim of his bonnet shadowed the top half of his face, yet there was something familiar about him . . . He sat between two women. On his left was an elderly one, the plumes in her hat a terrible distraction for the person sitting behind her; on his right was a sulky-looking woman wearing an elaborate coif and a crowned hat atop it. She was about his age, rather plump, with large, protuberant eyes. Her arms were folded over her ample breasts. She might have once been pretty, but her mouth was turned down, dragging all her other features with it. When she leaned over and said something to the man, he completely ignored her—that was, until she struck him on the cheek with her fan. Nodding frantically at what she was saying, he continued to look directly at me. I tried to ignore him and concentrate on the stage, but something drew my gaze back toward him again and again.

As he tipped his head back, revealing his face, we locked eyes and the space between us contracted. Everything around me disappeared in a great cloud of darkness—all except a pair of eyes and a leering mouth.

Oh dear God.

It was Raffe. Slightly older, his beard thicker, and staring as though he might devour me. I swear my heart ceased to beat; certainly I forgot to breathe.

"Are you quite well, mistress?" asked Lord Nathaniel.

"It's him," I whispered.

"Who?" asked Lord Nathaniel, earning a disapproving glare from the person in front of us.

"The man I called husband." The words left my mouth before I could prevent them.

"Husband?" He followed the direction of my gaze. He stiffened beside me and his eyes narrowed. "I thought you a widow, mistress."

Horrified I hadn't controlled my tongue, I rose swiftly and begged to be excused. Lord Nathaniel started to stand. "Please, my lord." I placed a hand on his shoulder. "I just need some air."

He reluctantly sat down and indicated Tace was to follow me. There were murmurs of annoyance from the other patrons as we cleared the benches, and Tace gave a click of disgust that I should choose the climax of the play to absent myself.

I stood at the top of the staircase, trying to gather my thoughts.

"Are you all right, mistress?" asked Tace, all annoyance forgotten. "You've gone awful pale, as if you've seen a ghost."

"I swear by Christ I have." I reached for my locket. What was Raffe doing here?

Behind us, the audience let out a collective exclamation of shock.

Tace and I swung to look past the seats and down at the stage. Dido was about to throw herself on a pyre of burning wood and sacrifice herself for unrequited love. There was a clatter of boots on the stairs and I didn't need to see the empty seat opposite to know who was ascending.

I looked for a place to hide before it occurred to me I no longer needed to. Raffe couldn't harm me, not anymore. He'd done his worst and I'd survived. I'd also confessed everything to Papa. It was time to face the demon and banish him once and for all. I owed it to myself; I owed it to my little boy.

Drawing a deep breath, I sought a semblance of composure. An inability to control myself, the feelings he stirred—the good and ugly—had always been my undoing with Raffe.

He reached the topmost stair, panting heavily, and started when he saw me.

"Mallory." He smiled and looked me up and down in a leisurely fashion. I'd forgotten how odd his pitch, how feminine. The face I'd once admired was mostly unchanged, though the sparkling eyes were crazed with broken veins. His doublet was finely made but tight and looked unclean. His breeches were stained; his boots needed buffing. Leaning against the railing, he gave what he thought was a rakish grin, running his fingers along the edge of his bonnet. The way his eyes grazed Tace and me revealed he saw something more—a need? No, not that—an opportunity.

"Raffe," I said, drawing on all my nonchalance. Castiglione would have been proud. "You're the last person I expected to see." I returned the slightest curtsey to his deep bow. "Ever. Again." Tace watched the exchange wide-eyed.

"I never thought to see you again either, Mallory, but God's will, I've been granted the pleasure. I'd forgotten how lovely you are. If it's possible, you're even more beautiful than I recall. And I do recall our times together, often."

Ignoring the crude way his tongue flicked his lips, I was pleased my unsteady heart and the scalding blood racing through my veins didn't prevent me from sounding almost indifferent. "God's will? Pleasure? Ah, I too oft recall our times together, but here's where we differ, sir. I hoped you dead."

Tace gasped. Raffe's eyes widened, then a slow smile appeared. He thought me indulging in a jest. Once his smile would have elicited a response. But I was older, wiser, and any charm those pursed lips once promised was spoiled by what I knew, what he'd done.

"You do not mean that," he said, stepping forward.

I gave a light dismissive laugh, stopping him in his tracks. "Oh, sir, but I do. I was clumsy. My thrust was poor."

His gaze swept me and he frowned. "You need to be careful what you say, Mallory."

"Not anymore, Raffe. You're nothing to me."

Much to my astonishment, he began to laugh. "Oh, but you're mistaken. I'm not nothing—to you or your family. If you do not show me respect, treat me in the manner I deserve, you will learn just how much I mean and to your detriment." He looked pointedly at Tace, who was staring aghast. I simultaneously wished I could send her away and was grateful she was there.

The man must be deranged. How could he babble in such a way—as if he still held my fate in his hands? Surely he could not have forgotten what had passed between us? Why was he being so bold, risking everything he had—wife, family and status—to torment me so?

Before I could question him, there was the sound of more footsteps as another roar came from the audience and many rose to their feet.

"Raffe," said a sharp voice. "What do you mean by disappearing like that? Mother is not at all . . . oh. Who is this?" The younger of the women who had been seated with him above the stage appeared. She halted on the step below him and peered over his shoulder. Her speech was slurred and she swayed upon the steps. She was clearly cupshotten.

"This, my dear, is an old friend of mine," said Raffe smoothly. "Mistress Mallory Bright. Mistress Mallory, if I might introduce you to my wife, Lady Joanna Shelton?"

The woman who took the name I'd been promised. She was welcome to it. Dropping a hint of a curtsey, I gave her the warmest smile I could muster.

"If you knew how I longed to meet you, Lady Joanna. Raffe has scarce made mention of you. In fact, it's almost as if you were a secret."

Lady Joanna's brown eyes squinted, her jaw wobbled. "Secret? Hardly. Not with three children and another on the way." She eyed me suspiciously. "Your name is familiar. Bright? How do I know that name, Raffe?" She struck him with her fan. Hard. He winced.

"If you recall, sweetling," he said, pushing the fan away, "I made mention of her father, Master Bright, the locksmith." His tone made the hair on the back of my neck stand on end.

All at once Lady Joanna gathered herself. She stared, her eyes narrowing. A cruel smile parted her lips. "Ah, that's right . . . Gideon Bright. Your cooperative, helpful friend . . ."

Friend? Helpful? Cooperative? What was this?

She placed a possessive hand on Raffe's arm. "But you made no mention of a daughter. What was your name again? Mally? Mallory? What sort of name is—?"

"That for an exceedingly lovely woman?" Lord Nathaniel appeared, ducking under the doorway to join us at the top of the stairwell. Forsooth, it was becoming crowded. "It's an observation I once made in the mistaken belief it wasn't perfect." He nodded for Tace to return to her seat. Torn between the stage and the theater taking place before her, Tace's shoulders slumped and with a curtsey she turned and slowly clumped back inside.

At Lord Nathaniel's words, Lady Joanna sniffed, clearly disagreeing with his assessment.

"This is Lord Nathaniel Warham," I said, introducing him. "Lord Nathaniel, this is Sir Raffe Shelton and his lady wife, Joanna."

Raffe gave a small bow. Lady Joanna tried to curtsey but almost fell down the stairs. If she hadn't grabbed the back of Raffe's coat, she would have taken a tumble.

"My lord." Raffe straightened his ruff and took a step forward. "Are you the same Warham who sailed with Drake?"

"I am."

Raffe gave another bow. "I'm honored." He was like a puppy next to a Queen's hound.

"Are you the same Shelton whose father was put in the Tower for harboring priests?" asked his lordship. I covered my mouth with my hand.

Raffe colored. "I . . . I . . . gentlemen do not discuss such things. That . . . it's in the past," he snapped.

Lord Nathaniel laughed. "I may be a lord, but I'm no gentleman.

After all, as you said yourself, I sailed with Drake. I'm more pirate than privateer."

Beads of sweat escaped the rim of Raffe's bonnet and trailed down his temple toward his beard. "You need to choose your acquaintances more carefully, Mallory, lest they offend those you'd do best to please."

"Sirrah!" said Lord Nathaniel. "I would caution you to choose your next words carefully lest I decide to pick you up by the scruff and show you the stairs."

Raffe's mouth fell open. Clearly he was unaccustomed to being spoken to in such a manner. This was the man I once wanted to wed so much that I threw away my virtue, my reputation and my family. Because of whom a little life was lost. I couldn't help but stare at him, this ordinary person. In my mind I'd given him a space and proportion he certainly didn't deserve. I felt foolish and so very ashamed. How could I have chosen so poorly? How could I have been so blind to my folly? To his obvious flaws? The cruelty that defined his features?

Mamma's words came to me: I should learn from my history, not repeat its mistakes. Aye, Mamma. I would not. I would never choose so badly again. This man almost destroyed me; the coward had destroyed our son. Yet his words, his thinly veiled threats, filled me with a deep unease. Why mention Papa? Why describe him as cooperative and helpful, let alone a friend? Papa would no more help this man than render assistance to King Philip. Why seek me out when I'd have thought he'd do anything to avoid the revelations my mere presence could portend?

His wife plucked at his sleeve, making no attempt to hide the fact that she wished to leave. No doubt she sensed how inadequate Raffe appeared in such company.

Raffe ignored her.

It was time to bring this act to a close, to leave the stage and lay this pathetic specter to rest. His wife struck him again.

"Raffe, I wish to go. Now."

With a solicitous smile, Raffe held out his arm for his wife to take. "It's been an unexpected delight seeing you again, Mallory, and meeting you, my lord." He lowered his head toward Lord Nathaniel, who said nothing. "Please, pass my regards to your father. Tell him it was always good doing business with him. I look forward to our next meeting."

Without waiting for a response, they left.

Discommoded by Raffe's last words, I resisted the urge to demand he explain himself. What meeting? What did he mean? Despite my promise I wouldn't let him affect me, my heart was pounding and cold sweat trickled between my shoulders.

Above the sounds of the audience, which was beginning to cheer, the play having ended, Lady Joanna's voice traveled up the stairs. "You never spoke of her . . . or her beauty. How long have you known—"

I went to the top of the stairs and gripped the railing, watching them descend. After all I'd been through, how could I still feel threatened by him? Or were there undercurrents of which I was unaware? I would have to raise Raffe and his threats with Papa as soon as I could. Warn him. Something was terribly amiss. I wrapped my fingers around the locket and held it tightly. Just when I thought I'd excised him from my life, my dreams, he had returned . . . I released a long sigh and turned back toward the seats, but found my way was blocked.

"Your choice of . . . friends, leaves much to be desired, mistress," said Lord Nathaniel dryly.

"Friends? They're no friends of mine. Or Papa's, for all he protested otherwise."

"Indeed. He seemed far too bold, his words discourteous." Frowning, he gazed after them. "You called him 'husband.'"

"Did I?" Heat crept up my cheeks. "I meant he knew my husband."

"Sir Raffe Shelton . . . knew your husband? How?"

I placed my thumb and fingers against my brow. How did I answer such a query? "Oh, aye, he . . . I'm not entirely certain. Something to do with sharing youthful follies."

Applause broke out through the inn, forcing us to raise our voices. Lord Nathaniel stepped closer. "I would like to learn how someone like your late husband, who clearly had good taste if he plighted his troth to you, could welcome one such as that man." He nodded toward the empty stairs. "I would sooner run him through with a sword than count him among my companions."

I struggled to respond. I wanted to tell him the truth. But Lord Nathaniel wasn't Papa; Papa who loved me unconditionally and could forgive my many sins. I could not bear to see Lord Nathaniel's admiration, his warmth, be replaced by disgust. God forgive my vanity. I'd made Papa a promise, and I intended to keep it.

Lord Nathaniel took my arm. I could smell the delicious scent he exuded, feel the heat of his body. My mind became giddy.

"Mallory, I know I spoke poorly of women who play a part to capture and torment men, who construct fanciful lines as a lure, but despite what I said, I know there are those who have just cause." His eyes flickered toward where Raffe had stood only moments before. "I would hear from your lips what your reasons might be."

I stared at the compassion in his eyes; eyes that dropped to stare at my lips, as if he might will the words from my mouth . . . or take them. We were standing so near to each other, I could feel his breath on my hair. He drew me closer still, his other hand circling my waist, pulling me into the shelter of his arms, against his wide, strong chest. I leaned into that long, solid body, felt the tremor that matched my own. We were two bows pulled taut, waiting for release. I tipped my head and he gazed down at my face, drinking in my features. The scars that so perturbed me had become things of beauty, badges that branded this man who he was—a fighter, a man of honor and justice. A man who did not tolerate fools or varlets, who despised lies and those who told them. Who, if he knew the whole truth, would despise me. This could not go on. I tried to break out of his grasp.

He wouldn't release me.

"Please, Mallory, you can trust me . . ." He bent his mouth toward mine and with a hunger I didn't know I possessed, I stood on my toes to reach his lips.

A crowd of folk poured through the exit, knocking us out of each other's arms. I gave a cry. People surged around Lord Nathaniel, as if he were a rock upon which their wave might break. He still had hold of my hand and pulled me to his side.

"Nate! Mallory, come!" cried Beatrice, collecting us both by linking her arms with ours, forcing us apart. "To the tiring room. I want to tell Caleb how splendid he was and admonish him for making me cry."

I glanced at her, grateful for her interruption.

"Cry? Was the ending sad?" I asked in as unaffected a tone as possible.

She waved her kerchief. "You did not see it?"

We clattered down the stairs in our pattens, the narrowness of the staircase forcing his lordship to walk ahead. Beatrice chattered. "How can it not be tragic when love is promised, taken and then cruelly denied? How can one not weep and rail and seek revenge when a dear life is lost?" She wiped her eyes.

"How indeed," I murmured.

We entered the tiring room to find the actors gathered around Caleb, slapping him on the back and congratulating each other. As I noted their dress, a mixture of togas, armor, regal robes and elaborate dresses, it was as if I'd traveled back in time, a sensation my encounter with Raffe also conjured. The young actor who'd played Dido was stripping off his slightly charred gown, bemoaning the damage done to his wig when a spark had caught in the hair. The book holder was talking to one of the other shareholders, the actor who played Anchises, the father to Caleb's Aeneas. When they saw Lord Nathaniel, they came over, huge smiles upon their faces.

There was no doubt, *Dido's Lament* was a triumph. A mixture of adventure, drama, a love story soured and the gods' revenge, it was also the tale of a strong queen, manipulative men, differences in faith, language and culture, courage and tragedy. It spoke to the audience and our times. Smoke drifted in from the stage as did the noise of patrons, many of whom were milling in the courtyard so they might discuss what they'd seen and buy drinks for the actors. By the time we arrived in the tiring room, some of the troupe were leaving to avail themselves of that generosity.

With a by-your-leave, Lord Nathaniel allowed himself to be led away by the book holder and one of the shareholders. Standing in the midst of the room, Beatrice and I watched as props were carted in, costumes quickly divested and hung, the stage beyond swept of debris and the musicians entered to collect their pay. The mood was bright and celebratory and I found my heart lifting.

Had I not also survived a performance? Aye, but so had the villain, and there were lines left unsaid . . .

Raffe's image was swiftly replaced by Lord Nathaniel's. His amber eyes, his mouth . . . I turned to find him watching me. Growing warm, I was relieved when Caleb came over.

"Lady Beatrice, Mallory!" He bowed and we both congratulated him. It had been weeks since we'd spoken but the worry that had etched his face of late was erased, and his eyes had their old sparkle. It couldn't just be today's performance, could it?

Perchance he read my mind, and as Sir Lance joined Beatrice, Caleb muttered something about wishing to test a line upon me and drew me aside.

"Well met," he said, smiling. We stood near a piece of wood shaped and painted like the prow of a ship.

"What's this line you wish me to hear, Caleb? I would it were one containing the words 'chest' and 'books.'"

"Hush," said Caleb, looking over his shoulder. "Must you demand a reckoning before you praise the play and my part?"

I folded my arms across my breasts.

Caleb gave an exaggerated sigh. "Very well. What I want to tell you is there's no need for you to concern yourself with either of those words or anything pertaining to them anymore."

Dread swept my body. "What do you mean?"

Putting his mouth to my ear, he whispered. "I mean, they're gone. The chest is empty, the books have been collected—everything."

I pulled away, the color draining from my face. "Oh, Caleb. No."

"No? There's no keeping you happy, is there, Mallory? First, I'm not to have such things, then I'm to keep them—" He tried to make light of my reaction.

"I told you not to do anything. To leave it rest until such time as I said it was all right to do so."

"You're not my mother to order me about so."

"No, Caleb, I'm your friend."

"Then, as my friend rejoice I'm free of such a terrible burden. Perchance it was the friend I told you of who saw to its removal. Turns out his friend was ready to receive it and, as a consequence, one burden has been replaced with another less dangerous one." He patted a bulge on his hip.

I stared at him, at the guilelessness and joy upon his face. "To whom did you deliver the books?"

Once more he made sure we were not overheard. Lord Nathaniel was looking in our direction and I gave him a reassuring wave.

"I told you, my friend did. Oh, I helped. What sort of friend would I be if I didn't? The man we delivered them to was most warmly recommended as being sympathetic to the ways . . . to the ways of your mamma, shall we say."

"When did this transaction occur?"

Caleb rolled his eyes. "Must you know everything? Why, last night. He came to the house—"

"To Harp Lane?" I wanted to shake Caleb, make him aware of the jeopardy he was courting. How could he be so oblivious? How could he do this to Papa?

"Where else? We've not fine dwellings in Knightrider Street from which to conduct business, you know."

I leaned against the ship's prow, wishing it was a real one I could board and take Papa, Beatrice and Caleb and sail away from all this. My eyes traveled to Lord Nathaniel, who was still watching us. He could board as well; I'd be foolish to take to sea without a real sailor among my mishmash crew.

"Can you describe the man to me?"

Caleb screwed up his face in thought, then suddenly his expression altered. It went from incredulity, to doubt, to panic, all in the blink of an eye.

"There's no need," he said, paling.

"Why not?"

"Because," said Caleb nodding toward a commotion at the entry to the tiring room. "He's here."

I spun around to see Sir Francis Walsingham's notorious agent Charles Sledd, alias Rowland Russell, striding into the room. Four constables and a sheriff followed him. His eyes swept the crowd before spying Caleb.

Caleb made a low guttural sound. "God help me," he whimpered.

Pointing to where we stood, Sledd cried out in a voice that was not out of place among the company, "There's the traitor, lads. Seize him."

FORTY-EIGHT

Shoved aside, I watched in horror as Caleb was struck repeatedly with fists, truncheons and the flat of swords. He fell to his knees, pleading as he tried to protect himself. Blood spurted from a cut above his brow, from his nose and mouth. Any who tried to help him were fended off with punches or blades pressed to their throats. It was only when Lord Nathaniel, uncaring of weapons or threats, wrenched the men off and grabbed the arm of one constable midswing, shouting for peace, that it stopped.

Panting, the men stood in a semicircle over Caleb, who was a bloody weeping mess on the floor. I wanted to go to him, but was prevented.

"Where's your warrant?" demanded Lord Nathaniel, refusing to move despite one of the constables trying to use his weapon to force him to stand aside.

With a sly smile Master Sledd pulled a piece of paper from his jacket. Ducking around the sheriff, I raced to his lordship and, to my dismay, saw Sir Francis's familiar sigil on the bottom of it.

Ignoring the drawn swords, I kneeled, wiping Caleb's brow with my

kerchief. He groaned and looked at me imploringly. I went to staunch
the flow of blood when my arm was knocked aside.

"Touch the lady again, sirrah," Lord Nathaniel growled, gripping
a young man by the throat, "and it will be the last time you lay your
hands on anyone or anything."

The man gulped, nodded as best as he was able, and mumbled an
apology. Shoving him aside, Lord Nathaniel indicated for me to continue. I resumed my ministrations, leaning over Caleb, placing my lips
close to his ear. "Do not despair, my friend. I will do whatever I can."

Caleb clutched my wrist. "Mallory, please, leave it be. It's not worth
the risk. I knew what the price of my folly would be. We both did."

We? His friend. I cared not for him. Only Caleb.

"There's nothing you can do." His voice broke.

Sir Francis's face loomed in my mind.

"Oh, but there is, Caleb, there is." I kissed him softly.

I stood back as he was hoisted to his feet and manacles were placed
on his wrists. "Do not abandon hope," I said.

The men dragged him out of the tiring room, the troupe parting
like soil before a plough. Jeers and cries of protest came from outside
as Caleb was marched past the shocked patrons who'd crowded into
the yard of the inn. Dear God, he hadn't even removed his costume
or makeup.

The room fell silent. The actors exchanged looks, uncertain what
to say or do. It was Lord Nathaniel who rallied everyone, ordering
the tiring room be cleared and the shareholders to go home. He then
asked Sir Lance to escort Beatrice and the maids back to Warham
House, sending the guards with them to see them safe. As folk swiftly
departed, horrified at what they'd witnessed, the general feeling was
that it must have been the subject of Caleb's plays that had brought
such retribution upon him.

There was some weeping, from the younger boys especially. Caleb
was beloved by his troupe and not simply because he was talented. I
was trying to console them when Lord Nathaniel came over.

"Come, I'll take you to your father. He must know of this."

"My thanks—"

"And on the way, you will reveal what you know"—he waved his
arm in the direction Caleb had been taken—"and what it is you pro-

pose to do. I'll not allow you to dissemble, Mistress Mallory. The time for pretense is over. Caleb's life is at stake."

My heart sank.

Once the troupe had left, we took to the streets and covered the distance to the river swiftly. Lord Nathaniel hailed a wherry and sat facing me, his back to London as the two boatmen rowed for all they were worth, his lordship offering to double their fare if they had us to Wool Quay before the sun disappeared behind St. Paul's tower.

"So," said Lord Nathaniel in a voice the boatmen couldn't hear. "Out with it."

Tilt boats glided past; fishermen, their lines taut, regarded our passage. Cries echoed across the water, and the splash of oars and the grunts of our sweating boatmen formed a counterpoint to the gulls screeching overhead. I did as his lordship asked and told him everything I knew. I told him of the chest in Caleb's room, how he claimed he was minding it for someone else. Then I told him what it contained.

When I finished, Lord Nathaniel stared at his hands twined together between his knees. Finally he raised his head. "Do you believe him?"

"Believe what?"

"That the chest belonged to someone else?"

"At first. I wanted to. But when he refused to reveal the name of this friend, and was in possession of the key, I faced the truth. I fear the chest is Caleb's, as are the contents."

Lord Nathaniel frowned. "I've known Caleb a long time—he is loyal and not inclined to untruths. In that regard I do not think he conveyed a falsehood. I do, however, think he's protecting this friend."

"Do you have any idea who it might be?"

Lord Nathaniel shrugged. "Caleb makes many friends. I would ask you the same question. But I fear the authorities will know his identity before us."

"It's not only Caleb I'm worried about. It's Papa, too. If Caleb is found guilty, then my father has been harboring a traitor beneath his roof. The punishment for that is—" I bit back a sob. Lord Nathaniel took my hand. We stared at each other, before turning away, deep in thought. He didn't let go of my hand.

"Mallory," said Lord Nathaniel after a while. "You told Caleb not to give up hope, that there's something you can do. Apart from break him out of a cell, which, forgive me, is beyond even your powers as a lock-pick, why would you imbue him with false confidence? I do not believe that is in your character. Please, I beg of you, tell me what is it you propose to do."

Lord Nathaniel had asked me to trust him. He was a friend of Caleb's, had given him work and defended him, even before the wrath of the law. Papa believed his lordship was a good man. Beatrice loved him and saw nothing but excellence in his character. Caleb was in grave danger, as was Papa. I needed a friend, someone in whom I could confide. It was time for me to have faith in Lord Nathaniel as well.

"I propose to go to my father."

Lord Nathaniel bit back a laugh. "Mallory, forgive me, your father is a fine man, a clever one, but what can a mere locksmith do? Caleb is being held for treason. Why, he faces death and your father will face—"

"Gideon Bright is not my father." There. It was said. My heart was fit to burst from my ribs. I waited for Lord Nathaniel to say something.

He locked his eyes on mine and let go my hand. "If Gideon is not . . . then who?"

"Sir Francis Walsingham."

If I'd hauled a stone from the riverbed and struck Lord Nathaniel with it, he could not have looked more surprised. His eyes narrowed and he tipped his head to one side, as if seeing me from a different perspective would help him accept my words. He gave a small, sharp laugh, gazed over the river, then slowly turned back and scrutinized me again from top to toe.

"Of course . . . of course. The height, your slenderness, the hair and, I don't know why I didn't see it before, but you do bear an uncanny likeness to Francis. Dear God." He slapped his forehead, almost sending his bonnet into the river. "How could I have been so blind?"

"If you're lacking in that faculty, then I must be also. Others as well. I haven't known for very long . . . It is a secret my family has kept. Though part of me suspects Sir Francis's lady wife harbors suspicion . . ."

"A secret? Is that so? And now you share it with me. I'm beyond honored, my lady. I thank you. I will hold it fast also. You're right. Your father might be able to help. By drawing on familial bonds, Caleb may yet have a chance. We will collect Gideon and make fast for Seething Lane, and pray Sir Francis is in residence."

If we hadn't been on the river, I would have thrown myself into his arms.

"Thank you, my lord."

"No need for thanks. I've done nothing yet and, indeed, this entire enterprise rests entirely on your delicate shoulders and the strength of the bonds you share."

Please, God, let them prove strong enough for this task.

We entered the workshop only to find it was empty. The forge was stoked, but the tools lay abandoned, a broom had fallen to the floor and a rag lay dangerously close to a burning candle left untended. There was no sign of Arthur or Galahad either. Astonished that not even an apprentice lurked within, I blew out the candle, locked the shop door and bid Lord Nathaniel follow me to the house.

It was in uproar. Comfort and Angela were weeping while Mistress Pernel and Gracious were tending the apprentices. Matt sported a puffy eye, Samuel and Dickon looked as though they'd been rolling in the mud. Young Simon kneeled on the stones, his arms around the dogs, who were whimpering, and it was clear he had been crying. Master Gib sat astride the bench, his shirt torn, his lip bloody and swollen. Upon the floor were broken plates and cups and the door to the main part of the house had been lifted off its hinges. All around was evidence of destruction.

I entered slowly, trying to take it all in.

Upon seeing Lord Nathaniel and me, Master Gib rose on unsteady legs. I ran to his side to assist him.

"They burst in before we even knew who they were. Tore the place apart," he said, lifting his arms to indicate the upper stories of the house as well. "Accused your pa of terrible things."

I went cold. "Papa? Where is he?"

Angela gave a howl and wept into her kerchief. Master Gib shook his head sorrowfully. I turned to Comfort.

"Where's Papa?" I asked again, more firmly.

It was Matt who answered. "They took him, Mallory. Dragged him away like a common criminal. Accused him of treason, of distributing seditious material."

"Oh dear God, no." My legs gave way. Lord Nathaniel grabbed me by the waist and lowered me onto the bench. He poured a drink and placed it in my hand as the story of the raid was told. A group of men purporting to be acting on behalf of the Privy Council entered the house and began searching, uncaring what they damaged or what distress they caused. Comfort had tried to stop them, Angela as well, but they would not listen.

Sending Gracious out to fetch Papa, Comfort had tried to make them listen to reason. "I may as well have been talking to the walls. They had hammers, metal bars and things the like of which I've never seen before," she said with a shudder. "They weren't only here to find evidence of heresy, but to ruin whatever they could as well."

"They've ripped apart the wainscoting, lifted floorboards," said Master Gib.

"They slashed Valentina's mattress," added Angela. "Gideon came running from the workshop, found them in her room and went wild. They beat him . . ." She began to sob uncontrollably. Comfort held her.

"Caleb's room had the worst of it," said Comfort quietly over Angela's head.

"They've accused Caleb and Master Bright of dreadful things," said Matt. "They took a huge chest out of Caleb's room. I wouldn't have believed any of it, only your father didn't deny a word, except to repeat that Caleb was innocent."

"Papa said that?" I glanced at Lord Nathaniel. How would Papa know? A terrible idea began to take shape in my mind.

"The sheriff said he could tell that to Sir Francis Walsingham and then they dragged him away," Comfort wailed.

"In chains, *bella*, in chains. I'm glad your mother wasn't alive to see this day." Angela wept into her kerchief.

"What do we do, Mistress Mallory?" asked Dickon. "What's going to happen to the master? Is it true?"

The servants quieted. Simon's howling ceased. The dogs calmed. Angela and Comfort sniffed loudly and looked toward me; so did the apprentices.

Unable to think clearly, I didn't respond.

"It's a nonsense," said Lord Nathaniel. "A nonsense they'll have to prove first," he said with such conviction, Comfort and Master Gib nodded. I prayed he was right.

"How can the master or Caleb be traitors?" asked Gracious through her tears. "They be gentlemen. They be no papists."

Comfort nodded in agreement. "Being a friend to one or feeling sorry for what they've endured does not turn you into either a Catholic or a traitor."

Angela, Master Gib, Mistress Pernel and Comfort exchanged looks. Mamma's adherence to the old ways had been kept hidden from the younger servants. The rosary, rood and other papist items had been buried with her. Angela didn't possess any. They couldn't have found anything to condemn her—or, by association, anyone in the room. The authorities and Sir Francis had always overlooked Mamma's stubborn refusal to convert; after all, she did no harm and Papa paid her fines. But what had been kept hidden in our house, those books and pamphlets, was something no one could condone—especially not Mister Secretary Walsingham.

My father . . .

And now my worst fear was realized: Papa was implicated as well. Or was it worse than that? Was Papa guilty? Why would he take such a risk? What could have persuaded him?

I had to seek out Sir Francis quickly and beg him to intercede on behalf of Papa and Caleb. With his help, his support—I glanced around the room, took in the tragic faces of our servants, the apprentices, Angela—my family could be restored. I would do whatever it took to ensure it.

In that moment, I foolishly believed anything was possible.

FORTY-NINE

*H*aving Lord Nathaniel by my side meant my reception at Seething Lane was very different to usual. I admitted us through the rear door and we entered the large room where the assistants worked. No one noticed us at first, so caught up were they in their work. There was tension and a frisson of excitement in the room that made the air crackle. No doubt the seizure of the seditious books and pamphlets and the arrests of Papa and Caleb would have brought the conviction that more of the papists and their pernicious plots would be uncovered.

Did they know it was my papa who had been taken? And my friend? Thomas had walked me home many a time and must have known. But it was their duty to protect the realm no matter who was the enemy.

Thomas was the first to spy us. He leaped to his feet, but approached cautiously.

"My lord, Mistress Mallory. What a pleasant surprise." His tone indicated otherwise. Of course, we were a distraction. "You wish to see Sir Francis?"

"Indeed, that's why I'm here," I said.

"He expects you." Thomas peered at me over his spectacles. Glancing over his shoulder, he lowered his voice. "Mallory, Sir Francis is most unhappy. It's apparent you've been hiding information from us; that your loyalty has been compromised." His glance included Lord Nathaniel. "While we might tolerate you protecting your father, this playwright deserves no such allegiance. I thought better of you. You've left Sir Francis with no choice but to act."

"Where is your master?" demanded Lord Nathaniel.

Thomas blinked. "Why, in his study . . ."

"Go to," said Lord Nathaniel loudly with a look that would have withered a rose, waving him away. "Cease your blathering and announce our presence immediately." The room momentarily stilled. The men cast wary glances in our direction before resuming their work.

Moments later, Thomas reappeared.

"My lord, mistress, if you would come with me. Sir Francis will see you."

I froze. Lord Nathaniel offered me his elbow. Placing my hand lightly upon it, I felt like a beldame approaching her own funeral.

"My lord, thank you for accompanying me thus far. I must do what remains on my own. I would speak to Mister Sec . . ." I lowered my voice, "my father alone." I held his gaze.

"Very well," he said, withdrawing his arm and again, I felt a rush of warmth that I didn't have to fight for this. He understood.

"I will wait for you out here. If you need me, call and nothing will keep me from your side."

My feet were leaden, my throat stoppered by doubt and fear. I gave Lord Nathaniel one last look before entering my father's office.

The door closed behind me and I saw Sir Francis bent over his desk, the candles throwing demonic light over his features. The teetering piles of paper were unchanged, except now they would contain reports of Caleb's movements—and, likely Papa's and my own as well.

"Mallory," said Sir Francis, gesturing to the seat on the other side of the desk. "We have a great deal to discuss."

"Where's Papa?" I asked. "Where has he been taken?"

"Where all traitors are taken—to the Tower."

I gave a small cry and sank into the chair. "Papa is no traitor."

Sir Francis neither answered nor sought to comfort me. This was no longer a father before me, but Her Majesty's spymaster.

I took a deep breath. "Sir, forgive me. I know I should have reported Caleb and the goods in his possession to you long ago. Verily, I was torn. But this has nothing to do with Papa. I beg you to release him."

"On the contrary, Mallory, it has everything to do with Gideon." He held up his hand to silence the protests I hadn't yet formed.

"Caleb has been released and even now is on his way to Warham Hall."

"Released? Why? How?"

"Your father and I reached an agreement. In return for the name of the person to whom the chest and seditious material belongs, and a full confession, Caleb Hollis was set free."

I shut my eyes. *Oh dear Lord, please do not desert me now.*

I opened them again. "To what has Papa confessed?"

"To treason." Sir Francis's voice was flat, lifeless.

No. I fought to stay calm. "Papa would never involve himself in Catholic affairs, in treason."

"Would he not?" asked Sir Francis gently. I knew he spoke of Mamma's recusancy.

"That was different and you know it, sir. In fact, you too turned a blind eye to Mamma's faith and her refusal to convert."

"Your mother wasn't involved in a plot to suborn good English souls. Furthermore, she kept her promise and raised you a Protestant."

"Papa is innocent. I know he is." I sat on the edge of my seat. "You do too."

"Innocent of plotting, mayhap, but he's guilty of being in possession of papist propaganda. He's admitted as much. Just as he confessed that he ordered Caleb to keep the chest in his room."

"I don't believe it. No. No. Papa would never . . . It cannot be."

"But it is. He's admitted this is the case. Your father is condemned from his own mouth."

Good God. This was worse than I suspected. No wonder Caleb couldn't reveal the name of his friend—it was Papa all along. No doubt he'd been sworn to secrecy.

God damn secrets. I buried my face in my hands. How could I have been so blind? I should have forced Caleb to tell me . . . only I didn't believe there was a friend, did I?

"Why?" My voice so small, the deed so large.

Sir Francis made a noise of disgust. "Because he was given no choice."

I raised my head. "By whom?"

"By the scoundrel Raffe Shelton."

My blood turned to ice.

Suddenly, the conversation earlier that day began to make sense. Raffe's snide references to Papa, to his profession; his suggestion that Papa was both cooperative and helpful; his thinly veiled threats to me. It's why Lady Joanna knew naught of me, but could speak of Papa. When did they meet? Why had Papa agreed to keep such material? Especially when he knew what it signified, and the consequences.

"The chest and contents are Raffe's?"

"Aye. We've known the Sheltons had papist sympathies—why, his father was arrested for harboring priests—but how far his son's networks extend, we're only now beginning to understand."

"I am afraid I do not."

"Mark me well, Mallory," began Sir Francis, taking his seat. "According to Gideon, some time ago Shelton wrote to him and asked for a lock to be made. Of course, your papa refused and threatened the scoundrel with all kinds of consequences. It was then that Shelton said if he didn't do as he asked, he would go public with what had happened between you and him. He would shred your reputation and make your name a byword. He would declare you weren't a widow but a whore."

I flinched.

"At first, your father laughed; he refused to listen and told him no one would believe him. Then the varlet hinted there'd been a child; that you'd ensured it didn't live. He not only claimed there were witnesses, but sent your father copies of sworn affidavits, said those who signed were prepared to swear in court it was God's truth. He claimed, and these testimonies supported him, that you murdered your babe."

I swallowed, drew a deep, deep breath and released it slowly.

My mind flew back to the moment I told Papa, the way he'd initially recoiled from me. Dear God. He'd been told the exact same thing by

Raffe. No wonder Papa was so enraged. No wonder he had been so
vehement in extracting a promise of secrecy from me. Raffe was black-
mailing him. He must have felt trapped. Oh, what must Papa have
thought when I'd told him? Even knowing how Raffe viewed events,
how he would represent me, Papa had exonerated me, tried to free me
from the guilt that consumed me. Raffe even claimed there were witnesses. Of course, Katherine and Agnes. The poor souls. What had
he done to them to elicit their testimonies? Anger and apprehension
rolled over me. I felt light-headed and fought for clarity. Dear God,
the man was a rogue of the worst degree—and a papist. How dare
he use my failings to blackmail Papa, to use our family to further his
subversive schemes.

Nonchalance, nonchalance. I worried my locket. I tried to think what
to say, to make sense of this tale.

"Was there a child?" The voice was cold as iron.

I stared at Sir Francis, the man who called himself my father.
Should I confess my sin? Did I trust him with such a secret? With little
Gideon's soul? No, I didn't—and I'd promised Papa. A promise, this
time, I intended to keep.

I rested my hand against my throat. "Raffe always embellished the
truth. There was no child, but there could have been." My words were
not exactly false . . . "It's clear he intended to ruin me for what I did,
not only for escaping from his clutches and threatening to expose him,
but also for wounding him. No doubt he threatened these so-called
witnesses as well."

Sir Francis nodded gravely. "I wish you'd never stabbed him." I was
about to make a bitter retort. "I wish you'd killed the blackguard."

Startled, I shrank into my chair.

Before I could respond, he continued. "Gideon couldn't, wouldn't
risk such a story getting out."

Especially not once I confirmed it. My stomach heaved.

"He agreed to Raffe's demands," continued Sir Francis, "even
knowing he courted peril. He said he'd no choice but to take Caleb
into his confidence. Hollis happened upon him the night the chest
was delivered and saw the contents. Shocked by what they found, but
knowing they could say nothing, they agreed to hide it. Your father
went ahead and made a complex lock. What Shelton still doesn't know

is that Gideon fitted it with a device that would spray ink upon any who tampered with the opening and who were not in possession of the correct keys. He wanted the authorities to be able to find the traitors more easily."

"You see," I said, leaping to my feet. "That proves it. Papa always intended you to find the real traitors. He worked with the government, not against."

"The Privy Council, Her Majesty, will not see it that way. Anyway, while that may have been his intention, something changed. It appears he gave the correct keys to the men he believed to be acting with Shelton when the chest was collected."

I knew what had changed. My secret. Oh dear sweet Lord. My confession had bound Papa even closer to Raffe, embroiled him further in the man's treachery.

"Then *you* must convince them otherwise." I strode up to him and grabbed his shoulders before releasing them quickly. "Forgive me, but this is my father's life. You must do whatever you can to have him released. Please, I beg of you. You know Papa is a good man, he would never do anything to hurt the Queen, to hurt this country. He's a Protestant, a devout man."

"Devout may be overstating it," said Sir Francis, indicating I should sit. "But he is a good man."

"He's your old friend, remember?" I dared, leaning over the desk. "If ever he needed a friend, one with whom he shares so much"—I paused—"more than most—it's now."

Sir Francis's eyes were unfathomable. "You think I would not do what I could for Gideon?" I refused to look away. "Mallory, you don't understand. This is too big. Someone must pay."

My stomach clenched. "Aye, Raffe Shelton. Not Papa."

"Shelton will pay. When we find him."

"He's not in custody?" My heart fell into my shoes. "I saw him today, in Southwark. At the Lewes Inn . . ."

"My men are searching but thus far he's eluded us. No doubt he is cowering in a Catholic safe house somewhere."

Sir Francis poured himself a drink. The splash of the liquid seemed incongruous during such a conversation. I wanted to pick up the goblet and dash it in his face. My fists clenched, I tried to draw on the *mediocrita* that had served me for so long. It was elusive. My passions were stirred, my fears as well. This was life and death. This was my papa . . . my father . . .

Sir Francis put his goblet down. "You should have told me about this chest, Mallory. In failing to mention the presence of these books, you've allowed me to waste valuable time and resources and thus enabled more Catholics to enter our shores. You've given them not only a sense of security, but made it genuine. All this time we've been looking in the wrong place, watching the wrong people." He leaned across the desk. "You've made us, made me, look like fools." He fell back into his chair. "I do not like being made to look a fool."

"Then I fear you will continue to look one, sir, for Papa is not your man."

Sir Francis gave a harsh, mocking laugh. "If you were not my daughter, I'd have you placed in chains for such a statement."

Here was my chance. "But I *am* your daughter." I came around to the other side of the desk and kneeled at his feet. "And, as your daughter, I beg you, please do not allow Papa to go to trial. We both know what will happen if it proceeds. The weight of evidence is against him. Yet all he is guilty of is protecting me. It's Raffe Shelton you want. It's Raffe Shelton who should be in the Tower."

Sir Francis was unmoved.

"Please," I said softly. "I've only ever asked one thing of you . . . Can you not do this as well? Can you not free him? For me?"

Without looking at me, Sir Francis replied, "No, Mallory, I cannot." He swung back. "This has gone further than I ever intended. There are too many in the Privy Council invested in the outcome of this for me to seek clemency—especially for Gideon. They know we share a past; that we're friends. If I treat him differently, it weakens my position. I've released Caleb, I cannot let them both go. Gideon knew that. He insisted Caleb be freed. As much as it pains me to admit it, we must let justice run its course."

I saw the truth of this statement in his eyes.

"This is not justice and you know it."

"Perchance I do, but that doesn't change anything. The best I can do is insist Thomas Norton go lightly on him."

"Rackmaster Norton?" The room spun. There were few who didn't tremble at the sound of that man's name. Caleb knew him as the coauthor of the play he'd performed so much over the last twelve months, *Gorbuduc*. To others, he was Sir Francis's principal torturer. "But Papa has confessed . . . ?"

"Enough. Mallory, as much as I might want to, I cannot change events already set in motion. This must play out to its conclusion. Your father was a fool, a well-intentioned fool, but a fool nonetheless. If only he'd come to me when Shelton first approached him, then none of this would have happened. He did not. You did not."

I knew why Papa had not. He feared Raffe's accusations were true, even then. Once I had confirmed them, Sir Francis would be the last person he'd seek out. Hadn't he made me swear to keep silent? Hadn't he sought to keep me safe, to protect me—even from my own father?

Understanding Sir Francis was about to leave and that my chance to plead would be lost, I threw myself at him. "Please, Father, please—"

He raised his arms, refusing to hold me.

"Do not beg, Mallory. And do not use our relationship to manipulate me. It does not become you."

Fury rose in me. I sat back on my heels, gazing up at him. "Why, sir, I seem to remember you using our relationship to strike your own bargains—and not only with me."

A look of anger flashed across his face then quickly segued into something else. Sir Francis shook his head, a grimace on his lips. "You will not sway me. Now, remain here while I see to final orders. I do not want you rushing about the streets trying to save Gideon, even if you do have Nate at your beck and call."

It was now night, and Lord Nathaniel was still outside. I wondered how much he'd heard, if our voices had carried.

Sir Francis left, turning the key in the lock as he did so. He would not risk me fleeing, though where I'd go, I wasn't sure. I could no more break Papa out of the Tower than I could stop what now seemed inevitable—his torture.

Cold gripped me; a great wall of ice formed in my middle, weighing me down. *Oh, Papa.* He would not be spared but examined by a master of the cruelest instruments known to man, instruments that would illicit answers from any who met them. I wanted to bang my fists against the door, scream my frustration, my impotence. Oh, to be a man, to be of Lord Nathaniel's stature and to force my way.

I scrambled off the floor, slumped into the chair and stared at the candles. What skills did I have? What could I offer? Papa, you foolish, wonderful man; I'm not worthy of your love . . .

The flames began to thicken and distort as tears filled my eyes. Marry! This was no time for womanly weakness. Brushing the tears away, I sniffed loudly, searching for my kerchief. It was then I noticed the piece of furniture Sir Francis took pride in above all others—his black cabinet. The repository of all his secrets. It had a complicated three-stage lock, a lock that Papa had designed and made.

As I gazed at it, my mind began working furiously. Did not Sir Francis accuse me of using my relationship with him to secure an outcome he disliked? Did I not accuse him of the same? Would Papa be granted a trial, a fair reckoning of the evidence and the right to defend himself? Or was he, as I suspected, to be a scapegoat? What if Sir Francis or one of his lackeys doctored the evidence, in the same way he'd doctored Sledd's dossier to include Campion's name? What chance had Papa then?

None. I could not risk letting this happen. An idea at once so awful and so incredible began to form. I dismissed it. But it would not lay dormant. Oh, dear sweet Jesus. Did I dare? Could I?

I glanced over my shoulder, suddenly grateful that Sir Francis had locked me in. It would give me a few seconds of extra time should I be caught. Though I had none of my tools, I was in possession of alternatives that would more than suffice. The day had been windy and I'd used a number of pins to secure my hat to my hair. Removing two, I ran one back and forth through the candle flame before bending one end into a hook.

I lifted one of the candelabras and held it over the cabinet so I might see the locks and their workings more clearly. It was as I suspected— behind the faceplate. Sliding the faceplate back, the main lock was exposed. At the side was another. There was also a small knob, easy to miss unless you knew exactly where to look.

Placing the candles atop the cabinet so the light fell downward, I slid back the rather plain panel to expose two rare trefoil-shaped keyholes. Papa had made only two of these kinds of locks, and though it had been years since I had unpicked them, I'd not forgotten. It was a triple mechanism. Inserting first the straight rod, I moved it around slowly, feeling the wards and tumblers inside. Confident, I paused. There were raised voices outside, and I worked swiftly. Sliding the bent rod beside the straight one, I matched movements, then hooked a tumbler. First one, then two, then three. Repeating this in the second keyhole, I used my mouth to hold the rods in place, reaching around the side to twist the knob. Turning it the opposite way to what would be expected, I heard the final bolt retract. Forced to breathe in and out through my nose, a sickly sweet smell emanated from the lock. With a start, I recognized it. Oh, Papa . . . how clever . . . how deadly. Withdrawing the rods ever so cautiously, I opened the door, extracting my instruments carefully as I did. If I made one wrong move, a blast of poison would strike me in the face.

In the shadowy interior, I could just discern the rows of drawers and shelves. I didn't need to move the candelabra; I knew what to look for. There, atop a stack of carefully bound papers, was Sir Francis's *Book of Secret Intelligences*. I placed it on the desk and quickly relocked the cabinet, respectful of the deadly substance lurking within.

I replaced the candles and, with my back to the door, moved to the other side of the desk and quickly shoved the book down my bodice. I rearranged the ties and buttons, so it sat flat against my chest, then used my partlet to hide the top. I put my cloak over my shoulders and clasped it at the neck, then sat on the very edge of my seat. I cast my eyes over the cabinet. There was nothing to show I'd opened it. Except . . . a tiny drop of pale wax, no bigger than a tear, perched on the very edge of the decorative capping.

I leaped to my feet, intending to scrape it off with my fingernail, when I heard the key turn in the door. I sat down again quickly.

I prayed he would not see it, would never imagine that I would do something so underhanded as to steal the most important book in his possession. A book that, if it were to fall into the wrong hands, would expose his network of spies, the codes they used, the information they'd uncovered and any plots, plans and people under suspicion. A book that could compromise the country.

If I could not bargain for Papa's life with this, then I knew not what else I could do. Wondering how I could make my exit without arousing suspicion, I heard Lord Nathaniel's voice.

"You locked her in the room? What sort of a man are you to do this to one of your own?"

Pushing past Sir Francis, Lord Nathaniel strode straight toward me and helped me up. With one arm across my chest, as if I was holding together a breaking heart, I adopted the most forlorn of faces.

"One of my own?" asked Sir Francis, glancing from me to Lord Nathaniel.

Oh please, I silently begged Lord Nathaniel, *do not reveal my secret now.*

I should have had faith. As he led me to the door, Lord Nathaniel used the most pompous of tones. "Did not Mallory work for you? Did you not trust her enough to recommend her services to me? Has she not been through enough today? For Godsakes, you arrested her father, her friend."

Sir Francis's face was a mask. "It's not a matter of trust, it's a matter of safety." There was an edge of cruelty in his tone. A reminder of the power he wielded—as my father and as Mister Secretary. Lest we forget. I shivered.

"I will see to her safety by taking her home," said Lord Nathaniel. *Not lock her in a room.* The inference lingered between them.

Sir Francis frowned. "Very well, but I would continue this conversation further. I will organize a time on the morrow and send for you, Mallory. With his lordship's permission, of course."

Lord Nathaniel hesitated then lowered his head in acquiescence.

"Marry, I'll look forward to it, sir," I said in a small voice. "May God give you good evening, and I most humbly ask you consider further what we have spoken of."

"I will, Mallory, and I ask you to do the same. Gideon will not suffer—not tonight. I can see to that at least. May God give you both good evening." Sir Francis held the door open for us to leave, then closed it behind us.

The outer room was empty now except for Thomas, who was busy writing.

"May God give you good even, Thomas," I said as we passed.

Without looking up, he replied, "Save your requests for the

Almighty, Mallory Bright. I don't doubt you'll be needing His benefi-
cence soon."

"I don't doubt we both will be," I snapped, earning a surprised look
from Thomas.

Laurence saw us to the horses Sir Francis had provided. He'd
always possessed a fine stable, as the two geldings attested. One of
Sir Francis's men led the way into Tower Street, a lamp held before
him. The streets were quiet at this time of the evening. As we rode, I
made the decision to tell Lord Nathaniel everything Sir Francis had
said—with the exception of the real reason Papa allowed himself
to be blackmailed. Among all the bad news was the welcome relief
that we could expect Caleb to be at Warham Hall. I also told him
that Raffe Shelton was implicated in what had happened and was a
wanted man.

"What is Raffe Shelton to your papa?" he asked suddenly.

Lord Nathaniel had the right to know, if he hadn't already guessed.
"To Papa, he's the man who seduced his daughter and stole her maid-
enhood. To me, he's the man I eloped with, only to discover, once we
reached his estate, that he already had a wife."

There was a great sucking in of breath.

"I . . . I'm afraid I deceived you, my lord. I am no widow. I am a
fallen woman."

"I see," said his lordship.

"If you wish to be quit of me at this very moment, I will understand."

He was quiet, but I could see from his glowering expression, the
way his hands held the reins, that he was working hard to suppress his
emotions.

"I really should have thrown him down the stairs," he snarled.

I gazed at him in surprise. He returned my look.

"You are not a fallen woman, Mallory, so much as one who was
pushed."

I knew not what to say.

A few stragglers disappeared down the laneways. The night watchmen tipped their caps when they saw his lordship and the insignia
on the guard's livery. Strains of music from a nearby tavern gave our
journey an artificially jovial air. A cool wind tugged at my cloak and I

struggled to keep it around me lest what I'd hidden beneath my jacket was exposed.

Divided between wanting to ask Lord Nathaniel if this new knowledge changed relations between us, if he no longer thought me an appropriate companion for his sister, and contemplating my temerity in daring to steal from Sir Francis, my thoughts churned. What choice had he left me? He had refused to listen to my pleas. When it came to Catholics Sir Francis was intransigent, unable to view them as anything but traitors—deadly enemies to be vanquished by whatever means possible. Even, it seemed, when they were old friends protecting *his* daughter. His indifference infuriated me and made me very afraid.

We passed the Baker's Hall and were approaching the workshop. I glanced at Lord Nathaniel. It was not only Sir Francis's reaction to my daring that gave me cause to fear.

"Do you wish to call into Harp Lane and inform Angela and the servants what has happened?" he asked.

I shook my head. "I'll send a note tonight and see them on the morrow. I want to get to Warham Hall and see Caleb."

"Very well. I'll have a messenger take the letter immediately when we get home." Lord Nathaniel let out a long sigh. "We can do little for your father tonight. I pray it will be different, but it seems Sir Francis is committed to his course."

"Perchance Sir Francis is, but tomorrow I'll have Papa free."

Lord Nathaniel gave me an indulgent, sad smile. "I would not wish you to be deceived in your hope."

I glanced at the guard ahead, slowed my horse's pace. Lord Nathaniel matched his own steed to mine. His lordship said I could trust him. Having already made one confession tonight, I was about to put that assurance to the test again.

"I do not believe I am, my lord."

Slowing his horse even further, Lord Nathaniel turned in the saddle. "Why, mistress, are you hatching some plot that will steer Sir Francis in another direction?"

"No, my lord—"

He appeared relieved.

"It is already in motion."

Lord Nathaniel let out a long whistle and shook his head.

"My lord, if I tell you, then you are complicit in a devious plot that could well see you in the Tower. Are you certain you want such knowledge?"

In the light of the street lamps, it was impossible to read his face. "You've seen fit to share with me a secret that must have caused you great anxiety, my lady. I'm yet to hear a full account and ponder the implications. You owe me that."

I lowered my head, my heart heavy. I did. No doubt he would ask me to leave so the reputation of his innocent sister wouldn't be sullied by my presence. Once I confessed to my theft, I'd have to work hard to convince him not to alert the authorities and have me dragged back to Seething Lane.

"Out with it then," said Lord Nathaniel impatiently.

"You must know, my lord, that the woman you hired to be your sister's companion is not only a woman of poor moral virtue, but a thief of the very worst order."

"There are degrees?"

"Aye, for I've stolen from my own blood."

"What is it you've taken?"

"In my possession I've something Sir Francis holds so dear, he'd sell the Queen's soul to have it back. I pray he will sell me Papa."

Lord Nathaniel stared at me with eyes that were huge and glittering. With disbelieving laughter in his voice, he drew alongside, his thigh brushing against mine.

"Oh, Mallory Bright, my little gull, my believer in churls and knaves who has plummeted from great heights and survived—tell me, what have you done?"

FIFTY

*U*pon our arrival at Warham Hall, Beatrice, Sir Lance and a battered and distraught Caleb besieged us. He'd arrived hours earlier, but thank God had revealed little of the situation except to say he'd been duped by a sly Catholic and stood accused of treason. Without exposing my theft or my plan for freeing Papa, Lord Nathaniel filled them in on the rest, including our failure to secure Mister Secretary's support. Caleb staggered and Sir Lance helped him to a chair.

"Oh dear God. Gideon, Gideon," he wailed.

Beatrice paled even as she tried to offer Caleb comfort. "Where has he been taken?" she asked.

"The Tower," groaned Caleb. "It's where we both were." One eye was swollen shut, and though he'd changed his clothing and had washed most of the blood away, evidence of his rough handling could be seen on his hands and face and in the way he limped to his seat and winced when he reached for a wine. Even lifting his arms was an effort.

He'd been bashed repeatedly on his way to the Tower and thrown in a cell. Fully expecting to be interrogated, he was astonished when, not long after he arrived, the warder had unlocked the gate and released him. Told he'd been cleared of all charges, he was ordered to get out of the Tower, make his way to Warham Hall and, as soon as he was able, get out of the city—and, if he had any sense, out of the country as well.

"I've little desire to remain here," he admitted. "But I'm not leaving until I know Gideon is safe—that you all are." His eyes filled with tears. Sir Lance propped on one arm of the chair and patted his hand gently. I sat on the other arm and stroked his hair.

"Your poor papa," said Beatrice, her eyes welling. "How can you bear it, Mallory? You are so strong, I admire your faith so much."

How could I reassure her? How could I tell Caleb I felt confident Papa would not be incarcerated for long? Though I'd committed a dreadful crime, I didn't fear Sir Francis's retribution—either upon myself or those who harbored me. This wasn't only about *mediocrita* and controlling my emotions. I was convinced that once Mister Secretary learned of my theft, he would no more send soldiers to retrieve his book than confess my paternity. After all, as he himself admitted, he did not like to appear a fool. If knowledge got out that a mere woman had bested Sir Francis by stealing the most important thing in his possession, a book that kept the realm and its queen secure, his reputation would not recover. He couldn't, wouldn't allow that. It was what I believed with all my heart; to consider anything else would catapult me into sorrow.

Sir Lance started to ask more questions, but Lord Nathaniel silenced him, saying all would be explained in good time. Aye, it would be. If I wanted his lordship's aid in all this, then the time to disclose my role as a watcher was at hand.

"I've already instructed Bede to see that bedding, fresh clothes, food and wine are sent to the Tower," said Lord Nathaniel. "God knows he'll need comfort tonight."

"I will visit him on the morrow," said Sir Lance.

"We both will," added Lord Nathaniel.

I knew I dare not try to visit myself, not while I had the book in my possession; not while I planned to blackmail Sir Francis.

We were a sorry group that evening. Every conversation eventually returned to the subject of Papa, his innocence, how neither the chest nor its contents belonged to him, that all he'd done wrong was store goods, the nature of which, Sir Lance and Beatrice assumed, he was ignorant. I didn't enlighten them on that score. Raffe was not mentioned, for which I was grateful.

It was late before Caleb, Sir Lance and Beatrice retired, leaving Lord Nathaniel and me in the parlor. If they thought it unusual that we remained in each other's company, no one said anything and there were no offers to chaperone us. Not that it was possible to ever really be alone in Warham Hall, with all the servants about.

After they had left, Lord Nathaniel rose and held out his hand. "Come," he said. Without a second thought I placed my hand in his and we went to his study. There, Lord Nathaniel sat me in his chair and placed his writing instruments at my disposal.

"Once you've written the letters, we will talk."

I gulped. "We will."

In my brief letter to Angela, I wrote of Sir Francis's intractable attitude regarding Papa, of Caleb's freedom and its cost. I also said not to give up hope and mentioned one avenue that remained to try. In the meantime I suggested that she, Comfort and the rest of the house pray, and signed with love and God's blessings.

I then began the letter to Sir Francis—a letter of extortion. Lord Nathaniel remained silent as I composed, and when I had finished, asked me to read it to him.

"If I'm to be a coconspirator, I wish to know exactly what it is I'm conspiring about."

"The release of an innocent man," I said.

He nodded slowly. In this man both Caleb and Papa had a brave and gallant ally. What I had remained uncertain. Lord Nathaniel had not yet denounced me or turned from me in disgust. I was both anxious to see, once more of my story was known, which way the ax would fall.

"Read it to me," prompted Lord Nathaniel.

I nodded. Lord Nathaniel was about to hear even more than he bargained for, and learn yet another aspect of the woman he had hired as his sister's companion. I began:

My dearest patron, parent and protector, Mister Secretary Walsingham, may God be with you now and always.

Mayhap, upon reading this, you will regret you ever took such a one under your wing, trained me in the ways of your men and honed the skills my papa taught me and of which you too were so proud.

I glanced up at Lord Nathaniel, who raised an eyebrow. "There's more to your story yet, mistress. I will have it." I continued.

I hope one day you will find it in your heart to forgive me, as I've abused your trust in the most wretched and underhand of ways that will see you disown me as soon as punish me.

Sir, I have taken a book that you hold most significant and secret. I will gladly return it in exchange for someone most significant to me—significant and, I know in my heart of hearts, innocent as well—my papa, Gideon Bright. By your own admission, he is an "old friend" and the man who raised and loved your daughter. I do not feel the need to insist upon Papa's innocence as your own heart will tell you it is true. I also require a guarantee of his safety. Lord Nathaniel informs me that once released it's unlikely Papa can remain in the country and I ask you provide him and Caleb with safe passage into exile and the means to execute this as well.

Father, I know I abuse the bonds I so greatly esteem and, in doing so, do myself no credit. Please understand I would never act in such a manner were my convictions not resolutely engaged. Papa is no traitor. Nor is Master Hollis an enemy. He is simply a playwright and actor who took the world to be his stage and misread his part. I ask you to allow both men to exit with their lives and dignity intact.

Your loving daughter,
Mallory Bright, SS

"SS?" asked Lord Nathaniel. "To whom or what does that refer?"
I took a deep breath.
"Another secret?"
Exhaling, I sealed the letter. "Aye. Another."
"Will you honor me by sharing?"
I closed the inkhorn, replaced the quill and sat back in the chair. Candles flickered between us, their light comforting. The shadows they cast upon his face softened his features, the look in his eyes. It occurred

to me that at some point, mayhap this very day, Lord Nathaniel had ceased to be my employer alone and had become my friend.

Swallowing the sensations that thought aroused, I decided to place my cards upon the table and see where the game went.

"SS stands for Samantha Short. It's my code name, my alias if you will. As you've long gathered, my lord, I was never a companion to Frances Walsingham—"

Lord Nathaniel raised a goblet in my direction, a smug look upon his face. I didn't find it nearly as offensive as I once would have.

"I worked as one of Mister Secretary's watchers."

Lord Nathaniel sat up. "Go to. A watcher? You—a woman?"

I could not help but grin at his reaction. "A woman. That was the point. Sir Francis included me in his network of agents because he believed no one would suspect me."

"Oh, I suspected you, madam, but not of being a spy. I thought you—"

"What?"

"Forgive me, Mistress Mallory, I'm mortified." He hesitated again. "There was a brief time when I thought you a woman of questionable virtue . . . I believed, against my own better judgment, that you were Sir Francis's mistress."

Shame swept over me, suddenly replaced by a modicum of irony as I looked at the discomfort upon his face.

"Not Sir Francis. But I did occupy that position with another man. As I mentioned, I lost . . . no, I gave—my virtue, my honor, to Sir Raffe. I did this outside wedlock." I then explained how I was gulled, and some of what I endured. "I am a fallen woman, my lord. Not, as kind as it was of you to suggest, one who was pushed. I tripped over my own conceit, my own foolish dreams."

"What you did was give that rogue your trust, your faith in his word, and he abused it. He deceived a young chit, and thrashed your reputation for the sake of his own base desires. He's of the worst kind."

He paced around the room, then stopped when he reached the hearth, gazing into its cheery warmth. "Mallory," he began, turning to regard me once more, "you're not the first woman to fall victim to a blackguard. Sadly, you won't be the last either." He came to the back of my chair and placed a comforting hand upon my shoulder.

"Your : . . your forbearance is more than I deserve, my lord."

"It is the very least you deserve. Though I do question your taste." I could hear the mirth in his voice. I lowered my head, burying a smile. I questioned it as well. If only I'd done so sooner.

"Anyway, how can I hold you to account when I too was coney-caught by declarations of love? When I too sacrificed my reputation and almost that of my family for someone to whom I gave my heart? Someone who didn't understand the gift it was and mistreated it most cruelly."

I tilted my head back to look at him. "Perchance we are both fools, my lord."

He gazed at me for a long moment. "Perchance we are," he said softly. "Fools for love." Bending over the top of my chair, his lips captured mine as he held my face between his hands, allowing his fingers to stroke my cheeks before they slid down my arms and drew me to my feet. Guiding me around the chair, he pulled me tight against his body. I didn't resist. Oh no. I did what I'd longed to do: I twined my hands around his neck and pulled his face closer, pressing the full length of my body against his hardness, his towering form. Staring into those golden eyes that claimed mine as surely as his tongue did my mouth. With a look I urged him not to stop, before closing my eyes and losing myself in the sensations rippling through my body that made me light-headed and weak-kneed. With a groan, his kiss deepened and a hot wave of longing spread from my center to inflame me. When his mouth left mine, I gave a cry of protest before his lips found my neck, his fingers the ruff which he drew away boldly, dragging the partlet free, unlacing my bodice, so he could claim my flesh, first with his searching fingers, then his warm, firm lips and scalding tongue.

In his arms, beneath his mouth and hands, I became the wanton he had believed I was. Pulling back his jacket, unlacing his shirt, I sought his skin, moved my mouth along his neck, eliciting a powerful moan from him. Pushing me back until my hips struck the desk, I felt the firmness of his manhood and for the first time since Raffe claimed me all those years ago, I longed to know a man inside me. A real man, whose desire not only matched my own, but whose intentions were not dressed in pretense. Who knew what I'd done, what

I was, and wanted me still. His need was evident and I did not want to deny him.

I don't know which of us heard the knocking on the door, but at some point as we clawed at each other's clothes, the rhythmic hammering at the door entered our consciousness. Breaking apart for a second time in a day, we stared at each other, registered the intrusion, then swiftly sought to repair the damage. I retreated to a corner while Lord Nathaniel sat behind the desk, his arousal untamed, his apparel as disheveled as my thoughts.

Checking first I was decently arranged, fixing his ruff, jacket and shirt, tucking the chair into the desk so his lower half was hidden, he bid enter.

It was Bede. "My lord," said the steward with a blank face, stepping over the pile of books we'd knocked to the floor and bending to collect the papers that, unnoticed, had taken wing from the desk. Replacing them, he bowed. "You asked me to collect some letters?"

"Ah, I did indeed." How could we have so swiftly forgotten? A guilty flush crawled over my cheeks and neck, so recently kissed. God, Papa, forgive me.

Lord Nathaniel stared at the disarray before him. He shuffled the papers on the desk. But the letters had fallen to the floor and lay at his feet. I swooped upon them and placed them in his hand. Our fingers touched, reigniting the heat. From the way his nostrils flared, I knew he felt it too.

"See this one to Seething Lane."

"Tonight, my lord?"

"Aye. Tell the courier it's for Sir Francis's eyes only. Make that clear, Bede. His men are not to read this. And this is to go to Harp Lane."

"Aye, my lord." Bede turned to leave the room, then paused and swung back. "Will there be anything else, my lord?" His eyes strayed toward me. "Would you like some hot water brought to your room, mistress? Something to wash away the stains of the day?"

Aware my coif had slipped and my hair had come unpinned, I became self-conscious. At Master Bede's solicitous but pointed inquiry, suddenly what Lord Nathaniel and I had engaged in, what I had relished, became unseemly. Why, I was like a cat on heat and no better than when I succumbed to Raffe's charms. Had I learned nothing?

Oh, but I had. And Lord Nathaniel was not Sir Raffe.

Aye, but he will treat you exactly the same way if you surrender to him, despite his claims. Women of your class are not for the likes of this man. And what of Papa? Can you so readily cast aside the reasons he's in the Tower? To protect the reputation you would willingly throw away—again.

I felt abashed. "That would be most pleasing, Bede. Thank you."

With bow and a long look at his lordship, the steward left the room, taking my letters and Papa's fate in his hands.

When the door shut again, Lord Nathaniel rose to his feet and stepped toward me, his intentions clear. "Now, where were we?"

"Wait," I said, holding out my palms. "This is not right; we must not do this."

Lord Nathaniel took one of my hands and brought it to his mouth. He turned it over and pressed his lips to my wrist with a warmth and tenderness that made my knees tremble and my heart pound. "My lord, you must not," I insisted. "We must not." I pried my hand away and hid it behind my back.

"Oh, but we must. Haven't we been denying ourselves for weeks now? From the moment I laid eyes on you, I dreamed of this, of seeing you with your hair tumbling about your shoulders, your beautiful mouth parted with desire and those wondrous eyes, eyes which have held me spellbound, fixed on me alone. Didn't you listen when I said I care naught for your past?"

Ah . . . but he did not know all.

"My lord, please. I beg you. Do not say such things to me. This is not right or proper."

"Proper? Right? You didn't object before. Do not pay any attention to Bede. He's discreet. No one need ever know about this."

"Oh, my lord, but I will. And I do not think I could live with the shame."

I put distance between us. He closed the gap. "You would be shamed to surrender yourself to me? Forgive me, Mallory, but of your own admission, I know you're no maiden to engage in blushes and trade on your virtue."

Though his words stung, they were true.

"No, I am not ashamed to be with you, my lord. How could I be given my confessions? I would be ashamed I let my passions control me when Papa languishes in prison, and I've engaged in theft. I've damaged what little remains of my reputation enough for one day without going any further."

Lord Nathaniel made an odd sound, but it was not harsh or demanding. "You misunderstand, your reputation is not only safe with me, mistress. It is assured." He did not try to touch me this time.

"You're right, you're right. Forgive me. I'm not thinking clearly. Your presence, your response to my caresses prevents such moderation." He paced the room, his deep voice wild and impassioned. I wanted to run after him, throw myself into his arms again and beg him to take me there and then. Yet I dare not.

"Oh, Mallory," he said, halting suddenly. "Don't you understand what you've done? You've bewitched me so I don't know whether I am lord or knave, man or animal. I want you in ways I've never wanted a woman before, but when I hear the tremor in your voice as you try to speak reason, to douse the fires you've lit within me, I see the desire but also the fear in your eyes, and it is a blow from which I may not recover. I do not want to see such an expression on your lovely face, not when you look at me."

I sank back into the chair. "My lord. I do want you and yet, I cannot. We cannot, must not. Not yet. Think of Papa, think of Beatrice; think of Sir Francis's possession, secreted in my room—"

Think of what Papa would do if he knew I'd given myself to another, albeit a lord, and with no surety. It would kill him.

Lord Nathaniel kneeled beside the chair and curled his long fingers around its arm. His rings flashed in the candlelight. "I thank God for your sense. For reminding me of my duties—to family and friends. I can think only of you and that is why you will rise and leave this room and not look back. Do you understand? You are my Eurydice and I'm your Orpheus—only this time, it's you who will leave me in hell."

As he kneeled at my feet, his face was almost level with mine. I held his cheek and wondered I'd ever thought his face arrogant, cruel almost. Even his scars, so deep and intrusive, were alluring, for they were his and his alone. I traced their journey, wondering at the fight that caused them, his bravery, his boldness. He shut his eyes, his long dark lashes sweeping his cheeks. I touched the bump on his nose, that long aristocratic nose, broken beneath a lesser man's knuckles. *How dare they.*

"Cease your caress, mistress, I beg you, or my assurance that you will leave this room untouched will be for naught."

God's teeth, it was I all could do not to tempt fate and withdraw my hands. Lord Nathaniel caught them. "You are as resourceful, brave and clever as you are beautiful," he said. "Forget whatever else you've been called and by those who don't deserve to utter your name. You're a loyal and loving daughter to your papa and a worthy one to Sir Francis as well. A watcher. A thief. My Mallory." He chuckled. "Taking his book is merely what he would have done to force someone's hand."

"I hope he sees it that way," I replied, a frisson of fear flaring in the pit of my stomach. It would not be the last.

"You're also the best of friends to Caleb. I would know one day what he's done to deserve such steadfastness. But, Mallory," he added, becoming suddenly serious, "in stealing the book you've also set events in motion that neither of us can foresee."

I nodded. "I know."

"What you must also know is whatever fate metes out, whatever the outcome on the morrow, you'll not face this trial alone."

I winced at his choice of words. I wanted no trial for Papa; just his freedom.

"Our destinies are entwined," he added.

"My lord," I said, pressing my fingers to his mouth in an effort to stop his words. "You do not have to say such things. You do not have to align your future with mine."

"Do I not?" He gave a broken smile and my heart leaped. "What if that is my greatest wish?"

I could not help it, I leaned forward and kissed his brow, right where the scars converged.

"You're a peer of the realm, a mighty lord. I'm but a locksmith's daughter, the bastard progeny of Sir Francis. A woman with a murky past who has made poor choices . . ." I hesitated. I was so much worse besides.

"Ah, but it's those same choices that led you to me," he said and drew me near once more.

I smiled. There was no help for it, though my mind and heart were in torment. Lord Nathaniel wished to know what Caleb had done to deserve my loyalty. God's truth, that was something I could never reveal. Though he tolerated my surrender to Raffe, a dead son he would not. No one could. Papa's words echoed in my mind: *Even the most considerate and understanding of men will find this tragedy impossible to reconcile without finding you guilty.* He was right. I would keep my promise to Papa. I must. But please, God, let me have this, Lord Nathaniel's friendship, his adoration, for now at least.

Tomorrow, after Papa was free, I would stop this madness before it went too far, before Lord Nathaniel knew the whole truth about me and his fiery ardor turned to ashes and his understanding to loathing. I could not bear it. "I do not deserve such from you," I whispered.

"That's for me to decide. Now is not the time; Bede is right. We must to bed. But I want you to enter the realm of dreams knowing you have all that is at my disposal and so much more besides." He stood. "We will fight for Gideon's freedom, for justice to be served, and we will fight together."

If I held any doubts, I knew in that moment I loved this man—this giant in heart and soul. Angela was right; Cupid's arrow struck when you least expected it.

He opened the door of his office and saw the servants he'd bade wait outside. Drawing me back into the darkness of the room, he placed a long, chaste kiss upon my mouth.

"Sweet dreams, my love. Whatever happens on the morrow, we face it together."

"Aye," I whispered. "Together."

"Now, go, and don't look back," he said and gave me a gentle push. I did not.

FIFTY-ONE

*T*he reply from Sir Francis arrived at dawn. Already awake and dressed, I had been pacing the hall in anticipation of its arrival, much to the bemusement of the servants. Mistress Margery in particular kept trying to coax me into the parlor upstairs. The footman took the letter from the courier, who refused refreshment and left even before the young servant had passed it formally to Master Bede. I could barely contain myself.

Nonchalance, nonchalance, I said to myself over and over as Master Bede took the letter and then proceeded to order the servants to their various duties. Spying me waiting impatiently near the stairs, he brought it over.

"God give you good day, Mistress Mallory," he said. "I trust you had a good night?" His kindly eyes twinkled.

"Thanks to you, Bede." My eyes dropped to the letter in his hand.

"I believe you're expecting this?" He passed it to me.

I took it slowly, noting there was also a second letter, addressed to his lordship. It was sent upstairs.

I opened my letter on the landing, in case Beatrice was already in the parlor. I wanted her to possess no knowledge of my intentions.

Be outside Middle Tower ere the bell strikes seven. Have the goods in your possession and the exchange you moot will take place and the means of escape will be enabled.

There was no salutation, no signature—not even his coded one. Nonetheless, I knew Sir Francis's writing. Cold and to the point, it acknowledged what had to be done. My plan was thus set in motion. But what had he written to Lord Nathaniel? I didn't have to wait long to find out.

As I was about to enter the parlor, Lord Nathaniel emerged from his wing of the house. One of his valets was fussing with his jacket, and young Nicholas was by his side, grinning at the antics of the valet, who Lord Nathaniel was doing his best to ignore. It was hard to imagine this richly dressed lord was the same man I first encountered in Harp Lane. I wondered if he ever longed for those simple clothes, for the society they included. Though he looked elegant in his silks, damasks and velvets, he never really looked comfortable. Perchance he yearned for the sea and the lack of propriety that London demanded.

When he saw me, he dismissed his valet and bade Nicholas enter the parlor, then drew me aside.

"God give you good morning, mistress. You don't look rested. While I would like to attribute that to thoughts of me, I fear your mind was otherwise occupied." He nodded toward the letter in my hand.

"In that, you, Sir Francis and Papa can claim equal shares." I kept my voice even and tried not to sound boastful. "Sir Francis has agreed to the exchange."

Lord Nathaniel grimaced. "Aye, but most unhappily. He urges me in the strongest language to dissuade you. He claims if you persist in your intentions, you will unleash forces not even he can control. The best course, he argues, is to bring him the book and allow justice to take its course."

"If I thought it would, you would not have to counsel me from my goal."

He compressed his lips. "I know. Where is the book?" he began, before changing his mind. "Hush. I do not need to know," he said. "But the exchange is a different matter. Where and when is it to happen?"

"This evening, outside the Middle Tower."

"Then that's where we'll go. Ah!" He rested a long finger against my lips. "I know what you're intending to say, but do not. You'll not do this alone, Mallory. Upon this, I insist."

Momentarily lost, I resisted the urge to kiss his fingers. I fiddled with my coif, fixing some imaginary strands of hair to give me a chance to regain my equilibrium.

He gestured for one of the servants to open the doors to the parlor. "After you, mistress."

The day was spent waiting. With my agreement, Sir Lance was brought into our confidence as Lord Nathaniel organized transport and guards to escort us to the Tower that evening. I granted Beatrice a day away from study; her despondency made concentration a chore rather than the diversion I'd hoped. I left her playing music and cards with Caleb, who was in dire need of distraction. When Lord Nathaniel and Sir Lance visited Papa in the Tower, I made a brief trip home, reassuring Caleb I would bring back his belongings.

Though I was offered a horse, I chose to walk, and Tace and a guard accompanied me. I kept my senses open and detected at least two watchers following us. There was little I could do. While the tricks for evading their eyes and ears were familiar to me, I couldn't very well invite the guard or Tace to duck suddenly into a shop, break into a run, climb a wall or knock on a stranger's door. A heaviness beset my limbs and a sense of foreboding I could not shake dampened my brief sense of triumph.

This was not dispelled upon reaching Harp Lane. Leaving Tace and the guard in the kitchen, I joined Angela in the parlor and invited Comfort to join us. I informed them Papa was to be released but would have to go into immediate exile. I also reassured them about Caleb, explaining he was at Warham Hall but would likely also have to leave the country.

"Thank God they're alive," said Angela, only just remembering not to cross herself.

"For now . . ." said Comfort, ever pragmatic, her brow puckered. The puffiness beneath her eyes revealed she too had not slept. Now here was a new worry: if Papa went into exile, what would happen to the household? For certes, I would give it consideration, discuss possibilities with Papa and Lord Nathaniel.

There'd been no more raids by watchmen or constables, and though the neighbors still gossiped and the destruction that had been wreaked was still evident, a certain calm, a sense of inevitability, had fallen upon the house.

When Comfort returned to her duties, Angela spoke her mind. "*Mio Dio, bella*, promise me, whatever it is you're up to, whatever it is you've done to bring this resolution about, you've not placed yourself in danger." She stood by the fire, her arms folded beneath her breasts. Her skirts looked as though they'd been slept in.

I shook my head. "I haven't, and Lord Nathaniel is supporting me in my endeavors to see Papa freed." I told Angela what I'd revealed to his lordship and his response. Angela clasped her hands to her bosom.

"I told you he was a good man, did I not? Not all men judge others by standards they cannot maintain themselves."

Aware my face was changing color, I suddenly found the fire needed tending. "Aye, you did," I replied. Angela stepped aside so I might poke the embers.

I stood and wiped my hands. "Verily, I admit, I was wrong about him—quick to judge and take offense. Though he was churlish and more than a tad cupshotten when we first met, and inclined to dispute. Then there was the matter of his attire. But, as I've discovered, clothes do not maketh the man." I thought briefly of Raffe and his fine garments. Oh, they did not. I returned to my chair. "His sister, Beatrice, says he found it hard to adjust to the losses his family suffered, as well as having been away so long and enduring so much at sea."

"*Allora*, it was what set you at odds with each other—recognition you'd both suffered, and suffered while you were away from those who loved you best," said Angela. "Losses and the gulf that time apart creates, even between loved ones, can make strangers of friends and friends of strangers."

I regarded Angela with astonishment. I'd never before considered Lord Nathaniel and I had that in common. But we did. Hadn't he experienced privations and violence for years on end, separated from hearth and home? And hadn't he seen death? So much death. Then there was the woman who had betrayed his trust—a betrayal so great it not only broke his heart, but forced him to leave his home and his country. We had a great deal in common.

Angela and I shared some soft cheese and wine, then went to Caleb's room and packed what we could of his belongings. I could not yet face sorting Papa's things. Angela promised to do it later.

"Where do you think they'll go?" she asked, shaking one of Caleb's shirts free from the mess upon the floor.

"I'm not sure." I sat on the bed, staring at the devastation the constables had left. We'd managed to clear a little, though there were still papers strewn about and the wood upon the walls had been jimmied away, leaving a rain of fine splinters and exposing the struts and beams of the house. Angela was doing her best to beat the soot out of a brocade jacket that had been flung in the fireplace. "A great deal of that will depend on Sir Francis—if he demands a particular location, how much money he provides so they can resettle. Whether or not Caleb wishes to remain with us. I imagine somewhere in France, maybe Italy."

"You will go with your father?" she asked softly.

"Of course. There's no question." Why then did the notion make me feel so very sad?

Angela sank down beside me, the jacket mostly clean. She folded it and stowed it in the burlap. "If it were up to me, I would go back to Italy," she sighed.

Papa had mentioned that Angela was struggling without Mamma, without someone to care for and talk to in her native tongue, someone with whom she could share memories of her youth. He said she felt a foreigner all over again, even though she'd lived here for nigh on eighteen years. He wasn't sure what to do. Switching to Italian, I asked, "Would you return? I thought you were happy here?" My gesture included the house, the city and country. "That when you left Italy, it was for good?"

Angela sighed again, this time from her core—long, sad and deep. "It was never meant to be this long. I think, as you grow older and the world changes, you yearn for the familiar again. Maybe it's your lost youth that makes you seek the places where you were young and happy. Perchance it's just I want to see home once more before I die . . ." She shrugged. "*Allora*, I would like to go back."

"To Padua?"

"I lived there only a brief time. I'm Venetian. It's to Venice I would return."

Something in her tone, in her lovely hazel eyes, alerted me. I recalled our conversation about love. I'd wondered then how Angela, whom I'd never known to have a man, could be so aware. "Is that where he is?"

She smiled, the corners of her eyes crinkling into familiar wrinkles. "Not much gets past you, *bella*. *Si*, that is where he *was*. Whether or not he is still there?" She shrugged. "I do not deserve such patience, as the good Lord knows."

"Patience?"

"*Si*. A man can only wait so long . . ."

Twisting slightly to face her, I began folding a cloak. Half in her lap, half in mine, we picked up the ends of it and met in the middle. Angela passed it over to me to pack in the burlap, then rose and began to straighten the paper and discarded quills on Caleb's desk.

"When Valentina asked me to join her in Padua, I was keen. When she asked if I'd like to go to England and help her with you, I was thrilled. Imagine, for me, a girl born in Venice who'd never been further than Padua, the very idea of sailing to England was an adventure I couldn't deny. My parents didn't stand in my way and Guido—*si*, that was his name, Guido Sapienti—didn't either. In fact, I went with his blessing."

"What happened?"

"Time. That's what happened. When we first arrived here, it was so exciting. A new place, new people, there was you, the locksmithing business, and Valentina was pregnant. Again. When it was time for me to leave, she lost the babe, so I could not. When I was ready to leave again, she lost another, then another and another. Soon, the misery of her losses far outweighed my own. She needed me more than I needed Guido. I wrote to him explaining the situation."

"And?"

She leaned on the windowsill and looked down into the yard. The noises of the chickens foraging drifted in. "I never heard back."

"Oh, Angela, I'm so sorry."

Angela turned around. "Don't be. Oh, I was sad for a while. Most forlorn, as Caleb would say." She gave a wistful smile. "I don't regret it, not really. By then I'd been here five years and Guido was but a memory. A lovely one," she smiled. "But faded. When I never heard from him, I imagined he'd found someone else. I prayed he'd find happiness. I hope he did."

"And what about you? Have you been happy?"

"I was, very. Now . . ." She screwed up her face. "Now, I am just tired. I'm scared. For your papa, *si*, but most of all I'm scared for you. I want to see you settled, with a good husband, not embroiled in plots and plans and working for that man, even though he is your father." She gave a laugh. "Now, look, I wanted to distract you from your sadness, make you think of other things, and I've just succeeded in making you melancholy again—and on my behalf. I do not deserve such sympathy. I made my choice. And God be praised, I'm alive to either live or change it."

"Oh, never fear, you did make me forget Papa for a while." I continued to pack things into the burlap: ink, paper, fresh quills, a knife to sharpen them, books, scrolls, gloves, an extra bonnet. "What's stopping you going home, Angela?" I asked suddenly.

"Why, you, you silly chick. You and your papa. You see, home is not just a place. It's people, too. You and your papa are my home. Wherever you go, so will I." She stroked my arm. "I'd be where I'm loved."

Why was love so difficult? Why did it always demand such choices of us? All or naught. I could face the truth. I'd lost my heart all right but I knew exactly where to find it—it was in the keeping of the man who both understood my sins and forgave them. All but one. Papa was the only man who could forgive me that. How could anyone but him, when I could not forgive myself?

PART EIGHT
Strange Visitors

We must pray to God to grant us
good masters, for, once we have them,
we have to endure them as they are;
because countless considerations force a gentleman
not to leave a patron once he has begun to serve him:
the misfortune lies in ever beginning: and in that case
courtiers are like those unhappy birds that are
born in some miserable valley.

—Baldassare Castiglione, *The Book of the Courtier:
The Second Book*, 1528

Gli sospiri ne sono testimoni very dell'angnoscia mia.
My sighs are true witnesses to my sorrow.

—Charles Bailly, servant of the Bishop of Ross, carved in the recess
of the northernmost window of his cell in the Tower of London

Without torture I know we shall not prevail.

—Sir Francis Walsingham to Lord Burghley

FIFTY-TWO

THE TOWER, LONDON
The 20th of March, Anno Domini 1582
In the 24th year of the reign of Elizabeth I

The moon was a sliver of white surrounded by dusty clouds as we rode through the streets toward Middle Tower. A cold wind snapped at our cloaks, making the horses more frisky than usual, and they shied at shadows and unexpected sounds.

The streets were mostly deserted. Some watchmen marched out with lamps and pikes held high, hailing those they spied to come forward. Trulls loomed in our path, hoping for custom, before vanishing again. We passed a group of beggars huddled together beneath the eaves of a church, trying to find warmth and comfort on this frigid night. I wondered how many of those we passed were Sir Francis's men. Had I not donned such disguises and pretended so I too might watch unawares? Watch and report. The sensation of being followed had not left me all day.

All too soon the vast dark ramparts of the Tower rose, the White Tower within them dominating the scene. The pennants snapped madly atop their poles, black figures moved between the crenulations, guarding those housed below. I cared for none but Papa and hoped and prayed he'd been treated well, though he had been marked as both traitor and enemy.

Earlier in the day Lord Nathaniel and Sir Lance had been refused admittance to the Tower and thus had not set eyes upon him. They received no explanation and were turned away at the point of swords and pikes.

"Knowing what was planned tonight, I didn't argue," said Lord Nathaniel, and I could hear what such a surrender cost him. "Brace yourself, Mallory, I fear it does not bode well."

Chick Lane came up on our left and we turned down Petty Wales and the steep slope of Tower Hill toward the gate Sir Francis had designated for our meeting.

Barely a word passed between us. Sir Lance and Lord Nathaniel were either side of me, their horses dark as midnight, the sound of hooves announcing our presence. Two guards rode with us, one ahead and one behind, each carrying a bright lantern aloft, their weapons on display to deter any thieves or rufflers—ex-soldiers who would turn their weapons upon travelers sooner than fight for their country.

League's Mount appeared on my left; Beauchamp Tower, where it was said the Earl of Leicester himself had once been held prisoner, peeped over the walls. We passed under a grand arch and arrived unscathed at the gate to Middle Tower. Behind us was Byword Tower, and between the two the black moat lapped the walls.

We reined in the horses and waited. Tower constables came through the main gate, lanterns aloft.

"Halt, who goes there?" demanded a deep voice.

Upon learning who we were, a messenger was dispatched back inside the Tower. Lord Nathaniel and Sir Lance dismounted. Lord Nathaniel spoke with the man who appeared to be in charge and pointed back toward the Tower and the complex of buildings and walkways swallowed by the darkness, which I knew so well from my work at Seething Lane.

The moon passed behind a cloud, plunging us into tenebrosity, and I shuddered. My spine turned to ice and the feeling of dread I'd resisted all day refused to be ignored. Just then, the bells tolled the hour. Seven of the clock.

On cue, guards emerged from beneath Byword Tower gate. They carried a man between them.

"Papa?" It could not be.

I slid from the horse and ran forward. Lord Nathaniel put out his arm to stop me. "We are forbidden to go any closer," he said.

The echo of the bells filled the night. The hollow trump of the soldiers' boots upon the cobbles was loud, offering a counterpoint to the churches' music. A raven launched itself from the parapets and went cawing into the night. I watched its flight, wondering if it was an omen. Light spilled from the constable's lantern onto the forecourt, making the cobbles appear wet and slick. They seemed to be moving.

I sucked in my breath and grabbed Lord Nathaniel's arm. Why, they had the wrong man. Whoever this poor creature was, it was not Papa. Blood dripped from the ends of fingers that were blackened and swollen. His clothes were in tatters, his face puffed, bruised and cut. His legs were useless, dragging on the ground. It wasn't until the guards came to a halt just feet away, their faces grim, that the person held between them emitted a heartfelt groan.

"Papa!" I cried.

He raised his head. One eye latched onto me. There was so much blood. "I'm here, sweetling," he croaked.

I tried to reach his side, but Lord Nathaniel caught me about the waist. "Mallory, wait." His lips were pressed against my hair. I could feel his heart beating. Its pace matched my own. Sir Lance had his hand on the pommel of his sword.

"Stay," Lord Nathaniel warned him. In a loud clear voice he addressed the constables, slowly releasing me as he spoke. "Who is overseeing this matter?"

"I am, your lordship," said a smooth and familiar voice. Looking like he was out for an evening stroll, Thomas emerged from under the gate, his yellow hair blue-gray in the moonlight, his pitted skin shiny. Behind the glasses, his eyes were unfathomable. "Mistress Mallory," he said, touching his cap. "Sir Lance Ingolby," he added, "and Lord Nathaniel Warham."

Somewhere, someone was taking note of our names, recording them for Sir Francis, for yet another chapter in the book that even now weighed heavily beneath my cloak. I scanned the darkness, but there were so many places to hide, windows and arrow slits from which we could be observed or fired upon. It was as if dozens of eyes were marking our every move, evaluating our motives. Had I not done the same? What would I have made of this tableau? How would I report it back to Sir Francis?

But this was my papa and I had to get him free. "Thomas," I said, and pried Lord Nathaniel's fingers away carefully, squeezing them so he knew I was once more in control. Drawing on all my strength, all the nonchalance I could muster, I walked toward Thomas.

"Do you have the goods?" he asked.

"I do indeed," I said. "But forgive me if I do not release them until Papa is safe with his lordship, safe and on the river."

Lord Nathaniel had organized his barge to be waiting at the river steps near the Traitors Gate. Fitting, but also convenient. Uncle Timothy would also be on board to offer physic. Dear God, Papa would need his care. From there, his lordship could have Papa rowed away— downstream, upstream, anywhere, depending how this played out.

"Mallory," exclaimed Lord Nathaniel, coming up beside me. "Give him the book. This is no game."

"I do not play, my lord, but follow the rules I know so well." I stared back at him, praying he would understand my intentions. "I know the man and how he arranges the deck. This is how it has to be. Trust me, my lord, I beg of you. Take Papa and get him to your boat. See him safe. It has to be you."

Lord Nathaniel glanced at Thomas, then peered at me carefully. About to say something more, he appeared to change his mind. "Very well." He turned. "Lance, you remain with Mistress Mallory and see she comes to no harm. I will collect you both from our agreed place."

"As your lordship directs," said Sir Lance. He moved closer to me and stood looking at Thomas with contempt.

"Will, Mark," said Lord Nathaniel to his men, pointing at Papa. "Take him. Gently." The men who'd accompanied us marched forward and, with great care, extracted Papa from the grip of the Tower soldiers. Papa let out a moan of pain before his head lolled, his eyes rolled back and he lost consciousness. Fury rose in me, fury and terrible presentiment.

Lord Nathaniel was not fast enough to stop me this time. I darted forward. The guard called Mark passed his halberd to Bill, and hoisted Papa over his shoulder. For all that Papa was not a small man, he was like a broken doll being carted about.

As Lord Nathaniel gave further orders to his men, I examined my father.

"How could you allow this?" I hissed at Thomas, my eyes full of tears, my words catching in my throat. I tried to lift Papa's head, smooth his matted hair back from his forehead. Even in the poor light, I could see the dirt and blood streaking his cheeks. His entire body reeked of piss and shit. How the guard, Mark, could bear it, I knew not. But he did. Papa would be so ashamed. I lifted one of his hands toward the light and saw his fingernails had been torn from their beds, some of his fingers were broken, nay, shattered. Likewise his feet, which were bare, were twisted and maimed. "How?" I railed. "I was assured he would be spared this. The poor man had no chance to defend himself. No trial."

"He is a traitor," said Thomas flatly. How could I have ever thought this man a friend? "He can be spared nothing."

"You don't know that," I spat.

"But you, apparently, do," he said calmly.

"I know injustice when I see it. I know cruelty. Does Sir Francis know what you've done?"

"Of course. He knows everything."

Dismay filled me, dismay and a deep, deep sadness.

"Mallory, do not say things you might have cause to regret," said Lord Nathaniel quietly. "As soon as I have Gideon in the boat, give the man the book. I want you away from here, away from this place." He gazed up at the battlements, an anxious expression on his face. "I want you with me."

"I will be," I said. "Go. Go. I will join you."

Gesturing for Mark to precede him, he paused and spoke to Thomas. "I have traveled the world and in that time saw little to match this for barbarity," he said.

"Then you did not look hard enough," said Thomas.

Deciding Papa's welfare was more important, Lord Nathaniel touched his cap, then his chest.

"Cleave to her, Lance, she has my heart in her keeping." He clutched Lance's shoulder. "Do not fail me."

Sir Lance nodded. We stood together and watched as Lord Nathaniel escorted Papa to where the boat waited in the darkness. At a signal, lamps were lit and it was rowed from the center of the river toward the edge of the stairs. The tide was high and Mark didn't have to struggle too far. Jumping into the barge, Will took Papa's unconscious body from Mark and they lowered it onto the deck. With a last look back at me, Lord Nathaniel leaped on board and ordered the boatmen to cast off.

Only when the lights appeared to be floating in some vast dark space, and the splash of oars had faded, did I withdraw the book from my cloak. I held it out.

"Here. Please, tell Sir Francis that if I thought there was any other way, I would not have acted so."

Thomas took it and gave a crooked grin. "I do not pass on messages from traitors."

"Traitors?" I gave a harsh laugh. "Why, I am no—"

"Guards," snapped Thomas. "Take her."

Before I could react, before Lance could draw his weapon, two of the Tower guards seized and disarmed him. His hands were wrenched behind his back and his own sword was held at his throat. Another guard grabbed me and pinned my arms.

"What's this?" I shouted. "What are you doing?" I began to struggle.

"Unhand her," shouted Sir Lance. "If you do not, you'll have Lord Nathaniel to answer to."

Noise appeared to erupt on the river. There were shouts and the smack of oars on water.

"We don't answer to Lord Nathaniel's authority here, sir." Thomas spoke with such respect, he could have been conversing in a drawing room. "We answer to the Queen, and it is by her authority that I hereby arrest you, Mallory Bright."

"What are the charges?" Sir Lance was enraged. Helplessly, he watched as I was wrestled toward the gate, the very same gate Papa had emerged from only minutes earlier.

"Why? Why are you doing this?" I cried to Thomas, who matched pace with me as we passed through the gate as if we were friends out for a stroll. "I had an agreement with Sir Francis—this was to be an exchange."

"And it is," said Thomas, ordering the portcullis closed behind us. "One traitor for another."

"There's been a mistake, I'm no traitor." I tried to yank my arms free, but the guard's grip was like a vise.

"Oh, but you are, Mallory Bright." The great chains of the portcullis groaned as they were slowly wound, the metal teeth descending like a giant maw closing. As I watched it, a great weight crushed my chest, an overpowering sense of doom that made it hard to breathe. This was a terrible dream from which I would awake. "Did you not," continued Thomas, "of your own admission, steal secrets from the Queen's Secretary, secrets that could endanger not only Her Majesty, but the entire realm?"

"I . . . I . . ." A wave of terror rose. I could not find words; my thoughts scattered, brittle leaves in a storm.

"And did you not use these same secrets to blackmail Mister Secretary into releasing a felon, a seditious filthy traitor?" Pressing his face close to mine, Thomas leered. "Though you're excellent at what we do, I always suspected Sir Francis was making a mistake employing a woman and that one day your duplicity would out. I was right."

The guards holding Sir Lance released him and slowly backed away, ducking under the portcullis before it closed. As the iron kissed the earth with an empty ring, Sir Lance threw himself against it.

"Let her go!" he cried, his arm reaching through the bars.

In reply his sword was flung through the gate and clattered on the cobbles, narrowly missing him.

I fought against the hands holding me with renewed strength.

"Conserve yourself, Mallory. You will need it for what awaits you."

I dug in my heels, trying to prevent the constable from taking me any further, and twisted and turned as I attempted to dislodge his grip. I slammed my head back into his face and there was a resounding crack, followed by sharp pain in the back of my head.

"You little bitch. I'll give you what-for for that," said the constable. The other guards sniggered.

"She be a fighter."

"She be a willful wench who needs a good swiving."

"Enough," snapped Thomas and gestured to them to keep moving.

Dragged across the cobbles, I let out a scream. "This is not right! Wait until Sir Francis hears of this."

"Hears?" Thomas spun to face me, walking backward, his cloak undulating about his boots. "Who do you think ordered this, Mallory? Who do you think signed the warrant?" Bidding the men stop, he unrolled a document and ordered a guard to lift his lantern. There, at the bottom of the page listing the charges against me and ordering my arrest, was my father's signature.

All the fight left me.

"Take her to the dungeons," Thomas ordered.

I cast one last imploring look behind me and saw Lord Nathaniel reaching through the bars, his face a mask of utter ferocity overlaid with trepidation. He was shouting, but the roaring in my ears, the pounding of my heart and the whispered threats of my jailer made it impossible to hear. But it was the man I saw in the moonlight behind my lord that caused my knees to buckle.

Touching the top of his dark head, whether in salute or surrender, was Sir Francis. My father. The man who had signed my death warrant.

FIFTY-THREE

THE TOWER, LONDON
The 20th to the 22nd of March, Anno Domini 1582
In the 24th year of the reign of Elizabeth I

*I*t was impossible to measure time in this dark, unforgiving space; the misery of thousands had leached into the walls, tainted the very air and sucked the goodness out of men's souls. One such man was responsible for my "welfare," as Thomas cooly termed it. I'd thought at first it would be Thomas Norton, the man who tried to persuade further confessions from Papa, but no. My "care" was reserved for a special sort.

I met him that night, when I was thrown into a dank, gloomy cell. I've no idea which part of the Tower I was in, only that I'd been led along the battlements and down many stairs. Any remaining fight in me had vanished at the sight of Sir Francis and the knowledge he'd not only ordered my fate, but witnessed it as well.

I'd passed other cells on the way. Voices rose and fell. There was the faint sound of crying as well as prayers being offered. Torches set at intervals along the corridors shed a little light, revealing damp walls, rats slipping away from the mighty tread of the guards' boots, and a thin rivulet of water flowing like a pungent vein, widening into puddles through which we waded. The smell was thick and nauseating:

odorous bodies, vomit, piss, shit and a strong metallic stench that I only understood later was blood. Old and freshly shed.

Thomas entered the cell with me. He snapped his fingers and one of the warders appeared with a blanket, two buckets—one filled with water, one empty—a cloth and a plate of what passed for food: a heel of dried bread, cheese and a lump of gray meat.

Sir Francis would not see me starve or freeze. I tried to be thankful but my capacity for gratitude was sorely diminished. Especially when Thomas ordered the men to search me.

One guard pulled off my cloak, barely allowing me time to undo the ties. Then they both began to pat my jacket and skirts, being sure to squeeze my breasts, fondle my thighs and arse, and place their filthy probing fingers everywhere. They found the dagger I kept in my boot, the very one Thomas had given me, and handed it to him.

My humiliation was complete when Thomas ripped the coif from my head and pulled out the pins that held my hair in place.

"It would not do for you to keep the means of your escape," he said wryly, holding my pins in his ink-stained fingers.

I stared at him boldly. "You will not keep me here, despite what you think. No lock or key can."

"Bold words." He passed the pins to one of the guards who began to clean his teeth with them. I grimaced.

"You will be visited shortly, Mallory," said Thomas, gesturing for me to sit upon the pallet of straw tucked against a wall. I obeyed. There was no point doing anything else. He ordered the guard to leave a lantern, so I was not plunged into total darkness.

"Sir Francis?"

Thomas gave a bark of laughter. "Sir Francis does not deign to visit prisoners."

My heart dared to hope. "Who?" Could Lord Nathaniel have been granted access? Surely by now he would have appealed to Sir Francis. But then, if Sir Francis was prepared to arrest and imprison me, his own flesh and blood, what effect would petitions from Lord Nathaniel have? Hadn't Thomas said the Queen herself had ordered my arrest? Hadn't Sir Francis watched as I was led away?

The hope I had beseeched Papa, Caleb and Angela not to lose fled to a place of eternal darkness.

"You will see. Till then, I suggest you rest. Think on what you've done." Squatting on the floor next to my makeshift bed, careful not to let his breeches or cloak sit in the muck, Thomas regarded me steadily. "How could you have been so foolish to think you could beat Sir Francis at his own game? You, a woman as well? Who do you think you are?"

It was on the tip of my tongue to reveal the truth, but I pressed my lips together. If Sir Francis would not declare me, I would not acknowledge our relationship; nor, truth be told, could I afford to anger him further. Anyhow, who'd believe me? Forsooth, not Thomas, who now only viewed me as a traitor to the Crown.

"I had high hopes for you, Mallory, despite my reservations. So did Sir Francis. Still," he said, heaving himself upright, "you'll have time to consider your actions and the choices that have led you here. Till then, I suggest you do what anyone in your position would."

"What's that?"

"Pray." With that, he left me, and the guards trooped out after him. The one I'd given a bloody nose to grabbed his crotch and waggled his tongue at me. I felt sick. Beyond sick.

Burying my head in my hands, I tried to think. I was a fool to believe Sir Francis would keep his end of the bargain. Had I so quickly forgotten what he had done to Edmund Campion?

I lay on the straw and pulled up the blanket, grateful for the scant warmth it offered. It was bitterly cold down here and my breath escaped in clouds of white mist before dissolving into the darkness. That's what I wished to do—dissolve, disappear, be anywhere but here.

But here I was and, as Thomas said, this was where my choices had led me. But not only mine—Sir Francis's too. Had he not trained me? Taught me the skills of watching, of staying one step ahead of the enemy? For, as God is my Lord and Savior, that's what my very own father had become: my enemy.

The man I hoped would one day announce to the world I was his daughter, the man I hoped would love and cherish me, was responsible for my current state. He did not love me, he never had and never would. It was Thomas, wasn't it, who had once said Sir Francis showed special care for me?

The truth was he cared nothing for me, only for his Queen and country. Only that the Catholic scourge and its supporters were wiped from the land. Forsooth, he'd imprisoned his old friend Gideon, the man who had raised his daughter. To know a Catholic was to conspire with one; dealing with Catholics meant you may as well be one. Whichever way it was construed, add popery to your alleged crime and the law judged you guilty.

Sinking into dark thoughts, I forgot to eat or drink and simply lay still, my mind a tangle, my heart broken.

A loud voice shook me from my misery. There was the clank of keys.

I sat up slowly and stared toward a bobbing lantern. Three men stood in its light. Two were guards, the taller man I hadn't seen before. Broadly if not brutishly built, he had thick hair that had turned almost completely white. Dressed in black, he wore a stylish bonnet and had a sword buckled to his doublet.

"Well met, Mallory Bright. You be Gideon's daughter, aye?"

"Aye," I said, cautiously, moving toward the bars. The door had still not been opened.

"I knew your grandfather; your uncle as well."

"I'm afraid you have the advantage, sir, for I know not who you are."

Removing his bonnet, the man gave a gracious bow. "I am Richard Topcliffe, one of the Earl of Leicester's Men."

I was confused. "How may I help you, sir?" I asked.

"Pretty manners for a caitiff, hey, lads?" said Master Richard, earning sniggers from the guards. "Almost as pretty as your self."

I bowed my head at the compliment. What was going on? Who was this man?

"I'm here to help you, Mistress Mallory."

I ventured closer. "Are you a lawyer, sir?"

"I entered Gray's Inn many a year ago, mistress, but alas, never had the inclination to practice. No, the help I offer you is of far more use than a lawyer's canting. Open the gate," he said to the warder.

Fumbling at the keys, the warder did as he was bid.

"Come, mistress, I've a great deal to show you."

Hesitantly, I slipped through the open gate, staring with wide eyes at a man I now began to think might be my savior. "What is it you wish to show me, sir?" I took the arm he offered, confused, not wanting to hope yet starting to think maybe, just maybe, fortune had not deserted me.

"This way," said Master Richard, and led me along the now completely silent corridor. The only noise was the rattle of keys, the belch of the guard and the incessant drip of water. "I would have escorted you to my house, but the nature of the accusation against you precludes such a venture, so we have to remain within these gruesome walls instead." He smiled and looked about him. "My apologies, mistress, it's not my preference. Forsooth, I find this place most inadequate for my purposes."

"And what might those be, sir?" I asked as we rounded a corner, went through a door and down a staircase so narrow, and with steps so uneven, I was forced to keep my hand upon Master Richard's back lest I tumble.

"You will see, you will see," said Master Richard over his shoulder.

The guards behind me mumbled something I could not catch. I ignored them. It seemed I had an ally in this Godforsaken place.

It wasn't until we stopped before a huge wooden door that I began to have doubts. Torches burned in the sconces either side of it. Stools rested beneath one, along with a brimming jug of ale and some leather tankards.

"Lads, let the warder through," said Master Richard. The warder found the key and unlocked the door, but left it closed.

"Thank you, Gerald," said Master Richard and slipped him a coin. The warder detached the key from the ring and passed it to Master Richard. I tried to read his face, but it was blank. With an obsequious bow, a flash of brown teeth and one last look at me, the warder mounted the steps.

"No one is to be admitted," Master Richard instructed the guards. "I'm not to be disturbed. Is that understood?"

"Aye," said the guards, and took up positions either side of the door.

"You wish to know my purpose, mistress?" Master Richard lifted the latch and pushed upon the door. "Here it is," he said and, grabbing my arm firmly, led me inside. Still holding me, he put down the lantern, then shut and locked the door.

The room was dark but I could see it wasn't large. There was a great deal of what I thought was furniture in it. Releasing me, Master Richard used the flame in the lantern to light the torches along the walls. Soon the room was brighter than the streets at midday and I was able to behold the place to which I'd been brought.

Dark brown matter stained the walls. The floor was a slurry, the stench of it made me gag. If I'd eaten anything in my cell, it would have been lost to the floor. Strands of hair, bits of what looked like teeth and God knows what else were splattered beneath the instruments lining the walls and the great, long wooden contraption in the center of the room.

I understood Master Richard's purpose. He was going to torture me. Seeing the alarm on my face, Master Richard began to laugh. I spun back to the door and threw myself against it, pounding my fists against the wood, crying for help I knew would not come.

"They'll not heed you, mistress," said Master Richard.

His words registered. Lowering my hands, I turned back toward him. He retained his friendly mien, which now seemed immeasurably sinister. He offered me his arm once more and I had no choice but to thread my hand through it.

"Allow me to introduce you to my friends, mistress."

"Friends?" I regarded the assortment of iron, wood and steel with perplexed eyes.

"Oh, aye, and soon they'll be yours too. No, that's not true. For you see, these wonderful creatures, these marvels of metal and nature's goodness"—he led me around them, stroking the chains, caressing the manacles, opening the clamps, running his fingers along the wood—"they will become like lovers. Certainly you will know their touch, the kiss of the fetters, the cold, smooth embrace of the manacles, better than that of the most intimate friends." He ran the back of his hand down my cheek.

A small whimper escaped. I pressed my lips together. This was a man who took pleasure from others' pain. I would not give him the satisfaction of seeing my fear. Not while I had some element of control.

Dear God, he was just like Raffe . . . Perchance he was worse. We paraded around the room like a couple out for an evening stroll and arrived back where we started.

"Marry, shall we begin?"

"I can't stop you torturing me, sir. You run to your own timetable. Do not offend me by pretending I have a choice."

"Torture you?" He gave a grin that made my stomach turn to lead. "Oh, my dear sweet lady, I did not bring you here to torture you."

I didn't believe him. "Then what's your purpose, as you put it?"

I saw the leery look in his eye—one I knew all too well. I began to shake.

"As lovely as you are, mistress, I'll not rape you . . ."

Not yet.

"Then why am I here?"

"I told you, I've something to show you."

"What?"

Before I could resist, he grabbed my hands and hauled me across the floor. With practiced ease, he enclosed both my wrists in manacles suspended from the ceiling.

"I intend to show you what will happen should you not cooperate; offer you a taste of what's to come. Think of me as doing you a grand favor; as sparing you untold misery."

The chains were heavy. I could barely lift my arms. Moving to a winch lodged against the wall, Master Richard began to wind it. The great snake of chain on the floor slowly untangled, straightened and, as he kept winding, began to grow taut. My arms were pulled above my head; soon, I was standing on tip-toes. Then I was hoisted into the air. My hands slipped, the only things holding me up were my wrists, jammed against the hard metal of the manacles. Spinning slightly, I tried to remain still. The iron bit into my soft flesh. My arms felt as though they were going to be wrenched from their sockets. Then my feet left the ground and my wrists took all my weight—my wrists and my knotted shoulders.

I groaned as pain seared through my body. Even my neck became weak, my head impossibly heavy.

Master Richard locked the winch and came and stood before me, his head level with my stomach.

"How does that feel?" He ran his hands down my bodice, clamping me about the waist, taking my weight, raising me slightly. For a moment, the pain eased. The chains loosened. An exclamation of relief escaped. Then he dropped me.

I let out a scream.

"Come now, come now. It's not that bad. Imagine hanging there for a few hours, days, even? Then you might have cause to complain."

I tried to lift my head to rest my neck. Below me, Master Richard bent over a strange metal contraption, undoing bands, opening the gauntlets attached to it. I watched in horror as he worked methodically, swiftly.

"Call it what you will"—I forced the words out, my body twisting one way then the other—"this is torture."

"Nay, lady, 'tis but trifles, something to torment me. If I'd my way, I'd torture you without blinking an eye. You who protect Catholic scum, you who would bargain a filthy papist life for the safety of our realm, for good Queen Bess. You deserve nothing but pain; pain and death."

"Papa is no papist," I cried.

"And what about his puking beetle-breasted wife?"

Shocked by the vitriol, the color flooding into his ruddy face and the deadly seriousness of his voice, I fell silent.

He finished what he was doing and unlocked the winch. With a series of grunts, he lowered me back to the ground. My arms fell to my sides, the chains cascading in a rain of metal. Tears began to pour down my face, not simply from the agony, but because of the situation I was in. Once again I was the plaything of a brute. Once again I was a puppet whose strings were controlled by a madman.

I knew his ilk, what he was after. How he derived pleasure and power from the pain he inflicted, the fear he instilled in others. God damn his eyes, I would not give it to him.

Freed from the manacles, I could do little but follow as he courteously led me to the next instrument. "I thought we'd try this one. It's called the Scavenger's Daughter." He looked me up and down and placed a hand on top of my head, then pushed me to my knees. "I might have to rename it Mister Secretary's Daughter."

I twisted beneath his hand, staring up at him in astonishment. "How . . . how do you know?"

"There's little I do not. You think your father—" He paused and made a scoffing sound. "Aye, let's call him what he is, shall we? You think your father is the only one with a network, the ability to forage for information, to pay for it as well? Not everyone who works for Sir Francis is loyal to him." He gave a bark of laughter. "Why, not even his own daughter. I told you, mistress, I'm one of Lord Leicester's Men and head of his network. As such, I look to his needs and, when the pay is right, to those of your father and even Lord Burghley too—especially when they coincide with my master's. Seems you've caught everyone's attention with your little exchange. But you see, Mallory—"

As he spoke, he forced me into a crouch and held me in place while he clamped bands around my body. Gauntlets were placed over my hands, irons were fitted to my feet. If I'd thought being suspended hurt, it was nothing compared to this. Furled into a circle, my chin touched the top of my toes, my spine was curved, my arse was thrust against the bars, as was my head. Unable to speak, barely able to breathe, I was forced to endure. Endure and listen as he taunted me.

"Women should never try and gainsay men. You will always lose. You are weaker, smaller, slower of wit and lack heart. All you're good for is bedding and bearing." As he said this, he thrust his fingers under my skirts, lifting and tugging and tearing the fabric as it wrestled with the metal. Finding skin, he crawled his way up the back of my thighs, across my arse, until he was able to spread the cheeks and move lower. Oh dear God, no. Muttering, he thrust his fingers in and out, making grunting noises as he did so. With his other hand he undid the laces of his pants. Out of the corner of my eye, I saw him extract his member and begin to rub it, looking at it with narrowed eye, his tongue poking out of the corner of his mouth. He pushed his cock between the bars, in front of my face, so I might see it. I shut my eyes tight. "Open your eyes, slattern, see what a man is, hey? Feel me. This is what you don't possess—yet."

He rubbed it over my cheek. If I could have, I would have turned and bitten it off.

"Would you like to suck on this, mistress?" *If only he knew.* "I'll bet you would, hey? Take it in that pretty mouth and lave it with your tongue? If I could put it in your sticky quim, I would, shove it deep inside you and make you moan. All bent over. Shove it up your arse. Some women like it there too. But this will have to do, hey . . . Come on, moan for me, hey? Moan. Oh God, oh God . . ." A warm jet of seed shot onto my face and down my bodice. With one last push, he extracted his fingers, shoved them under his nose and inhaled, then placed them in his mouth, sucking noisily.

"It's not all torture, mistress," he said, tucking himself back into his trousers and lacing himself up. "But next time when I tell you to moan, you will, understand?"

I did, but I refused to do those things I could control. Between bouts with his "friends" I was slapped and punched for not complying. At least one tooth flew out of my mouth. My lip split and, after the fourth slap, one of my eyes began to swell shut. At least I wouldn't have to watch him pleasure himself. Over the ensuing hours, as he placed his fingers inside me again and again, I relived the moment I stabbed Raffe, only this time it was Topcliffe on the receiving end.

I can't recall how long I spent in that room, nor how many instruments he practiced upon. I only knew I could not let this man break me; if I did, his would be the victory and he would have my soul in his keeping forever. I refused to think about what he was doing, refused to succumb to the weight of his evil. Instead, I thought of the good in the world, of the people I knew who had sacrificed so much—not because they were forced to, or persuaded by cruel means, but for love: Papa, Angela, Lord Nathaniel, Caleb, Beatrice. I thought of my little son, dead because of a man like Topcliffe. Then I thought of Raffe, who might have escaped justice for now, but was trapped in an eternal prison with a virago for a wife.

When I was taken back to my cold, dirty cell, I found it had become a place of refuge. Sinking onto the straw, I was aware of Master Richard standing over me, staring at me, willing me to look at him. My entire body ached. As I was unable to walk, he'd carried me back to my room. My wrists were rubbed raw, my ankles too. I was drowning in an ocean of pain.

"Tomorrow, we'll meet my friends again, and the day after. Then you will choose which among them you'd like to be intimate with. I know my preference," he chuckled. "Of course, you can always confess before we get to that."

"Confess to what?" My voice was dry, rough.

"You know," he said, lowering himself, placing his hands on either side of my body. I could smell his fetid breath.

I opened an eye. "If I did, I would not ask."

"To being a papist plotter; to the treason in your heart." He cupped my left breast. I'd not the strength to throw him off. "And when you do,

I'll rip it out." He twisted my nipple as he stood. I bit my lip. I would not scream. No more.

Topcliffe ordered my cell to be locked and stormed away, his promise to see me on the morrow filling the room.

I rolled over and began to assess my injuries. I could taste blood on my lips, in my mouth. My groin ached from Topcliffe's obscene attentions. I stank of his seed, his saliva and my own sweat. I reeked of fear. I had to wash, to cleanse the stain of that man away.

Forcing myself upright, I crawled to the bucket. Dipping the cloth in, I wrung it out. The water smelled dreadful. Lifting the cloth to my nose, I quickly cast it away. The bastards had urinated in it. Not once, but many times while I was gone.

Slowly, I made my way back to the bed and, with sharp intakes of breath, feeling every single clamp, pinch, gouge of metal, rake of iron, fist and palm that struck me, lowered myself back onto the straw. I could not even pull the blanket over me. It was too much effort.

There was no light except the lamp, no sounds except the faint caw of the ravens, the whistle of the wind and the drip of water. Even the rats had left.

I tried to conjure up thoughts of Papa, of Lord Nathaniel, Angela, Beatrice and Caleb. I could not. Like my courage, they too had fled this terrible place. I dared not examine my thoughts too deeply, I was too afraid of what I'd find—a father who allowed this rogue to manhandle, threaten and foully abuse his daughter.

All I could think was, if this wasn't torture, then, God forbid, what was?

FIFTY-FOUR

*F*or more than a day, I begged for fresh water and food. A shambling servant eventually delivered the water. There was no food. I was able to wash and drink. My mouth was dry, my body one enormous site of suffering. What little sleep I'd managed was racked with visions of a white-haired man, of Raffe sneering as he was whipped by a fan, of my dead son's sweet face, Mamma's deathbed, and whispered threats. Waking banished the nightmares, but plunged me back into the dismal truth of my situation.

I shuffled around, sat, listened to the sounds of the dungeons: the somnolence of the stones, the rasp of my straw pallet, the chittering of the rats and the percussive drop of water. I tried to discover if the cells near me were occupied and called softly into the semidarkness. No one replied. Apart from the warders, who refused to engage with me, I was alone.

My thoughts traveled to the outside world. I wondered how Papa was faring and prayed the grievous injuries he'd suffered were not permanent. For certes, the attentions he'd endured made mine but trifles. I tried to raise my arms but could not. My ankles were banded by raw marks, the flesh broken in parts and weeping slightly. It was more than trifles.

I prayed Papa would not sicken himself with worry for me. I pondered whether Lord Nathaniel had spoken to Sir Francis. Was help on its way or was I as doomed as Topcliffe would have me believe? I prayed Caleb and Beatrice fared better, Angela too.

I tried to measure time, imagine the weather—anything to distract myself. Despair threatened to break me and send me into a paroxysm of tears and anguish. I would not permit it. Though I hurt in ways I'd not thought possible for a long time, I'd received much worse from someone who used love as an excuse for it. Topcliffe loathed me and that made his attentions easier to bear, even if it did not lessen the suffering after.

My inner thighs ached. My ribs and breasts. My dignity should be in tatters, but it was not. I considered what the man had done: his base treatment of me, his coarse lust, his disregard for me as a woman, as a human—all designed to instill terror and break me. I would not allow it. I was no innocent. Raffe had subjected me to far worse. For once, I was grateful to the man.

Love hurt far more than hate.

Though I would try not to let Topcliffe destroy me, my mind or the knowledge of the goodness I knew existed beyond these walls, it was his so-called friends I was more concerned about. The instruments of torture he'd lovingly introduced me to—the rack, the Scavenger's Daughter, the iron maiden, the collar, the gauntlets, irons and fetters in which he'd briefly trapped me, treating each manacle and chain as though they were jewels to adorn his mistress. Placing me in each of his instruments, he'd had me endure only minutes of what they offered—the stretching, crushing, pushing, pulling and, above all, the pain. He explained each and every time what they could do if I didn't confess, the hours I'd be forced to endure. The very idea of more time in any one of them turned me into a quivering mess.

On the way back to my cell, he'd paused and shown me the Pit, a deep, dark hole, and Little Ease, a cramped space in which no one, not even a child, could stand. The implication was clear—there were more friends for me to "meet."

I could not prevent him breaking my bones, but whether he sapped my resolve was something within my control. For all Castiglione offered, he did not tell a prisoner how to cope with torture. How was one to affect indifference to a man who was a master of the art? How could one not break under the sheer weight of injustice?

I had to discover the answer to that, and fast. I flexed and stretched my limbs, ignoring my hurts, forcing myself to walk, quoting poetry and Caleb's plays to sustain my spirits.

Some time after the midday bells tolled, Topcliffe paid another visit. He was alone. Standing by the bars, he was so still I wasn't aware of him at first. I was sitting upon the pallet, breathing in and out, recollecting an afternoon spent with Beatrice where we quoted excerpts from Ovid to each other. That led me to think of a time Lord Nathaniel and I had done the same.

"You're stronger than I gave you credit, mistress," said a friendly voice, interrupting my reverie.

My heart hammered, but I kept my back to him and shrugged. "I'm oft underestimated, sir, like most women."

"I think tonight I will allow you longer with my friends, give you the chance to get to know them better."

"Say what you want, sir, do what you will. If Sir Francis, my father, knew for certes all you did to me, I think he would be most . . . displeased."

"Displeased?" The tone made me turn. "The man who says your very existence is a threat to the realm? That with those pretty long-fingered hands and that sly mind"—he poked a finger through the bars, as if he were pressing it into my head, pinning my palm to the ground—"you think you can open any lock, steal any secret? Even under the noses of the most cautious and highest ranking folk? I doubt that, mistress. Possessed of a papist mother, you're a curse, a blight he wishes he'd never brought into the world. He'll be glad to facilitate your exit. So will I. The sooner the better."

He struck the bars and left.

I sat with my back to the wall and rested my chin on my knees. I forced my mind blank and shut my eyes. It was impossible. Once more, I was a blight—Mallory Blight.

Please, God, my Lord in heaven, save me from that man; from the men who would bring about my doom.

As the hours ticked by and the bell tower's faint chimes resounded gently through this mighty fortress, I began to think that everyone, even the decent men, had forsaken me: Papa, Caleb, Lord Nathaniel— even God.

Sir Francis, despite all I'd hoped and all he'd done for me, had never really wanted me. Mamma had warned me: *Trust not Sir Francis,* she'd said. *Just like you, he's not what he seems.* Nothing, not even a daughter, would interfere with his lofty goals.

That's exactly what I'd done. Interfered. Worse, I'd made him appear a fool, unable to protect his secrets, to keep his queen safe from a mere chit. And now Topcliffe had added another sin I hadn't really considered: a papist mother. Whether Valentina or Lucia, it mattered not.

To think I'd once relished the idea of possessing two fathers. That Sir Francis might be more to me than a master . . . and I more than his servant.

Forgive me, Papa. Forgive me, Mamma.

I was a selfish, dim-witted buffoon. Why should I have two fathers when people like Beatrice, Lord Nathaniel, and so many more besides, had none? If he'd loved me, Sir Francis would never have given me to Papa and Mamma. For certes, he would have claimed me as daughter, not encouraged me to work for him, sent me into danger and kept me a secret. That was not love—forsooth, it was not what a father did. Just like the good Lord, a father protected and forgave his children even the worst of their sins. He didn't mistreat them or deploy them for his own ends.

A real father risked being called a traitor and facing certain death for his wayward child.

But the way Sir Francis coddled the miniature of his daughter Mary—didn't that suggest a modicum of feeling? I tried to recall if he'd ever shown any to me. Alas, in this cheerless space, I could not.

Fighting against the sobs building in my chest, I began rocking back and forth, back and forth, ignoring the pain in my spine, in my hands and feet and sides.

As the time passed and my next appointment with Master Topcliffe drew nearer, rescue became less likely. No doubt Sir Francis would have Papa and Lord Nathaniel watched; he would place obstacles in their way, make himself elusive. There was no conceivable way they could help me. But did they even want to? Was I not a blight on their lives as well? Was this not a way to be rid of me once and for all? Though he'd been released, Papa had not escaped unscathed because of my actions. As far as the authorities were concerned, he'd concealed papist propaganda, colluded with a traitor—never mind raising one. Exile might not be enough. As for Lord Nathaniel, he'd kept me beneath his roof. He too would be tarnished by my blight. As would Beatrice. Oh dear God, had I condemned her future as well? Though Lord Nathaniel reassured me that my affair with Raffe didn't reduce his esteem for me, and had even aided me in my scheme to free Papa, he'd have had time to reconsider his words and actions by now. No doubt he regretted both.

It was better for everyone if I was left here to meet my fate. My wits were becoming addled if I thought they could facilitate my escape. Was I not locked in the most secure prison of them all?

No one was coming. It was just me, this cell, Master Richard Topcliffe and his friends. If I wanted help, I had to provide it. Us women, we had to look to ourselves, did we not, Mamma?

Raising my head, I studied the room once more. The lantern was guttering and though I'd tried to conserve the flame, I doubted it would be replaced. All I had was poor light, a bucket for drinking and washing and another for toileting, a cloth, a blanket and a plate of uneaten food. The walls were thick, the gate securing me possessed of a simple lock. However, without a key or picks to force it, I was still a prisoner at the mercy of my jailers. I shivered.

Wood, metal and cloth, much like Master Richard's special room. Wood, metal and cloth . . .

A burble of laughter rose. Of course. When there was no metal, a solid piece of wood would often suffice, no matter how thin. If I could make the bucket splinter, then mayhap, mayhap, I had a chance.

Tipping the food off the plate, I drank some more water, gave my neck and face one last wash—my inner thighs too, anything to cleanse myself of that man's touch—then poured the rest on the floor. Sitting on the pallet, I began to use the edge of the plate to dig away at the edges of the bucket. It was old, had seen many uses and in parts the wood was soft. Large pieces and splinters came off with ease.

Where the metal bands girded it, there was solidity, strength. Gradually I whittled the wood down to the first of the bands. It clanged to the floor. I waited to see if the noise attracted attention, then I picked up the metal and studied it.

Without tools to refashion it, it was no good as a pick, but it was a sturdy weapon. I concealed it beneath the mattress and kept working. I needed to get to where the wood was firmer.

As long as the light lasted, I dug away, prying off bits of wood, testing pieces that were long enough in the lock of my cell. My fingers were cut and bleeding, already damaged by the gauntlets. I ignored them.

None of the pieces were quite firm enough, not yet. They snapped as I pushed them into the keyhole, forcing me to use others to dig them out.

How long I worked at this, I'd no idea. All I knew was that the hour for my reckoning with Topcliffe was approaching. I was tired, hurting, hungry and soul-sick. Urgency made me work faster. Shards of wood scattered about my feet. Still I tried, until a splinter too thick to be useful broke off halfway in the lock, and no matter what I did, how hard I tried to force it out, it only became embedded further in the keyhole.

Tears welled. I sank to my knees, my face pressed against the bars. If I could not get out, perchance Topcliffe could not enter. It was a small hope, but a fervent one.

Before long, I heard voices. Scrabbling about, I collected the wood and threw it in what remained of the bucket, pushing it into the darkness. The iron band that circled the bucket I concealed behind my back.

I stood, brushed off my skirts and waited. He would not find me broken and trembling, though I was both those things.

There were footsteps, whispers. Silence. Then some more footsteps. Something was amiss. Topcliffe stalked these corridors as if he owned them.

Oh dear Lord, what new horror was being sent to test me?

There was the clink of a key, the sound of latch being raised. The outer gate was breached. My fate marched on.

"Mallory?"

It could not be.

"Mallory?" A different voice this time. A woman's.

I ran to the bars. "My lord? Beatrice?"

There was the sound of running feet and then the face I most wanted to see in the world appeared. Attired in the very clothes in which I first met him was Lord Nathaniel. Larger than life, solid and oh so real, he reached through the bars and pulled me to him, kissing my mouth so hard I cried out.

"What have they done to you?" He cataloged my face; rage contorted his. "My God, they'll pay for this."

"Mallory, my sweetling," said the woman. It wasn't Beatrice. The voice was familiar, but the long golden hair, the bright red lips, dark brows and flushed cheeks were strange. Yet the disheveled dress and coat were not . . . I'd seen them upon the stage . . . The woman pushed her arms through the bars and found my hands. "Mallory, it's me."

"Caleb?"

He pushed his face against the bars until I could rest my forehead against his. It was a moment of sheer peace and stillness amid this madness. I began to weep. God curse my womanly weakness.

"Mallory," said Caleb again, his voice breaking.

"Come," said Lord Nathaniel. "We've not much time."

Caleb touched my cheek and moved to the gate. "Here, here," he said, waving me over and thrusting a leather pouch through the bars. It was my lock-picking tools. My heart soared. Opening it, I extracted two picks and with unsteady fingers began working. Caleb closed one eye and attempted to peek through the keyhole from his side "Something is blocking it."

"'Twas me," I said. "I tried to fashion picks out of wood. Here, quick, if I give you one, try and lever the last of it out from your end." I passed a rod through the bars.

"Wood?"

"Aye." It seemed reckless now. "It was mostly rotten and broke." Tears coursed freely. Was my ambition also to be my own destruction? Was I about to ruin my chance at freedom and imperil Caleb and Lord Nathaniel as well?

Scraping at the lock, I managed to get all but the smallest bit out. Reinserting the metal rod, I put my ear to the lock and listened as Caleb extracted the last of the wood and struck metal. Passing me the rod back, I reinserted it alongside the first and, bypassing the wards, I finally heard the click for which I'd longed. The latch popped, Caleb wrenched open the gate. I flew into his arms.

Turning, I sailed into Lord Nathaniel's embrace. "Mallory," he said. His voice was a dangerous purr.

Relocking the cell, I checked it could not open without a key.

"Come, let us away from this terrible place," said Lord Nathaniel and took my hand.

"How did you get in here?" I asked as we crept back up the corridor. "Where are the guards? The warder? Where is Topcliffe?"

"Lord Nathaniel will explain," said Caleb. He hadn't let go of my other hand.

"We still have to get out," said Lord Nathaniel. "Till then, explanations can wait. Just do as I ask and pray all goes well."

We reached the top of the stairs.

There, upon a small table surrounded by three stools was a pile of clothes. "Quickly now," said Lord Nathaniel. "Put these over your garments."

Shaking out the gorgeous skirt and jacket, I quickly pulled them over what remained of my own clothes. They were slightly too big for me, but gorgeously decorated, strewn with seed pearls and embroidery. There was also a beautiful hooded cloak, lined with fox fur.

"What is this? Whose? Why do I have to dress so?" I asked as I hurriedly dressed. "Where are the guards?"

"The guards have been sent searching for a prisoner who escaped," said Caleb wryly.

"Who?"

"Your father—the traitor. But in case they find you gone, you're disguised as a lady."

Lord Nathaniel peered up the stairs. Faint shouts could be heard. Running feet. "Sir Francis made a fatal mistake with his exchange. He only told those yeomen in his pay. Sir Owen Hopton, the Lord Lieutenant of the Tower, a man who bears no love for Sir Francis, had no knowledge Gideon had been released. Once we learned that, we were able to use it to our advantage—that and my friendship with him. They are searching for your papa now. As for these guards"—he waved a hand at the empty seats—"the pay is so poor that a few coin to look the other way was gratefully received. They know not why we wished admission and absented themselves to help in the search before they found out. Their ignorance will at least be genuine."

I thought of Topcliffe's fury when he discovered what had happened. He would never accept ignorance as a reason for my escape. But I could hardly feel sorry for the men. Hadn't they been complicit in allowing him to hurt me?

Though Caleb helped, I finished dressing with some difficulty. My arms were aching, every movement was agony. I tried to spare Caleb and Lord Nathaniel my complaints.

Lord Nathaniel looked me up and down. "Well met, my lady. My mother's clothes do become you. No one will question two sisters visiting the Lord Lieutenant, nor their humble servant." He had a sword strapped to his hip. He drew it now. "We must confuse the yeomen who will surely be thoroughly questioned once your escape is noted. If we encounter anyone, and I pray we do not, you are Emma and Lettice. Do not refer to me by name."

"But my lord," I whispered. "You need to do more than adopt diverse dress and omit a name to confuse anyone. Your height trumpets your identity."

"Let me worry about that. I'm not patron of a troupe of actors for nothing."

"He can play his part, Mallory," said Caleb.

The footsteps above us faded, the cries grew more distant. "Come," said Lord Nathaniel. He took a torch from the wall and began to ascend the stairs. As we climbed, Lord Nathaniel outlined the plan. Avoiding the guards, we were to make our way to the outer ward and the river. A boat was waiting to row us to a ship. From there, we would sail to safety. I did not want to point out the flaw in the plan—where in England would we be safe once my escape, and his lordship's and Caleb's complicity in it, was discovered? The authorities had already released Caleb once—they would not show clemency again. I tried not to think about it and followed his lordship, unable to quite conceive that here he was before me. Caleb, as always, looked to my back.

Dousing the torch and discarding it, we emerged into the darkness between the stones of the Bloody Tower and the wall that separated

Tower Green and the Inmost Ward. The White Tower rose ahead, spectral in the gloom. The shouts of the yeomen became louder. Torches lit the battlements and the space near the chapel. In the darkness at the top of the stairs we waited while two guards ran past, then moved swiftly up the slope toward Tower Green. There we turned and, keeping to the wall, ran toward St. Thomas's Tower. We paused to catch our breath beneath the very tower in which I'd been imprisoned. I inhaled the cool air, enjoying its freshness, sending prayers of gratitude heavenward and supplications we'd not be caught. Above us, men's voices rose in anger. One in particular turned my blood to ice.

"Check the cells, you fools. Bright has not escaped. The highest authorities endorsed his release. This is but a ruse." There was a grunt followed by an expletive. A door slammed and more shouts and the hollow echo of footsteps followed.

"What's that pizzle-headed rogue Topcliffe doing here?" whispered Lord Nathaniel.

I didn't know I'd made a sound until his lordship sucked his breath in. "By God, I'll kill him." I wondered if he meant Topcliffe or Sir Francis. At that moment, God forgive me, I wished them both dead.

We levered ourselves away from the wall and waited until another group of guards had passed. Then we ran across the Outer Ward toward our destination—Traitors Gate. I knew it well, as did all Londoners who glided past it upon the river. The irony was not lost on me. While I may have denied being a traitor before, in fleeing the Tower and the justice of the Queen, no matter how unfair, I had indeed become one. As had the men beside me.

At the entrance to Traitors Gate stood a huge wood and iron doorway. To my right, I could hear water lapping the banks and see the shadowy outline of a boat. Beyond that, the portcullis was raised and the Thames glimmered in the moonlight. My God, we were so close.

I withdrew my picks once more, as Lord Nathaniel kept watch, his face contorted into an expression that rendered him nigh on unrecognizable.

"Hurry," hissed Caleb.

"Guards approach," whispered Lord Nathaniel.

I risked a glimpse. Torches marched relentlessly along the Outer

Ward, indistinct figures breaking away to prod the shadows, searching the darkness for the missing prisoner.

There were bellows from within the walls of the Bloody Tower.

"Mallory," urged Caleb, looking over his shoulder. There was no light, my hands were trembling.

A voice exploded into the night. "Sound the alarum! Sound the alarum! The traitorous bitch has escaped." God in heaven help us. "Find the wench Mallory Bright, bring her to me." Richard Topcliffe shouted my name over and over from the parapet of the Bloody Tower, turning in every direction so he could be heard by all. Like the tolling bells, my name echoed across the entire Tower fortress, down to where we stood upon the wet cobbles, trying desperately to gain admission to the waterway and our escape.

Guards paused, then leaped to action.

In the boat below, Lord Nathaniel's men gazed at us in silence, willing us on.

Though I shook like a tent in the wind and I swear my heart was in my throat, I concentrated hard. The lock was not that complicated. In seconds the tumbler lifted, the gate clicked and soundlessly swung open.

"Inside, inside." I pushed Caleb through, he almost stumbled over his skirts. With one last look at the approaching guards, Lord Nathaniel, still hunched over, scrambled to my side, hurried me through and slammed the gate.

"Lock it, Mallory. Our lives may depend on it."

Quivering so badly I almost dropped the pick, I locked the gate, jamming the rod and bending it for good measure. By the time I finished, the boat had moved forward, its prow against the water stairs. I slipped and fell against Lord Nathaniel, stifling a cry as my shoulder was wrenched and my ribs struck his sword. Standing once again at his full height, my lord lifted me in his arms and swung me over the side of the boat. His men reached up and helped me to a seat. Already aboard, Caleb found my hand and held it gently. Under his breath, he was praying.

The men wasted no time and pushed off from the stairs and through the gate. The portcullis began to lower just as guards burst through, their torches turning them all into silhouettes—deadly ones. As soon as they sighted us, they kneeled on the stones and began firing arrows.

"Take cover," cried Lord Nathaniel, throwing himself over me and Caleb. "Heave to, men," he shouted.

Never before has a boat moved so fast. It was as if we sped above the water, so swift was our passage. Across the currents, we rowed south, toward the opposite bank. Arrows rained overhead, most missing. Shields were held above our heads and to our sides.

We hadn't pulled away very far when a shot rang out. A chunk of the boat exploded and water doused us.

"Keep your heads, men," said Lord Nathaniel. Adjusting his position, he turned so he could keep an eye on the receding bank. St. Thomas's Tower rose, the arrow slits and wider windows glowing with the light of torches. In one, a tall, white-haired man could be seen issuing orders. He watched us depart and I could imagine his expression. He would pretend indifference, embracing Castiglione's notion of the perfect courtier, never letting those under his command see just how rattled, how furious he was. The thought we might both share such a notion and strive to hide our feelings sickened me.

Rage and fear filled me as I stared at the figure in the window. Not even Dante could find a place in hell deep enough and dark enough for such a one.

The rain of arrows began to fall short and I dared to think us safe at last. Then another shot rang out. At first I thought it too had missed its mark, until I heard a sound I never wish to hear again issue from my lord's lips. The world slowed as Lord Nathaniel fell, his hand pressed over his heart, dark liquid welling between his fingers and spilling from his mouth.

"Nathaniel!" I screamed as he toppled backward into his men, who with cries of woe tried to prevent him hitting the deck. Scrambling over them, I collapsed beside him, pressing my hands over his, trying to stop his lifeblood draining away. I ripped my ruff from my neck and pushed it against the wound only to watch helplessly as the pale fabric changed color.

Ahead of us, a huge ship was lighting its lanterns and readying its sails. Dark shapes flitted from prow to stern, throwing out ropes ready to bring us on board.

"We are almost there, Nathaniel. Please, please, hold on. Do not leave me." Tears ran down my face, great heavy tears that fell from the end of my nose onto his face. His beautiful, kind face; the face that filled my dreams and captured my soul. "Please, God, his heart cannot cease. I'll not let it, not when it's in my keeping."

As if from a distance, I heard Caleb shouting for a doctor.

Confusion and anger filled his lordship's eyes before they were replaced with a look of wonder. "Mallory Bright, do my ears deceive me? Or did you just confess affection for me?"

"Aye." I placed my lips against his, breathing life into his cold ones. "Affection that doth fill me from the top to the toes—all for you. Only you."

He reached up and stroked my cheek, found my hair and tried to pull me closer. His fingers were heavy, clumsy. His breath came in short sharp gasps, his eyelids flickered. "Can it be that I, your boorish knave with the manners of a cur, have found the key to unlock your heart?" Moonlight glimmered in his laughing eyes before they closed.

"The very same," I said, pushing the hair from his forehead. A sob shuddered from me. "Hush, hush, save your words, save your strength."

"Beloved," he whispered, and did not speak again.

PART NINE
The Last Lock Opened

If our courtier happens to find himself in the service
of one who is wicked and malign, let him leave him
as soon as he discovers this, that he may escape the
great anguish that all good men feel in serving the wicked.

—Baldassare Castiglione, *The Book of the Courtier:*
The Second Book, 1528

Videna: A father? No: In kinde a father, not in kindliness.
Ferrex: My father? Why? I know nothing at all,
Wherein I have misdone unto his grace.

—Thomas Norton and Thomas Sackville, *Gorboduc or The Tragedie*
of Ferrex and Porrex, 1561

Private confessions were not enough for Elizabeth's government.
Any malefactor, from the humblest offender to someone
as symbolic as Edmund Campion, had to recant, to be seen
to recognize his error and then to repent of it.

—Stephen Alford, *The Watchers: A Secret History*
of the Reign of Elizabeth I

FIFTY-FIVE

ABOARD *DODONA'S DREAM*,
THE THAMES, LONDON
The 24th to the 30th of March, Anno Domini 1582
In the 24th year of the reign of Elizabeth I

*H*ow do I describe the events of these last few days? They are not easy to recall and more difficult to tell.

Upon reaching Lord Nathaniel's ship, which lay ready midstream, not far from the Tower, we were hauled aboard swiftly and carefully, especially his lordship. His men, upon seeing his condition, did not fall victim to despair as I feared, but carried him to his cabin and summoned one among them who knew physic.

Nicholas was barely able to contain himself, moving from joy upon seeing me and Caleb, to tears when he learned his lord had been shot. He wept as he lit lamps and candles, casting much-needed light upon the darkness enveloping us.

Caleb and I crammed inside the cabin, trying to remain out of the way, but ready to offer whatever assistance we could. Caleb quietly told Nicholas all that had befallen us. Sniffing loudly, Nicholas nodded and tried to be stoic.

God bless him, I felt his anxiety.

As the sails were unfurled, the anchor weighed and we set off downstream toward the sea, a rough-looking man entered the cabin. He bore more scars than hairs on his head, and carried a satchel over his shoulder. This was Jim—the crew member versed in physic. Using a grim-looking dirk, he cut away his lordship's jacket and shirt, peeled away my ruff and examined the wound.

"It's missed the heart, that much I can tell," he said, his eyes betraying his concern.

I clasped my chest with relief.

"But he's not out of danger. The shot is still in there, as far as I can tell." He signaled Nicholas. "Help me roll him over." Nicholas and the physician grunted as they positioned Lord Nathaniel on his side. There was no exit wound. They lowered him once again onto his back and Jim scratched his pate.

"I've no choice but to remove it lest it travel about his body and kill him." Dropping my ruff onto the floor, he rummaged in his bag, producing a mortar and pestle, a flask, a few vials of powder, clean cloths and a wad of dark brown matter that looked like a dying plant and smelled just as bad.

"My lady," he said, "be so good as to grind up the powders I put in here"—he held up the mortar—"with some of this." He held up the flask. "You"—he said to Caleb, ignoring his woman's attire—"hold this." He handed over the pestle. First pressing some of the brown substance onto the wound (it was dried moss, he explained), he then opened the vials and poured the contents into the mortar, muttering as he did.

"Seeds of henbane, juice of poppy head, cassia lignea, some seeds of scalage, fennel and Macedonian parsley. There, that should do it. Now, grind it up and mix it with this. His lordship will be in need of something for the pain—and soon. You"—he said to Nicholas—"help me undress him."

As gently as he could, Nicholas held his lordship and helped Jim remove what remained of his shirt and jacket. By the time they'd laid him back down again, the potion Caleb and I had prepared swam in the mortar.

"Pour that into a cup," ordered Jim. Caleb obliged while Jim grabbed one of the lanterns, opened it and held the blade of the dirk to the flame until it changed color. As I stood in the center of the cabin,

I was transfixed by Lord Nathaniel's body. Strong and lean, his chest was muscular and covered with a down of dark hair that was matted with sweat and blood. The wound was raw, purple, crimson and black, a weeping eye out of place on that bronzed body. Despite its scars from other battles, his form was a thing of beauty.

I went and sat at the top of the bed and took his head in my lap, holding the sides of his face firmly, stroking his temples with my thumbs.

Jim bade Nicholas and Caleb hold his lordship down. Persuaded the patient was tightly held, he counted to three, then pushed the heated dirk slowly into the wound.

Lord Nathaniel groaned. The further Jim pushed, the louder the sound became until his eyes flew open, his back arched, and he ground his teeth together.

"Hold him. Hold him," said Jim, fixed upon finding the shot, his fingers prying the wound apart as he twisted the knife even more.

Lord Nathaniel's face became worryingly red, the noises strangled. Sweat poured into his eyes. Using my skirt, his mother's, I wiped it away, whispering what I hoped were comforting words.

"God's wounds, Mallory!" he spat. "Cease your prattling and forgive a man his cussing!" He proceeded to curse and profane in a manner that would have made the devil himself blush.

The ship lurched as the wind took the sails. Above us, cries rang out, followed by more shots.

Reassured Lord Nathaniel was in possession of his wits and would remain still, Caleb withdrew his arms. "I'll see what's happening," he said, his face white. First ripping off the wig and divesting his skirts, he left the cabin.

Fully awake now, Lord Nathaniel didn't move, and allowed Jim not only to make the wound bigger, but finally, with a levering of the dirk and a terrible sucking sound, to free the shot. It clattered to the floor and rolled under the table. Nicholas retrieved it, holding it between thumb and forefinger with a whistle.

Immediately, Jim poured wine over the bubbling blood and torn skin, the hole laid bare. Reheating the knife, he pressed the blade against the open flesh, searing it, filling the small space with a smell I hoped never to inhale again.

Lord Nathaniel shut his eyes tight, hissed, then grew pale and quiet. His usually bronzed skin was clammy and gray. I wiped his brow, eventually earning a small smile. "Forgive me," he said.

I smiled back. "Forgive you what?"

Placing the rest of the moss against the wound, Jim pointed to the clean cloths. I passed them to him, my hands trembling. Placing them on top of the moss, he bound his lordship's chest and shoulder.

After a while, Jim helped him to sit up and Nicholas propped him with pillows, then forced him to drink the potion I'd helped make. Pulling a face, his lordship didn't object too strongly.

Caleb came back into the cabin, a cold gust biting his heels, making the lanterns dim and the candles gutter.

"We're being followed," he said grimly. "Three boatloads of soldiers, armed and angry." Upon seeing Lord Nathaniel bandaged and sitting up, he beamed. "Good to have you back again, Nate," he said. I prayed he was not being too optimistic, that his lordship was indeed back. As Jim said, the danger had not passed. The wound could become infected; perchance the shot may have done more damage than we could see. There was so much that could still go wrong . . . It did not bear thinking about.

"The man with the white hair who shot you," continued Caleb, addressing Lord Nathaniel, "is leading them. He has not stopped shouting since they came within range. He is like a trumpet inciting them to battle."

"Fear not, Caleb, this ship can outrun the boats. We do but play with them. Order the cannons fired, Nicholas," said Lord Nathaniel. "A louder musket will silence theirs."

"Are you sure, Nate?" said Caleb. "Once we fire upon the Queen's men, there's no turning back."

Lord Nathaniel gave the grin I'd grown to love. "Once we helped Her Majesty's prisoner escape, it was never an option."

With a bow, Nicholas left.

I was desperate to ask about Papa, about Beatrice, Angela and Sir Lance, but resisted. Lord Nathaniel had grown so very pale again. Answers could wait. There was a jug of water on the table and some clean cloths, and with them I washed his lordship's face, then washed the blood from his body and the unharmed parts of his chest. I was as gentle as I could be.

Grabbing my wrist, Lord Nathaniel stilled my action. "Jim," he said, his eyes fixed upon me. "See to my lady's hurts as well, would you? None other than Richard Topcliffe, the white-haired whoreson who blusters from the boats, attended to her in my absence. She will not admit her injuries, but I fear what that scoundrel has done. Caleb, make sure she allows him."

"My lord," said Caleb with a mock bow, one hand resting on my shoulder.

From where he sat on the bed beside his lordship, Jim eyed me with respect. "You enjoyed that fen-suckled canker's attentions and yet you aid Nate? And without a murmur or a fit of the vapors." He nodded approvingly. "She be a mate worth keeping, my lord," he said.

Lord Nathaniel lifted my hand, clicking in dismay when he saw the welts that ringed my wrist. He pressed the most gentle of kisses to them. "You read my mind, Jim. You read my mind."

Before long, he drifted off to sleep.

I was given the only other cabin and left to Jim's ministrations. Caleb and Nicholas stayed on deck, helping where they could, measuring the growing distance between the Queen's men and the ship, watching the moon move in and out of the clouds.

Jim kept his face neutral as he examined me, but the way he pressed his lips and furrowed his brows revealed his thoughts. Gently he bathed my wrists and ankles, tended the wounds on my arms and legs and gave me a balm to rub on the more tender parts of my body. He said the external hurts Topcliffe had inflicted would heal. I knew this to be true. It was those unseen, which I did not mention but Jim seemed to guess at, that would take longer. Knowing Lord Nathaniel and Papa were alive, that his lordship and Caleb had risked so much to save me, that the love I felt for all of them was returned in abundance, was all the physic I needed—for now.

I refused the potion we'd administered to Lord Nathaniel, then washed and, knowing I would be unable to sleep, went on deck. There was no sign of pursuit. Caleb and I returned to Lord Nathaniel. The physic had carried him into a pain-free slumber. In repose he appeared so young and untroubled. It was hard to resist the urge to kiss his brow, stroke his face.

Caleb gave a sad, sweet smile. "You do love him, don't you?"

"Aye. I do. I know, I know. No good can come of such emotions." I sighed. "Though they are so different to the affection I thought I had for Raffe, this too can only end in disaster. Lord Nathaniel is so far above me, I may as well reach for a star than have him acknowledge me."

"I'm not sure he would see it that way," said Caleb. "You've always underestimated him. He has given up his home for you, and more."

"What do you mean?"

"In helping you and Gideon, in aiding me, he's sacrificed everything—his position, his lands, much of his wealth. He can never return to Warham Hall or his estates, not while Elizabeth sits on the throne."

My eyes remained fixed on his lordship. He'd sacrificed all that for me? "I thought because he was a noble, with court connections, he'd be spared the punishments of lesser folk." Caleb shook his head. "What of Beatrice?"

It was then I learned the rest of Lord Nathaniel's plan, his folly. The ship we were upon, *Dodona's Dream*, named after the talking forests of myth and legend that were said to offer prophetic utterances, was making its way to Plymouth. There, Sir Lance would meet us, bringing Papa, Beatrice, the maids Alice and Tace, Angela and any of Lord Nathaniel's men who weren't currently on board but wished to join us.

"Where is he intending to go?"

Caleb looked at me in bewilderment. "Don't you understand? Just as he can no longer remain in England, neither can you."

I knew that. But to think my rashness meant others could not return either . . . It was too great a burden, too great a responsibility. I couldn't think upon it. Not tonight.

"How is Papa?"

Caleb smiled. "He is well. At least, he will be. Your uncle Timothy saw to his wounds. They were dire. He'd been racked, his fingernails torn out, his hands broken. I fear he'll never be able to make his beautiful locks and keys again."

My heart was rocked. How could Sir Francis have been so cruel? It wasn't enough to take his daughter, he had to take his friend's livelihood as well. I wanted to feel rage, but it would not come. Sir Francis had arrested Papa, failed to intervene in his torture, and all I could feel was an overwhelming sadness. Poor Papa. It was not his eyes that would end his locksmithing days, it was his old friend . . .

No matter, for was I not the locksmith's daughter? If I could be his eyes, then I could surely be his hands and anything else he needed as well. It was the least I could do after all he'd sacrificed for me.

"Where is he? Where's Angela? I cannot conceive they would still be at the house. Were they troubled by the constables or the sheriff again?"

"They were not. Even so, we took precautions. Nate sent them to Timothy's." I nodded. Bless Uncle Timothy. "Sir Lance will find them there."

"Much occurred while I was . . . while I was incarcerated."

"Aye," said Caleb. "Are you going to tell me what happened to you?"

"One day . . . maybe."

Caleb took my hand ever so gently. "I'm here whenever you're ready."

"I know."

He let my hand go and glanced at Lord Nathaniel, his eyes lingering upon his fine chest, the way it moved up and down. "In the blink of an eye, our fortunes change. I still cannot credit Sir Francis had you arrested. Myself and Gideon, well, it was not unexpected. But you? When Nate and Lance told me . . ."

I lowered my head. I could barely believe it myself, that he had given such an order—or that he'd given Topcliffe permission to hurt and threaten me in the way he did.

"Do not look so despondent, dearling," said Caleb softly. "Sometimes, change is for the better."

"Change? It's not change that disheartens me, not when we seek it ourselves. But Caleb, this is exile—enforced exile . . . Where do we go?"

There was a sound from the bed. Without opening his eyes, Lord Nathaniel spoke.

"That is up to you."

I fell to my knees by his side. "We've woken you."

"And I am glad."

Caleb, showing uncharacteristic decorum, cleared his throat, mumbled something about checking we were sailing in the right direction, and left.

When the door closed, I turned to Lord Nathaniel. "Can I get you—?"

He drew me down and halted my question with a kiss. A long, slow one that parted my lips to admit his tongue. Hot waves of longing flowed over me. I rose slightly to meet his ardor and the pressure of his lips increased.

"Ouch," I exclaimed against his mouth.

He pulled away. "Mallory, forgive me, I forgot. Your poor mouth. What that brute did to you."

I touched the bandage wrapping his chest. "What he did to you, my lord."

"Ah, but he didn't kill us, did he? And please, my love, can you cease calling me my lord and call me Nate?"

"I fear I cannot." He looked taken aback. "You will always be Nathaniel to me."

With some difficulty he slid over and patted the bed beside him. "Come, lie with me. Oh, I'll be chaste, do not concern yourself." I sat upon the edge of the cot. "You know, my mother always called me Nathaniel."

Careful not to hurt him and stifling my own cries of pain, I wriggled until I was comfortable, removing my coif so my hair fell about him. "I'm not your mother," I said softly, tipping my chin to gaze at him, one hand splayed on the unbandaged portion of his bare chest. His skin was warm and smooth.

Pulling me closer so I felt his manhood stirring, he laughed. "Oh, I know."

"Does it hurt terribly?" I asked, my hand suspended over the bandage.

"Not now." He put a finger under my chin and tilted my face toward his. "And you?"

"Not now."

We lay in silence for a while. The rocking of the boat was soothing, the sound of the river water as it streamed past reassuring. It took us further and further away from London, from the Tower, Topcliffe and, above all, Sir Francis.

"So, where shall we go? In which country do you wish to live out the rest of your life?" Nathaniel grazed my hair with his lips.

"If you'd asked me that question a week ago, I would not have known. Now, it's easy. I would go to Venice."

"Why Venice?"

"It's the place Angela calls home. It's also a city tolerant of different faiths, of different people and customs. I've had enough intolerance to last me a lifetime."

"Aye, me too."

"And then there's the matter of her heart."

"Angela's heart is of interest to you?"

"Not as much as yours," I said, shyly. "But aye. She left it there a long time ago and I think she should at least try to retrieve it."

"A lost heart is a good reason. The best. We will settle in Venice."

"We? You would stay too?"

With a muted groan he lifted himself up onto one elbow, causing me to fall back against the pillows, my hair spread beneath me. Lord Nathaniel stared in disbelief. "You addle-witted goose. Did you think I did all this"—his gesture encompassed the cabin, the ship, the river itself as he sucked in his breath at the pain—"for the sake of adventure? Uprooted my sister and household, got shot, so I might taunt the Queen and rescue a maiden in distress?"

"I'm no maiden, nor in distress."

He dropped a kiss on the tip of my nose. "No, you're not. And I'm no knight in armor. But, Mallory Bright, Mallory Walsingham, whatever it is you're called, whoever you are—watcher, spy, lock-pick, daughter, widow, fool, liar, prisoner—you are mine."

It was a while before we spoke again. As he drifted off into much-needed sleep, his arm around me, it occurred to me that when he described me with such love in his voice, such pride in all the roles he listed, he omitted two: mother and child-killer. The darkest secret of all, which I had promised to keep, even from the man I loved most in the world.

Papa may have had it in his heart to understand and forgive me, but he was my father. Once again, his words of warning rang in my ears, squeezed my heart: *Even the most considerate and understanding of men will find this tragedy impossible to reconcile without viewing you as guilty.*

I would rather imagine what could have been between his lordship and me than have my dreams and his destroyed. In order to ensure that never happened, I had only one choice.

FIFTY-SIX

ABOARD *DODONA'S DREAM* AND
IN THE MERMAID'S TALE, PLYMOUTH
The 31st of March to the 4th of April, Anno Domini 1582
In the 24th year of the reign of Elizabeth I

We sailed into Plymouth Sound on the last day of March, past the Isle of St. Nicholas, and dropped anchor midstream, parallel to the main dock. A veritable forest of masts surrounded us, swaying like ghostly limbs in the wind and only partly obscured by the fine curtain of rain. Plymouth was a vibrant and surprising place, filled with industry, shops, warehouses and shipyards as well as people of all colors, ages and occupations. It was also the township where Lord Nathaniel had begun his voyage with Sir Francis Drake all those years ago.

Standing on deck, still pale but determined not to be an invalid, despite Jim's warnings, my lord ignored the drizzle and pointed out various landmarks to Caleb and me. Above all, this was a place where we could disappear for a few days, at least until Papa and the others joined us. Over the last week, Lord Nathaniel's wound had shown no sign of infection. Jim had been excellent in his care, replacing the bandages and applying fresh moss twice a day.

"I've seen men die simply because wounds weren't kept clean," he explained. "A lot can be learned from the Musselmen and Turks. I don't care about a man's color or faith. It's what's in his head and his heart that counts. If you ask me, we condemn folk too readily because they don't look like us or worship as we do."

I could only agree.

Leaving a basic crew on deck, we rowed to the docks. The men went to seek supplies and entertainment in town, and we hired rooms at the Mermaid's Tale to enjoy the luxury of some space, comfortable beds and hearty meals.

There were soldiers in Plymouth as well as various port officials. Leaving Lord Nathaniel to rest, and ignoring Jim's recommendation that I too should rest and remain in my room, I was accompanied by Caleb and Nicholas as I went to an apothecary's and, following Jim's instructions, purchased medicinal unguents and herbs with which to treat Lord—I mean, Nathaniel.

I studied all who lingered under shop awnings, beside vendors' carts or in doorways; those whose eyes alighted upon us for any length of time. I was not concerned about the uniforms as much as I was about those who wore an air of indifference and appeared to blend in. Any one of these raggedy men, battered sea-salts, fences or vendors could be in Sir Francis's pay. I could imagine them scribbling a note to him as soon as we were out of sight, revealing the whereabouts of his wayward daughter, the traitor, the woman who had sought to hold the nation to ransom.

For three whole days we waited as the rain fell. Nicholas went backward and forward to the ship, and Lord Nathaniel rotated the crew, ensuring all men had time ashore.

Unexpected sounds, the tramp of boots, the clop of hooves, all had the power to unsettle me, and I found it hard to know peace. Nathaniel urged me to relax, but I felt responsible for everyone, my guilt knew no bounds. I expected us to be arrested at any moment and longed to depart . . .

My physical aches had long diminished and my bruises were all but gone. Even the memories faded, as I passed the days with Caleb and Nathaniel playing cards and chess, discussing poetry and faith. It was only at night that recollections of Topcliffe and my time in the Tower dungeons returned, and the pain of his various instruments would visit me anew. I would also remember his assaults—his and Raffe's.

Blurring into these were memories of my infant son, my son who died because I was not brave enough to want him from the outset, or brave enough to leave, or brave enough to stop Raffe's assault before it was too late.

I would awake with my hand tight around the locket, my face wet with tears. While I knew that each day brought Papa, Beatrice and Angela closer, it also brought my leave-taking nearer too. It was increasingly difficult to smile, to remain lighthearted so Nathaniel would not suspect my intentions. For I knew in my heart I must go.

And yet . . . I also wished Sir Lance delayed; that the incessant rain would make the roads impassable; that the horses would throw their shoes, become lame; that all manner of other dreadful, but not dangerous, mishaps would befall them.

For all my efforts at dissembling, Nathaniel knew something was amiss. So did Caleb. When I told him of my intention to leave, he wanted to tell his lordship immediately. I dissuaded him.

"You're set upon this course?"

I hesitated. "There's no alternative. I cannot tell him of little Gideon, of my complicity in his making and unmaking. I simply cannot. My shame, my sin is just too great. Revealing what I did almost cost you and Papa your lives. I would spare my lord if I could."

"But you can," said Caleb, taking both my hands in his, "if you tell his lordship all. You do him a disservice by not speaking out. He will understand. I know he will."

"Understand, maybe, but will he forgive?"

"Forgive? We've spoken of this many a time. There's nothing to forgive, Mallory. You did nothing wrong except trust a rogue. You were gulled."

I raised welling eyes to Caleb's. "Oh, Caleb, how can you of all people say that? You of all people know—I did everything wrong. That's why little Gideon died. Oh, Raffe may have dealt the blows, but it was me who, when I first knew I was with child, did all in my power to expel him from my womb. His death is as much my fault as Raffe's, for all you and Papa believe otherwise, and I bless you for that. Then there's the real reason I was living beneath Lord Nathaniel's roof—not to be his sister's companion, but to spy on his troupe. I kept a dossier, Caleb—a dossier of all those who came into his compass. Up until you

were arrested, my loyalty was still with Sir Francis. How could Lord
Nathaniel or Beatrice stand to have someone like me in their lives
once they knew? Especially when his lordship has already tolerated so
much? When another woman had trampled his heart with deceit? Had
caused his babe to die as well? I would rather disappear from their lives
and keep them ignorant than lose their goodwill, see their faces and
hearts change."

"You could stay and keep silent," said Caleb.

I stared at him.

"All right," he admitted. "You could not."

"I would rather go without admitting it. I know it's cowardly, I
know it's unfair. But Caleb, I do not have it in me to act otherwise."

Caleb shook his head. "You're wrong. You do. You do Nate a huge
disservice by not telling him. You're both my friends. I would you
were at peace. I would he knew the truth. You understand all too
well the damage secrets between loved ones can do. We all do."

He held me at arm's length, forcing me to meet his gaze. His blue
eyes were earnest and loving.

"Caleb, I promised Papa . . ." I told him about the day I finally
confessed everything, about what Papa had made me swear and why.

Caleb shook his head and gripped my shoulders tighter.

"You goose," he said, shaking me. "Gideon didn't mean for you
to sacrifice someone like Lord Nathaniel. He was terrified someone
else would learn and support Raffe's claims, that's all. He begged your
silence lest you be convicted of murder. He never meant your promise
to cost you your heart."

Dear God, I wanted to believe Caleb. "But who could love a woman
who's done what I have?"

"What Shelton did," corrected Caleb.

"And what of my watching?"

"That is such a small thing and, in the end, caused no harm to the
Warhams. Not every secret needs to be shared."

"I would not have any betwixt him and me . . . but how could he
love me knowing what I've done? The woman I really am?"

"Doesn't Nate love you now?"

"He says he does, despite everything."

"No, *because* of everything. All you've done and experienced has made you what you are: a woman worthy of love—worthy of *his* love. Just as he deserves your affection. Mallory, listen to me. You're so afraid Nate will judge you, you've lost sight of what you are doing to him. You are judging him intractable and unable to forgive when he is the opposite. You're cutting him to fit Raffe's cloth and measuring by Sir Francis's standards—it's you who is being unjust."

God in heaven. I'd not considered it that way before.

"If you intend to leave him," continued Caleb, "you may as well give him a reason. He deserves that, especially seeing what he stands to lose. Consider this: if he behaves as you predict, you've lost nothing except a dream."

Though it weighed upon me worse than a sea anchor, I pondered Caleb's words and decided he was right. Of everything I owed Nathaniel, the truth must come first, even if it meant breaking my promise to Papa.

Even if it meant losing Nathaniel, at least there'd be no more secrets.

It was our fourth night in Plymouth. The rain was heavy and the wind howled and shook the shutters. The candles were lit in the parlor set aside for our small group. Caleb and Nicholas went to the taproom downstairs for an ale, promising to have some wine sent up for me and Nathaniel. Caleb was trying discreetly to give us time together. Time for me to confess to Nathaniel what I'd only so recently told Papa. The greatest of my sins.

Nathaniel was seated near the fire, a goblet of wine in his hand, his shirt open at the neck, his hair ruffled from falling asleep earlier. He looked content. Color had slowly returned to his face and he had regained movement in his shoulder. He was not as fast in his actions and, for certes, spent longer sleeping than he was accustomed to do, but he was healing and his strength was coming back. Perchance he was ready to hear what I had to say. If I didn't tell him now, it would be a huge secret between us—a lock never opened—and it would keep us apart as surely as a physical separation.

"Mallory?" he said, his voice low and sonorous. "What is it, my love? What is it that perturbs you so?"

I tried and failed to smile. "I've something to tell you."

"Uh-oh. Come, sit beside me."

I came nearer, but sat just out of arm's reach. "I'm afraid once you've heard what I have to say, you will demand I quit your sight for good."

He sat up and put down his wine. "You'd best begin."

The entire time I spoke, Nathaniel's eyes never left my face. Once, they narrowed and, I swear, darkened. His hands gripped the arms of his chair so hard his knuckles turned white. My voice began to quiver and I thought my boldness would fail me. Thoughts of Little Gideon and Papa and Caleb's frank blue eyes sustained me.

I told him how, just as I determined to run away from Raffe, I discovered I was pregnant. While I first sought to rid my body of the babe, I grew to love my child, and believed it would alter relations between us. Then I told him what happened the night Raffe discovered I was with child, the night the babe was born. How he never had a chance to draw breath and his little life was snatched away. How I, the greatest of transgressors, through my terrible sins, cowardice, pride and vanity, had caused the murder of my babe.

I didn't shed a tear. Had I not already cried an ocean?

Then I confessed to stabbing Raffe. How, in sheer rage, I had tried to kill him. How, in that, I also failed. I was a woman who, denied her child, was also denied revenge.

"So, you see, my lord, I'm not who you think I am. I never have been. You were always right about me. Like the women you despise, I play a part and thus good men are gulled; they misread me for one thing when I am truly another—a Jezebel, thief and murderer by any other name."

There. It was done. I waited.

The fire spat. A gale shook the walls and slapped great sheets of rain against the glass. The limbs of the trees bent and snapped. Inside the small room, we were still.

Finally, when I thought my heart would burst and I must make my exit and never look back, Nathaniel spoke.

"I only wish you'd told me sooner."

I lowered my head in remorse. Of course he would never have risked everything for me, sacrificed his life here in England, and that of his sister, if he'd known. He never would have wasted another moment upon me and my family. For now they were tainted with the same blighted brush I had so readily wielded.

"Forgive me," I whispered, unable to look at him, such was my guilt. Hauling myself up, I dropped a curtsey. Though Caleb was right in persuading me to speak, he was wrong about how his lordship would react. Papa had been right all along. He was disgusted.

Just as I moved past him, his hand shot out, gripping my wrist so tightly I cried out.

"For, if you had," he said, "I would have run that son of a mongrel Sir Raffe Shelton through with my sword not once, but a hundred times. He would never have left the Cardinal's Hatte alive. As it is, I hope when Francis finds him, they hand him over to Topcliffe to do with as he pleases."

Finally I raised my head and looked at him.

"Oh, Mallory." He drew me toward him, ceasing only when I was standing between his legs. "You foolish woman. Did you believe me so unfeeling that I would reject you because of this? Abandon you?"

"It's what most men would do."

"I am not most men."

"Aye, you're not. It's what most men of sense would do, my lord."

"Stop attributing to me qualities I lack, Mallory Bright."

My lips twitched as he pulled me down onto his knee.

"I'm not so insensitive that I could not see, from the moment I met you, that you'd endured something terrible. Beneath your fire, the beauty you tried so hard to hide, behind those magnificent eyes, it was evident you'd been made to suffer."

I let out a small sob. He tightened his arms about my waist.

"Now, I too have a confession."

I swear, my heart stopped.

"My lord?"

"Your sorry story was known to me before I even met you."

Of all the words I thought might leave his lips, they were the last I expected. I stared in shock, then horror.

"How . . . ? Oh dear God, Caleb."

Why, that underhanded . . .

"Ah, before you become enraged and seek to injure his person, know this: he simply told me a tale, an idea he had for a play. It was about a beautiful woman who, convinced she was in love, fled a good home and took up with a rogue. This rogue maligned and abused this woman and then murdered her child. He admitted someone he knew and cared for deeply had inspired it. His sorrow and great affection were apparent. When I met you, I wondered if you were that woman. Later, I persuaded myself you were not—that instead you were being improper with Sir Francis. Afterward, as I came to know and love you, I could not but cast you in the role Caleb had created, and saw not a fallen woman but a heroine who, like Dido, had suffered for love."

"A heroine?" *Did he say he loved me?* I could scarce believe it. My heart quickened.

"And when you confessed to me your rash elopement, I knew the second part of his story must also be true. You were indeed the woman at the center of his tale. All I needed was for you to trust me, to love me enough, to complete it."

What had I done to deserve such understanding? What had I done to deserve Lord Nathaniel? *Thank you, God, thank you.*

"Did . . . did Caleb have an ending?"

"He said she takes a terrible and just revenge upon the varmint . . ."

"How?" I asked in a small voice.

He pulled me to him. My eyes filled, as did my heart.

"He did not know." He pushed the hair from my face, collected the tear rolling down my cheek. "He said he was waiting for the muses to speak to him—perchance he meant you." I gave a burble of tear-filled laughter. "But, Mallory Bright, I know how it ends . . ."

I dared to look at him. "Please, my lord, enlighten me, for I do not."

Stroking my jaw with his thumb, he smiled. "She takes her revenge by uniting with a powerful lord and becoming the happiest woman in—where was it? Ah, Venice—and spending her years making him content, giving him lots of babes and growing fat and ugly—"

"I will not grow fat—" I went to strike him but remembered his injury. "Or ugly." The enormity of what he was saying struck me. I lost the ability to speak.

He grabbed my hand and brought it to his lips. "Now, that's what I wanted to see, a smile, indignation, joy, anything but these doldrums you've been trapped in the last few days."

I rested my cheek against his palm. "I thought you would turn from me in revulsion." I lifted my face. "I'm a woman who has borne another man's babe . . . and lost that child. I'm no widow, no innocent, though I have pretended to be both. You loathe any deceit and those who play false. As a watcher, what was I but the very embodiment of all you detested? And, my lord . . . Nathaniel." I took a deep breath then spoke in a rush. "My sins continued. I was watching for Sir Francis while in your home. I was employed to watch your men and report their goings-on to Mister Secretary. Though I saw nothing, heard nothing, I felt I could not remain in your company while I still carried such secrets locked within me. I could not bear to have you reject me. I was sad because I believed our time together must end."

"End? You thought to leave me? Over watching Lord Warham's Men? Over what Shelton did?" His indignation and bewilderment were almost comical.

"As much as I might desire to, I cannot blame Raffe for all. For what I did. For what I concealed. I thought I'd no choice but to go. I believed it was the penance God demanded for my sins. All of them."

"We all have a choice, and if you think I would have allowed you to escape me, my lady, you're sorely mistaken—God's will be damned." We looked into each other's eyes and he ran a finger the length of my nose and placed it against my lips. "When are you going to understand, my beautiful, stubborn Mallory, that I don't care what you've done in your past, so long as you can forgive me mine. I don't care that you ran away like a three-inch fool of a chit, that you gave birth, though I ache that you endured such punishment at that cur's hands, that he took the life of your child. What's done can't be undone. Do not be heavy, beloved. We've both made mistakes, made choices and done things we're not proud of, but doesn't that make us perfect for each other? I will follow you, chase you if I have to, to the ends of the earth. You must understand: you are mine and I am yours."

Lightness filled me. My hands crept to my locket. "You don't have to go to the ends of the earth. I'm here."

"You are," he said, and proved it with a tender kiss.

At some point we left the parlor and, hand in hand, retreated to his lordship's room. My body burned.

"Lock the door, beloved," he said from the bed. "I want no squire of mine or Caleb interrupting us."

Eagerly, I did as I was bid. Having confessed all, I was not going to pretend a virtue I didn't possess. I wanted Nathaniel as much, if not more than he wanted me. I'd been touched by hands that only knew how to pretend love or mistreat me with raw brutality. All I wanted was the touch of the man to whom I'd unlocked my secrets and laid my soul bare. I wanted him to explore every part of me, teach me anew what love and desire were.

I could not have picked a better teacher.

As he sat on the end of his bed, he pulled me to him once more, watching as my eager fingers tugged at the laces of his shirt, laughing and crying out in mock pain as I carefully pulled it over his head, trying not to disturb the bandage, so that magnificent chest was bare once more. As I did so, he pulled the partlet from my bodice and undid my laces.

Just as he was about to open my smock, I stopped him. "Please, Nathaniel, I must warn you. I've not the body of a maiden either. I've borne a child and bear the marks of it. I also bear his—Raffe's." I didn't mention Topcliffe; as Caleb had suggested, some things would have to remain a secret between us. Topcliffe had already harmed my love and, knowing what Nathaniel would do to him if he learned what had happened to me in the Tower, I would rather keep my peace and him safe.

In answer, Nathaniel scooped me into his arms and lay me on the bed. Gently he finished removing my clothes and stood over me, examining every inch as the color rose in my face and I fought the urge to cover myself. Then, reaching for my locket, he opened it and gazed in wonder at the lock of dark hair curled within its center. With a poignant smile, he closed it, pressed it to his lips, and replaced it over my heart. Then he lay beside me and with gentle lips began to kiss every inch of my body, from my small (but perfect, he said) breasts, to the white lines that traced my stomach and hips, my map of motherhood, and the scars he later found on my back and legs, which drew exclamations of anger and pity. He placed his mouth everywhere and

I relished every kiss, every liquid swirl of his tongue. All the while he spoke words of such love, such devotion it made my chest swell, my eyes fill and my body quiver.

Tangled in my hair, in the sheets, we wrapped our limbs about each other. So gentle and yet not. I tasted myself upon his lips, the sweet saltiness of my womanhood, and heard him sigh with pleasure at the response his attentions elicited. God and all the angels, I was indeed blessed to find such a one.

Returning his ardor, I forced him to lie on his back and did what I longed to do; with my lips and tongue I explored every part of his perfect body. The satin of his skin, the silkiness of his hair, the velvet warmth of his manhood as it slipped first into my mouth and then inside me.

The room disappeared and I was transported to another place, a place of sweet meadows and flowers; I was plunged into turquoise waters and dipped in vats of warm wine. Drunk with desire, filled with starlight and sunshine, I touched the heavens and returned only to find they'd taken up residence inside me.

We slept and woke, hungry for each other. Greedy beyond measure, we feasted again . . . and again . . .

FIFTY-SEVEN

A long, heavy leg pinned me to the bed as a gentle finger traced whorls on my body. I slowly opened my eyes and smiled into the face that dominated my dreams.

"Am I awake or asleep?" I said groggily.

Nathaniel laughed and the sound matched the sunlight striking the pillow and the warmth expanding beneath my breasts.

"Awake—as I've been these last minutes, most perplexed and eager."

I looked down at his manhood. I would not admit to being sore, though I was. Sore and not yet sated.

"Not only for that, my love," he smiled. "But for the answer you avoided giving me yesterday."

I frowned. "You have the better of me, sir. I do not recall a question."

"You do not remember me asking you to marry me?"

Placing a hand over his, I stilled his attentions. "I think I would recall that, my lord."

"Verily," he said, "I didn't ask formally but thought with your clever mind you would understand what I believed I made clear."

I gaped at him. "Clear?"

"Do you not recall me telling you your reputation was assured with me?"

"I . . . I . . ."

"And that my heart was in your keeping?" His leonine eyes grazed my form.

"I . . . I do . . . But you do not have to marry me because I surrendered my body to you."

Nathaniel sat up. "You gave me this gift"—he gestured to me—"thinking I would not?"

"Verily, my lord." I sat upright, pulling up the sheet to protect a modesty I could no longer claim. My throat grew dry. My heart skipped wildly. "I . . . did not expect such an offer nor think I would be suitable for such an honor. Please, my lord, if this is a jest it is most unbecoming."

I tried to get out of the bed, but he pulled me back and planted a kiss upon my bruised lips. When I was unresponsive, he smoothed my hair back from my brow.

"Mallory, I jest not. Banish that frown, do not regard me like that with those magnificent eyes of yours. I ask you in all seriousness. I've intended to for many weeks. Did I not say I hoped you would see yourself as part of my family? I meant it. Would you do me the honor of being my wife?"

Unable to speak, I simply stared.

"When are you going to understand, woman? I care not whether you be Mallory Bright, Walsingham or—what was the name Sir Francis gave you? Samantha Short. You are Mallory, the woman I love, and I would make you a Warham. What say you?"

Is it possible to know such happiness that you think, like the fireworks on Lady's Day, you will explode into a thousand brilliant stars and be scattered all over the skies? With shining eyes and shining heart, I tumbled into his arms.

"If you would have me, my lord, the honor would be all mine."

We did not leave the room for some time.

Though I know Papa would have disapproved of my wantonness, when news of our engagement was shared, joy overcame the terrible context of our togetherness. Caleb was the first to be told (and was overjoyed and mouthed a triumphant "I told you"), followed by Papa, Beatrice, Angela and Sir Lance, who all arrived that day, travel-weary and a little afraid, along with Tace and Alice, the cats and the dogs, who barked and scampered about the place with delight.

For a brief moment, we snatched at happiness—as we'd learned, it could be short-lived. Ours would prove to be no exception.

Though Papa bore grave injuries from the torture he had endured in the Tower, he was healing. He did not wish to discuss what he had been through, and I respected his wishes, though every time I saw the stick which he now depended upon, the fading bruises upon his face, the blackened nail beds and twisted fingers that the bandages could not disguise, I was filled with dark rage. I still didn't understand why Papa had had to suffer, and it would take a long time for me to accept that I never would.

Sir Lance had been charged with bringing papers that would allow us to leave Plymouth unimpeded by the authorities, but he arrived empty-handed.

Nathaniel lowered himself into a chair. Papa, Sir Lance and I formed a grim semicircle around him. Near the fire, Angela, Caleb and Beatrice chatted excitedly, the three dogs at their feet. Angela and Beatrice had become firm friends on their journey. Oblivious to the setback, they cast glances in our direction but knew better than to join us.

"What does this mean?" I asked.

"It means," said Nathaniel, "that we must leave tonight, under cover of darkness, and pray the authorities don't discover our intentions or stop and question us. I'd hoped that, knowing what I've done in aiding you, and knowing that you, Caleb and Gideon would be leaving the country under my care, they'd want to be rid of me and we'd be given papers. I was a fool." He regarded Sir Lance gravely. "Were you followed?"

"I feared at one stage we might have been, but after we remained at an inn for two days, the courier didn't dally. We didn't see him again on the road."

Lord Nathaniel nodded. "Very well then. A change of plans. I'm sorry, Lance, but we'll be abandoning you here almost immediately."

"Abandoning me?" Sir Lance scoffed. "Nate, you can hardly abandon me if I'm on the ship with you."

Understanding registered in Nathaniel's face and he reached for his friend's arm. "The second-best bit of news today." He flashed me a look, a look that took my breath away with its bold desire. Sir Lance saw it too and turned aside to wink at Caleb.

"So," continued Nathaniel, "I will ask you and Nicholas to order any crew still in Plymouth to make their way back to the ship before nightfall. We've learned the port watchmen's shift changes around nine of the clock, so if a boat is ready at the end of the south dock it can take us to the ship where we will board. All being well, we'll weigh anchor and be gone with the change of tide."

"It's risky, Nate," said Sir Lance.

"Aye, but what choice do we have?"

And so as the moon began to rise, casting far too much light for Nathaniel's liking, we stealthily made our way along the waterfront toward the dock that would lead us to freedom. If we were caught without papers, we'd be arrested. Because both Papa and I were escaped felons, traitors, no less, I would join Anne Askew and become the second female commoner to lose her life in the Tower. Whereas I would die at the order of Queen Elizabeth for being thought a papist conspirator, the Queen's father had killed Mistress Anne because she was a Protestant. How swiftly those who govern change the manner of their allegiance to the Almighty, forcing their subjects to follow. I wondered if our rulers would face a reckoning when they met God in heaven. If they did.

Timing was everything. We kept to the darkest part of the street, avoiding the pools of light cast onto the cobbles by alehouses and taverns, trying not to attract the attention of the many trulls and sailors. Around us grunts of lust sounded in the darkness. I heard two men pissing in a ditch, one man in close relations with another, choruses of singing, shouts, and even a fight that spilled onto the street. We turned our heads away and prayed these people were what they seemed, not soldiers in disguise or watchers waiting to pounce.

The watchmen on the dock began to leave their small wooden office, lanterns held aloft. They stood awhile with their pipes to greet their colleagues and exchange news before heading home. The smoke and conversation drifted into the night. Downwind of them, Nathaniel ordered Jim, who'd come to escort Beatrice, Angela, Caleb and Sir Lance, to go ahead. Tace, Alice, the cats and the dogs had been taken aboard earlier that day, along with pieces of luggage. Any watchers would dismiss the servants out of hand—they would be searching for a group of noble felons, a crippled locksmith and his daughter. Nathaniel had wanted me to go with them, but I refused, and not merely for fear of being observed. I would wait with him, Nicholas and Papa.

With bated breath we saw them pass the watchmen in the darkness. The pier they crept along was slightly below and behind where the guards stood, their backs to them.

When they were out of sight, Nathaniel took my hand. "Ready?" he whispered.

"Aye," I said. Papa gripped his stick and nodded.

Just as we left the shadows a figure detached itself from the wall opposite and came across the street to cut us off. There was something familiar about the walk, the way he held his hand out to silence us. Nathaniel moved to draw this sword, but I bade him stay his hand.

"Who goes there?" he asked instead.

"Samantha knows."

It was Thomas. Dressed as Peter Halins the merchant, he wore the same cap and dun-colored clothes he'd donned at Deptford. We were undone.

I strode toward him, angry, terrified, but determined not to show it. "You cannot stop me, Thomas. *He* cannot." We both knew of whom I spoke. How dare Thomas, how dare Sir Francis.

"Hold, Mallory," said Thomas softly. "That's not my intention."

I came to a halt inches before him, Nathaniel on one side of me, Papa on the other. Nicholas stood watch. "Then why are you here?" I asked.

"To give you these," he said. From the satchel slung across his shoulder he extracted a batch of papers and a large purse.

"What is this?" I asked, eyeing the items cautiously. I did not trust this man, the man who had handed me into the Tower and put me at Topcliffe's mercy.

"Passports, the paperwork you need not only to leave here, but to ensure his lordship's lands are not seized, and that you are welcomed wherever you decide to go." I glanced at the papers before passing them to Nathaniel. He quickly scanned the pages, holding them to the moonlight.

"These seem in order," he said. The relief in his voice was palpable.

"And there's this too," said Thomas, handing over the purse. It was heavy. "Consider these wages owed and a debt paid."

I balanced it in my hand. I did not thank him for what was my due. I still wanted to strike him. I gave the purse to Papa. "Did *he* send you?" I asked finally.

"Aye. But I wanted to come, to explain my actions and his."

There must have been something in my expression, for Thomas stepped nearer. Both Nathaniel and Papa went to prevent him.

"I do not seek to harm her," he snapped. "I never did. Don't you see, Mallory? Of all the things you could have taken, you chose the book that would have undone Sir Francis—after everything he's sacrificed—and the entire country. You could not just walk free with a simple scolding or slap on the wrist. Nor could you have your own way and just leave with your father. Your thieving could not be rewarded. It would have set a poor example, one others may well have sought to emulate. But he would have done that—let you saunter away. Sir Francis was prepared to do all you asked and more. I told you, he cares about you, Mallory. He cares about you." He nodded toward Papa. "Now I know why."

So, Sir Francis's secret, our secret, was out. I felt Papa's fingers curl around mine.

Thomas latched his satchel. "It never made sense why he admitted a woman into our network, training you and giving you tasks only a man should be given, or why he took such pride in your work—pride he never took in ours." There was a slight note of jealousy. "It wasn't until he reacted the way he did when I said you needed to be punished, that I understood. You were more than a watcher to him, more than a spy to ferret out information and pass it on: you were his daughter. His bastard daughter." He spat the words.

"Soft, Thomas," said Nathaniel in a voice that made me tremor.

Thomas looked up at him. "You do not frighten me, my lord. I just have to say one word and soldiers will pour into this area, boats will row to your ship and prevent it leaving. I can have you interred faster than you can snap your fingers."

"But not as fast as I can draw this knife across your throat." I stared at Papa. When had he learned to wield a weapon so quickly? To drop his stick, my hand, and lunge with such speed? When had he learned to overcome a man like Thomas Phelippes, to press a knife to his neck with broken hands and speak in such deadly tones?

"Stay, stay," said Thomas, his hand held before him, his head tipped toward the sky, his neck vulnerable and white above his ruff. Papa withdrew the knife slightly.

I took the opportunity to get answers. "Are you saying it wasn't Sir Francis's intention to imprison me?"

"Of course not," said Thomas. "But when I suggested a small example was necessary to deter you from such foolish behavior, that it would act as a lesson to any others who sought to blackmail him, he listened and conceded a few nights in the Tower could not do you any harm."

I almost choked. "Oh, but he was wrong."

Thomas inhaled sharply as Papa's knife pressed deeper. "Topcliffe went too far, of that there's no doubt, and I am sorry."

Nathaniel growled.

Thomas spoke faster. "When Sir Francis found out, he was furious. He ordered you to be released, came to see to it himself. By then, his lordship here and Master Hollis had gained entry. Under normal circumstances, they would never have been admitted, nor would you have escaped. Sir Francis saw an opportunity and simply ensured you'd succeed. Unbeknownst to any of you, he ordered the guards to admit any visitors to Mistress Bright, then ordered them to hasten to different parts of the Tower. He tried to confound Topcliffe's intentions, but the man was obsessed."

Obsessed. Aye, that was the word. A man who saw the world in two colors only. "He knows I'm Sir Francis's daughter."

Thomas pushed the knife from his throat, his fingers testing the skin. Papa allowed it, and bent to retrieve his stick.

"Feared as much," said Thomas. "It's what I worked out for myself. But here's the rub, Mallory. As long as you're alive, Sir Francis and his secrets will never be safe. There will always be someone, somewhere, who will use you as leverage against him and thus the Queen. You are his one weak spot. He knows it now, too. England is not safe while you walk the land."

I stared at him in disbelief. "But I'm a woman, I'm no one."

Thomas shook his head. "Not no one—you are the spymaster Mister Secretary's daughter and privy to his secrets—even those he would keep from you." *The book.* "Unable to order your death, which would solve everything, Sir Francis is in your thrall. While he is, we all are. You make him weak, Mallory, and thus you make England weak."

There was a gust of wind, a spray of water. I shivered. Thomas glanced at me. "Sir Francis wants you to leave—for your sake as much as his. But he wants you to go with his blessing and help." He nodded toward the papers and purse. "He told me to tell you how sorry he is for everything. He hopes one day you will understand why he acted the way he did. Why he can never acknowledge you. He wants you to know, however, that though you cannot have his name, you have his undying affection."

As Thomas spoke, it was almost as if Sir Francis were standing there, offering the words himself. I heard the voice of my father, the man I thought had betrayed and abandoned me. I was wrong. What he had done, he had done in a misguided notion of love. That the lesson was wrested from his control was not his fault.

I searched Thomas's face. "Thank you, Thomas. And thank my father. Tell him I don't need time to understand. I do."

Thomas swept off his bonnet and bowed. "I will."

We stared at each other a moment longer. We'd shared adventures, a connection, an understanding of the intricate and intuitive work of a spy. We had shared something very few ever did, and that joined us. I couldn't hate Thomas, though I suspected he hated me. But I also knew he loved my father, Sir Francis. Well, he could love him for me as well. Though I felt a deep fondness for the man, I could never love him or call him father. My father was the man who raised me, forgave me, risked his life for me and held a knife to the throat of a man who dared to threaten me; the man who would give up one country so I might share another with him.

Gideon Bright was my father. Blood counted for nothing.

I turned to go, when something occurred to me. "Tell me, Thomas, how can I leave under my own name when I'm an escaped criminal? Will I not be detained?"

Thomas gave a crooked grin. "You're listed on your papers as his lordship's wife. You're used to playing a role. Surely that of a lady is not difficult?"

I slipped one arm through Papa's and the other through Nathaniel's. As laughter rang along the wharves we strode boldly to the waiting boat. No more shadows or darkness; no more hiding or lies and secrets. The port authorities demanded papers and we presented them. As they farewelled us, I'd a taste of my new station.

"Safe voyage, my lord," called one, who'd clearly had a few ales. "And you too, Lady Warham."

We approached the waiting craft.

"My Lady Warham," said Nathaniel. "I like the sound of that."

Oh, so did I.

I tucked my head against Nathaniel's chest and drew Papa closer as well. I knew if I was going to be anything from here on in, it was both safe and loved.

Above all, loved—as a wife and a daughter.

EPILOGUE

VENICE, ITALY

The 12th and the 13th of July, Anno Domini 1590

In the 33rd year of the reign of Elizabeth I

I thank God I am endued with such qualities that
if I were turned out of the realm in my petticoat
I would able to live any place in Christendom.

—Elizabeth I

*I*t was one of those glorious, sultry days when the sky was a dome of blue, the waters a deep turquoise and the light softly diffused. A gondola drifted past, its occupants seated in the *felze*, the small cabin, the curtains drawn despite the heat as the gondolier sang sweetly, his oar carving the canal. He saw me upon the terrace and lifted his arm. I returned his wave.

The children played around me. The sound of their bright voices as they argued over a toy Angela had made them caused the life within me to stir, as if he too wished to join his siblings.

"Not long, *mio bambino*," I whispered, my hands resting protectively upon the swell of my stomach.

This was to be our third child and I knew, just as I had known the sex of my other two, that this was a boy. This would be Gideon, named in honor of the little life lost, and for Papa.

It was Nathaniel's idea. Caleb was to be the godfather and I prayed he and Lance would return in time from their tour of Padua and the northern towns with their new troupe of players. Caleb had adapted to Italy with ease, no doubt helped by the partnership he had formed with Lance. With no desire to be a devout Catholic or Protestant, only to worship God in his own way, he regularly produced plays of such quality his work was in demand.

Caleb was slowly coming to grips with the language, but in the meantime, I translated his words into Italian and gave him and Lance lessons.

As well as translating for Caleb, I helped Nathaniel with his business and taught the children, ensuring they were fluent in English and Italian as well as Latin and French. In addition, I spent most of our first few years working for Papa. He never really recovered from the injuries he sustained when he was tortured, and his eyesight continued to fade. Papa entrusted me with the designs of his locks and to oversee the apprentices he hired to make them. Thrilled to have Papa among them, the Venetian guild of locksmiths admitted him as a member, and he would pass many an afternoon enjoying the *vino* with the other men, reminiscing about the great locks they'd made and opened, and proffering advice to any who sought it. Papa was beyond content.

Then he died one day last spring. He'd stood after a glass of *vino* with his friend Guido, clutched at his chest and fallen, never to rise again. I thought perchance our idyllic existence on the lagoon would come to an end once Death had visited. For certes, my heart broke. I wept and fell into a profound sadness.

But life conspired to force me to count my blessings, so that in the midst of the deepest grief, of feeling my heart had been torn asunder, a child's smile, the loving caress of my husband, the happiness in Angela's face as she enjoyed the love she once thought lost to her forever, the way Caleb and Lance could lose themselves in a shared and loving glance (oh, aye, I was wrong about Lance and Beatrice—'twas Caleb for whom the knight pined, and the feeling was thrice returned), the bark of sweet-tempered old dogs, and lazy aging cats stretching to capture the sun on hot cobbles—all these things slowly mended my grief.

I still mourned Papa and wished he was alive to meet his name-sake. Our son Jonathan Benet, named for Nathaniel's brothers, and our daughter Lucia Valentina, had brought him such joy, just as they did to Nathaniel and me.

Our house seemed to be filled with children, both ours and Gui-do's grandchildren. I looked at Guido and Angela, the way they bent together over pots of herbs and flowers on the terrace, their hands in the soil. Angela was a different woman now.

The voyage to Venice had been long and hard but as we stepped ashore near Piazza San Marco, greeted by flocks of pigeons, it was as if she burst into life. Returned to her home, she was restored, and her restoration presaged ours. We leased a *palazzo* on the Grand Canal and made a home. Angela took charge, hiring servants, organizing the purchase of supplies, and ensuring we had a gondolier at our beck and call, for you could not go far in this water-laced city without a boatman.

It was during one of her forays to reacquaint herself with the city that she found Guido—or rather, he found her. The father of seven children, it was his eldest daughter, Angela, who, learning about the *Inglese* family (though I was Italian by birth, I would forever be an *Inglese* to the Venetians) and their Venetian cousin who happened to possess her name, suspected the connection. Scurrying home to her father, she insisted he pay a call. Reluctant at first, not daring to believe it could be his Angela returned, it wasn't until Guido saw her upon the *fondamenta* one day that he knew it was her—his first and, as it turned out, only love. Guido had enjoyed his marriage to Baptista, a cousin of Angela's. She'd given him four sons and three daughters, including the dark-haired and strong-willed Angela. Aye, his beloved Angela may have disappeared to England, but her memory lived on in his daughter and his eldest son, Angelo. Baptista had died giving birth to her youngest child and Guido never remarried. He rowed the canals, put food in the mouths of his family, and nourished himself with memories of his wife and her cousin who'd once promised to share her life with him.

I watched Angela brush some dirt from Guido's face. Older, sturdier, but glowing, they lived in an apartment above the *piano nobile*—our upper floor. Beatrice, or Contessa Faliero as she was now, and her husband Cesare and their lovely daughter, Fiora, had rooms above us too. Well, they were Caleb's really, but he liked to tell people they belonged to the Conte. He felt it imbued him with significance, having important relations, and opened doors that would otherwise remain locked. Perchance it did.

Beatrice, Cesare and Fiora divided their time between England, Venice and Cesare's family's domains in Padua, and we saw them often. When in England, Beatrice, under the careful stewardship of Bede and Mistress Margery, ensured the Warham estates continued.

Nathaniel thrived in Venice. *Dodona's Dream* was now one of a fleet of ships he owned, and he traded with more countries than I could count. Working with the Muscovy Company, among others, he strode the docks, examining his warehouses, the stock that comprised his imports and exports, ensuring his interests were cared for and his men well compensated.

Yet while he liked to jest that the sea was his other mistress, he claimed he was most content when he was at home. Nathaniel loved his children—and the companionship of his wife, who adored his company too.

I'd grown older—I prayed not ugly, though I was currently very fat—and within a few weeks Gideon would come into this blessed world and distract me with his needs. And so I too was content.

Long ago I learned to abandon *mediocrita* and embrace my emotions. As I matured, I learned the real meaning of happiness: it came through others, through the love you bore them, and which they returned. It came from family and friendship. It was not something to be doled out or carefully measured, but something that grew and expanded. Like a garden, it had to be tended and nurtured. But happiness could not be achieved without some sadness, without sacrifices, or without truth. That was real equilibrium; embracing opposites was how genuine balance was achieved. Not through pretense or denial.

"Mamma, Mamma!" I turned at the sound of my daughter Lucia Valentina's voice. She ran toward me. "It's Papa!" she cried, her dark straight hair flying out behind her.

I stood and allowed her to lead me to the railing where Jon, his eyes shielded against the sun, watched our gondola approach.

Already, at the age of seven, he was so tall. Pointing at the canal, he picked out our craft among all the sleek black vessels gliding upon the waters. Even if our colors were not so bold, my lord made his own statement. Considered a giant in England, he was a colossus here among the Venetians. They called him *Il Inglese Mammut*—the English Mammoth. He was a spectacle that turned heads wherever we walked. As I ruffled Jon's black locks, I suspected he would one day be the same.

As the gondola drew closer and the gates at the water stairs below opened to admit our craft, Jon and Lucia Valentina called out, their little voices full of excitement, their Italian accents no end of delight to their father. I encouraged them to practice their English, and they switched with ease from Italian to English and back again, and from French to Spanish as well. Their Papa was welcomed home in many tongues.

The children raced downstairs. I returned to my seat to find that Angela and Guido had organized *vino*, bread, cheese and other delicacies to be brought onto the terrace. With a contented sigh, I reclined and turned my face to the sunshine.

A shadow fell and a kiss was bestowed and returned. The children giggled at our open displays of affection.

"Beloved, how goes it?" asked my lord, placing his hand against my stomach then sliding into his seat. He pulled Lucia Valentina onto his lap and slipped an olive into her mouth. Jon leaned against his father. I smiled at the picture they presented.

My family. Something I once thought forever denied me.

Then I saw the package on the other chair.

"It goes well, my love. But what is this?" I gestured to the parcel.

"It arrived this morning from England." Nathaniel looked at me gravely. "It's for you."

"For me? But who would send me a parcel?"

I'd maintained correspondence with Comfort. After selling our house and dividing the profit among all the servants and apprentices, as Papa insisted, thus ensuring Dickon, Samuel, Matt and Simon had new masters and the others coin to tide them over until they found employ, Comfort had returned to Bath. I could think of no one else who would send me a parcel.

"I believe it's from Seething Lane," said Nathaniel quietly.

The sun dimmed. The world darkened. My heart leaped as I pulled myself upright.

Angela, who had been listening, came forward with Guido. "Come, you two," she beckoned to the children. "Let's go to the market, shall we?"

With squeals of delight, the children took Angela's and Guido's hands and, touching my shoulder briefly, Angela led them away.

"*Grazie,*" I whispered, staring at the package as if it contained poison.

"Mallory." Nathaniel stretched across the table for my hand. "It arrived with some tidings. Brace yourself, my love. Sir Francis is dead."

The color drained from my face. "Dead? When? How?"

"April. He'd been ill a long time."

I nodded slowly. Verily, I recalled his many stomach complaints, how he'd endure so his work might be done. Though I'd never written to Sir Francis, news of him reached us from England—how could it not, when Nathaniel was invested in our homeland and our hearts were as well? We knew that though Raffe had initially eluded capture, he was caught two years later when he was embroiled in another plot against the Queen. He died in the Tower. Of his family, we knew naught.

For all I'd once believed Sir Francis was blinded by his faith and fear of Catholics, seeing plots and treason where often there was none, I was proven wrong. Throckmorton, Babington and many more plotters besides had all sought to bring down the Queen, hand England to Catholic forces and, in doing so, justified every single one of Sir Francis's actions. All except what he had done to Papa. And what he had done to me. Many died on the scaffold—Jesuits, lay priests, traitors, and, I'd no doubt, innocent souls as well.

The thought made me sad. It also made me incredibly grateful I'd avoided such a fate.

Three years ago when Mary, Queen of Scots, was beheaded as a traitor at Fotheringhay Castle, I wondered if Sir Francis might be able to rest now the Catholic viper in England's bosom was dead. But it wasn't to be. Just as one head was lopped, another rose in the form of the Spanish Armada. Against all odds, the Queen drove them back and England triumphed.

But Sir Francis had suffered his own losses—not just deteriorating health, but the death of his beloved son-in-law, Sir Philip Sidney. Frances was a widow at the age of nineteen. I wondered how she fared. Somehow, I felt that woman would make sure life did not shortchange her.

"Are you going to open it?" asked Nathaniel quietly, squeezing my hand.

I sighed. "Aye. I'd better. It looks like a book."

I lifted the parcel onto the table and tore the paper. When the contents were revealed I gasped.

"God's wounds," I exclaimed. "I never thought to see this again."

"What is it?" Nathaniel half stood as I lifted the book from its wrappings and held it up.

It was *The Book of Secret Intelligences*. Nathaniel took it from me and as he did so, a page fluttered out. I snatched it before the breeze could take it.

It was a letter. I glanced down at the signature. It was from Thomas Phelippes. The terrace blurred, Nathaniel became a gray, hulking shadow, his voice distant.

"Mallory," he said. "Mallory. Are you all right?" He put the book down and kneeled at my side, pushed the hair from my forehead and smoothed my cheek.

"It's just shock, 'tis all. After all this time . . ." I looked at the letter still in my hands. "Can you read it to me?"

I passed it to him with shaking hands.

Nathaniel took a sip of *vino*, cleared his throat and began.

Mallory,

I know this letter will find you well, as our informants tell us Venetian life agrees with you and his lordship and for that I give praise to God. I write to let you know that Sir Francis passed away on the 6th April at the eleventh hour. He'd been unwell for a long time, as you well know, and in his final week suffered fits and much discomfort. He is in the Lord's arms now, with Jesus Christ his Saviour and into His infinite mercy his spirit was given. He was buried the following day, according to his instructions, "without any such extraordinary ceremonies as usage appertain to man serving in my place." He rests in the north aisle of St. Paul's, the noise of the operators and booksellers sing to his soul. Dame Ursula and Frances chose to bury him with Sir Philip. Know there is no effigy, nor tomb. There is, however, an inscription, to which I thought you should be privy . . .

Nathaniel paused.

"What is it?" I asked, my eyes full, my heart sore. Though he was no father to me, his loss was still a blow and I felt it keenly.

"It is in Latin. Yours is better than mine." He passed the letter back.

I read aloud, translating as I did so. It told of how Sir Francis worked diligently to ensure there was peace, protected the country from danger and served state and sovereign. Of his role as father, husband, of any love borne for him by his wife or daughter, there was no mention.

"Thomas says there's an English epitaph as well." I scanned it quickly, only reading a part.

In foreign countries their intents he knew,
Such was his zeal to do his country good,
When dangers would be enemies ensue,
As well as they themselves he understood.

We sat in silence. I stared over the water then back at the page.

"Look," I said to Nathaniel, holding the letter out. "It's an acrostic. The first letter of each line spells out his name."

"Clever," said Nathaniel.

I gave a half-smile. "He would have liked it, I think. Wait. Thomas has more to say." I blinked back the tears.

His will was found in his secret cabinet. Among the papers was a bequest to you. While you have no inheritance as such, I believe Sir Francis is giving you what meant the most to him. On his death bed, he asked I send you this book that you once stole and over which you nearly lost your life. He wrote you would understand why and what to do.

I glanced at Nathaniel, who was frowning.

May God bless you and keep you . . .

I put the letter down and picked up the book. "How very strange."

"Is it?" Nathaniel poured me a *vino* and slid it across the table.

I drank. "This was Sir Francis's life's work. It's a record of every agent, every code, every plot and particular. Why, he wrote it so those who came after him would know what he did, and know what to do."

"Perchance he felt that was no longer necessary? That he'd achieved accord?"

I shrugged. "More like he felt it wasn't worth it. After all, he lost his health, he had no relationship with his family to speak of. He lived only to serve. To serve Queen, country and faith."

"He also lost a daughter," said Nathaniel.

"Aye, her name was Mary. If you mean me, he could not lose what he never really had. He gave me up so he might become the man he did. I don't think he had regrets; they were not within his compass."

"Then why give you that?" Nathaniel gestured to the book.

I frowned. "I'm not certain."

That night, I could not sleep. Dreams I'd not had in years arrived to torment me. Sir Francis featured strongly and yet, for all he appeared to be trying to tell me something, I could not grasp his meaning.

In the still hours before dawn, I rose. Slipping on a nightgown, I walked to the *piano nobile* and gazed out over the canal, over the tops of the buildings opposite to watch the sky lighten. Birds took wing, vendors wheeled their carts across bridges to market, gondolas launched out onto the water. Though aware of them, my mind was elsewhere.

What are you trying to tell me, Sir Francis? Why give *me* the book? I wished Papa were here to ask. Though he'd no doubt have insights, Caleb was not due back for weeks.

As the sun's golden rays struck the windows, admitting a triumphant blast of light and slow-building warmth, the truth came to me. Of course. I understood.

Racing back to the bedroom, I woke Nathaniel and, dressing fast, scurried to explain to Angela what I must do and asking her to help Tace and Alice with the children. Then I went to the terrace and grabbed the shovel she'd been using yesterday, broke off a small piece of the rose bush, and, placing some of the soil from the pot in a bucket, put both the cutting and shovel carefully inside.

In less than an hour we were gliding out of the water gate and toward Isola di San Michele. We'd sought permission from the Camadolite monks who dwelled there to bury Papa in their cemetery. I couldn't bear the thought of him being crammed into an overcrowded city plot, not when he craved the open spaces the lagoon allowed. He'd loved visiting San Michele, admired the church with its lustrous Istrian stone and bold curves, and had even supervised the making of locks for the crypt. In burying Papa among this Catholic community, I was persuaded I'd reunited him with Mamma.

We reached the small island midmorning. Nathaniel helped me clamber up the stairs and paid a toll to the gatekeeper, who admitted us with a pleasant *buon giorno*. I knew him well from my regular visits to Papa's grave.

As we moved along the weed-strewn path, Nathaniel and I spoke softly, not wanting to disturb the monks who wandered among the distant cloisters, lost in their quiet contemplation.

"Now, tell me why you think Sir Francis sent you the book?"

Drawing a deep breath, I touched where it sat beneath Nathaniel's arm. "Because I think he wants me to dispose of it."

Nathaniel stopped in his tracks. "Dispose of it? His life's work? The tome that contains the secrets he held so dear and fast? The book, as Thomas points out in his letter, you nearly died for?"

"Aye." We walked a bit further. "Do you remember what Thomas said to me when we left Plymouth?"

"It's hard to forget."

"He said my very existence was a threat to Sir Francis and to England—that people would use me as leverage against him and undermine all that had been done to make England safe. I made Sir Francis weak and thus the country. Don't you see? This book is exactly the same. This book is another me."

"Perchance, but without your sweet curves, my lady," he grinned.

I waved away his humor. "But there's more to it than that. Sir Francis sacrificed everything for what's contained in that book: he gave up his relationship with his wife, his daughter; he gave up me. Even Her Majesty didn't like him much, for all that she used him."

"She threw a shoe at him once," said Nathaniel. "Humiliated him before the entire court."

"She let him use his own monies to keep her and the country safe—by rights, that was her responsibility. The richest woman in England

and she ruined him." I sighed. "I believe by sending me the book, something he always intended to pass on to the next Secretary, he's telling me it's not worth it. Not to make the same mistakes he did. He's imparting a last lesson."

"What's that, my love?"

I swallowed and forced back the tears biting my eyes and threatening to clog my throat. I ignored the pain in my back, my head, the heat of the sun.

"That love, family, are more important than politics or faith. After all, without them, what are you fighting for? Sadly, what he doesn't know is that through his own actions, he already taught me that . . . So did you."

Nathaniel stopped in his tracks and stared. "Mallory, though I never underestimate you, I do forget sometimes how sharp that mind of yours is." He held me against him briefly and kissed my lips before we resumed walking. "Apart from reminding you what's of real value, as long as this book exists, England and the Queen are never safe. What do you intend to do?"

"I'm going to give it to the only member of our family who can keep it secure. I'm going to give it to the locksmith so he might protect its secrets forever."

"Ah," said Nathaniel, and lifted the bucket and shovel. "Now, I understand."

And so we buried *The Book of Secret Intelligences*—the record of years of labor of one father—and put it to rest beside another, just by the ground near his tombstone. If any of the religious men thought our actions strange, they didn't say. Perchance they believed the small cutting I placed in the soil was another memorial that would one day grow into a bush. Little did they know that there, beneath the tiny piece of rose, a beautiful flower replete with sharp thorns, lay some of the greatest secrets ever recorded—secrets that could bring down a Queen and her realm.

Nathaniel patted the soil down then stood and placed his arm around me. "Thomas was right. Forget coin or houses, he left you the greatest gift of all. Maybe in his death Sir Francis became the father he never was in life. He trusted you, his daughter, with the safety of the country he loved, the country he died serving."

I wiped the dampness from my brow. "And no one will ever know. It will be as if the book never existed."

I said a prayer over Papa's grave—for him and Sir Francis. Nathaniel added his own words. As we walked back to the waiting gondola, a thought occurred. "I'm mentioned in that book. I don't know whether Sir Francis ever admitted I was his daughter, or used my real name, but I'm there. I saw him write me in." I glanced over my shoulder. "It will be as if I never existed—not as a Bright or Walsingham."

"Then I'll write you into another book. Write you back into existence."

I laughed. "You, Nathaniel, write a book?"

"You doubt me?"

"I don't doubt that you can do anything." I stroked his face. "And what would you call this book?"

"What else? I would call it *The Secrets of Lady Mallory Warham*."

I pulled a face.

"You don't like it?"

"I've my own book to confess those in, remember? The one Papa gave me long ago. Anyhow, I do not want my story told. Some doors should remain locked." I paused and took a deep breath, pressing my hand into the small of my back.

Nathaniel gave me a look of concern. "Are you well, my lady?"

"Well is such a strange word," I said. Thoughts of Papa sprang to mind, bringing with them unexpected tears. This was not the time for sadness, but great joy. I pulled Nathaniel's arm, urging him forward. "We must hurry home."

"Why the sudden haste?" Nathaniel easily matched my stride.

"'Tis not for me, but for your son."

"Jon?" he asked, when I stopped again and puffed a few times, grimacing as the aches I'd been experiencing but trying to ignore became acute, demanding my full attention.

"My lady?" Nathaniel paled. "Have your pains begun?"

I could not help but smile at his expression, and his choice of words. "Aye, my love, our Gideon Francis has taken this as his cue, but I would prefer he arrives upon a different stage and without an audience— though I doubt even a woman in my state would be a distraction for the holy ones."

Without further ado, Nathaniel dropped the bucket, hoisted me into his arms and ran to the gondola, earning stares from all we passed. "Just like his godfather," he gasped. "He knows when to make an entry."

I was gently placed into the boat and crawled in a most ungainly fashion into the *felze*. Nathaniel promised our gondolier a reward for a speedy passage before joining me.

"Did I hear aright? Our son is to be named for Francis as well?"

"Do you object?"

"On the contrary, I think it most fitting. Gideon Francis Warham."

I watched the island retreat into the distance, the church's grand facade shrinking, the sun striking the water, making it appear as if diamonds had been cast over the surface. "Sir Francis denied me a place in his family . . ." I took a deep breath, gripping the edges of the seat as a cramp took over my body, "but I would not deny him a place in ours, through a grandson. Not now."

Nathaniel held my hand and wiped a cool cloth across my forehead. I smiled at him. "The book changes everything," he said.

"It does," I agreed. "Even so, for all Sir Francis tried to make amends, to reach out beyond the grave, for all he attempted to train me, mold me in his image, present me with opportunities denied most women, to be a father in the only way he knew how, I am and always will be the locksmith's daughter."

"Don't forget my wife and mother of my children."

My stomach tightened and pain flowered, the world turned white, the air hot, and I grimaced.

And my lord, what did he do, but laugh and fold me in his arms.

AUTHOR'S NOTE

$\mathcal{W}$henever I read a work of historical fiction, I love learning how the author integrated fact with fiction—how their imagination intersected with real events and figures from the past. In case my readers are similarly curious, I thought I'd explain how I used known events and people to create the world that is *The Locksmith's Daughter*, as well as share some of the fabulous sources I used, including those about locks and keys.

The idea of writing a book featuring a locksmith, or more accurately, a lock-pick, came to me unexpectedly one day in 2012. My husband, Stephen, had broken the key in the ignition of his car. It was late Friday afternoon, so I fetched him in my vehicle and we left his car parked overnight outside the major brewery where he then worked (as a tour guide) and met a locksmith there the next day. It was when I was watching the locksmith, Bruce, repair the damage (he had to replace the entire ignition barrel and craft a new key) that I began to discuss with him his training and what drew him to it. Realizing he had a keen audience, Bruce shared his excitement about locks and keys, showing me the instruments he used and how they worked. I returned to my car and, as I drove home, the story of a young woman who was a lock-pick began to form. As usual, she came with an era—it was like a package deal. Somehow, I knew not only must she be using her skills during Elizabethan times, but the book also had to involve Sir Francis Walsingham, a historical figure who has long held me in thrall. So, a female spy named Mallory Bright was born.

I knew nothing about locks, but I was adept at losing keys. My son's first words were "car keys." Seriously. When I complained to a friend about it, she screeched with laughter. "Is it any wonder?" she said. "Have you heard yourself?" I stared at her, confused. "Every time you go somewhere, the first thing you say is, 'Where are the car keys?' Over and over . . . 'Has anyone seen my car keys?'" True story. My poor son. I also had a habit of locking myself out of the house. So, until this book, I had an inauspicious relationship with locks and keys.

Unperturbed, I began my research. This, I have discovered, is often the time when incredibly generous and knowledgeable people unexpectedly enter your life and share their expertise and passion. My search for information about locks was no exception. A wonderful man from the US named Scott Klemm, who is also the author of two terrific books on locks (*Unlocking the Portals of History Through the Lock and Key Collection of Scott J. Klemm* and *Ancient Locks: The Evolutionary Development of the Lock and Key*), answered my many questions, as did others whom I thank properly in the Acknowledgments. Other great resources were Vincent Eras's book *Locks and Keys Throughout the Ages* and Martina Pall's *Prunkstücke Art Treasures from the Hanns Schell Collection*—both of which Scott recommended. I also found Eric Monks's *Keys: Their History and Collection*, Stephen Tchudi's *The Secrets of Locking Things Up, In and Out* and John Chubb's *On the Construction of Locks and Keys* incredibly useful. As James Forrestor in his marvelous novel *Sacred Treason* writes, "locks tell you where secrets are hidden." What better way to explore the notion of secrets, lies and deceptions than through the motif of locks (which were as much works of art as they were cunning and sometimes deadly devices) during the era when, according to many historians, modern espionage was born.

In terms of actual history, the major events depicted in *The Locksmith's Daughter* are entirely accurate: from the movements of all historical figures such as Sir Francis Walsingham, the Queen, Lord Burghley, the Earl of Leicester and the various Jesuit priests mentioned to the executions (of Campion and the others) and the names and actions of the other spies in Walsingham's network. Likewise, all the works of fiction or nonfiction mentioned actually existed—from the books used to educate Mallory when she was a young woman to those she reads for pleasure, the various letters between Spain, France, Rome and Reims, the publications and pamphlets (including Campion's "Brag" and *Raciones Decem*—though there were only 400 copies distributed, and only in Oxford), and the dossier written by Charles Sledd, which was interfered with by Walsingham (or under his instructions). The only exceptions are the plays by Caleb Hollis—they are my invention.

Sir Francis Walsingham bore witness to the St. Bartholomew's Day massacre as he was Elizabeth's ambassador in Paris at the time. He showed remarkable bravery in the face of terrible danger and protected not only many English nationals, but French ones as well. Some of his biographers believe this bloodbath and the treachery of the Catholics against the Huguenots both scarred and changed him for life, and cemented his inflexible attitudes toward Catholicism and his own Puritan-based faith. I take this notion further to explain his unbending attitude as well.

Walsingham did live in Padua during the time described in the novel. In various nonfiction accounts of his life and biographies (the most popular, and most often cited by other writers, is the three volumes by Conyers Read written in 1925, to which I am indebted as well), they are described as the "missing years." It's known he attended university in Padua then traveled to Switzerland, but exactly what he did and the date he returned to Padua is not—only that he did return. I asked the eternal question of all writers—what if?—and speculated a love affair resulting in an illegitimate daughter and what the consequences of this would be for an ambitious yet devout man with a promising future.

The agreement to supply munitions between Elizabeth and the Sultan of Turkey that Mallory steals from Captain Alyward Landsey aboard the *Forged Friends* is also true—though the captain and his ship are not. The Queen and selected members of her government agreed to supply arms for coin. If word of this had reached any of the major Catholic powers in Europe, never mind some of the Privy Council and leading nobles of the time, it would have resulted in huge civil unrest and war. The correspondence was kept very secret.

The Book of Secret Intelligences did actually exist. According to various contemporary records and some biographers (including Read), it was kept in Sir Francis's special cabinet (which is also a real object) and contained the type of information described in the novel. When Sir

Francis died, it was never found, and to this day no one knows what happened to it. It's quite the mystery and I could not resist weaving it and a conclusion into my tale!

All the boxes described in Sir Francis's study existed and had the labels I have given them. The other watchers and secretaries working for Sir Francis were also real people—Thomas Phelippes (who also used the alias Peter Halins, as well as John Morice), his servant Casey, and Charles Sledd (who, among many aliases, used Rowland Russell)—as were Sir Francis's second wife, Ursula St. Barbe, and his daughter Frances. Frances Walsingham went on to marry the poet Philip Sidney. She was widowed and a mother by the age of nineteen and remarried the infamous Earl of Essex (stepson of Leicester), Robert Deveraux, who was put to death under orders from Elizabeth for, among other misdemeanors, trying to stage a coup. After he was killed, she married her lover, Richard de Burgh, the Earl of Clanricarde, and went to live in Ireland.

Contrary to popular belief, though Elizabethans were very religious, the schism that erupted during Henry VIII's reign—when he became head of his own church, the Church of England, and designated the Pope a mere bishop of Rome, so he could divorce Katherine of Aragon and marry Anne Boleyn (Elizabeth's mother)—took a long time to heal. After all, just because a king (and later, a queen) orders you to change the manner of your faith, the rituals you've known your whole life and that have been practiced for generations, doesn't mean you automatically do. There was, naturally, a great deal of confusion, resentment and (oft-times militant) resistance. Henry also ordered the translation of the Bible into English, so ordinary literate folk could read God's word for themselves. This was an enormous step. When Henry's son Edward became king, he introduced further reforms and was intolerant of Catholic ways. After his brief reign, Henry's eldest daughter, Mary Tudor, a devout Catholic, took the throne and earned the sobriquet "Bloody Mary" because she killed many English Protestants who refused to recant their beliefs and return to Catholicism.

When Elizabeth became ruler upon her half sister Mary's death in 1558, she promised she wouldn't "make windows into men's souls," inferring tolerance toward Catholicism despite her firm Protestant beliefs. The Thirty-Nine Articles of Faith, introduced in 1563, demonstrated this was tolerance with strict caveats. After Pope Pius declared his Bull

against Elizabeth (which, at the opening of the novel has just been reinforced by Pope Gregory XIII in 1580—again, all facts), priests started
to surreptitiously enter England with the intention to undermine Elizabeth, the English faith, her rule and laws and to align people with Rome
and Catholic Europe. Schools to train Jesuits, overseen by Dr. William
Allen, as referred to in the novel, were established in various parts of
Europe and young, ardent Catholic men flocked to them. Even knowing it could result in their imprisonment and possibly death if they were
caught, the priests (often accompanied by devout lay people) traveled
to England and were given refuge by recusant families and individuals.
And so this fragile official tolerance was dashed. Between the years 1580
and 1590 especially, laws were tightened. Heavy fines, arrests, jail terms
and severe punishment, torture and horrific executions resulted. Suspicion was rife and propaganda flourished. Religious prejudice was profound on both sides. In many ways, parallels between what happened in
Elizabeth's reign can be drawn with the world today where assumptions
are made about people on the basis of faith—a person's religious beliefs
have become synonymous with their politics, calling into question an
individual's patriotism and loyalty to their nation and fellow countrymen and women. Just like Elizabethans, we're being taught to fear an
"enemy within."

It fell on Sir Francis Walsingham's shoulders, as Elizabeth's spymaster and secretary, to do what he could to keep her and England safe
from what was seen as the Catholic scourge. In order to do that, he
kept himself informed using an incredible network of informants. Historian Alan Haynes likens his network of agents to a "Secret Service,"
conjuring images of "spooks." Walsingham's men did utilize aliases and
disguises, infiltrated enemy quarters in England and abroad, spread
false information, developed secret codes and deciphered them as well
as exposing themselves to great risks and danger. This all occurred
under the watchful eyes of Walsingham, who determined not only to
bring down Catholics, but one in particular—the "viper in England's
bosom," Mary, Queen of Scots. He achieved this in 1587 when Mary
was beheaded at Fotheringhay Castle.

Walsingham wasn't above embellishing evidence or falsifying it to
get a result. Edmund Campion's name *was* belatedly added to Charles
Sledd's dossier, and while Campion's fate was likely already sealed,

placing his name alongside known traitors and inferring he traveled widely with these folk definitely removed all doubt as to the priest's purpose in England. Likewise, evidence was falsified or added to further condemn Mary, Queen of Scots, thus attempting to silence any who doubted her guilt.

Yet despite this perception of Catholics as traitors and plotters, even seminary-trained Catholics such as Edmund Campion didn't see themselves as terrorists or troublemakers so much as liberating English souls from the shackles of heretical Protestant reform. As Robert Hutchinson says in his book *Elizabeth's Spymaster*, "Today's dictum that "one man's terrorist is another man's freedom fighter" was just as true in the 1580s." He argues,

> *To Walsingham, faced with a succession of plots against his Queen and state, the many English Catholics covertly practicing their religion were potential terrorists and assassins.*

While some Catholics had benign intentions, others certainly didn't. The equivalent of terrorist cells existed, and small groups of Catholics plotted assassinations, bold shootings, poisonings, the overthrow of the government (and killing of leading figures within it), bombings (the Gunpowder Plot that occurred during the reign of Elizabeth's successor, James I and VI, being an extreme example), and general disruption to good governance. There was even what Hutchinson calls the first internment camp in England—Wisbech Castle in Cambridgeshire—where Walsingham sent unyielding Catholics to suffer deprivations in the cold, damp and isolated dungeons of the north.

Walsingham also didn't hesitate to use whatever means at his disposal to put an end to Catholic treachery and stamp out the faith for good. This included torture, payment for information and the infiltration of embassies and prisons where Catholics languished. His spies and informers were drawn from all walks of life; many were from the lowest echelons of society, others from the higher strata. Some did it for coin, others for adventure and a sense of importance, or because they truly believed in the cause. Haynes describes them as being motivated by "belligerent conviction, self-interest, family necessity, vanity, desperation and perhaps a low threshold of boredom." Some, like

Charles Sledd, Thomas Phelippes, Francis Mylles, Robert Beale and even Malyverny Caitlyn, among others, were very good at what they did. Others were clumsy, ill-informed and poor at their tasks. Some became double agents, so there was often doubt cast upon information received, especially from agents overseas. Elizabethan England was quite the police state in many ways, especially during the 1580s, engendering fear even among those who had no cause to be afraid.

In the novel, I allude to the fact that while many of these spies were promised recompense for their work, and would write copious letters demanding it, often they weren't paid. It's true that Sir Francis mostly funded the network out of his own pocket and died heavily in debt as a consequence. His pleas to the Queen for funds to support his work (mostly) fell on deaf ears.

Despite the propaganda about Catholics and religion, it was not all black and white. There were debates, confusion and sympathy for Catholics and tolerance for their beliefs among all classes of society. Despite the threat people were told Catholics posed and the constant stream of (mis)information, arrests, tortures and deaths—many of them public, and as gruesome as those described in the book—a blind eye was often turned toward benign recusancy, meaning neighbors' lack of church attendance wasn't always reported, information about known recusants wasn't necessarily passed on to authorities and priests were protected. Many priests, like Edmund Campion, insisted, even until death, that they were not in England to incite treason but to succor the faithful and mend wounded souls.

This was especially true in the early part of the 1580s, when this novel is set. As the decade wore on, and attempts to assassinate Elizabeth increased, understanding and tolerance diminished, and subsequent searches for the traitors in England's midst became more pressing and fervent.

London was the city where suspicion and fear thrived. Informants found a great deal of work and neighbors could turn on their own for coin, revenge or other base motives. Others believed it was the right thing to do—and feared the consequences if they did not.

One of the cruelest of consequences for breaking laws—especially treason or even suspected treason—was torture, which was endorsed and practiced with no small degree of skill and, according to many accounts, sick pleasure during Elizabeth's reign. Thomas Norton, who earned the sobriquet "Rackmaster Norton" because of his expertise with the rack and his ability to prolong pain while keeping death at bay, was considered an expert in extracting confessions. He did rack Campion—twice. He was also a playwright, as noted in the novel. But he was nothing compared to Richard Topcliffe.

Topcliffe's name became a byword and people feared him. These days we'd probably call him a sexual sadist, a psychopath at best. He was known to take great pride and joy in his work, inflicting shocking pain upon his victims, deforming them, threatening them and taking pleasure from their pain. Claiming friendship with Queen Elizabeth, he did have associates in high places and was protected—so much so that he was given permission to have his own torture chamber in his house. He also had an assistant and, together, they often sexually abused the women in their "care." The abuses I have him inflicting upon Mallory are tame compared to some of the records of Topcliffe's activities and his known proclivities. Rape, abuse, destroying bodies and minds were his specialties. It's no wonder that in later years the mere mention of his name evoked terror.

On a lighter note, the incident at Deptford where the Queen manipulated the French ambassador into knighting Drake is true (it was done so the Spaniards couldn't take offense that she'd rewarded a man who'd recklessly plundered their ships), as is the breaking of the gangplank, which flung so many of the crowd into the muddy waters.

To the best of my knowledge, all street names and churches existed during the period and are where they should be according to contemporary maps. I also walked the streets that still survive, and stood outside where Sir Francis Walsingham's house would have been on Seething Lane, crossed the Thames back and forth, and walked to the Royal Exchange, St. Paul's, and where I thought Lord Nathaniel's town house would be. I also navigated through many tourists and experienced the Tower, which is daunting, incredible and a testimony to the power of fear. However, when I visited the Bloody Tower and the dungeons in the Clink and saw the instruments of torture on display there, I felt quite sickened by our capacity to inflict pain upon one another. The real Topcliffe did give his instruments of torture names as he does in the novel.

Attitudes to homosexuality were mostly extremely intolerant and based on religious beliefs, and sodomy (a term which at that time encompassed a number of things, including what we now call bestiality) was punishable by death. But there were those who, like Mallory and Nathaniel and others in the book, could see beyond entrenched prejudices to the person. It is not a modern inflection to include their forbearance. As Liza Picard notes in *Elizabeth's London*, "There are indications that it [homosexuality] was tacitly accepted in London. Otherwise, the 'male stews' would have been quickly closed down." Many known homosexuals of the era were accepted and even lauded for their talents despite their sexuality by friends, family and even the royal court. What they did in private was conveniently overlooked and never publicly discussed.

Contrary to the popular belief that everyone in this period married young, the average age for a first marriage among the general populace was twenty-four for women and twenty-seven for men, so Mallory was considered quite young to be eloping. Her engagement to Isaac would have lasted a few years—at least until he was a qualified lawyer. There were exceptions. Some people did marry very young; a girl could be married and a mother while still in her teens. The nobility and gentry tended to marry younger, but not as young as we sometimes think. Contracts of marriage between royalty could be ratified while the bride and groom were mere children, but that didn't mean they were wed or the marriage consummated (though some were). A person under twenty-one years of age needed permission to get married.

Women in those days didn't have much to barter with. Their social currency was dependent on limited means—their father's wealth and position, and their own virtue. Lose one, and all else lost its appeal. Of course, this could change contingent on the dowry and the prospective husband's needs—but a child born out of wedlock, and without a father to acknowledge him or her, tarnished the mother and potentially damaged all hope of a future, regardless of how the child was conceived (as in medieval times, if a woman accused a man of rape and subsequently fell pregnant, it was then believed she hadn't been raped but had consented to the sex and was therefore little more than a whore).

While there were no doubt many happy marriages in Elizabethan times (it was the goal of most women—as Alison Sim states in *The Tudor Housewife*: "A woman was brought up to be a wife, to the extent that this was seen as her calling from God"), the notion that a woman had a subordinate status and was akin to a possession (not unlike a piece of livestock) was enshrined in law and generally accepted in society. As Thomas Becon wrote in *The Christian State of Matrimony* in 1546, "Women and horses must be well governed." Women were also understood to be "the weaker vessel," fragile and incapable of inner strength of the mind or outer strength of the body (despite the example to the contrary of the Queen herself). Their primary roles were to keep their husbands sexually satisfied, produce children and keep the household running smoothly. A *feme sole* (single woman) was regarded with suspicion, often open hostility, and could be exposed to all sorts of gossip, bullying and even charges (such as witchcraft). Married women were subject to their husband's rule, while widows had the opportunity (albeit sometimes brief) to experience independence.

Men were encouraged to respect their wives, but also to control them. While there were diverse marital relationships and degrees of accord and discord, women were raised from childhood to perceive themselves as inferior and men superior. Women—single or married—could be publicly punished and thus shamed for something as simple as nagging (being a scold), being disobedient or generally subverting their father/brother/husband/master's power. For wives, this was especially the case. Retha M. Warnicke writes in *Wicked Women of Tudor England*, "Reinforcing each other, the legal systems, medical lore, and religious instruction contributed to this ethos . . . That wives should be in some sense subject to their husbands' control." It was not forbidden (or uncommon) for men to beat their wives—or their servants or children—and no one had the right to intervene when such punishment was meted out. Some men, such as Thomas Howard, the third Duke of Norfolk, even imprisoned their wives in the home, took away their clothes and jewels and made their lives a misery—fortunately, these men were in the minority. For a man to slap or even beat a woman in public, as Mallory witnesses in the streets of London, was not illegal or even necessarily frowned upon—provided the beating was not unusually severe. There were also women who went beyond being "scolds" and beat their husbands, but just like today, stigma was attached to a man who couldn't control his wife. Like the women, he bore his marriage stoically, as best he could.

Just as it does now, terrible violence of the kind Raffe metes out to

Mallory happened behind closed doors. Shamed, her self-esteem battered as much as her body, Mallory is so ready to blame herself for her son's death that when she is accused of infanticide, she accepts the responsibility. I never intended to write a story that included domestic abuse, but as I read about the lives of Elizabethan women of all classes, it made its way onto the page. The more I write about the past, the more I understand that I am, in a sense, also writing about the present. Mallory, like so many other brave and remarkable women past and present, is a survivor who succeeds in spite of what has happened to her.

For those of you who would like to explore the period and learn about the real people who appear in the novel, here are some more books I found particularly helpful and fascinating. I cannot express my admiration and gratitude to their authors strongly enough. I hope that by listing their books here (many more are reviewed on my website), they will know how much their work is appreciated.

A fantastic book that explores not only the ambivalence during this era toward faith and the laws that upheld it but also Catholic sensibilities and the lengths some families—who never posed a threat to the Crown—went to in order to maintain their faith, is Jesse Child's award-winning *God's Traitors: Terror and Faith in Elizabethan England*. Another terrific book that outlines the work done by Walsingham and his network is Stephen Alford's *The Watchers: A Secret History of the Reign of Elizabeth I*. There's also *Sir Francis Walsingham, A Courtier in the Age of Terror* by Derek Wilson, and *The Queen's Agent* by John Cooper. I have previously mentioned Conyers Read's three-volume biography, simply entitled *Sir Francis Walsingham*—detailed, fascinating and insightful. For a quicker, lighter read, try *Her Majesty's Spymaster* by Stephen Budiansky. More detailed efforts are *God's Secret Agents* by Alice Hodge, *The Elizabethan Secret Services* by Alan Haynes, and *Danger to Elizabeth* by Alison Plowden. *The Pirate Queen* by Susan Ronald was also very useful, while *Elizabeth's London* by Liza Picard and *The Time Traveller's Guide to Elizabethan England* by Ian Mortimer were brilliant, colorful and completely indispensable—as was anything by Peter Ackroyd. Also essential were *The Writer's Guide to Everyday Life in Renaissance England* by Kathy Lynn Emerson, and *Daily Life in Elizabethan England* by Jeffrey L. Singman, and *The Elizabethan World Picture* by E. M. W. Tillyard—an oldie but a goodie.

There were also many, many other books and articles I accessed about religion (special mention here for Eamon Duffy's *The Stripping of the Altars*), clothing, medicine, food, weather, torture, houses, streets and major incidents, such as the Spanish Armada and the imprisonment and death of Mary, Queen of Scots, even though these events aren't included in the novel except tangentially. Likewise, the early years of Elizabeth's reign and her relationship with Robert Dudley are endlessly fascinating, and I highly recommend Chris Skidmore's *Death and the Virgin* (which explores the suspicious death of Amy Robsart—Dudley's first wife), Christopher Hibbert's *Elizabeth I*, Sarah Gristwood's *Elizabeth and Leicester*, Alison Sim's *The Tudor Housewife*, the plays and sonnets of Shakespeare, and Michael Wood's excellent *In Search of Shakespeare*.

For information about Elizabethan theater, I used *The Shakespearean Stage, 1574–1642* and *Playgoing in Shakespeare's London* (third edition), both by Andrew Gurr. I also thoroughly enjoyed Neil McGregor's delightful *Shakespeare's Restless World: An Unexpected History in Twenty Objects*. Revisiting the work of the bard and his contemporaries such as Kit Marlowe, Ben Jonson and the poet Philip Sidney, just to name a few, was such a pleasure. So was rereading Dante's *Divine Comedy* and Castiglione's *Book of the Courtier*.

While I'm loathe to single out one author from all the wonderful fiction I read set in this period—both before and after the years *The Locksmith's Daughter* covers—the work of Patricia Finney (who also writes as P. J. Chisholm) was sensational. But so are the books of Edward Marston, S. J. Parris, Rory Clements and Alison Weir (her nonfiction, too), among many other authors whose writings enthralled me and which I review on my website and, often, on Goodreads.

Researching the times in which my novels are set is almost as joyous as writing about them. It's always a wrench to leave an era, especially after you've done what you can to bring it to life. Because this period has so much to offer, I hope I get the chance to return soon.

Any accuracies in the novel are due to the brilliance of these and other writers; any mistakes are entirely my own, and I beg your forgiveness and cry "artistic license."

ACKNOWLEDGMENTS

This is probably one of the hardest and nicest parts of writing a book—the moment when I get to thank, in print, all those who directly and indirectly supported the writing of the book; those who inspired me to keep writing and those who knew when to drag me away and when not to be offended by my refusal to come out and play but instead patiently awaited my return from the 1580s. I love acknowledging my gratitude, but I also find it really hard because I'm so fearful I will leave someone out! If I do, if I have, please, please, forgive me.

First and foremost I want to thank my agent and dear friend, Selwa Anthony, for her constant support and belief in this book. After reading some early chapters Selwa gave me sage advice that I followed, and she continuously encouraged its slow birth. Thank you, Selwa. Thanks as well to her gorgeous daughter, Linda, and to Selwa's husband, the kind and ever-patient Brian. I love being part of your extended family (the fur-kids do as well).

To my Australian publisher, Harlequin/MIRA, who championed this book when it was just an idea and who have been incredible in their communication, support, acts of random kindness and morale boosting. Whether it was the lovely Sue Brockhoff with her enthusiasm and timely phone calls, or wonderful Annabel Blay with her considered, wise and generous words and insights, Michelle La Forest, James Kellow, Adam Van Rooijen, Cristina Lee, and the rest of the marvelous Harlequin/MIRA team! I am one lucky writer to be in such fabulous and capable hands and I know it.

The lexical attentions of my incredible editor, Linda Funnell, a woman with an uncanny ability when it comes to shaping a sentence into its best form and polishing a plot until it shines, are unparalleled. It's hard to express how much I appreciate the work she did with and for me on this book and how much gratitude I feel. Thank you, Linda. It's been such an utter and sincere pleasure working with you again and I look forward to the next time. As I have said before, you are a gift to writers and I am so glad you were given to me (again!).

I also want to thank my US agents, James Frenkel & Associates—in particular Catherine Pfeifer, for advocating for my work and making the deal, and Jim Frenkel, for his incredible support, wonderful emails and his enthusiasm. He's an utter delight to work with, and I feel very fortunate to be part of his literary family.

My US editor, Rachel Kahan, has been a great champion of my work from the outset. I'm so very grateful to her for believing in it and for shepherding this book to publication in the northern hemisphere. Along with Rachel comes a marvelously talented team. I'm greatly appreciative of the effort and care they've given the novel—from Rachel's assistant, Alivia Lopez, to Jeanie Lee, the production editor, to Alicia Tatone and Mumtaz Mustafa, the cover designers who created the beautiful package in which this story comes, and to Jennifer Hart, the paperback publisher who was responsible for so much as well. Thank you all for your help and support.

In my Author's Note, I mention the amazing Scott Klemm, an American whose knowledge of locks and keys and whose generosity in sharing that knowledge has been phenomenal. Scott came into my life when I ordered his books via the internet. Curious as to what a "young" (bless him) woman wanted with what he thought was a fairly dry subject, we began corresponding. Excited by what I was doing, Scott offered to answer any questions I might have regarding locks and keys . . . I hope he didn't ever regret that. Certainly I sent him many questions in the early stages of writing and he always provided full and insightful responses—sometimes including photographs with labels! I cannot thank you enough, Scott, and what I really like is that this book has unlocked a new friendship.

Another kind and knowledgeable person was Richard (Rick) Leigh, the branch manager of Jacksons, a locksmithing business here in Hobart. I met Rick through my husband Stephen's brewery. Rick had asked Stephen what my next book would be after *The Brewer's Tale*, and when Stephen mentioned it was on locks and keys and spies, Rick offered to help in any way he could. As good as his word, he gave up his time to show me the inner workings of old locks, explain how various mechanisms functioned and show me how to pick a lock. He also, very kindly, asked after the book and its progress every time he saw me. Thank you so much, Rick.

Traveling to the UK in 2014, I stayed with my darling friend Dr. Lesley Roberts, who subsequently accompanied me around England, Scotland and particularly London, as I did on-the-ground research for this novel (and fact-checked my previous one). We discovered many astonishing places and people, walked so many miles, laughed, cried and uncovered stories and wonders galore (including the basis for my next novel). Thank you, Lesley, for an incredible adventure. Here's to many more.

I also want to thank Puddleduck Winery here in Tasmania for allowing me to walk their charming grounds and collect, of all things, goose feathers. When I explained what I needed them for (to practice writing in the manner of the Elizabethans—as well as making my own invisible ink), they were so enthusiastic and made helpful suggestions about the best sort. Their delicious wine went a good way to making my experiments more fun and, I'm sure, was the reason they were mostly successful.

I also want to offer loving and grateful thanks to one of the people this book is dedicated to, Kerry Doyle. Kerry, Stephen and Kerry's beautiful husband, Peter Goddard (whom this book is also dedicated to), and I have a friendship spanning many, many years and some trials and tribulations. It's so very, very special. Treasured. Kerry and I also happen to share, among many other things, a passion for books and "stalk" each other's reading. Kerry is such an astute and insightful reader and early on offered to be a test reader for drafts of my novels, something I gratefully accepted. It's a huge ask to not only request a friend read a manuscript and offer honest feedback—it's an even bigger leap of faith to accept. Kerry read an early version of this book and gave me some invaluable suggestions that I know made the work stronger. Not only that, she also sent me little texts of encouragement when I flagged or doubted during the initial writing and rewrites, which bolstered me in ways I find hard to explain, except to say that's what the love of a dear friend can do. Thank you so much, Kerry.

Books might be written in isolation, but the sharing of ideas, the interest in the work in progress, needs good friends and, along with Kerry and Peter, I am so blessed to have people in my life whose love, forbearance and enthusiasm for what I do is abundant. Here, I want to thank them:

Thank you to our neighbors and dear, dear friends, the darling Larks—Bill, Lyn, Jack, Kristy and David—your support has been wonderful. To the rest of the Single Malt Motorcycle Whisky Club— Mark Nicholson, Clinton Steele and Simon Thomson and their beautiful partners (and my friends) Robyn, Rosie and Lucy—thank you so much. To Bob and Chris, thank you as well.

To the wonderful Stephen Bender, my partner in former careers (we're both ex-Army), our invaluable assistant in the brewery and go-to person for fun times, the man who makes me and Stephen laugh, think and is a sounding board for all things beer and bookish as well as political and personal—a huge and loving thanks.

Same to Christina Schultness, who was one of those thoughtful people who would drag me away with an invite to w(h)ine, as did her partner PJ, Danny Matheson, Kazuo Ikeda, Ali Gay, Terry and Rebecca Moles, Robbie Gilligan and Emma Alessendrini. I also want to thank the gorgeous Dr. Kiarna Brown, her fantastic husband, Chris, and son, Jake, for the joy they've brought into our lives and support they've given both Stephen and me. Thanks also to Dr. Lisa Hill, Sheryl Gwyther, Dannielle Miller, Katherine Howell, my extraordinary editor at the *Courier Mail*, Margaret Wenham, the amazing and learned Professor Jim McKay, Dr. Liz Ferrier, Dr. Helen Johnson, and Professor David Rowe as well as Dr. Frances Thiele, dearest friend, historian, sensational harpist, teacher and audience for many of my ideas. I also want to thank my Facebook friends and supporters as well as many of our simply terrific patrons at the brewery for their interest in my books and their kind and wonderful words. You are the best.

I also want to thank my fantastic little sister, Jenny Farell, and my mum, Moira Adams. They do what families do: love you, prod you and tell you—in not so many words—when you're being a dick. Also, a special shout-out to the brilliant writer and person, Kim Wilkins—thanks, my love.

I also wish to acknowledge my absent friend, the beloved Sara Warneke (Douglass) who, though she is no longer with us, I swear dwells in my study. I often talk out loud to her—testing notions, expressing frustrations, celebrating a light bulb moment—causing my fur-kids (the dogs Tallow and Dante and brew-dog Bounty, as well as the cats) to twist their little heads and listen intently. They are my furry muses, but I still miss you every single day, Sara.

I also want to thank my readers—where and what would I be without you? We share a love of words, reading and imagination and I am grateful for your support and passion. Thank you so very much.

But of course, without my beautiful and amazing kids, Adam and Caragh, and my husband—my partner in life and love—Stephen, I would not be in a position to write at all. Without their ongoing love, ability to make me think in ways I might not otherwise, their endless teasing, encouragement, reminders to live a little and put things in perspective (they tell me candidly to stop being stupid), belief and ability to boost me when I am crippled by doubt (which I often am), then I could not and would not write. I wouldn't want to.

I love you, Adam and Caragh—thank you for being you and letting me be me (except when I shouldn't be!).

And, lastly—but only in this list—thank you, Stephen. You hold the key to my heart, a key that's opened doors which, holding hands, we've stepped through together. I know there'll be many more we'll open and explore.

Thanks, my love—this book, like all those before and to come, is for you.

LIST OF CHARACTERS

denotes an actual historical person
Mallory Bright: daughter of Gideon and Valentina Bright
Caleb Hollis: Lodger with the Brights, playwright, actor and shareholder in Lord Warham's Men
Angela: cousin of Valentina's
Gideon Bright: locksmith, father to Mallory
Comfort: housekeeper at Harp Lane
Gracious: maid at Harp Lane who replaced Nell after she was dismissed
Latch: cat
Arthur: dog—Cocker spaniel
Galahad: dog—Cocker spaniel
Master Fodrake: Mallory's former tutor
Master Gib: general help at Harp Lane, married to Mistress Pernel
Mistress Pernel: cook and general help, Harp Lane
Valentina Bright: Mallory's mother, Gideon's wife
***Sir Francis Walsingham**: Secretary to Queen Elizabeth I and spymaster
Sir Raffe Shelton: knight with estates in Durham
Ellis: Sir Raffe's squire
Matt Culpeper: apprentice locksmith
Kit Jolebody: eldest apprentice of Gideon Bright
Samuel Blackstone: apprentice locksmith

Dickon: apprentice locksmith
Benedict Thatcher: former apprentice of Gideon Bright
Nell: Mallory's former maid
Widow Dorothy: neighbor of the Brights
*__Timothy Bright__: brother of Gideon, uncle to Mallory and doctor of Bright family and Sir Francis
*__Thomas Phelippes__: secretary to Sir Francis Walsingham
*__Casey__: Thomas's servant
*__Robert Beale__: secretary to Sir Francis Walsingham
Laurence: Sir Francis's manservant
*__Ursula Walsingham__: wife to Sir Francis Walsingham
*__Frances Walsingham__: daughter to Sir Francis Walsingham
*__Mary Walsingham__ (deceased): daughter to Sir Francis Walsingham
Lord Nathaniel Warham: lord of the realm, privateer who sailed with Francis Drake
Nicholas: Lord Nathaniel's squire
Swithin Hattycliffe: weaver and counselor, father to Isaac
Isaac Hattycliffe: junior lawyer, son of Swithin and former betrothed of Mallory
*__Edmund Campion__: Jesuit priest
*__Robert Persons or Parsons__: Jesuit priest
*__Dr. William Allen__: head of Jesuit schools on the Continent
*__Ralph Sherwin__: student priest
*__Alexander Briant__: priest, condemned to death with Campion
*__King Philip of Spain__
*__Stephen Brinkley__: owner of Oxford printing press that published Campion's *Ten Reasons*
Baldassere Zucchero: master locksmith and Mallory's grandfather
Lucia Zucchero: Mallory's aunt (deceased)
*__Amy Robsart__: (deceased) first wife of Robert Dudley
*__Lettice Knollys__: second, or possibly third wife of Robert Dudley
*__John Stubbes__: printer who lost a hand on Elizabeth's orders
*__John Foxe__: author of *The Book of Martyrs*
*__William Charke__: pamphleteer who wrote a scathing response to Campion's "Brag"
*__Meredith Hammer__: Oxford theologian who wrote a response to Campion's "Brag"

Captain Alyward Lindsey: captain of the *Forged Friends* and traitor to his country

*Sir Francis Drake: privateer who successfully circumnavigated the globe, sacked many of Spain's ships and ports and brought back great wealth for himself and Elizabeth

*Mary Drake: Sir Francis Drake's wife

*Queen Elizabeth I

*Lady Jane Grey: the "Nine-Days Queen," beheaded by Mary Tudor

*King Edward: younger half brother of Elizabeth and Mary

*Mary, Queen of Scots: under house arrest by Elizabeth; one of the banes of Sir Francis's life

*Mary Tudor: staunch Catholic who ruled England before Elizabeth, her half sister, and was known as "Bloody Mary"

Lady Beatrice Warham: Nathaniel's sister

Merlin: Lady Beatrice's puppy

Bounty: Lord Nathaniel's horse

Tesoro: Lady Beatrice's horse

Bilge Rat and Barnacle: the cats of Warham Hall

Rebecca: Beatrice's nurse

Alice: Beatrice's maid

Master Bede: Lord Nathaniel's steward

Mistress Margery: wife to Master Bede and housekeeper to Lord Nathaniel

Sir Lance Ingolby: best friend to Lord Nathaniel

Mary: maid at Warham Hall

Tace: maid to Mallory at Warham Hall

Master Connor: cook at Warham Hall

Virtue: Master Connor's wife

Missy: daughter of Connor and Virtue

Gully: servant at Warham Hall

Simon Thatch: new apprentice for Gideon

*Anthony Munday: watcher for Sir Francis and talented writer

*Anthony Tyrell: priest

*Earl of Leicester, Robert Dudley: greatest love of Queen Elizabeth's life, courtier and investor in privateering

*Lord Burghley, William Cecil: one of Elizabeth's closest advisors

*Robert Cecil: William's son, who would replace his father in the

Queen's service and later serve King James in the same capacity; was said to also run a formidable network of spies

*Charles Sledd, alias Rowland Russell: agent of Sir Francis Walsingham

*Arthur Gregory: secretary and agent of Sir Francis Walsingham

*Duke of Anjou: French prince who sought Elizabeth's hand in marriage

*Lord Vaux: a well-known Catholic

*George Eliot: Sir Francis's man, hired to track and arrest Edmund Campion

*Pope Gregory XIII

*Guise family: powerful and very influential French family

*Doctor Dee: well-known astrologer and physician

*David Jenkins: Sir Francis's man, hired to track and arrest Edmund Campion

*Yate family: known Catholic family who hid Campion and others from authorities

*Thomas Sackville: playwright

*Thomas Norton: playwright and torturer—because, of course, the two go hand in hand

Master David Smithyman: bookholder, Lord Warham's Men

*Richard Topcliffe: sadist and torturer who worked for different nobles and claimed a close relationship with the Queen

Reverend Bernard: parish priest, Harp Lane

*Sir Edmund Tilney: Master of the Revels

*Will Kempe: famous actor—a comedian

Mistress Bench: housekeeper, Billiter Lane

Agnes and Katherine: former nuns, beholden to Shelton family for protection

*Sir Richard Worsley: Ursula Walsingham's first husband

Guido Sapienti: Angela's beloved

*William Harborne: negotiated the agreement with the Ottoman Empire on Elizabeth's behalf

*Sultan Murad III: ruler of the Ottoman Empire

*Francis Mylles: secretary to Sir Francis and watcher

*Marquis de Marchaumont: French ambassador who knighted Drake

Lord Jonathan Warham: eldest brother of Nathaniel (deceased)

Benet Warham: older brother of Nathaniel (deceased)
Father Mark Forwood: parish priest, St. Katherine Coleman
Master Hamon: servant at Oxford University
Mistress Bakewell: laundress in Billiter Lane
Goody Clara: Father Forwood's cook
Mistress Roach: parishioner, St. Katherine Coleman
George Cooper: parishioner, St. Katherine Coleman
Harold Pinchwite: deacon, parish of St. Katherine Coleman
Goodwife Mabel: parishioner, St. Katherine Coleman
*****Thomas Ford**: Catholic priest
*****John Colerton**: Catholic priest
*****William Filby**: Catholic priest
Beth Oldswain: parishioner, St. Katherine Coleman
Rose: parishioner, St. Katherine Coleman
*****Richard Bristowe**: author of the tract *Motives Inducing to the Catholic Faith*
*****Nicholas Sanders**: Catholic priest
*****Luke Kirby**: Catholic priest
Lady Joanna Shelton: Raffe's wife
*****Sir Owen Hopton**: Lord Lieutenant of the Tower

About the author

About the book

Insights,
Interviews
& More . . .

Meet Karen Brooks

Stephen Brooks

Australian-born KAREN BROOKS is the
author of nine novels. She is also an
academic, a newspaper columnist and a
social commentator, and has appeared
regularly on national TV and radio. Before
turning to academia, she was an army
officer and had dabbled in acting. She lives
in Hobart, Tasmania. ⌇

Reading Group Guide

1. When Angela tells Mallory to ignore the man who bullies her, Mallory responds, "A coward and a bully he may be, but there's many would argue my actions created him— Mamma among them." Why does Mallory believe this? Is it a fair assessment?

2. Mallory has a radically different relationship with her father the locksmith than with her mother. Why is that? Does your view of either relationship change as the story unfolds?

3. Mallory speaks several languages, knows mathematics and can pick any lock. She is unique in an age when women of her class were rarely educated or taught a trade. But in what other ways does Mallory defy traditional gender roles of the time? Are there instances when she does conform to what's expected of a woman?

4. "Uncommonly tall, slender as a willow stick but with olive-toned skin and jet-black hair, I was most often described as ungainly and teased as a spawn of a blackamoor or a Romany." Mallory's mother uses lemon juice and cosmetics to lighten her daughter's hair and skin. What does this say about sixteenth-century beauty standards? Are they similar or different from those of the twenty-first century? ▶

3

5. From Mamma remaining a faithful Catholic until the end of her life to Sir Francis's unwavering allegiance to Queen Elizabeth, loyalty drives many characters in the novel. How does their loyalty to various causes—and each other—impact the characters' lives, for better or for worse?

6. After witnessing the grisly torture and execution of Catholic priests at Tyburn, Mallory says: "It was even easier to commit atrocities when they were enacted in the name of justice; when you believed you were working for the good of the realm, for the security of the sovereign and your people. It was easy when you didn't see the consequences and others performed the retribution for you. It was easy to be ruthless when you ceased to think of those convicted as human, and saw them as enemies. In that way, anything—any kind of action—could be justified." What other examples of this do we see in history? Or in our present time?

7. How does what Mallory sees at Tyburn change her view of her work for Sir Francis? Is it a turning point for her?

8. Nathaniel says to Mallory: "You are not a fallen woman, Mallory, so much as one who was pushed." What does he mean by that? Do you agree? How do you view Mallory's relationship with Raffe and its fallout?

9. What do you make of the complicated relationship between the locksmith and Sir Francis?

10. Why does Sir Francis leave his book containing his life's work to Mallory? Does the book "change everything," as Nathaniel promised?

11. What do you think becomes of Mallory and her family ten years following the end of the novel? Do you think she's using Sir Francis's book in the way that he intended her to use it? ∽

Author Q&A: Karen Brooks on
The Locksmith's Daughter

This interview originally appeared on www.betterreading.com.au.

Q: All your occupations seem to start with "A": acting, army, academic and author. Is there a particular "A" job that you'd love to add to that list?

A: It's funny how all my jobs ended up starting with "A"—it certainly wasn't deliberate on my part. If I had to add one more, it would be Assistant Brewer at my partner's brewery, Captain Bligh's Ale and Cider in Hobart—a job I do love. But, if I could add anything to that list I wish I could do, providing it starts with "A," it would have to be archaeologist. I've always been fascinated by archaeology and while I know it's usually fairly mundane and that archaeologists are not all Indiana Jones (could you imagine!), there's something about the painstaking unveiling of the past and deep understanding about how our ancestors lived by examining the traces they left behind that's so compelling and utterly fascinating. I think I could be happy with some dirt, a trowel, brushes, camera, buckets of knowledge and traveling to various historical sites—oh, and Indiana Jones for company.

Q: What was your fascination with locks/locksmiths?

A: It seems strange, doesn't it? I wasn't always interested in them, even though I have a long and not very distinguished relationship with locks and keys. You see, I'm always misplacing or losing my keys. My son Adam's first words were actually "car keys." When I expressed concern that he didn't say "dada" or "mama" like other children, my friends laughed uproariously and asked if I was serious. When I appeared confused, they said, "You should hear yourself. You're always running around asking, 'Where are the car keys?' 'Has anyone seen my car keys?' 'I can't find my car keys!' No wonder Adam said those words first. He hears them more than any others." True.

But, the idea for the book happened after I watched a locksmith, named Bruce, replacing the ignition barrel in our car after a key snapped in it. His tools, the way he worked and how he answered ►

my questions had me hooked. Researching locks and keys, I became
fascinated with the entire process. After all, locks were invented to
keep people out of places—houses, rooms, cabinets, chests etc. Why?
Not only so precious material objects could be kept secure; but to
keep certain things away from prying eyes and to protect secrets—
even if that secret was the accumulation of fortune, love letters,
betrayals, treason and so on. Locks are a fantastic metaphor for
secrets, whether they're of a personal nature or political. During
and prior to Elizabethan times, locks were not only ornate and quite
beautiful works of art, they were often deadly, being infused with
poison, dyes, sharp metal that could sever fingers and worse. As
the person tasked with designing locks and the keys that opened
them, locksmiths played a very important role; particularly the
more secrets a government or individual had to keep, the more
possessions they wanted to secure. Spies, secrets, locks and
locksmiths seemed to go hand in glove—especially with Tudor
times and the birth of modern-day espionage.

Q: *What was your inspiration for Nathaniel?*

A: Ah . . . Nathaniel, he's a contrary, wonderful, misunderstood
bloke. Like many of my characters, he's an amalgam of good
men I know, naughty men too, who is then sprinkled with a bit
of perfection dust. I also imagined him to look a little like the
actor Chris Hemsworth, in terms of size and movement. It wasn't
hard to project the notion of the good, clever and provocative
buccaneer when I had such a clear physical idea of the man.

Q: *How much research went into* The Locksmith's Daughter?

A: A great deal in that I immersed myself in the period for at
least a year and kept researching while I was writing (I do love the
research!) for another year and more. I read numerous nonfiction
books by marvelous academics, journalists and historians, spoke
to locksmiths and experts on keys and locks here in Australia and
the USA. I traveled to England and walked the streets and places I
wrote about, went to the Tower, into dungeons, walked up and down
Seething Lane and various other alleys and snickets. Went to see
some productions of Shakespeare's plays, toured the Globe and so

much more. Inhaled the period as best I could. Went to Elizabeth I's various palaces, explored Hampton Court, rode upon the Thames, and went to Deptford as well. I also read some wonderful fiction set in the period and watched films and TV documentaries. I found the entire era just mesmerizing. It was difficult to tear myself away from!

Q: Who are the Australian and international authors you most admire?

A: Gosh, I admire so many. I just read Melina Marchetta's latest and, like all her work, it just filled me with admiration and wonder. I love Liane Moriarty's books; Michael Robotham's fabulous, suspenseful books I devour; Katherine Howell's works; Candice Fox and so many more (we have some stellar crime writers here, we really do). I think Kate Forsyth is astounding, and long for her next book to be published. Kim Wilkins is an amazing writer whether she writes under her own name or as Kimberley Freeman. Shirley Hazzard and Geraldine Brooks are also sublime. I also love Garth Nix, Juliet Marillier and Sara Douglass. In terms of international writers, I will try to be brief(ish), but, in no particular order: Margaret Atwood, Johan Theorin, Elizabeth George, Jo Nesbo, Khaled Hosseini, Sharon Kay Penman, Anya Seyton, J. K. Rowling (and as Robert Galbraith); Elizabeth Gilbert's *The Signature of All Things* is a simply magnificent book. I am also partial to Edward Marston, adore C. J. Sansom's work, Ken Follett, Ian Mortimer, Philippa Gregory, Peter Robinson, Peter May Lewis's books, S. J. Parris, Hugh Howey, Liza Picard and Robin Hobb . . . Gosh, I am finding it hard to stop. So many great writers and books and so little time.

Q: What do you hope readers take away from this book?

A: I hope readers take away a sense of pleasure, of having invested in something really worthwhile that lingers in their hearts and minds for ages afterward. Also, I would love them to feel a sense of history, but particularly, the humanity that links us across the eons—how, for all our differences and so-called advances we are more alike than not—we still love, laugh, make silly and great decisions and gestures, suffer, long, grieve and triumph. I really hope my readers enjoy the book. ▶

Author Q&A: Karen Brooks on
The Locksmith's Daughter (continued)

Q: What is your attraction to historical romance?

A: I love giving voice to the past through strong but, hopefully, realistic characters and allowing them to speak to us in the here and now. Historical fiction becomes the means of inviting readers to go on a journey back into time with my characters, no matter how dangerous and wonderful. The romance element adds a particular and delicious frisson that I hope they relate to and love as much as I do writing it. "Romance" is a broad church: it's not just about people falling in love, it's about taking risks of the heart, that most precious and fragile of organs. It's about emotional investment, not just between the characters, but from the readers as well. When a reader does that, gives you his or her heart, loses it to your characters and the story, there's nothing better.

Q: What's next for you?

A: I am currently writing a book set in the early years of Charles II's restoration, 1660s England. It's called *The Chocolate Maker's Wife* and is about a young woman who comes to London just as chocolate houses are being opened. They were select establishments where the wealthier citizens could imbibe the new beverage, the deliciously sinful "West Indian" drink called "chocolate," and places where gossip, gambling and sexual misconduct thrived. The 1660s was a period when everything was changing and the British Empire was expanding; it was also the post-Puritan era, so a great many of the restrictions upon social and public behavior were either lifted or being challenged. Chocolate drinking as a rich person's popular pastime also coincided with the rise of slavery, journalism, women entering theater, war, and huge religious and political upheavals and tensions. I thought the Elizabethan era fascinating, but the Restoration is a revelation—never mind all the dark and sinister secrets around chocolate! ∾